WOMEN TALKING DIRTY

GIVING UP ON ORDINARY

Also by Isla Dewar

Keeping up with Magda

WOMEN
TALKING DIRTY

GIVING
UP ON
ORDINARY

Isla Dewar

LONDON NEW YORK SYDNEY TORONTO

CONTENTS

WOMEN TALKING DIRTY

To Sibyl and Gordon for always
– in their own way – being there.

1

Ellen

Chapter One

There are women whose eyes lock momentarily in bars, across crowded rooms, in the street and, though they are strangers, they recognise each other. They go through that female summing up thing, the subliminal eyeflick, the quick look from shoes to haircut, and for a second their eyes meet.

I could be friends with you, they think. There goes a fellow smoker, drinker, slut, slag, domestic failure, neurotic, whatever, they think. A fellow traveller, a soul mate, they think. Sometimes they leave it at that, a moment's wondering and speculation. They do not act upon that look and make friends. But sometimes they do.

When Cora O'Brien's eyes met Ellen Quinn's across the crowded living room at one of Jack Conroy's parties, Ellen thought: Who is that vividly dressed woman? And Cora thought: I could be friends with you. And she thought: There sits one of the most insecure women I have ever seen. And she thought: Still, she's a soul mate and a fellow traveller. Cora was like that, a romantic. She went over to chat.

She had thought to say to Ellen that she was meant to enjoy it. Meaning parties, life, everything. It always amazed Cora that people forgot to take pleasure in things. 'Pleasure,' she'd say, 'it's even a nice word.' But she thought the better of it. Wasn't it always a bitch when people said things like, 'Smile, it may never happen'? Instead the first words she ever spoke to Ellen were, 'You look like you could do with some serious corrupting.' Over six years in Edinburgh had not shifted the Highland lilt. She sounded like a mist, soft, enveloping.

Ellen said, 'What makes you think that about me?' She didn't want this new woman in her life to leave her side. She wanted to listen a little longer to that voice.

3

'Oh, I don't know. I just thought it was a flash thing to say, I suppose.' Cora sat down beside her and looked longingly at her cigarette packet. Ellen offered her one. 'No. I'm a smoker at heart, I always will be, I just don't do cigarettes any more. Pity. I used to love it. I must say, though, how good it is to meet a smoker who does not disappoint. So many opt for cheap brands with ghastly packing and huge boxes of matches. I think that when you smoke you smoke for all of us who took fright and have given up. You should do it boldly. Carry an illuminated sign, "Smoking and proud". These however,' and she picked up Ellen's pack, sniffed at it deeply, 'remind me of someone. His flat smelled of these, and garlic. And sour milk.' She drifted into memories and from that momentary distance smiled to Ellen. A confiding smile it was – one day I will tell you everything. Ellen's heart was won. A small curve of the lips, a fleeting fix of eye contact was all it took.

'It's good for irritating people,' Ellen said. That, after all, was why she'd started. And why she'd chosen French cigarettes. They were so obviously smelly. She had wanted to shock her mother, who had been suitably horrified, sneering, 'Disgusting habit.' Ellen's moment of adolescent glee was, however, long past. Now she was addicted. 'If I die with blackened lungs,' she defiantly said, 'I like to think I blackened them with style.'

Cora knew when she saw Ellen sitting fiddling nervously with her cigarette packet, dressed completely in black, hair and dark glasses concealing as much of her face as possible, that she would have to be the one to introduce herself. Looking at Ellen, she knew she was looking at someone who had never once in her life made the first move.

But hell, Cora made first moves all the time. Thought nothing of it. She had beads sewn into her hair, and a black velvet band at her neck. She wore a red silk jacket and her nails were loudly lacquered plum. She raised her small self by wearing stiletto heels. Now her eyes were level with most men's chins.

She was a teacher. She taught seven-year-olds. And she knew she was a very fine teacher indeed. She loved it. Her pupils adored her. 'Come come, Billy Mackie. If you're going to grow up and marry me you'll have to learn to tie your shoelaces.' The child looked at her, and squirmed with embarrassed pleasure. Along with his class-mates he jostled to be head of the line every Thursday morning when Cora took them to the swimming baths. 'Any girl who wants to hold my hand, Laura Sutton, better be able to multiply five by three.'

'Fifteen, Miss O'Brien.'

'Good girl.' Cora held out her hand. A little sweaty palm squeezed it. Wide eyes looked in awe at her shiny red nails.

Cora found seven-year-olds a delight. She thought they were like a litter of warm-tummied animals, friendly, friendly and only friendly. At the peak of their careers as children. They had not quite learned to snigger and rant. Innocents. It would not last. Soon they'd be sneering and lying. 'Don't know, Miss.' 'Wasn't me, Miss.' They'd be greedy – like the rest of us, she thought. They'd be eyeing electrical goods and watches. Thundering through a childhood of burgers and baseball hats, desperate to become grown-ups. Desperate, too, to grow into the big, loud, foul language they'll have learned from videos. As the years passed, each new batch of infants seemed more sophisticated than the last.

'I swear,' she said to nobody in particular in the staff room, 'seven-year-olds are getting older and older. Soon they'll be like a class of forty-year-olds.'

'And what,' her headmaster asked, 'will forty-year-olds be like?'

'Same as ever. Looking back at their childhoods and wishing they'd had the gumption to enjoy being seven when they were there.'

The children in her present class had a full and active range of swear words. 'Oh fuck,' someone cried when his pot of blue paint toppled to the floor. Cora looked up mildly and shook her head. Pity. It used to be such a handy little stinger of an Anglo-Saxon outcry, but overuse had rendered it bland. Now it was a Black Forest gateau of a swear word; common as cake and completely without meaning.

She had the gift of enthusiasm which, to their parents and grand-parents' dismay, she passed on to her pupils. She was regularly accosted in the street by aggrieved mothers and fathers who believed their children were being given ideas above their station.

'Hey you, Miss O'Brien! I want a word. What's all this nonsense you're filling our Billy's head with? About being a New York cop? He's staying right here. He'll be a plumber like me. What's wrong with that?'

'Nothing, Mr Mackie. As long as it's what Billy wants.' She sighed hugely, clasping a batch of jotters to her chest. 'Mr Mackie, he's a child. He's seven. If you don't get to dream about becoming a New York cop when you're seven, when do you get to dream about it?'

Mr Mackie did not know. Cora's voice, words woven in a soft Highland accent, always stopped people in their tracks. She could be giving them a recipe for beef hash or reading the Kama-Sutra. Who cared? Just so long as she kept speaking.

Sitting by her side with the party humming round them, Ellen felt the same. She wanted Cora to keep speaking. Cora, however, was considering Ellen in close-up. She was younger than she appeared to be from a distance. Her nails were chewed. A worrier, Cora thought, and smiled at her, hauling her back from the little world she was plainly prone to drifting into when left to her own devices. Together they gazed across the room, watching the party. People in small gatherings, drinking and smiling, chatting and smiling, bitching and smiling and looking idly round checking that there was nobody more interesting, smiling more than they were.

'Here we are then,' Ellen said suddenly, 'trembling on the edge of the awesome world of jackets and haircuts.'

'Well,' said Cora, 'I don't think you need to tremble,' she stroked the sleeve of Ellen's jacket, 'not with this on. What do you do?'

'I write,' she said glumly. She hated telling people what she did. 'Write!' they'd exclaim with interest. 'Oh, what?' Then she'd have to admit that she was no Kafka, Virginia Woolf wouldn't have to roll over and Iris Murdoch had nothing to worry about, Ellen had nothing fabulous to say. She wrote comic strips.

'Oh,' said Cora. 'Who are you? What do you write?'

'I'm Ellen Quinn. I do some of Jack's strips. Two of Jack's strips.'

People nearby switched from surreptitious eavesdropping to blatant eavesdropping.

'Which ones?' Cora wanted to know. Jack Conroy had output. It seemed he never stopped working. Nobody quite knew how many strips he drew. There was from his drawing board (at which he sat, perched like a little gnome on his high draughtsman's chair) a constant outpouring of action-packed, slam, bam, kapowee exquisitely drawn stories of tumbling-haired, pouty-breasted, warm-lipped women and steel-jawed men saving the world.

'I do *Gangster Women* and *Engels of the Forest.*'

'Ah,' said Cora. She had no idea what Ellen was talking about. She had never in her life read a comic strip, and had no intention of ever doing so. But the eavesdroppers nodded amongst themselves. They'd heard of Ellen Quinn. *Gangster Women* and *Engels* weren't bad. In fact they were almost good. In the awesome world of jackets and haircuts almost good was as good as anything got.

'Do you work at Starless, then?'

'Yes. With Stanley. Do you know him?'

'We nod. Actually I know where you are because it's round the corner from where I live.'

'Really?' Ellen was pleased. 'You live in Giles Street?' This was a fine coincidence.

'With my two boys,' said Cora. 'You must drop by for coffee sometime.'

'I will,' said Ellen. Then, changing the subject because she absolutely hated talking about her work: 'Jack Conroy has a corn on his bum,'

'I know,' Cora replied smugly.

'Aha,' they said in unison and exchanged mutually knowing smirks. Ellen worked round the corner from Cora's home. They had both had intimate access to the Conroy bottom. This could be a basis for friendship. A couple of things in common. They could be chums.

It was not until this evening at this party that Ellen had considered fucking Jack Conroy as anything other than a sophisticated and rather raunchy thing to do. It was the look of loathing Jack's wife, Black Fingernails – Maureen, actually, but known as Black Fingernails because, well, she painted her fingernails black – flashed at her as she came into the room that changed her mind. She knows, Ellen thought. And flushed shame.

One day she had taken some work to him. She stood in his studio, awed by its fascinating messiness. There were jerseys, tapes and

CDs spread on the floor and the sofa. It was as if someone had opened the roof of the house and poured in a fifteen-year collection of newspapers, magazines and books. They were everywhere. There were shelves, sagging at the centre, cluttered with a vast selection of reference books, old jars filled with pens and glossy plants. His drawing board was covered by bits of paper: measurements, letters, scripts, memos, reminders, and jottings from Jack to Jack. There were rows of inks along the top, a jar of murky inky water, ceramic palettes and the floor was a thick mass of rubbings. Jack drew his strips in pencil first, inked over the approved rough, then feverishly rubbed over the finished job, removing all extraneous pencil lines. He then pulled the sleeve of his battered, stained sweat shirt down over his hand and swept all the minuscule bits of rubber from his board to the floor. He'd been doing this for years but Black Fingernails and her vacuum cleaner were never allowed into his studio. His work then, was perfect. His surroundings approached post-holocaust devastation.

'Let's have a chat,' he'd invited Ellen over the phone. But they hadn't chatted, had they? Jack Conroy's bed smelled of Musk. Jack Conroy's bed smelled of Jack Conroy's wife. Maybe that's what turned Ellen off. Maybe it was Jack Conroy's wife's silk underwear draped over the chair beside the bed. Maybe it was his breath on her face, the unashamed maleness of him. He was sure of himself, knew what he wanted. When he took her wrists and held them firm on the pillow above her head, she panicked, squirmed and kicked. 'Let go. Let go.' Then, maybe, it was that when she ran her fingers down his back, over his bum, she felt, small and hard, the corn.

'How was it for you?' she stupidly asked when they were done.

'I didn't think anybody actually asked that,' Jack said. 'You don't want an answer, do you?'

'Yes,' said Ellen.

'How was it for me? Truth or bullshit?' He was sitting on the edge of the bed casting hopefully around for his boxers which he had kicked off. Naked from the back, Ellen decided, Jack Conroy was more exciting than naked from the front. He was hairy. This man was not born, she thought. He was knitted by his grandmother on a cold day.

'Bullshit,' she said.

'There,' said Jack. 'That's how it was for me. I don't want the truth either. Good way that of telling how you're doing. When things are fine you can fearlessly face the truth. When they're not you want a little comforting bullshit.'

'I asked for bullshit,' Ellen insisted.

'Oh, the earth moved,' Jack said flatly.

Now Cora hooted a great guffaw from her tiny body that cut through the brittle and glittering socialising that was going on all around them. 'What an arse he is! A corn on the left buttock! That's what happens when you spend too long sitting at a damned drawing board doing those comic strips. He never stops, I swear. It's just little.' She indicated the size with her fingers. 'The corn I mean, ha ha.' She had fabulous nails. Ellen considered them with envy. Hers were shamefully chewed. She worried too much. When she'd nothing to worry about, she worried about worrying. It was as bad a habit as smoking.

Cora smiled at her. 'I'm Cora O'Brien. And what's that you're drinking?' she asked.

Holding up her glass Ellen said, 'White wine.'

'White wine? What sort of uptight middle-class drink is that?' Cora asked, noticing as she did that behind her dark glasses Ellen Quinn had been crying. She took the glass from Ellen's hand and, before she could protest, opened an abandoned handbag and emptied the wine into it. 'You want some vodka.'

'No I don't.' Ellen waved her hands, dismissing this suggestion. 'I can't drink spirits any more. They make me ill.'

'Nonsense.' Cora would have none of this. 'You have to learn to drink. You must master the vices. You know that if a thing is worth doing it's worth doing well. If, however, a thing is not worth doing then it's worth doing fabulously, amazingly, with grace and style and panache.'

She fetched a bottle and poured them both a huge drink.

Ellen stared at hers. 'I can't drink this. I get drunk. I get headaches. I feel wretched. I hate not being in control.'

'Ah,' said Cora. 'It isn't getting drunk you fear, then. It's getting sober again that scares the shit out of you.' She raised her glass. 'To

9

being out of control,' she said. 'Best feeling in the world.'

Ellen drank but she did not agree. 'To being in control,' she said. She knew, however, that it was not the best feeling in the world.

Chapter Two

Ellen's mother, Janine, always worried about her. Ellen was distant and secretive, like her father. There was no real knowing what went on in her head.

'Douglas was the same,' Janine said. 'He had a wayward mind. You'd be trying to talk to him about the phone bill or if the lawn needed mowing and he'd be nodding his head and agreeing but he'd be looking up at the light thinking about goodness knows what. You could never pin him down.'

Janine had a straightforward mind. She liked to think she was a straightforward sort of a person living a straightforward life. Mondays you washed. Tuesdays you ironed. Wednesdays you did the bedrooms, cleaned out the bath and polished the sideboard. Thursdays you baked and Fridays were for all the things you couldn't fit in to the rest of the week. Janine liked routine. She felt it kept her right. She had routines within her routines. Ironing: cool iron first, then hot iron. Clothes then towels, sheets, etc. She liked ironing, the rhythm of it, the comforting creak of the board. If it was Tuesday she would be ironing. If she was ironing it would be Tuesday. You knew where you were with routines.

She shook her head, thinking about Ellen and her father. She did not know how they got by. Them with their dizzy minds, dreaming and messy. She did not understand either of them. Sometimes she thought when she saw one of them gazing silently at the wall or out of the window that she would like to smack them out of their dreamings, reminding them that she was here and she was the one who did their ironing and cooked the food they ate. Then again sometimes she thought it best not knowing the nonsense that went on in those drifting minds. It would, she concluded, drive her daft.

It always surprised Ellen when she returned to the leafy,

11

suffocatingly polite Edinburgh suburb where she was brought up that as a child she had seen these streets of quiet boredom as a seething hotbed of low life, intrigue and tribal rituals.

She was convinced Mrs Paulo three doors up was a film star. And if she wasn't a film star she definitely had dazzling connections and lived the film star life. This because once Ellen had seen her standing at the window speaking on the phone. Not only did her phone have a cord long enough to stretch to the window, but it was white. A white phone – only film stars had such a thing. Ellen kept a beady young eye out, keen to spot Audrey Hepburn or Rock Hudson should they come by. She was sure they would one day. Of course they'd call first – on the white telephone.

Mr Martin, four doors down on the other side, was a spy and Mrs Robb next door to him was a witch. But better than all of that, Ellen knew beyond a shadow of a doubt that a whole Sioux tribe lived on the golf course at the end of the road. For an entire summer Ellen rode out nights to the great plains on that scrubby municipal golf course and led the Sioux nation. Nobody knew about this except, of course, in time, when she became Ellen's closest friend, Cora.

'God, Ellen,' she said when she was told, 'you must have been born stupid. I just had stupidity thrust upon me. Well, I more rushed towards it, the way you do. Marriage, men, life, children . . . and such.'

'You have never been married,' Ellen said.

'OK. Men. Life. Children. That's stupid enough. I don't go the whole hog.' Cora would not be put down or corrected.

Ellen told her everything. But then she would. She was one of those people, a puppy at heart, who had not mastered the simple art of thinking before she spoke. Dressed in black, looking shyly out at the world from behind a thick fringe, she was not as distant and dark as she seemed. Give her a crumb, give her a smile, give her a sliver of affection, a kindly word, and she was yours, she was anybody's. She was easily won. This is me, she would say. And, pouring out a pile of emotional rubble, this is my life. Look at it, what a mess. Look at this bit, I really screwed up there. She was as enthusiastic about her failures as her successes. It never really crossed her mind how judgemental people would be with the

12

information she freely dished out. That was why she was loved, if only she'd known it. Cora's outrageousness, her vividness, on the other hand, was a façade. She only told Ellen almost everything. Some of her shame, some of her rage and most of her regrets were secret. She believed in holding a little of herself back.

That summer, the summer of the Sioux, as Ellen thought of it whenever she brought it to mind, she climbed from her bedroom window almost every evening when her mother and sister were sleeping. She wore her pyjamas under her dark blue, elastic-waisted corduroy trousers and hand-knitted polo-neck jersey, her playing clothes. On her gleaming black horse, Thunder, she trotted under sodium lights down the middle of Wakefield Avenue, reins jingling, saddle creaking. Thunder was, of course, part of that play. He was only real to her. Beloved imaginary horse, for that small part of her life he was the only thing she could cling to. The only thing she allowed to be real to her. Her father had just died. As she went she sang songs of the day, favourite tunes from the radio. She listened to her own whisperings, 'Hey Jude, too-ti-too-ti-too.'

It was one of the silliest things she ever did. But when you're eight and the Sioux are waiting on the eighteenth green, danger is the great iron horse steaming over your hunting grounds, the long knives, the rolling wagon trains of white men who do not know the ways of the buffalo. It is a mountain lion, a renegade Pawnee, nothing that would faze someone mighty and wise, who does not realise she is only eight summers tall, and who has the ear of Sitting Bull himself.

'I was happy then,' she'd say wistfully to herself in those mindless moments when, idle-brained, she'd be washing the supper dishes, or just vacantly staring out of the window. Then she'd draw herself up sharply. 'No I was not.' Of course she wasn't. When a child takes to wandering a golf course at night with a whole tribe of imaginary companions something is wrong, very wrong indeed.

Thinking back it seemed like another time, when she'd been another person – the human being she was before Cora was in her life, before Daniel, Emily Boyle and Chippy Norton. Chippy, of course, was only a figment of her imagination. But of all the characters she created he was her favourite, and he was also the

13

most successful. So in his fat, dreamy and fictional way, he was the most important of all. It was he who paid the rent, bought all the clothes, footed the grocery and fuel bills and kept Ellen in French cigarettes and Russian booze.

It started in March. Daniel Quinn was a long time into her future, she was Ellen Davidson then. She remembered the night her father died well. Every moment, every look – her mother's furrowed concern, her sister's goody-goody smirk as she finished every scrap of her liver and wiped the plate clean so that now she could have her almond slice; every sound – the muted babble of the television her sister, Rosalind, had left beaming into the empty living room up the hall, the clatter of pots in the kitchen; every scent – burned liver, that fresh air smell of just-ironed clothes – was with her always. It was a snapshot, mindbite memory she could take out and relive whenever she was low and needed to go even lower.

It was Tuesday. Tuesday in the little two-bedroom bungalow in Wakefield Avenue was liver and a bath. Ellen hated liver and always ate slowly, carefully cutting the dread meat into tiny bits and shifting them about her plate, waiting for her mother to leave the table. Then, with her disapproving sister watching, she would with one swift practised move empty the liver into the plastic bag she always kept handy on Tuesdays. She'd scrunch it into a little roll and shove it up her jersey. It lay warm against her tummy. Later she would bury it in the garden. Even now the sight of liver lying flaccid, bleeding slightly on the butcher's slab, could cause her to retch.

Her father came home late that day. Still wearing his tweed car coat he slumped on the armchair by the fire that was his armchair and nobody else's, complaining that his head hurt.

Her mother laid his liver on the table and looked at him, with furrow-browed concern. 'You won't be wanting your supper, then?'

He shook his head.

'Go wash the dishes, Ellen,' her mother ordered. Ellen protested. She'd cleared the liver from her plate, eaten the regulation piece of bread and was planning to have an almond slice. 'Wash the dishes,' her mother ordered in that final flat voice mummies had when no arguing would be tolerated.

Ellen went into the kitchen, filled the sink with hot water and washing-up liquid, and started to play submarines with the plates and a cup. The cup, pink with a thin gold rim, was the enemy lurking in the deep, waiting for the innocent plate to pass overhead. It would strike. Boom, whoosh. Torpedoes on the port side. The liver in the bag was getting cold as she pressed against the sink keeping it in place. She would have to get rid of it.

'For heaven's sake, Ellen, can't you do anything properly?' Her mother came into the kitchen and, shoving her from the sink, took over. 'Go have a bath.'

'But it's early. What about my programme? I want to see my programmes on television.'

'Have a bath.'

Her father groaned. She watched him as she passed on her way to the bathroom. His face was grimly grey under a filmy sweat. He had just been sick. His head lolled back, mouth slightly open. He held his hand on his chest, his breathing sounded pained, rattled in his chest. He looked at her and called her, ' . . . Um.' He always called her that. There were so many little girls running around his house – his daughters, his daughters' friends, neighbours' children – he lost track of them. He knew of course that Ellen was his. But he was weary. His job took all of him. So he couldn't always single out her name from the mass of little girl names that flooded into his mind whenever he saw her.

' . . . Um . . .' he said. That was the last time she saw him.

She filled the bath, dutifully took off her clothes and folded them according to her mother's strict guidelines. Janine Davidson's great achievement in life was the acquisition of a bungalow. One hundred and ninety-two Wakefield Avenue was a bungalow in a mystifying maze of post-war bungalows and from the time she and Douglas moved in, Janine had spent all her time and energy living up to the sanctified respectability she imagined was the stuff of bungalowees. She was too rigid with the fear of getting found out – found out that she was from poor working-class stock, from tenement housing, and shouldn't really be living in this hallowed, badly heated, insufferably clean little house – to relax and enjoy her life, her family.

15

There was, then, according to Ellen's mother, a right way and a wrong way to do everything. In the Davidson household everything was done the right way, even folding of the clothes prior to getting into the bath.

Ellen hid the liver under the perfect pile. Now she wouldn't be able to bury it in the garden. She'd hide it in her schoolbag and drop it in a litter bin on the way to school. Her tummy gurgled. She was hungry. She thought longingly of her almond slice still on the table, waiting for her to come to claim it. Still, baths were good. She resumed her game of submarines. The sponge was the enemy waiting in the rocks – her left knee – for the face cloth carrying a load of bananas and sugar cane to sail by.

'Hello, Dr Phillips? Mrs Davidson here, a hundred and ninety-two Wakefield Avenue . . .' Ellen heard her mother's voice. It was her posh voice, the one she used for the doctor and the insurance man who came by on Thursdays.

Ellen liked her address. It rhymed. One hundred and ninety-two Wakefield Avenue. A wide street, well lit. A row of houses amidst rows and rows and streets and streets of houses all the same. Wakefield Avenue was posh though; it led onto the golf course.

'It's my husband, Douglas. He's not well. He's having trouble breathing and . . . yes . . . in his chest. Thank you. The house is on the right-hand side of the road, just past the bus stop . . .'

Dr Phillips would come in his Jaguar. Ellen held her breath, something was happening. If you held your breath when things happened people forgot you were there and you could watch the grown-ups being grown-up. She was Ellen Davidson, she was eight years old, she had straight browny-black hair, brown eyes and a small face. Her favourite person in all the world was Burt Lancaster. Her favourite things were a luminous yo-yo that shone in the dark and a bumper book of the countryside. But the thing she wanted most was a horse. If she only had one she'd be happy, and she'd never ever ask for anything else ever again. Every year she wrote to Santa asking for a shiny black stallion, but she never got one. Every Christmas morning she would run through to the living room and peer into the garden. 'Please let it be there. Please.' She dreamed it would be standing on the lawn, just behind the lilac tree, black and

16

magnificent, pawing the ground, snorting and waiting for her to come to him. She would call him Thunder.

'Ellen, we can't possibly have a horse,' her mother repeatedly told her. 'Where would we keep it?'

'In the garden. In the shed when it rains. It could fit in beside the lawnmower. I'd look after it. Brush it. Ride it. I'd ride it on the golf course.'

Every Christmas she and her mother went through this dialogue. Every Christmas Ellen hoped wildly and every Christmas her mother sighed. She would disappoint her daughter yet again. Games compendiums, new frocks, a dolls' house, a little pocket radio – nothing, absolutely nothing would ever be as good as that black horse, glistening and tossing its mane out past the lilac tree.

The doctor arrived. Ellen heard him booming down the hall. Why did doctors have such big voices? She held her breath. She could hold it for a count of two hundred and forty-seven, though the last sixty or so had to be rattled through, top speed. This would be handy should she ever have to hide underwater from renegade Pawnees.

'An ambulance, please.' The doctor was on the phone, using their phone. Would he have to put the money in the little box like Mrs McKenzie across the road when she phoned her mother in Inverness every Sunday afternoon? ' . . . a hundred and ninety-two Wakefield Avenue. Heart attack . . .'

Ellen looked at her fingers. They'd gone all white and wrinkly. The water was cold, but she was scared to get out. She didn't want to appear at the bathroom door in the middle of all the fuss. They wouldn't want her there. Best stay put. She stopped her intricate little sponge and face cloth games and sat absolutely still, listening. She could hear herself breathing here in the bathroom, hollow, throaty against the damp. Further off, house noises: the television, the pipes clanking. Somewhere in the distance a dog barked, Mrs Barr next door came out, put some rubbish in the bin, slammed the lid down and went back into her kitchen. Ellen was getting goose pimples. It was cold in here.

'I wish I had a horse,' she said. 'I wish, I wish, I wish . . .'

The ambulance arrived. The doorbell rang. Her mother went out.

Ellen heard the fuss, the rush of footsteps thumping down the hall. Ten steps it was from the front door to the living room. It never changed. She counted every day.

'Davidson? Ambulance. Where is he . . . ?'

'Down the hall . . . down the hall . . .'

They left the front door open and the chill rushed in under the bathroom door. Ellen shivered. She imagined the ambulance outside in the dark, light whirling, flashing blue across the night into neighbours' living rooms. They'd come to their windows to watch surreptitiously. 'Something going on at a hundred and ninety-two.'

She heard the stretcher being carried back out the door, down the path. The ambulance men would be big. Her mother said she'd go with them. 'I'll get my coat and bag.' She sounded strange. 'Rosalind, look after Ellen. See she goes to bed. And go to bed yourself at ten o'clock. I don't know when I'll be back.'

'Where is Ellen?'

'Oh goodness, in the bath. She's been in the bath all this time.' Bang bang bang on the bathroom door. 'Are you all right, Ellen?'

'Yes,' small, squeaky voice.

'I'm going in the ambulance with Dad. You go to bed. Do what Rosalind says.' Her sister would bully her. She'd have to be careful with the liver.

Shivering Ellen climbed from her bath, dried herself. She went to bed without saying her prayers.

Every night Janine Davidson insisted her daughters pray before sleeping. It was what respectable people did. Every night, then, she reinforced in Ellen the conviction she was going to die before morning.

> Each night as I lie down to sleep
> I pray the Lord my soul to keep.
> If I should die before I wake
> Take me to heaven for Jesus' sake.

Alone in her bedroom, muted noises of living-room life sounding through the wall, Ellen would lie waiting for death to come for her.

Death was a man in a hat with a thin moustache, glittering cruel
eyes, pointy two-tone shoes and a little black, gleamy gun that he
would use to shoot her. Or, he might strangle her with his strong,
black-gloved hands. And death was a lady in a white dress that
rustled in the hall just beyond the bedroom door. She had a thin and
taunting face, white like her frock. In her hand she held a silver
stiletto that she would plunge into Ellen's heart shrieking, 'Die. Die.
Die, child. Die.' Ellen spent the hours between bedtime and
morning in a state of terror. She slept with the blankets over her
head so that when death came it would take her unawares. She
would not hear the approaching tiptoe of pointy two-toned shoes or
the abominable rustle of the silken white frock.

Her mother got home after midnight. She stood leaning against
the door, stark, ashen. Her face had been painfully stripped of its
old expressions and stamped deeply with a new look of shock,
horror and grief.

'He's dead,' she said, leaning forward, clutching herself. 'Your
father is dead.' She started to cry, deep, deep sobs. She couldn't
breathe. Her shoulders shook and she gulped air with a huge
sniffing, yelping sound, like an animal. In their pyjamas, still warm
from sleeping, Ellen and Rosalind watched. Ellen froze. She didn't
know mothers did that. She didn't know mothers hurt, cried.
Hesitantly, she stepped forward to put her arm round her. But her
mother, face streaked with sorrow and sudden surprising loathing,
looked at her.

'Not you,' she spat, shaking her head. 'Not you. I don't want
you.'

It was dark in the hall, cold. Rosalind stepped forward and
pulled their mother to her. 'Sssh,' she said. And, 'It's all right.'
Cradling her. Rocking her. Patting her. The unnerving yelping
stopped, calmed into weeping. The two locked in that embrace
walked down the hall, disappeared into the living room.

Ellen stayed alone in the dark, her private chaos fixed on her face,
small, shiny with the need to please, creased with anxiety. She felt
her flesh crawl. Self-loathing moved through her, over her. She
wasn't loved, her mummy didn't want her. Should she stay here for
ever in the dark and cold or go into the living room? She didn't

know what to do. An icy draught swept under the front door. She shifted slightly from chilled foot to chilled foot. She looked hopelessly down at her arms and at her unwanted body. Then went back to bed. Her life hinged on this moment. It shamed her, and she couldn't bring herself to tell anybody about it.

Later, much much later, when all the crying and mumbling and chinking of teacups was over and her mother and sister were sleeping, Ellen rose. She took the crumpled bag of liver from amongst her clothes and crept out of the window to bury it in the garden. What with her father dying and her mother not wanting her and everything, she thought she'd better get rid of it quickly. If her mother found it now it'd be too much. Goodness knows what she'd do. It was a perfect night – a thousand stars in the sky and the lawn frosty under her feet. Ellen stood in her pyjamas and blue furry slippers and looked about in wonderment. She hadn't known that as she curled in terror under the blankets all this was out here, waiting for her. It was not scary here.

She fetched a trowel from the garden shed and dug a small hole on the far side of the lilac tree that was not visible from the living-room window. She entombed her guilty parcel in it and smoothed it over, patting the loose earth down. There, now nobody would ever know. She turned round and that's when Thunder came to her.

Had anyone been watching they would have seen a little girl in blue polka-dot pyjamas standing on tiptoe in furry slippers in a small, frighteningly tidy garden. They would have seen her stretch out her arms in ecstatic greeting into the chill empty air, patting and stroking nothing, nothing at all. They would have had to have seen the world through Ellen's eyes, been part of her little world, to know that she was embracing the love of her life, a muscled and magnificent black stallion that gently stamped the perfectly mown, immaculately edged lawn.

Prancing across the garden, gleaming and gorgeous, mane tossing, he came to her. Snorting gently he nuzzled her and she put her arms round his neck and kissed him. His mouth was velvet, shoving gently into her hand. She loved him and he loved her, only her and nobody else – ever. Nobody knew. Nobody in the whole world knew the friend she had.

Chapter Three

Sometimes Ellen ran through her life, the edited lowlights, a series of ifs. If she had not been such a harum-scarum child, running about the golf course at night on a pretend horse, she might have been more alert during school hours. If she'd been more alert during school hours she might have developed the habit of paying attention to what her teachers were saying. If she'd paid attention to her teachers she might have passed more exams and left school with a few more qualifications than she did. If she'd had more qualifications she would have been able to get a better job than the one she got in the stationery and book department of a large store. If she had not got that job she would not have started reading the comics they sold and she would not have met her friends and soul sisters Karen, Sharon, Alice and Katy. If she had not met them, she would not have thought up *Gangster Women*, her first comic strip creation – 'Hit the streets, Gangster Women, we have sisters to avenge' – and sent it to Stanley Macpherson, sole proprietor of Starless Enterprises, entrepreneur and dreamer, and she would not have been given a job writing science fiction scripts. If she had not been given a job, she and Stanley would not have been lunching in the Oyster Bar, and she would not have noticed Daniel Quinn leaning on the bar, staring at her. If she had not gone through the small flirtatious routine of noticing him noticing her, then pretending not to notice him noticing her, he would not have come across to chat and she would not have gone out with him that night, gone to bed with him that night, married him six weeks later and lived through years of absurdities, guilt, swearing, good sex, bad sex and long convoluted arguments that he always won. She would not have been the constant butt of his energy and fury or witness to his frenetic search. Search for what? Neither of them knew.

Sometimes Ellen thought that all she was searching for in life was another moment to match those of sheer joy she'd known that summer, the summer of the Sioux.

She first slipped out for another meeting on the lawn with Thunder on the night of her father's funeral. She brought him a piece of shortbread and a salmon sandwich, which she ate herself. Next night she went again to find him. Then a couple of nights later she slipped out again. By that time she was becoming addicted to her late-night sorties. Every night she lay in bed resisting the temptation of the night outside her window, the stars, the soft spring grass, the fabulous horse. Every night she gave in to it, till at last she was lost in her fantasy.

When Thunder became real to her, she thought that the little lawn was not big enough for him. After all, he lived a secret patient life waiting by the side of the house for her to come home from school. He needed a larger expanse of grass, somewhere to gallop. It seemed natural to trot out of the garden gate, down the street to the golf course. Once there she took the horse at a canter, then a gallop down the fairways and across the putting greens. She moved further and further into her dreams. Once when she was riding she turned round and there they were, the Sioux. Feathered and proud on painted ponies, they were gathered behind her. She was not alone. She had a whole tribe of warriors with her, looking after her. She was quite safe now. After that they were always there. Ellen painted her own body with her mother's lipstick and eye shadow, red and blue whorls and daubs that spelled out the story of her life: her father, the mighty chief's, glorious death; her tepee with her mother; her sister; the smack she'd got from her teacher because she was always falling asleep in class. With the night life she had it was hardly surprising she dropped off in the classroom. But she could not resist the night. Bareback and semi-naked she rode, arms spread into the air, yelling and whooping. She was a little girl, tamed and house-trained in the daytime, feral at night. A wildness came reeling from the depth of her and as she galloped across the summer grass it turned to exultation. When she was grown-up and returning to the scene of her imaginings, Ellen would stare out over the golf course and long to know such uninhibited freedom again.

22

* * *

After her father died Ellen's family became dowdy. Or rather dowdier. They drifted into a quietly harmonious gloom. It was undemanding and it suited them. Though they ate supper at the same time they would have, had they been waiting for him to come home from work, mostly they carried on as if Douglas Davidson had not existed in the first place. They never spoke about him. Only sometimes, at four or five in the morning when Ellen was arriving home after her adventures with the Sioux, she heard, drifting sorrowfully from her mother's bedroom, the muffled sound of sobbing. But in time even that stopped.

Her mother found solace in a dreary culinary routine: Monday stew, Tuesday liver, Wednesday mince, Thursday mince again and Friday fish – though they weren't Catholic. Saturday they heated a pie and Sunday was roast beef. The house became bleak, comfortless. They came together over Janine's grim meals. The woman had the knack of taking good nutritious food and turning it into cardboard. 'Set the table, Ellen,' she would call.

Ellen would obediently leave the television. Put on the tablecloth. Then forks and knives at each place, salt and pepper in the middle and sugar and milk at the head of table, where the man sits, though the man didn't sit there any more. Nobody was going to take his place. They ate and they rarely spoke except to say things like, 'The fish is good.' 'Better than last week.' 'Tasty.'

Then, and now, Ellen couldn't understand such conversations. Why talk about boring fish when there were so many fabulous things in the world to discuss? She couldn't, of course, tell her mother and sister about the movement of the buffalo on the golf course, or the heron frozen still on one leg silently waiting for eels that swam the great water beside the bunker at the tenth hole, or the wild ponies, or the war dances or the furious gallops on Thunder over the prairie. But there were other things.

Clutching her fork, she leaned over the table, little eyes gleaming deep in her small, pale face. She had the mark of an unfed and sleepless child. Her mother, however, was too absorbed in her mourning to notice. There was so much Ellen wanted to say, so many stories from the little life she led after school finished and

23

before supper was served she was desperate to share, she did not notice her jersey trailing in her ketchup.

'Jumper,' her mother said, waving an exasperated hand at the little indiscretion. Ellen stared down at the gaudy stain and lifting her jersey to her mouth sucked it clean. Her mother sighed in despair. That child would be the death of her.

Ellen shrank into herself, hiding from the disapproval and hiding, too, who she really was, her thoughts. Now they would never know the things she knew. Mr Martin was a spy – she was sure of it. She'd seen him one day last summer in dark glasses and a white hat. And Mrs Robb across the road was a witch. How could she tell her mother these things? Her mother did not want her. Best keep quiet. Best not make a pest of herself.

Ellen had discovered she could crawl into Mrs Robb's back garden through a hole in the hedge. She spent hours huddled behind the gooseberry bushes watching the old lady bustling about her kitchen. She imagined she was cleverly hidden. But, of course, Mrs Robb knew she was there. Poor child, she thought, I hate to think of the nonsense that's going on in her head. She knew Ellen. She had seen Ellens before. She was a small, underfed suburban waif who rode everywhere on a glorious pretend horse. Nobody cuddled her, nobody tucked her up at night. And nobody had ever told her she mattered.

Looking back on it, and she wasted a deal of time looking back, recriminating, regretting, Ellen realised that crouching low in Mrs Robb's garden and riding out at night was when she started inventing lives for other people and for herself. That must have been the beginning of me – this me that I am now, she thought. But then she was prone to sudden bouts of indulgent self-examination.

The three lived separate lives. Janine Davidson disappeared into her head, coping with her grief and guilt, mourning the man she married, chastising herself for not knowing him better, not trying to understand or communicate with him more. Ellen rode out on her beloved Thunder, and Rosalind, seven years older than her sister, discovered sex. She was, then, the only sane one in the house. Friday and Saturday nights she would come home, her neck covered with lovebites.

24

'What a mess, Ellen. I told him not to do that. Don't tell Mum.'
The only sisterly thing she ever did was show Ellen how to reduce
the glaring redness by rubbing the lovebites gently with Janine's
Nivea cream, then covering them with pan stick makeup. Ellen sat
on the bath watching. This was fascinating. What she longed to
know, but didn't dare ask, was, how did they get there? And why?

What she did know was that it was part of the huge secret that
her mother knew and her sister knew and all the smart and popular
people in the playground knew and she didn't. Oh, what a tortured
soul Ellen was then. And oh, what a tortured soul she was still.

Chapter Four

Every day after school Ellen rode to where Mrs Robb's garden backed on to the golf course. Leaving Thunder tethered to the flagpole on the second hole, she squeezed through the gap in the hedge to do some spying. She was keen to spot some actual witchery, spells in the making. Maybe there was a cauldron in the kitchen where toads were stewing nicely with nettles, slugs, cat's spit and school dinners. Blech. Sometimes she craned up hoping to catch a glimpse of a pointy hat or a broom, though she knew for a fact not all witches had such things. Perhaps this was the sort of witch who stuck needles into little dolls whilst chanting in a scary drone. Maybe she could make things move just by glaring at them.

To her surprise Mrs Robb grew fond of the little solemn face peeking from behind the gooseberry bush. Ellen was a skinny child peering at the world from under a thick dark fringe. Her hands and feet were large. She was going to be tall and needed feeding. Mrs Robb could see that. Though she warned herself that no good, no good at all, would come from interfering, she decided a few scones and some chocolate cake of an afternoon would not go amiss.

She lured the girl into her garden as she lured bluetits and sparrows, with titbits. Ellen found small brightly wrapped parcels hanging from the gooseberry bush, like baubles on a Christmas tree, waiting for her when she took up her daily vigil. At first they confirmed her suspicions. Aha, she thought, a trick, some sort of witchy ploy. I'm not falling for that. Next day there was another parcel. And the next, and the next. In time they became irresistible. She opened one and found three sweets glistening in transparent purple wrappings. She wouldn't eat, though. They might make her float above the ground gushing fountains of sick. Oh yes, she was a match for any witch, any time. But there the sweets were, lying in her hand, chocolate-covered and overwhelmingly tempting. She unwrapped one and slowly put it into her mouth, then lay back on the ground watching the world turn purple through the paper.

Each day, then, she went to the garden, and each day a new surprise, brightly wrapped and tied with gold ribbon, was waiting for her. She crouched low, sucking home-made toffee or chocolate fudge, patiently waiting for witchy doings, breathing in the brown smell of earth, listening to the sounds of the suburbs; a dog barking, blackbirds in neighbouring gardens, Mrs Rush two doors down taking in her washing, Mr Johnson noisily revving his car engine, distant children playing. Ellen knew everything that everybody did. On chilly spring afternoons she watched her breath splay out into the late frosty air as she whispered her favourite word. The one her sister said when she dropped her lipstick down the lavatory. Over and over she said it. 'Bugger.' It was a fabulous word. 'Buggery-buggerybuggerybug.'

She listened to the sounds of the golf course. Two golfers in checked trousers and tweedy caps strode by trundling their trolleys, discussing their game. Far across the fairways she heard a wagon train roll, the whistle and shout of drivers encouraging tired horses. It's a might late for 'em to be movin', she thought. They ought to be getting bedded down. Get some fires lit. Let the wimmen folk rustle up some beans an' coffee.

A group of boys going home, dragging sticks, passed nearby. She could hear their strange conversation. Boys were tricky. You never could understand what they were talking about. They seemed to provide their own soundtrack when they spoke. 'Then the black car spun over and over, eeeee, boom, spadoom . . .'

A lone brave rode slowly by, a deer slung over his horse. They'll be mighty glad to see that back at camp, Ellen thought.

The world was budding, too cold still for blossoms. Ellen looked at the buds on the gooseberry bush, and on the silver birch tree by the fence. Little greening knobs waiting to happen. Did it hurt? Did plants breathe and cry like the women she'd seen in cowboy films on Sunday afternoons on the telly? 'There ain't time to git her to the doctor. The baby's acomin' now. Fetch some whisky an' boil up water, and jes' keep it comin'. We'll be aneedin' plenty of it. Give her somethin' to bite on.' There'd be a close up of the mother-to-be's face, twisted in agony. She'd be gripping the brass bed, knuckles white, sweat dripping from her face. Her hair would be matted. Then the action would switch to the father, walking anxiously to and fro whilst his wife screamed from the birthin' bed. Screamed and screamed and screamed. Ellen wasn't going to do that. Oh no. She was never going to have a baby, never ever. It was nippy. It hurt. It hurt worse than getting the strap at school or falling down on your knee. She did not like, even, the idea of growing up. Becoming a woman frightened her. Did it mean she'd be like her mother? Would she have to wear a girdle? And curlers in bed? No. No. No.

After a week of shiny little gifts, Mrs Robb knocked on the window. Ellen froze. She was not expecting this. Obviously the witch knew she was out here spying, but she didn't think she would ever actually speak to her. Also, she was beginning to suspect Mrs Robb of being disappointingly ordinary. But you never knew with grown-ups, especially witchy ones. The witch held up a plate of chocolate cake and beckoned her in. Ellen knew she shouldn't go. Her mother often told her to beware of strangers. But a look round the witch's kitchen, a chance finally to see if there was a cauldron or a black cat or anything witchy at all, was too good to miss. Besides, the chocolate cake looked like real chocolate cake, large and fluffy with proper icing on top and gooey stuff in the middle. It was the sort of thing children in storybooks ate and was also, therefore, too good to miss.

It was a strange kitchen, not at all like the one at home. Gleaming copper pots hung from a beam above a white Aga. Ellen's mother cooked on a three-ring Belling using two big pots, one little pot, a chip pan and a frying pan for everything. Here the walls were lined with shelves, cluttered with rows of blue and white plates, jugs and bowls. Cups hung in perfect order from neatly spaced hooks. But there was no sign of anything evil. Ellen peered round. There were no dubious brewings, no toads, no foul-smelling weeds, no tiny bottles of rancid liquid. She'd hoped there might be a huge book of spells, ancient, leather-bound, stained with years of dire spillages; rat's blood, horn of unicorn, eye of crow sort of thing. But no, the house smelled of lavender polish and baking. Ellen felt let down. This woman led a warm and comfortable life. How dare she?

'Is this a potion?' Ellen asked at last.

'A potion?' Mrs Robb looked mildly surprised. 'It's tea. Tea and chocolate cake.'

Milky tea lapping in a wide-brimmed blue and white cup, a glistening slab of cake – such treats, such riches, such difficult crockery. It would need two small hands to steady such a vessel from saucer to lips. Should she, though, drink the witch's brew? Eat the witch's fare? What might it do to her? Turn her into a hat stand or a creepy-crawly? Then what would happen? Would anybody miss her? She would go bustling home tiny, so tiny it would take a week to cross the road, and nobody would know she was there.

'Where's that child?' her mother would snap. 'She hasn't been home for four weeks. Well, we'll just have to sell her bed and forget all about her.'

'But I'm here. This is me in the larder,' Ellen would say smally, voice whisper-shrill vanishing unheard into the air around her, tears in her eyes. But nobody would know it was her. They'd stamp on her or chase her out into the cold waving brooms and pokers.

'So,' said the witch sitting opposite her, 'why do you spend so much time in my gooseberry bushes?' Her voice was deep and old, cracked with use. Like her cups, Ellen thought.

'I'm watching,' she said.

'Watching what?'

'You know. Everything that has to be watched. Birds, starlings.'

'Ah. I see.'

'Don't you get scared?' Ellen asked suddenly. 'On your own?'

Mrs Robb shook her head. 'I like my own company.'

'Don't you have children? A husband?'

Mrs Robb shook her head again. Her children were long gone, they rarely came to see her, and her husband died over ten years ago.

'I get scared when I'm alone in the dark,' Ellen confessed. 'At night there's people coming to kill me.'

'Nonsense.'

'No. Not nonsense. You don't know. I'm alone, aloner than anything.' Out riding with the Sioux she wasn't alone. She was lonesome. There was a difference. 'There's a lady in white and a man in a hat. Sometimes they fight about who is going to do it. "Let me," says the lady,' Ellen shrilled her voice, ' "No, me," says the man,' a deep voice for the man, chin down. ' "You did it last night. It's my turn." '

'Goodness,' said Mrs Robb, reaching over to pat the child's hand. 'You need a brave.'

'A brave?'

'Yes, lots of people have them. A guardian angel who looks after you. Imagine him standing at the end of your bed, arms folded whilst you fall asleep, and promising to stay watching over you all night.'

That night Chief Golfing Moon stood at the end of her bed. Ellen did not fight to stay awake watching out for manic murderers or waiting till it was time to ride. She slept deeply from eight thirty at night to seven in the morning. Maybe it was the brave keeping her safe. Or maybe it was Amy Robb's magic potion – food.

All summer Ellen rode on Thunder. 'Ellen, for goodness' sake will you stop galumphing about on a pretend horse,' her mother chastised. 'Soon you'll be nine. You're an embarrassment.'

Ellen shamefully looked at her feet, scuffed tennis shoes. Soon as she left the house she heaved herself on to Thunder, yanked the reins and headed off.

Summer evenings she was allowed out after supper. She trotted up Wakefield Avenue along Wakefield Road to North Broadway. She loved that name, Broadway. This could be America. Maybe one day she'd see Ben E. King with his steel guitar that he could play so he'd be a star on Broadway. But it wasn't just the name attracted her. There was the chip shop. Ellen spent evenings Gene Kellying round the lamppost outside it, utterly happy. The air was magic, the scent of chips in the making mingling with the roaring jangle of early sixties favourites on the juke box: 'Da Doo Ron Ron', 'Leader of the Pack', 'Then He Kissed Me'. Ellen swung and sang along. 'Met him on a Monday . . . too-ti-too . . .' But her constant waif-like presence annoyed Enrico Ross, the owner.

'Go away. You can't hang about here. You're putting off my customers.'

Ellen hung her head.

'Piss off. I'll tell your dad.' Enrico waved her away.

'Don't have a dad.'

'OK. I'll tell your mum.'

'Don't have a mum. They're dead. In a car crash. My leg got hurt.' She began to limp. 'I have to go into hospital to get it fixed.' She was tempted to tell him that she was going to have it sawn off, but realised that would stop her coming. He would notice the leg was not missing. And, she would miss that fabulous vinegary waft and thick blast of Detroit music. 'They're putting a pin in it.'

Enrico felt terrible. How could he tell such a tragic infant to piss off? He believed her. Pale, thin child looking up at him. She had too much hair and was growing out of her clothes.

A tear slid down Ellen's cheek. She believed herself. She could imagine the crash vividly. The car was overturned, a pool of petrol spread across the road. Her father lay crushed behind the wheel and her mother, who had been thrown clear, was lying splayed out, arms wide, legs apart, clutching her best black handbag. She was wearing her green coat with the velvet collar buttoned to the neck. Her mouth was wide open. She had a faint look of surprise on her face.

'Hey,' said Enrico, 'have some chips. On the house, OK? Good for the leg.'

Ellen took them. They were hot in her hand. She was a poor orphan child, and was almost too choked with grief to eat them. Grief and giggles. She thought something hugely funny about the vision of her mother spread-eagled on the tarmac, astonished and, well, dead. Heartened at the chip coup she decided to go see her new best pal, Mrs Robb.

They had formed, Ellen and Mrs Robb, an instant and deep understanding, isolated child, lonely old lady. They fell easily into a little pally world of private jokes and small secrets. 'Come,' Mrs Robb would say, 'put on my other apron and we'll bake flapjacks.' Or, 'Let's put crumbs out for the birds.' Then she and Ellen would sit by the window watching the squabbles on the bird table and making up stories about ebullient sparrows and cheeky bluetits. Mrs Robb knew of Ellen's desperate struggle with long division and her constant failure to leap over the horse at gym.

'No mind,' she'd comfortingly pat Ellen's shoulder. 'Albert Einstein couldn't leap a horse as far as I know. And I'm absolutely certain neither could James Dean, Maria Callas, Leonardo da Vinci or Dostoevsky or—'

'Who?'

'Never mind. Just know that leaping a horse is no sign of future achievement. In fact, I'd go so far as to say those who can leap a horse at nine may well be peaking. This could be as far as they go. Downhill from now on for them, I'm afraid.' Ellen had no idea what she was talking about, but knew it was heartening. She wasn't the failure she thought she was.

Tonight the garden was silent. The house was still, deserted. This is a new sort of quiet, Ellen thought, creepy. She licked her salty lips and wiped the grease from her hands on the seat of her pants before setting off across the lawn. She crouched. You never knew. This sort of silence needed careful investigation. She peeped into the kitchen window. Mrs Robb sat in the chair by the Aga. Ellen knocked heartily on the pane and waved. Mrs Robb did not move. Must be sleeping, Ellen decided and rapped more heartily. Still nothing. Ellen pressed her face to the glass. Mrs Robb stared ahead. She did not see her. She did not, Ellen realised, see anything. Her arm dangled by her side. She seemed strange, all lop-sided. Dead, Ellen thought, tremblings starting in her stomach, tears glazing her eyes. Damned folks are always dying.

She knew enough to get help, but didn't dare fetch her mother. 'What are you doing sneaking about other people's gardens?' she would say. She ran next door and rang Mr Martin, the spy's, doorbell. Together they peered into Mrs Robb's kitchen.

'I'll have to call the police,' the spy said. Then he shocked her deeply. He turned and snapped, 'You bugger off.' There was that word – bugger, bugger. Fancy a grown-up actually saying it. As she turned towards her bolt hole in the hedge Mr Martin, suddenly, as if he had been waiting to get hold of her, said, 'I see you. I see you running about this golf course at night. What do you think happens to little girls who do things like that? Silly little cunt.'

It was the worst word she'd ever heard. It curdled into the

33

evening and hung between them, still ringing with the coarseness
and malice in his voice. Ellen fled. But that word – it penetrated her
innocence. She instinctively knew she could not ask her mother
what it meant.

She watched the departure of Mrs Robb from her front room
window. The police came and broke down the door. Shortly after,
an ambulance sirened down the avenue. She wondered if it was the
same one that took her daddy away. There was fuss and people in
uniform being important. And then they brought out her friend on
a stretcher, cosily tucked, Ellen thought, in a bright red blanket. She
could see that the old lady's face was not covered. 'Not dead, then,'
she comforted herself. That, however, was the last time she ever
saw her.

A few days later, she overheard her mother discussing the
business with a neighbour. 'A stroke,' they said, shaking their
heads. 'She'd been sitting there all day till Mr Martin found her.
Poor old soul.' Ellen didn't like that. Mrs Robb, she knew, wasn't,
never would be, a poor old soul. In time, though, Mrs Robb's family
turned up and emptied the house of all its treasures – the blue and
white cups, everything. In time new people moved in. Ellen didn't
like them. Whoever they were, she didn't like them.

She was a Jesus-stricken child, Ellen. There were Bible readings
in class first thing on weekday mornings, and on Sundays she was
sent out, buttoned and polished, in her best clothes to Sunday
school. Hardly a day passed, then, that she was not warned that the
Lord was watching her, knew all her thoughts and deeds. There
was no doubt then about who'd been spying when she'd lied to the
chip shop man and giggled at the thought of her mother lying
hugely splayed out on the road. The big Who, that was who. And
now He'd smote down Mrs Robb as a punishment. That was what
He did. He was always smiting folk. He worked in mysterious ways
and she felt awful about it, just awful. It was quite obvious. She'd
done a terrible thing. She'd sinned, a right piece of sinning and Mrs
Robb had copped the blame. Poor old bugger. At night she lay in
bed wondering about Mrs Robb and wondering if Mrs Robb,
wherever she was, lay in bed wondering about her.

Then there was the Sioux. She hadn't been out to see them for weeks now. She was torn in two about all her imaginary friends. She knew, of course, that they were not there. But at the same time she thought they might be missing her.

It was round about then she started to stammer. It had been bad at first, a fierce impediment which put a panicked, gasping gulf between what was in Ellen's mind and what was on her lips. Red of face and shaking with frustration and embarrassment, she would stumble and stop at hard letters and sounds. 'P-P-Pass the salt, pl-pl-pl . . .' That, and her skin, which began to flake and scruff from her face and hands, made her the object of a deal of horrible, hurtful whispering in the school playground. Her mother took her to the doctor.

'Has she been under any stress lately?' he asked.

'No,' Janine told him. 'Well, her father died. But that was months ago and to tell the truth she showed no signs of upset when it happened. And now she's started wetting the bed, too.'

'Delayed shock,' the doctor nodded. 'You never can tell with children. You just don't know how they turn things about in their little minds.' They spoke about Ellen as if she wasn't there. As if she wasn't real. Ellen watched them exchange views about her, little head moving back and forth, as if she was at a tennis match.

'Don't worry,' the doctor said. 'It'll pass. Vitamin C and time. Great healers, you know. She'll grow out of it.'

That was the sort of doctor he was. The age of him, the times he'd lived through, he believed in Vitamin C, time and massive doses of antibiotics. He was convinced she would grow out of the stammer. She didn't. The spluttering calmed after a year. But in moments of distress that unconquerable gulf between what she wanted to say and how it staggered and lurched from her lips came reeling back.

In time fortunes in the depleted Davidson household improved. There was, after all, nothing else for it. Money ran out and Janine was forced to get a job. She was taken on at the local supermarket where she started out stacking shelves, worked up to the checkout till and ended up as under manageress. She wore a green and white striped overall and she made friends. Ellen saw her laughing and telling jokes and could hardly believe her eyes. Her mother was a person after all. And the cuisine cheered up. There were super-market treats – fishfingers, hamburgers, beans and packets of chocolate biscuits. The supper time conversation moved beyond the tastiness of fish to her mother's anecdotes about work.

Going out to work suited Janine. To her it was just another routine. And she did like her routines. She was good at them. Now it was wake, get up, put on underwear, wash available uncovered bits, finish dressing, make toast and coffee, get children up, fed and out the door. She matter-of-factly did this every morning. At night she came home, took off her overall, snapped on the radio in the kitchen, stuck something under the grill, opened a tin of beans. She clung to the rhythm of her ways. It stopped her thinking. It was thinking got to you, she decided. If you could keep your thoughts at bay you'd get through.

Sometimes, though, she could not help herself. She'd watch couples at the supermarket making their way up and down the aisles, choosing what they were going to have for supper or bickering over breakfast cereals and she'd wonder: Had Douglas lived, would we have been like that? As years passed she replaced the quiet, bookish, somewhat grumpy husband she'd had with the jolly, outgoing, even-tempered one she secretly fancied. She imagined the things she might have done with this fantasy husband. They would have watched favourite sitcoms on the telly. They would have gone for drives on Sunday afternoons. They would have had a cup of tea together on the back doorstep Saturday mornings as they made up the week's shopping list. They would both have been fond of a nice bit of salmon (tinned, of course, they couldn't be doing with real) for a treat. Anniversaries and birthdays he would bring her a cup of tea in bed. All in all she was happy with her daydreams. One thing she was sure of, it was a lot easier to mould a dead husband into your perfect man than it was a live one.

In time Ellen started to leave her childhood behind. She still banged into doors and apologised to them. When her mother was about she dropped cups and mumbled. But time was distancing her from that moment when her mother, grieved and scorned, had said to her, 'Not you. Not you.' The horror, the loneliness of it faded and Ellen rarely thought about it. The rift between her and her mother became part of her life. It was simply how things were. They didn't talk about it.

Sometimes, sitting on the bus going to school, and later going to work, she would gaze out over the golf course. There was that special little valley where golfers played blind over a high ridge from the sixteenth to the seventeenth hole. She used to ride along the small canyon and look up at that ridge. There the Sioux stood in a long magnificent line, silhouetted against the sky, waiting for her, watching over her. Looking back at it from her almost-adult standpoint, it was hard to come to terms with how vividly real they had been to her. She could only shake her head at how silly she'd been. It was time to get on with the business of growing up.

Chapter Five

When she was eighteen Ellen left school and started work in the stationery department of a city store. She loved it. She could play with the pens, practise writing her name over and over in different coloured inks. She could watch the folk who came and went into the store, what they bought, what they wore, listen to what they said to each other. She could pore over the comics on the newspaper and magazine counter. Lunch times she went to the staff canteen and sat drinking foul tea from a thick white mug, eating ham sandwiches and listening to the shop girl gossip. It was wonderful. Girls getting together and talking dirty. The fabulous world of sex was new, or newish to them. They took to it with relish. They discussed men's cocks; size, shape, the difficulties of sex in the back of a car, difficulties with gear sticks and ashtrays, and how to get really drunk really quickly and really cheaply. They laughed bawdily, ate low-cal sandwiches because they were always watching their weight, followed by huge puddings, apple pie and custard, chocolate cake, crisps and bars of Dairy Milk, because wasn't weight-watching a bore? They spoke about men as sex objects, accessories, necessary nuisances, messy pets and objects of ardent and utter adoration. They took their love lives more seriously than anything else. Their conversation was incandescent. They chirruped in unison like sparrows roosting in an evening hedge, nudging up to each other. Ellen sipped her tea, ate KitKats, eavesdropped and was happy. But she did not, could not, join in. All her life joining in was a problem.

Occasionally one raw voice would break free of the giggling chorus and tell a tale of derring-do and sexual extravagance. 'I was in Jimmy's car an' he wasn't gonney take my pal Norma home. He was going to leave her at the end of the street. It's dark, I says, she could get attacked. An' he says, who'd attack her? Well, I'm not havin' that. I got his balls. He's thinkin' he's in for a treat. But I says, you'd better take her to her door, look what I've got . . .' There were guffaws of approval for that. Ellen was impressed.

'Hey, Ellen,' Alice from Hosiery asked once. 'Ever been clubbing? Louie the King's?'

Ellen shook her head.

'Oh, come on Friday night,' Alice said enticingly. 'It's great. Good laugh.'

Ellen shrugged. 'Maybe.' She was surprised to be invited. She didn't think they liked her. But then, she didn't think anybody liked her.

'The girls in the shop have asked me to go out with them on Friday night,' she told her mother.

'I hope they're not going to that dreadful disco in Leith. What is it? Louie's or something.' Janine stiffened with sanctimonious censure.

'Louie the King's,' said Ellen. That disapproval, however, was what Ellen needed to hear. She went.

Friday night and they'd just got paid and, arms linked, shrieking youth and cheek and freedom, five abreast they went looking for sex and booze and rock'n'roll. But mostly sex. The girls were barely recognisable out of their shop outfits. Hair spiked, lips painted brown or black, skimpily covered thighs flashing, they strutted to the pub, found a table and set about smoking, talking filth and drinking themselves into oblivion.

'Five Bacardi and Cokes, please.' They rummaged in their purses and were histrionically democratic about who paid for what. 'No, Ellen. You bought the crisps. I'll get the peanuts. And another round. Ha, ha, ha.'

The night was beginning to reel. They made lewd comments to men, innocent bystanders who simply had the misfortune to be standing in the wrong place at the wrong time, mildly sipping a pint of lager. 'Ever had a blow job, mister? Well, you're still not gettin' one. Ha, ha, ha.' Ellen didn't know where to look.

Now and then, suddenly it seemed, they'd used up all their conversation, so they filled the vacant spaces in their minds, singing

snatches of favourite songs. Shoulders moving in rhythm, fags
drifting smoke, they had such sweet voices. Nobody thought it rude
that someone would suddenly turn vacuous and start singing, mid-
sentence. 'No woman, no cry. Oh I love that.'

At eleven they went clubbing. 'We switch to cider now,' Ellen's
companions and bebop cohorts ordered. 'Spirits cost too much
here.' The night stopped reeling, started to colour and rage. Ellen
was scarcely capable of standing up. She lurched into the club,
handbag flapping, hair askew, eyes glazed, face flushed, mascara
streaming. Lights roared. Music more than roared. It was a hard
presence. When she moved she moved through and into the sound
that filled the whole building. For days afterwards her ears were
hot. She was hot-eared from the disco. Love is the Drug, blast, blast,
blast. The noise blew her thoughts away. She could not speak,
communicated by mouthing wildly and pointing. 'Another drink?'
waving at the bar.

Her friends put their bags, shapeless from the weight of junk
within, on the floor and shifted from foot to foot round them. If they
were dancing together nobody could tell. They shut their eyes, sang
along and moved, waving their heads and haircuts in rhythm.
Lights flickering jarred and splattered the movers and shakers on
the floor like light through splintered glass, and everyone was
dancing in action replay. If a boy was foolish enough to ask one of
them to dance, he was mouthed, 'Fuck off.'

Ellen went to the loo and, opening the door, entered a Fellini film:
a wall of noise and the air was impenetrable – smoke, hairspray,
perfume and swearing. There were girls on the floor fighting,
rolling over and over, scratching, biting, kicking and screaming,
'You shite. You fucking shite. If you go near my Pauly again I'll kill
you. I'll kill you.' Over and over they rolled, pale little arms flailing,
fists flying. Nobody paid them any attention. Bloodied and bruised
they staggered to their feet and glared. Nobody won.

Girls stood in thick ranks making pouting lipstick faces in the
mirror and squished gallons of Charlie scent on to every available
bit of their bodies under the arms, behind the ears, down the
cleavage, wrists and up their skirts, 'You never know I might get
lucky. Ha, ha, ha.' Howls of laughter. The veil of hair lacquer

squishing from spray cans was thick. Girls were gluing not only their hair but the air surrounding it, cigarette smoke was caught and stuck in blue waft fug. All the cubicle doors of the lavatories were open. Girls sat, knickers round their ankles, roaring drunken angst to friends leaning on the wall, legs crossed, waiting their turn. 'I love him, Sandra. I really, really love him.'

Ellen thought she was going to die. She knew she would never get to pee. She wanted to lie down. Bacardi, cider, vodka, lager and she thought perhaps some brandy were coursing vilely through her veins. She slumped to the floor, sat, legs splayed before her, gazing at the carpet which, close up, was not as plush as it appeared from the upright position. It was dark blue nylon and pock-marked with cigarette burns.

'Are you all right, darlin'?' one of the wrestlers asked. Ellen didn't even have the strength to nod. 'Here,' the wrestler grabbed her by the hair. She really was going to die. This was it. 'Put your head between your knees. Best place for it, ha, ha, ha. Stop anyone else's getting up there. No. Only joking, darlin'. Deep breaths. Fresh air'll help.' Fresh air? What fresh air?

And at three in the morning they hit the streets again. Arms linked again. Singing. 'Here we go. Here we go. Here we go. Here we COME. Here we COME. Ha. Ha. Ha.'

Alice and Katy needed a pee, disappeared top speed up an alley, and reappeared squealing in triumph. 'Alice's pee won,' they shouted. 'We had a bet about whose would run down to the litter bin first and Alice's won.' They all bawled and laughed and bent double with mischief. Vulgarity? Wasn't it lovely?

'I love you, Alice,' Katy wept. 'No, I mean it. You're my pal. And no man could replace that. I mean, you need men, but you need women to be your pals. Women are best.' They all agreed and cried. And Alice was sick.

'Great night,' she said. 'Brilliant. Best night ever. Are you coming next week, Ellen?'

She shook her head. 'No,' she whispered weakly. She felt brittle and frail. The very sound of her own voice was too much to bear.

On Monday, tamed and pale, they'd appear at work again. Next

Friday they'd be out here again, screaming and drinking. Always after that, when she was sitting at home watching television, or working late in the office, and the shrieks of women out on the town came careening through the night to her, Ellen thought it would be them lifting their skirts, running down the street, yelling. She thought them wild and wonderful. They made her feel she was not very good at life. She rolled wearily home and fell asleep unwashed, half dressed, battered and beleaguered, under the knowing black-and-white eye of Humphrey Bogart on the poster above her bed.

It did not take her long to reinvent her new friends and what she imagined to be their savage sisterly love. She had seen the name Starless Enterprises on some of the comic strips in the local Sunday newspaper. It was the brainchild of Stanley Macpherson. He was the regular subject of interviews. He appeared colourful, and his characters made an interesting splash on dull pages.

Dear Mr Macpherson, *Ellen wrote a month later.*

    I have written a comic strip story about four gangster women who live in an old tower block and who vow sisterly love and seek to save their fellow women from the injustices of living in a man's world. I've called it Gangster Women, and I am sending it to you to look at . . .

Then she dried. What did people say in this sort of letter? She abandoned her plan and left the letter lying in her bedroom drawer. Two weeks later she added, 'Hope you like it.' Then, before she could change her mind she swiftly posted it and expected to hear nothing. She always expected the worst.

'You can't work in a shop for ever,' her mother worried. 'You have to decide what you are going to do with your life.'

'OK,' said Ellen. 'I will. Soon.' She walked out of the room, banged into the doorpost and apologised to it. 'Sorry.'

Her mother rolled her eyes. That girl, what was she to do with that girl?

Two weeks after she posted her letter, Ellen got a reply.

* * *

Dear Ellen,

Loved your scripts. Come and see me, four o'clock next Monday afternoon.

Look forward to it.

Yours, Stanley.

PS: Give us a bell if this doesn't suit.

Chapter Six

Stanley Macpherson was scruffy. Ellen hadn't imagined that. She had him in a suit answering phones, making decisions, being ruthless. His office was a heap. There were heaps and heaps, and heaps bundled into more heaps. Heaps of papers on his desk. Heaps of files on the shelves behind him. More heaps on the window sill along with an ivy plant, dried and clinging to life. His phone rang constantly. He wore a sweat shirt with a hole in the sleeve. The crotch of his jeans was about to collapse under the constant strain of containing his thighs. The threads that held it together were worn and tired. He drummed his fingers as he spoke, and when he moved he moved quickly, in short enthusiastic bursts.

Ellen delighted him. She was exactly what he'd been looking for since he started up. There was something about her uncertainty and indecision that pleased him. She was immature, inhibited and wildly imaginative. Here was a writer he could mould and shape. Furthermore, here was a writer he was sure would stay put. His last two had moved on, one to work for New York comics from London, the other to San Francisco.

He rubbed his stubby beard and felt only slightly guilty about his motives as he offered her a job. He would in time, he knew, take her home to his family. He would feed her, introduce her to food and wine she plainly knew nothing about. He'd show her a new world of books, music and films. He could see it already. He'd done it time and time before with other writers, artists and, well, just people he took a shine to. He was shrewd and he was kindly. He, however, thought he was jaded and a soft touch. He was never particularly kind to himself.

'You can't take a job like that.' Ellen's mother clasped her hands in dismay. 'What will become of you? There's no future, no security.'

It was just what Ellen needed to hear. Her judgements and decisions were always measured by her mother's disapproval. The greater the disapproval, the more likely Ellen would do whatever was disapproved of. She took the job.

On her first day Stanley took her to 'meet the gang'. She stood uncertainly in the doorway, gazing round.

'This is Ellen,' Stanley said. 'And,' gesturing the room with a sweep of his arm, 'Ellen, this is the gang.'

They were all men. Ellen was shocked. She hadn't expected this. Nor, apparently had they. They shifted in their seats and tried to look welcoming They were all young. There was a script editor, and a central-casting designer/art editor with wire glasses and pony tail. He spent hours poring over typefaces, constructing words – different typeface for every letter. It looked odd, Ellen thought, likeably odd. There was another writer, Don, and Billy who did things. He sold advertising space, unloaded bundles of comics from the van when they arrived from the printer, answered the phone, fetched sandwiches, nipped to the bookies to place bets and probably worked harder than anyone else. And, whilst all the others would, eventually, move on, Billy would in time combine his job as fixer and fetcher with that of script editor. He'd stay put, then – along with Ellen.

They all stared at her suspiciously. A woman writer was a creature rarely glimpsed in the world of comic strips. This wasn't right. Women were, well, women, weren't they?

Ellen nodded hello and sat at her desk. Her hair was drawn over her face, she smelled of patchouli. Apart from that first hello she hadn't a clue what to say. For two weeks she sat quietly, scarcely moving. If she needed a pee she waited till she could wait no longer, she felt so awkward and embarrassed just walking across the room. Her shoes squeaked, or so she thought. She felt the faint rustle of her thighs to be thunderous. People stopped work and looked at her, she imagined. Her shyness came wheeling from deep within her. She sat considering her fingers, did not want to look up, and when she spoke, she mumbled.

She arrived dutifully at nine, left at five. Her lunch lasted precisely one hour. It took a while for her to realise she was the only one closely observing office hours. Though she relaxed enough to let her lunch hour roll on past two o'clock to three, or half-past, she never relinquished that hour between nine and ten when she had the office to herself. That was when she did her best thinking.

In time her quiet presence was accepted in the office. She learned to join in the banter, discussed television programmes, favourite songs on the radio, and the best way to dunk a biscuit. She won ten pounds betting that Stanley's jeans would last till the end of the month, if not for ever. 'It's physics,' she said. 'Stressed thread and thighs. The thighs are not going to get any bigger so the threads will not be stressed any further.' Everyone was impressed. They took her in. She might be a woman but she did not speak of womanly things. She did not spend hours putting on makeup or fiddling with her hair. In fact, Ellen hated her face. She thought it absurdly eager and shiny, as it had been on the night her mother said, 'Not you.' She looked at it as little as possible and was fairly adept at putting on foundation and lipstick without a mirror. They forgave her the patchouli. She was, they agreed, as near to a bloke as a woman could get. She'd do.

Stanley gave her the desk next to the window, nearest the door. He figured that if she was smitten by a sudden bout of femaleness – which could be, he knew from experience, messy – or if the maleness of the office got too much for her, there were escapes. She could either run out of the door and away. Or she could leave them all behind staring out the window. Mostly she chose the window. She looked out at people in the street below. Other people's lives always fascinated her. Often Stanley would pass the office door and catch her sitting watching the world, and he'd smile. The fruit of her starings would soon be written down, incorporated in her strips.

Though fat and scruffy, Stanley Macpherson was no fool. His life plan was to be a millionaire by the time he was forty. He had the ideas and energy. But his heart's gentle reputation kept his bank balance low. He left the writing of story strips to others and concentrated on what he could do best – the quick three-framers. He had a knack for them. They were simple, he explained. 'You start at the end with the joke and work forwards to the beginning.'

He'd been doing this reverse thing for years and years. 'Man and boy,' he smiled. But he was beginning to think he was doing this in reverse, too. He was sure he'd been a man when he started. Now, though, working back, he was beginning to doubt his maturity.

His wife, Brigit, visited him at work regularly trailing children. It never seemed to Ellen that it was the same children she brought along.

'How many children do you have, Stanley?'

'Five. Brigit had two before she met me, then we've had two, but the new baby, Jackson, isn't mine.'

'Goodness. Don't you mind?'

'What has minding got to do with things?' he said. Sadly. 'I believe in monogamy but the woman I'm monogamous with doesn't.'

He had, however, an impressive way with a business plan. His idea was to specialise in small, joky strips for advertising companies and local newspapers. It was only after he met Jack Conroy that he moved into science fiction. These he sold to Sunday supplements and freebie papers, then syndicated on. Jack Conroy drew his stories, usually double layer, eight-frame serials for an agreed sum, took standard syndication fees, and got slowly richer and richer. Stanley ran the office, met people, shook hands, paid bills, handed out money, supported children he hadn't fathered, kept his wife in clothes and a Volvo and struggled.

He'd started out writing all the strips but in time got too busy running his business to do what he started his business to do. He knew most of the writers he interviewed were ambitious and he had spent some time looking for someone who, like him, would stay put. Someone who would sit behind a desk for years and years and one day would look up and notice time had passed. Ellen was a find to him. He knew she was the one the instant he read her bawdy script and the shy little letter that went with it. He suspected, however, that in time he'd end up looking after Ellen and sorting out her life, just as he looked after and sorted out just about everyone he employed, married, befriended or, it seemed, happened to sit next to in the pub. He was a soft touch's soft touch.

Women Talking Dirty

He was right about Ellen. She had not meant to stay working at
Starless Enterprises for long. She had intended to raise enough cash
to see her through university. But she got comfortable behind her
desk. She liked the monochrome view from the window and the
people she shared the room with. She slipped into a laconic
relationship, slow lunches and small talk, with Stanley. And she got
paid to daydream. She had landed on her feet. Though *Gangster
Women* palled on her – their strutting and posturing bored her – she
continued to write them. She was convinced that one day she would
come up with a character she could give her heart to. Someone
humane and kindly and yet real. She knew it was there, somewhere,
waiting for her and one day she would come to it.

Stanley liked Ellen. Her lunch time company was refreshing. She
still hadn't mastered small talk so her conversation was a mass of
speculation and daydreams. Also she did all the speaking, leaving
him free to eat and dream. 'What would you do with five hundred
pounds to spend on yourself, Stanley?' 'What's the most boring
evening you ever had, Stanley?' 'Have you always been faithful to
Brigit, Stanley?' 'Have you ever wondered about God, Stanley?'

'Christ, Ellen. I don't know. There have been so many boring
evenings they all seem to blend into one these days. Brigit – no. No,
I haven't. Don't ask about that. Anyway, I'm not as bad as she is.
And no, I have not and will not ever wonder about God. Why do
you ask that?'

'I was reading an article that said God is a woman. It's an old
idea, but I'd forgotten about it.' Ellen had been working for Stanley
for four years. 'Only now I don't think He can be a woman.' She
yanked at her T-shirt, peered glumly down at her body in there.
'Look at me. No woman would do that to another. God's a bloke or
a cat.' Across the room at the bar a man was looking at her. His stare
made her uncomfortable. She did not like men staring at her. She
felt her chin was too big and her forehead shone luminously if she
did not keep it covered. Bryan Ferry was searing on the juke box,
'Over you . . .' A saxophone crooned.

'A cat?' Stanley sighed and eyed her sandwich left abandoned on
her plate as she keenly conversed, a pursuit she found more
absorbing than eating. He, however, was more of an eater than

49

talker. His wife had recently been warning him that if he did not do something about his weight she'd leave him. He was in a quiet torment. Brigit or the sandwich? The sandwich won. It was nearer. 'Do you want that?' he asked. She shook her head, a gesture he took as meaning he could have it. 'Why a cat?' A shower of crumbs flew from his mouth as he spoke and landed in the middle rumple of his sweat shirt. The sole was coming off his training shoe.

'I knew this old lady, Mrs Robb. She had a cat. She fed it chopped liver and bits of fish. It lay in a basket by her Aga. I never saw anyone or anything so adored. Cats are made to be adored. Yes, a giant celestial cat in a huge gleamy basket.' She was pretending not to notice the man who was very openly and obviously noticing her. 'Don't you ever feel, Stanley, that your life is being messed about for no real reason? It's the celestial paw playing with you, the evil way cats do, batting you around, then leaving you alone only to turn and pounce again. That's cats for you. That's God for you.' The man was walking across the room. He wore a black suit with a white T-shirt and grubby baseball boots.

'Presumably the great cat in the sky only gave us thumbs that we can operate tin openers,' he said.

He was like that. He joined in the conversations of complete strangers if they interested him. In the years to come he would often leave Ellen alone in bars twiddling a glass whilst he went to sit with people he did not know to marshal their arguments or participate in discussions he found too amusing, too puerile, silly or fascinating to miss. Sometimes he made new friends. Sometimes he got a smack in the mouth.

'Absolutely,' agreed Ellen.

Daniel picked up her drink and drained her glass. 'If I wait for you to finish lunch time will be over and you'll be gone. And I won't be able to buy you another.'

'I'll have a pint, too,' said Stanley. Then whilst Daniel was at the bar he told Ellen she'd better watch herself with that one. But Ellen was charmed. She was ripe for a spot of adoration.

That night, after the first meeting in the pub, Daniel was standing in the street waiting for Ellen to finish work. He was leaning on the barrier at the edge of the pavement, smiling at her, looking fabulous. He took her for a drink, bought her a pint of Guinness and a cheese sandwich. And he took her back to his flat – to bed.

Years later, remembering, feeling vaguely cheap, she complained to Cora, 'A Guinness and a cheese sandwich and I'm anybody's. It didn't take much. I was easily won.'

'*Was*,' said Cora. '*Was*? I just love your use of the past tense.'

It rained. When they got to Daniel's flat they were both soaked. He brought her a towel.

'I'm all right,' she only feebly protested.

'You're wet,' he said.

'I've been wet before. It doesn't hurt.'

'You're shivering,' he pointed out.

'I'm a woman of the world. I've shivered before.' She thought that such a clever answer. She was twenty-two. She thought she was cool. But she did not know as much as she thought she knew..

She worried that first night with Daniel that she would not be good enough for him. She hated her body and did not want him to see her without her clothes. She was under the impression that everyone in the world was better at sex than she was. She slipped uneasily out of her T-shirt and bra and looked glumly down at her tits. 'Do you think one's bigger than the other?'

'Perhaps,' he agreed. He was older than she was. He could not count how often he'd had this conversation before. 'Which one do you think is larger?'

'The left.'

'Is that your favourite tit?' He thought he could tell a great deal about a woman by how she answered that question. But then it was hard, sometimes, to understand women. They were all far more intimate with their own bodies than any man was. A woman would always have a favourite bit of her body. If she went through life believing she had a fabulous arse she was usually outgoing, vibrant, confidant. But an awful lot of the women he'd been with just liked their wrists. He supposed this was the bit they saw most, or maybe it really was their best bit. As they got older many women seemed to think one side of their face wrinklier than the other. Then again a woman might break her nail and cry out in dismay, 'Oh, it was my best nail, too.' They had things like that, women – one eye baggier than the other, and favourite nails.

'No. I like the small one best,' Ellen said.

'Ah.'

She was frightened of having big tits. She stood holding them, considering them. He knew who she was when he first approached her. That comic strip woman, Ellen something-or-other. She was sort of famous, locally famous, though she plainly did not know it. He sensed money. If she did not have any now, she would in the future. Seeing her chatting to Stanley, he recognised a glistening chance and hated himself for his opportunism. But he couldn't help himself. She was not without experience, he could tell, but lacked the self-confidence to relax and enjoy the pleasure her body could bring her. He was the man to put that right. He ran his hand slowly over the favourite tit and surveyed the other with critical care. 'Perhaps this one is the nicer. Let me consider it from another angle.' He moved round to the back of her, and, kissing her neck, reached round, continued his research. He told her to take off her jeans. But please leave on her knickers. He'd like to take them off himself.

Afterwards she lay listening to the building. People who were soon to become her friends were moving about, getting on with their lives. Had they heard her? Ronald and George upstairs had finished supper and were washing up together. She could hear them walking back and forth across their kitchen. Mrs Boyle downstairs opened her door and called for her cat, 'Fergus!' Her deep and fruity tones echoed down the corridor. The cat came running, yowling. Ellen loved this. She could lie in bed eavesdropping on the people around her. There was something comforting about the nearness of neighbours. She did not feel alone.

In the bungalow of her childhood where she was for ever alone, neighbours kept themselves private. When Ellen wanted to spy on them she had to climb on their garden fence and stare through the window. In her glory days this had been a favourite game, but she no longer indulged. Well, a person gets too old to gallop about on a pretend horse. Thunder, then, was no longer around for swift getaways when people furiously burst from the sacred isolation of their living rooms waving fists and bawling, 'Bugger off! Nosy little brat!'

Daniel fetched them some bourbon and said he hoped she wasn't going to do anything boring like get up and go home. Ellen phoned her mother and lied. She said she was staying with a girlfriend. She found lying to her mother a very easy thing to do. As she spoke Daniel ran his hand up the insides of her thighs. They drank and when the bottle was empty Daniel went down to the pub for another. She paid.

'What do you do?' she asked when he got back.

'Stuff,' he said.

'Stuff?'

'I'm working on my PhD.' He hadn't looked at it in years. Doubted he'd ever finish it. 'I do a few bar shifts. Three evenings, a couple of afternoons.' Since he spent so much drinking, it seemed reasonable to make some cash doing the odd stint on the other side of the bar. 'I pick up a bit on the horses.' He gambled. Mostly he gambled.

In the kitchen the phone rang and rang. Daniel paid it no heed. Neither did Ellen. She was in love. She loved Daniel's flat; the lumpen corduroy-covered sofa in the living room, the postcards and bills stuck behind the clock and candlesticks on the mantelpiece, the multi-patterned rugs, the clusters of unwashed cups and glasses everywhere, the small collection of jackets and coats hanging behind the door. The pictures throughout the flat were all framed and all of women, women by men – Man Ray, Degas, Aubrey Beardsley, George Grosz and in the hall there was a part of a Robert Crumb strip cut out and blown up. She loved the strange musky, joss sticky smell and the ragged chenille curtains. An entire wall in the living room was taken up by his record collection. The only thing that was cherished was his stereo system. There was nothing about Daniel's flat that Ellen didn't love. There was nothing about Daniel that she didn't love. His body was soft. When he took off his shirt, she saw he had a mole under his left nipple. He was skinny like a boy. His ribs showed.

He turned to her, took her glass and laid it on the floor by the bed. Then he kissed her. They both tasted of Jack Daniel's. His mouth was soft on hers, his tongue moved, and probed into her. His hands slid over her, over her back. She loved that. She felt him between her legs and desperately wanted him, pushed herself up towards him.

'No,' he said. 'No. Go on top. Sit on me. Let me look at you.'

'I can't.' She hung her head. She was embarrassed. She didn't like anybody to look at her.

'Leave the light on and let me see you,' he whispered and he pleaded and she could not resist him no matter how awkward she felt. She sat on him, feeling high up and vulnerable. But then the pleasure of it took hold of her. He moved up into her and let her curl her legs round him. He kissed her neck and the lobes of her ears, stroked her hair. 'You are beautiful,' he told her. She was, too. For the first time in her life in that flat with summer rain splattering the window and starlings from the park roosting and chorusing and complaining outside, in the quiet nine o'clock gloom she thought she was beautiful. In the morning she'd re-join the world, bang into doors and apologise to them, say sorry to strangers when they stood on her foot. Move along streets, eyes down, shoulders slumped.

The phone rang again. And again. Behind the door, swept against the wall, there was a huge collection of unopened letters and bills. Ellen was dealing with a rogue. All the signs were there, but she did not recognise them. She was twenty-two. She was ardently working on her cool. And she *really* did not know as much as she thought she knew.

Chapter Seven

Her mother hated Daniel. 'What do you see in a man like that? Can't you tell he's the worst sort of man? Too good-looking for you. What does he do anyway?'

'Stuff,' said Ellen.

'What sort of stuff?'

'He's working on his PhD.'

'Pah. Nonsense.'

'He works in a bar.' Her mother thought it beneath her to say anything about that. Ellen didn't mention the horses.

Daniel wasn't enthused about Ellen's mother. It was plain to him, however, that the more she loathed him, the more Ellen would adore him. He felt he'd be letting himself down if he did not exploit the situation. When Ellen and her mother were standing face to face chatting he would get as close to Ellen as possible and slip his hand up her skirt, down her knickers, round her bum. He would stare Janine in the eye and do secret intimate things to her daughter. 'She is mine,' his look of derision would say. 'She is mine and you can do nothing about it. I am groping her arse as you speak to her about the macaroni and cheese you ate last night.'

Once, after supper, when he and Ellen were washing up together, he suggested she bend over the small Formica-topped kitchen table so that he could take her from behind whilst her mother was in the other room watching *Sale of the Century*. And, though she refused, Ellen was surprised at how much the suggestion turned her on.

'Well, if you won't do that, marry me,' Daniel said. 'You'll be Mrs Quinn. The fabulous Mrs Quinn.'

It was as overwhelmingly tempting as the purple-wrapped sweets in Mrs Robb's garden. Daniel scarcely looked at her. He was drying some forks, slowly laying them out in a neat row. He wanted

Ellen to be the fabulous Mrs Quinn. He felt he deserved a fabulous Mrs Quinn in his life. He could take her, mould her. Show her all the things she knew nothing about – art, films, books, food, sex – life, dammit, life. He could shape her into the wife he longed for. He, of course, had no intention of becoming the fabulous Mr Quinn. He wanted a wife, but no way was he going to become a husband.

'It will be wonderful,' he persuaded. 'Just as long as we don't start acting like husband and wife. That's the sure-fire way to kill a marriage.' She hadn't a clue what he was talking about but she agreed with him willingly. She finished washing the dishes, wiped the sink, folded the dishcloth and placed it neatly between the taps, and went through to her mother.

'Daniel has just asked me to marry him,' she said.

'He what!' Her mother was appalled. 'Marry him? Marry a man like that? You can't. I forbid you . . .'

That did it. She married him.

Chapter Eight

Ellen and Daniel got married, and, too broke to afford a honeymoon, they drifted into their own world of comfort and passion. A sort of second childhood, only with sex. They cocooned themselves in Daniel's flat for a fortnight, dining in, and in bed, on carry-out fish and chips, Chinese or pizza. They made alcoholic concoctions with vodka, rum, Kahlúa and Coke, and sat on the lumpen sofa scarcely dressed, drinking, eating Chocolate Olivers and prawn cocktail crisps. They bought champagne, shook the bottle jubilantly and ran round and round the sofa spraying each other. They got sticky. They whooped and laughed and danced, a slow semi-naked shuffle, draped over each other listening to Roxy Music. They fucked themselves to a standstill. Towards the end of their fortnight of junk food and love a spot of actual fresh air seemed tempting, and sane. Hand in hand they set out across the park. Shaky-legged and pale they made it to the nearest bench. They sat a while staring bleakly ahead before heading home.

Watching from the upstairs window, Ronald said to George, 'Oh look, our young lovers have shagged themselves witless. They can hardly walk.'

George said to Ronald, 'Oh, jealous.'

Next day the two tried to make it over the park again, and still couldn't. It became a joke: if they ever could make it over the park together their love would be finished. They sat on the bench.

Daniel kissed her. 'My tongue's having a better time than I am,' he said, slipping his hands up her T-shirt.

She loved that, loved his hands on her. In years to come when the big fights started he would turn his back on her, leaving her helpless. She never could deal with rejection, 'Not you. Not you.' 'Touch me, you shite,' she'd scream at him. 'T-T-T-Touch me.'

She loved to be touched. The people she held dearest were touchy, feely people. George upstairs, who would grip her hand in the pub and say, 'Now, Ellen, you must tell me what you've been up to. Lots of naughty things, I hope. And if it isn't naughty don't bore me with it.' Mrs Boyle downstairs, who would link a frail arm in hers and say, 'Come, Ellen. We'll go on a mushroom quest to the Italian deli on Elm Row. Mushrooms and wine. You'll pay.' Cora, who would tidy her hair, fix her collar and say, 'Ellen, you can't possibly go out like that. Let me sort you out.' And Daniel, of course Daniel, who more than fucked her, he cuddled her. It was the cuddling that more than anything kept her married to him. Sex was, of course, a fabulous bonus. But she loved having him next to her in bed, arms round her, clinging to her. She loved to hear him breathe.

In times to come friends would show Ellen pictures of their honeymoons. She would look at pictures of people as they had been years before, thinner, smilier, looking enthusiastic and slightly foolish in luminescent beach outfits and straw hats.

'What did you do for your honeymoon, Ellen?' they would ask.

'We went to bed for a fortnight,' she'd say. There would be silence. Was it disapproval? Or maybe envy? Ellen never could tell.

After two weeks of hectic bliss she went back to work, a relief really. She needed the rest.

The initial burst of married life over, Daniel thought his life would continue as before. He did not think of himself as a husband. He had a fixed notion of husbands. They were dull people who faced south-west.

'Husbands,' he explained to Ellen, 'are people who stand outside shops, wearing tweed caps, vacantly facing south-west, whistling vague tunes through their teeth whilst their wives shop. That's not for me.'

He was adamant about that. At the time, Ellen had no wish to have a man in her life wearing a tweed cap, whistling vaguely, whilst facing south-west. Daniel in her bed was more than enough. She brought in food, and, in a martyrish sort of way, thought she was making her relationship work when she did not, in any way, impose her taste on his flat.

'Don't be bringing pink things in here,' he ordered. Actually until he mentioned it she hadn't thought to bring home something pink. After that she was constantly tempted. When she discovered that Daniel slept regularly with Friendly Mary, who owned the fruit shop at the end of the road, she painted the bedroom the colour of tinned salmon. 'Have that, you bastard.' That she loathed the effect as much as he did made no difference. This was not a piece of design. This was an act of vengeance. She was only just beginning to consider their flat as much her home as it was his. She'd been paying the rent since she moved in.

On her first afternoon alone she spent a gruelling couple of hours going through the pile of mail that she'd seen lying mouldering behind the front door that first night with him. She settled on the sofa with a cup of coffee, thinking this a glorious opportunity to discover more about her new husband. She wanted to know everything about him. There was so much he did not tell her. She imagined there were mysterious businessy things, deals and intrigue, that she would not understand. She was thinking Humphrey Bogart in *Casablanca*, a man with a past and a gritty integrity. This was not naïveté, it was stupidity. She opened eviction notices, dire threats from the electric company, police warrants about his parking fines – she was not even aware he had a car – and warnings that the bailiffs had obtained a warrant to enter the premises and would be doing so unless payment was received within seven days. There was a letter from Daniel's mother – he'd told Ellen she was dead – pleading with him to get in touch. Where are you? Why don't you call? There were hysterical outcries from credit card companies and a letter from Daniel's bank manager demanding he hand in his cheque book and card.

Ellen had no idea that the simple act of opening mail could have such a foul effect on the digestive system. She sat in the lavatory, rocking back and forth clutching her stomach. Her beloved was not a man of gritty integrity after all. Any moment now the door might be battered down and heavy men in porkpie hats would remove all their furniture. Oh God.

She put the sordid mess into a box and next day poured it dramatically on to Stanley's desk. 'What do I do, Stanley?'

He always knew what to do. 'Run away,' he suggested. 'Leave

the bastard. I did warn you. That first day – remember?'

Then with a heaving intake of breath he pulled the financial ruin towards him. He sat her beside him at his desk. Together they slowly sorted out the mess. At the end of a churning day Ellen had taken charge of her husband's finances. She handed over most of her savings to clear the back rent. She agreed monthly sums to pay his credit card debts. She settled with the electric company, and had the phone connected again. She didn't know what to do about his mother. Though she no longer had anything to fear, the chill of the threats and the panic they set up within her remained. The dread sounds in her life were no longer the awful rush and swish of silken dress or the slow menacing fall of pointy shoe on chilled lino. They were the simple sounds of morning mail tumbling through the letter box or the sharp insistent tapping of someone knocking at the door.

None of this really changed her feelings for him. She would lie in bed watching him move about the bedroom vaguely humming some favourite song of the moment, and she would think how beautiful he was with his boy's body and his perfect haircut and she would wonder what such a person saw in her. In the end it didn't matter what he did, what debts he brought home for her to sort out. All he had to do was kiss her; all he had to do was touch her; indeed, all he had to do was walk, smiling, across the room to her and she was his.

The notion of just was lodged in the depth of her psyche. She was just . . . She was just a plain sort of a person with short dark hair and big hands who never thought someone like Daniel would ever look her way. She was just a person who wrote silly comic strips. When Stanley told her she was beginning to have a following she thought: It's just me. They must all be wrong. Or they must have terrible taste. If she told Stanley her plans for a new script he'd say, 'Sounds good.' She'd think: Sounds good. Only sounds good. But *is* it good? It's just a comic strip.

Chapter Nine

She did, of course, challenge Daniel about his heap of hate mail and debts. But he was unrepentant. In fact, he couldn't understand why she was so upset by it. She let her resentment grow and fester within her for a week before she said anything. She was not used to confrontation. In her bungalow days, confrontation had not been on the agenda. It did not fit into her mother's emotional routine, which was a round of smiles, frowns and disapproving hostile silences directed at anybody who stepped out of line.

Daniel wasn't one for confrontations either. He didn't really reckon any of life's biggies – birth, marriage or death. Birth – well, he'd done that obviously, but what was it to him? He could remember nothing about it. Death – well, he didn't mind really. As long as it took him by surprise. And marriage was just something he'd done. He liked Ellen, he fancied having her around on a regular basis, but he'd no intention of letting this marriage thing interfere with his gambling, his hanging out with his mates, working at the bar – his life, in fact.

'You have a mother,' Ellen accused.

'Yes, don't we all?' He raised his eyebrows. Why should that surprise her?

'But she's alive. You didn't even invite her to our wedding.'

'So? You have a problem with that?'

'Yes I do. I should imagine she would too.'

'Nah.' He shook his head. He was adamant she would not have a problem about missing his wedding. 'She doesn't like me. I'm not her sort. I didn't grow into the person she planned. I think she'd rather forget about me.'

Ellen stared at him. She found it hard to take in what he was saying. 'Your own mother. You never ever go to see her.'

He shrugged again. 'She doesn't ever come to see me.' There was always something reasonable about Daniel's arguments – no matter how atrocious he was being.

'I go see my mother once a week.' Ellen was fairly saintly about this. Priggish, almost.

'But that's another of your lies,' Daniel told her. 'You don't want to go. You just kid yourself you're being a dutiful daughter. Don't even bother to open your mouth to tell me you enjoy it or she enjoys it. I won't believe you.'

Ellen shut her mouth and left it at that. A few days later, however, she phoned Daniel's mother and introduced herself.

'Um,' she said when she heard the voice at the other end. 'Um . . . Mrs Quinn? Um . . . I'm Ellen. Daniel's wife.'

'Who? Who's this?'

'I'm Ellen Quinn. Um . . . I married your son the other week.'

There was a long silence. Breathing. Then, 'Well, well. There's a turn up for the book.' Ellen could almost hear her battling against making scathing comments. Eventually she simply said, 'Well, there you go. You never can tell with Daniel. You can never accuse him of being predictable, I'll say that for him.'

'Um,' Ellen said again. 'Um . . . would it be all right if I came to see you?'

Ellen could tell that it wouldn't. But Daniel's mother was too polite to say so.

'Yes,' she said stiffly. 'Why not? I'm sure we've lots to talk about.'

'Tomorrow?' asked Ellen.

'Tomorrow,' the older Mrs Quinn agreed. And did Ellen hear her say – let's get it over with?

She was tall, straight back, hair that had once been blonde but was now just pale, palely grey. It was obvious where Daniel got his looks. She was still beautiful, though she wore her beauty badly. It irritated her. People stared, or they were absurdly polite to her.

She showed Ellen into the living room. This is where Daniel sat as a child, Ellen thought, looking round. It was infinitely more comfortable than the living room she'd sat in as a child. Through the window she could see the garden. All the love Daniel's mother had left in her was lavished on that quarter-acre or so. It was lush and vibrantly blooming. The little patch that came with the bungalow Ellen grew up in had been tamed and clipped, mowed and tidied into bland submission. A polite row of lupins grew along by the far hedge and some pansies lined the flowerbeds by the lawn. The only thing that flourished was the lilac tree and now Ellen's mother was talking of having it chopped down. The brutishly vigorous way it bloomed every year offended her. 'Chop it down,' she muttered. 'That'll show it.'

'I'll make us tea,' Mrs Quinn offered. She brought them a pot of Earl Grey and a plate of exquisite home-made almond biscuits. Ellen ate an abstemious one and refused a second though she longed to take more. She didn't want her new mother-in-law to think her greedy.

'Perhaps you'd like to see Daniel's room?' Mrs Quinn asked.

Ellen nodded. 'I'd love to.'

It was up a small staircase. Ellen could imagine Daniel as Christopher Robin coming down these stairs wrapped in a blue dressing gown, dragging a favourite teddy, bump bump bump, behind him. The room made Ellen draw her breath. It was perfect. A shelf of stuffed toys – a white cat, a hen, several teddy bears, a scruffy dog. There was a wooden yacht for sailing on the park pond, several model vintage cars, shelves and shelves of books – all the classics. Ellen writhed in envy, remembering the sparse and linoed bedroom where she lay waiting for the man in pointy shoes or the lady in the white dress to come to kill her. Look, he had *Winnie-the-Pooh* and *The Wind in the Willows*. She'd been past twenty when she discovered them.

'He had an idyllic childhood,' she gasped.

'I like to think so,' his mother said. 'It goes to show, don't give your child everything. It simply isn't enough for them. Shall we go downstairs? We'll have more tea and see if we can find something to talk about other than Daniel.'

They didn't succeed. By the time she left Ellen had seen his school reports, the cards he made for his mother for Valentine's Day, the holiday seaside snaps of him in blue swimming trunks sitting on a beach donkey, the breeze ruffling his hair. His dream childhood was packed neatly into three shoe boxes and a few photograph albums.

'Where's his father?' Ellen wanted to know.

'He left,' Mrs Quinn said with withering finality. Ellen didn't dare push for more.

When she got home she told Daniel of her visit. 'She wants me to go see her again. Next week if I can manage.'

'Does she?' He didn't seem to mind at all. 'I bet she liked you. You're much more her sort than me.'

'What do you mean by that? She's your mother, you could go see her sometime.'

'Oh, she wouldn't want that. She doesn't really want to see me. Not now that I'm no longer the perfect son. Actually, I'm not her sort.'

'Not her sort! Not her sort!' Ellen was exasperated with him. 'How can you say that?'

'Look, Ellen, just because someone gave birth to me, it doesn't mean to say I'm the kind of person she'd like to have round for tea.'

On Thursdays Ellen went to the pub where Daniel worked to watch him hold court. He moved up and down the bar serving opinions and drinks. 'A tequila and a half of lager. You didn't buy that album, did you? There's only one decent track, third one in side two. The opening riff's pure early Hendrix.' Then down the bar, different punters, different booze, different opinions: 'Two pints and two Bells. No, I didn't bother with Misty Morning. Not on that turf. He's had a bad season.' Back down the bar: 'A Glenfiddich and a Guinness. Thing about David Lynch is his weirdness, that's why you go to see him.' Daniel knew about things she didn't. He knew about proper things.

Once she overheard some boys discussing him.

'Bastard,' said one.

'Fuck never paid us,' said another.

They sat in a pathetic row on bar stools. They were all much younger than she was. And they were paler than she, thinner, raggier, grubbier and hungrier. They were a band, Five Believers. Daniel had hired them to play in the bar. Though the owner had left cash for them, Daniel had pocketed it.

Ellen was shocked. 'These poor boys.'

They had holes in their jeans, long bony hands dangling from

64

denimed sleeves, spots on their faces. They had that well-honed weirdness of youths who were sure they had something to say if only they knew what it was; multi-coloured hair, pierced noses, shaved and tattooed heads. They spoke Scottish, but they dreamed in American. But then, Ellen thought, didn't everyone everywhere do that at some time or another in their lives.

When she and Daniel got home she berated him. 'How could you? How could you treat these boys like that? They're children, Daniel. Children.'

Daniel scratched his head laconically. He was unrepentant.

Shocked at how little he seemed to care, Ellen continued her tirade. 'That's a terrible thing to do. You didn't just steal their money. You stole their dreams. You took their dreams and turned them into some sleazy gain for yourself. These boys want to be musicians.'

'They're not musicians,' Daniel said. 'They're not even dreamers.' He crossed the room pulled out a Charlie Parker album. 'This is a musician, and a dreamer.' He threw down a tattered copy of *Electric Ladyland*. 'And here's another. What are these boys? Greedy. They want to be stars. They want to be in the pop charts. They want little girls to call their names and unzip their flies. They want sex and booze and big cars. They want adoration.' He turned to Ellen, face gleaming and saintly. 'I have done them a favour. I have shown them what it's about. The disappointments, the graft. That's what evolution's about. Adapting to the facts. Getting real with the truth.'

'Is it?' Ellen was sure there was something wrong here, but Daniel at full stretch could convince her grass was blue and dogs didn't bark.

'They should thank me,' he decided. He threw his arms about, ran his fingers through his hair, paced the room. He even started to have faith in his own rant. 'Greedy. Greedy. They're all greedy. They want. Everybody wants. They want now. They don't want to work. Perfecting a craft? Forget it. They are filled with the hysteria of having. They look round at jackets and haircuts and mobile phones and hi-fis . . . and . . . Jesus Christ, I don't know what else. And they think, I want some of them . . . some of them . . .'

'Apples?' suggested Ellen weakly.

'Apples! Apples!' Daniel screamed. 'Fuck apples. We all got apples. Tasteless. A ruined fruit. No, they want kumquats and papayas, passion fruit and mangoes. Juicy exotic things.'

Upstairs Ronald said to George, 'Daniel's on the rant again.'

Downstairs Mrs Boyle raised her eyes to the ceiling and turned to the cat and tutted, 'Such bollocks, Fergus, don't you think? Well no, I suppose you've quite forgotten what bollocks are.'

But Ellen was impressed. Hysteria of having. Kumquats and papayas. Oh yes, she was impressed. Considering Daniel's hero and his hero's writing on his bookshelf, *The Origin of the Family, Private Property and the State*, she sat in the office next day and wrote *Engels of the Forest*. She had not, of course, actually read anything Engels had ever written. And had, in fact, no intention of ever doing so. Well, she was just . . . just an ordinary writer. It was, she thought, well beyond her understanding. So she imagined what it was about.

In her version, Engels came from his hermit retreat in the Amazonian Forest to save the world. A chicly shabby soul in a white baggy suit and black T-shirt, he stood high on the parapet of the multi-storey car park where he slept on a small rush mat that he unrolled nightly. This was his only shelter. 'I do not seek comfort,' he cried. 'Comfort weakens me.' He spread his arms in despair and, Jesus style, wept for the world. 'We are consumed by the hysteria of having,' he sobbed. 'What has become of us?' He was a martial arts champion. He lived on junk food, unwrapping a chocolate bar: 'Oh God, sugar, chemicals, additives. I must have them. Junk food. Street nutrition.' The first story, 'Engels and the Five Believers', was an instant cult.

Stanley read it and said to Billy, 'Do you know, I believe this is Daniel. This is how the silly bugger sees him.'

But Billy said, 'No. I mean I know she's a bit ingenuous but she's not *that* bad.' Then pausing a moment, thinking about this: 'Is she?'

One Sunday morning Mrs Boyle waylaid Ellen when she and Daniel were returning from the newsagent's, arms laden with newspapers. 'I have been lying in wait for you,' she said. She had a deep and fruity voice. She hung on to words as if she loved them, and wanted them to last a long time on her tongue. 'It's time we got to know each other. I'm Emily Boyle, your neighbour downstairs. You must come for a chat. Sometime soon.'

'Yes,' Ellen smiled. 'I'd love that.'

'You must tell me all about yourself,' said Mrs Boyle. 'I want to know it all – how you met Daniel, everything.'

'We met in the pub.'

'That's right,' said Daniel curtly. He did not like Mrs Boyle. He sensed she had the measure of him.

'You spied her across a crowded room,' crooned Mrs Boyle. 'And you had to make her yours.'

'Something like that,' said Daniel. Ellen carried on up the stairs. She was eager to study her horoscope for the week ahead.

'You came, you saw, you conquered.' Mrs Boyle eyed Daniel – a challenge.

'Something like that,' Daniel repeated, making sure Ellen was out of hearing range. 'Wrong order,' grinning now. 'I saw. I conquered. I came.'

'Ah,' said Mrs Boyle. Wasn't it always the same? These young people thought they could shoo her with shock back into her flat. As if the very hint of sex would set her scuttling to the safety of her own fireside. As if she, in her time, hadn't had her share of shagging. 'Oh Daniel,' she said, 'you came. I know you came. Ronald and George upstairs know you came. I do believe the people who live on the other side of the park know you came.' Daniel said nothing. Ellen appeared looking over the banisters at the hostilities below. She did not realise what was happening.

'Come for coffee this afternoon,' Mrs Boyle called up to her. 'Come chat to me, my dear.'

'You're not actually going?' Daniel demanded when they got inside the flat.

Ellen considered this. 'Are you telling me what to do?'

'No,' said Daniel. 'Just I didn't think it was your scene to spend afternoons with old ladies.'

'As a matter of fact . . .' Ellen said, 'as a matter of fact it is.'

Mrs Boyle was delighted to see her. 'Come in. Come in.' Ushering her down the hall to her living room, a sunny south-facing place: a dark green velvet sofa covered with cushions, long green curtains, blue walls, white ceiling, bookshelves, pictures, a tiled fireplace with actual fire flickering and, centre stage, a Steinway grand piano.

'You play?' asked Ellen.

'Of course I do. Less and less these days. But I play. You don't really want coffee?' Mrs Boyle asked. 'It's such a bore boiling a kettle, checking for clean cups, finding milk. We'll have sherry.'

'Sherry?'

'Absolutely,' pouring as she bossed. 'I do not allow myself gin before teatime. It's my rule. So I have sherry.'

Ellen knew she was dealing with an older, superior digestive system.

'So,' Mrs Boyle sat on the sofa looked at Ellen and said, 'tell me about yourself.'

Ellen shrugged. 'I write. I'm married to Daniel. I live upstairs. That's it, really.'

'What do you write?'

'Stuff. Comic strips.' She looked glumly out the window. She was always slightly ashamed of what she did.

'I know you,' Mrs Boyle pointed triumphantly. 'You do that *Gangster Women* thing. I read that.' Then, qualifying her little admission of bad taste, 'Normally I wouldn't, but I quite like that. It's rude. I like rude. Are you famous?'

'Good heavens no. I haven't got the face for fame. It's not thoughtful enough. Deep. You need to look deep, even if you're not. Don't you think?'

'No,' Mrs Boyle spoke slowly, 'I don't think so.' Young people said such young things. 'How old are you? Though that's only a technicality really. Well, with women anyway.'

'Twenty-three.' Ellen felt suddenly shamed by youth. She was only just twenty-three.

'That would make you seventeen, then.'

'Twenty-three.'

Mrs Boyle grinned, old teeth. 'I have this idea that woman reach seventeen and stop. They still thrill at men and long for love. They stay seventeen till they get to thirty-five then they panic about

68

becoming fifty one day. So they have a tense few weeks facing the future, giving up cigarettes, coffee and wine. Then they get fed up and go back to seventeen again. It's more fun. Of course, in between they are all sorts of ages. Depends on the time of the day. Me now, I'm seventy-three. First thing in the morning I'm well past ninety. At noon I'm fifty without the panic. Just capable with warmed up semi-functioning joints. At night I'm me again. But there's a spot in the depth of me that's for ever seventeen. Eager to please and wondering about it all.'

Ellen smiled and looked down. 'At seventeen I was too busy rebelling against my mother to thrill at anything. Besides, women have careers. They take themselves seriously. I don't think they bounce about from one age to another these days.'

'Oh,' said Mrs Boyle. 'Perhaps. But I think most of us feel seventeen inside all our lives. In my heart there is still the spark of what I once was. And sometimes when I look in the mirror the face I see surprises me. The creature I used to be haunts me.' Then, changing the subject: 'I think you need bringing out. Perhaps one day I could teach you how to behave badly.'

'I don't think I need to be taught that.'

'Oh you do. I can see you do.'

'I do not need to be taught to behave badly,' Ellen said. This conversation was not what she wanted. She wanted to chat like she chatted to Mrs Robb. Then with the sherry, in the warmth of the fire, she relaxed and confided. 'Actually I always wanted someone to talk to who was handy with the free advice and Kleenex tissues. That sort of thing.'

'Oh,' said Mrs Boyle. 'That sounds like a surrogate mother. I'd avoid that at all costs. One mother is hard enough. Far better to behave badly. I mean, you might choose someone for your surrogate mother and find yourself rebelling against and speaking back to some poor person who simply imagined she was your friend.'

'This conversation is a bit sudden,' said Ellen. 'We've only just met.'

'I'm seventy-three,' Mrs Boyle reminded her. 'I may well pop off at any time. I have no time for sodding small talk.'

Chapter Ten

There was, Daniel decided, something wonderfully unashamed about Friendly Mary's bedroom. Everything was pink. Pink wallpaper, pink curtains, pink sheets, pink duvet, fluffy pink rugs on pink carpet. Christ, he couldn't live here. But the odd afternoon lolling in bed, dreaming, was wonderful. Across the room, on the pink dresser, lay a formidable collection of pots, jars, tubes, tubs, mascaras, lipsticks, blushers, eye shadows, mousses, lotions, creams and gels. Mary spent a deal of time on her complexion. Which was also pinkish.

There was, too, something unashamed about sex with Friendly Mary. It was sex and only sex. Sex with gusto and lust, but nothing more. There was as little conversation as possible. Mary just wanted to get on with it, then sleep for half an hour. Actually Daniel suspected his attentions were only part of Mary's intense complexion care, but obliging her had its compensations. There was time to himself afterwards to lie back wallowing in all that wonderfully horrible pink and consider his life.

His most vivid memory of his childhood was of himself, six years old, standing on a high wall that he had climbed up but couldn't climb down again. His father stood below. He was wearing his holiday sports jacket, tweed check. The collar of his shirt was open. There was a small triangle of tan at his neck. His arms were spread open. 'C'mon, jump. I'll catch you.' Daniel jumped. His father dropped the welcoming arms and stepped back. Daniel landed on the tarmac at his daddy's feet, a small crumpled body. There was screaming, such a terrible noise that it took Daniel a moment to realise the howling was coming from him. It was more than the pain, though the pain was awful, it was the hurt and confusion. Why?

His father loomed over him. 'Let that be a lesson in life. Never trust anybody.'

His mother came running, 'Oh my God, Bill,' she screamed at his father, beating him with clenched fists. 'What have you done?'

'I've taught the lad about life. A short sharp lesson. He'll thank me—'

'You've broken his leg, you idiot.'

It was true. The crumpled crying child was bawling in agony. The pain was huge and engulfing, and through it he saw his mother and father argue. She hit him, over and over she hit him. 'You fool. You fool.' He turned. Shoulders hunched, hands plunged deep into his pockets he walked off. Neither of them paid any attention to Daniel and his awful pain.

He was in hospital for weeks, lying in striped pyjamas, plastered leg covered in autographs and silly rhymes. His mother visited, bringing toys and books and fussing round his bed. Nurses cuddled him, stroked his hair, ran their fingers round his chin and smiled lovely smiles whenever they caught him looking at them. 'Oh,' they would softly say, wrapping him to them, 'he's such a gorgeous boy. I think I'll take him home with me.'

He changed from a boisterous, ebullient infant, the hero of the football park and playground leader, to a bookish boy, mummy's darling. He became a nice lad. 'Ah Mrs Quinn,' neighbours and friends would say, ruffling his hair. 'You must be so proud of your son. What a nice lad he is.' Feeling safe and approved of, Daniel would grin sheepishly.

All his life he'd done as he was told. In fact, his mother had him so fine-tuned she didn't have to say anything. A look, a sigh, a firming of the lips was enough, and if he really did not come up to snuff, if he failed an exam or was home late from school, his mother would stiffen. Stiffen and turn her back. Sometimes she would not talk to him for days.

This loss of affection made his stomach ache and he trembled within. Thinking about it now, he decided it made him soft. He was a man now, but he did not know what kind of man. Macho bored him – he did not want to run about a football field and he had no interest in fixing cars. If he had to define the sort of macho he sought, it would be more than a man's man. It would be a thinking man's man. Robert De Niro in *Taxi Driver* or *Goodfellas* would do. Daniel thought yes, he could be my hero and pal.

Daniel had been a nice lad through his school days and on through university and a double first in psychology. And then . . . and then . . . he did not know how it started, or when. He found himself walking faster, jaw constantly clenched. Once he went to a dinner party at his professor's house and, finding the conversation shrill, pretentious and utterly unbearable, he grabbed a bottle of Rioja and emptied it on to the table. 'I can't stand this. I can't stand this.' Horrified at himself, he stood listening to the gloop gloop of escaping wine, watching it soak into the perfect Irish linen table-cloth. Then he left.

Not long afterwards he'd written a passionately rude letter to the head of his department. When he'd finished it he rushed out to post it. He hung about the mail box waiting for it to get lifted. As soon as he saw the postman collect the pile of letters and put them in his sack, Daniel decided he was doing a very foolish thing. He should not send that letter. He should get it back. He ran shouting, waving his arms after the post van till his legs shook. He stood heaving and sweating in the middle of the road, hoarsely repeating, 'I've changed my mind. I've changed my mind.' Remembering now, he covered his eyes and whispered, 'Christ. What got into me?'

Whatever it was, it now got into him regularly. He behaved badly whenever the opportunity presented itself. But since he nutted his father, his rages had calmed. Seeing the man standing before him crying and bleeding and saying, 'Well, that was a pretty laddish thing to do,' had made him feel both horribly satisfied and horribly guilty.

Not long after he had written his famous foul letter to his professor, he'd been drinking and thinking about his childhood. He missed the laddish child he'd been before he broke his leg. Remembering how he'd trustingly leaped into his father's out-stretched arms, and the shock when he hit the tarmac filled him with wild loathing for the man. 'Shite,' he said through clenched teeth. 'Bastard. Shite. Shite.' He'd been in the Café Royal at the time,

73

drinking too much malt. Whisky always brought out the worst in him.

He shoved on his raincoat and set out east across the city for his father's flat in London Road. It was raining. He did not fasten his coat. It flapped and flew out behind him as he strode, eyes fixed, staring insanely ahead, hair flattened against his head. 'Bastard. Bastard,' he said. People moved aside to let him past. Passengers on the city's maroon buses watched him, faces pressed against the window. He could have jumped on one as it trundled past him. But sitting still on a bus would do nothing for his rage. No, a bit of fierce striding was called for.

His father was alone when he arrived. He was usually alone. He didn't make friends easily. His marriage had fallen apart not long after he'd stepped aside and let his son fall. 'I break things,' he said when he was drunk. 'I break everything.'

He was surprised to find Daniel on his doorstep. His son was soaked and obviously enraged.

'Daniel,' he said pleasantly. 'What brings you here this time of night?'

'You bastard. You bastard, why didn't you catch me?'

'I didn't mean to hurt you,' his father said.

'Well, you did. Look at me.' Daniel stepped back, let his father view his lean body. 'I used to be one of the lads. Look what's happened to me. I'm soft. A wimp. Bastard.' He nutted his father. Heard his nose crunch under his head. 'Oh God. What have I done?' he cried. 'Oh sorry. Sorry.'

But his father waved away his apologies. That was when he'd said, 'That was a pretty laddish thing to do.' Blood streaming down his face. He'd been consumed with guilt about his son for years. Now he was released. Well, almost. And now, though Daniel rarely saw his mother, his father was a regular at the bar where he worked. The two got along together.

Now Daniel was being disgraceful again. Three weeks married and screwing around already. Not that he found women easy. They scared the shit out of him, and they confused him. No, women found him easy. Brought up by his mother, denied access to his father he did not talk man talk. He was not threatening. He understood about favourite fingernails and beloved lipsticks. It did not demean him to walk down the street carrying a bunch of flowers, and he thought nothing of going into the chemist's to buy Tampax. Women found it easy to tell him what they wanted, 'No. No. Touch me there. And there.' He did not think it a problem to give them exactly what they wanted.

When he wasn't gambling or dealing in the pub Daniel wandered the streets. He loved street life. The insistent thud of rock'n'roll blaring from shops, lead in the air, the chunter of buses, gleamy windows draped with stuff to buy with money he didn't have, the boozy waft from pubs, the hot blast of junk food flooding from restaurants. He breathed it in. He couldn't get enough. He moved with a young man's recklessness keenly through crowds. People always stared. His sudden handsomeness shook them. Looming through the throng at Woolworth's pick'n'mix he stood out. Women nudged each other asking, 'Isn't that . . .' 'Wasn't he in . . . ?' 'Didn't he . . . ?' 'Who is that . . . ?' Daniel ignored them. He hated the attention. Some people seemed to be on the point of adoration. He detested them for it. Once, two teenage girls, pale and thin in this week's style, swooned when he went by. Then burst into giggles at their silliness.

Daniel thought them sweet and reached out to stroke the cheek of the nearest one saying, 'I forgive you. I forgive you.'

The girls were outraged. 'What an arse,' they whispered.

Daniel heard and turned to them grinning, 'So I am. But I'm so good at it.' He was gentle with women, he was sweet to them. Then he could not help being hateful.

He sighed, sniffed deeply at Mary's perfumed sheets. In half an hour he'd be back out there. What he enjoyed most about sleeping with Mary was her rudimentary approach to the act. She liked the missionary position. She didn't feel herself or pant urgent instructions, habits he'd noticed in younger women. And she never, absolutely never, indulged in any sort of post-coital conversation. She fucked with abandon. She came. She rolled over and slept soundly for half an hour.

She lay beside him now, breathing deeply, a slight snore. He had ten minutes left to consider her back before she woke. A fine back.

75

It should be fat but heaving sacks of potatoes, crates of apples and oranges kept the flesh firm. Fascinated, he ran his fingers through her frizzed and bleached hair. Friendly Mary was deliciously tarty. Ellen rarely bothered with the frilly fripperies of being female. But he loved them; the smell of makeup, perfume and hair-spray. Ellen's female fripperies were the dark and messy sort that turned him off: old tights strewn across the bedroom floor, abandoned knickers, tangled hair embedded in brushes, empty Tampax packs on the bathroom shelf.

The clock beside him flicked over another minute. Daniel chastised himself for his day so far. He had risen early that he might take Ellen a cup of coffee in bed, a small considerate act to relieve his conscience. The night before he had taken money from her handbag. He regularly took money, so regularly he had rules about it. He never took big notes, something she'd miss. He took sums made up of coins and small notes. He reckoned she never knew how much she had anyway. He always swore to himself that the money was for food. And always in the racing pages he found an irresistible horse which always let him down.

Recently Daniel had developed a new approach to his gambling. Once he had studied form. Had in fact taken life as a gambler as seriously, as scientifically, as he had his life as an academic. Now, however, he trusted to luck. But he was meticulous about it. He kept a lucky book. In it he noted winnings and losings and set against them the exact pattern of the day.

Today he'd written: '7.45 rose. Ellen coffee. Wore white sweat shirt, red boxers, tennis shoes. No socks. Breakfast me: coffee, black, two cigarettes. Didn't shave. Played old Springsteen. Watched breakfast telly, got pissed off.'

He detailed every moment right down to putting money on Small Wonder. At the end of the week he'd study it all and try to discover some link. Did he perhaps own a shirt that was luckier than the rest, or was there a pair of loser's underpants in his drawer? Was there a winning breakfast? If he could unravel a common denominator constant through his losings he could eliminate it from his life and build up a winning routine from that.

Mary woke, rolled over and groaned. 'Make us a cup of tea, love,' she said.

She was a bad waker. It was on Daniel's mind that when he, if he, returned to academic life he might write a book, a paper at least, on how women of different body types and from different socio-economic backgrounds behaved after sex. He considered himself an expert. Some women were depressive, some joyous, some silly and some just liked throaty low talk, a kind of verbal replay on the action that had just taken place.

Ellen had quite a line in post-orgasmic prattle. She always spoke about sex. Sex speculative: wonder what divas are like in bed. Wonder what they sound like when they come. Sexual lament: do you know, we've never done it in a car. Sexual inquisition: have you ever done it in a car? Who with? Was she better than me? Sex on a heightened intellectual plane, almost: Isn't sex clever? If I was God I'd never come up with sex. I'd have people exchanging eggs orally, some sort of disgusting party game type thing.

She was so withdrawn, but when she opened she really opened. He smiled, remembering Ellen.

Last night he had found her sitting on the sofa yanking at her hair, crying. 'Look at my hair,' she wept. 'It's been cropped. I look like Martha Klebb in that James Bond film.'

'You do not.'

'I do. I do. I'm never going out again. Everyone will laugh at me.'

'Why did you let him cut it like that? Why didn't you tell him what you wanted?'

'I don't speak hairdresser,' Ellen wailed.

Daniel had a rush of rage. How dare some absurd hairdresser person treat his Ellen like this? He longed to protect her. He had a flash of himself as a New York Italian, De Niro, in a perfect suit, holding the hairdresser by the collar and instructing him with chilling good manners, 'When the lady wants her hair cut you cut it the way she says. Know what I'm sayin' here?'

'Will you fetch us a cup of tea?' Irritated, Mary reached over and punched Daniel's thigh.

'Sorry. I was thinking.'

'Too much of that'll give you hairs on the palm of your hand.'

He walked naked through to the kitchen, a yellow room. Whilst he waited for the kettle to boil he rummaged through the cupboards for food. A meal for Ellen was expected of him this evening, and he'd lost all his money on Small Wonder. Was it the red boxers?

He always left his jacket behind the front door so that he could fill his pockets as he made the tea. Two packets of soup into the top inside pocket, a handful of chocolate biscuits and a tin of sardines into the right-hand side pocket, a wedge of cheese into the left. Everything had to be flat. But, that should do it. A teabag into each of Mary's sex'n'chocolate mugs and still time to read his horoscope in her newspaper. 'Aries: a problem that has been plaguing you will soon be solved. A windfall will relieve stress on a close relationship.' Cheered he took the tea back to the bedroom.

'You've been ages. What have you been doing?'

'I was reading my horoscope.'

'What did it say for me, Pisces?' Mary wanted to know.

'It said,' Daniel told her solemnly, 'that you should watch your friends closely. One of them is taking more from the relationship than you realise.'

Chapter Eleven

On the Saturday after their first meeting Emily Boyle invited Ellen to go shopping. 'We shall go on a mushroom quest to the Italian deli, and I shall teach you how to behave badly.' She linked arms.

Ellen did not quite know how to say that she did not want to learn how to behave badly. 'Why would you want to do that?' she asked.

'Because I can. I have been waiting all my life to get away with being naughty. Who is going to throw out a little old lady? I love behaving badly. It's my hobby.'

Ellen didn't have a hobby, didn't really understand hobby culture. However, when she went to work in the stationery department she'd been asked to fill in a job application form. Name, address, age and hobbies. The first three were routine. But hobbies? 'Tennis,' she wrote (a lie). 'Squash' (another lie). 'Learning new languages' (complete and utter bullshit). 'Reading, writing and appalling my mother' (the truth). As soon as she had it down on paper she regretted it, but as it was in ink, she could not rub it out. Still, she got the job. She wondered if management thought that was what shop girls did, or if they even bothered to read the form. But it was official, then, and noted down for posterity in some filing cabinet somewhere. She was Ellen and her hobby was appalling her mother. Perhaps it would be slightly less adolescent to take up behaving badly.

They went first to buy some fish. Emily fiddled with the trout that lay gaping vacantly in the window.

'Please don't handle the fish,' the assistant called.

'But I will handle it. I am going to buy it. I'm allowed to fiddle with it.'

'No you're not. Please leave it alone.'

'I will not leave this trout alone. I intend to be very intimate with this trout.'

Other shoppers turned to stare. Goodness, what was she going to be doing with the fish?

'I am going to eat this fish. You don't get more intimate than that. Well, not at my age you don't. I want to look at it. I want to see if its eyes are bright, its scales shiny. I want to know if it has been a happy little trout before it came into my life.'

They glared at each other, the fishman and Emily. The fishman took a sharp intake of breath and heatedly said, 'There are other folk interested in my trout. And they'll not be interested in something you've had your hands all over.'

Emily snorted, tossed the trout back on to its tray and rounded on the fishman. 'Have you the vaguest idea who you are talking to? Have you the vaguest idea who I am and what these hands have accomplished? Fiddling with your trout is beneath them. Beneath them.'

She waved her hands in front of him. Ten fine fingers flapping before a man who plainly did not know superior merchandise when he saw it.

Ellen looked round. Did anybody know they were together? Was there some way she could slip into the street and wait round the corner? She hated scenes.

'I am Emily Boyle,' Emily Boyle crowed.

Emily Boyle? The fishman was baffled. He turned for support to the queue. 'Emily Boyle?' he mouthed and received a unanimous shrug. They hadn't heard of her either. But she said her name with such withering authority they all felt they must be wrong, must be missing something not to have heard of her.

'I am a concert pianist. And these hands that you so deride have played a duet with Rachmaninov.' There was a hush. Emily played an air piano, little, strong fingers dashing over an imaginary keyboard, head moving to the music in her head. 'Rachmaninov, I tell you. And he did not find my hands to be anything other than magnificent.'

Defiantly then, she picked up one trout then another and decided in the end to have some plaice. As they left Ellen overheard the fishman say that if effing Rachmaninov came in he wouldn't let him fiddle with his trout either.

'Did you really know Rachmaninov?' Ellen asked.

'Indeed I did.'

'And did you really play a duet with him?'

'I did.'

Ellen was impressed.

Emily linked arms again and proposed they continue the mushroom quest. 'I suspect,' she said, 'that you have never eaten a proper mushroom in your life.'

Ellen suggested they go to Friendly Mary's fruit shop, but Emily Boyle refused. 'That woman is too friendly by far. No, we shall go to the deli on Elm Row and we shall listen to *opera* as we choose. How dull life would be if all there was to buying a mushroom was just buying a mushroom. So, mushrooms and Puccini it shall be, and a bottle of Barolo. You'll pay.'

It had been a good day for Daniel. He had, he was sure, finally cracked the lucky routine. Up at eight, coffee to Ellen, white boxers, putty-coloured chinos, black sweat shirt, baseball boots, no socks. Breakfast, two cups black coffee, two cigarettes and the Atlantic Soul Classics – Otis Redding, Wilson Pickett, Aretha Franklin. He did a small jive as he drank his coffee and read the racing section. Urban Domino, he thought. It'd been a black and white sort of a morning so far. He walked down the left side of the street, stuck his head round the door of the fruit shop to see if there was anything required of him. Mary dismissed him with a small decisive flick of her hand.

At noon he grazed in the supermarket. A croissant from the pick'n'mix bread section, eaten with a couple of slices of salami from the deli as he slowly wandered the aisles eavesdropping on shoppers and reading the labels on ketchup bottles. He opened some ginger biscuits took out three and replaced the packet behind the others on the shelf. He'd return to it tomorrow and eat some more. Then he wiped his mouth, brushed off any telltale crumbs, and bought a can of Coke as he passed through the checkout. All this he noted carefully in his lucky book before he went to place his first bet of the day.

He put the five pounds he'd taken from Ellen last night on his chosen horse. It won. He put his winnings on Monochrome City. It won. Now he put all his winnings on Two Tone Alley. It won. Daniel had a simple gambling system. He simply put all the money he had on his fancied horse to win. He didn't really gamble to make money, he gambled for thrills. This simple all-or-nothing method made his blood rush, heart pound, palms sweat. He loved it. Now, scarcely able to breathe he scanned his paper for another likely horse. Metropolitan Black And White was running in the four thirty. It was too good to miss. He put everything he had on it.

He couldn't stay in the place. Couldn't watch the race. Couldn't even bear to hear it. He sat on the pavement outside the bookie's drinking his Coke. He knew how he looked. His hair stuck on end from the excited way he ran sweaty fingers through it. He was wild-eyed and mumbling to himself, 'I'm right. I'm right. You bastards, I'm right. It'll do it. It'll win. Win. Win, you fucker, win.' People passing walked wide of him. His face was streaked with sweat. His Coke can caved in under his wild grip, Coke flowing over his fingers on to the pavement. He hardly noticed. He didn't care. Didn't care about anything. The lucky gods were with him. There were angels at his side. The good planets were shooting through his sign. Everything was going for him today. He couldn't lose.

When he got home, he emptied his pockets on to the sofa. He had a thousand pounds. 'A grand,' he said. 'I did it. Me.' Actually he'd turned his fiver into one thousand and fifty-seven pounds and forty-six pence. But he'd rounded it down to a neat sum and spent the difference on wine and steaks and records.

Unable to contain his excitement he paced the room, fists clenched saying, 'Yes. Yes. Yes,' over and over. He'd cracked the lucky routine. He knew how absurd this was. And he knew too that he'd have to go with this new flow. Thing was, when he started on this lucky routine he'd nothing. Now he had all this money. Plainly he had to start every lucky day with nothing, or at least five pounds pinched from his wife's purse. He couldn't have money. He couldn't let Ellen know he had money. She would want to do sensible things with it. Pay bills, save up for something nonsensically sensible, like a holiday or a new car. Oh no, he was having none of that. 'Hide it,' he urgently told himself. 'Hide it from me, and hide it from her.' He unzipped one of the cushions on the sofa, stuffed in the notes, plumped it furiously and replaced it. 'Now,' he said, 'pretend it hasn't happened. Don't talk about it. Don't acknowledge the luck and it won't leave you.' This was lunatic. He was logical, sane with an above average IQ. He didn't believe any of this, not really. But what could he do? He was hooked. 'Put on some music,' he urged himself.

He keened across the room, ripping a new record from its sleeve, put it on the turntable and skipped frantically through it, moving the needle from track to track, searching for the sound he needed. A rock'n'roll fix. He needed that. Gambling was not his only craving. Sometimes he'd leave home and not make it to the end of the road before he was filled with some kind of howling angst, a teenage thing, a great hole in his psyche that could only be cured by hearing – and hearing at full blast – certain bits of certain tracks. It started with Jimi Hendrix, those first few bars of 'Burning of the Midnight Lamp' and moved on in time to Neil Young's 'Like A Hurricane'. On it went through the years – now he was dozing on brain-numbing smashes of James Brown – live. He flirted with Little Feat. Had a through-the-earphones affair with Talking Heads, 'Letting the days go by. Watching the river . . .' Then it was 'Rock the Casbah', 'London Calling' or 'Transmetropolitan', 'Yes aye yeah,' he'd sing along. When he'd finished deifying The Clash and The Pogues he went in search of new heroes. The ache, then, ran constant through his life. U2, Public Enemy – the more music he bought, the more he was addicted. He'd stand beside his precious stereo still in his thin raincoat, eyes shut, 'Ah, yes. That hit the spot.' He'd have enough to get him through the next few hours. Then he'd come reeling back, needing more, telling himself the while that it was time he grew out of this.

Today's acquisition was discarded. He shoved it back in the sleeve and would probably never play it again. 'I'm too old for this,' he said to Ellen when she came back. 'Somewhere out there, on some album is the ultimate track. I'll find it, play it and be cured of rock'n'roll for the rest of my life.'

'Did you know Mrs Boyle downstairs knew Rachmaninov?' she said.

'Oh that. She didn't tell you that old story, did she? She tells everybody that.' He groaned indifference. 'You didn't believe her, did you?'

'Of course I did. She played a duet with him.' It was Ellen's turn to play the air piano, demonstrating.

'Oh, bollocks,' Daniel sneered. 'Rachmaninov's dead. All these old classical boys are dead.'

'Rachmaninov died in 1943,' Ellen said. 'He was born in 1873.'

'Did he?' Daniel was surprised. He vaguely imagined that everybody who wrote symphonies lived in an age of frilly shirts and powdered wigs and that they all knew each other. Rachmaninov, Mozart and Beethoven, he thought, probably lived next door to one another. They'd be chums. 'He was born exactly one hundred years before Lou Reed recorded "Walk on the Wild Side",' he said. 'We've come a long way, babe.'

Ellen was angry at being so dismissed. 'I believe Emily Boyle did meet Rachmaninov. She did, too, play a duet with him,' she said hotly. 'I was impressed.'

'I am a siren. I am a woman,' she had written in her notebook. 'I am timeless, sister. I have played violin with Paganini. I have sung with Caruso. Danced with Vaslav Nijinsky. I have been carved in Carrara marble by Michelangelo Buonarroti. I have spanked Freud's bum, taught Einstein sums, discussed scansion with Keats, dined with Escoffier and droned along with Leonard Cohen. But it is my time now. Time to strip the centuries from my face and I am Boudicca, Queen of the Iceni, warrior. I am Jeanne d'Arc, sanctified seventeen-year-old, scourge of the English at Orléans. And I am Patti Smith, godmother punk, chemical dreamer and abuser. Hit the streets, gangster women, we have sisters to avenge.'

'Good script,' Stanley would say. 'Loved the old woman.'

'We shopped for mushrooms and pestered the fishmonger,' Ellen told Daniel.

'Sounds fun,' he sneered, running his fingers through his hair.

The collar of his shirt opened as he did, so Ellen saw the mark on his neck.'What is that?' she said.

'What is what?'

'That mark on your neck.'

'I've got a rash. Dunno. Maybe it's this shirt.'

'Shirt my arse. That's a lovebite, you bastard. I know a lovebite when I see one. At your age. How gross, Daniel.' Ellen was eight again, sitting on the edge of the bath again, getting lessons in lovebite camouflage from her sister. She stayed eight for a few moments, before the full implications of the mark on her husband's neck sank in. 'You've been with someone else.'

Daniel did not look at her. 'Fancy some sardines?' he asked.

'You've been with another woman,' Ellen told him. 'Who is it?'

'You wouldn't know her. God, Ellen, there's no need to make such a fuss. It's only sex.'

'What do you mean, it's only sex? Only sex. What else is there? You shite. You shite. I've been shopping and you've been fucking another woman.' She glared at him. 'I had a lovely time. I bought mushrooms,' she cried. 'I bought mushrooms and you were doing that.'

'No I wasn't,' he said. 'I was . . .' No, he couldn't tell her he was winning. He tapped his neck. 'That was yesterday.'

'Yesterday,' she howled. 'I was working and you were . . .' she pointed accusingly at the guilty patch, ' . . . you were doing that.'

She wanted to hit him, wanted to hurl herself at him and punch him and punch him till he hurt and she didn't. But she couldn't. She had never in her life hit anybody. She had hardly ever lost her temper. So, unable to deal with confrontations, she turned her face to the wall and slowly banged her head over and over. 'Bastard. Bastard. Bastard,' she moaned. 'I hate you. I hate you.'

She picked up her best black leather jacket and left. 'I'm going out. Cook your own effing mushrooms.'

Hands deep in her pockets, she wandered back streets, sniffing and choking. Tears spread mascara down her cheeks. 'Bastard, bastard,' she blubbed to herself. She was cold, but that was good. Cold was good. It served Daniel right that she was so cold. Maybe she'd get a chill that would spread to her lungs and develop into pneumonia. She'd palely lie on a chaise longue, glittery-eyed, dying a tragic, operatic sort of death. That would show Daniel. Then he'd be sorry.

Eventually a small gang of boys, cottoning on to how defenceless and low she felt, started following her, calling to her, 'Hey, darlin'. C'mon over here. Hey, wait.' She heard their steps quicken. She moved faster and eventually broke into a half-walk, half-run with them hard on her heels, hollering into the night. 'Bitch. We're going to fuck you.'

Heart pounding, she stumbled and started running. She did not turn to look at how far behind they were. She just headed for Leith Walk, hailed a taxi, climbed in and gave Jack Conroy's address.

It was his birthday. 'I'm having a party, young Ellen. Come and bring that dreadful man of yours.' She had imagined herself sipping wine, Daniel by her side in his white linen suit. He was gorgeous in that suit. He'd worn it to their wedding. Everyone agreed, though nobody actually said it to her face, the groom was prettier than the bride. She stopped at Oddbins and bought a bottle of chardonnay to take with her.

Black Fingernails opened the door. She was not pleased to see her, Ellen could tell. When she slept with Jack she thought she was oh so cool, oh so sophisticated. Just a swift roll in the hay, a bit of an afternoon frolic with a married man. She was a woman of the world. She did that sort of thing. Now she knew. She was a cuckold too. It hurt. Sinners had fun. Those sinned against felt stupid, inadequate and naïvely trusting. That feeling of standing in the dark and cold, unwanted and her face shiny with the need to please. 'Sorry,' she whispered as she was let in. Not that Black Fingernails understood. Well, Ellen was always apologising and saying sorry.

So Ellen found a corner, sipped her drink and fiddled with her cigarette pack. Across the room a vivid woman flirted and laughed and watched her. At last she came to her. At last she sat down beside her. 'You look like you could do with some serious corrupting,' she said.

2

Cora

Chapter Twelve

When she was ten Cora O'Brien ran away from home. She packed her school bag with a few of life's essentials and took off, top speed, along Tobermory's main street, past the lavatories and past the distillery and up the brae. She hadn't an exact plan as to how she was going to get to the terminal at Craignure and on to the Caledonian MacBrayne ferry that would take her off Mull to Oban and the mainland. She figured she'd deal with that when she got to the top of the hill which was steep, extremely steep. The faster she tried to go up it, the steeper it got. Running made her heart pound. She gasped for breath, but kept going.

That was the first time her father saw her run. He was driving down the hill into the village when he saw her. The speed of her shook him. He stopped the car, got out and called to her. 'Cora! Cora O'Brien, just where are you going battering up the brae like that?'

'I'm running away,' Cora wheezed.

'Oh good for you,' her father said mildly. 'I'm all for that. Could you not have taken one or two of your brothers with you? Only it gets a bit crowded in the house with you all around.'

Cora was part of a sprawling family. Her oldest sister was twenty and her youngest brother six. She was in between, along with two older brothers and a younger sister. Bill and Irene had six children. Sometimes Cora thought her life too crowded by far, hence the bid for freedom.

Cora shook her head. 'I'm not doing that. If I hadn't all those bloody brothers and sisters I wouldn't need to run away.'

'Too right. I quite agree,' her father nodded eagerly. Like his daughter he had the gift of enthusiasm. He leaned towards her, smiling. And she loved his face, such a comfortable face, her dad's.

You could curl up in one of its little curves, that gentle rounded place where cheek reached down to chin, where the smiling happened – you could curl up there and sleep for ever, Cora thought.

'Let me come with you. Let's run away together. Have you brought enough for two?' Her dad unzipped her school sports bag, peered in. 'Oh yes,' he nodded approvingly. 'You've got everything a person could need.' And so she had. She'd packed a copy of the *Beano*, two Mars Bars, a spare pair of socks, a torch and two extra pairs of knickers. What else could a person possibly need in life?

'No,' Cora shook her head. 'You can't come. It isn't running away if you come.'

'Sure enough,' her father agreed. 'Well,' he extended his hand, 'goodbye then. It's been lovely knowing you. And I'll miss you.'

Cora shook the proffered hand. 'You won't do anything silly like cry, will you?'

'Oh, Cora, when you're gone I think I will. I'll cry.'

She couldn't bear the thought of her precious dad weeping. Just imagining it brought tears to her own eyes. 'Don't cry. Please don't cry, Dad.' Tears flowed now. Great fat, wet drops of sadness for her father's sadness ran down her little freckled face, gathered at the point of her chin and actually splashed to the pavement.

'Tell you what,' said her father. 'Stay home and I won't cry.'

So she did. She stayed till she was seventeen. But it was ten years and two children before she went back. Meantime she drifted into and out of her father's enthusiasms.

In the summer of the great escape, Bill O'Brien, having seen the speed that she was taking her leave of Tobermory, decided that Cora had the makings of an athlete. Actually, not just an athlete, but a famous athlete, a fast and dazzling athlete. He was famous, fast and dazzling with the hyperbole.

He bought her a tracksuit and a pair of running shoes. He devised an athlete's diet that consisted mainly of bananas and steak. He took her every evening out to the fields behind the house to train. When it was raining they did squats together in the back bedroom to strengthen her thighs. Had he known the mischief she'd later get up to with her strengthened thighs and the pleasure they'd bring, he would not have bothered. At the time he simply thought he was covering all the angles. His training advice was short and sweet. 'Blister and hurtle, Cora,' he'd say. 'Blister from the starting blocks and hurtle for the tape. Don't look round. Don't think about anybody else, just go for it. Blister and hurtle.'

Cora's running career was short and, well, spectacular. That summer she blistered and hurtled her way to becoming star of the school sports. She won two cups, a medal, and a box of Dairy Milk. Cups and medals bored her, but the chocolates were worth the effort. Heartened by their success her father entered her for the 100 metres at the Oban Games. Most of the village was on the ferry going across to the mainland. A party afloat. For Bill O'Brien it was forty beer-filled minutes. He was more nervous than his daughter.

The track was part of the main arena, cordoned off by ropes. When they were not in the beer tent, people sat on bales of hay, watching. They took their drinks into the sunshine to lubricate this watching. Cora attracted some interest. There was her tracksuit, bright red and covered with butterfly badges she had sewn on. But it was her height that caused most nudges and grins and knowing nods. As soon as the entrants for the first heat were lined up it was plain there was a good six inches' difference between Cora and her nearest rival. That six inches was all leg.

'A fiver on the wee one,' someone said. Cora flinched.

'Never mind them,' her father whispered. 'Go for it. Blister and hurtle.' He reeked of alcohol. Cora shrugged. All this bored her. She had no real desire to run faster than anyone else. Just running was enough. As the starter lined up the competitors, she handed her dad the orange lolly she was eating at the time and received some rapturous applause from the crowd for that. She took her place, heard the gun, shot from the blocks and flew for the tape. And won. It was easy. Very, very easy. She won the next heat. And by the time she hit the quarter finals she had a small following.

'Come away, the wee one.'

At the semis the now ritual handing over of the lolly was received with whistles and roars of approval. Her father took it with pride, gave it a lick for luck, and held it aloft to the crowd. Cora stepped back from the fiery blast of his breath.

'You know what to do, darlin'. Just do it. Know what I mean?' he reeled, pointing waveringly at the tape. Cora adored him. Sober he was wonderful, drunk he was more wonderful. Drunk he always cried. She looked at that special little bit of his face where she would curl up and lie if only she were tiny enough and she promised to win. Bill O'Brien was high. He was a man on the make. Why, he had a knack for this. Cora could, he drunkenly believed, go all the way – whatever that meant. And he would go all the way with her – wherever that was.

As the afternoon moved on, the waft and fumes of booze filled the air above the park. The very air was alcoholic, and the mood was jubilant. People sang. There was a new heroine to sing for, 'Come away, the wee one.' They were Scots, and they would all their lives root for the wee one. It was part of what they were, automatic underdogs. Those who were not naturally small had delusions of smallness. Tall people could not enjoy with grace and style their height, they longed to be down there blistering and hurtling with the wee ones. They wept for Cora and her courage, and bought her Cokes and ice creams and chocolate, all of which she ate with relish. A small euphoria was cooking, people were betting on the wee one. Money was changing hands, drinks were being got. And was everybody happy? You bet your life they were.

Come time for the final Cora was, naturally enough, awash with confectionery and fizzy drinks. Though she was a bit worried about how tired she felt, Cora did not think her alarming consumption of Coca-Cola, raspberry-ripple ice cream and Mars Bars would, in any way, slow her up. They lined up.

Her father was incoherent with joy, hope and whisky. 'Do it, Cora. Do it, my lovely. You can do it.'

Strategies, sadly, meant nothing to them. They both thought a strategy was something a general did to manoeuvre an army. It had more to do with winning wars than races. Cora did not know about holding a little back, or saving her best till last. She heard the starter's pistol and felt the rush and bustle of others passing her, the desperate urgency. It was the urgency of those who knew to blister and hurtle only when it mattered, only when the real winning was at stake. She came last, then. But last to a wild roar and thunderous applause. She bowed and opened her arms to the crowd as she crossed the line. 'Come away, the wee one.' That cheer was for her and she imagined people would hear it miles away. It would sound clear across the water to Tobermory, a yell like that. She lost. But only gloriously.

'You humiliated her,' Irene O'Brien scolded her husband on the ferry home. 'How will she ever live this down?'

Bill hung his head. The fool he was. But Cora slipped her hand into his and told him not to worry, she'd had a lovely day. 'The loveliest of my life,' she said. She had learned to play a crowd. She'd had more goodies than she thought she could ever eat. And she knew that there was joy in moving. She could listen to her body as she went, her heart and her breathing. All her life, then, in joy or sorrow, she ran. But winning meant nothing.

When her children were old enough to leave unattended she would run through the Edinburgh mornings by the Water of Leith, watching starlings, listening to the rhythm of her feet and the sounds of her breathing, thinking about her father. It was the only time she managed to mull over the things she found in her head. The only time she had herself to herself.

Chapter Thirteen

When Cora arrived in Edinburgh she was seventeen. She was dressed for safety. Her hair was pinned back and she had one of those faces that looked like an infant's drawing, two bright eyes, small nose and a tumble of auburn hair. All that was on her face was a child's candour. It was innocent, waiting for life to happen to it. Waiting for a few expressions to add to its repertoire.

She had a place at Edinburgh University. She was going to be a chemist. Chemistry came easily to her, she had a natural understanding of the mixing of solids, liquids and gases. Ever since her teacher at Tobermory High had explained about the nature of matter – anything that occupies space and has mass.

'Matter can go through physical changes – ice melts, solid to liquid; water boils, liquid to gas,' her teacher said. 'These changes are easily reversed. Chemical changes, now, chemical changes are tricky. They are hard to reverse.' Cora thought it easy. Chemistry was a delight, its precision a comfort, its colours a delight, its changing forms, reversible and irreversible, a constant fascination. It had a kind of poetry for her. That, and she fancied she cut a dash in her white lab coat.

She went home for Christmas. She was changing. The life she was living was on her face. Irene saw it right away. A firmness about her daughter's jaw, a resolve. All Bill saw was the shorn hair, the pierced ears, the extravagant eye makeup. He saw the short skirt and huge boots. Neither of them saw the moth tattooed on her bum. Neither of them would ever know about that.

'Don't you ever tell your grandmother about my tattoo,' Cora warned her boys when they were still little enough to be allowed lingering looks at her backside.

'Why not?'

'You know,' she nodded to them. 'There are some things you just don't tell your mother.'

'But you're our mother.'

'Well, don't tell me, then.'

'Don't tell you what?' Children were so persistent.

'Don't tell me whatever it is you don't want me to know when the time comes for you to have things you don't want to tell your mother.' They stared at her, baffled.

'How're the studies going?' her father asked.

'Oh fine,' she lied.

'Well, that's all that matters, isn't it?' he smiled. Irene looked at him witheringly. Men were such fools. What on earth was going on in that dim head of his? Didn't he see? Didn't he see anything? God, she could see it. She turned the glare on to Cora. Cora winced.

'The girl's got in with a bad crowd,' Irene told Bill in bed that night.

'Oh, she'll be fine,' Bill said. 'Cora's got a good head on her.'

Irene tutted and turned over. He just didn't see it. And Cora was his darling. How could she tell him? Cora wasn't a girl any more, was she? Cora was a woman now. And furthermore it was plain to Irene that Cora was turning into the wrong sort of woman. The naughty sort.

The next morning Cora went round to see her grandmother. Irene phoned an advance warning.

'The child's had a mental aberration,' she said. 'If that's what university does for you, you can keep it. Strikes me education only makes you daft.'

'Well, I wouldn't go as far as that.' Gran O'Brien always felt Irene was too dismissive of everything and everybody. 'It's a child she is.' She was from Orkney, had met Bill's father in Inverness over sixty years ago and had lived here in Tobermory since she married. As a child she'd been beaten in class for speaking Gaelic, the tongue she spoke at home. It had left its mark. Now she spoke English, thought in English, but dreamed as a Gael. And her everyday linguistic constructions were the ones she'd learned almost eighty years ago from her own mother: 'A child she is.'

But when Cora arrived in her kitchen her grandmother saw a

child she wasn't. 'Have you walked here through the streets dressed like that?'

'Yes.' Cora was proud. 'We all dress like this. Well, all my set anyway.'

'Is that the style?'

'Yes.'

'It'll be a reading you're after.'

Cora nodded. 'Yes.'

'Well, put on the kettle.'

Cora's grandmother read tea leaves. As far back as Cora could remember her grandmother had been peering into people's tea cups, telling them their lives. As a little girl she'd played with her favourite doll under the huge table in her grandmother's immaculate kitchen listening to the readings.

'I cannot tell the future,' her grandmother said. 'It's the present I'm making sense of. Help you see the broader view.' They'd drain their cups, keen to know what was happening to them. Many an afternoon was spent standing by the window holding a cup up to the light, making mystic sense of the shapes in the gathered leavings, dredged at the bottom. Cups would be passed to young Cora that she would stare in and say what she saw. 'Stars,' she'd say. 'A tree.'

'She has the child's eye,' her grandmother would explain. 'She sees what she sees. We see what we wish we saw. Ah now, look. Right enough. A tree. Great branches reaching out. It's good fortune you'll be having.' Then again, when the news wasn't good, the bad tidings were delivered gently. 'Oh my, now. Things are getting away from you. You're not at all happy at the moment.'

It always seemed to Cora that people would know what was happening to them without her grandmother peering into a cup. But they liked it. It was a comfort. Her grandmother offered people understanding, sympathy and hope, always hope. She never charged. She saw trips across water (considering they lived on an island this was hardly surprising), lucky dark strangers. She saw more than people knew – black crows and dogs, deep depressions.

'You have to ask the person to drain the cup. And it's good tea you use. Proper tea, big leaves. And it isn't just the cup you read,' Cora's grandmother told her. 'It's the people behind the cup you look at. It's their moods you're interpreting. Then again, you're letting them know what other people think of them, and what they think of themselves.' She sighed. 'Women,' she said. 'They're always looking for something more. A deeper meaning. "This can't be it," they say. How can I tell them it is?'

She understood this desperation well. Like the drinkers from the cups she read, she imagined she had dedicated a good part of her life to the elimination of dirt and was, like them, seriously doubting the validity of such devotion. She imagined she was a domestic despot declaring war not only on dust and muck but on the bringers of filth into the house – but she was wrong. Her house was old-fashioned clean. Kept pristine, not with aerosols, but with polish and elbow grease. It gleamed darkly, smelled of polish, and soup simmering and home baking. Visitors lingered, savouring its old-fashioned warmth and safety. Still Cora's grandmother regularly chastised herself for bustling through life duster in hand. She was a wiper and a guardian of household surfaces.

'It'll all be here long after I'm gone,' she said, indicating the sideboard with a sad flap of her hand. Then, realising the finality of that remark, 'Long after I'm dust. Everything . . .' This time she indicated the world beyond her dresser with a dramatic sweep of both arms. Everything, the furniture, the house, the street, the village, all the towns out there she'd never visited. Streets and streets of houses with wiped sinks, gleamy draining boards, shiny baths, perfect skirting boards and all the dust. All that dust that she and a million other women vigorously worked to eradicate would return to settle on picture frames, television screens, whatever, for ever. 'I'll be the dust. It'll be me getting wiped off mantelpieces, shaken out the window only to come back and settle again.' Shocked by this vision she slumped on to her perfectly plumped sofa. The truth? God, you could die from it. 'Maybe that's why women search for something mystic – a meaning. There must be more to life than just getting on with it. Men now, men think getting on with things is the meaning of their life. That's what they do, they get on with it. What do you think, Cora?'

'Yes,' she answered, though she hadn't a clue what her grand-mother was on about. Well, she wouldn't, she was four at the time.

But she always remembered those words. It helped her later to understand the indestructibility of matter and the uselessness of a life as a guardian of household surfaces.

It was inevitable that Cora should pick up her grandmother's gift. Now she was earning quite a reputation as a mystic back in Edinburgh. Her friends considered themselves sophisticated and cultured. They wore their rebel clothes, listened to outrageous music but couldn't resist a bit of no-nonsense, down-to-earth mysticism when it was on offer.

When Cora left, clumping down her grandmother's tiny front path in her boots, Jenny O'Brien phoned Irene.

'Well, I did a reading. She's just finding a new way. A road for herself to follow.'

'I suppose it's natural at her age,' Irene said. 'Was there anything else?'

'No,' Jenny lied. She could hear Bill scoffing in the background. 'Voodoo rubbish,' he was shouting. 'Bloody women with their horoscopes and tea leaves and mumbo jumbo.' Jenny did not say that she'd seen a dangerous road in her granddaughter's cup. She knew when to keep her mouth shut.

'The girl can read cups for herself.' Bill could hardly believe this cup business. 'She could make a cup of tea, drink it, look at the stuff at the bottom and think, goodness me, I'm behaving like a prat.'

'You can't read your own cup,' Irene scoffed. 'Surely after all these years you know that.'

'He knows nothing,' his mother said down the phone. 'Someone like Cora, the way of her, she'd only ever see sunny roads and winning posts. It's an optimist she is.'

So knowing nothing about her family's worry and the grandmother's secret gleanings from the bottom of her cup, Cora returned to university. She was longing to get back to her new life and her new friends. Her family came down to the ferry to see her off. They stood in a straggled row in the car park watching the boat and the girl on board it sail away. Cora leaned over the rails waving and waving. She had her chemistry books in her bag, was still wrestling with the nature of matter, the nature of things. But irreversible chemical changes were happening in her.

Chapter Fourteen

In April Cora phoned home to say she wasn't coming home for Easter. She wanted to be with her friends. 'And,' she said, 'there's nothing up there for me. Oh,' she added casually in a detached disinterested manner, 'by the way . . .'

Irene gripped the receiver and held her breath. Something dire was coming. Through her parenting years Irene had learned to beware the words 'oh by the way.' Oh by the way, Mum, someone's thrown a lump of coal down the lavatory and water's pouring over the sides. Oh by the way, I've failed all my exams. Oh by the way, I've crashed the car.

' . . . I'm moving out of hall. I'll be sharing a flat with a friend,' Cora said.

Irene stood in her long green candlewick dressing gown, clutching the phone. 'Oh no, you don't my girl. Oh no, you don't,' she shouted.

She stormed into the kitchen where Bill was mildly drinking tea and reading the paper. 'That young madam thinks she can do what she likes. But she can't. Oh no, she can't.'

To Bill's surprise they were within the hour rattling down the road to catch the nine o'clock ferry. 'You're surprised,' Irene thundered. 'Just wait till you see the look on her face.'

But it was she who was shocked. The changes in Cora, eyebrow-raising at Christmas, were now, four months later, dramatic. Her hair was purple and green, shaven at the sides and worn in a long vibrant tumble down the middle. Her ears were multi-pierced rows of chain-and-charm-laden hoops. She wore black lipstick and her eyebrows were plucked almost out of existence. She openly smoked, blowing rebellious blasts of smoke past Irene. Her right eye was ornately made up. She seemed to be scowling out from the

101

depths of a five-pointed star. There was a black spider drawn on her left cheek.

'Is that a tattoo?' Irene pointed, horrified.

'It washes off,' Cora heaved the words out. The trial it was speaking to people over twenty-five. 'Actually,' she added, 'I was thinking of changing my name to Spyder.'

Irene felt her knees tremble, though she didn't know if it was shock or rage.

Cora took them to the pub round the corner and introduced them to her turbulently clothed friends, who all looked at them briefly and nodded.

'My parents,' Cora said. Wasn't it awful and embarrassing to have two middle-aged people in tow? she said to her friends with a slight movement of her eyebrows. And her friends shot her sympathetic glances.

Bill bought drinks. Cora, to Irene's horror, asked for a pint of Guinness but hardly touched it. After a while she went to the bar and bought herself a Coke.

'It's a pity they don't have sneering at the Olympics. We'd have a roomful of champions here,' Irene said to Bill when Cora left their table. 'And our daughter is turning into the queen of the lip curl. Where did she learn that?'

They sat slowly drinking, communicating occasionally across their silence with sudden questions and bits of information. 'How's Gran's flu?' 'We had the hall painted.' 'Can you walk in them boots? Are they not heavy?'

'They're very comfortable. They last.'

Cora's friends across the bar rose to leave. They waved laconically. ''Bye, Cora. 'Bye, Cora's parents,' someone said. Irene seethed. She felt old. She felt frumpy. An outcast in a lurid world of wild music and rebel clothes. All around her were people in leather jackets and T-shirts. She was an old fool in her best navy coat. She was sitting in a strange bar drinking a glass of wine at two in the afternoon when she'd rather be having a cup of tea and a sandwich. These people, she thought, would know nothing about a nice cup of tea. They'd all be drinking or taking drugs or listening to funny loud music. In the end, though, she had nothing to say to Cora about her moving out of hall. She and Bill both realised that their daughter would just do what she wanted to do. More than that, she would really want to do what they didn't want her to do.

'Did you hear them?' Irene said on the way back to the car. She was hoarse with indignation. ' " 'Bye, Cora's parents." Parents. They called us parents.' And though she never swore, now she lapsed and delivered what she considered a mouthful. There was no other way to say what she felt. 'Bloody children. You bloody give birth to them, then one bloody day they bloody turn bloody round and bloody call you their parents. The cheek of it. I may be a mother but I'm nobody's parent. I refuse to be a parent.' She grabbed the car door handle and rattled it furiously, waiting for Bill to come to open it for her.

Bill shrugged. He too felt old and foolish and past it and envious. He thought that they didn't have youth when he was young. He had a sports jacket and a Gene Vincent record. Somehow it wasn't the same. 'They'll all grow out of it,' he said. 'They'll end up accountants and they'll look back not in anger, but sheepishly.'

Irene had looked at her daughter long and hard. She'd changed. The girl who had left home dreaming of becoming a chemist had grown up, gone away. Irene could tell, didn't know how she could tell. But she could tell. It was the swelling of her daughter's breasts. The curve of her stomach. The consumption of fizzy drinks. The lowering of her eyes. The shame. Irene saw it all. The physical changes in Cora, the clothes, the hair – were easily reversed. But the other change was chemical and at four months was becoming irreversible.

'That child's pregnant,' Irene said to Bill when they got back to the car. She sat heavily in the passenger seat, put her handbag on her knee. She was not going to get comfortable for the long drive home. She refused to get comfortable. Her daughter was behaving like a wanton fool, and – dare she even let the word flit through her head? – a whore. She could not possibly allow herself to get comfortable. She rounded on her husband. 'It's all your fault.'

'Me?' Bill pointed to himself. 'Me? Don't be disgusting. I won't be accused of that. You're not blaming me there. God. She's down here and I'm miles away. I haven't even seen the child—'

Isla Dewar

'No.' She was exasperated enough to hit him. 'No. You with all that running nonsense. It started then. We lost her then. It turned her head.'

Dear Cora, *she wrote when she got home.*

I know all about you. You can't hide such a thing from your mother, you know. A woman knows. I don't even want to imagine all the nonsense you are getting up to. But it was plain to me, if not your father, that you are pregnant. I only hope you know who is the father of your child. But I'm so disappointed in you. It didn't take you long to go off the rails, did it? Obviously we will support you. But I have to tell you this – you have broken your father's heart.

'You have broken your father's heart.' Cora read and reread that phrase. All day she turned it over and over in her mind. 'You have broken your father's heart.' Did he cry? She shed tears for her father's tears.

Dear Mum, *she wrote back.*

Of course I know who is the father of my child. He is Claude, a Frenchman I met at a party. I love him very much and I know he loves me. I am proud to be having his baby. This is the best thing that has ever happened to me. Having a baby is more important than any education. I am bringing a new life into the world. Nothing can surpass this . . .

Her handwriting swept and curved deeper and deeper the more she expressed her passion. Before she signed off she added: 'I'm sorry I've broken Dad's heart. Tell him that I love him.'

All her life she remembered that letter, and no matter how hard she tried to forgive herself for writing it, she never could overcome the cringe inside it brought. There is no fool like an old fool, what bollocks, she thought. There is no fool as dire as a young and headstrong fool. They are the biggest fools of all.

'But,' she would cry in the night, years later, when remembering and cringing kept her from sleeping, 'but, what the fuck are you

104

meant to say when your mother says, "A woman knows"? How dare she?' And she would pummel her pillow before banging her head on it, furiously trying to sleep.

Years and years later, after a night lying awake staring into the dark plagued by memories and cursing herself for the fool she'd been when she was young, she sat at her kitchen table sharing wine, cigarettes, regrets and New York cheddar crisps with Ellen.

'I think,' Cora said, 'that I live a lie.'

'You? Rubbish.'

'No. Really. My mother used to say, "A woman knows". Know what I mean?'

Ellen nodded. 'I know the saying. I just don't ever say it. Because I don't know what it is I'm meant to know in my capacity as a woman.'

'I said it myself just the other day,' Cora confessed. ' " A woman knows," I said to my class. Knowingly, I said it, arrogant even. But what does a woman know? How to bake a sponge? How big is a ball of string? The meaning of life?'

Ellen shrugged.

'No good will come of it. I'll be found out. I know nothing,' Cora said.

'I don't think that's true.'

'I know nothing about the knowing thing that women are meant to have. I look about at women in the street and I wonder if they know what it is we are meant to know. If it's only me that is ignorant about the secret business of being a woman. I had children too young. I left home too young. I rushed at everything and I didn't stop to learn. And now, even though I do a job and I have brought up two sons, I still think I know nothing. There's so much I'm ashamed of. Do you think that's what women know? That in the end we'll shame our parents?'

After her father learned about the baby he sent money every week. It came on Thursdays in a brown envelope, always with a small note: 'Everyone's well here and thinking about you. Take care, Cora, and don't you go thinking we've forgotten you.'

She never found out if her mother knew about this money. 'You broke your father's heart.' She knew of course that she hadn't. But

105

she knew how broken-hearted he'd have been if he ever found out about the things she did. It wasn't Bill's heart she broke with her fatherless babies and her wildness. It was her own.

Chapter Fifteen

Cora met Claude at a party. She was standing leaning on a wall, drinking Guinness, smoking dope, rolling her head from side to side in time to a cracked and overplayed copy of *Pretzel Logic*. Her mind was numb. But she was watching him, and thinking she would get to know him. The way she did. When he eventually came over to speak to her she realised how befuddled by chemicals she was. She'd quite lost control of her lower lip.

Conversation was limited. He said, 'Hello,' and she said, 'Uh-huh.' He said, 'Can I get you another drink?' and she said, 'Uh-huh.' But she thought, isn't it a bitch? Just when you need them most your brain and your tongue abandon you. However, with a debilitated lower lip and malfunctioning brain such a thing was far too complex to say. But her uh-huhs must have been more alluring than she imagined. He took her back to his place and showed her everything he knew about sex. Which was a great deal more than she knew.

His flat in the Grassmarket, three floors up, was the filthiest place Cora had ever seen. It smelled damp and she did not know if the floorboards were up to the strain of her walking across them. She tiptoed when she made her way to his bed. She drunkenly thought that way there might be less of her.

There was a cooker, a grubby rug, a table, a chair, a frying pan and a small pot. And, of course, the bed. It was unmade, sheetless, that tangle of blankets he'd left when he rose in the morning. Or, as Cora would discover, in the early afternoon.

As soon as they got in the door he kissed her. They had been kissing and groping a bit all the way home. Now they were alone, in private, and free to really kiss. And grope. Though when Claude did it, it wasn't like groping. He knew how to make a woman squirm. It was what he was best at. He ran his hands up her thighs, and removed her underwear as if that was what underwear was for. Removing. He set Cora moaning, 'Oh please. Oh please. Touch me there.' She was just eighteen. When he entered her, and they were still just by the door, he did not move, did not shove or thrust. She was against the wall, legs curled round his waist. He pressed against her. He smelled of garlic.

'I could stay like this for ever,' he boasted. 'We could die like this.'

'You couldn't. You couldn't,' Cora said. Or panted. 'Bet you couldn't.'

'I could.' Then facing the truth, 'No, you're right. I couldn't.'

In the morning she lay, arms spread, his head between her thighs. This was lovely. This could replace running. She started to count the milk bottles lined up beneath the window, beside the cooker. They were unwashed, stained, milk streaked and they only slightly glistened in the sunlight, smelled sour. There were hundreds and hundreds of them. A little army of them. 'One, two, three, oh. Four, five, oooh.' Her counting got to seven before she was distracted.

She moved in with him. She bought sheets and started a Get Rid Of The Milk Bottles campaign. She rarely went to lectures. She'd made a significant discovery about herself that was devastatingly to waylay her progress in life. She was horny as anything.

When as a teacher she considered the scattering of wriggling infant, tiny beings in constant motion, in her class, she thought: Shame, most of them are going to get waylaid, too. And she thought: Damned hormones. They've had such a diabolical effect on my life and I don't even know what one looks like. God, I really, really needed sex. I couldn't understand why people studied or worked when they could be shagging. It was more than throbbing hormones. I was a teenage hormone.

And though she was not prone to recriminations she knew it was a pity that she had discovered sex for real, so important and so grown up, when she was eighteen. She could not sit still for thinking about it. She took up serious shagging when she was supposed to be making lifetime career decisions. She supposed lots of other people were similarly caught out. No wonder folk got to forty and started to scream and cry. They'd got distracted a couple of decades earlier and were feeling the chill of naff decisions, heated doings.

But she'd been more than distracted. Something had got into her. A thing. A wildness. She couldn't, now, properly define it, but remembering sometimes made her reel. Not with shame. No, it was relief she felt. Thank heavens she hadn't got caught. Her mischief came screaming back to her when she hadn't got a proper grip on her thoughts. She'd be wiping the kitchen unit, peeling a potato, hoovering the carpet and the boredom of it would numb her mind. It was then the raw naughtiness of her brief life with Claude would come back to her.

There they were, furiously fucking up some alley, high on the rush of shoplifting. It was too exciting, thieving, too exciting by far to wait to get home before they started their celebrations. Adrenalin belted through them, the spoils of the day spread at their feet – well, Claude's feet. Cora's were always well and truly off the ground.

'Oh my God,' she would moan. 'A fool, me.'

Then rounding on her boys, 'I don't want either of you growing up to be like me.'

They would dismiss this with a sigh. Considering the life she led – the noise, the constant blat of music that she had to have with her in the car, in the kitchen, in her bedroom, the irritating musical sizzle that eeked from her earphones when she set off running; her mess, the tissues, nail varnish, lipsticks, scatterings of female stuff and God knows what under the bed, her relationships – men who never reappeared, thrown out at one or two in the morning because she could not bear to let go and actually sleep, dip into unconsciousness, with somebody – considering everything they knew about her, neither of them had any intention of growing up to be like her. Though they loved her. Oh yes they did that. That was what made her mess tolerable.

'I mean,' Cora continued, 'what's the point of me making all those mistakes if you're going to make them too? The very least you could do is make some new mistakes. That'd be interesting for me.'

Cora knew her mistakes. They visited her often. She had crammed all her youth into two years. Blister and hurtle, Cora. She threw herself at everything. She thought she was still suffering from some lingering adolescence she hadn't got out of her system – the music and the mess. She didn't think having two children before she was twenty a mistake – a vast and absurd inconvenience, yes. But they weren't a mistake. There was the shoplifting, big mistake that. And then there was the breaking of her father's heart. Oh, she did not want to think about that.

'You have broken your father's heart,' her mother wrote. Cora caught hold of those words and locked them within her. When she was torturing herself about her wrongdoings she brought them out to increase her torturings. Her biggest mistake, though, was not challenging it. She should have blistered and hurtled to the nearest phone and demanded of her mother, 'What the hell do you mean by that?'

Chapter Sixteen

'What's the worst thing you've ever done?' Ellen asked once. They were drinking where they usually drank – Cora's kitchen, having one of those best and worst confessional conversations. Best sex ever. Worst dinner party. Most embarrassing date. Silliest outfit. Worst buy.

'Oh,' said Cora. 'Hard to say.' Was it all the stuff she stole? Or lying about what she saw in tea cups? Or was it forcing a lifestyle she did not cherish on her children? There was so much.

'What's the worst thing you've ever done?' Cora asked Ellen.

'Dunno. I slept with two men at the same time once. But that's not so terrible really. They were my love slaves. I quite enjoyed it. But it's sweaty. If you fall asleep you have to be careful not to be the one in the middle. You wake in a terrible lather. Damp, hungover and ashamed of yourself.'

'Oh that,' said Cora. 'Yes, we all know that.'

Ellen met her lovers at a comic convention in London. They were fans. She didn't know she had any and was quite delighted with them. They were younger than her, but very presentable. Well, presentable enough for someone who'd decided it was time to avenge her husband's philandering. They didn't wear back-to-front baseball caps, that was enough for Ellen. They'd gone for a drink in the hotel bar and one thing led to another, and another. She couldn't choose between them so they'd all ended up in her bed. That seemed fair.

Stanley had looked at her coolly when they appeared all three in the morning, rumpled and bleary. 'Behave yourself,' he told her.

'I know. Sleeping three in a bed is tricky,' said Cora. She'd had two boys in her bed for years. They slept like a heap of puppies, Cora and Sam and Col. She hadn't needed to chase them away.

111

They each decided when they were too grown up for such cuddles and each went his own way to his own bed. Let them go, Cora thought. And having a bed to herself was lovely. She did not wake with a damp biscuit sticking to her thigh, or a brutally hard little car wedged at the small of her back. Nor did she wake at three in the morning hanging uncovered and shivering over the side of the bed whilst two little people in Peter Rabbit pyjamas spread themselves in the warm, snoring sweetly.

But there was a time in Cora's life when she had not felt complete unless some little body was curled comfortably against her, little lips pursed, little fists clenched – such serious sleepers, children. And then when they'd left her bed they still came back to it every morning, icy little feet on her naked thighs, to relate to her their adventures whilst sleeping. The dreams they had.

It was Claude's elixir of life that got them started on their shopping sprees.

'This is the secret of perfect health, good skin and a sturdy heart,' he said, scraping crushed garlic into some extra virgin olive oil. 'Take this every day and nothing will go wrong with you.' He thumped his chest demonstrating the healthy sturdy thing beating within. And coughed. Cora adored him. He was pale-skinned, thin and fragile, like a poet, she thought. And she was robust. She could run up the three flights to their flat, whilst he came slowly behind. He was sensitive. He had beautiful dark eyes and was prone to night sweats. His life was pained and he was misunderstood. She was coarse and too healthy by far. She felt crude beside him.

He could withstand the Scottish weather, but the food drove him to distraction. The only time Cora saw him lose his temper was during their first week together when she cooked for him. She lovingly prepared her speciality.

'What's this?' he said, looking in horror at the plate before him.

'It's sausages and eggs and beans. A fry up.'

'This isn't food. It's pig shit.'

Cora was hurt. How could he insult her cooking like this? How could he speak to her like this?

'I will not eat this,' he waved at it in disgust. 'Take it away.'

'No. This is good nutrition. I won't see it wasted. I hate waste.'

'You don't hate waste as much as I hate pig shit.' Peeg sheet.

He opened the window and hurled the food, plate and all, out into the night. She heard the faint whistle as it took to the air, then seconds later the smash as it landed on the pavement below – cries of protest from passing pedestrians who'd just had a narrow escape from flying food.

'What was that?'

'Good grief! It's a plate of sausage and egg. God's sake. Where did that come from?'

Cora and Claude, three floors above, did not dare look out and declare themselves. In the morning it was still there, lying on the pavement, one smashed plate thick with congealed fat. Some night creature, human or four-legged, had eaten the rest.

It was, then, the need for the elixir of life and the lack of money to buy it that started them shoplifting. It was so simple. Claude in the delicatessen simply slipped a bottle of olive oil up his sleeve as Cora bought a single croissant. They left. Burst jubilantly on to the street.

'Did it. Got it. Aha.' Neither of them had ever felt such wicked glee. They walked, stifling their delight, carefully from the shop. Don't run. Running's a sign of guilt. Walk. Walk quicker. And quicker. Faces glowing. No smiling. No running. Control. Quicker then. Till they were tanking up the street. Till they had to run. Racing away, then. Laughing. They'd been naughty and got away with it. It started there. It started then.

Within weeks they were both hooked on the rush it brought them. Their little grubby room filled with nonsensical goodies. What had started as an act of survival – neither of them had the money to eat properly, and certainly couldn't afford to eat the sort of food Claude wanted – became a thrill.

Every morning they lay in bed together promising each other not to do it today. That's what they called it, doing it. They couldn't bring themselves to say 'stealing' or 'shoplifting'.

'We won't go to the shops today,' he'd say.

'No,' she'd agree. 'Better not. Someone will spot us. They're bound to notice us. We can't keep doing it.' Nor did they voice the words, 'get caught'. Neither could bear the thought of what might happen to them if they did.

They'd rise around noon, and, after several cups of coffee to wake them and set their blood flowing, they'd breakfast on the remains of last night's dinner, the previous day's spoils. Bits of garlicky chicken picked from the carcass, straight-from-the-pot spoonfuls of Claude's daube, dark chocolate biscuits, wine, brandy. They'd dress in their acquired outfits, splash on acquired colognes, and, vowing they weren't going to take any more risks, they'd set out for their day's adventures.

Always they'd hit the department stores in the centre of town, heading first for the food hall. 'We have to eat,' she'd say. 'We'll only take what's necessary.'

'What we need. What we have to.'

'We have to eat.'

But there were such natty things to have, tasty jars of grainy white wine mustard, jams and jellies, pralines, quails' eggs, cheeses. They'd walk together slowly, staring, quietly discussing, scarcely breathing. Just beneath this control, their hearts were beating wildly. Hammering. Cora had the knack of looking about, watching whilst not appearing to be watching. The casual, yawning gaze rather than the furtive guiltily wild look about. 'Take it. Take it now.' Claude would hand over a couple of things at the checkout. Cora, carrying the loot, would wait for him. They'd walk through the rest of the store, fingering this, ogling that, shoving whatever into their pockets. Didn't matter what, scarves, earrings, a tie or two, and out the door. Along the street into the next store.

Sometimes they'd split up. Claude would wander, she would wait by the door. Her heart would pound when she saw him through the crowd, heading for her. Then she'd wander and he'd wait, till their exuberance got the better of them. It was a high that hit each of them simultaneously. They would gather speed. Out the door, walking. Along the street. Don't run. Don't draw attention. Pushing through the afternoon crowds. Faster, faster. Till running became inevitable. Cora in front, blister and hurtle, he some way behind, panting. But both faces lit with the glee, triumph. 'We did it. Did it.' If they could have raised their arms and taken a bow they would have. 'Yes. Yes. Yes. Yes. Easy.'

Running top speed was the only way to express the wildness of it. Head back, Cora went. Claude, pale and eventually breathless, followed. Off Princes Street into Rose Street and into the dark of its little lanes, back doors of pubs and restaurants. The smell of food and booze. Cora off the ground against the wall and he on her, fucking. They'd pull at each other's clothing, kissing, licking, touching, desperate to consummate the rush. 'Oh please, please, now. Do it.' Drained and shaky with exhaustion they'd stagger wanly home, pockets and bag filled, sometimes – often – with rubbish. They'd get home, pour out their prizes and always, always be surprised with what they had.

'We'll have some brandy. I need some brandy,' Claude said.

But Cora shook her head. 'No. I don't want that.' She was consumed by new needs that she didn't understand. She felt that her body was bossing her about. She wanted brandy. It didn't. She wanted coffee. It didn't. 'I need something fizzy. And none of your Perrier. I want something sweet and fizzy.'

Cora got ill. She lay in bed mornings, moaning and throwing up. Her breasts hurt. She was bloated and couldn't run. Going to the shops with Claude to *do it* no longer interested her. In fact she found all that excitement nauseating. 'I can't, Claude. I just can't. Look at my legs. I'm all swollen and horrible. I hate myself.'

Claude stroked her leg. 'It's just as well, really. We'd get caught. What do they do to shoplifters?' There, he'd said it. They were shoplifters. They'd get caught. The spell was broken.

'I don't know,' Cora said. 'Prison? Probation? My mother and father would make me go back home.' She turned and faced the wall. 'I don't want that.'

She was, of course, pregnant. Nine weeks, the doctor said. He offered her an abortion which she refused. She thought it was her punishment for behaving so badly. Or maybe it was a bit of reality come to save her from the horrors her wildness would bring. However, except for when her children had nothing to eat, she never stole again.

'Do you have a worst dread?' Ellen asked her once. 'I have. A sound. After Daniel and all his stuff, you know? I dread the sound of the mail box in the morning, and sometimes the sound of someone knocking on the door gives me a chill.'

Cora shrugged. The sound she dreaded was simple. When she went to Princes Street shopping she always worried that someone had spotted her on her stealing rampages and would recognise her. To this day she worried about it. The sound she dreaded was a simple belligerent cry, 'Oi you!'

Chapter Seventeen

It was Ellen who first interested Cora in the movement of starlings. 'Look at them,' Ellen said. 'They are not what they seem. You'd think them dowdy. But they're little dandy birds, tricked out in all colours. They glisten. And you'd think them cheeky, pushy. But they're worse than that, they're little mobsters. They're only happy in a gang. Watch them. When they take to the sky and fly, they all fly together. There isn't a sergeant major yelling, "Yo, starlings, right wheel, left turn." How do they know which way to go? Why is there never one, just one, banging into the others, causing mayhem, going left when everyone else is wheeling right? For there sure as hell always is with humans.'

'That's you,' Cora said. 'Always turning the wrong way.'

When the day faded Cora would stand in the park watching starlings cluster in the trees. As darkness turned the leaves and branches to silhouette, the starlings would chatter. Their wheezy chirrupings went unnoticed. People passed but they did not comment. The raspings of starlings were, like the rattle of cars and the whoosh of lorries skimming by too close, so common they went unheeded. Come full evening blackness, the starlings would silence. Nobody knew they were there. But if you clapped your hands, or blew a whistle or yelled and waved your arms, flapping and complaining hugely they would rise, squalling from their evening branches, and take to the air. They would start their panic flight as individuals but would, within seconds, flock. Every one would be part of the whole flight. As one they would pass in their thousands over the tops of trees. As one they would wheel one way, then the other, and when the shock and danger were gone, as one they would come in to land. How did they do that? Cora always watched them, trying to identify one that was the leader of the flight. A chief

117

starling that yelled, 'This way, lads.' Or, 'Right turn at the last tree and wheel sharp left at the steeple across the road, lads.' But no. Each one knew the ways of the whole. The movement of starlings was not for individuals. There were no rebels.

If Cora hadn't been so young she might have known that Claude was ill. He must have been ill when they met, and slowly, without her noticing any change, got more and more sick. But she had no experience of the nature of illness, how it smelled, the colour of it. Thinking back she knew she noticed that there was a difference in Claude, she just didn't make much of it. She was too taken up with the dramatic changes in her own body. The lump within was getting larger and lumpier. She could feel its bits, elbows, feet and knees – or so she imagined. Nights she could feel it wriggle and dance, little feet pattered inside, and sometimes she could see the little thing banging in there, blips on her tummy. 'Goodness look at that.' She had settled into being pregnant. She had not grasped the reality of it – that it would end with an actual baby.

After three nauseous months, Cora bloomed. Pregnancy suited her. Her skin was clear and lovely, hair shiny. She was filled with a new vibrant energy. She scrubbed the little flat, painted the walls – three a pale buff colour, one dark red. She pinned up purloined posters and record sleeves. She washed the window and cleaned the cooker with Brillo Pads. Her energy was boundless.

Claude lay in bed watching the nest-making, saying nothing. The whole business irritated him hugely. When he wasn't yelling at her to stop, he sullenly smoked Gauloises and drank brandy, neither of which he could afford. His ulcerous temper and malice surprised him. When he swore at Cora, he meant it. He wanted to hurt her for existing so healthily when he felt so constantly tired. His back and chest ached so much sometimes he could not stand up.

'Stop it, you stupid shit woman,' he cursed her.

'Stop what?' She had only been sitting by the bed listening to the radio.

'Stop being there. Stop it. Get out. Get away from me. Just stop existing. You're so . . . so . . . smug, so content. I hate it. You. I hate you.'

118

He hit her. She put her hand to her face, surprised and wounded, unwelcome tears spilling down her cheeks. He was vile. Why was he doing this? He hated himself and hit her again.

He was beginning to suspect there was something wrong with him. When they ran Cora sweated copiously, youthfully. Fresh, it smelled fabulously human. His sweat was slow and thick, smelled shrill. He could not stand the foul rancid taste in his mouth every morning. He was so thin, he hated Cora to see him naked. 'Don't look at me,' he spat. Often he was overcome with a sweeping exhaustion; face pale, he'd heave air into his lungs trying to overcome it. He thought this exhaustion was caused by the strain of his finals. The pains that, without warning, suddenly shot through his stomach were excruciating, but it was just nerves causing them, surely. He noticed all this, but said nothing. It made his heart stop. Waves of fear surged though him. Cancer, he had cancer. He knew it. Maybe it would all go away. Maybe there was nothing wrong really. His shit was black.

One night he woke up screaming. He curled into his pain, held it and shouted for help. Something from within was cutting him in two. Cora dressed and ran down into the street to the phone. She could not persuade her doctor to come to him.

'It'll be a spot of indigestion,' he patronised. 'Give him some Andrews Liver Salts. He'll be fine in the morning. You students and your curries.'

Cora went home and stood at the end of the bed, chewing her fingers as Claude howled. This wasn't like any indigestion she knew. Still dressed she got in beside him. Quiet now, lost in his pain, he clung to her. At six when a slow light crept into their room she rose, went out into the street, found a taxi and took him to hospital.

Cora always thought of the days that followed as a time of corridors. Confused and anxious she rushed along endless municipal miles, following signs, breathing in the nervy medical reek that pervades all hospitals. On that first morning she stood with Claude. He was stretchered and waiting for something to happen.

'What's going on?' he said. She could hardly hear him.

119

'We're waiting for the doctor. They're going to admit you to the ward.' She held his hand.

'What's wrong with me?'

'I don't know.' The words sang out. Scared little Highland voice amidst the rattle and thrum of medical doings. She was wearing a lurid green T-shirt, coffee-stained and crumpled. Her jeans were skin tight, worn through and calculatedly ripped down one leg. They didn't fasten over her pregnancy. Her multi-pierced left ear hung with rings, small chains that rattled moons and stars. Her boots were scraped and grubby. Her choice of hair colour this week was defiant strands of black and purple. She wore no makeup. When the doctor arrived he did not spare her his look of disapproving loathing before having the nurse usher her from the cubicle. She sat outside whilst Claude was examined and admitted. She watched as he was wheeled off into a lift. Other people were taking over the life of the one she loved.

A nurse told her, 'Your . . . ?'

'Boyfriend,' said Cora.

' . . . is being admitted to the ward. He has a duodenal ulcer that has burst. We'll be operating later this morning. It must have been bleeding for some time.' She looked accusingly at Cora.

She shrugged. 'I didn't know. Can I see him?'

'After he's been admitted to the ward we'll be preparing him for the theatre. Why don't you go home? Phone later this afternoon.' She wasn't unkind. She just had a lot to do. And she didn't reckon someone who looked like Cora. Not many people did.

Cora didn't go home. There was nothing there. She sat stranded amidst the rush and whisper of people who had things to do, and who always, always ignored her. All day she sat. At four she went to find out how he was. Corridors. Stares. They would not let her on the ward. Claude was recovering. She could see him tomorrow at visiting time. She walked home slowly, making her journey last. She watched her feet move against the pavement, dreading that moment when there would be nothing left to do but go into that empty room. Then there would be no escape from the thought that was running, unwelcome, through her head. *Claude is going to die.*

She went back next day. Walked fearfully down the ward

searching each face for that one she knew, his face. He was not there.

'He's down in ICU,' the sister told her. Cora looked at her vacantly. 'Intensive care,' the sister smiled.

Cora knew then something was wrong. Suddenly someone was being kind. Something was definitely wrong. She had never known such worry. It hurt. It pained her face and neck. She did not trust her legs to make it through the corridors any more. She was shown into a little waiting room and offered tea. They were being awfully kind. She hated it. I can't deal with sympathy, she whined to herself. A male nurse came to talk to her.

Cora's memory of that time was of sounds, colours – mostly green and red – and expressions. The expressions on the faces that moved through that small part of her life stayed with her for the rest of her life. She had been delivered into the hands of people who had made a lifetime's calling dealing with the seriously sick. The bewilderment and fear of relatives and friends were routine, part of their day-to-day dealings. She felt safe. She sat on a red plastic seat. The nurse was wearing green. He sat by her, turned towards her as he spoke gently, looked her in the eye, smiled. Claude's condition was more serious than they first thought. The ulcer had exploded inside him. Would she like to see him? He was attached to a monitor and there were tubes attached to him draining the poison. She must not be alarmed.

Cora was finding this sudden kindness increasingly hard. If it continued she was going to give in to it and cry.

She was helped, childlike, into a sterile gown – one arm, good girl, now other arm. Looking back, she thought he even fastened it for her. He led her into the unit. Six beds, widely spaced, red blankets, a nurse at the foot of each one. A guardian angel, Cora thought. A television softly beamed bland afternoon shows to a bed in the corner. There were defibrillator paddles, red, centre of the ward.

For an insane moment Cora was tempted to take them up and clamp them against her own heart. 'Clear. One. Two . . .' It was all so familiar from visions in soap operas and trips through movies. Cora had been here a hundred times before. A huge sign on the wall, white on green, 'DO NOT CROSS YOUR LEGS.' She thought vaguely that was exactly what she should have done six or seven months ago. But it was calm here, serene. People had left their lives and were battling within themselves with the business of staying alive. The sun streamed in. She thought she would like to sit here, quietly warm, for hours and hours if only they would let her. It was the first time in her life that Cora felt round her, and breathed, humanity.

She sat neatly by Claude's bed, hands folded in her lap, listening to the clack clack of the ventilator attached to a patient across the room and the insistent bleep of Claude's monitor. Claude lay still. A gunge-like bile seeped along a tube that snaked down from under his light blanket to a bottle on the floor. He was not sleeping. He just turned to her, gazed a cold moment, then turned away. She didn't think, she listened to her own body. Nerves, and the occasional kick and squirm of infant within.

Once, the monitor stopped. A loud alarming constant squeal shook the room. This was it. Cora knew this moment. Her own body throbbed fear and dread. It always happened in films. The nurse moved efficiently from the end of the bed, raised her fist, thumped, not Claude's arrested heart, but the monitor. The comforting bleep started again.

'That one's always doing that,' said the nurse. Then seeing Cora's frantic look, 'Don't worry. He's going to be fine. This is only a precaution. We're only keeping an eye. He'll be back in the ward tomorrow.'

And so he was. Almost to Cora's regret he was removed from the comforting tranquillity of intensive care to the frenetic bustle of the ward. He lay, thin and pale, seemingly lost, in the high little bed. He looked furious when she came to him. There was a flask of water and a glass on his locker.

'I have to drink this piss,' he said. She had never seen him so tired or angry. Before she could reply his anger continued, 'They have sliced me open. There's a great fucking zipper down my front.'

'I always wanted a scar. Like Zorro,' Cora stupidly said. She thought she was being cheering.

He stared at her cruelly. 'I'm a mess. It's all your fault. You did it. You with your let's do it today. Let's shop. All that strain and tension did it. Look at me, you bitch. Look at me.' He pulled up his gown. The cut, deep and straight, stretched from his groin up to his chest. He was stitched up, great black stitches, deep red surgical welts where the healing thread tightened and dug in.

Cora was shocked. 'I'll bring you Evian,' she said. These were the only words exchanged till it was time for her to go. She made to kiss him, but he waved her away.

Every day, then, for a week, she walked the long way from the Grassmarket to the Royal Infirmary. Every day she moved, raddled with anxiety and fear, along the corridors to the ward. Every day she sat by his bed, scarcely ever speaking. He still wore the open-backed institutional hospital bed frock. He had nothing else. Every day he was bullied from bed and forced to spend some hours sitting up. Every day he protested in French. It did not take any imagination at all to know that what he was saying was vile. He could not bear what had happened to him.

After six days of harrowing visits – blistering resentment, silent rages – Cora walked up the ward. In a few days Claude would be allowed home. Fresh sheets on their bed, roses in a milk bottle. She had spent the last of her money on a bottle of Evian and a purple African violet. She scanned faces looking for her favourite face, that set of features that was beloved. It was not there.

'Where's Claude?' she asked a passing nurse.

A shrug, a shake of the head.

'Isn't he here?' Cora indicated the bed, empty, stripped, scrubbed and regimentally tidy.

'Ask Sister,' said the nurse.

Cora looked wildly round. 'Where's Claude?' she said again. There must be some mistake. He must be here. She just couldn't see him. The nurse walked off. Cora ran after her. 'Where's Claude?' She was aware of how absurd she looked. A vivid little person blistering and hurtling down the ward. A raging splat of colour in an orderly world. She was beginning to shout. 'Where is he? Where is he?'

She saw the sister rattling down the ward, anxious to get to her, shut her up. Her arms were spread before her, pleading for quiet.

'Please, please. We can't disturb the patients.'

Everyone was staring. But then everyone stared at Cora anyway. She ran past all the beds, little gaudy speeding figure, spiked hair, hugely pregnant on skinny legs yelling, 'Where is he? Where is he? What have you done with him?'

This was her worst moment. This was her dread. He'd died, hadn't he?

The sister and a passing nurse caught hold of her and took her to the office. Cora was sobbing hysterically, mascara melting down her face.

'Fetch some tea,' the sister ordered, then, turning to Cora, switched her voice to concern. 'He's gone. Didn't he tell you?'

Cora shook her head. 'Gone where?'

'Back to France. His parents took him last night. You didn't know?'

'No.' Cora was quiet. This was a mistake. Claude was there. He was waiting for her. He hadn't left her. He wouldn't do that. Would he? 'I don't believe you,' she said finally.

'No, I expect you'd like to think it isn't true. But I'm afraid he's gone.'

'Is there a note?'

The sister shook her head.

'Nothing?'

'Nothing.'

They looked at each other. Cora was embarrassed. This woman knew she'd been abandoned, knew the failure she was. It was something Cora would prefer to be a secret.

'Is he the father of your baby?'

'Yes,' Cora nodded.

'It wouldn't have been easy. He would have needed a lot of looking after. You might not have managed.'

'I would have.' Cora was indignant.

'Yes. You probably would.' The sister recognised a valiant soul when she met one. 'I'm so sorry.'

Cora looked at her defiantly. There were tears in her eyes. Her throat was blocked and lumpen. 'Don't you effing be sorry for me. I don't want your sympathy. I can't stand all this fucking kindness.'

The sister smiled. There was, it seemed to Cora, not a thing she did not know about the business of being human. 'Yes. Kindness is a bitch, isn't it?' She handed Cora a box of medical tissues. 'Here. I'll leave you a minute to get yourself together. Then someone'll bring you some tea.'

Cora, trying to contain, or at least understand, her loss, put her head in her hands. The nurse reached out, touched her shoulder and that was all it took. That tiny bit of human contact broke Cora's resolve. She could hide her hurt no longer. She let go and wept.

The sister walked from the room. Shut the door. When she returned a few minutes later, Cora was gone.

For the rest of the day Cora walked. She walked through old Edinburgh, cobbled streets, ancient grey and fume-blackened buildings. Maroon buses grumbled past her. She moved with the bustle of the day. Stared down tiny darkened lanes, saw sudden bright signs, brilliant against the drab of the rest of the street, braying about galleries, pubs and shops she'd never noticed before. Haunted by her sadness, she read menus pinned outside restaurants: salmon with something or other wrapped in filo pastry, pan fried thingy in redcurrant coulis. 'I'll never have stuff like that,' she moaned. 'Life isn't that good to me.'

She looked at the glossily fed people on the pavement outside who, stuffed with bonhomie, were busy being interesting, making a fine public show of being fabulously happy, linking arms, putting gorgeous haircut against gorgeous haircut. They would briefly stop their display to watch gaudy Cora glumly pass, 'The state of that.' She decided that when her time came to join the greedy people on pavements outside restaurants hooting fruitily about holidays and glorious puddings whilst watching the less fortunate go by in their less fortunate outfits she would not laugh. 'I'll have been there,' she would say. 'Nothing to laugh at.' All the time the shock of what had happened lay within her. It was a twist in her stomach. A lump in her throat. It was an ache waiting to course through her if only she'd let it. But she kept it at bay, walking.

She walked through the Grassmarket past her flat. 'I'm never going in there again.' Past unshaven old men, long-term drinkers, who greeted her and other passers-by from the depth of their derelict lives with a cough, a lump of phlegm, and a 'Yumph.' They sat, multi-overcoated heaps on benches, against a backdrop of plush boutiques, pizza joints and antique shops. Only a few yards down the road and now she'd abandoned the notion of ever joining the glossy, greedy people. That was not for her. No, it would not be long before she joined the forsaken, drinking Eldorado wine, looking for fag ends in the gutter. She'd be a bag lady. She'd wear luminous socks and carry her life around in a selection of battered Tesco's carriers.

She walked up West Bow. She walked past the comic shop, a visual blast of wham and splat windows where men in masks and capes flew to save the poor and lowly. But not her. Past the joke shop – fat red false noses, fart powder and whoopee cushions, silly times. But she couldn't join in. And the coffee shop – air laden with the thick waft of a dark and tempting brew that she couldn't afford.

Down the Mound now, dragging her hand against the railings. She went into Princes Street Gardens and trailed with tourists, watching squirrels. She sat on a bench, mesmerised by the fountain, eating an ice cream that gave her heartburn. Children played at the swings beyond, little Pollyannas. She walked across the railway bridge, stood in mild shock, feeling through her the rattle of a train thundering beneath her. Panting now, she climbed the hill, went through the gate at the top of the gardens on to the Esplanade, then through the Castle. She stood staring across the top of the city – glittering roofs, spires and chimneys – to the river beyond, that expanse of pewtery blue water, shining. She loved it. But today she watched the view and knew the first real fear of her life. It had never once crossed her mind that Claude would leave her. Even while he was ill she stayed in their room alone at nights knowing he'd soon be back. Love, for some people, is the fear of losing the loved one. Love, for Cora, was the knowledge that she and Claude would never part.

'What am I going to do?' she barely whispered. All day she'd held her fear in. She'd walked the city, bent, huddled against her misery, clutching her stomach, refusing to acknowledge the dread growing within her. Now she stood up, breathed deeply and said out loud, 'I am well and truly up shit creek.'

She still could not face going back to their room. It was so full of him, his things. Out here there were people she could follow around, listen to their touristy small talk. She could pretend to be with somebody. Back home she'd have to face the start of her life alone.

Instead, when she was too tired to walk, she leaned in the doorway across the road and stared up at her window. As night came she crouched low. 'I am not going back there. I am never going back there.' In a doorway nearby a tramp coughed. People passed and momentarily stopped their laughter and chat to look at her.

'I will never go back to that room,' she vowed. 'Never. Never. Never.'

To ease the pain of this night, she did what she had done as a child to ease other pains, other dire moments; a nightmarish trip to the dentist to get her back teeth extracted, making space for her wisdom teeth; a long wait for the doctor to come when she broke her arm; a slow walk home with a dreadful report card. She took refuge in her beautiful moments past. The time she'd seen a lone swan come flying from behind a clump of trees. White it was against the forest green, wings whooshing and whistling. The perfect air on the top of a mountain, standing in that clean chill with the heathered grass wind-mown and lush like Wilton beneath her feet. That line on her father's face where, as a child, she wanted to curl up and lie for the rest of her life. Her life with Claude.

They had reached a time in their sex life when they could do it and chat. He would reach for her, lick her tits. Kiss her, tongue moving in her mouth. He'd put his hand between her legs. Watching her. And she would stroke him. Take him in her mouth sometimes. He liked her to move her tongue over his chest, his nipples. Then he'd enter her. Moving together they'd talk. It was their special trick. They'd worked at it. Oh, nothing mundane. He wouldn't say that they were out of washing powder and toothpaste. She wouldn't tell him the bulb in the light above the bed was gone. Nothing like that. This was when their conversation became fabulous.

'I saw a blue stone on the beach once,' he might say.

'I love blue. Sometimes if you climb a mountain the air is blue.

127

You feel you are walking through blue.'

'It was perfect. Round and perfect. I didn't pick it up. I don't want anything perfect. And I have seen a purple heron on a hill and a golden bird with soft yellow fronds flying lazily through larch trees.'

She might say, 'Oh.' Then a longer, 'Oooh.' He would watch her face.

'The loveliest thing I have seen was swans, seven white swans, only they weren't on a lake they were on grass,' she said, struggling to speak, working at controlling her body. She would finish this. 'Swimming on a deep green moist sea of grass, they were. It was twilight, and the trees were darkening in front of a promising sky. There was a slip of a moon.' She always remembered that moment. Then oh. They would move off into their private worlds. Glad to be with each other, aching for pleasure.

By four in the morning Cora could hardly move. Groaning, she rose from her despair. Cold knotted her bones. Her eyes were gummed shut and she felt her feet were glued to the floor of the world. She was chilled, shaking with chill. 'This is not good for me,' she told herself. 'And this is not good for the lump either.' She went slowly home. Slowly, for stiffness made moving problematic. She shuffled. Shuffled home.

Inside the flat she took off her boots and, still clothed, shaking like an old wino from cold and hunger, she crawled into bed. Not for Cora, then, the comfort and closeness of starlings. She was alone.

Chapter Eighteen

When Ellen and Cora were at Cora's they drank at the kitchen table. When they were at Ellen's they sat on the sofa, legs curled. Their conversations, though, always went the same way – long visits to their separate pasts, justifications, explanations and pontifications. On the sofa one night, a bottle of chianti wedged in the cushions between them, and the bottle they'd just finished lying on the floor, Ellen said, 'What happens to you when you marry? You go through this absurd ceremony. Do you, Ellen Frances, take this Daniel to be your lawful wedded husband and promise whatever it was I promised. I wasn't paying attention. Blah blah blah. And a few days later you find yourself in the supermarket queue buying Vim. There was no mention of Vim in that ceremony. I never bought it when I was single.'

'You must have been really filthy,' Cora said.

Ellen considered this. 'Do you know, I think I was. I think I was born filthy. I don't think you develop. I think you are born what you are.'

'Maybe it's to do with conception. Maybe you take on the mood of the moment you were conceived. Happy people will have been conceived in orgasm. Miserable people not. And those crazed, unsatisfied, frustrated folk – well, say no more. We've all been there.'

'So what's all that got to do with me being filthy?'

Cora pulled a face. 'Knowing your mother, she was probably worried about the sheet getting rumpled and stained. Now I come to think about it, Sam was conceived in absurd passion, and with Col I was looking for a little comfort. And look, Sam's all hot-headed and difficult to deal with and Col is the easiest human being alive. He's a joy.' Warming to her theme, she was convincing herself that there was some substance in her theory.

'What about you, then? How do you explain yourself, Cora O'Brien?'

'I was conceived in a warm marital bed by two loving parents. I have no excuse for myself. Unless of course my mother was faking it. There's that. Maybe that explains everything.'

When Cora had been in labour for four hours she phoned home. There was, she realised, nothing else to do.

'Mum,' she wailed down the line, 'I think the baby's coming.'

There was a brief terse silence before her mother gave in to her maternal concerns and heaped Cora with questions.

'Where are you? Are you at the hospital? How far apart are the pains? If you're not at the hospital, did you get in touch with your doctor? Where's that young man of yours?'

'I'm not at the hospital. I haven't phoned the doctor. And my young man has gone back to France.'

'What do you mean, gone back to France?'

'Just that. He's gone.'

'Are you on your own?' Her mother sounded horrified.

'Yes.'

'What have you been doing?'

'Reading paperbacks. Eating baked potatoes and going to the clinic. That's about it.'

'We're on our way.'

Of course Cora could not hold on. By the time Irene and Bill packed the car, got someone to look after the rest of the family and drove to Edinburgh, they were grandparents.

There is nothing like a baby, a grandchild, to heal family feuds. If Irene left home still bristling disapproval at her errant daughter's behaviour it took only one glimpse of the infant for her to forgive Cora her naughtiness, her hairstyle, her makeup, her big boots, her pierced ears – everything.

'Oh, what are you going to call him?' she crooned.

'Sam,' said Cora. 'Sam William O'Brien.'

'That's lovely,' Irene wept, great tears falling from her eyes. A grandchild was lovely. Cora was lovely. Life was lovely. Irene was hugely happy and was planning to go out and spend as much as possible on baby things. Baby things were lovely.

'What have you been doing all alone?' Bill asked Cora. 'That's a terrible thing to be – alone. When you're having a baby and all.'

Cora shrugged. Alone, she'd discovered, was not as bad as she'd thought it would be. Besides, she hadn't really been on her own. She'd formed quite a relationship with the child within, chatting to it, reading to it, planning with it, discussing songs on the radio. 'Oh, that's my fave of the moment.' In fact, after a while she'd become hooked on alone. But alone was not to last long.

Claude wrote to her. He wept on to the paper that he did not want to leave her, and he did not want to stay any longer. 'I would not get well staying in that room. I need space. I need time. Food, wine. I need air.'

'Huh!' Cora was incensed. 'Air indeed. We might not be so hot on the food and wine but we've got air. We have got air. Air we have aplenty,' she told the room. A week alone and she was already talking to herself. It was a habit that would stay for the rest of her life.

She'd find herself the subject of strangers' stares and smirks in the supermarket when looking through the veg. Picking up carrots and onions, carefully squeezing them and tossing back the unacceptable. 'We're not having you. And you're too soft. You'll do. And you. But *you're* not coming home with me.' If the starer got too critical Cora would turn. 'Speaking to the carrots and to myself,' she'd say briskly. 'Well, mostly to myself. I like speaking to myself. I know I'm not going to give me an argument.'

'How are you?' Claude asked in his letter. 'Are you well?'

'Ha,' Cora cried out loud. 'No, I'm not well. I'm effing up the spout with your baby. I've got constant indigestion and I'm spending my days sitting by the window retaining water. That's all I do these days – retain water. I'm all puffy and squishy,' she howled.

'Take care,' he wrote. 'Please take care of yourself.'

'You don't mean take care of me,' Cora said. 'You mean take care of it. The baby you are working hard at not mentioning. You haven't told your folks, have you? They don't know about me, and they don't know about it. Damn you.'

Isla Dewar

She threw down the letter. But that was not enough; he deserved rougher treatment than that. She stamped on it. Still not enough. She jumped on it. Then she picked it up and tore in two. Then two again. And two again till tearing it became too difficult. Feeling a little tired she threw it in the bin and sank on to the bed.

He sent money which she held now. He must have got it from his parents. She considered throwing it away too, but didn't. There was too much of it to toss aside temperamentally. She was furious, but she wasn't daft. She needed all she could get. He had, he told her, posted to the landlord money to pay the rent for the next six months. If she needed anything, anything at all, just write, just ask. She never did. After Sam was born she never even told him he had a son. She suspected he was relieved she never got in touch.

She washed the junk from her face, let her hair grow and joined the library. She ate sensibly, drank milk and read. Every night she sat by her open window watching summertime people passing below, listening to songs on her radio, a book in her lap.

One day, walking home with this week's armful from the library shelves, she was overcome with an urgent need to stop feeling scared and alone. 'I have to do this,' she told herself. 'I have to get a grip on myself. I will cross the road and the fear and loneliness will be over,' she said. 'I will be fine.' She crossed the road. Stood and took stock of herself and her nerves. No. She was still scared, still a wreck. 'Cross back. The moment my feet hit the other side, I will be fine. I will be fine.' She crossed again. It came from nowhere, a feeling of calm. My goodness, she thought, I'm almost happy. Only almost, of course. But if this is as good as it gets, it'll do. It'll have to do. She walked on. 'I matter,' she said. And knowing the truth of her condition, 'I have to matter.'

After Sam was born Cora's mother was convinced she would come home. 'She'll have to,' she said to Bill when they went to visit her on her last day in hospital. 'She can't go back to that room. It's not right. It's not hygienic.'

Bill shook his head. 'You better not be telling her that.' He knew Cora would not come home. 'You don't understand, do you?' he said. 'She feels she's let us down. And she thinks she's let herself down. She'll not be coming back till she's redeemed herself.'

132

'Redeemed herself!' Irene had never heard such rot. 'She'll not have a lot of time for that sort of thing. She's a child to rear. She better put redeeming herself out of her head.'

But Bill knew the truth of it. 'All I'm saying,' he said, 'is she's ashamed to go back. She left with high hopes and she's not likely to return with bloody pierced ears and a bloody baby till she's got her dignity. So if you want to see your grandson you better get used to long journeys in the car and not sit tutting and sighing for miles and miles with that damned bag on your knee.'

Irene allowed herself one last tut and sigh and turned on Bill. 'Damn you and your "blister and hurtle, Cora". You started it. Now here you are with your redemption and dignity.' She feebly hit his shoulder. 'I hate it when you're right. She'll need a fridge.'

'What,' said Bill, sensing that his flash of insight was going to cost him money, 'has that got to do with anything? And why does everything end with me paying out?'

'Dignity and redemption are all very well but she's got a young baby, she can't go running out for food whenever. She'll need a fridge. And I'll bet the silly bugger hasn't even got herself down on the housing list.'

Cora came home to a little room transformed. There was a cot in the corner, an armchair and a fridge full of food.

'Oh,' Irene withered defensively, 'I know it's not to your taste. It's all pinks and blues and babyish. And that chair's not your sort of chair. But you'll be glad of a proper sit down soon enough. And it folds down into a single bed so there'll be somewhere for you to sleep when your father and me come to stay.'

'I know. I know,' Cora said, vaguely dismissing all this. She had her baby home and she was anxious to get on with being a mother, whatever that entailed. She wasn't sure.

Oh no, Irene thought. You don't know anything.

Cora was to discover in the next few weeks the difference between knowing and *knowing*.

'It's like,' she told Ellen, 'knowing that if you shove your finger in the electric socket you'll get a shock, and actually doing it. Then the *knowing* starts. You are flung across the room, land on your bum, hair on end, heart shuddering and stomping. And you think:

133

Right enough that's what happens. That's when the *knowing* starts.'

She spent the first six weeks of Sam's life at full hurtle. Milky, stained, bleeding and knackered, she zombied from feed to feed, carrying bundles of laundry. It hurt to sit. And it hurt to stand. She lived on bacon sandwiches and the only thing she did for herself was make the bed the instant she got out of it. She knew she'd be too wrecked to do it when it was time to crawl back in. Every four hours it seemed her breasts filled up, itched and ached. Sweet, nutty milk dribbled down her front. Hot and sticky, she could not wait for him to take his fill, empty her out. It was her pleasure, so, so nice, that little mouth on her nipple, the small noises he made, tiny perfect hand clenching on her as he fed. But she cried a lot. She did not know it was possible to feel this tired. When the baby cried, and oh how he cried, she cried. They howled together. When he cried the sound of it, the pitch, cut right through to the depth of her. She had to stop the noise, she had to. When feeding, comforting, changing the nappy did not stop it the only relief she could find was to cry along. She stood clutching him to her, patting him, rocking him, wailing too.

'What a pair of major dweebs we are. Scream along with Cora and Sam,' she snivelled.

Once a day at first, then once a week, the health visitor called. She worried about such a young girl alone with a baby, so she fussed and looked discreetly around for signs of Cora not managing. But Cora wasn't going to let her weariness show to anybody official. Every time she called, Cora could not wait for her to go away.

There was nobody but the baby in her life. Sometimes she longed for someone else to talk to, someone else to pick him up, to feed him so that she could sleep, just sleep. She felt she was moving, wall-eyed with despair, through a bad dream. 'Please let it end.' She was slave to a tiny, incontinent, hairless, toothless master. Then one day in mid-nightmare, the baby smiled. The little bald and gummy face lit up when she came looming into view. She felt like a star.

'Good job you did that,' she said to him. 'Things were getting a bit one-sided between us. Know what I mean? I was beginning to feel I was doing all the running.' The baby smiled again. Her heart turned over. She didn't know it could do that. They stood, mother and baby, beaming at each other, rock 'n' roll tinnily blaring from the little tranny on the sink, babygros dripping, traffic rumbling in the street outside.

'We can do this, kid,' she said.

By the time Sam was six months old she'd sung him her entire range of Neil Young and Van Morrison. She explained to the little face in her arms that people like her who could not properly sing a note could do Neil Young for, truth be told, he couldn't properly sing either. In the pubs of her days of abandonment her old friends were sneering still.

It mattered not one whit what she read him. When she was stuck it was the leader column in an old newspaper that she'd brought home wrapped round a pound of carrots. A sweet soft whisper lilting through the evening. He seemed to like Robert Frost – 'And miles to go before I sleep, And miles to go before I sleep' – but Kerouac was the one. *Big Sur* was never intended as a lullaby but set him sleeping every time, didn't let them down. The sea was the sea wherever it was – California or the Inner Hebrides. Cora read and remembered picnics at Calgary Bay years ago. White sand hot between her toes, clear green water, salt on her lips, and Irene sitting on a tartan rug waiting with the family's huge blue and white towel for her children to come shivering and wet to her. She'd wrap them up, rub them dry, then dish out ginger biscuits and American cream soda. In her little room Cora read and drifted back to softer days when sand coated her skinny legs and the sea cooled and slipped over her. She moved her tongue over her lips and could have sworn she tasted salt. The movement, the surf, Cora's endless rolling whisper and little thumb moved into little mouth, eyes rolled back and there it was – the most precious moment of the day. The baby slept, leaving her free to do whatever she wanted, which was mostly sleep, too.

By the time Sam was nine months old they had games they played, hiding and making faces and zooming the aeroplane full of boiled egg in through the air to the mouth. 'Here it comes. Here it comes.' Zigzagging the laden spoon across the sky, little mouth open wide. Going out for walks Cora would charge the pushchair along the pavement top speed, baby laughing. Blister and hurtle,

Cora, blister and hurtle. If shoppers and tourists got in her way she'd yell, 'Peep, peep. Toot, toot. Stand aside please, incontinent person coming through.' She'd shove the child forward. Coming home they would, when traffic allowed, always walk on the cobbles. The rough roads suited them. Battered through them, 'Ah. Aaaaah . . .' they sang. Jagged and rough like the road, their song would rattle out of their throats.

Once a month Irene and Bill came to visit. And at last, after nine visits, Irene admitted that her daughter was managing. To her surprise, their grandson was beaming and healthy.

'You seem to be managing,' she accused.

'Oh yes,' said Cora. 'We're doing fine.' She did not mention the nightmare time before the smile when she'd been tempted to place a soothing pillow over the howls just for a second, just for some peace. Just for a small guilt-free, silent moment.

'And,' Irene said eventually – as if this was a continuation of some previous conversation. It wasn't. It was the worry that had been rattling round her head since she'd discovered her daughter was pregnant – 'what are you going to do now? What about money? How are you going to manage?'

'I get social security. I get my rent paid. Family allowance. You send me money.' Every week they sent her money. 'But, I was thinking,' Cora said, 'Sam could go to a nursery and I could go back to college. Otherwise I'll have to get a job.'

'What doing?'

'What can I do? Wait tables? Wash dishes? I'll have to take what I can get.'

Cora sulked. For nine intense months she'd been cocooned in this little room with her child, hiding herself away from her wrecked ambitions, refusing to face up to the looming fact that she had the rest of her life to get through. Now here was Irene confronting her, the world was out there and it was time to get back to it. She had responsibilities now. She tutted and huffed.

Irene responded with a piece of disapproving breathing and told Cora she should get out for the night. They would baby-sit. She was so adamant about it, so eager to be left in charge of her first grandson, Cora didn't like to spoil her fun. A baby needed a grandmother, she figured. She couldn't bring herself, then, to tell her mother that she'd lost touch with her friends. She had nobody to go anywhere with. For the first time in months she dressed up, did her hair, painted her face, and set out. She couldn't say she had no money and nowhere to go. For an hour she walked up and down outside then, feeling the cold, went to the pub across the road to spend tomorrow's lunch money on a pint of Guinness.

She thought she would make it last. She would sit in the corner unnoticed, sipping slowly till ten, then she could go home. She worried about the baby. Longed to check that her mother was doing everything right, going through his little routine. Was he crying? Would she read to him? And what about his bath? Could her mother cope? She fretted. And fretting made her drink.

It was not part of her plan to get picked up. But it was nice to be noticed as a woman again. She'd quite forgotten she was one. She thought he said his name was Michael. He slipped into her life so easily, sitting opposite her, starting that flirtatious small talk that's so exciting because, well, you never know where it's going to get you. Was she alone? Was she a student? Well yes, she said, sort of. Not exactly any more. But she was going to get back to it, definitely that, yes. She did not tell him about Sam. Later, remembering, she was ashamed of herself. Did she want another drink? Oh no, she shook her head. I'm fine. She indicated her glass, noticing for the first time that it was empty.

'I'll get you another anyway,' he said. And that went down so easily, so quickly, he got her yet another. She felt the tension ease from her shoulders, and knew she was smiling too much. It was that pleasant drunkenness when she knew she'd had too much to drink and was too drunk to care. She realised though that it had been a while since she'd touched alcohol. She wasn't cool any more. It rushed to her head.

He lived in Jeffrey Street, and took her back to his place. It smelled of curry. There was a view of the railway from the back window. The only drink he had was cherry brandy and they were both drunk enough to think themselves sober enough to drink it.

It was so nice, so nice to be touched again. 'Put your hands on my back,' she said. 'Touch me.' They made love in an inebriated calm.

It was wonderful. So wonderful to feel someone next to her, on her, in her. She put her head on his chest. Kissed his neck, slid on top of him and made love again. 'It's the comfort,' she said, whispering in the dark. 'I just want some comfort. Someone to take my mind off it all.' He was happy to oblige. 'Sometimes,' she told him, 'it gets so lonely. It's nice to have someone who talks back. He likes Dylan, but my favourite is Van Morrison. Do you like Van? Say goodbye to Madam George,' she sang. 'I like your skin,' she stroked him. 'I love it. Look at me, pale and unhealthy. You're fabulous,' she laughed. She was very, very drunk. He hadn't a clue what she was talking about. 'How was it for you?' she asked.

'Wonderful,' he smiled. He was so polite. Such a gent, she thought.

'And how was it for me?' she asked.

'From the sounds of it wonderful too,' he told her. After they made love a third time they slipped into an alcoholic void.

Oh, the shame when she woke. She brought herself to life with her own snoring. Naked, she sprawled across the bed, and for a moment she did not know where she was, or who it was snoring next to her. There was a blissful blank a few seconds before she remembered. 'Oh no,' she said. 'Oh, please no.' Her head hurt, her mouth was dry and horrible. 'Oh God,' she whispered, for speaking any louder would be too painful. She looked about the room for her clothes. Then went to find the lavatory.

She was sick and lay on the floor, curled and clutching her knees, thinking the thing to do would be to stay like that here on the floor for the rest of her life. This unsanitary place smelling of pee is all I deserve as a resting place. Why do men miss? She lay gazing at the Harpic and the loo brush, and hanging just above her a greying comfortless towel. Someone somewhere was playing Steely Dan, 'Rikki Don't Lose That Number'. She wept a little. 'I have done a dreadful thing,' she said. 'I'm not fit. I'm not fit . . .' to be a mother, she thought.

Four o'clock in the morning she ran through the streets though she wasn't dressed for speed. Her heels stormed the silence. There was panic in her throat, her heart pounded. Oh God, oh God, oh God. What if something's happened? What if the baby's ill? What if they're waiting up for me? She ran, handbag banging on her leg, and conjured dread scenarios in her head. Her mother had dropped the baby and they were all in hospital but they couldn't find her. Now she'd turn up at this time and find the police waiting. Her mother and father had waited up for her and would be sitting bolt upright, looking grim. They'd declare her an unfit mother and look at her and know from that one glance the mischief she'd been up to. Oh God.

Normally she enjoyed being up early. She liked the feel of having the city to herself and a moment's easy breathing when the air is clear, unleaded before everything wakes and the bustle and rush starts up again. Not this morning though. This morning her throat was tight and lumpen; several times she had to stop and lean on a doorpost, gasping and panic-stricken. She reached her doorway, ran up the stairs, then stopped outside her door. Silence. She straightened her clothes and worked at her breathing, hauling great draughts of air into her lungs. Calm down, she told herself. Then she went in.

There was only people sleeping. There was a curtain pulled round her bed, behind it Irene and Bill snored. In his cot the baby lay, fists clenched, head to one side, a small sweat damping his head. Cora let her fingers trail across his brow. Then she slipped from her clothes and crawled into the bed her mother had made up in the fold-down chair.

At seven she heard her mother move about the room. She lay watching her.

'I can't lie,' Irene said. Irene, it seemed to Cora, had the knack of knowing what other people were thinking or doing seemingly without casting even the smallest glance in their direction. How did she do that? Without turning her head Irene knew Cora was awake. 'I know I should, but I can't lie. Soon as my eyes are open I have to get up. Did you have a good time?'

'Yes,' said Cora. 'Wonderful.'

'What time did you get back?'

' . . . Um,' said Cora. 'Don't really know.'

Irene turned to look at her daughter. 'Goodness, you look awful. Are you all right?'

'I'm fine. I've got a bit of a headache. I think I've got flu coming on.' Cora coughed a bit and sniffed. Irene sighed. She knew a hangover when she saw one. Why did her children always pretend to her? She tutted and turned to switch off the kettle. Was there, perhaps, something naïve about her that her children always put on this absurd display of innocence? 'This'll sort you out.' She gave Cora a cup of tea and a long piercing look. Cora winced.

'I hope you haven't been up to what I think you've been up to,' Irene accused.

'What do you mean by that?' Cora was defensive but, sipping her tea, avoided eye contact.

'You know fine what I mean,' Irene said.

Cora shrugged. 'No I don't.' She hid her face behind her cup, drinking. She wondered if, when her son grew up, she'd be as perceptive as Irene. Would she accuse with fierce glances and tight-lipped silences? Oh no, not her. She'd be the perfect understanding mother. She was sure of that.

Remembering – and how could she forget? – she said to Ellen, 'One day you wake with the hangover that is a hangover too far and you realise your time has come. The reckoning is no longer nigh. The reckoning is here.'

The reckoning was there for Cora six weeks later when she threw up first thing in the morning, when her breasts felt tingly and she had that old familiar longing for a sweet and fizzy drink.

'Oh Christ,' she said to Sam, 'I'm fucked.'

'Fucked,' said Sam, clear and loud, ten and a bit months old. It was his first word. And considering the times ahead, very appropriate.

Cora picked him up, held him aloft. 'Oh cool,' she crooned. 'I love it. You're so clever. What a clever boy.' Then, realising the word he'd mastered, decided this was when the swearing had to stop. 'Pity, I like a good curse. There are some things you just have to swear about. Like being pregnant. Oh God,' clutching the child to her, 'what am I going to do?'

She ignored it. For three months she vaguely hoped it would go away. But when plainly it was here to stay she went to the doctor and had her condition confirmed. By then it was too late to do anything about it. She did not, however, confess her folly to her mother and father. More than she worried about her pregnancy, she worried about them, what they would say. She had let them down again. She was about to break their hearts again. Every time she phoned home she meant to mention it, but couldn't.

'How are you?' Irene would breezily ask down the phone. 'And more important, how's my boy?'

'Fine,' Cora would say. 'We're both fine.' She told them that Sam had started to talk, but didn't mention what he'd said.

'Any word on the nursery? Have you tried to get Sam in anywhere? Have you gone to see about getting back into college?'

'Um . . . not exactly. Soon. I'll do it soon.'

When she was five months into her pregnancy the terror set in. The what-ifs started. What if social workers found out about her and took her babies away? The room could not contain three people. How was she going to live? What was to become of her?

'Only one thing for it,' she said to Sam. 'Face up to it. It's a bitch but there you are.' She went to the council offices to see about getting rehoused and found to her astonishment that she was already high on the list. Her mother had put her name down months ago.

'With another one on the way you'll be a priority,' she was told. 'It won't be great but better than one room.'

'Anything,' said Cora. 'Anything.'

Two weeks later she got word that she'd been allocated a three-room flat in Leith. 'Near the water,' she said to Sam. 'We'll love it.'

They got the bus, riding upstairs for the view, and went to explore. She found her new address in Giles Street. One floor up and along a lengthy balcony. There was a motorbike under construction outside her door, bits of oily things lying scattered. She was aware of curtains moving in flats nearby. Children stopped playing to stare blatantly.

'Look, Sam, pals. You'll have friends here.' She was working hard at convincing herself.

That night she phoned home to tell her mother and father she was moving. Bill insisted they come to help.

'No. No.' Standing in the phone box Cora shook her head, waved her hands. 'No, really. I don't need help. It's too far to come. I'll be fine.'

141

'We'll be there,' Bill said.

A week later Irene took one look at Cora, turned and walked out the room.

'How could you?' she yelled when, seconds later, she returned. She had too much anger battering through her veins to cope with stairs or the street. She wanted to throw something. She wanted to hit someone. Cora. 'How could you?'

Cora shrugged. 'It was easy,' she said. 'The tricky bit starts in a few months. And it goes on for the rest of my life.'

'Good glib remark,' said Irene. 'Don't get smart with me. I know when this happened. That night. That night we baby-sat. You were doing this . . .' She waved her hand at Cora's pregnancy. 'What kind of slut are you, anyway?'

'The best kind,' said Cora simply. 'I enjoy it.'

Her mother hit her. The baby started to howl. Bawl. Bill picked him up and walked him up and down. Cora glumly rubbed her stinging cheek.

'There's no need to smack the girl,' Bill said. 'What's done's done.'

'What's done's done. Just like you. Just like a man. You have no idea. Two children, no father. There is nothing to be philosophical about. She'll need a cooker.' She turned on Cora again. 'I don't suppose you've even given that a thought.'

'Actually I have. But I didn't give it much of a thought.' She was frightened of moving from her room. For months she had shared it with her son, and in it they had built up a small world of their own. She felt safe here, bricked in, tucked away from her worries which she knew were out there beyond her four walls waiting for her, refusing to go away. Nights now were starting to crowd in on her. What am I going to do? No money and in that place. Me, a pushchair and two bleating infants needing their noses wiped. That's what will become of me. Miles and miles with shopping and tired moaning babies. Miles and miles.

'I will not trudge,' she said.

'Well,' said Irene, 'it will take all that passion of yours to stop yourself. Trudging with babes, we've all done it. When you've two little ones and miles to go before you shop, trudging comes naturally.'

142

And miles to go before I shop, And miles to go before I shop. Cora's brain was running on empty. It was the first time she had heard her mother speak as if passion were normal, a part of her. It was the first time she realised her mother had passion too. It was the first time they'd spoken as women.

'I'm scared,' she said.

'Yes,' her mother heaved, agreeing. 'I'd be scared if I were you.'

It was a grubby day, struggle and woe. They took Cora's few possessions from her room. Sweating and swearing, bitterly blaming each other as they wedged round corners and bashed fingers, they got everything into the hired van. Cora listened to her father and mother battering down three flights, arguing all the way.

'It's you can't carry furniture.'

'No, it's you.'

'You can be married to someone for umpteen years,' Irene scathed, 'but it isn't till you carry an armchair down three flights of stairs with them that you discover the truth about them.'

Cora wandered about her room touching things for the last time. Saying goodbye. Goodbye to everything, her little life with her son and the times she'd had with Claude. He wouldn't come back, she knew that now. She'd spent weeks, months, thinking that any moment he would burst in carrying goodies. When she went out she always wondered if when she got back he'd be there lounging on the bed, waiting for her. She looked at the spot under the window where the army of milk bottles had stood. He'd be leaving other messes in other flats now, nothing to do with her. She'd never see him again.

At the other end, bleary with effort and scarcely speaking, they carried her bed, Sam's cot and her armchair up past the skeletal motorbike and in the main door, painted yellow, wire mesh in the glass, a heavy-duty spring that creaked hugely whenever it opened.

There was a comfortless institutionalised hallway with a begrudging and bleakly clean smell and a constant wind that swirled up skirts, flapped jackets. It was a low-rise grey stone block with bright doors and windows, unsubtle slabs of colour – blue, orange, yellow – a municipal notion of cheerful. Someone somewhere had conjured a life that worked well on a drawing board, on a cardboard model. It was the living of it that was the bitch.

Cora's flat was first floor left. Every room was painted orange. The tiles in the kitchen were grey marl filthy. She wandered through her three rooms saying, 'This is fine. I can do this.' Over and over she said it, ignoring Irene's scrutiny

'Where are you going to plant the hollyhocks?' Irene asked, staring out the window at the building across the road.

'Oh,' said Cora. 'Down at the bottom where it gets the sun. I'll have a herb garden just beyond the croquet lawn and beech hedges. I'll wander the flowerbeds snipping lupins and delphiniums, laying them gently side by side in my trug basket. In summer I'll snip a little fresh mint to put on my new potatoes. And I'll have honeysuckle at the door so I can get the scent in summer. It'll waft in. Waft. Waft. I'll breathe it in as I sit on the back step shelling peas and singing lullabies.' She indicated the flow of scented breeze with a soft wave.

'Oh well. If you can still dream . . .' Irene's voice trailed off.

Next day, driving home, she said, 'I think Cora might be all right.'

And Bill, enthusiastic as ever, said, 'Of course she'll be all right. She won all those races, didn't she? She's got fire. She would have won the final only she pushed too soon.'

'It seems to be developing into a lifetime's bad habit,' Irene scathed. Then, softly, after a small silence: 'She'll be fine. As long as she doesn't look at other women.'

'Why would she be doing that?'

'Women look at each other. They watch. They judge. If Cora looks at other women she'll see herself as they see her, and it'll break her heart.'

Cora, meantime, was setting about her kitchen floor with a bucket of hot water, some Flash and a deal of optimism. Sam watched.

'Look!' she shouted. 'It isn't grey marl at all. It's black-and-white tiles. I can live with this.' And she scrubbed with even more fervour.

Halfway across the floor her enthusiasm waned. She fell forward, laid her face on her arms, bum in the air. 'This is hell, Sam.

Sodding floor. I know, I know. Don't swear, you'll only pick it up.'
She sighed deeply, took up her brush, did a single swift two-handed
scrub and collapsed once more. She fell into a human heap, then
rolled on to her back, stared up. Sam, seizing the moment, as
children will, climbed on top of her. He was clutching a bright
yellow plastic squeaky hammer that among all his toys had become
beloved.

'I can't say I think much of your taste in toys, Sam. I prefer the
red bricks. Is this a statement of your maleness, this hammer?' She
took it, squeaked it violently. Gently batted his forehead. 'You can
see the sky from here, Sam.' Then a confession, a swift relating of a
few truths before he was old enough to understand what she was
saying to him.

'I have led a scrawny life, Sam. My successes are all unmention-
able moments of pleasure. I don't even know the name of the man
who is father to squidge number two. Know what I mean, Sam?
Shameful. I have let my folks down. Oh, I have climbed a few
mountains, and won a couple of races. Other people are doing
worthwhile, happening, career-motivating things and I am lying
here on the floor on my back looking out at baby clothes flapping
on the line. I have ruined my chances.'

The child took his hammer, and sucked it. He put his little arms
round her neck. She kissed the warm top of his blonding head, held
him to her. 'Still,' she said, 'we've a new cooker arriving in the
morning. The tiles are black and white. You can see the sky from the
kitchen floor. The social security will get us a sofa. Is this as good as
it gets? What do you think? Someone up there likes us? Ha ha. Some
boozer angel perhaps has put in a slurred word for me. God, Sam,
how are we going to cope?' She would have cried but pregnant,
hormones and all, she seemed to have left tears behind. Pity, crying
helped. 'How do you do that again?'

Four months later Col was born. Three days before Cora went
into labour Bill and Irene came to stay. Bill took Cora to hospital,
stayed with her, then chickened out just before the birth, backing
out of the delivery room waving his arms saying, 'No. No. I don't
think so.' And, 'Please don't ask me to stay. I couldn't. I just
couldn't.'

When he took his second grandson into his arms all he said was, 'He's gorgeous, Cora. You make a beautiful baby, so you do.' Next day Irene took the child to her and gazed down with unreserved love. 'Hello you,' she said. She turned to her daughter. 'Well, Cora, never a dull moment, eh?'

'What do you think?' said Cora. 'As we are conceived so we continue? Sam's all passion.'

'Blister and hurtle?' suggested Ellen.

Cora ignored her. 'And Col is a constant comfort, smiley and sweet-natured.'

'And they both love their mum,' said Ellen.

'The sex and drugs and rock 'n' roll I gave up for them, they better,' Cora blistered. 'They bloody better.'

Chapter Nineteen

'What's the most important thing in your life?' Ellen asked.

'Moisturiser,' said Cora.

'Apart from that.'

'There is nothing else. I have my children. And the pleasure of being me and just me – not mother, not daughter – just Cora, now that I have forsaken sex. And I had to give up swearing in front of the children, smoking on account of the children. So there is vodka, and there is moisturiser. It has come to that.'

'Swearing's good,' said Ellen. 'I seem to swear more now that I'm getting older.'

'Yes, you're getting angry. You get angry young men who are furious about all the things they'll never have. And angry middle-aged women furious when they realise all the things they might have had.'

'We will not trudge,' said Cora. 'We will buy some cornflakes and some potatoes and milk and bread.' We will walk there and back and we will not look at people, she thought. I do not want to see myself in their faces. She noted the fear of it in her diary.

She'd started writing down her feelings in a small notebook. She thought that since giving birth, which was the biggest thing that had happened to her, her feelings had become smaller and smaller, and were now on the same scale as the book. She thought about laundry and feeds. She was aware that she was demanding absurd standards of herself. 'Each day,' she wrote, 'I try to give my children love, fresh air, clean clothes, some education, chocolate, play, a bath, stories . . . So who do I think I am? God? Is this what they call coping?'

She thought it silly, but living as she did with only two small

147

children to talk to and neighbours who did not indulge in the sort of brutal self-scourging she did, it was really a conversation with herself.

A year in her new home and Cora knew every lamppost between her house and the shops. She knew a million shades of grey. Blue-grey, green-grey but always grey. Walking with children, eyes constantly at child level she was keenly aware of the concrete bases of lampposts. 'And God created man,' she sighed. 'And man created lamppost bases. And you do not guide yourself through the maze by the stars. Forget them. Guide yourself home to safety by the graffiti. Left by the big red "Fuck off", left again at the third sprayed blue "Shag" and on to the end of the road.'

The grass was grey. Not the grass in the little postage stamp patches of garden between pavement and house, that were either vibrantly, greenly neglected or defiantly tamed and nurtured. It was the municipal grass that scrubbily grew along the outside edge of the pavements and in the small parks that never made it to lushness. Underdog grass, Cora thought. Trampled and peed on, denied the right to be green.

Every day she walked down to the river. She found it wasn't as far as she'd imagined to the shops, which were an eclectic mix of delicatessen and corner newsagent. There were new restaurants, striped canopies alongside old pubs. She liked it here. She belonged. Every day she sat on a bench staring out at the water. There were new buildings heaving into the skyline. It wasn't like home. At home the water was bluer, cleaner. There were fishing boats and all sorts of sailing boats. There were mountains. She ached to see them again. 'But I will not go back. I will not go back till I can face them again.' Sometimes she'd sit till the cold cut through her – she almost enjoyed the chill. Only her children's protesting howls – they were cold and they were hungry – made her get up and go back to her flat.

Cora had a brown carpet on her floor, a sofa of sorts in her living room, a cooker in her kitchen. And she had the thin and terrifying Mrs Lawrence across the hallway looking out for her. Mrs Lawrence arrived at Cora's door two days after she moved in.

'Just called to introduce myself,' she said, ducking her head from side to side so that she could see past Cora, openly nosy. 'I'm Betty from across the way there. You're all settled, then?'

'As much as I can be,' said Cora. Betty had already noted her new neighbour's condition, her child and the obvious lack of a man in her life.

'On your own, then?'

Cora shook her head, looked her new neighbour in the eye. 'I've got Sam.'

'Great age,' said Betty. 'I love them that age. Pity they have to grow.' Then smiling, 'Come and have some tea.'

Wasn't it odd, Cora thought. One minute you were charging about stores getting hot and horny shoplifting, or fucking some bloke for all your worth with Steely Dan playing somewhere off stage. And the next here you were sitting taking comfort in some shiny yellow kitchen, breathing in the fumes of Mr Sheen and Jif, sipping milky tea, talking children. How did that happen? And what was it about having children that you found such a moment soothing when it should send you screaming for the horizon, waving your arms and bawling, 'Let me outta here'? Why, this was almost pleasant. Only almost, though. Keep a grip on that almost, girl, Cora warned herself.

Betty drained her cup, rose to take it to the sink and rinse it out. But Cora reached for it, and gazed deeply in.

'You're safe,' she said. 'There's an umbrella here. You've been in some sort of danger. Exposed. Some worry perhaps. But you're safe now.'

Betty cried out, 'Amazing. How did you know? I've just had the all-clear. Just this morning. That's why I came, really.' Lowering her voice, about to confide a truth, she said, 'I needed to talk.' She brought a letter from her apron. 'They thought it was cancer. But it's not. A benign lump. I've been worried. There was nobody to tell. Oh, I could tell my husband, Will. But he's a man.' A man – what did he know about lumps?

Betty clasped her hands and considered Cora anew. 'You read cups,' she said delighted. What a find. What a fabulous friend. There was awe in her voice.

Cora nodded. 'My grandmother taught me.'

'Amazing,' said her neighbour. Cora smiled. She was made. She had a baby-sitter for life.

Word spread. Cora became, in a small street-to-street way, famous. Every morning brought a new invitation to tea. Every morning she was handed cup after hopeful cup. Tell me how it is, Cora. Tell me what I want to hear, Cora. Sometimes women would knock on her door at eight or nine at night and hand her cups with strange tea leaf patterns brought gingerly through the dark.

'What does this mean?' she'd be asked. 'What's going to happen to me?'

Cora would take the cup, turn it to the light, look into it and give her verdict. 'Tea leaves do not predict the future,' she would always say. 'They only tell you what is. It helps you realise to the full the time you are living through. That's all.'

Afterwards she would throw herself on her battered sofa, loudly declaring her despair. Sam, and later Col, would watch quietly. They were used to their mother's outbursts.

'What do they want? What can I say? Oh, I know what to tell them. Everything's fine, that's what. Everything's fine. God's in His heaven and your mummy still loves you.'

Still, being a soothsayer she was forgiven her sins. Nobody mentioned her children's lack of a father or her strange clothes. In fact, strange clothes were now expected of her. Nobody minded what they considered to be smelly and oily French cooking. And nobody minded her strange daily wanderings, crisply telling her children not to trudge.

'We're off to explore the neighbourhood. No trudging.'

And on the way home, Sam and Col would plead, 'Please, please let's trudge. Trudging's best.'

'OK. Just this once, you can trudge for three lampposts, then walk three, then trudge three.'

She was forgiven the weird things she brought home, goodies liberated from skips carried triumphantly home in the pushchair whilst behind her back her children defiantly trudged. Stamp, stamp, stamp of little feet. Gleeful looks, there is no pleasure finer than not doing what you're told. Well, Cora knew all about that.

'Look, an old oval mirror. A picture frame. A bentwood chair needing stripped.'

'Christ, Cora. My granny threw stuff like that out.' The rubbish Cora brought home puzzled Betty. It mysteriously stopped being rubbish and would appear transformed and desirable in Cora's kitchen, living room, or bathroom. In lieu of daily tea cup readings Betty lent Will to help paint over the orange walls. Cora rescued roots and cast-off bits of plant from dustbins and skips, a more legitimate plunder than her earlier thievings. She planted them in pots out on the balcony outside her door. At first they were dug up and tossed on to cars parked in the street below. But Cora just planted more. Things grew for Cora. In time her tiny potted garden became part of the backdrop and it was for most of the time left alone.

Every day she walked to the play park or the shops and every day she and the boys played games. The bears, Sam's invention, lived behind the wall with 'Shag' sprayed blue and they wore checked trousers and red caps, and they were watching them. There were thirty-three manhole covers between the house and the play park. Stamp on each one and count. Look for a four-leafed clover in amongst the weeds, we need all the luck we can get. Catch a drifting seed and you could get a wish. Watch all the wishes you didn't catch floating away into the autumn air. Wasted wishes.

'What do you wish for, Sam?'

'I wish for a motorbike and an orange lolly.'

Whirl on the roundabout and watch the sky whirl. There was a life. You just had to find it. But never say: is this it? Is this all there is? Through it all Cora listened to the radio. Songs of the day, chart toppers, filled her kitchen. She could tell the time of day by the direction she had to turn her radio to catch the best reception.

Once on her way back to her flat she noticed that a church round the corner had been turned into an enterprise scheme. There was a list of projects on a board outside. One was Starless Enterprises.

'What's that?' she asked a fat scruffy bloke coming out of the building. 'Starless Enterprises, what on earth's that?'

The bloke looked at her and her two children. 'Comic strips,' he said. 'Some for syndication, some one-off ideas for adverts.'

151

'Why call it that? What a depressing name?' She was incensed.

Stanley Macpherson smiled and indicated the sky. 'City nights. You can't see the stars any more – starless.'

'And enterprises?' Cora asked crisply, noticing the bloke's jeans, straining at the crotch and rumpled. He had a beer stain on his sweat shirt and one of his baseball boots didn't have a lace. What a mess, she thought. He's worse than me.

He shrugged. 'Yes, enterprises. Starless, yes. But I'm not going to let it get me down – enterprises. Starless Enterprises.'

'Right,' said Cora. 'I see. That sort of figures.'

So Cora got to know Stanley. They weren't friends, didn't say hello. They acknowledged each other with a nod. Not nodding acquaintances. Just mutual nodders.

When Sam was two and Col one, Cora took a job wiping tables and serving in a local pub. Patsy Cline and Hank Williams twanged sorrowfully on the juke box, 'Yore cheatin' heart . . .' and men flirted. But Cora was having none of it. She had done with men. Still, the chat was occasionally cheering.

'Ah, Cora, a woman like you won't be used to a place as grand as this.' A customer looking round glumly at the drab vinyl seating and stained red carpet.

'Oh, bugger off. Thing to say. Hope there's more going on between your legs than there is between your ears. That'll mean you're not totally useless.'

'Ah. You've a mean streak in you.'

'I need it. A mean streak keeps a woman alive.'

Cora started to go to night school three times a week. She read tea leaves to pay for baby-sitting. Baby-sitters would arrive with cups wrapped in plastic bags, keen for an update on their lives. Was something good in the offing? Cora always took time to look meaningfully at the patterns in the leaves. She twisted and turned the cup, considered the possibilities. She always gave out good news. She figured nobody would want to stay alone in someone else's house, looking after someone else's children deliberating grim prospects and a murky future.

She did English Literature and French. Afternoons, after the park and before work, she studied. At work she kept a book under the bar and sat chewing gum and reading. She wriggled as she read, rattling through her consciousness the constant twang of Tammy Wynette or Johnny Cash. Customers bought her drinks and asked about her books.

'What're you readin' there, Cora?'

'*Pride and Prejudice*.'

'Any good?'

'I like it.'

'Any good bits?'

'Not in the way you're thinking.'

'Why are you reading it, then?'

'There's more to life than cars, sex, shopping and cheap thrills.'

'What?'

Cora chewed and solemnly stared ahead. 'Love. Honesty. Dignity. Stuff like that.'

'You have them, then. I'll have the sex, shopping, cars and cheap thrills. Wouldn't you rather have them. Really now?'

'Yes. But I'm working on it. See, that's honesty.' She beamed enthusiastically.

'I'm getting there.' She fetched drinks, emptied ashtrays and carried on chewing, wriggling and reading.

Still when scrubbing her kitchen floor, and she very occasionally did, she would lie back and stare at the sky. And sigh, 'What in the name of hell am I doing?' One day she stopped and sat up. 'This floor,' she said, thumping the black-and-white tiles with hatred, 'will be here long after I'm gone. I'll be dead but this floor will go on and on.' A horrible bout of truth hit her. Her hands came slowly up to her cheeks. 'God, who does that sound like? I have skipped a generation. I haven't turned into my mother. I've grown up to be my grandmother.'

She wanted to start screaming, but relieved the tension her revelation set up in her by running through the rooms stripping off her clothes. She ended up in the bathroom where she filled the bath and climbed in. Her sons joined her. They sat side by side at one end watching in amazement as Cora furiously scrubbed at herself saying, 'That's it. That's it. That's definitely it,' over and over. She caused a small tidal wave by suddenly standing up and stepping out. She wrapped herself in a towel and strode the flat once more. 'When you find yourself turning into your granny it's time to do something.' She slumped on the sofa. 'What do I want?' Then slowly: 'I want to teach. I could do that. What do you think of that, Col?'

Col smiled and handed her a towel. 'Dry me.'

'What do you think of that, Sam?'

'It's crap.'

'Don't say crap.'

'You say crap.'

'Yes, but I'm a grown-up.'

'Why do grown-ups get to say rude words and children not?'

'Dunno, Sam. I think we need it more.'

'Well, that's not fair. And all the other children round here get to eat fishfingers and beans when we get olive oil and horrible French stuff. And also when I go to nursery when you're not there I trudge.'

'Ah,' said Cora. 'Well, trudge away. I'm sure you do it magnificently.' It was dawning on her that her children weren't children really. They were people. And the two people she'd landed with both seemed to be a lot smarter than she was.

She phoned Irene and Bill. 'I'm going to be a teacher,' she said. 'I've decided I'd be good at it.'

Irene was tempted to say she hoped this would last, remember when she wanted to be a chemist, but she held her tongue.

Bill was enthused. 'That's great. You can do it. Just go for it.' Blister and hurtle, Cora.

She passed her exams in night school, applied for and got a place in teacher training college. Betty picked up the children from school and fed them secret fishfingers and oven chips. Evenings, Cora studied. It took her mind off her great longing and it helped her to keep at bay those shameful memories that floated back to her when her brain was idle.

Whilst her children watched television she worked, earphones on, jaws working out the rhythms that thrummed through her head on Wrigley's Spearmint Gum. Keep going, Cora. Don't think, Cora. Thinking's a killer, Cora. Thinking will be the end of you. But sometimes the memories battered through the noise and gum.

They'd walk the length of Princes Street. Where shall we shop today? They could both feel the heat, a sizzling glee that started in the groin and rose up through them. They had to do it. Had to. Into Marks and Spencer and start small. Don't get greedy. A pair of tights, one swift, fluid movement. Chat to each other, quietly, like proper shoppers, and inside the blood is hurtling through the veins. Then a shirt. Grinning and getting hot. The thrill of it, looking about, checking that nobody was watching them. Through the food department, a quiche, some cheese, a pot of apricot jam, a funny-looking raisiny cake that neither of them would eat. But this wasn't about wanting or needing. It was the rush. The rush. Back through the store, just look at the door, chat and laugh. A scarf, a pair of socks, a single shoe, ah ha. Be still my hammering heart. Slowly walk to the door. Relax. Relax. Can't breathe. Hit the street. Walk, chat. Laugh. Then move faster, through the crowd. Laughing louder. Thrilling. Oh yes. Oh yes. Oh yes. She was always miles ahead, miles ahead. Running and yelping glee. Up Frederick Street, into Rose Street. Find an empty alley round the back of some pub. Bottle banks and bins. They'd kiss. Too thrilled to speak. That wild fanatical kissing that has nothing to do with love, it's the only way to blast the last of the rush away. Hands on each other, pushing aside clothes. She'd feel him. Oh yes. Oh yes. He'd be far from her on his own high, moaning. He would always have some extra thing she hadn't seen him take, up his sleeve. Olive oil, wine. Claude was a far, far better thief than she was.

When she'd stopped going with him he went out alone. He'd approach wealthy shoppers outside Marks and Spencer, offering to plunder the food department for them for twenty pounds. 'Fifty pounds of food for twenty,' he'd smile. There was always someone who took him on. He squandered his takings on cognac, wine and Gauloises which he'd toss flamboyantly in front of Cora when he got home.

'Where did you get the money for all that?' She'd point at the booty accusingly.

'Somebody has to keep us going. And it's not going to be you, is it?'

Oh God, what might have become of them. Done for shoplifting, done for indecent exposure, lewd behaviour in public, and her pregnant at the time though she did not know it. Sam might have been born in prison. She imagined the phone call home. 'Hello, Mum. I've been arrested for shoplifting and shagging a bloke in public.' They would never have forgiven her. Their kindness would never have stretched that far.

'Oh no,' she would call, yelling loudly above the roar in her earphones into the quiet of the room. 'Oh God, no. I did that.' Her sons would exchange a look across the room, eyes lifted. Their mother, God help her, was always doing that – shouting out, squealing and squirming. Cora would take her head in her hands and shake it from side to side trying to shift the shame from her head. Sometimes she would bang her head on the table. 'Oh no. Oh no. Please no.' There was nobody in the world could give Cora a talking to that was worse than the regular beating up she gave herself.

She bought a tracksuit and started running again to see if a spot of vigorous exercise would help.

'You're not off running again, are you?' Betty looked horrified. Running was no fit thing for a woman to do.

'Yes,' said Cora. 'It helps.'

'What does it help with?'

'If I effing knew that, I wouldn't have to do it.'

But really she knew her two main problems. There was her shame, and her great longing. She needed sex. She wanted a man in her bed. She sighed and sighed and when she could no longer keep the longing away she remembered Claude. Her nights with him. The things they did. He could take her to extremes and when she was moving with joy he would stop.

'Don't,' he'd say. 'Don't you dare come without me. I want to be with you. In you. I want to feel your pleasure.' For that time they had together he filled all of her. She thought of nothing other than pleasing him. There would, she knew, never be anything like it again.

'Thank heavens for that,' she'd say. 'I couldn't stand the pace.'

'Think, Cora,' he would say. 'Think about all the world. Everyone coming at once.'

'They couldn't. People are doing all sorts of things.'

'Imagine the roar.'

'What are people doing now, right now when we're in bed doing this, you inside me?' Gasping and trying to hold on, they'd list the doings of the world.

'A child in Brazil is stealing a watch from the arm of a driver parked at the traffic lights.'

'A woman in Minneapolis is hanging out her washing.'

'Pigeons in Trafalgar Square are flapping and shoving aside as a bag lady in orange luminous socks walks through them.'

'A man in Australia wears torrid shorts as he rides a wave.'

'There are blizzards of butterflies in Burma.'

'In the paddy fields of China people are making dirty jokes as they plant rice.'

'A woman in Pakistan is singing her baby to sleep.'

On and on they went. 'Oh God,' Cora would cry when it all came flooding back, 'what a precious pair of pretentious wankers we were.' Hollering from the isolation and the din in her earphoned head, she was unaware of how loud she shouted. Her boys would exchange the pitying look. Mother was torturing herself again.

There were, of course, very occasional one-night stands. Men Cora brought home, shushing and holding her finger to her lips as they tiptoed past the children's bedroom. They got coffee, sex and a small snooze. They were her indiscretions. But they never got to stay all night. If they wouldn't leave, Cora would phone Betty Lawrence across the hallway and ask if her husband, Will, would mind doing a bit of bouncing.

'Is he bothering you?' Will would say, struggling to hold his pyjamas together, and shooting Cora a disgruntled middle-of-the-night look.

'Just leaving,' the indiscretion would say, cramming himself into his clothes.

Cora couldn't bear for anyone to be there when Col and Sam came rushing through in the morning to greet her as if they hadn't seen her for years, to sing and slap hands in the air and shout at her Van Morrison tapes. 'Van the man.'

Cora's fleeting lovers always got turned out into the night. But she was more than protecting her sons from the shock of learning that their mother was only, after all, a human being with needs and lusts. Well, hell, they were finding that out every day. She found she could not bear actually to sleep with someone. Intimacy was lovely. Oh yes, she'd say. Give me that. But dipping into unconsciousness with someone she didn't know, going through the graceless business of snoring and farting and dreaming with a stranger seemed, well, somehow sort of rude. And she'd no intention of ever doing it. Eventually she had to put a stop to her indiscretions. Betty's uninhibited show of disapproval became too much to bear.

'What's got into you, bringing these men home? You never know where they've been.' She made them sound like some dubious sweet she'd found in the gutter and was about to pop into her mouth. 'It's got to stop.' Betty was adamant. 'You can't go waking folk up in the middle of the night . . .'

Cora raised her hands, stopping her flow. 'I know. I know,' she said. It was bad enough taking the scoldings she gave herself without receiving another from her neighbour. 'You don't have to tell me. It'll never happen again.'

When Betty left, Cora leaned glumly on the window, looking out. 'That's it for me, then. My youth is over. No sex, no drugs. There's only rock 'n' roll left. They'll not take that away. Oh no.'

The songs on her radio played on and on. She was listening to the music she would have danced to had she gone to clubs, jumped about to at gigs, had she gone to gigs. These were the tunes that would have marked dates, picnics, dinners, holidays, nights at bars. She was listening to the life she would have had, had she been available to live it.

Cora graduated. She started work and within a year was earning enough to move. By then, though, something had happened. She had grown up here, made friends here, felt oddly safe and accepted here. She survived here. Cora did not want to leave. She was ensconced, comfortable here. And besides, her children were growing. 'The sticky years are over,' she said. 'Thank God.'

One day Sam brought in his first single. 'Listen to this,' he said. It sounded odd to her, disjointed.

'You like that?' she asked.

158

''Course. It's great.'

Cora went quiet. Then: 'You young bastards. You've changed the tune.' She sighed hugely and let her arms drop by her side. 'I don't like that. It's your music. God dammit. What do you get up to listening to that? You're not doing any of the things I did, are you?'

'What did you do?'

'Mind your own business.' Then, examining his face fiercely for lies, she demanded, 'You haven't got a tattoo on your bum, have you?'

'Of course not.'

'Do you know what you've done? You've turned me into a mother.'

'But you are a mother.'

'I may be one, but I never wanted to feel like one. Actually, I was thinking of resigning from motherhood. I want to be me again. I've been waiting all my life to get to do all the things I missed, bringing you two up. I wanted to be young again. And now just when you're old enough for me to get to do it, you go and change the tune and youth doesn't seem so juicy any more.'

Sam put his arm round her, roughly squeezed her shoulders, kissed the top of her head. 'Too middle-aged to be young and turbulent. Too young and turbulent to be middle-aged. Life's a bitch.'

'You're not sneering at me, are you?' Cora asked.

'Yes. But only because I'm young and turbulent,' said Sam.

In summer swallows dipped, swooped and cried. Children, kicking a football in the street, called to each other. And in small gatherings on the balcony women stood, arms folded, gossiping and laughing. That was Cora's favourite sound. That moment on summer evenings when women standing arms folded, discussing men, children, parents, stopped being wives, mothers, daughters and relaxed. That indiscreet cackle of women talking dirty.

That summer, though, she denied herself that indiscreet cackle. She bought a car. Yellow and rusting, it was, but with the necessary tape deck and radio. She called it the fartmobile. It moved grudgingly, fartingly, from place to place. She packed the boot, put the boys in the back and with some semblance of dignity, slightly redeemed, she went home.

3

Cora and Ellen

Chapter Twenty

Ellen often dropped into Cora's after work. Cora's kitchen was sunny and cluttered, an organised mess that she hated people meddling with, tidying for her. When it was messy she knew exactly where everything was. It was her mess and she loved it. Being in Cora's kitchen was calming. Soothing, Ellen thought. She felt the stiffness and tension drain from her shoulders. She got drowsy.

Cora always made a fetish of preparing a pot of tea. Warm the pot, two spoonfuls of Earl Grey, boiling water, leave to infuse then pour.

'Tell me, Cora,' said Ellen, 'what do you want out of life? Do you ever stop to think?'

'What an adolescent question. What do I want out of life, truth or bullshit?' Cora said, giving Ellen a cup of tea. She sat across from her and started to paint her nails. One glossy chestnut, the one next to it plum.

'Truth,' said Ellen.

'I want,' sighed Cora, 'instant gratification, constant adoration and to find a bottle of quality drinkable plonk on Safeway's shelves that costs less than two pounds. Mostly I want the wine.' She waved her hand at Ellen. 'What do you think?'

'Plum,' said Ellen. 'More dramatic.'

'Yes,' agreed Cora. 'If Sarah Bernhardt painted her nails, and she probably did, this'd be the colour. Tonight's the big night. You are remembering it's my school play? You have to come.'

'Maybe,' said Ellen.

Cora pressed her palms together, a small prayer. 'Please,' she said. 'You must come. You're my best friend. It's your duty. I need somebody of my own there. Somebody rooting for me, calling my

163

name – if only silently. There's no point asking either of the boys. They'll only look frightful and sulk.'

'Oh all right. Though I hate going back to school. And you'll be all bossy. I hate it already.'

'And I hate your absurd conversations. Tell me what you want out of life, then? If we're talking profound.'

She was slowly spreading plum on to her remaining nails. Tonight she'd have beads in her hair again. She'd wear pointy-toed patent mules, her scarlet silk jacket and orange T-shirt with 'Vulgarity Thy Name Is Woman' vividly in purple across her tits. She liked to look alarming. She still got an adolescent buzz out of the unchecked expressions of surprise that fleeted across the faces of her pupils' parents when they caught their first glimpse of her. She liked people to know she was there.

'I want my very own placid dumpling,' said Ellen.

The radio across the kitchen played a selection of rock music that was familiar enough to be nostalgic. Cora was sure it was never meant to be that. From another part of the flat came the relentless thud of more agonisingly disjointed music. Now that they were nineteen and eighteen, Cora's sons were heard but rarely seen. Ellen could more than hear it, she could feel it thumping up through the floor, through her chair, through her. Though it only contained three people, Cora's was a noisy household, tackily noisy. Silence unnerved her. She did not care for the thoughts that the absence of noise allowed into her head. She looked at Ellen, alarmed. 'You want what?'

'You heard,' said Ellen, taking a ponderous sip of Earl Grey. 'I want my very own placid dumpling. You know, those women you sometimes find at supermarket checkouts. They smile and smile and look concerned for you and your Brussels sprouts and toilet rolls and think nothing of themselves.'

Cora blew softly on her nails. 'You mean you want a wife?'

'Sod that. I was a wife. I know how awful a wife can be.' She shook her head. 'Oh no, I don't want anyone like me in my life, other than me. That's enough. I want a placid dumpling. There was one in Safeway's today. She said, "We'd better get you a double bag for your wine, luvvy." And I felt wanted. I thought how nice if she took me in and stroked my hair and made me puddings or cocoa. Cocoa would do.'

Luvvy, the placid dumpling had called her. Luvvy. Ellen couldn't resist her after that. She was a sucker for affection, any kind of affection.

'Ellen, you hate cocoa.'

'I wouldn't if a placid dumpling made me some. Anyway, today I got my stuff together in the trolley and went to the kiosk to buy some cigarettes. Then on my way back to the main door there was my placid dumpling being kind to another. She was saying, "We'd better get you a double bag for your wine, luvvy," to someone else. I felt betrayed. She broke my heart.'

'Why?' Cora was exasperated. Ellen always exasperated her. 'Can't you just do your shopping like everyone else in the world and stop looking for love and acceptance everywhere you go?'

Ellen shrugged, drained her cup and stared at the formation of tea leaves left at the bottom. Cora stretched over and took it from her.

'It's still the black dog. You're still depressed.'

'I know that. I don't need tea leaves to tell me that. I'm depressed about my life. My on-off marriage. I have to do something about it. I just drifted into it. I always thought it would sort itself out. But it's not going to do that on its own, is it? What about my future? Will I ever get my act together and do something about Daniel?'

'Tea leaves only reveal your present. And you know what to do about Daniel. Throw him out. The man is unfaithful and when he's finished losing his own money, he'll start on yours. Nobody else would put up with him. I'll pick you up at six. Be ready. None of this appearing half dressed and borrowing my mascara. I have to get there early. I have some serious bossing to do,' Cora said briskly. She was warming up, getting ready for the fray.

Col came into the kitchen and started to rummage through the fridge. 'There's nothing to eat,' he complained.

'Of course there is,' Cora said. 'There's yoghurt, apples—'

'That's not proper food.' He took a banana.

Cora watched him. 'Your legs are awfully hairy,' she said. 'When did that happen?'

He shrugged. 'It's been happening all my life. Leave my legs alone.'

'One day you notice them,' Cora said, 'and their legs are all hairy and they've got stubble on their chins and their skin is suddenly clear and it's got nothing to do with Biactol. Then they kiss you goodnight or give you a cuddle and you notice they're no longer handling you like a scrum half. There's someone else out there that you're not being told about yet. Some female someone. It's all so . . . so . . .'

'Normal?' suggested Ellen.

'I'm not taking any sort of comforting sanity from you. You are the last person in the world to dispense sanity. Anyway, it just makes you feel old.'

'You would have got to this age anyway even if you hadn't had them.'

'But I wouldn't have looked it,' Cora said. Then, 'Six, OK?'

'Can't wait.' Ellen sounded morose. 'You know some parent is going to come up to you and say something utterly insensitive and daft. You'll get all upset, probably be sick afterwards and it'll all just break my heart, Cora.'

'What with your two-timing placid dumpling, that'll be twice today your heart will have been broken.'

Ellen nodded glumly.

'Only twice,' said Cora. 'This will have been a good day for you.'

Ellen nodded glumly.

At six Cora knocked on Ellen's door. True to form Ellen was still in her underwear. She led Cora through to the kitchen and continued to eat the bowl of cornflakes that was her supper.

'Look at you,' cried Cora. 'Look at how you're dressed. Look at what you're eating and look at the time.'

'It's only half-past five,' said Ellen. 'Well, it was when I looked at the clock.'

'When was that?'

'Dunno. Half an hour ago, I suppose. Before my bath.'

'You expect it to still be the time it was when you looked at the clock?'

'No,' Ellen sighed. 'Not really. It's just sort of surprising the way it keeps on moving. Relentless.'

'You're so dreamy.'

'What's wrong with that?'

'Nothing, if you're the one doing the dreaming. But really irritating to everyone else. Please get dressed.' Cora was nervous.

Ellen pulled on a pair of black jeans and a black silk shirt. Took a black jacket from the hook behind the door and followed Cora down the stairs.

'You don't have any problems deciding what to wear, then?' Cora said.

'I hate decisions. You know that. They take too long. They can cut into your dreaming time.'

A trip in the fartmobile was always thrilling. At full rattle the wind howled through the gaps between door and sill, and through the windows that would not properly shut. The car roared and shuddered. In third and fourth gear there was such a vibrating feeling of energy, speed, rushing air, it always came as a surprise to both passenger and driver to glance at the speedometer and discover they were only travelling at thirty-five miles an hour.

Cora had driven up Leith Walk to pick up Ellen. Now she was driving back down again.

'Bloody red light,' she swore, and wrestled with the gear stick. First was always sticky. And if she didn't watch it, it would slip into reverse and they'd shoot back into the Jaguar behind. 'Bloody Jag's right up my arse.' A Volkswagen pulled up alongside. Revved. The lights turned orange. The fartmobile revved. Green. They both shot forward. Cora triumphed. She beat the Volkswagen across the lights. 'Have that, you short-arsed, cheap jacket, nasty-haircutted shite,' she yelled as the rival car pulled easily ahead and shot on to the next set of lights.

'Cora!' Ellen was horrified. 'You're bossy in life and a hooligan on the road.'

'Oh bollocks. I'm just judgemental like everyone else. It doesn't do to be racist or sexist but all the advertising I soak up makes me full of other sorts of bigotry. I have my own istnesses? Istosities? Like everyone else these days I'm haircuttist, jacketist, small dickist when judging male drivers. Get in your car and throw political correctness to the wind, baby.'

The lights were against them, they couldn't surf on green and ride without stopping. So they did the traffic light dash. Draw up alongside a superior car (every car on the road was superior), swift eye contact with driver, swear and challenge. Screech of tyres and on to the next set of lights. Not exactly heat and rage in the city, just an early evening metropolitan swagger as they plunged into the depth of Leith.

Cora loved Leith. Edinburgh was style and patter, haircuts and jackets in bars. But Leith was full of folk. People spilled from pubs. Of an evening the air was boozy. You could get drunk from passive drinking. It was a place to live out a recession. And, though it was filling with bistros and bars with their names gold lettered in Palatino on their windows, low times still suited it.

Ellen normally spent trips with Cora with her hands on her head screaming, 'Stop! Brake! Pull over! Let me out! Behave yourself!' But tonight she sat rigid with nerves, chain-smoking.

'I don't know why you do this,' Ellen said as they drew up outside the school and started to reverse, exhaust at full howl, into a parking space.

The poster pinned to the railings glowingly said, 'Panto Tonite. *Jack and the Beans Talk*, a spectacle on Been Hur scale, orchestra conducted by that well-known German Heinz Bean. Starring Warren Peas. Written by Miss O'Brien and the Kids of Class Three.'

'You've been busy,' Ellen said.

The playground was already full of infants, heads and feet sticking out of red and green cardboard pods. 'The beans,' explained Cora. 'Everybody has to get a part. Casting is a masterpiece of diplomacy. Some of these kids have absolutely no self-confidence at all. Being a bean helps. If you can be a convincing bean at seven, then the rest of your life should be lived with style.'

'You think?' Ellen laughed.

'Not really. But you know us teachers – we have to wrap up everything in psychobabble nonsense.'

The air thrummed excitement. Beans sped up and down the corridor, faces aglow with glee. Jumping up and down, waving their arms, they chanted their lines. 'I'm a bean. I'm Green Bean, and this is my friend,' pointing at vacant air. 'He's a has bean.'

168

'These kids are as high as kites.' Ellen looked round at them. 'They'll never sleep tonight.'

'I have been busy for nights and nights and nights. Have you any idea how much paracetamol and vodka has gone into this production?'

'Yes,' Ellen said weakly. 'I have a very good idea. I contributed a deal of it.'

'Well worth it,' said Cora. 'It's surprising how many of them remember these plays.'

'It's you they remember,' Ellen told her. 'Who is Jack, anyway?'

'Melanie Johnston.'

'The one with the mother . . . ?'

'The very one,' said Cora.

Cora had once given her class the task of drawing what Mummy did all day. 'I know we usually draw what Daddy does. But mummies are busy people. Have a think about yours – what does she do all day?'

There were drawings of mummies at work behind word processors or at supermarket checkouts. There were mummies carrying home shopping, mature student mummies falling asleep at their books, angry mummies, smiley mummies, mummies wracked with PMT, mummies ironing and mummies collecting children from school and there was Melanie Johnston's mummy. She was lying on a sofa, wearing a pink dressing gown and fluffy slippers. In front of her was a huge television set and by her side a box of chocolates and a glass of wine.

'Melanie Johnston,' Cora shouted, 'this can't be what your mummy does all day.'

'Yes it is.' Melanie Johnston nodded as she spoke.

'It is, Miss.' Other children who had obviously witnessed this indolence agreed.

'I wouldn't mind but she looks great on it,' Cora protested to Ellen. 'Feminism seems to have passed her by. She feels no guilt.'

'Maybe she has reached a plain we're all striving to get to. Maybe she knows something we don't. Freedom from guilt and everything,' Ellen mused. They spent a deal of time speculating about Melanie Johnston's mum.

Walking into the school with Cora Ellen said, 'You have to point her out to me. I must see this woman.'

Cora led the way into the gym hall and indicated a seat in the front row to Ellen.

'Aw, Miss,' Ellen cried. 'I want to sit at the back.'

'At the front,' Cora ordered, waving Ellen into a chair. 'I want to keep an eye on you. No slipping out to the pub. And here's a programme. That'll be fifty pence.'

'How long does it last anyway?'

'An hour and a bit, with sandwiches, cakes and tea afterwards.'

Ellen felt herself go limp. That feeling that she'd be in this gym hall for ever. That her buttocks would go numb sitting on the hard school seat. 'Numb buttocks,' Ellen said. 'Why are municipal seats so hard? That'll be why I didn't achieve at school – I was too preoccupied with my bum. Maybe if schools had softer seats a whole different set of people would emerge as professionals and leaders of society. Maybe that's why society is such a mess, the people who have shone at school are merely the ones with insensitive backsides. Maybe—'

Cora leaned over and touched her arm, a shut up gesture. 'I have to go,' she said. 'I'll leave you to your theories. I have to switch into hyper boss.'

She disappeared behind the curtain. Ellen could hear her imperiously shrill cry. Every now and then she stuck her head out, checking Ellen hadn't slipped away, and that the hall was filling up. People were going to turn up, weren't they? They did. Of course, they did. Mothers, fathers, grans and granddads, sisters, brothers, neighbours and friends sat in expectant rows, waiting to cheer on their own little star.

At last she appeared on stage, smiled, and thanked everyone for coming tonight. 'We need all the support we can get,' she said. She was wearing a long skirt so that nobody would see the dramatic effect standing before a crowd had on her knees.

Ellen fixed her eyes on Cora's throat. It was flushed with anxiety. Her eyes shone, glassily shone. She had been working on this play for weeks and weeks. The curtain behind her billowed with little lives. There were urgent whisperings from the side of the stage, sniggers and semi-hysterical titterings. These children had been rehearsing every day since, it seemed to Cora, the beginning of time. She knew it didn't matter. Glowing parental pride, people would come and watch their own children change their socks on stage. OPCs, as Cora called other people's children, were of no interest at all. Camcorders whirred, cameras flashed. They were off.

The school spotlight wavered across the curtain, Mrs Grundy, the visiting music teacher, beefily thumped the piano, upper arms aquiver, and a cancan of beans danced on stage, kicking little legs, little faces (mostly toothless) grinning inanely, singing 'Happy Talk' from *South Pacific*.

When she was a child, Ellen recalled, school concerts were dour affairs. The choir sang 'Swing Low, Sweet Chariot' with stultifying suburban politeness, pronouncing every syllable. 'Sweeng low swe ... ee ... tt chaario ...ttt'. It wasn't actually her voice but her height that got her a place in the choir. Her music teacher had a keen sense of symmetry. Ellen had fitted perfectly into the middle of the back row.

This, though, this was ebullient. The audience joined in, clapped, booed, hissed and sang. When she was little Ellen had longed to be in a school play. She had squeezed to the front when parts were being cast and stared, maniacally she now thought, at the teacher. But she was never chosen. She was considered too quiet, too distant, too dreamy to carry any starring role – any sort of role, in fact. But Ellen knew that somewhere inside her was a star trying to get out. In fact, she was quite sure the only reason she hadn't made it to Hollywood was that she was never in a school play. She hadn't been given the right sort of break. Not the sort of break the beans and Jack were getting now. They were dressed up and dancing. They were having a lovely time.

This, Ellen realised, was their first fifteen minutes. She didn't believe people only got one set. She didn't think she'd had one yet, though. It was a small glimpse Cora was giving them of what a fifteen minutes could be like. Standing backstage, prompting and bossing and organising, Cora was giving these children the chance she had had years ago when she ran in front of all those drunken cheering people – 'Come away, the wee one'. She had sensed the thrill of having a go. These children were blistering and hurtling.

At one point the excitement got too much for Jack. She tumbled from the stage. A woman rose, slowly, majestically from the mid ranks of the audience, chocolate wrappers scattering. She was tall and wearing a coat with a huge fake fur collar. She raised her hand and, pointing at the child scrambling to get back under the spotlight, roared, 'Get back up that beanstalk, you little bugger.'

Ellen stared. So that was her, Melanie's mum. Our lady of the sofa and fluffy slippers. No wonder nobody criticised her lifestyle.

By nine it was over. The volunteers who had contributed cakes, shortbread and trays of sandwiches clustered round to clear up. With an efficient snapping of yellow rubber gloves, the following of trusty mums set about wiping and cleaning. They displayed a clear upmanship over those who were sloping off home, hand in hand with infant beans. Children trying to make their moment last were refusing to take off their costumes and were walking to their cars through the evening still dressed for the show. Some of them would refuse to take their stage outfits off when they got home. They would sleep as beans tonight.

Wasn't upmanship strange? Cora thought. People will take on a bit of rivalry about anything. Cars, jeans, CDs, the neat cut of their lawns, the flatness of stomachs, food – anything. Once they had a visiting American student who expressed horror when she saw little children who lived only a street away set off for home alone. 'That wouldn't happen in the States.' The student couldn't believe her eyes. 'We got child abductors, muggers and murderers there.'

'So do we,' Cora hotly defended her country. How dare someone suggest it was, in any way at all, inferior? She was about to add that muggers and murderers over here were as good as anywhere in the world. But wondered if she was perhaps taking patriotism a tad too far.

'Can we go now?' Ellen asked.

'Oh please, let's. Oh God. What did you think of that?' Cora wanted to know. Then, 'No, don't tell me. Doing it was enough. I can't take criticism.'

'I loved it,' Ellen told her. 'Really, it was fun.'

But Cora was a wreck. She had been writing this panto for weeks. Then rehearsing it, nagging mums into making costumes and bringing along food, rounding up other teachers to help make the stage set and work the lights.

'It's over,' she said. 'It's over. Till next year it's over. Thank God . . . Oh my . . .' Her chest heaved. There were tears in her eyes. 'Quick, for Christ's sake, hold my shoes.' She swiftly freed her feet from her stilettos. 'I have to . . .' she started off down the street, ' . . . run.'

Head back, stocking-soled, she ran along the street, and disappeared round the corner. She threw herself forward and flew. She flowed, gaudy in her producer/director outfit, over the pavement. She was still fast. People saw her coming and stepped aside, turned to watch her go.

'Cora,' Ellen called. 'Cora. God damn you, Cora.' She stood holding the shoes, staring in amazement at the empty street, the space where Cora had been. Every time, every single time, Cora had a concert she did this. And every time the speed of the woman amazed Ellen. She got into the car, and started at full throttle after her. But by the time she got round the corner Cora had disappeared. She crawled kerbside, clutching the steering wheel, peering up alleys. No Cora. At last she stopped and stuck her head out through the sunroof and yelled. People stopped to stare, looked round for signs of Cora, believing Ellen to be summoning a naughty dog. Some young boys out pubbing took up the call, howling, 'Cora. Cora. Cora,' into the night as they moved from one drinking place to the next. Long after they'd gone Ellen could hear them still laughing and bawling Cora's name through the dark.

At last Ellen found her. She caught Cora in the full glare of her headlights. She was bent over, panting and gasping for breath. Her hair hung down covering her face. She gripped her sides, and wheezed, 'Oh God, I hate all that. I hate it. I hate it. I hate it.'

'Then why do you do it?' Ellen spoke quietly.

'Because I have something to say.' Her wild breathing calmed. 'I really do believe I have something to tell these children about life.'

'What?'

'This is what I have to say. Aaaaaaaaaah.'

173

'I don't think they heard you. They were having such a good time. Your feet are bleeding. God, you're such a fool.'

'If you truly loved me you'd bathe my bleeding feet in your teardrops and dry them with your hair,' Cora sniffed.

Ellen handed Cora her shoes. 'I'll buy you a drink.'

They went to the Oyster Bar, settled at a table. Ellen bought the first two rounds, then Cora the next two, and by then she was feeling mellow. Drinking another seemed like more than a good idea, a necessary thing to do to keep the mellowness going. She took off her jacket so that her 'Vulgarity Thy Name Is Woman' tit message was boldly on show.

'Oh God,' she said. 'All this has to stop. All this drinking.' She put her head in her hands. 'Shit, Ellen. I'm too old to be young.' She lifted her glass and half emptied it. 'Look. Look what I can do. I shouldn't drink like that. Me. I'm an old woman in the making. Droopy tits. Thighs to weep about.' She beat them ineffectually. 'I don't know.' They drank some more.

'When I worked in that pub the women all used to sing "Staynd by Yore Mayn". I used to think it'd be wonderful to have a mayn to staynd by. But now I think you only stand by your man because it saves you the awful responsibility of standing by yourself.'

Ellen nodded and said nothing. When Cora prattled it was best to let her prattle till she was all prattled out. Then she would start to sing. Then they would have an argument. Tomorrow they'd make up and be pals again. This was what was going to happen. She knew it.

'Of course,' Cora prattled, 'I don't understand men.'

'Neither do I. They are perplexing and mysterious creatures who think they can drive cars fabulously – especially backwards. Why do they go so fast in reverse?'

'See, women,' said Cora, 'women, by and large, quite like themselves but hate their bodies. Men just can't get the hang of having a body. Every month women come to terms with their body and how it behaves. Women all over the world, whoever they are, know about themselves and each other. Men don't have that. They have a bit of their body that does what it wants. It behaves badly on its own.'

174

Cora's face was flushed. She went to the bar, brought another round to the table and continued, 'See, if women had penises, they'd have penis encounter groups where we'd all sit round and bring them out and come to terms with ourselves. Of course we'd be bitches. "Oh, Helen," we'd say, "it doesn't matter that yours is so small." Then when she was gone, we'd say "Poor Paul, Helen's is so small. Size is everything." '

Across the room a group of young girls shrieked and laughed. They ate crisps and drank tequila. Their earrings jangled and anyone could tell just by looking at them, they were talking dirty. There goes Karen, Sharon, Alice and Katy, Ellen thought. She imagined they were out there still, running the streets, howling and calling, for ever young and free. And, of course, they were – maybe not that particular Karen, Sharon, Alice and Katy, but another lot, a new lot. They'd always be out there, Ellen thought.

'Look at you,' Cora accused. 'Drifting off. Dreaming again. You never stop.'

'I was just thinking about some people I knew years ago. I always imagine they've stayed the same whilst I've got older.'

'Ah well, that's surely the way of it,' Cora said. Her face creased with mischief. An unbounded exuberance and love of humanity filled her, booze flooded her bloodstream. The world was a lovely place full of lovely people and did anyone want to hear her doing Marlene Dietrich? Every woman over a certain age, Cora thought, could do Dietrich. She did Dietrich. Then she did Leonard Cohen. Then she deepened her voice, adding a couple of chins to her existing one and a half, and did Dietrich doing Cohen, and flatly sang, 'Oh ze zeesters of mercy.' She dipped a soulful finger into the froth of the half of Guinness that had appeared from goodness knows where, goodness knows who. Women, soul mates, fellow travellers who all longed to be deep and mysterious and loved, from here and there about the room joined in.

'Why do you do it?' Ellen asked when they staggered out. The night hit them, that whammy blat of fresh air, scorching through boozed brains and lungs. Walking was suddenly tricky. 'Why do you do it? Go drinking and, dammit, take me with you? You corrupt me.'

'I'm only abusing someone I've been trying to get fond of all my life. Me,' Cora explained.

Ellen stopped and leaned on a wall. 'I'm drunk,' she confessed. 'I'm so drunk. And you did it. You got plastered and took me along.'

'You could've said no.'

'By the time I realise that I've drunk too much I think, might as well carry on. I love you, Cora. But sometimes you're too vibrant for me. You rush at life too much for me. Blister and hurtle, Cora. But leave me at home.'

Cora was offended. 'Don't blame me if you've drunk too much. I'm fine. I'm not drunk.'

'Yes you are. You always deny it. It's so weird because you are Cora and the thing that you mostly are is honest.'

'Oh no I'm not.' Cora was hurt. She was a woman of mystery and depth. She wasn't honest. She had two sons, different fathers, and when they asked about their dads she skirted the truth. 'Oh, Sam, your father was French. We just lost touch before you were born. People do. He got ill. Don't ask.' Then feeling bad, 'Well, ask, but not now, OK?'

Ellen knocked on Cora's forehead. 'You're hiding something. Hiding. Are you in there, Cora?' She waved to Cora from the other side of the gulf, Cora's guilt.

'Oh bugger you,' cried Cora. 'What do you know. You've got it all. Stanley Macpherson sorts you out. He fixed the mess you got into with Daniel. You've done nothing for yourself, Ellen. You know nothing about life. Tucked away. Dreaming.'

'I'm not tucked away. You're the one with secrets.'

'Secrets,' Cora screamed. 'A person should be allowed their secrets.'

Start at the top of the store and work down. Scarves, lipsticks, nail varnish, chocolates, gloves, a perfume tester. Take it, take it. Above the lift, the sign to watch out for – two lights flashing. They are calling for the store detectives. Quick, quick. Time to go. Only that was when it was best. Eyes wild, crazed with the thrill, danger set the blood buzzing.

'You are bricked in, Cora. I tell you everything. I expose myself

176

to you. And you tell me nothing,' Ellen shouted. They were yelling at each other. Drunk and yelling. It drove Ellen wild that Cora knew everything about her, and she did not know everything about Cora. She felt cheated. And they were getting older and older. Time and worry showed on Cora's face. There were valleys on it that had not been there that night when she came fabulously across the room. 'You look like you are in need of some serious corrupting,' she had said.

Oh, corrupt me, Cora, Ellen thought. Make me like you are, take me to the vile places you have secretly visited and show me how to sin marvellously like you did.

And it was true. Stanley Macpherson did look after her. Ever since she had shown him Daniel's mess he had cared for her. He sorted her accounts. But then everyone knew that Stanley, being Stanley, would have sorted Ellen out had she walked in off the street with her problems in a shoe box. Stanley had started pension plans for Ellen, Billy and Brigit. He had trust funds and savings plans for his children. The only future Stanley hadn't provided for was his own.

Stanley never left the house without a pocket full of change for the beggars he'd pass on the way to work. Stanley's living room was full of waifs. Waifs of the living room storm Ellen called them – people from his past who turned up to sit at his table, eat his food, borrow money and disappear from his life for another decade or so. He syndicated *Gangster Women* and *Engels* and all her other characters and invested her share of the profit. She was thirty-seven, comfortably off, protected and cosseted by Stanley.

'I still think you're hiding. I hate it,' she said. 'You've locked me out.'

'Not you,' her mother said when she stood in the cold bungalow. 'Not you,' on the night her daddy died and the draught rushed under the front door, freezing her feet. All her life, then, rejection had terrified her.

'And you think there isn't part of you that's locked away in your dreamings,' Cora retaliated. 'You shut yourself off. And you are so privileged. So lucky. Everybody likes you. You don't realise. You are so cool you can wear sunglasses indoors at night. At your age. I hate that.'

'Oh good one. I'm privileged and you've had it tough. I know nothing and you're worldly. You're a mother, an empowered woman . . . and . . . and I'm . . .' Ellen stopped. She was what? She was a wimp, tucked away from the world. A dweeb, geek – she had a vast selection of derogatory descriptions of herself.

'A mother,' Cora shouted. 'I'm a mother. You think that makes me something special? Guilt trippers of the world unite . . .'

A mother, me a mother, she thought. Some mother. A boss, a nag, purveyor of proteins and vitamins, clean socks and quick, gravure, easy-access philosophies.

'Who was my father?' Col asked.

'He was my love,' she replied. She lied.

'Why did he go away?' he asked.

'Sometimes people have to go away,' she said.

'Other children have fathers,' he said.

'Well, you've got me. And I've got you. We don't need a father.'

Oh good one, Cora, she chastised herself. You really tackled the issues there. That'll see him through life's ups and downs. He can cling to that. You've done the lad proud. Watch him face the world.

Sometimes she would stand in the hall outside her children's room listening to them sleep. And she was filled with shame. She had brought these boys into the world and what could she give them? She had little money. She had worked through their early childhood. She felt she had missed out on part of their infancy, and they had not had the mother they deserved. And their mother's sins had denied them both a father.

'I have failed. I have failed,' alone in the dark she accused herself.

And here she was, nearly forty, wearing an absurd T-shirt and bawling at her best friend in the street. Why stop at shouting? Why didn't they let go and fight? Why didn't they just start battering each other with their handbags? Passing cars were already slowing so that passengers and driver could stare and enjoy the show.

'I'm too old for all this,' she sighed. 'Where's the car?' She was jealous of her friend and hated herself for it. Furthermore, her head hurt. She was sure she was going to have an embarrassing bruise where Ellen had knocked on her forehead. 'I think you have injured me.'

'Have I? Oh sorry,' said Ellen. 'And I can't remember where I left your car. Can't drive anyway. Get a taxi.'

'I'm so pissed. And I have to get up in the morning and go to work. Unlike some,' Cora said pointedly.

'Sorry,' said Ellen. 'Sorry I don't have to turn up at exactly nine o'clock and I can lie in bed when you can't. Sorry I'm such a wanker.'

'So you should be.' They shared a taxi and parted in the glum reckoning of throbbing and painful sobriety. Sore hearts and tears, parched mouths and a headache coming searing in.

Chapter Twenty-one

Daniel didn't leave with one wild flamboyant sweeping farewell. He drifted out of Ellen's life. Then back in again. And out again. In again. Out again. Their parting took a lot longer than their getting together. They became expert at arguing with each other, and could slip with ease from bickering to quarrelling to full-scale screaming and throwing things. And then make love. They could yell foul things at one another. Stop. Go to bed. Make love. Fight lying down. Stop. Make love again. Get up in the morning, and still be fighting. It was draining.

The disintegration of the relationship started with Friendly Mary's lovebite and never recovered. Daniel often came home with an armful of fruit and veg. With shrinking heart she remembered on the night of the lovebite Daniel came home with a huge bag of apples. Once she got up after sleeping with Daniel and ate a particularly juicy pear.

'Where do you get all the fruit you come home with?'

He shrugged. 'Here and there.'

'Don't lie to me,' she cried, throwing an apple at his head. It hit – a beautiful strike just above his left ear.

'Jesus.' He rubbed the damaged spot. He was astonished. He was surprised that someone as utterly non-confrontational as Ellen should suddenly start throwing things. Then there was the devastating accuracy of her aim. Thank heavens she did not know about Louise, his old tutor – not only were the pickings from her flat more up-market, they were also heavier. A bottle of claret from her wine rack fitted into the deep pocket of his raincoat, a couple of frozen veal cutlets from her freezer that they'd eaten the other night – with apple sauce – things like that could, when thrown over a six-foot distance, cause some serious damage. He felt aggrieved.

Ellen had no idea the trouble he went to.

'Bugger you,' he snarled. It never once crossed his mind that what he was doing was wrong. It was just the way he was. Evenings on his way home he'd stick his head round the door of the fruit shop. A big smile and a wave and Mary would fill a bag with this and that. 'Oh take it. They'll not be worth putting out tomorrow,' she'd say, dismissing his protests.

Daniel would say, 'Ta,' and smile again at her. It was part of his life, his job. If he didn't smile and wave and take, he'd have to buy food. His money was far too precious for that. He needed it for horses, music and booze. But mostly for the horses.

Ellen did not understand how much he needed to gamble. It was winning that did it. Just winning once was enough to make up for losing twenty times. If he got really low, he knew just one little win would bring him back up again. He just had to have that moment when his horse was flying at full canter past the winning post. 'Yes,' he'd shout to himself, an inward and silent roar of triumph, fists clenched. 'Yes. Me. Me. I picked that horse. I did that. Have that.' In his head he'd line up his mother and father, old teachers, tutors, lovers, people who doubted or mocked him, and, these days, Ellen. 'Have that, all of you. I knew that horse would win. Me.' He'd take his winnings, and, if he didn't put them on another horse, he'd lavishly squander them. Saving money, being sensible, would break the lucky flow. You had to laugh in the face of the lucky gods.

The thing he hated most about sharing his flat with Ellen was that she found out about his lucky routine. She had no sympathy with it at all.

'You've washed my red socks,' he screamed. 'I need them today. They worked for me last week. Got up nine thirty. Grey striped boxers,' he waved his lucky book in front of her, 'white shirt, Levi's, red socks. Look, *red socks* . . .' rapping the page with his finger, pointing, 'played The Smiths. Coffee. Walked down left side of street. Ten pounds on Heartbeat. Won. See that? Won.'

She looked dumbfounded at his precise, absurd notes, his small neat writing, listing every event in his diabolical life. Said nothing.

'Now you've ruined it. I can't repeat last week's lucky routine. You've broken the divine flow.'

Realising she might read his own carefully documented evidence against himself he snapped the book shut and shoved it into his back pocket. His lucky jottings included no mercy details of who he slept with, positions and what he'd filled his pockets with as he made post-coital tea or coffee. Ellen would not appreciate knowing that his other lovers provided her meals. Especially when they caused her so much trouble. She did not have his iron digestive system. The other night she'd lain in bed, complaining and belching – and there was nothing worse than a woman belching – put him right off.

'What was that we had tonight?'

'Chicken,' he said. Casually he thought.

'I know it was chicken. But how did it get red like that, and so sweet?'

'Oh, it's an old recipe of mine.'

'What was it?'

He'd stolen a bottle of white burgundy from Louise along with some frozen chicken thighs, a carton of yoghurt and a can of Coca-Cola. He'd planned to drink the Coke as he cooked the chicken in the wine. But somehow as he chopped onions and mushrooms (a gift from Friendly Mary) he'd poured and drunk a glass of wine, then another and before he knew it there wasn't any left to put in his casserole. Congratulating himself on his inventiveness, he cooked the chicken in the Coke instead. The result he thought surprisingly interesting. A culinary discovery, he decided. The chicken went fascinatingly red, and tasted sweet.

'It's Thai,' he told Ellen.

'Oh clever,' she enthused. He could tell she wasn't keen on eating it, but was, as ever, too polite to say so. It wasn't quite vile. In fact, he thought, a little garlic and ginger and it could be palatable.

He blamed this sudden throwing of fruit on old Mrs Boyle downstairs. Her and her damned mushroom quests that were now a regular Saturday afternoon outing were turning Ellen's head. But he was wrong. It was Ellen's dreams that were driving her to distraction.

She dreamed she was in a boat and the sea was heaving, a huge swell. The vast, heavy wall of water washed over the land, over small single palm tree cartoon islands, sent them rocking and sinking. The boat was still but everything around was going under. She dreamed she was walking through a city that had a vast canyon in the middle of it, a sudden plunging gap that stretched the full length of the ancient, worn paving slabs. To cross the gulch and get to her friends Ellen had to use a narrow, shaky rope bridge. People were bustling across easily back and forth, but it scared her. She couldn't bring herself to cross it. She dreamed she was driving to a park and suddenly realised she did not know the way. She stopped the car and ran into a huge building where she confessed to the man at the counter that she did not have a driving licence. They took her out right away in a car covered with gaudy signs, one neon lit on top, and a PA that boomed, 'Keep back. Learner.'

'What do they all mean, Stanley?' she asked at lunch one day.

'Overwhelming odds, feeling of inadequacy,' Stanley said. 'You've some sort of crisis you're not facing up to. Something you feel you can't cope with. That sort of thing.'

'Ah. My dreams are a bit obvious, aren't they? Not intricate and Freudian – well, if Freud wrote for the *Beano*, I suppose,' said Ellen.

'Only you would offer an apology for your dreams,' Stanley said. 'It's that bloke of yours, isn't it?'

'No,' she lied.

'Thought so,' said Stanley. He sniffed, took her bacon and brie sandwich and chewing it, told her. 'Brigit has left me.'

'No. Why?'

'I eat too much. I'm never home. I get agitated and fret if I take a day off. I annoy her. Not as much as I annoy me, I can tell you.'

'What are you going to do?'

'Eat too much. Stay at work too late and get agitated and fret if I take a day off. I don't have to change now, do I?' Staring glumly ahead, they shook their heads in unison.

'I really think Daniel cares for you in his way,' he said.

'Oh yes. I think that. But I can't stand him being with other women. I mean,' she lowered her voice, 'among other things, the unfaithfulness and the holding and kissing someone who isn't me. Well, frankly, I don't want to share him. You know . . .'

184

Stanley finished her sandwich and considered going to the bar for something else to eat. 'No, what?'

'His thing. His thing.' Ellen never mastered talking frankly about intimate parts of anybody's body – her own included. Stanley looked blank. How irritating. 'His thing,' louder now. 'I think about where he's putting it. What he's doing with it. What these other women are doing with it. And I don't want it near me.'

'It'd be a little more than near,' said Stanley seriously, wondering what it was about him that women always confided in him. Whatever it was, if he knew, he would fix it. He didn't want to know this.

'I think I'll have a pork pie,' he said.

Ellen burst out crying. It hurt so much. She thought Daniel was hers, her prize. He was so beautiful. Nights she waited – straining to hear his footfall on the stairs, his key in the lock – for him to come home to her. He always arrived bursting in, his marvellous life pouring from him. He'd carelessly toss his jacket over the back of the sofa and sit down, hands clasped behind his head. He'd tell her his day. She thought his life mystical and wild. He met this geezer who ... knew a bloke who ... he had a drink with, and ... there was this deal brewing, and if ... he put thirty quid on Joker's Wild and had won this ... look. He'd hold up a wad of notes or he'd bring out something – a silk scarf, a pair of earrings – to give to her. He was so fabulous, and look at her. What did she do? She came and she went. She left for work at half-past eight. She came home again at six. She knew nothing of geezers and blokes and deals. She sat at her desk writing comic strips, correcting proofs, having the odd script conference – whatever. She ate lunch and in the afternoon she did it all over again. I'm so boring, she thought. So ordinary. I live a little life. Give me my Nescafé, give me a Twix and watch me go.

Every Saturday afternoon Emily Boyle would link arms with Ellen and they would set off on a mushroom quest. They rarely returned with mushrooms, they rarely returned sober. They weren't drunk, of course, just drunkish, deliciously touching the gigglish edges of silliness. Enraged, Daniel would hear them coming along the street, laughing, and there was always the telltale clank of bottles in their Oddbins bag. Emily would invite Ellen in and cook for her. It was the only decent meal she ate all week.

'I'm not teaching you to cook,' she said. 'I'm teaching you the meaning of food. It brings sanity and wellbeing. Never make decisions or love on an empty stomach. In other words, if you are ever in the position of having a man propose to you again, insist, absolutely insist, on having a bacon sandwich before you reply.'

They sat in Pierre Victoire's eating dish of the day, drinking wine. They'd order more wine, drink it and smoke. They'd be there all afternoon. Cora too.

'Oh,' said Emily Boyle. 'People accuse Rachmaninov of being romantic. Yet the Rhapsody on a theme of Paganini was quite terse, completely devoid of any overblown nonsense. And,' taking one of Ellen's cigarettes, 'the ending begins with consecutive fifths. That's hardly nineteenth century, is it?'

Cora and Ellen shook their heads.

'Did you sleep with him?' Cora asked.

'Sleep with Rachmaninov? Me? For heaven's sake, one didn't sleep with a man like that. He was so dour. Tall and glum. And devoted to his family. Oh no, I had other lovers.' She had a special way of saying Rachmaninov and piano. She rested her voice on the As. Prolonged them, as if she loved saying them and didn't want to let go – Raaachmaaaninov. Piaaano. Ellen loved it. Alone, in the bath she often imitated the old lady. 'Rachmaaaninov. Aaaaabominable. Aaan aaabsolutely aaadorable aaarse.' She thought Mrs Boyle's a golden voice.

'No, I just played a duet with him, that's all,' Emily said.

'I know you did that. You told me.'

'And I will tell you again. You can depend on it.'

'Ah,' said Cora. 'I just wondered.'

'I'll have a vodka martini.' Emily flapped her hand at the waiter. 'Will either of you join me?'

Cora and Ellen shook their heads in unison. But they were dazzled by Emily's drinking bravura.

'Oh I know,' Emily said, abashed at her consumption, but only slightly. 'I shouldn't. But at my age what can possibly happen to me? My liver is as old as I am. Things I've already put it through, another few years of abuse is hardly going to matter. Thank God I never have to look at the thing. Oh, I give myself the odd ticking off, tell myself to stop. But it's so lovely being naughty. The spirit has always been willing, and so has the flesh. So I'm at one with myself.'

She was holding court, expounding her theories about life. Half a bottle of barolo and a couple of vodka martinis and her life story and philosophies were anybody's.

'You people, you young people are all the same. Every generation of young people, all the same. You think you invented sex. I don't know. My goodness we used to have a lovely time. All the better because we weren't as lewd as you lot. You're so explicit.'

Ellen drank. Cora switched to Evian, espresso and inhaling the smoke from Ellen's cigarette.

'During the war there was such urgency – the shagging that went on. Let me tell you. We thought we were going to die. Or we thought the ones we loved were going to die. Of course we made the best of what time we had. Ah . . .' she was remembering, 'it all stopped in the fifties. People bought bungalows and sat inside neatly with their hands clasped in their laps – front doors shut. It was trauma did it. They were stressed, traumatised. No doubt about it. Philip Larkin says sexual intercourse was invented in 1963. But that's nonsense. People just came to themselves. They just noticed there were jolly tunes playing on the radio and they thought, time to get shagging again. And that's what they did. Time to get shagging again.'

Her golden voice hung gloriously on to the A. Shaaagging. She took an expert swig of her drink. 'That's the sexual revolution according to Emily Boyle.' She finished one vodka martini, ordered another and said, 'He never made faces as he played.'

'Sorry. Who?'

'Rachmaninov. He kept his face still. I never saw that in anyone else. Everyone else showed the emotions that were running through them with the music.'

Ellen said, 'Ah. Fancy that. I never knew.'

'Practice. Practice. Practice. That's what does it. That's how I spent my nights for years and years. Four, five hours a day. One day

I looked up and my life was hurtling past me. You people with your sex and drugs and rock 'n' roll are so lucky. I wish I'd had that.'

'So do I,' said Ellen. 'It kind of passed me by.'

'I was too busy with children. It all went on without me. Sex, oh yes, did that, smoked a little dope but it was mostly rock 'n' roll for me, other people's sins,' Cora sighed. 'Not that I didn't enjoy what sinning I managed. Sinning was fine. Loved it. But look what happened: two children, no father. And look at the environment I gave them.'

Emily gazed at her, ancient eyes. She reached her veiny old hand across the table and patted Cora's. 'Look at my hand,' she said. 'I have watched my life passing on the back of my hand. There it was, getting older and older in front of my eyes, whilst I stayed the same.' Then, 'You give yourself such a hard time. You don't see it, do you? *You* were your children's environment. Your body at first. Then your thoughts, your presence.'

'I wasn't there that much. I was working,' Cora said.

'Oh, stop chastising yourself. You worked for them, didn't you? Your stuff was there. Your taste. Books. Music. Give yourself a break. Children are tough. It's you middle-aged people who are fragile and broken.'

Chapter Twenty-two

Sunday lunch time, Cora put a plate of cauliflower soup before Ellen. 'There. Eat that.'

Still recovering from yesterday's hangover, Ellen stared glassily at the bowl before her. 'Women should take up physics,' she said.

'Is that some kind of incomprehensible comment on my cooking?' Cora asked. She did not take kindly to any kind of criticism.

'No. It's just soup. I mean that men are nature's physicists. Women are natural alchemists. The alchemy of our bodies and the alchemy of the mixtures we brew. Potions we put on our hair, moisturisers on our skin.' She sniffed deeply. 'Doubtless men invented the bow and arrow. Women, soup. Definitely, soup.'

'Hmmm,' said Cora.

'So I was wondering – what if,' Ellen said.

'What if?' Cora said. 'Do I have to listen to this? Your life is a mess of what-ifs and maybes.'

'What if Einstein had been a woman? Even better, what if Oppenheimer had been a woman? What if a woman had split the atom? Think about that. A man split the atom and he unleashes this abominable power. What does he do? He takes it to other men. "I have unleashed an abominable power," he says. And the other men, who are politicians and soldiers – the worst sort of people to have access to abominable power – say, "Abominable power. Does that mean we can destroy the world, then?" I ask you,' Ellen was getting quite heated now. 'I ask you, would a woman do that? "Destroy the world?" a woman would say. "You're not going to do that, I've just paid my phone bill. I've just had the curtains dry-cleaned." Oh no. If a woman had split the atom and unleashed that power she would have taken it to other women. To Helena Rubenstein or Coco Chanel and told them to see what they could do in the way of producing the ultimate moisturiser. Alchemy's creative.'

'Ellen,' Cora said, 'do you ever have any logical thought progressions? I sometimes think you are lost in some sort of dreaming. You hide in your head. Mostly from yourself. And you'll do anything rather than face up to your problems.'

'Yes,' said Ellen. 'I know. Whenever I have a problem I drift off into daydreams, vaguely hoping it'll sort itself out without me. I walked into this life I lead and sat down thinking: This'll do. I never planned it. I never plan. People look at me and think: She's OK. She's got an interesting job. But I don't know. I don't know what I want to do when I grow up. It's all right for you, you just know me. But I am me. I'm in here, and, frankly, I'm confused.'

'You need to get away. Ideally from yourself. We could go walking next Saturday. Give you a rest from Emily. She's as bad as you. Her and her mushroom quests. Have you ever bought any?'

'Once. Years ago.'

'She's leading you astray.'

'If anyone is going to lead me anywhere, astray is where I choose. I can't go anywhere on Saturday. I have to go out with her. I have to listen to her stories about Rachmaninov. I'm hooked. I have to find out if they're true.'

'Of course they're not. She is a bullshitter. I don't believe she ever met Rachmaninov. Do you?'

'Yes. I know her stories are unlikely, but I believe them because I want to. I'll go walking on Sunday if you want. I'd like to go watch geese coming in.'

'Well, we'll go on Sunday.'

They drove up to Cameron Loch. Hammering up the motorway, singing and dancing in the seat, playing at being Tina Turner.

'That's who I want to be when I grow up,' said Ellen.

'I'm going to be your Mrs Boyle. Over seventy, drinking everyone under the table and full of wonderful lies. I'm going to tell people I knew Jimi Hendrix.'

'Aren't you going to say you slept with him?'

'No, that's what's so wonderful about your old lady. She doesn't say she slept with Rachmaninov. She played the piano with him. I

190

love it. I jammed with Jimi. I did lyrics with Jim Morrison. I sang doowop oooh in Tina Turner's backing group. I'll reinvent my life for the young and gullible people who were not around to witness my youth. Fill my glass, child, and I'll tell you a story. I'll lie and I'll lie and I'll lie and it'll be wonderful.'

They left the car in the car park overlooking the glassy expanse of icy water and set off up the tamed side of the loch along a wide track that Cora took at a brisk pace. Ellen trailed a couple of yards behind. They cut a dash in the countryside. Cora drowned in a dark green jersey, a multi-coloured selection of scarves and beads round her neck, a grey chenille hat wedged on her head, jeans tucked into striped socks, walking boots. Ellen was in black. The further from the city she got, the more of an urbanite she looked. Walking through muddy places in black jeans and black jersey, black scarf wrapped round her neck, she seemed awkward. She stuck her hands in her pockets and bent forward watching the ground as she walked. Open spaces worried her. No matter how many layers she put on she always looked cold. Her cheeks glowed chill, her lips moved slowly when she spoke. Her nose was red. She hated that.

Across the loch huge pine trees loomed into the sky. A heron stood skinnily still at the edge of the water watching them approach. When they got too near, it grudgingly took off, flying low over the water, huge wings lazily spread, a loud irritated gravelly cry.

'We really pissed him off,' said Ellen. 'He was comfortably settled there. Enjoying his daydreams. You could see him thinking: Oh bugger them. Now I'll have to fly away. Wonder if he's like us, lying in bed, putting off the moment of getting up. Does he delay the moment of flying off because he's ensconced?'

Cora shrugged.

'I love it when I wake early and realise I've another hour before I have to get up. It's my favourite pleasure,' Ellen wittered on. 'So warm and soft and I'm all relaxed. It's best if it's raining. Even better if it's pissing rain and I can hear people outside walking about in the wet and cold whilst I'm still fabulously in bed. Hee, hee, hee, I think, I'm in bed and you're not.'

'There's a nasty streak in you,' Cora said.

Ellen ignored this. 'Then if there's someone with me, someone I can wake to share my bonus hour, well, that's perfection.'

Across the water pine trees woodily creaked and moaned. Pigeons clattered unseen in amongst the deepest branches and exchanged throaty cooing. The Sioux could live here, Ellen thought. I could come see them. They'd ride along that far bank, single file. And they'd know everything – where rabbits hide, where the deer drink, the fox runs, everything.

'Who'd be in your bed rainy mornings?' Cora asked.

'Ideally all sorts of men. In reality Daniel.'

'You can't let go, can you?'

'Doesn't seem like it.'

After Ellen threw the apple at him, nursing his bruised head and ego Daniel left. He stayed away for three days. Ellen sat alone at night waiting for him to come home. Every time she heard someone on the street outside she thought it was him, and she brightened. She'd arrange herself on the sofa with a book, a cup of coffee and the television on across the room, looking, she hoped, as if she hadn't really noticed him missing. But when at last he did reappear she was out at work. When she got home, he was there, looking cool.

'Hi,' she said. Casually, she hoped.

'Hi,' he said. A better sort of casually than her. He got it right. He had no problem sounding as if he didn't care. Damn him. He was the one sitting with a coffee watching telly, looking as if he hadn't noticed her missing.

'Have you eaten?' she asked.

'Yes,' he said. Well, sod him. She malevolently hoped he had eaten the prawn salad she was planning for supper. Then she could pick a fight with him about it. But he hadn't. And now she didn't want it. She did not ask where he'd been, but knew he hadn't been alone and hadn't been with one of his mates, the interesting blokes and geezers he mixed with. They said nothing about their fight. They watched television, were polite to one another. And when they went to bed, made love. They fell easily into sex together because it was what they did best together.

Two weeks later they argued again, about Daniel's sex life again, and this time he stayed away for a couple of nights. Then he began staying away for a week, or a fortnight. In time she stopped listening for his coming home. He moved odd bits and pieces of his furniture to Friendly Mary's flat and Louise's house. Ellen replaced them with her own things. The flat started to look as if Ellen and not Daniel lived there. Neither of them addressed the overwhelming sadness they brought out in each other. This went on for years.

Once Ellen had seen him with another woman, someone blonde and thin she did not know. A soft wind, a central casting sort of wind that only added to their mutual gorgeousness, flapped their clothes and wrapped her hair round her face. Ellen could tell that they had, by unspoken agreement, decided to walk and laugh together and cast not a glance at the lesser beings who, peeping at them from the depth of their ordinariness, wondered who they were. They had the gift of celebrity. They looked famous. Daniel was carrying her shopping and, as they crossed the road, he put his arm round her shoulder to steer her safely through the traffic to the far pavement. He never did that for me, Ellen thought. Her heart was breaking. Then Daniel reappeared, letting himself into the flat late one night. She could not help but accost him.

'Who was that you were with? I saw you. You bastard. I saw you.'

Daniel shrugged. 'It was nobody,' he told her. Was that how he spoke about her? To them? His other women? 'She was nobody. A woman I once knew. Someone I married'?

'You shit,' she said. 'You shit. You are so nice to these other women. You put your arm round them. You carry their shopping. You look at them and smile. You were never that nice to me, Daniel. Never. Why couldn't you be nice like that to me?'

He picked up the jacket he'd thrown off, put it on and walked out the door. As he went she heard him say, 'Because you matter.' That hurt more than anything. She raced after him down the hall and caught him by the sleeve just before he left. 'What the hell do you mean by that? "You matter." How can I matter when you treat me so badly?'

'I never pretended for you,' he said flatly. 'I never let you believe I was the ideal bloke other women always think I am. Want me to be.' He shrugged, looked at her sadly.

'Oh thank you for that,' she shrilled. 'Just what I needed, someone who was totally honest about his affairs. Thank you for that.'

He shrugged again. 'I'm sorry,' he said.

It was not what she wanted to hear, an apology for refusing to be perfect for her when he worked so hard at being perfect for everyone else. This was some kind of privilege? She should thank him?

'Bastard,' she said. 'Bastard. I love you.' It was the only time she ever said it to him. As far as she could remember he never once said it to her; she didn't ask it of him. He slipped out the door, shut it against her tirade and stood, head down, listening to her.

'Bastard. Bastard. Bastard,' was all she said over and over. He did not know what he was hearing. The demented howl of a worm turning. But she did not run after him, or call him back. She returned to the living room, curled on the sofa and wept instead.

After that he stopped coming by so often. When he did he no longer let himself in, but rang the bell and waited for her to open the door. A small thing, but it meant a lot. It said, I no longer live here. I am a visitor. And yet she couldn't resist him. If he was there in her living room, she had to have him. No matter what ideals she set herself – I will send him packing, I won't give in – when he was there, when he was for the having, she would have him. Afterwards she always felt that she'd let herself down.

Daniel kept coming back. He came back when she was at work. And on Saturday afternoons when he knew she'd be on mushroom quests with Mrs Boyle. Yesterday as he was leaving he'd met her on the stairs and she'd let him know she was going walking with Cora. Right now, then, though she did not know it, he was standing in her bedroom breathing in the scent of her, slowly going through her things. He did it all the time, visited her when she was not there to receive him. He'd let himself in and wander through the rooms, touching her things, keeping himself informed about the details of her life. He'd scrutinise her cheque stubs, look at her supermarket receipts, read her mail, eavesdrop on the messages on her answering machine, thumb through her books, criticise her records. He noted she'd developed a taste for opera, something he knew nothing about. He blamed Mrs Boyle for that. He'd rake through her kitchen cupboards, stare into her fridge. He'd look at her dishes in the sink, and in the bathroom open her scent, sniff it deeply, splash a little on. He'd read her notebooks, check on her plots and characters and the fast-flowing speeches she planned for them. He'd lie on her bed and touch the tumble of clothes she always left draped on the chair. He listened to her silence.

He always thought Ellen had wonderful silences. She was, by and large, content with what went on in her head; plots, dreams, memories. Her silences, then, were deeper than his – more profound, mature, grammatical, more glossily silent. His silence was always the same – a wild syncopated clamour, bits of songs, racing facts, things people said to him years ago, that went battering round and round, a mind out of control, no matter how he tried to make it stop.

When he left, he always took something. He knew better than to take food. She bought so little she'd notice. There was so much else she would not miss. He could take an earring and she'd think she'd lost it in the street somewhere. A CD and she'd think she'd lent it to someone and had forgotten who. A cup, a glass, and she'd think, I'm sure I had more of these. A lipstick and she'd think she'd mislaid it. Once he took the soap she washed with and knew she'd only be momentarily puzzled by its disappearance. 'Funny,' she'd say, looking vaguely around. Thinking of her, he smiled as he wrapped it in toilet paper before slipping it into his pocket. Today he found her favourite silver ring lying on the dresser in her bedroom and couldn't resist it.

He would put it in a box he kept in the room across from Short Price Frankie's, the bookie, where he now lived. It was a small bedsit but it suited him. He had his records and his stereo and a bed to lie on. Not that he used it much. There were other beds. He would sleep with Louise and take her mangoes and prickly pears that Mary gave him. He would sleep with Mary and take her white wine and Belgian chocolate that he stole from Louise. Mary wore a necklace he'd taken from Louise's jewel box and growing on Louise's kitchen window sill was a white begonia that once had been growing on Mary's. Daniel slept with them, made them tea or

195

coffee and made up cheering horoscopes he pretended to read from their magazines. One day he knew he'd be found out. Meantime, what the hell, they all enjoyed it. Still, he thought about Ellen. He could not leave her alone. In her way she drove him crazy – if anybody, anything could drive him crazy. He could not get through to her. He could not penetrate the wall she'd put up years and years ago. He'd talk to her then notice she wasn't listening. She'd be staring off into the distance, a slight smile moving on her mouth. She'd be dreaming. She'd be off somewhere with someone else, visiting some moment from her past and creating in her whimsy a moment better than the one she was having with him. He hated that.

Cora and Ellen walked along the dam at the top of the loch, a wide grassy path. Swans came whooping across the water, dipping their necks, watching them. Their calling cut through the afternoon chill, spread eerily to them. Ellen was beginning to long for the city. She did not like to spend too long walking on untarmacked surfaces. She was uneasy with horizons. There was something about built-up places, city smells, music playing in streets, international wafts from restaurants, the drift of booze from pubs, heavily leaded fumes, that made her feel safe. They walked down the far side of the loch, moving slowly through long grasses, thick bushes. Shoving branches of trees to one side as they went. It was getting dark, a textured velvet black in amongst the pines.

'Are you sure you know where we're going?' Ellen asked.

'There is one path that leads round the loch,' Cora said. And pointing back, 'That is where you've been.' Pointing forward, 'That is where you're going.'

Chaffinches cheesed in thickets and occasional rabbits thudded out of view.

'There're scuttly things here,' Ellen protested. 'I don't like that.'

'Oh shut up. I always forget what a pest you are when we walk. I always forget that I vow never to take you again.' Then she heard the first geese. Her stomach fluttered, as it did when walking at a favourite estuary on north Mull she'd seen five o'clock eagles take to the sky. Every evening for years she'd cycled to her spot to watch them. Two of them rose straight up calling, declaring their presence.

Vast magnificent beasts they were, occupying a huge piece of sky.

The first geese flew in a small skein high above them.

'They've overshot,' said Ellen, 'they'll never get down.'

'Of course they will,' said Cora, pushing forward to hide in amongst some trees so that she could get a closer view of them. 'They're scouts come to check the going's safe for the main party coming along behind.'

'Like the Sioux,' said Ellen.

They seemed to stop overhead. Ellen imagined one calling out, 'That's it, chaps. We're here. Everyone down.' They wheeled, almost fell out of the sky, tumbling they came. The noise they made. Jostling and hooting they formed ranks on the water, settling their wings and shoving up to make room for others. Then they'd float, heads high, dignity regained, acting as if the nonsensical fiasco of landing hadn't happened. Yammering and honking another skein came, and another, thousands of them surging up the loch just below the line where trees met sky. Floating, lookout geese called to flocking new arrivals with a wheeling urgent passion, anxious for them all to be together again. The cacophony of hoots and cackles vibrated the air. When they'd all landed they looked from a distance like one vast floating raft, only their mewling and humming gave them away. A gang they were. Constantly calling and communicating, they knew nothing of silence.

Ellen knew that the urge to fly somewhere safe for the night came to them all as one and as one they'd take to the air as if landing didn't matter. 'Now there's a trick to master,' she told herself.

'They're monogamous,' said Cora. 'When a goose dies, his partner flies alone for the rest of her life, back and forward from feeding place to resting place, morning and night. And then when spring comes, she flies all the way to Siberia alone.'

'Poor old lone goose.' Ellen was quite distraught. Cora turned to look at her. There were tears spreading across her eyes. Her nose was chilled. She'd slipped her arms out of their sleeves and shoved her hands up inside her jersey to warm them in her armpits. Two hours out of the city and the woman was a wreck, weeping openly for lost geese in a lonely sky. Widows and orphans.

'For God's sake, Ellen. They're geese. They don't ache. They are all instinct. They don't ponder what might have been.'

'You don't know that,' Ellen said. It always surprised Cora how soft Ellen was. Her gentleness was boundless. She'd lift spiders from the bath and set them down to safety on the bath mat. 'There you go.' In a crowded room hers was the lap cats chose to settle on. Strangers told her their life stories. If beggars and drunks approached her for money in the street they were never disappointed. She spoke to her plants. She had a ruined relationship with a man who had broken her heart. But she could not find it in herself to reject him, completely, utterly. It hurt her to think of him alone. So she always let him come drifting back.

'Well,' Cora sighed, 'look at it this way. Widows and orphans and all sorts of single geese join the skein. They take their place in amongst the others, and nobody minds them. They do not discriminate against those that have lost their loves.' She remembered years ago Ellen putting the boys to bed and, wondering why it was taking so long, she'd gone through to the bedroom where all three of them were in tears over an Edward Lear poem. Edward Lear, for chrissakes, this woman would weep buckets at Edward Lear.

'They never came back. No, they never came back. They never came back to me.' Ellen read and it seemed so utterly, utterly sad. The boys found it unbearable. They pleaded that Ellen never put them to bed again. 'Please don't let Ellen read us a story again. It's too sad.'

'I don't know why we're such friends,' she said now, handing Ellen a tissue. She knew Ellen would not have one of her own. 'We have absolutely nothing in common.'

'Each of us is a lone goose. We take our single place in the human skein of things,' Ellen said.

Chapter Twenty-three

'I have reached an age when I don't like anybody to see my naked face. It's a bad habit, makeup. You get uncertain about yourself without it,' Ellen said to Cora. 'Some people have defensible space round their house, a smallish mowable area complete with hedge that is theirs. It is what they need to protect and to protect them from the world, from aggressors. I don't have a lawn. So this is my defensible face. This is what I protect and what protects me. The ever thickening layer of gunk between my face and the world.'

It was just after five. Ellen had just finished work and had popped round for a swift visit.

'You need taking out of yourself,' Cora said.

'I need taking out of myself and putting into Lauren Bacall. Somebody snazzy.'

Later that evening Emily Boyle considered Ellen and agreed with Cora. 'You need taking out of yourself,' she said.

'You're always saying that,' Ellen said. 'I'm fine the way I am. I don't want to be taken out of myself.'

'Rubbish,' said Emily. 'Everyone needs to be taken out of themselves once in a while. Me. You. Cora. We shall have a dinner party. Well, you shall.'

'I can't do that.' Ellen was horrified at the thought. 'I can't cook.'

'What's cooking got to do with it? We're going to drink and chat and eat and tell stories.'

'If it's a dinner party don't I have to supply food?' This seemed to Ellen like one of the essentials of any dinner party.

'Absolutely. If you're stuck for what to serve at a dinner party you can always do my old faithful, the edible Bloody Mary.'

Ellen had a good idea that this was not a dish to be taken lightly.

'Thing about it is,' Emily enthused, 'once you've served it

nobody is capable of eating pudding and they certainly don't remember if they've had starters, or not. It requires minimal cooking. No need to bother with salad, nobody notices it. Just some celery as a salty side dish. Oh yes.' She drifted off smiling slightly, remembering glory evenings of yesteryear.

'So what's the recipe?'

'Oh yes. Olive oil in a pan, a biggish pan, I'd say. Not huge. Large drink on the side for Cook. No ice cubes, the heat dissolves them. Melt garlic and anchovies in oil with a chopped chilli. Or two. Add onions and once they're sort of melty and transparent pop in some bacon, celery and grated carrots. Not too many carrots. But lots of garlic. After all, everybody's going to be eating it so everybody's going to be smelly, aren't they? And, by the way, it's good for vegetarians. Everyone knows they love bacon really. Add some tomato pulp to this mixture. Oregano, if you like. Let it simmer. Top up Cook's drink. Season your brew. Salt, pepper – lots of pepper – a pinch of sugar. Let it simmer some. Now pour in lots and lots of vodka. Lots and lots. Do not stint on the vodka. Some Tabasco and a good dash of Worcester sauce. A squish of lemon. You could even pop in a dash of sherry. And more vodka. Serve as a sauce for pasta.'

'What sort of pasta?'

'Do you honestly think anybody is going to notice or care? Plain spaghetti, linguini, penne, what difference does it make? And a side dish of celery with salt. Or you could make a salad with lettuce hearts and celery in a sour cream dressing. But that's a bit complicated for you.'

'What sort of wine do you think?'

'When I had it in Paris in the thirties it was served with vodka. But wine, yes why not?'

'Red? White?'

'Absolutely.'

'Do you put Parmesan on it?'

'Child, this is a recipe guaranteed to disguise the fact that you can't cook. Parmesan yes, Parmesan no. Trust me they won't know the difference.'

So she cooked it, and invited Ronald and George to share it with

Emily and Cora. On a whim as she was leaving the office on the Friday, she asked Stanley if he'd like to come along.

'I don't do dinner parties,' he grumped.

'Neither do I.'

'Will there be food?

'Of a sort. I'm not good at food.'

He looked at her suspiciously. 'What are we having?'

'The edible Bloody Mary.'

There was a long, long silence. 'I don't do much since Brigit. She's pregnant again, by the way.'

'Is she ever anything else?'

He shrugged. Ellen knew he'd end up supporting this child like he did all Brigit's offspring though he'd only fathered two. She missed him since he separated from Brigit. She'd been a regular visitor to their house, a rambling, messy place filled with children, their noise and their tawdry plastic clutter and filled with Stanley and his books. Visions of Stanley at home were of a man, child in one arm, shovelling oven chips and fishfingers on to Peter Rabbit plates, eating as he went. But now he lived alone, she didn't drop by to see him any more. It wasn't the same.

'You'll never be a millionaire if you keep carrying on like this,' she softly ticked him off.

'It isn't me carrying on, is it? I don't know, life keeps intervening with my plans. I'll bring some food. Your menu sounds dubious.'

It was a drunken evening. The edible Bloody Mary steamed on plates, drizzled with olive oil, glistening with olives, Parmesaned and parsleyed. It was extraordinarily good. The room was candlelit. Conversations staccatoed. People started to say something, wandered off mid-sentence, mid-thought and ended up saying something else.

'I don't mind what we talk about,' Emily was adamant, 'as long as we don't talk about death. When you get to my age all the people you know talk about death. Who has gone, is going, will go next. It's very depressing.'

Candles flickered and the wine bottles dwindled.

'Have you always been faithful to George?' Ellen said to Ronald when George was out of the room.

'What in Christ's name was in that sauce?' Stanley wanted to know. 'It had a real depth of flavour. And I feel . . .'

'Of course I have,' smiled Ronald, though somehow Ellen didn't quite believe him. 'Darling, I'm far too insecure to be anything else but faithful. I don't take risks.' He smiled wickedly.

'Have you ever thought about getting a new pair of trousers?' Emily eyed Stanley's crotch.

'You are treading in dangerous territory when you cast aspersions on a chap's trousers,' Stanley said. 'A chap and his trousers are, well, close. I'm a stout trouser sort of a chap.' Stanley was drunk.

Emily beamed to Ellen. 'See. I told you the edible Bloody Mary worked. Stanley is being gorgeously affable. I love him. I have a trouser theory, too.'

'What could that be?' asked Stanley.

'That people always go too far. You can tell that by the state of women's heels and men's trousers. Look at them in the seventies. Vast flapping things. People went round with yards and yards of material waving round their ankles. Then they went all tight. You can tell the state of the world by the width of men's trousers and the height of women's heels. I tell you.'

Cora put a familiar hand on the intimately straining threads of Stanley's jeans. He always wore jeans, but had, for the evening, abandoned the stained and dubious sweat shirt for a denim shirt and spotted tie. 'These aren't as stout as you think, Stanley,' she told him. Her face glowed. Umpteen glasses of wine and more vodka than she knew about made her more forward than she planned to be. 'I think you give your trousers qualities they do not possess.'

He looked at her with unreserved longing. He adored her. Always had. He'd first spotted her marching along the shore, crisply ordering her sons not to trudge, and had desperately wanted to introduce himself and say if she would love him for ever he wouldn't trudge either. Then one day she'd been standing outside the building when he finished work. 'What does that mean – Starless Enterprises?' she'd officiously asked. He told her, then she'd gone on her way before he could declare himself. When she'd turned up at the office visiting Ellen he couldn't believe his luck.

'You know her?' he asked. In a loose disinterested fashion, he hoped.

'Yes,' said Ellen. 'Cora O'Brien. A chum. Do you want me to introduce you?'

'No. No,' he shook his head. 'Life is complex enough.'

'You don't have to have a relationship. You could just buy her a drink. Have a chat.'

'I can't afford a drink. I can't afford a chat.'

'Cora isn't like that,' Ellen hotly defended her friend. 'Cora is wonderful.'

Stanley didn't dispute it.

They opened more wine and cooed over his runny Camembert and provolone.

'Cora,' George said, 'I declare you have a chip on your shoulder.'

'Jealous,' said Cora, 'because you're too old to have one. Your shoulder's past it in the chip stakes.'

'How did you guess?' George smiled. It was a joke they had. They did not greet each other with a 'how are you?' or a 'hello'. It was always, 'You've got a chip on your shoulder, Cora.' George was always amused by the replies. She never let him down.

'You've got a chip on your shoulder, Cora.'

'Of course I have. Where would a low-class girl like me be without one.'

'You've got a chip on your shoulder, Cora.'

'It suits me. It is me. I am that chip.'

'You've got a chip on your shoulder, Cora.'

'And you haven't with your murky past, George? I'll show you mine if you show me yours.'

'Cora, my sweet, I don't think that would be a treat for either of us.'

'Have you always been faithful to Ronald?' Ellen to George when Ronald was out of the room.

'Oh for heaven's sake, how old-fashioned you are,' George sighed. 'Of course not. Darling, who is? If not in fact, then in daydream, in longing. I, of course, am far too insecure to be faithful. I have to know I still have what it takes. My ego, my libido depends on it. My insecurity, you could say, does the relationship proud.'

'Oh that old thing,' Emily derided him.

George beamed at her. 'You no doubt have heard it all before.'

'Absolutely,' said Emily. Aaaabsolutely. Then, when Ronald returned to the table, 'Our Ellen has been digging into the intimacies of your relationship.'

'Good heavens,' said Ronald. 'I hope the child has a strong stomach and a stout heart. It doesn't make pretty telling.'

They all smiled. Ellen often watched Ronald and George walking home from the pub, summer evenings, close, so close. Their quiet, constant almost rhythmic bickering cutting through the soft air. She envied them. I'll never have that – a chum, lover, companion, she thought.

'She wants to know if you have been faithful to George and if he's been faithful to you.'

'And now she knows,' said George.

'See,' said Emily. 'Their neuroses match perfectly. It makes them friends. They know all about each other. Unlike you and Daniel.'

'What about me and Daniel?' Ellen refilled her glass and other glasses nearby.

'Your neuroses match disastrously,' Emily told her.

'What do you mean by that?' Ellen wanted to know.

'Well,' Emily cut herself a wedge of Camembert and heaped some grapes on to her plate, 'Daniel simply hasn't learned to give.'

'You can say that again,' Ellen nodded, a kind of hypernod, a nod of someone who has had far too much undeclared vodka and declared wine.

'You on the other hand,' Emily looked at her sternly, 'have never learned to take.'

Cora pointed a loving finger at her friend. 'She's certainly got the measure of you,' she said.

'I'll make coffee,' Ellen said. Rising unsteadily from the table. She was concentrating on the long drunken walk from table to kitchen and the heroic effort needed to make it. She returned in time with her cafetiere and only five matching cups.

'Funny,' she said. 'I used to have six of these. I don't remember breaking one.'

Stanley and Cora shared a taxi home. He got out, paid, and walked her to her door. He leaned on the front door. In those golden days of yore before satellite dishes and mountain bikes, when her children were young and sleeping, Cora used to lean here to listen to and breathe in other people's lives. The Robinsons upstairs were making chips, the Lawrences were arguing. A low moan somewhere – someone was making love. And she would shut her eyes, trying not to envy them – them all – arguers, chipmakers and lovers. None of them was alone.

'I have a theory about bad housing and anoraks,' said Stanley.

'Oh, this housing isn't that bad. There is an odd comfort in the closeness of other people.'

'If it wasn't for sex,' said Stanley, 'there would be no housing schemes and no anoraks.'

'You'll have to explain that,' Cora said.

'You grow up. You get horny. You screw somebody. She gets pregnant. You need some place to live, you've got no money, you move into a housing scheme – two rooms and a kitchen four floors up, no furniture except a bed, a sofa and a telly. What else is there to do but screw? You have more children. They use up all your energy and sense, so the only thing you can bring yourself to do in the evening is watch crap on the telly. Then you're so bored when you get to bed you screw some more. You have more kids. They use up all your money. No energy, no sense, no money, the only thing you can afford to wear is an anorak. And you're stupid enough to think you look good in it. If there was no sex there'd be no tower blocks, no housing schemes, no shit on the telly and no anoraks. We do it to ourselves.'

'Stanley!' Cora chided. 'You old cynic. Life isn't that bad.' She was laughing, but still she felt a flicker in her stomach. It was registering some sort of truth. No energy, no sense, no money. She recognised herself in some of this outpouring.

'No. I know it isn't that bad,' he said.

She reached up on tiptoe. 'I have to go. It's late.' She kissed him. It was just a small peck on the cheek but she surprised them both. 'Sorry,' she said. Then, absurdly, tried to rub it off, wiping the kissed spot with her fingers. 'I don't know what came over me. It's a reaction. Just something I do. Please don't think I mean it.' Then realising how awful that sounded, 'Well, don't think I didn't mean it. I mean . . .' She was being silly now. 'Oh good night,' she said. And left him leaning there, smiling vaguely, with his nonsensical theories and his damp cheek.

Two in the morning and all that was left was debris. A wine-stained tablecloth covered with crumbs. There were dishes piled in the sink, and dishes on the unit and dishes on the table. Candle wax drippings, overflowing ashtrays, remains of soggy salad, grape stalks, grubby glasses, burned pots and a pristine lump of Roquefort left, drunkenly neglected, in the fridge. Oh, someone's had a dinner party, Ellen thought, glumly looking round. I'll deal with it in the morning.

She was feeling a little leftoverish and liverish herself. Her mouth was raw with smoking, her head ached and just beneath the deepening ache of her hangover were the scatterings of vodkaed conversation; relationships and sex, holidays abroad, critical pronouncements about films she hadn't seen and books she hadn't read. She'd deal with it all in the morning.

She climbed naked into bed, said, 'Never again, never again. Oh, please, please, never again.' Over and over. The night she'd had, a lucid memory of drunkenness spread before her and she could see it as clearly as if her follies were lying in full view on a sheet of black silk. 'Never, never again,' she promised herself again before falling into a deep, dirty sleep.

Two hours of unconsciousness she got before she woke. There was someone in the room. Her head hurt, and she was numb, still, with fragments of dream humming in her head. It took a moment before she realised what was happening, before she could interpret into reality the rustle and movement that had woken her. She saw him, dark against the window, standing by the bed looking at her.

'Daniel?'

'You bitch,' he said. 'You bloody bitch.'

She could not think of what to say. She could not sort out her confusion.

'Daniel?'

'You've had a party and you didn't invite me. You didn't even think of me, did you?'

'We're separated, Daniel. I get to have a life.'

'You get to have a life. You. You've just taken over my life. This used to be my life. This. In this flat.'

It hurt. He imagined everyone sitting round the table drinking and laughing and never even mentioning his name. He'd lived here for years and Mrs Boyle had hardly spoken to him. Ronald and George passed him on the stairs and barely said hello. But Ellen, oh yes, his wife, with her black clothes and hair and dark glasses and shy ways, everybody wanted to know her. 'What do you do?' they'd say. 'Um. Write comic strips,' she'd answer in that deferential way of hers, and they'd ooh and aah. 'How wonderful. What fun.' And they'd invite her to tea. Or something.

'You took my life. You took my books and my music and my things and I made you. I told you things. Books, films. You knew nothing when I met you.'

She struggled to rise, propping herself up on her elbow. Her hangover took hold. Oh God, she didn't need this. She really didn't need this.

'I don't need this, Daniel. Please go away.'

'Please go away,' he mimicked her. 'Please go away. Just like that. Go away, Daniel. I'm finished with you. And away Daniel goes like a good boy. Does he bugger.'

She sighed. Their arguments were always the same, a childish peeved hurl through Daniel's anger and pain.

'I took nothing, Daniel. I picked up the tab for a year's back rent. You were lucky not to get thrown out. I paid all your bills. I got your phone reconnected. I paid your parking fines, though I still haven't seen any car.'

'I pushed it into the river.'

'God help us. And I paid your back poll tax. It was years overdue. Daniel, you'd have ended up in prison. I bailed you out.'

'Oh fuck you.' Fuck you, always fuck you when he couldn't think of anything more dire to say.

She lay down. Pulled the duvet over her head. 'Leave me alone.'

'I will not leave you alone,' he fumed, yanking the cover off her, throwing it across the room.

Naked, she squirmed, pulled a pillow over her. 'Stop this, Daniel.' It was horrible. He was horrible, out of control and unable to contain his hatred. It would be easier to deal with if he hated her and not himself. He leaned over her. Whiskied breath. He was drunker than she was. He took her wrists, held them on the pillow over her head, climbed on to the bed, on his knees over her. She hated that. Hated it. Writhed and fought. Pushed and kicked. 'Leave me, Daniel. Leave me.'

He held her, said nothing, such a vicious silence. He shoved his knee between her legs.

'Daniel, please. Please. Let me be.'

Then he fell on top of her. She felt his lips on her neck. His breath on her. He was moving on her. 'I've been watching you. You could have asked me if I wanted to come. You don't even think about me. Well – here I am.'

She felt him. He took her. Inside her. 'This is me,' he said.

There was never a time when she did not want him. But now she shouted, 'Not like this. Not like this. No.' His body always entranced her. It was not like a man's body. It was a boy she loved. A boy. Men scared her. Men were big. Men were huge and they called you cunt.

'Daniel!' she screamed. 'Don't. Leave me. Leave me be.' But her legs curled over him.

He moved and heaved into her. 'This is me. This is me. Me, here. Me.' He came. Not his usual roar of joy and release. This time he just howled, a cry of such anguish, Ellen almost forgave him. Spent, he collapsed on to her. Then rolled away. Held his knees. Shamed, he clutched his head. 'Sorry. Sorry. Sorry. I didn't mean that.'

'Oh yes you did,' she said. She lay beside him. The room was cold but she did not move to cover herself up. She would get really, really cold, blue with it, shivering. That would show him what a bastard he was. 'Oh sod this,' she said out loud, realising how foolish she was being. Daniel lay by her, quite still. Sniffing occasionally, staring ahead.

'Stop this,' she said to him. 'Either go or get into bed and sleep. I need to sleep.'

He turned to her. She had decided never to forgive him, but she still took him in her arms, stroked his hair. Kissed his head. She never could bear his pain. 'You bastard. You're such a mess. Worse than me.' She put her lips on his neck, licked it slightly. Salty, it was. He'd been sweating. 'You're all sweaty,' she told him. 'Take your things off.' She helped him out of his clothes. 'That's much better.' She surprised herself, she sounded so maternal. She didn't think she had such feelings in her. They lay entwined.

'When I was little my mother told me she didn't want me,' she told him.

'She didn't mean it,' Daniel said. 'I bet she didn't.'

It was their old game. They always bet each other pathetic absurd bets that she always lost. Listening to the radio she might say, 'I bet you a blow job to fifty pounds the next record will be U2.'

'OK,' he'd say. 'You're on.' She never won. Not once.

'You know nothing about gambling,' he told her. 'It takes you shuddering and shaking to the brink of yourself. You have to risk losing everything you have for the thrill of winning something you don't really want. It isn't the gain, though. It's the winning. I can't tell you what it's like. You have to take yourself to the edges of not just who you are, but what you have and how little you care about it. And yourself.'

'What's wrong with you?' she asked.

'I'm a shit,' he said. 'You know that.'

He hung on to her. 'We could just lie here and hold each other. Just touch. People can do that. You don't have to have sex.'

She didn't believe him. 'That has never worked for us, Daniel.'

She reached down to touch him. 'I always thought this was mine. I couldn't stand other women sharing it,' she said. She moved down him. 'It didn't need to be like that,' she said. She closed her mouth over him. Everything seemed louder, more than real. The rustle of bedclothes, the soft slap of their bodies touching. His breathing. She wanted him so much, and he was a shit, always would be. There were tears in her eyes. He pulled her back up to him, and lay on her. Stroked her, kissed her.

'I bet you,' she said, 'I bet you everything – this flat, everything I have – that after this you will never come back to me.'

He did not reply, did not take her on. He just lost himself in her. She opened her eyes. All of Daniel's Madonnas were round the walls, watching. They'd seen too much, she thought, all the nonsense that had gone on in this bedroom through the years. They with their permanently serene faces. And her with her legs in the air.

Chapter Twenty-four

Still drunk, naked and holding on to Daniel, she slept again. He was gone when she woke. The morning hurt her eyes. There was something relentless about early light, the way it bled into the room glimmering and seeping round the edges of the curtain. Stiff and shivering cold, she wrapped herself in the duvet, pulled it over her head. And hiding, remembered.

For weeks and weeks she had not visited the Sioux. They must be sitting by the campfire thinking about her. Little White-eyes has not ridden out from the bungalow to see them. She missed her old friend Mrs Robb. Maybe the Sioux would be missing her. Maybe they'd be wondering where she was.

Only, they did not live on the golf course. She was just a silly little girl that everyone laughed at because she galloped about on a pretend horse. She knew that by day. Standing up in the sunlight she could see the golf course was just a scrubby over-used expanse of grass. But at night, lying down in the dark listening to the television through the wall and trying not to think about the man in the pointy shoes and the woman in the white dress coming to kill her, she could not resist imagining them.

She could see their faces, those wise features, calm, honest eyes. She could hear the sound of their horses as they moved across the plains. School was starting tomorrow. She knew after that there would be no riding out to see them. She would be back in her gymslip and cruel schoolgirl knickers, her garters would dig into her leg and her school shoes would be heavy on her swift summer feet. She would no longer be fleet.

Summer lay outside her window. Stars in the sky. Her mother went to bed; Ellen could hear her snore. The Sioux were out there. She imagined them riding in slow single file through the golf course gates, down Wakefield Avenue to her front gate. She could hear them. A certain jingle, a clip of hooves on tarmac. Right now they'd be lining up on the pavement, standing still, pooled in lamppost light, waiting for her.

She slid out of bed, dressed and climbed out of the window. Thunder was there, of course, faithful and still as she leaped on to his back. Bareback, tonight, she gripped his mane and rode down the garden path to greet the Sioux. The chief, feathered and proud, raised his hand when he saw her come to him. Side by side, with a whole tribe coming behind, they rode down the centre of the avenue and into the golf course.

Summer had warmed the earth, the air was still and soft. She did not need her jumper. She took it off, threw it to the ground. Wanting to feel the grass on her feet, she slid them from her shoes then set off towards the hunting grounds. The night was glorious, stars above and a fat moon shining. She sang a little song as she went, a little song that was her own. 'Toot-ti-too,' breathy singing. A deer drinking at the great water lifted its head to watch her go.

The chief at her side, the tribe behind her, the night soft on her body, she was happy. Deliriously happy. She stopped. Trembling, she listened. She thought if she concentrated she would be able to hear the stars move, thump, dunt, in the sky, or the grass crushing beneath her feet. And there was a breathing. She turned. Screamed. He was standing behind her. The spy, Mr Martin, in his yellow V-neck jersey, checked trousers and a raincoat. The blood drained from her heart. She paled and shook.

'Look at this,' he said. He opened his coat. There was between his legs a huge pink thing. Heaven's sake, what was that? It was horrible. Horrible. Amazed, she took another look before she set off away from him. Running. And where was Thunder now? And where were the Sioux? Gone. All she had was her little leggies that fear turned leaden. She could hear him lumbering behind, feel his hand clutch at her shoulder, rough on her bare flesh. 'C'm 'ere,' he said. 'Don't you want to touch it?'

'Leave me. Leave me.' She opened her mouth to call for help, but nothing came. She threw herself over the grass towards the hole in Mrs Robb's fence.

212

He, breathing behind, called her name. 'You'll like this, Ellen. You'll enjoy this. It's what you want, isn't it? Running about alone at night.'

She couldn't find the hole in the fence. Ran up and down like an animal, searching for it.

'They've fixed the fence,' Mr Martin said, catching up with her. 'Your little bolt hole is all fenced up. Look at it. Look at what I've got for you.' He showed her again the huge pink thing. Lunged at her. She turned and ran, fled towards the golf course gate. Battering, pelting without looking back. Her face was frozen with fear and effort. Little fearful noises, yelps, came from her throat.

'What in the name of God are you doing, girl?' Her mother. Her mother standing on the sacred Sioux hunting ground in pink candlewick dressing gown and fluffy bedroom slippers. Ellen stopped, panting and trying to catch her breath, pointed back. But there was nobody there. Mr Martin must have his own bolt hole that he used when he saw Janine storming furiously towards them.

'The man,' Ellen said. 'The man was after me.'

'What man? There is no man.' Janine took her daughter by the arm and marched her home.

'The man,' Ellen cried. 'The man.'

Her mother smacked her hard and sent her to bed. 'You're more trouble than you're worth, my girl. Stupid . . . stupid . . . stupid . . .' Aching, trembling and filthy, Ellen curled up under the blankets. She was stupid and more trouble than she was worth. There really were no Sioux, and there was no gleamy black stallion.

Chapter Twenty-five

The best thing for a hangover, Cora thought, was a walk. On the Sunday after the night of the edible Bloody Mary she got up at six, filled a flask with coffee, packed her rucksack and headed for the hills. It took almost three hours from Edinburgh to reach Glen Doll and Jock's Road. A favourite walk because, whilst she liked to be alone, there were always lots of other walkers to smile and nod to in passing. Being too alone in lonesome places wasn't always advisable.

She parked the car, put on her walking boots and took the path at a lick. She liked to get some distance between herself and the rest of the world and she knew that when she started to think, as she always did when walking, her pace would slow. The more tortuous her thoughts, the slower the pace. Then when her memories came full flow she would stop, hold her head and groan, 'Oh no. Oh no. I did that.'

She chastised herself daily for the mother she'd been. Looking back it seemed to her that all she'd done was boss and nag. 'No, you can't have . . .' and, 'Just where have you been till this time of night . . .' and, 'You are not leaving this house till you've done your homework . . .' and, and, and. The trouble with having children was they turned you into a mother against your will, she thought. Nobody really mentioned when she had a baby that it would grow up. She strode and listed out loud the things she hated.

'Training shoes,' she said. 'I didn't bargain for them.' She passed through the gate of the deer fence and started up the path. Huge trees, a deep, green pine smell, and a chill in the air. Deer tracks on the soft mud at the side of the path. 'Things,' she said. 'There were all those childhood things I'd never heard of till they were demanded of me. "Oooh," they'd lie. "Everyone's got one except

215

me." Nintendo, transformers, mountain bikes, shoes that pump up. God. Nobody mentioned any of that to me.'

The path branched off, up and up through the trees or along the wide forestry track. She took the hard way, started up the long steep slope through the trees. Breathing hard, calf muscles starting to ache.

This morning, before she left, Sam had found her kneeling on the kitchen floor, head inside the fridge, looking for food.

'What are you doing?'

'I'm kneeling here searching for food and swearing like a trooper. I'm a mother, what do you expect?'

'From you, Mother, nothing other than that.'

'Don't you mother me.'

'Sorry.'

'Don't speak to me like that.'

'Like what?'

'Patient. You're being patient with me. Don't you dare be patient with me.'

He laughed.

'There's nothing to take on my walk,' she sighed. He brought her a Mars Bar and a bottle of water from his room. 'There,' he said. 'Don't you go eating it till you arrive. I know what you're like. You can't wait, can you?'

Last year he'd left home to live with his girlfriend. When they split up he came back. But he wasn't Cora's any more. She couldn't boss or bully him. She missed him for that. It meant Col took the brunt of her bossing. She liked having someone to keep right.

Panting, she carried on up through the trees. There were fabulous views ahead, a reward for all this climbing. 'Parents' Day,' she yelled. 'I hated that. Sitting on hard seats waiting to get spoken to as if you were ten years old.' Pant, pant, stride. 'God, though, boys. Grubby little buggers.'

Out of the trees at last, and there was the whole fabulous world she'd been denied by the thick pine barrier. The river, hills – brown and only vaguely purple now that September was gone. A little wind crept over her, bringing the smell of peaks she would not reach today, peat. She was moving easily now, that fluidity she loved. It came, too, when she ran mornings over the Links, a moment when movement was all. A purity in that moment that was clear and simple. She did not think. There was only her body and the world it was running through. There was only her heart beating, her lungs heaving in air and the regular thud of her feet hitting the path. She loved that moment. It cleaned her out. It kept her sane.

'They peed in old Coke tins. Ugh. Clammy hands, dangerous underpants. Ugh.'

Cora was steaming up the mountainside now, the rubbled path quaking and scattering in her wake. Great lumps of quartz jutted from the hills, a mountain hare scudded up the huge slope above her. 'Alphabetti spaghetti,' she hollered, voice bouncing off the mountains, 'goodbye to you.' She sniffed. 'Potato waffles, oven chips, Wee Willie Winkie sausages, beans – goodbye to you.' Bye to you. Bye to you. Bye to you. Her farewell echoed up the valley. Highland voice, beaming softly away from her. She sat considering the view. 'Burgers,' she said sadly, 'milk shakes, toffee yoghurt, tomato sauce flavour crisps, cherry cola, fishfingers, chunky chicken bites – goodbye to all you sticky things. I will not miss you.'

Eating her Mars Bar she started back. It was two o'clock. Two hours' walking to the car park, then three hours' driving. It would be dark when she got home, and she did not trust the lights on the car.

She listened to Rachmaninov as she drove, a new addiction. Emily Boyle played the Third Piano Concerto on the table most Saturdays after the mushroom quest, and listening now Cora realised how well the old lady played it. Why, you could almost hear it as her fingers hit the wood.

'See,' she'd say. 'Three movements and the opening theme pops up in them all. Clever, huh?'

Cora and Ellen would nod. 'Yes,' they'd say. 'Fancy that.'

Without glancing at them Mrs Boyle would smile and say, 'I suspect you two are making a fool of me. But you'll see. You'll see.'

'Maybe she did know Rachmaninov,' Cora said. The car battered down the glen, through Kirriemuir then right turn at Glamis, on to Perth, down the motorway and home. 'Not long,' she said. Music poured into the car. Cora wondered how long Mrs Boyle had been alone. And who was Mr Boyle? Soon she'd be alone. Her boys would go, and if she would not miss all the mess, and stickiness and stuff they brought, she would miss them. She would definitely miss them. The tape ended. Snapped out and the radio came on. 'Golden Oldies,' some disc jockey burbled, bending his voice round his enthusiasm. 'Blasts from the past.'

'Oh no,' said Cora. 'Not you. Not that. No more past blasts for me.' She turned the tape; Rhapsody on a theme of Paganini.

'Opus forty-three,' Cora boomed. Like Ellen she had started imitating the old lady. Would the house seem empty when the boys left? Would they come back to her? 'They never came back, no they never came back to me. Oh God, shut up.' She'd had only the Mars Bar all day and wished she'd stopped for some more chocolate. Her work with the boys was done. 'They don't need me now.' Rachmaninov's terse melody hummed out. She turned up the volume, opened her window. Put her foot down. 'I could die now,' she said, suddenly emotional, pre-menstrual, foolish. 'I could die to this tune. Die now.' Hurtling and blistering, Cora. 'I'll die to Rachmaninov.'

She hammered round a bend that the fartmobile was not up to hammering round. On two wheels, then over. Over and over. The hideous grind of aching metal, the roar of ungeared engine, before it cut out. She crashed and tumbled. Though she was in it, she could stand apart from it. She could see it. She could tell what she looked like, spinning and rolling. A car coming towards her stopped. People got out, were running towards her. Then it stopped. The car landed on its side in a ditch. She thought: Oh. This is a strange view. The cassette spat out of the machine, the radio came on: 'A blast from the past, remember this? "Bohemian Rhapsody".'

'I'm not dying to that.' Cora was appalled. 'I hate "Bohemian Rhapsody".' Hanging sideways and almost upside down, desperately reaching for the radio switch. ' "Scaramouche, Scaramouche . . ." Get stuffed. I refuse to die to that.'

She could only have hung there for a couple of minutes. Was aware of hands getting hold of her, cutting the seat belt and heaving her out of the car. She was pulled to safety through the open window. And as soon as she was free from the wreckage she got to her feet, stepped back and politely asked if someone could please switch off the bloody radio. The car was ruined, but she was fixated on stopping the music.

'You were lucky,' one of her rescuers said.

Cora considered him calmly. 'I will not die to that tune,' she told him.

She was taken to the local doctor's, declared fit, given a lift to Perth where she caught the last bus back to Edinburgh. It was after midnight when she got home.

'Where the hell have you been till this time of night?' Sam was furious with worry.

Cora was amazed. Why was he so bothered? 'I had an accident,' she said quietly. 'The car's a write-off.' She sat down to take off her shoes and rub her feet. 'I think I'll have a bath.'

'Are you all right?' She could tell he'd worked himself into a lather imagining all sorts of things. 'You might have phoned. I was going to start ringing round the hospitals.'

'I'm fine,' she said, icily calm. 'I'm absolutely fine. Nothing wrong with me. I just will not die to "Bohemian Rhapsody".'

'What do you mean, "Bohemian Rhapsody"?'

'I mean it was playing when the car went off the road and rolled. And I will not die to that tune. Rachmaninov, I'll consider. But not that.'

Shaking her head she went through to the bathroom. He stood, scarcely believing what she'd said. The scent of her ylang-ylang bath oil floated through to him, mingling with steam and her cool assurances. 'Oh no. Not that.'

He thought she'd finally gone off her head. 'She's bust her string,' he said to nobody but himself. 'Off her rocker.'

Next day Cora rose early, put on her tracksuit and running shoes and took off at a mild jog. She did not think. She felt so serene, removed from herself, as if she was standing outside herself, watching. She chose Mozart for her Walkman. Can't face rock 'n' roll, she thought. I need something perfect. Rock isn't perfect. It's a howl to match your mood. And moods are rarely perfect. She looked down at her body. 'I'm fine,' she told herself. 'No aches. No

219

pains. No bumps or bruises. Well, look at me.'

She didn't run so much as float. The car crash was vividly with her every step she took. The colours of it – the yellow rusting bonnet, grass, road and the sweep of her mediocre lights as she rolled. Then everything spun round; cans, cups, papers showered from one side of the car to the other as she landed. Crashing past her.

'I'm fine,' she said.

The morning was crisp and raw, first frost. She had run through other mornings when the cold air rushed and burned down her throat, but this cold was a perfect cleansing chill. 'This is what I want,' she said. 'This perfection.' She got to Leith Links and did not jog. She took off, running and running over the grass, music in her ears, tears in her eyes, pouring down her cheeks. 'I'm fine.' It was the first time in her life she'd felt it. Ecstasy.

She moved through her day. She showered, dressed, went to work. She walked through corridors to her room, watered her plants, wiped the board, laid out books. She marked the register, wiped noses, tied shoelaces, marked sums and read stories. She did all her usual things, she thought, in her usual way. Only her pupils said, 'Miss O'Brien was in a funny mood today.' Friends in the staff room said, 'What's up with Cora? She's being weird.' She told them all that she'd been in a car accident and held out her arms, displaying her soundness to everyone in the room. 'Not a scratch on me. I'm so lucky.' Thinking back she recalled vaguely talking at length to rows of baffled, but polite, little faces about the joys of climbing mountains. 'It's the only place you'll find air that is totally unleaded and not recycled, that has not previously been breathed by others. Free-range air.'

Next day Melanie Johnston's fabulous mum phoned to complain to the headmaster about Miss O'Brien and the nonsense she spoke. 'My Melanie came home bright red and all but fainted. She tried to walk from school without breathing in any old air. What is the woman on about?'

Feeling positively smug about herself and her luck in the face of death she went shopping. Even the blessed have to eat, she told herself. She wandered the aisles clutching her basket, wondering what on earth it was she'd come in for.

'I nearly died,' she said out loud. People debating the merits of cornflakes over Weetabix looked round and pretended she was not there. 'But it would not matter if I did,' she continued, wandering past the toilet rolls. 'The boys wouldn't miss me,' she said. Then, considering this: 'Yes they would. I mean,' to a woman loading up with cat food, 'Col kicks off his shoes and never can find them. Every day, every single day we wander about looking for them. And I ask you, would either of them touch a vegetable if I was not there? And they don't get up in the morning without nagging. They need me. They still need me and I could have died. I didn't care. Death, I thought, take me. Take me now. This is it, now. Only "Bohemian Rhapsody" came on and I'm buggered if I'm going to die to that.'

A small crowd gathered. Cora dropped her basket. She could see her accident clearly again. The car hanging in the ditch as she calmly told her rescuers to switch off the radio. It clanked and groaned and crumpled down, and as it did the roof flattened. Had she still been in it, she would have been killed.

'I would have died,' she said. She was shaking now, visibly shaking and crying. She was completely out of control.

Stanley Macpherson always shopped on his way home. Every evening he glumly drifted past the frozen food section muttering, 'Something to eat. Something to eat. Steak pie? Frozen peas? What?'

He heard the little fracas but paid it no heed. Life was grim enough without witnessing other people's grief. If he had not remembered that he needed to wash his boxers and socks he would not have gone up the pet food and cleaning stuff aisle and he would not have seen Cora standing, ashen and weeping and passionately declaring to an astonished crowd of shoppers that she wanted to live. He pushed through them to her.

'It's all right, I know this woman.' He took her arm.

'Oh, Stanley,' wailed Cora. 'I was in an accident. The car crumpled to nothing. And . . .' she spread her palms, tears streaming freely down her face. She quite forgot what she wanted to tell him. ' . . . And I just realised now that I don't really want to die. I nearly died. Died, Stanley, died.'

Anxiety stretched her voice so that he could hardly make out what she was saying. He was not good at this. Emotional moments worried him. He would have liked to run away but couldn't leave her standing weeping and wailing between the cat food and washing powders like this. He put an awkward arm round her and clumsily pulled her to him. She buried her head in his shoulder. He smelled of soap and beer. His hand was on her head, fingers through her hair.

'There, there,' he said.

In her whole life, she thought it was the nicest thing anyone had ever said to her. There, there.

He took her to his car, held open the door, sat her inside.

'Thank you,' she said. 'You're kind.'

'Manners maketh the man,' he said.

'And mistakes maketh the woman,' she said. 'Is this your car, Stanley? It's quite nice.'

'Not everyone drives around in a fartmobile, Cora. Some of us think safety, you know.'

'I'd forgotten cars could be comfortable.' Then remembering her shopping. 'I came for olive oil and garlic. I can't not have them.'

'All right,' he soothed. 'Sit here. I need some food anyway.'

He returned twenty minutes later with her shopping. 'It's in the boot,' he said.

'No. I need it. I need to see it,' she fussed.

'OK.' He fetched her shopping and placed it on the floor of the car, between her feet. 'I'll take you home.'

'I don't want to go home.'

'I'll take you for a drink.'

'No. I don't want that. I don't want to sit somewhere public.'

'OK,' patiently, 'I'll take you to my flat.'

She thought about that. 'All right.'

She sat on his sofa drinking tea, shivering slightly. 'It just suddenly dawned on me, the finality of it all. It came to me in the supermarket there, I wanted to live a little longer. I could have died. And for a moment I welcomed it. This is it, I thought. This is it and I don't care.' She blubbered. Then howled. 'But I do.'

'You realised you were mortal, then. Bummer, isn't it?'

'Yes,' she nodded.

He reached over and took her cup, put it on the table.

'This flat isn't bad, Stanley. I thought it'd be all messy. But it's nice. High ceilings. I like your stuff.' She patted his sofa. She was talking quickly, her tongue and brain out of control. So he kissed her. He didn't mean to take advantage of her distress. He just thought he might shut her up. He kissed her and she let him. Such a comfort, human contact. She slipped her arms round his neck and drew herself to him. It was a gentle kiss, a may-I? kiss. Nothing passionate. A little exploratory touching of lips and tongue. But he slipped his hand across her breast and discovered that whatever was going on in her head, her nipple, at least, was willing. He'd take it from there.

He took it from there to the bedroom because fumbling about on the sofa, unbuttoning and groping, was a bit adolescent for them both. She was pleasantly relieved to find his brass bedstead was not, as she'd imagined when she realised she was inevitably on her way to it, surrounded by old beer cans, abandoned underpants and socks worn – as were socks of the men in her life so far – to the point of crispiness. It only creaked tellingly, but as there was only the pair of them in the flat it didn't matter really. All those years of silent sex, sssh, sssh, muffled pleasure, she'd almost forgotten the joys of really letting go, yelling out loud.

'I can't remember the last time I did that,' she said, surprised at herself. 'The older your children get the less privacy you have.'

'Teenagers are irritatingly omnipresent,' Stanley said, thinking glumly of Brigit's two older children. 'They hog the phone, the bathroom, the fridge and they gather in the dark outside the bedroom when you want to spend some serious knickerless time with your wife.'

'There is nothing puts you off more than a loud kitchen full of lager-raddled giants eating all your food,' Cora agreed. 'Is that what happened to your marriage? Not enough knickerless time?'

'My wife said I was never home. But I objected to the knickerless time she spent with other men. We worked up a real recipe for disaster.'

The curtains moved against the window, voices from outside

223

floated up, people out there embarking on their evening. Early laughter floating through the night. In a few hours, a few drinks, the laughter would be darker. She knew that. She'd done that.

'They're off pubbing. They'll drink and wish and play eye games with strangers. They're hoping to get lucky.' She judged his silence before she said, 'Like me.'

He turned and smiled to her. 'Are you hungry?' Then pushing back the duvet: 'I'll fetch you something.'

Love in the early evening, or love in the afternoon, lying in bed while the rest of the world went on with its business, was bliss. She was stretched out in a stranger's bed taking sneaky peeks at the life he led; the books he read, his pictures on the wall, shirt draped over the back of a chair, letters from credit card companies and lawyers – a divorce in the offing. His boots were lying askew where they had been kicked off, and his CDs were scattered over the floor. She leaned out of bed to examine them. Charlie Parker, Thelonious Monk, Wardell Gray, Duke Ellington, 'Oh no,' she sighed, rolling back. 'Not jazz. I hate jazz.'

There was something hugely comforting about lying in Stanley's bed. She bummed across into his bit that seemed, somehow, warmer, comfier than hers. He'd put the light on in the kitchen; a muted glow filtered up the hall into the bedroom. He clattered, whistled a bit, nothing intrusive. It was so calming to lie there with the drifting sounds of someone caring doing things for her in another room. For a few moments she let go of the tenacious grasp she'd always held on her life and allowed someone else to take responsibility for her. When Stanley came back to her, she was sleeping. He ate a bacon sandwich, drank coffee and stared out of the window before joining her.

The emptiness of his bed woke him. It was two in the morning and chilly. Cora sat in the chair across from the bed, staring at him. She had his sweat shirt pulled round her shoulders. That was all she wore. He shut his eyes, hoped she hadn't noticed him wake. He was relaxed and warm, wrapped in sleep, and was not willing to keep his eyelids raised, but he knew, he could tell, a serious conversation was coming up.

'Stanley,' Cora said. 'I hate jazz. Is that all you listen to?'

'Mostly it is.' He still was not going to open his eyes. 'I'll get you earplugs. All right?' With any luck that would be it.

'I have to go, Stanley. I know it's the middle of the night, but I have to go.'

'I didn't think you were the type to get up and go home.'

'Well, no. I never go to other men's beds. Until tonight, that is. Before that I used to make the men get up and go home. But then, that stopped.' She sighed. 'Years and years ago, when the children were little, I stopped. I didn't want them to come in and find a strange man in the house. And Betty Lawrence gave me a ticking off. And—'

'Please don't ask me to drive you. I'm tired.'

'Sam and Col will be wondering where I am.'

'I phoned them. They know you're with me.'

'Stanley, I have this thing. It's nothing to do with you, really it isn't. It's just sleeping with someone. I don't do it. I like the sex, love it. But afterwards sleeping – know what I mean? Drifting into unconsciousness whilst your body keeps on functioning without you keeping an eye on it. Snoring and farting and dreaming with someone seems somehow – I don't know – intimate.'

'Isn't that what relationships are about? Not the sex. The snoring and farting and dreaming together afterwards?'

'I don't know. It scares me.' For a while she said nothing. She sat considering the man in his bed. 'What do you think about relationships, Stanley? Do you think they work?'

'I don't know.' Then knowing he wasn't going to get away with that negativity: 'Yes. If you want them to.'

'It's just that in a relationship you become and . . . Stanley.'

He gave up. 'And? And? Now you've got me. I'll have to open my eyes. What do you mean – and?'

'People have billing in relationships. One person remains the same, the other becomes and. Daniel andEllen. Only that's sort of become Ellen andDaniel, hasn't it? Fred andGinger. Laurel andHardy. Lennon andMcCartney. You'd be Stanley. I'd be andCora. I've been Cora for years now. I don't want an and.'

'Cora, if we have a relationship, and Christ we've only just slept together, but if we do I promise you top billing. On all our

225

Christmas cards and in our cheque book you can have top billing. You stay Cora, I'll be andStanley, OK? Now will you fucking come snore, fart and dream with me? I need someone to hang on to in the night. Stop me drowning in my sleep.'

She couldn't move when she woke. Accident damage had set in. She was raw and stiff, bones knitted, a slow bruising was welling round her eyes and purpling down her cheek. Her neck felt as if it had been rammed down into her spine. Turning her head was impossible. To look right or left she had to turn her whole body.

'Oh God. What's happening to me?'

'You've been in a car crash. What did you think – you wouldn't hurt? The unbruisable Cora.'

'But I didn't hurt yesterday.'

Stanley shrugged. 'It took a whole day before you reacted emotionally. Here's your body having its turn.' He heaved himself into his trousers. 'I'll bring you some tea.' He brought her tea and toast on a tray and a pile of books. 'Stay in bed,' he said.

'I can't stay in bed,' she protested. 'I have to work.'

'I've phoned and said you won't be in for a few days. They weren't in the least surprised. Sleep,' he instructed, 'is what you need.' He reached across and pulled out a fraying, ancient hardback. 'I found this the other day when you were striding about the hills and defying death. Have a look through it. See if you can see what I saw.'

'Oh mystery,' she sounded sarcastic.

'No, really. You'll love it.' He pulled his sweat shirt over her bare shoulders, put the tray on her lap and kissed her.

'Stanley,' she said.

'Oh God, no. Here we go again. You can snore and fart and dream to your heart's content, I won't be here. I'll be andStanley and I'll wear headphones when I listen to jazz. What more can I do?'

'Stanley, I have to tell you something. I've done dreadful things,' she confessed. 'You brought me tea. I can't not tell you.'

He looked at her. His hands were deep in his pockets, worried about getting to work, but knew this was not a good moment to look at his watch.

'My children have different fathers,' she confessed.

226

'Cora, anybody can see that,' he said.

'I've done other things,' she said, fiddling with her cup, not looking at him. 'Terrible, terrible things. I can't not tell you about them.'

'Goodness,' he said.

'I went on shoplifting sprees. I loved it. I got such a high, I can't tell you. I didn't do it for the gain. I just did it for the doing of it. We'd sometimes stand outside a shop and one would send the other in to come out, say with something green from the third floor. Or something pink from the second. Didn't matter what it was. We were so naughty.'

'Oh that,' said Stanley. 'With that French bloke. Yes, naughty gets it.'

'You know about that?'

'Yes.'

'How do you know about that?'

'Daniel Quinn saw you. He told me.'

She looked astonished. 'He saw me?'

'Yes. You know what a telltale he is. He was probably up to the same thing. It's no big deal. Kids steal all the time. Christ, Cora, please don't tell me you are still recriminating about this. Please don't tell me you have been living in shame all these years. What, nineteen years?'

But she had been. She was crying. 'Not all the time. But it sneaks up on me and I feel such remorse. Then there's the boys, they deserved better.'

'Better than what?'

'Than what I gave them. You know that house. I never had any money.'

'Cora, you did fine.'

'You knew. You knew. Oh, don't tell me everybody knows.' She hid her head in her hands. 'Everyone knows, don't they?'

Sighing he lifted the tray from the bed and sat beside her. He put his big bear arm round her. 'Cora. You brisk through your life bossing and nagging. Don't trudge. Behave yourself. What's five times three. Sew your crotch, Stanley. Brush yourself down before you leave the house, Ellen. Don't eat all the biscuits, boys. I do not

227

have a chip on my shoulder, George. If we did not know you were smouldering underneath there somewhere, and that you had a mischievous past do you think we'd put up with you?'

'Oh God, Stanley,' sobbing. 'I'm so tired. So tired. I wish I was sleeping. I think it's my preferred state.'

And gently rubbing her shoulder, lips on her hair, staring at the curtain moving, worrying vaguely about getting to work, Stanley said, 'Tell you the truth, Cora, I'm beginning to prefer you that way too.'

He arrived late at the office. 'I don't know, Billy,' he said. 'Why do we bother with women when we can send out for a fat tart in nylons with a carry-out?'

Billy shook his head. 'Fucked if I know.'

'And,' Stanley waved in frustration at the empty desk across the room, 'where's Ellen? She hasn't phoned in, has she?'

Billy shook his head. 'Nope.'

'Sodding dinner party, sodding drink, sodding people. I could be happy but for these things,' Stanley said. But he picked up the phone, dialled his number, checking on Cora.

Chapter Twenty-six

It was a week before Cora was well enough to leave Stanley's. She could, of course, have gone home, but she allowed herself the luxury of having someone look after her. It was addictive. It was a week, then, before Cora got round to visiting Ellen. She battered on the door. No reply. She creakily dropped on to complaining knees and shouted through the letter box, 'Ellen. Ellen. I know you're in there. Stop being an arse and open the door.'

She heard the sound of a city door being opened. The rattle of a chain, the thick slide of a bolt, the heavy rumble of sturdy key in lock all before the doorknob turned and there was Ellen. Her childhood doors had not been like this. In the village of her youth doors were never locked. There was nothing, she fondly imagined, to lock them against.

Ellen was wearing a huge T-shirt, an ancient cardy – hardened tissues barrelling out the pockets – black knickers, rumpled grey socks. Her face was pale, washed out pale. As she stood in the sudden daylight she wiped her nose with a small stub of used tissue.

'What the hell happened to you?' Cora asked.

'I might ask the same thing,' Ellen said. 'Look at you. Who beat you up?'

'The car. It died. Unfortunately I was in it at the time.' She followed Ellen up the hall and into the bedroom. Ellen climbed back into bed.

'You are wearing the alluring outfit of a woman who sleeps alone,' Cora said.

'You should know,' said Ellen.

Ah, no longer, Cora thought. But was astute enough to know this was not the moment to mention it. She climbed carefully on to

229

Ellen's bed, sat beside her and said, 'So tell me.'

'Nothing,' said Ellen. 'It's nothing.'

'Doesn't look like nothing. Are you all right?'

'I'm fine.'

Cora looked at her witheringly. 'No you're not.'

'I said I'm fine. Why don't you believe me?'

'Only your lips are saying that.'

'Well, tell me which bit of my body you're reading that I can correct its language, and make it lie too.'

Cora looked round the room. Daniel's pictures, all his women – Man Ray's, George Grosz's, a Matisse – the faces who had for years looked down on Ellen's bedroom life were on the floor, looking, now, at the wall.

'They've seen too much,' Ellen said. 'I can't bear what they know about me.'

Cora said nothing. They sat side by side on the bed in the quiet silence friends develop. At last Cora took her hand. 'What happened?'

'He came here after the dinner party. He let himself in. He was so angry at me.'

'What for?'

'Having people in and not inviting him.'

'What! How did he know you were having a party? If that's what it was.'

'He watches the flat. He stands outside. And when I'm not home he comes in and hangs about.'

Cora put her hand on her stomach, controlling her sudden queasiness. 'Horrible. Horrible.'

'He forced himself on me,' Ellen said. 'At least I think he did. I don't know.'

'He raped you?'

'No. Not exactly. He forced himself on me. And then, I let him. I always let him. Is that rape?'

'Yes,' Cora was adamant. 'Surely you know?'

Ellen shrugged. 'I know. It was rape. The first time it was rape. Then we made love.'

Cora despaired. 'You're a fool, Ellen.'

'I know. But he was lying there all crumpled and rejected. I couldn't stand it. It was so sad.'

Cora threw her hands in the air. 'Pack it in, Ellen. Pack him in.' Then remembering the absurd realities of Ellen's life, 'I don't suppose you have any food in the house, do you?'

Ellen shook her head. 'I think there's an old bar of chocolate in my jacket pocket. I'll get it.'

'I'm not eating something that's been in your pocket for weeks.'

'I know. But I will.'

This was a woman, Cora well knew, who would often stand by the window staring out whilst eating cornflakes straight from the packet. Her clothes were lying in a tangled entwined heap, jeans, tights, knickers, T-shirt, jersey, where they'd landed after she'd removed them in one or two rapid unpeelings and tossed them away.

'Do you know what I remembered?' Ellen said. 'I remembered running across the golf course and being chased by the old man who lived across the road. He was flashing. I always thought he was a spy.'

'Well, you got that wrong,' Cora said.

'Yes. Then my mother came and she didn't see the bloke. She was so angry at me for running around on my own in the middle of the night she smacked me. Really hard.'

'If you'd been mine I think I might have smacked you too,' said Cora, shaking her head. She reached over and took Ellen by the hand. 'You are such a fool, sometimes.'

'I suppose. But I needed her that night. I needed a mother. I have always thought my mother didn't like me. I've always had difficulty with that. I went to terrible lengths to shock her. I really was horrible. If she disapproved of something I'd do it. Smoking, drinking, marrying Daniel. Shame on me.'

'Indeed,' said Cora. 'Is this taking stock what's made you hide away all week?'

'That, and that effing edible Bloody Mary gave me a three-day hangover.'

Cora shivered. 'It's freezing in here.'

'Central heating has softened you.'

231

'Well, certainly, I don't go to bed looking like Captain Oates.' She climbed under the duvet and, chittering, pulled it up to her chin. 'I've been sleeping with Stanley.'

'Stanley! *My* Stanley?'

'That isn't how he defines himself. But, yes, your Stanley.'

'Goodness. How did that happen?'

'He found me having a nervous breakdown in the supermarket. I thought my accident hadn't bothered me. Then suddenly as I was walking down the aisle between the pet foods and washing powders it hit me. I realised how close I had been to death or serious injury, and I started to – well – gibber. Yes, gibber gets it. He came along and rescued me. He said something lovely.'

'What?'

'Mind your own business.'

'OK, I will. But after you've told me what he said.'

'He put his arm round me and said, "There, there." There, there. Isn't that lovely? Pass it on.'

They huddled a while. At last Ellen said, 'A nervous breakdown? In the supermarket? Between the pet foods and the washing powder? God, Cora, you've no style. You could have hung on till you got to the Haagen Daz.'

They lapsed back into silence, staring ahead. Thinking.

Then Ellen said, 'Do you want a drink?'

Cora said, 'Have you any wine left?'

'Wine?' said Ellen. 'Wine? What sort of uptight middle-class drink is that? You're getting all comfy and middle-aged. You could do with some serious corrupting. I'll get you some vodka.'

Cora grinned. 'Oh, vodka. I don't drink spirits. I can't. They give me a headache. I feel wretched. I don't like not being in control.' She considered this. 'Actually, that's true. I don't like not being in control these days.'

'Not being in control.' Ellen got up and headed for the kitchen, boogieing slightly to a tune in her head as she did. 'Best feeling in the world. Really. I mean it. Really.'

'What've you got to be so happy about?'

'Dunno,' said Ellen.

232

Chapter Twenty-seven

'Don't you dare ask me what Stanley's like,' Cora said. 'Just don't.'

'OK,' Ellen said. She sat at Cora's table, looking vacant, saying nothing. Then: 'So, what's Stanley like?'

'Lovely,' Cora said.

'Do you think sex gets better as you get older, then?'

'Perhaps. Less urgent. Maybe. Less of a whoosh. He stops, rolls over and falls asleep. But you're sort of like a car with a dicky timer. You shudder on going ah-ah-ah on your own. 'He gave me this.' She handed Ellen the book Stanley had showed her weeks ago on their first morning together. 'See if you can find it.'

'Find what?'

'What Stanley found. And isn't he clever to have spotted it? When you were lying hungover, trying to decide if you'd been raped or not and I was dicing with death, he was poking about an old bookshop in Victoria Street spotting this.'

Ellen took the book and gently turned it over. *The Travels of Rachmaninov* by C. L. MacDonald. 'Clodagh MacDonald traces the life, travels and undiscovered music of a pianist and composer who became one of the first international performers in the age of modern communication.' Ellen opened at random and read ' . . . as early as 1907 Rachmaninov was producing work that would evoke mystery and romanticism. His *Isle of the Dead*, for example, has a quintuple rhythmic quality that matches the rich orchestration . . .'

Ellen snapped it shut. 'You've read this?'

'Well,' Cora shrugged, 'I'm more of a one to look at the pictures.'

Ellen opened the book again, and looked at the photographs. Distant times frozen for ever, people in hats looking stiff and uncomfortable in their New Age life. Rachmaninov himself was standing looming above his entourage, tall and taciturn. Nature seemed to have endowed him with more elbows than ordinary mortals. It was not the man himself, however, who caught Ellen's eye. It was the small enthusiastic woman standing behind him, wildly waving. She was exquisitely beautiful and seemed to be leaping up and down, boundlessly gleeful. Ellen pulled the book closer. 'Who is that?'

'Who do you think?'

'Is it?'

The same cheery character appeared in several other photographs, never actually playing with the man, but always looking, in the face of the great man's glumness, joyous.

'It's Emily Boyle. It is. Surely it is.' And they gave a quick burst on the air piano, a small homage to an exuberant liver of life, teller of tales and inventor of the edible Bloody Mary.

'Isn't Stanley amazing?' Cora said. 'He fixes lives, rescues me from a nervous breakdown and solves mysteries.'

Ellen was impressed.

'Chippy Norton ace detective,' she wrote, 'is shrewd and he is kindly.' She adored this character already. He was chubby, wedged into an old tweed jacket. He moved slowly through his life – by bike if possible, looking somewhat like a plum on a razor blade. And he solved his crimes by observing the trivia in his suspects' lives; their shopping, choice of television viewing, the contents of their bathroom cabinets, the books on their shelves, their laundry. He spent as much time as possible gossiping, eavesdropping, staring and eating biscuits. He was comfortable. His jeans were complaining of the strain at the crotch. The juicy and the curious might get lucky and cop a swift peek of his Calvin's.

Jack Conroy loved him. Ellen delivered it personally, stood in the midst of his clutter as he looked it over.

'He's lovable,' Jack cried. 'You don't do lovable. Neither do I. But this is different. He's so familiar, Ellen, I feel I know him.'

'Yes,' Ellen nodded. 'He has that effect on people. Do you ever vacuum, Jack?'

Jack's carpet was still thick with rubbings. 'No. Never. My wife vacuums the house, but not in here. Oh no. If she tidied in here things would get lost.'

Ellen looked round. 'I do believe you are even messier than me.'

'Really?' Jack was proud of that. Ellen's untidiness was legend. 'I take that as a compliment.' He slid off his chair, and came to her. No need for words, the look in his eye, a certain purpose in his movement said it all.

'Oh please,' she said, dismissing him. 'Not that. We've been there, done that and frankly . . .' She made a face. 'You know, frankly, the earth didn't move.' She spread her palm on her chest. She'd been feeling awfully nauseous lately. 'I don't know why they say the earth moves. If it did, you'd stop, wouldn't you? You'd think: Hold on, better stop, the earth is moving. Maybe that's why modern women prefer to go on top. If the earth moves he'll fall into the hole first. You'll have a soft landing.'

Jack looked bemused. Ellen's burst of wittering reminded him of how disastrous their attempt at sex had been. If he remembered correctly she'd spoken through it, in that shy meandering way of hers.

'Besides,' Ellen explained, 'I've been awfully queasy lately. All the time queasy. I don't know. Something I ate.'

Jack nodded. Queasiness, women. He had a feeling he knew what that was all about even if Ellen did not. He smiled to her.

'What?' she said sharply. 'What do you mean by that smile? Every time I tell somebody about my nausea they look like that. Smile. Smile, they go. And they don't say a word. I hate that.'

It was true. She'd mentioned it to Stanley.

'Sick?' he said. 'Right.' And he'd smiled.

'Queasy?' George had said. 'All the time? A sort of all over, constant sickness? Goodness.' And he had exchanged a knowing look with Ronald.

'Nauseous,' said Emily Boyle. 'Well, that's not so good. Perhaps you should stop drinking for a while.'

Cora simply said she should see a doctor.

The doctor looked at her. He did not even try to hide his surprise.

'You have sore breasts. Tingly. You feel bloated. You're being sick in the mornings. Can I ask you how old you are?'

'Um,' said Ellen. 'Thirty.'

'I have your notes, Mrs Quinn. I can see you're older than that.'

235

'OK. Thirty-five. Six . . . ish. I always feel ashamed of how my life has passed and I haven't got round to doing what I planned. I sort of drifted into everything, you know. Not one serious well-thought-out and planned decision. Work – I was in the right place at the right time—'

'The reason I ask,' the doctor interrupted her, 'is you seem rather old not to have considered you might be pregnant.'

Ellen looked astonished. 'Oh no. Can't be, it's ages since I had any sex.'

'How long?'

'Three months.'

'That'd do it. When was your last period?' the doctor continued.

'Gosh.' Ellen scratched her head. 'Yes, it must have been a while ago.' She measured her life by Daniel's visits. And she hadn't seen him since that night. A little churn in the stomach. That night.

'I don't know,' she whined. 'I can't remember.'

'Why don't you hop up on the bench over there and we'll take a look.'

Doctor speak. Ellen hated it. She felt doctors must do a special course in euphemism. Hop up on the bench – heave yourself on to his bench, paper towel under the bum and lie with her legs open. Take a look, he'd put on his plastic gloves and poke about her innards, whilst gazing contemplatively ahead saying, 'Relax. Relax. Let your knees drop.'

'You're three months gone, I should say, Mrs Quinn. Congratulations.' Ellen walked home in a daze.

It was over, then. Her life of late nights and drinking had to end now. After years and years of abuse she had to come to her senses. And she would spend the next five months worrying about the damage she might have done in the months of not knowing the babe was there within her.

'I suppose,' she sighed, 'I can put it down to youth. To growing up. All that time taking vodka, smoking, sitting up late listening to music, eating absurdly at absurd hours and now it's over. Oh well. It's been good. I can just put it down to an extremely long adolescence.'

She went to tell Daniel. He was holding court behind the bar and looked only slightly abashed when he saw her. She should have known when he didn't take on her bet that night, the terrible night of the Bloody Mary, that he wouldn't come round any more. He held up a glass and pointed to the vodka.

She shook her head. 'Mineral water,' she said. 'I'm off drink.'

'Goodness,' he said. 'It won't last, of course.'

'Yes, it will, Daniel. It'll last for another five or six months anyway.' She gave him her best purposeful look. 'Know what I mean, Daniel? I'm pregnant, Daniel. *We're* pregnant, Daniel.'

The colour drained from his face. She knew what he was feeling – as if his circulation had suddenly been cut short and was doing overtime in his gut, leaving his legs without support.

'And you are going to take some responsibility,' she ordered. 'None of this getting to know another woman who has a child and stealing from it to give to your child. You are going to chip in.' She'd thought about this a lot. 'If not with money, then time. Time whilst I work. Know what I mean, Daniel?' She was prodding the bar with a decisive and bossy finger. 'I won't let you get away with it.'

She thought she had, at last, come to terms with the truth about Daniel. There was some rage in him, yes. But mostly he just didn't consider the consequences of his actions. He wanted so he took. And in turn he expected others to do the same to him. When they didn't he thought them mugs, easy picking.

She could tell, though, that Daniel didn't want a baby. It would pee, he thought. It would puke. It would shit vilely into a nappy, green shit. Babies did that. He'd seen it in other people's babies' nappies. He shuddered. But worse than all of that, much much worse, it would look at him. It would look at him the way babies did, like Buddha, with their perfect faces and their terrible innocent eyes. And it would know.

It knows, he always thought when he came face to face with a baby, whingeing under its constant gaze. And he always felt shame. No, he did not want a baby.

Chapter Twenty-eight

'Cora,' Ellen said, 'what will you do when your children leave?'

'Cry,' said Cora. 'It will break my heart when they go.'

She considered this. There was, for example, the dire consumption of food in her house. There was the noise, the roar of television and CD player. There was the mess, the decaying training shoes in the middle of the bedroom floor, the damp jumble of towels in the bathroom. There was, also, the toilet roll situation. Cora had not realised the importance toilet rolls would play in her life as a parent. Their husks lay on the bathroom window sill as if nobody in the household was admitting to ever using them and therefore did not see it as up to them to throw them out. Before that, toilet roll husks were delivered to the play group and nursery in large plastic bags and were returned crudely glued to cornflake packets, roughly painted and were now, she was assured, space stations and lost planets. The constructors of space stations and lost planets were grown now, but still thought she was on constant duty as a mother. When she was in the lavatory glumly considering a cardboard heap of toilet roll husks they would bang on the door demanding, 'Where is . . . ?' and, 'Have you seen . . . ?' and, 'Is there anything for eating . . . ?' and, 'What are you doing in there?'

'Leave me alone,' Cora would cry out. 'I'm a woman. I demand to be left alone.'

Now, of course, her boys were grown and she could annoy them, bang on the bathroom door. 'What are you doing in there, Col?'

'Leave me alone.'

'I will not. I have been waiting for years to irritate you. You've got a lot of irritation coming before I'm avenged.' Yelling through the door now, 'Just wait till you leave home. I'll come round to your perfect flat and leave Smartie marks round your walls and I'll jump

239

on your sofa and when something wonderful is on telly I'm going to whine and demand we watch old *Sesame Street* tapes. Oh yes, my boy. Just wait. Parent's revenge.' Battering on the door, both fists.

'Bugger off, Mum, will you?'

'Yes,' Cora admitted to Ellen, smiling. 'It will break my heart when they go. But sometimes I cannot wait for my heart to be broken. Though I'll cry, and it shall be wonderful, they will not be around to ask why I'm crying. Or what I'm crying about. I will have peace at last to cry and cry and cry. And when I'm finished crying for my lost children, I'll watch sad old black-and-white movies and cry some more. I've a bit of crying to catch up on. Looking forward to it.'

'You're lucky. I don't cry any more. Last time I did was when I first discovered about Daniel and his women. I think I've forgotten how.'

'Nonsense. All your tears are there. One day you'll open up and have the most fabulous howl of all time.'

Did her mother cry, Ellen wondered, now she was alone? Did she sit in her living-room gloom with fat tears rolling down her withered cheeks as darkness deepened around her? Outside in the garden a late evening blackbird would cluck a warning that night was coming. In the street a bus would rumble by. Her mother would hear the sounds of suburbanites coming home for tea. But nobody would clatter through her door, nobody would call her name. Ellen was shaken. She almost made fat tears roll down her own cheeks imagining her mother's loneliness. She phoned home.

'I'm fine, dear. How are you?'

'I'm OK,' Ellen said.

'I really can't stop,' Janine went on. 'It's my bridge night. And I've only just got rid of Rita and Betty, and Peggy's calling at seven. So I haven't long.'

Wrong again. Wasn't she always? Ellen had forgotten how many friends her mother had.

'I thought I might come over to see you tomorrow.'

'Tomorrow. That isn't your usual day. But that would be lovely.'

She was doing the washing up with her mother when she told her about the baby. She was washing, Janine wiping and putting away.

240

'By the way,' she said. 'I'm going to have a baby.' She looked into the soapy water.

Janine stiffened. 'When?'

'I'm four months gone.'

'Is it Daniel's?'

'Yes.'

Her mother busied herself with the plate in her hand, wiping it vigorously. 'Well,' she said at last, 'that'll learn you.'

'Learn me what?'

'Not to be silly. To start taking life seriously. To do all the things people have to do when they have babies. You'll find out.'

'Ah,' said Ellen, 'I plan to be a very good mother.' She plunged a cup into the water, let it fill with water and sink. Then she floated a plate on the surface. The cup would be lying in wait for it. She remembered that. Torpedoes on the port side, boom, whoosh.

'Don't we all,' Janine sighed. She disappeared into the pantry with a pile of plates and clattering, put them away.

'I always thought you didn't want me,' Ellen told her. She vaguely thought her mother was out of hearing range, or the clattering would drown her accusation.

'What on earth made you think that?' Janine appeared at the pantry door, astonished.

'You told me. The night Dad died you were standing at the front door and when I came to you, you said, "Not you. Not you." I've always remembered that.'

'Did I do that?' Janine took a stack of cups and started to hang them on their hooks. 'How awful,' she said mildly. She did not think it so dreadful.

'My feet got cold,' Ellen said.

'It was a cold night.' Her mother looked at her. 'You were always such a strange child. So removed. I never knew what was going on in your head. Then there was the night I found you on the golf course, half naked. What were you doing?'

'I was riding with the Sioux,' Ellen told her, grinning, squirming in embarrassment. It sounded so silly now. 'I thought they were out there waiting for me. I imagined them coming for me, riding down the avenue. The whole tribe of them. I could see it. I could really see it.'

241

Janine stopped her cup routine and looked at her daughter. 'Have you any idea how lucky you are? The rest of us just see a grubby, yellowing municipal golf course and you see hunting grounds complete with the Sioux nation. Other people see a bunch of silly girls and you see Gangster Women. Daniel, for heaven's sake, a man like that, you see an avenging philosopher. Now this Chippy Norton chap. No doubt it's some perfectly ordinary person going about his business but you see an adorable fat detective. You can imagine a Sioux tribe coming to ask you out to play in the middle of the night. You are so lucky. I am so envious.'

'You? Envious?'

'Me. I'm an ordinary oldish woman in an ordinary suburban bungalow. I know who I am. I have no illusions.' She tutted. 'Oh damn. I promised myself I wouldn't do that when you told me you were pregnant just then. Don't tut, I said to myself. Now I have. Sorry.'

'That's OK. I wouldn't have felt right if you didn't tut.'

'When you work you'll need someone to look after the baby,' Janine offered.

'Yes. Thank you,' Ellen said. 'Actually everyone's been super. Ronald and George are keen to baby-sit. And Emily is going to teach her the piano.'

'I'm having a baby,' Ellen had told Mrs Boyle.

'I know, dear. We all know. Isn't it wonderful? I shall teach her to play the piano.'

'Her?'

'Definitely. It looks like a female sort of a bump.'

'You'll teach her the good old EGBDF,' Ellen said. 'I remember that. Every Good Boy Deserves Football.'

'Football?'

'That's what my old music teacher said.'

'It's fun, dear. Fun. Favour. Frolics. Fornication? Oh, I'm sure you don't need me to fill you in on any more effs. But as you get older the effs just get better and better.'

Ellen smiled to her.

She turned to Janine. 'There's Daniel . . .' she said weakly.

'Oh goodness me, Ellen. Don't talk rot,' Janine sniped. 'Still, it's good to see your absurd imagination is still functioning. You're going to need it now you have someone to support. Daniel is not getting ready access to any grandchild of mine. I mean, daughters you have to let go. But grandchildren, oh no.'

Chapter Twenty-nine

'I don't think I can do this,' Ellen said. 'I don't think I can be a mother. How did you manage, Cora?'

'I just did it. To anyone in my position I'd offer the advice: learn to love your duffel coat – you'll be wearing it for years and years and years – and keep your eyes down. Avoid the eyeflick.'

'The eyeflick?'

'That look women give each other. You know, that swift recce women give each other. The gorgeous one looks at the dowdy one and thinks, Nah-ne-nah-ne-nah-nyah, thank Christ that isn't me. I haven't let sex and doughnuts ruin my thighs and reduce me to living my life in a duffel coat. And the dowdy one looks at the gorgeous one and thinks: If only I'd taken life and sex at an easier pace I wouldn't have become the woman in the duffel coat trudging around, trailing children, taking comfort in doughnuts.'

'You're an excellent mother. I have no maternal feelings at all. In fact, I don't think I like children.'

'Other people's children, nobody likes other people's children. Your own are different,' Cora assured her. 'Becoming a mother is easy. You just do it. It's stopping that's a bitch.'

'But you're a boss. You are naturally bossy. If you hadn't anyone to shove around you'd get withdrawal symptoms.'

It was true. Recently Stanley had borne the brunt of her verbal bruisings. 'Stanley, you have never embraced the concept of leisure, have you?'

'No. I don't know what it is. Actually, it scares me. It's since I saw leisure pants in a catalogue, stay pressed leisure pants. Though these were spelled without the Y, sta-prest leisure pants. I had this vision of myself wearing them with an open-neck leisure shirt and I hated it. Terrifying. Terrifying leisure. I can't deal with it . . .' He

245

was walking round the bedroom expounding, waving his hands about.

'Come to bed, Stanley. I just thought we should go visit my folks. You're the first decent bloke I've ever had, I thought it might do them good to see I've sorted myself out.'

'It's taken you a while.'

Cora nodded. 'You won't have to put on any sort of leisure wear, I promise.'

'So how do you do it?' Ellen said.

'Guilt'll get you through.'

'Women are good at guilt.'

'That's why they make better mothers than men. Men have no sense of stoicism,' Cora said wistfully.

They thought about this. Life without the urge to be stoic. 'Bastards,' they decided in unison.

When Ellen got home Daniel was there. He was standing in her living room with a friend, one of the people – a bloke, a geezer – with bit parts in his life. The life she had once considered fabulous, but now thought wasted, and, as he got older, sad.

'What the hell are you doing here?' she demanded. 'How dare you keep coming into my flat like this?'

'I just came for the sofa,' Daniel said, smiling. He made it sound natural. A normal sort of thing to do – uplift a person's sofa without asking.

'That's mine. You put it down.' Ellen was horrified.

'Actually,' Daniel sounded superior, 'it's mine. I bought it.'

'I love that sofa. You're not having it. You have left this flat. Get out.'

'Not till I have the sofa.'

Ellen sat on it. Thumped her body on to it, claiming what was hers. 'I bailed you out, you bastard. I paid off the rent. I—'

'I know, I know.' Daniel was beginning to turn nasty. He wanted that sofa. He had, after all, thousands of pounds, years of winnings, stuffed into the cushions. Ellen knew nothing of this.

Over the years Daniel had been through many lucky routines. And though they were not all made up of the same combinations of breakfasts, socks and boxers, two common factors ran through them all. He always had to start out with a small sum of money stolen – or as he saw it, borrowed – from the purse of whatever woman was in his life when he woke in the morning. He'd fetch her, whoever she was, a cup of coffee in bed. And when he was waiting for the kettle to boil, he'd take something from her purse. His second common factor was that he could not use his winnings, so he always put them into the cushions of the sofa that had once been his sofa, in Ellen's flat that had once been his flat. Now he was moving from his bed-sit opposite the bookie's to a larger flat. He wanted the money. He also wanted the sofa.

'I want that,' he said. 'And I will not leave without it.'

'Oh yes you bloody will.' Ellen was more adamant than he'd ever heard her before. Perhaps that's what pregnancy did for women – made them adamant. Bummer. Ellen sat harder on the cushion, pressing herself into it.

'Come on, Jake.' Daniel indicated to the bloke, geezer, he'd brought with him to take one end of the sofa as he lifted the other.

Jake was hesitant. 'I don't know about this. Whose is it?'

'Mine,' said Ellen.

'Mine,' said Daniel.

Claiming her territory, Ellen lay down. 'You are not having this,' she boiled and raged. 'You bastard. You took and you took from me and you're not getting this sofa. I love this sofa. Get out. Get out and don't ever come back.'

Daniel, remembering her accuracy, years ago, with the fruit, stepped back.

Filled with bile and venom Ellen sat up again. 'Get out.'

Jake headed for the door. 'I'll leave you to it, then, Daniel,' he said. 'See you outside.'

Daniel stood his ground. 'That sofa's mine,' he told her. 'I bought it.'

'You bastard,' she said. 'You absolute bastard. It's mine now. God, the money you took from me. I paid you for this over and over. You're not getting it. It's mine now. First time I ever came to this flat I sat on this sofa. And you seduced me on this sofa. I told you I thought one of my tits was bigger than the other. And you asked if the small one or the big one was my favourite tit. I loved that. You've made love to me on this sofa. And when you first left me I waited for you on this sofa. I've been lonely on this sofa and I've been really happy on it. I watched our favourite videos on this sofa and got drunk with Cora on this sofa. We had our honeymoon here. Drinking dubious concoctions, spraying champagne. I have lived on this sofa.'

Daniel stood quietly. His hands were deep in his pockets. He did not look at her. 'I'll leave it with you, then,' he said, and turned to go.

'In fact,' she softly told his departing back, 'I'm going to play with my baby on this sofa. Feed her. Let her lie and sleep on it whilst I work at the table there.' She was silent, contemplating her life on the sofa.

'I have plans. For the first time in my life, plans.' She affectionately patted its beloved, worn arm. A cloud of dust sighed into the air. She stared at it. 'I'm planning on getting it cleaned next week. Furthermore,' she added when he reached the front door, 'don't bother coming back. I'm having the locks changed.'

Later, when Daniel phoned her, he said that he wouldn't advise her to get the sofa cleaned without first checking inside the cushions. Puzzled, she put down the phone, crossed the room, unzipped the cushion and found a wad of notes. Ten minutes later she was still pulling out money, wads and wads of money. When she had yanked out the last of it she could hardly believe her eyes. It lay spread across the floor, a huge haul. She sat amongst it, fingering it, lifting it and putting it down again. 'Money,' she said. 'Heaps and heaps of money. See, I knew I was right about this sofa. It's lucky.'

She phoned Cora.

'What are you going to do with it?' Cora wanted to know.

'Dunno,' said Ellen. 'I just dunno. I've never seen a heap of real money before. A vast pile of cash. Daniel's winnings.'

'Is he going to get some?'

'He doesn't want it. He's decided it would break the flow of his lucky routine.'

'You can have it all.' Cora suddenly got greedy. 'You could go on a world trip. Buy a new car. A really new one that hasn't belonged to several other drivers before you. You could get amazing clothes. You could—'

'I could get one of those really, really good, expensive bottles of vodka you can get these days,' Ellen joined in.

'Vodka?' Cora roared. 'Thousands of pounds and you're going to buy a bottle of vodka!'

The force of her voice thundered down the phone. Ellen held it away from her ear. Turned it over, considering it from underneath her thick fringe. It was an old phone and sort of past it. Faded and used. Years and years, she'd been speaking to Cora down this phone. Years and years.

'I could buy a new phone,' she offered suddenly.

'Vodka and a new phone.' Cora couldn't believe it. 'Is that all you can think of? You must be really happy. I keep telling you that. You're secretly happy.'

'Happy?' Ellen whined. 'Me? Happy? How can you say I'm happy. I can't even do a backflip. I always wanted to do that.'

'A backflip,' Cora said flatly.

'Yes. I may have a job and a flat and a baby on the way, but I always wanted to be able to do a backflip. You know, you leap up, twirl round a couple of times in the air, backwards. Land. Spread your arms, shout, "Tra-ah!" and get wild applause. That. Oh no. How dare you say I'm happy? What's happy? I'm not happy. I wouldn't go that far . . .'

And Cora said, 'Bye, Ellen. Speak to you tomorrow.'

GIVING
UP ON
ORDINARY

With love to Nick and Adam, for all the socks, books and funny chewed plastic things they selflessly left lying everywhere for me to pick up, without which experience this book would not have been possible.

Chapter One

'I belong on a train,' said Megs. Dreaming of movement, she shut her eyes, sank deep into her bath. It was the best bit of her day. Her life had become so routine that week to week, day to day – minute to minute almost – she knew what she'd be doing. There was, these days, a strict timetable to her existence: get up, get children up, feed children, feed dog, clatter, bang, wipe, sigh, go to work, come home from work, feed children, feed dog, clatter, bang, wipe, sigh, slump, go back to bed. Sleep. If you can.

It was a fight against grubbiness and clutter. She hated it. Still, at least she knew when the good bits in her day were coming round. She savoured and looked forward to them. Leaning back in the bath was one. After this, there was that moment when she spread herself, unfolded herself into bed, alone in the soothing dark, waiting for sleep. That was the best bit. She was the sort of person who saved the best till last. It was a lifetime's habit.

Sleep to her was a perfect thing. But then, she wasn't very good at it. She cherished that moment of waking, realising she'd been dead to the world, tranquillised by tiredness, for a few hours. The only thing she regretted about sleeping was that she was not awake to enjoy it. She longed to relish it, like she relished anything she did not get enough of. She got through night after night in a series of two- or three-hour bouts. This made her regard with envy and wonder those people who managed a sweet eight to ten hours every time they hit the sack. Her children, for example, especially little Lizzy, who was four. Nights, Megs would stand looking at her daughter – head on pillow, eyes shut, lips pursed – breathing sweetly. Megs loved to watch her lying there, making sleep seem simple.

253

'Definitely a train. I do not belong in this dusty box I live in, surrounded by bits of paper – bills, half-read newspapers, wrappings, supermarket receipts – paraphernalia of a life I did not plan. Oh, bugger ...' Cursing, she stiffly heaved on to one buttock and removed from underneath her bruised, raised cheek the cruelly sharp little white Corvette she'd just sat on. 'Bloody kids.' She idly sent it wheeling away from her, heading for the taps.

Lorraine, on the floor across from her, chin on knees, back against the wall, said nothing. She was used to her friend's flyaway declarations. Megs had always been this way. Megs's mother, Vivienne, worried about her. But her Aunty Betty said, 'Let her be. A bit of dreaming never did nobody no harm.' 'A bit, maybe.' Vivienne shook her head. 'But she goes too far. Everything she does, she goes too far.'

The room was thickly steamed, damp towels hung limp from the rail. There was a pile of magazines by the lavatory, an awesome row of fruit and herb shampoos, moisturisers and deodorants – avocado and glycerine, coconut and jojoba, papaya conditioner, camomile and marigold hair strengthener – on the shelf by the mirror. At the end of the bath was a multicoloured heap of sodden toys – a dumper truck, a beloved, balding one-eyed doll, a pull-along sheep. Shameless, the dog, was lying on the floor, head between his paws. He gave a single indolent flap of his tail whenever Megs spoke. She was his love.

Down the hall in the living room Megs's son, Jack, was sitting, legs draped over the arm of the chair, watching *Ren and Stimpy*. He drank Nescafé from a chipped A-Team mug that had been his and his alone since he was four, and that had survived Megs's umpteen attempts to see it off. It bounced on the kitchen floor whenever she accidentally dropped it. Till at last she gave up accidentally dropping it. 'This damn thing will survive the holocaust. I'll emerge after the blast toothless, balding and in rags, and what'll I see? This hideous thing spotless and untouched on top of a pile of rubble.'

Every time a shriek of laughter howled out of the bathroom Jack raised his eyes in horror. He was seventeen. Parents were embarrassing.

Megs and Lorraine were drinking white wine from a box. They were discussing their day and complaining about life. Recently it seemed whenever they got together – and they got together most days – the conversation, when it wasn't about men, children or sandwich fillings, turned to, wait a minute, how did this happen? And, how did I get here? And, this wasn't what I planned.

'Oh yes.' Megs warmed to her theme. 'I belong on a train rushing across distant continents.' Rushing, she said. Rushing. She liked that. She lifted her arms, dripping camomile-and-lavender-foamed water, and made a train-like movement. 'Rushing,' she said again.

Lorraine tutted. 'You do not have one iota of sense in you.'

'Sense,' Megs scoffed. Throughout her growing years sense had been held up as a desirable goal. A virtue to be worked for and treasured. But now she was having doubts about it. 'Comes a time in your life when you have to abandon sense.' She turned on her side, causing a small, scented wave to sweep over the edge of the bath, soaking the floor, and indicated the room and the flat beyond with a dismissive flap of her hand. 'This is what sense gets you. A box that costs a fortune. A small cluster of undistinguished rooms that you fill with your consumer goods and your arguments. Sense got me an ex-husband and a small brood of children whose only accomplishments as far as I can see are growing and eating. Sense! Fuck sense.' With a deep, throaty sigh she leaned back in the water. 'I love baths. You can do some serious thinking in a bath.'

She had spent the afternoon washing Mrs Terribly-Clean Pearson's kitchen floor, waxing her coffee table and matching pine bedside cabinets, wiping down her stair banisters, hoovering, cleaning her bath, squishing blue stuff down her loo, polishing the windows, changing the beds and ironing half a dozen identical white shirts for Mr Terribly-Clean Pearson to wear to work. After all that effort the place looked exactly as it had when she arrived three hours before.

'I really deserve this. A glass of something alcoholic and a hot tub.'

'Maybe you just belong in a bath,' Lorraine offered. She drank her wine. 'God, this is vile.'

'Well, go buy a bottle of something better, then.'

'You go.'

'I can't. I'm in the bath.'

'Well, I can't be bothered. I'll just have to put up with this. Anyway

255

I don't feel so guilty about drinking this early in the day if I'm drinking something I don't really like.'

'Well, you've got to feel guilty about something. You're a woman, it's your job.'

Megs knew about guilt. She was good at it. Every night in bed she'd do a rerun of her day – what she'd eaten, things she'd said, what she'd done, what she'd not done. Tomorrow she'd make up for her failings. Tomorrow, always tomorrow, she'd exercise, first thing – fifty squats and a hundred sit-ups every morning as advised in the 'Gorgeous Thighs in a Fortnight' article she'd read in one of Just-Keep-It-Above-the-Dysentery-Line McGhee's magazines. Tomorrow she'd allow herself absolutely no chocolate or biscuits or anything in any way likely to do unkind things to her hips. Tomorrow she'd clean the kitchen floor and remove the decaying thing, whatever it was, that was lurking damply at the bottom of the fridge. Tomorrow she'd keep her cool and she would not bawl at her kids. She wouldn't stay up late, sitting bleary-eyed on the sofa, drinking too much coffee, watching dreadful old films on television, keeping her feet warm the while by shoving them under the dog. Oh yes, tomorrow she'd get her life in order. 'Sod guilt,' she said before slipping down under the water. She rose, soaked and gasping. 'I'm back on my train.'

'Rushing?' Lorraine asked, reaching for the box.

'Rushing.' Megs smiled. 'Over strange terrains, watching new colours, listening to wonderful languages that I shall never learn, and feeling always, always slightly afraid.'

Lorraine leaned through the steam to refill her glass. She was taller than Megs, thin-faced, dark-haired. 'Fear?' she said. 'You? You don't know the meaning . . .'

'Being slightly afraid isn't fear. It's wonderful. A certain uncontrollable trembling in the tummy. It's dealing with mystery, strange destinations, the unknown. Fear isn't like that. It's a sweat that reaches into your palms. It's knowing your knees aren't going to hold. It's a vile curdling in your stomach and it's humiliating.'

Megs looked at her, dark eyes, mascara oozing in the heat and damp. She smiled, a perfect row of gleaming ceramic caps. A present from Megs to Megs on her thirty-sixth birthday. Time, an absurd diet that she inflicted on herself while insisting her children eat healthy veg

256

and pasta, and a bitter, tear-sodden fracas with her ex-husband had ruined her natural set.

Lorraine and Megs had met thirty-four years ago on their first day at school. They'd been best friends by lunch time, sharing a desk and, at break time, a KitKat and a bag of roast chicken crisps. In those days that was all it took. Bonding only needed a shared smallness in a vast and scary world and a mutual passion for American cream soda and raspberry ripple ice cream.

'Do you like American cream soda?' Megs asked.

Lorraine nodded enthusiastically. 'Yes, it's my favourite.' This was serious.

'Mine too,' Megs agreed. 'You can be my best friend.' She added, 'For ever and ever.' It seemed like a fine idea to Lorraine, who was looking for someone to be her partner in the line out to the playground. Years passed and shared experiences on the way to being grown-up – first boyfriends, first bras, first cigarettes, first sex, first love – deepened the relationship. Now, here they were, facing forty, still best mates, and not a drop of American cream soda had passed the lips of either for years and years and years.

Friendship was so simple then. The older Megs got the harder she found it to make new friends. If only she could ask some stranger she thought had pal potential what was her favourite drink – vodka and Coke? gin and tonic? wine? What was her favourite ice cream – pralines and cream or Belgian chocolate? Favourite sandwich filling? Favourite television programme? Favourite sexual position? If you could ask someone you fancied for a chum these things and found some common ground then maybe you could make new friends easily. As it was, though, meeting new people always involved small sorties into emotionally safe conversational ground: the weather, holidays, the infrequency of buses. No wonder folk were lonely.

Lorraine thought Megs the bravest person she knew. All those years ago, first day in class, their teacher had said, 'Hello, boys and girls. I've still got to learn all your names. But I'm Miss Watson and when you talk to me, you put your hand in the air. You only speak when I tell you to. And you call me Miss.' She leaned back brightly folding her hands on her desk. That was clear and simple, was it not?

Megs stuck her hand in the air. 'Why?' she said, eager to be told, little voice, shiny eyes. This was puzzling, putting your hand up, calling someone who plainly had a proper name Miss.

Miss was stumped. 'Because you do,' she said. 'It's the rule.'

Megs's hand shot up again. 'Why?' she asked.

'Because it is. We need rules, you know.'

Up went the hand again. 'Why?' Again.

'Because we do. Without them there would be anarchy. Absolute anarchy.' She shook her head at the thought of it.

'Miss.' Megs raised her hand. 'What's an . . . an . . . that thing you said?'

'I'll tell you later, when you're old enough to understand.'

'I'm old enough now. I'm big. I'm at school.'

'You are disrupting class.'

'No I'm not.'

'You are. And do you know what happens to people who disrupt class? They get put in the corner.' So, within an hour of starting her education, Megs, the budding anarchist, was put in the corner.

'There is always one,' said Miss.

Megs was the one. She was the one then. She was still the one. Her bravery went on and on, Lorraine thought. Christ, she hadn't the nerve to do half the things Megs did. The only braveish thing she'd ever done was to run away from her husband, Harry, with a poet she convinced herself was her one true love. The heated romance hadn't survived the poet's arrogant disregard for regular meals or the chill of his unheated squat. She took Megs's glass. 'Ready for a refill?'

'When am I not?' Megs said.

Megs drank too much. She knew it, worried about it and warned herself regularly that she ought to stop. But she never did. She tempered it, controlled it, recognised that moment when she should place one firm hand over the top of her glass and with the other wave away refills. But she still could not deny that longing, when faced with a glass of something alcoholic, to drown herself in it. She was in constant pursuit of that moment when the spirit took hold and her feelings lifted. A sip and she felt better. Another, even better. Then she would feel it – for it was a real thing to her – that moment when she didn't care. When she smiled and laughed and thought perhaps she wasn't such a failure after all. That wonderful, alcohol-induced twinkling when she actually liked herself.

'You drink too much,' Vivienne, her mother, worried.

'Rubbish,' Megs countered.

'You should be ashamed of yourself. You sleep around and you drink all the time.'

'What a slut you must think I am. And you brought me up, too. Nothing out of ten there.'

'How dare you speak to me like that? I'm your mother.'

'I know, Mother,' Megs said. 'You certainly don't seem to think very much of me, do you? So who's failed – you or me?' Then before Vivienne could answer, Megs corrected her. 'Actually, you've got it wrong. I don't sleep around. Haven't ever, as a matter of fact. No, I drink around and sleep alone. It's the healthy option, don't you think?'

'No, I don't. I'm not so stupid as you think. I've seen a thing or two in my time. I'm sixty-three, you know.'

Hardly a day passed when Vivienne did not, in a fiercely indignant tone, tell somebody her age. Sixty-three, how dare that happen to her? Sixty-three years, and she'd spent the last thirty-nine of them watching her daughter career through a life that was not a planned, step-by-step journey to some sort of sane, safe destiny but was instead a set of furious impulses.

Megs had left school at seventeen and turned down a good university place to sing with a rock'n'roll band. When that had fallen through, when the dreams of stardom and riches did not materialise, Megs married and started a family. When the family needed money, Megs started work at a mail-order market garden. A job she loved and was good at. Then she'd succumbed to one of her outbursts. She'd been swept along by the undertow of rage that bubbled constantly just beneath the cheery façade she showed the world. The fury and frustration she felt at living a life she considered a failure came hollering out. Megs had lost that job, and now she cleaned.

Vivienne shook her head when she thought about it. Her son, who'd worked so hard at school, had gone to university, then, as soon as he graduated, or so it seemed, had gone to live in Australia. He'd married and now had two golden-haired, bronzed children whom she hadn't met and who called her their Scottish Granny Megson. Her beautiful daughter, who had bounced so gleefully in her morning cot, whose first tooth was wrapped in tissue in a tiny, dark-blue padded box in her dresser drawer, who'd fallen from a swing and broken her arm, who had worn a frilly pink frock covered with pale blue daisies to her first school party, who had won the local church talent contest singing 'People', 'Peepole, peepole who need peepole', when she was seven, who had brought home hand-made cards covered with hearts and stars every Mother's Day, who had handed over glowing school reports that said, 'Megs has a natural musical ability' and 'Megs's use of language is both imaginative and creative' – that daughter went into other people's houses and cleaned them. It broke Vivienne's heart. She grieved for her daughter's dreams and she grieved for her own.

Vivienne could never fully understand her daughter's lifestyle. It was the lack of a man that puzzled her. In my day, she'd think, for she knew better than to say this out loud, a man was what you wanted. You got married and that was that. But Megs got married and that plainly wasn't that. She got divorced. 'Men,' she'd say. Huffing the word out as part of a sigh. 'Men.' There was no derision in her tone. It wasn't men she didn't trust. It was the embroiled tangle of emotions that came with sharing her life with one that brought out the worst in her. She came from the Groucho Marx school of relationships. She didn't want to have a relationship with the sort of person who would have a relationship with her. 'Men,' she rasped, mostly to herself, 'you win some, you lose some, and some just stay to tea.'

Vivienne hated to imagine her life without a man in it. A man made her feel safe. She had to admit that her man, Walter, had banished himself to the garden shed when he couldn't cope with the depression she'd suffered after her hysterectomy, and had – it seemed to Vivienne, anyway – spent a deal of his life in there ever since. She wished Megs and Walter would become close. They couldn't make up their differences. There were no differences to make up. It was their isolation from each other they had to resolve. Walter hadn't bothered much with his daughter when she was small, preferring instead to dote on his son. Vivienne had taken charge of Megs's upbringing.

Before retiring, Walter had worked shifts on the railway, so

Vivienne hadn't seen much of him. But still, he was there most evenings, in the armchair on the opposite side of the fireplace from her armchair. He'd read the paper and smoke. Then, about nine o'clock, there would come from behind the paper a deep breathing, then a deeper breathing, then a snore. Round about eleven they'd have a cup of Ovaltine, then bed. Walter would never admit that he'd been sleeping.

'Thinking,' he'd protest night after night. 'Having a bit of a think.'

But his evening sleeps were an important part of his day. If for some reason he was denied his two or three hours slumped in his chair, he'd be grumpy all the next day.

Sometimes, when she was cleaning the living room, Vivienne would stare at the two chairs on either side of the fireplace. One day one of them would be empty. Either she or Walter would sit alone in the evenings. In the depth of the night she would reach out for Walter and put her hand on his chest, checking that it was still rising and falling softly with sleep. Checking he was still alive.

She was older than him, two years. He was seventy. She had been declaring she was sixty-three for almost a decade now and, funnily, nobody seemed to notice. If you say something firmly enough, she discovered, people will believe it. Perhaps if Megs dreamed with a little more conviction, she'd believe herself and make something happen.

Megs never abandoned her dreams. She added to them, elaborated them. Her enthusiasm seemed boundless. Only occasionally did she suffer uncontrollable bouts of reality. A running rush of truth. The grim reality of the life she led, the job she had would arrive in her head and refuse to go away. 'This is me,' she would say. 'Thundering towards forty, three living children, one not living any more, a cluttered, noisy flat with a view of the cluttered, noisy flat across the road, a mucky job that does nothing for my nails, a cantankerous car that does not love me, a cantankerous mother who does and wants too much of me, and . . . Oh God.'

It was all too much. If she got a gushing bout of truth when she was at home she'd pour herself a glass of cheap plonk and wish it away. If it hit her when she was at work then she'd shout out, 'Oh God, no.' Or, 'Sod all that.' It was whilst suffering one of these truth bouts that she lost her job at the market garden on the outskirts of town. But that was a bout that could be forgiven.

It was after Thomas died. Six years old, he suffered for his wild imagination and impulsiveness. He had not waited at the school gate for her to come and collect him and had set off for home alone. Swinging his purple and black canvas school bag and mumbling to himself, he walked to the crossroads. Without properly checking the traffic, he stepped from the pavement. He had not made it to the other side.

For months after the funeral Megs sat all day at home on the sofa, staring. She wasn't even aware of the silence that filled her life. Neither Lorraine nor Vivienne could get through to her. They felt they stood on the edge of her life, watching her from across the room, whispering concern. 'Has she eaten?' 'Did the doctor give her something to make her sleep?' 'Has she taken it?' After the initial flood of sympathy cards, friends stopped calling. The doorbell stopped ringing. The phone was lifeless. On the rare occasions she did go out, people crossed the road when they saw her coming. They did not know what to say to her. Her tragedy was beyond their conversational range.

The pain, it seemed, was always there. First thing in the morning it was there. Sometimes when she woke and grief was rumbling through her, as it had been all night, even when she slept, she'd think: Why do I feel like this? Then she'd remember and start sobbing and rolling her head back and forth on the pillow. 'Oh no. No. No. No.' For months and months the only relief she got was that small moment between waking and asking herself what it was that made her feel so bad.

She couldn't accept the child was dead. Couldn't say the word. She'd look at the clock. 'Ten past three,' she'd say. 'Time to go fetch Thomas.' Or she'd serve up four plates at supper time instead of just three. Hannah and Jack, her other children, would stare at the plates and say nothing. But neither would they eat.

The pain was physical. It made her stoop. At last she went to the doctor.

'I think there's something wrong with my heart,' she told him. 'I think I'm going to die.'

He listened to the pain, and touched her chest. Long fingers, cool hands.

'You're not going to die,' he said. 'I know you want to but you're not. I'm sorry, but you're not.'

For a moment she looked mildly surprised at him. 'Is that where my heart is?'

He nodded.

'I always thought it was lower down.'

He smiled. 'No, your heart is there and it's fine. It's doing well.'

'But it hurts. It really, really hurts.' She thought she was going to cope with this conversation, but lost control of her voice. It slipped off the rails into grief. Her throat blocked and she cried.

'You thought a broken heart was a metaphor, didn't you? It isn't. Sometimes people suffer real pain as if the heart was ruptured.' He looked at her. A healthy heart he knew would chunter on. Stomachs were different. Stomachs actually went pale with loss, bled with anger. 'Are you eating?' he asked.

'I should. Somehow I've forgotten how. Lost the knack of it.'

He gave her something to help her sleep. She refused anti-depressants and returned to her sofa.

Vivienne phoned Aunty Betty. 'She just sits. It's not right. She's got other children. I can't fetch and carry any more like I used to. I'm sixty-three, you know.' She and Lorraine had been taking care of Hannah and Jack between them. They worked out a routine. Lorraine dropped them off at school in the morning on her way to work. Vivienne brought them home. Lorraine shopped, Vivienne cooked.

'Leave her be,' Aunty Betty said. 'She'll come to herself.'

But in the end Vivienne did not leave Megs be. 'Snap out of this,' she said stiffly. 'You have other children. Remember them? They really need you. All you do is sit about all day in that old dressing gown. Moth-eaten thing.' She tugged at the sleeve of Megs's pink towelling robe.

'You may not have noticed, Mother,' Megs sighed. 'But the style police don't come round this neighbourhood.'

'I hate you in it. And you have the baby to think of.'

Megs stared at her. It was the first time either of them had mentioned her pregnancy, though it was daily becoming more and more obvious. The baby was as yet a bulge. But it was a bulge that caused small signs of disapproval – stiffening of the shoulders, tightening of the lips – in everyone who observed it.

Vivienne did not ask who the baby's father was, and neither did Lorraine. They both knew. It was Mike, her ex. There was something about the shifty way he and Megs eyed each other whenever he came round to collect Hannah and Jack on Saturdays. He would cast a slow, shameful eye across her stomach, and she would sigh, that small, resigned sigh of hers. Fine mess you got me into now, sort of thing, Vivienne thought, watching her.

Four days after the funeral Mike had come to the flat. He wanted some pictures of Thomas. He wanted something that had been Thomas's – a toy, a drawing from school – something to treasure. And he wanted someone to talk to.

Denise, his new wife, tried to share his sorrow but she could not reach him. He was in a turmoil of bewilderment, rage and sorrow that was beyond anything she had experienced. She could not plumb the depths of his wretchedness. When she saw him go to Megs, she felt glad, guiltily glad. She could watch a soap or laugh at a sitcom without suffering any self-recrimination. After he left she settled down to indulge herself with a video, a gin and tonic and a few hours free of torment.

Mike and Megs sat side by side on the sofa, looking through a photograph album. He chose as a token of remembrance of a lost love a picture of Thomas, three years old, wearing his navy cord dungarees tucked into his shiny red wellies, and his little duffel coat, offering a lump of bread to some belligerent ducks in the park.

'That's Thomas. Nothing put him up nor down,' he said, putting the photo on the table beside one of Thomas's drawings from school, an illustrated list of his favourite things, a crayoned, childish scrawl. 'My favourite things are – Shameless, toffee pudding, purpl things, football, trees, my frend Brian and cartoons.' He'd drawn Shameless looking large and shapeless beside a tree – thin brown trunk and rounded fuzz of green leaves atop.

Megs held the slightly tattered bit of paper. 'We should have looked after this. It's precious. You never know. Never know.'

Mike put his arms round her. Held her, put his lips against the top of her head. They rocked together, a slow, woeful movement. Hannah and Jack were with Vivienne. She brushed his neck with her lips. There was solace in the way he gently stroked her back.

The sex they had started as a comfort. The nearest thing either of them had got to sucking their thumbs in years. They were two despairing souls momentarily losing their sorrow in each other. There was a moment when they each lost control, started to shake and cry out. Not an ecstatic howl, just an anguished shriek from within. When they were done, they were weeping. It was quickly over. Afterwards they sat like guilty teenagers, adjusting unbuttoned shirts, crumpled skirts and tousled hair.

'Oh God,' said Megs. 'What a thing to do.'

Mike said, 'Sorry.' Then he asked if she had anything to drink in the house and went to fetch some whisky and two glasses.

'I sometimes think that was the only thing we ever did well together,' Megs said.

Mike did not answer. He finished his drink, gathered his photo and drawing and left, saying sorry again. 'And sorry about the tooth. Sorry.'

On the day Thomas died Mike had come round deranged with grief. When he discovered that Megs had been late picking Thomas up from school he'd swung at her. And missed. Megs stepped back, lost her footing and hit her mouth on the sink on the way to the floor.

'Oh God,' Mike cried when he saw the blood streaming down her chin. 'Oh God, I didn't mean it.'

'It's all right,' Megs said. She felt she deserved a smack in the mouth. But the pain her collision with the sink brought did nothing to relieve the guilt she felt.

He apologised for swinging at her, and for the sex they had. Looking back, she thought that all he did during their marriage was alternate between acting aloof and apologising. She never could figure it out.

They were too guilty, too shamed to discuss their moment of tormented love, even when the evidence of it became obvious. Even when Denise called Megs a disgusting, thoughtless slut for becoming pregnant so soon after her son's death, Mike said nothing.

At last, at Vivienne's insistence, Megs took off her pink towelling robe, the moth-eaten thing, and returned to work. She only lasted a day.

She'd been asked to pot on some geraniums. When she got to the greenhouse the air was heady with their tart green smell. There were more small plastic tubs of tender, tiny geraniums than she'd ever seen in her life. If she put her eyes level with the table top they stretched to the horizon.

'Can't I have some help here?' she asked Mr Hammond, her boss.

He shook his head. 'No, we're short-staffed. I need Jean in the office. Lorna has deliveries, and Cara's on the winter-flowering pansies.'

Megs sighed and started work. She gently removed the seedlings from their tiny pots and put them into larger plastic pots where they would settle and grow into saleable, robust geraniums. She held the frail tendril roots, dipped them in lukewarm water, then trailed them a second in sand. That slight weight made them sink straight, undamaged, into the hole she'd made for them. 'There you go,' she whispered to them, from a place so deep in her, her lips moved but no sound came out.

At four o'clock she once again put her eyes level with the table top and decided that the acres of geraniums still stretched to the horizon. She'd made no progress at all. 'I'm no further forward with this,' she wailed.

'Oh,' said Mr Hammond casually. 'I put another couple of hundred pots down when you were at lunch.' He jingled his car keys as he spoke. Megs looked at him mournfully. Soon he'd be driving home in his BMW. She'd take the bus, almost an hour's journey back to her flat in Stockbridge, because her cantankerous car had decided to take the day off and refused to start. The bus driver would stare rudely at her nails as he took her fare. She could never get them properly clean till she got home to her own sink and her own nail brush. Her cantankerous mother would be in the flat when she got back and would be walking round and round the kitchen table telling the children to eat their supper. 'When I was your age we didn't have lovely things like frozen hamburgers, you know,' she'd be nagging. The house would smell of overheated insides of grill pan and the television would be roaring. If nobody had remembered to take the dog out, there would be a huge damp patch by the front door. And she'd be potting on geraniums for the rest of her life. She could pot on a geranium in the dark. She could do it whilst sleeping.

Her arrival back at work after almost five months' absence caused a ripple of gossip and surprise. She found it hard to live with the silence when she arrived in a room and the whisperings when she left. There was a look, she'd seen it first in the hospital where they'd taken Thomas. A slow movement of the eyes away from her eyes. It said, that look, that death has touched you and you must keep away. As if tragedy was infectious. It was, also, plain that nobody approved of her condition.

'I do not need this,' she muttered furiously to herself. 'I do not need this.'

Jack, her oldest, seemed recently to have absented himself from the world. He disappeared to school early, came home late and spent his time at home earphones on, lost in his own rhythmic space. Hannah, two years younger than Jack, had decided two weeks ago that she was a vegetarian and that the rest of the family were gross for eating meat. She wanted to eat on her own.

Now Megs's pregnancy was bulging, and she was dreading the time ahead when the baby came. She knew well the unavoidable, draining routine that came with babies. She hated herself for how she looked. She hated herself even more for not wanting the child she was expecting. All that, and Thomas would not be there. He would not come banging down the hall. He would not argue with the others about his television programme. Or rattle through the kitchen cupboards demanding food.

'I do not need all this,' Megs said. Louder now.

Mr Hammond, on his last key-jingling round, popped his head round the door.

'Nearly done?'

'No,' howled Megs. 'No way. God, what a question.' Then she gave a full-throated protest. 'I can't stand this,' she yelled.

Her voice, always one of her best features, carried well. She was heard throughout the five greenhouses, across the gardens, in the salesroom and office, and down the phones. Several customers asked in alarm as they ordered their summer bedding plants – lobelia, dwarf marigolds, begonias – what was going on. Mr Hammond boomed that Megs may have gone through a hard time but she was here to work.

'Oh, bugger you,' Megs screamed. 'I hate this. It's too much to bear.'

'Well, if you want to work here, young woman, you'll just have to bear up like the rest of us.'

Megs always wondered how people got to be the way they were. How did this man turn into such an absurd bully in a suit? She would try to imagine people in authority as they might have been years and years ago in primary school. This patriarchal man had once been a spiky-haired, skinny-kneed boy who snivelled at the gate when his mummy let go of him. He had been a whisperer of tales to teacher and grubby rumours to his pals. Now here he was, a grandiose being in a suit who got irritated simply at her presence in the world, who could not even tolerate her relatively inconsequential refusal to do what he wished her to do. To pot on geraniums, smiling. And grieve politely.

'Oh, bugger you,' Megs spat.

'Just what are you going to do if you lose this job?' Mr Hammond wanted to know.

'I don't need you.' Megs was sure of this. She banged her chest defiantly with her fist. 'There are millions of things I can do,' she bawled. Remembering this moment would, for years and years afterwards, embarrass her. 'I can scrub floors,' she boasted.

'You said what?' Vivienne could not believe it when Megs told her. 'That was a good job you just threw away. And you in your condition.' She considered the absurdity of her daughter's outburst, and the state of her kitchen floor. 'You have never scrubbed a floor in your life.'

'I could learn. Don't tell me there's any great knack to scrubbing a floor. Any arse could do it.'

'In that case you qualify as a floor-scrubber.'

Next day, then, Megs put an ad in the local paper. 'Scrubber seeks floors. Will also wax, wipe, dust, launder, iron and polish. Well-greased elbow. Distance no object.'

A couple of months later she was waddling heavily through strange houses, watching new lifestyles. Cleaning suited her. Or at least the mindlessness of it, the repetitiveness of it suited her mood. She was in too much despair to want to do anything more taxing than wiping, dusting and ironing. She, who rarely lifted a finger in her own home, did not mind cleaning up after strangers. And her strangers did not mind her, her grief or her pregnancy.

Six weeks after Lizzy was born, Megs went back to work. The baby went with her. She cleaned for Mrs Terribly-Clean Pearson Wednesday afternoons and Monday and Friday mornings; Mrs Emotionally-Deranged Davis Tuesday mornings and Thursday afternoons; Ms Just-Keep-It-Above-the-Dysentery-Line McGhee Tuesday afternoons and Thursday mornings; and after today Hundred-Miles-An-Hour Wednesday mornings and Friday afternoons.

Megs moved her arms in the bath, making small ripples waft round her. 'I feel life returning,' she sighed. 'I'm beginning to think I may be human after all.' She soaped her arms and hummed a snatch of a song that had drifted into her head.

Lorraine drank and joined in. 'Brie and chopped apple,' she said, 'on a bed of shredded lettuce, with a light vinaigrette and a slice of crispy, maple-flavoured bacon.'

'That'd be nice.' Megs nodded dreamily. 'Chicken marinated in soy sauce and ginger, grilled and chopped, mixed with a lightly curried mayonnaise and bamboo shoots.'

'On a wheaten bun?' Lorraine was keen to get all details perfect.

'No, sesame. Sesame with chicken.' Megs thought. She returned to her tune. Then, 'We could call it the Dixie Queen.'

'I like that.' Lorraine nodded and hummed along. They were still dreaming of sandwiches. Their sandwich bar plans were endless. It made them happy.

Megs stopped humming, reached for a towel and heaved herself, dripping from the tub.

'Hey, guess who I'm cleaning for now.'

'Who?' said Lorraine.

'Hundred-Miles-An-Hour.'

'Really?' Lorraine was thrilled. 'Have you been to his house? What was it like?'

269

'Full of things,' Megs said. 'Walls covered with pictures. Books. Clutter. Staff your granny threw away. He's a messy bugger, though.'

'And have you been to his bathroom? Does he have a comb?'

'Lorraine, I just had a quick look round. We only spoke for about ten minutes.'

Everyone knew Hundred-Miles-An-Hour. He was famous about town, well, at least their bit of it. He cycled uphill to the university in the morning and downhill going home at night. Uphill in the morning the effort creased his face and shoved his hair towards the heavens. Downhill in the evening the force of the prevailing wind pushed his hair even more dramatically upwards. He never seemed to think to fix it. He had, then, a constant expression of surprise, hair swept back as if he were travelling at great speed. Hundred-Miles-An-Hour. Gilbert Christie he was, but people only called him that to his face.

'He's a bit professorish. Know what I mean? Distracted if you're being kind. Daft if you're not. He's not my type.' Then, changing the subject, for she did not enjoy talking about her work, 'Hey, Lorraine, pour us another before my mother comes home with Lizzy and Hannah.' She put on the towelling robe her mother hated so much, and considered without mercy her body. 'Christ. Look at me. All cellulite and flab. I'm drooping. Gravity is cruel.'

'Middle age,' said Lorraine. 'Soon you'll have to start walking around with your arms folded under your tits to keep them up. You'll be standing at the door gossiping with your tits propped on your forearms. And walking along the street the same way. And running for the bus.' She demonstrated. Folded her arms and ran up and down the room, though it took only four steps to get from one end to the other.

'That'll be me.' Megs folded her arms and went into the hall, where she would get a full six steps. Up and down she ran, and into the living room. 'Look at me.' She danced, arms folded, tits propped. 'It's the middle-aged woman's jig. Arms folded, tits ahoy, here we go.'

Jack sneered, aimed the remote at the screen, switched off the set and left the room. Lorraine joined in, sashaying up and down to bump folded arms, then back down the room again. Back up again and bump again. They giggled.

'The pair of you. What are you up to?' Vivienne said. They had been too busy dancing to notice her coming in.

'It's a jig,' said Megs. 'Arms folded, saving-tits-from-gravity sort of thing.' She stopped dancing and panted.

'Will the pair of you ever grow up?' Vivienne looked at them witheringly. She stormed across the room, put on the television and showed Hannah and little Lizzy the sofa. 'Sit,' she ordered. Then, rounding on the two drunken dancers, 'And you,' pointing at Megs, 'shouldn't you be ready? Isn't it Glass Bucket night? I'm here to baby-sit. And your father will be along in a couple of hours.'

Megs always thought her father came to see his grandchildren, not her. He was especially fond of Lizzy. He'd call her name and hoist her into the air. 'Where's my little girl then?'

Vivienne heaved in her breath and disappeared into the kitchen. 'Wait till I tell Aunty Betty about this. I have never seen the like in my life. And I'm sixty-three, you know.'

Chapter Two

Every Friday night Megs sang at the Glass Bucket. She sang the songs Aunty Betty taught her when she was little: 'Sippin' Soda', 'Paper Moon', 'I've Got a Crush on You', 'Manhattan'. She did all sorts of jigs and toe-tapping tunes, 'Marie's Wedding', 'Star of the County Down'. Everyone joined in. She sang songs from the sixties and seventies, 'Here Comes the Night', 'Honky Tonk Woman', 'Something In the Air'. And how the crowd loved that. They swayed in their seats, drank till the booze and noise they were making helped them forget all the things they had come to the Glass Bucket to forget.

As the night wore on and people clustered round their tables to drift into little worlds of sudden relationships, moods, sighs, tangy cheese Doritos and the small truths alcohol helped them disclose, Megs switched to the blues. She sang Bessie Smith, "Tain't Nobody's Bizness If I Do' and 'My Sweetie Went Away'. But mostly she sang Billie Holiday, 'Good Morning Heartache' and 'Speak Low'. When she sang about heartache people nodded and drank: yes, they knew about heartache. They'd been there. And when she sang 'Speak Low' and moved her hips to its jazzy rhythms, pouted and smiled, they all knew what she meant. People would smile and reach out to touch knees, naked shoulders – whatever was available to touch. They were going to get lucky tonight. Megs's voice, once pure and clear, was cracked and frayed around the edges; time and grief had taken their toll. It fitted perfectly the songs she sang.

Round about eleven o'clock, when the air was thick with smoke and thrumming with chat, Megs always sang 'God Bless the Child'. Everything would stop. People stopped drinking, stopped buying chicken in a basket, stopped touching, hoping. The crack stopped,

273

the laughter. There were only sad spirals of cigarette smoke and the slow movement of glass to lip. She sang it the way Billie did. She didn't sound the 'l' in help. 'Hep,' she sang. 'God hep the chile'.

After Thomas died, when Megs poured her despair out across the room, the silence that greeted that song, then, was the sort of silence a bar manager dreaded. The till did not chime. There was no rustle of notes, no chink of coins. Women burst out crying. So Dave Roberts, manager of the Glass Bucket, sacked her.

'You're no good for business,' he said, poking her with a stubby, nicotined finger. 'I can't afford you. People come out for a good time. They don't want you bringing them down.'

For three weeks Megs stayed away. Then she went back to the bar. She was wearing her snakeskin shirt and tight black jeans. On her feet silver strappy high-heel sandals. Her toenails were painted bright red. Her hair, long and bottle-blonde, moved across her face as she spoke. She thought she ought to get it cut. Stop bleaching it. 'I'm too old for my hair,' she told Lorraine. But she never did anything. Drastic hair changes were too taxing.

'I need to come back,' she said to Dave. 'I need the money. Hannah's got to have new shoes, Jack has grown out of his school trousers and people need to be fed. And I have a baby. If you don't take me back I'll go sing at the Black Bull and everyone'll go there.'

'You upset folk,' Dave protested. 'They get depressed.' He knew she had him. He knew she was right. He'd lose his customers.

'A bit of sadness goes a long way,' Megs said. 'Especially if it's someone else's. Mine. They all listen to me and think, thank Christ it's her and not me.'

'OK, Megs,' he said. 'But when they stop drinking, switch to something happy. Stop reminding people of what they're waking up to in the morning. He stuck his hands into his pockets and stared at her. That was his deal, no 'God Bless the Child'.

'Do some of those jigs, Irish songs Aunty Betty taught you. People clap and stamp, work up a thirst.' He clapped and stamped, a small, joyless demonstration. His jacket moved perfectly with him. He spent a fortune on clothes. A girlfriend once told him that women laughed at men's trousers because they smelled of stale fast food, petrol and God knows what else. So he changed his clothes at least twice a day, got discounts at the dry cleaners he was such a good customer.

'I will for a bonus,' she said. 'I need the money.'

He stared at her. 'I bet you do.'

She had three children and no man to take care of her. That was how he still saw relationships, at least the relationships of the people who drank at the Glass Bucket. Women had babies and men brought in money – usually in cash in brown pay packets. He knew this wasn't true. People got paid the same way he did – money transferred straight into his bank account – but he liked to think he was a cut above his customers. He knew he was a cut above Megs. As well as singing on Friday nights, she cleaned five days a week and waitressed for Clark's Catering, banquets and official functions, whenever she could.

'Tell you what,' he said, 'sing those jigs and I'll give you five per cent of the increase in the take.'

'Ten,' she said.

'OK. Ten.' He shrugged. He didn't care. He was planning to give her an extra twenty pounds whatever happened. How would she know what the increase was? Business was slower without her. Furthermore, customers were asking for her. He had not realised how popular she was.

The following Friday, Megs, wearing her favourite short black dress, was back on the little stage again. She held the mike close to her lips, shut her eyes and moved in time to her songs. The life she led – cleaning, cooking for her kids and worrying – this was the only time her mind emptied enough for her to find some contentment. It was when she did a little forgetting of her own. Once she'd been a singer in a band. Now it seemed long, long ago – such a distance she had travelled since then – a different time when she was a different person. Life had been – hopes, dreams and spangled lights – fleetingly like a fairytale. She could almost say it was once upon a time. 'Once upon a time I sang with First Degree Murder. Remember them?' To her enduring surprise some people – not many – actually did.

She knew, of course, that she was rewriting her history in her head. She was romanticising what had been a time of long, kidney-jarring journeys bundled and bumping in the back of a van with dubious suspension. It had been years of broken dreams, frustration, sore throats, chilblains, boredom, noise, quarrels that started as squabbles, ended with full-blown fisticuffs, frustration and cruelly suspicious carry-outs from nightmare fast-food joints that all ought to have been called House of Diarrhoea. She still thought about those days, sometimes she even sighed for them. And sometimes she heaved herself from the gilded depth of her romanticising and admitted the truth. 'Giving birth to four children and battering about in that bloody van for years have taken their toll on my bladder for ever.'

Mike, her ex, was bass guitarist and the driving force whose ambition took them bumping, clattering and dreaming through ten thousand Saturday nights (or so it seemed), over a million miles of motorway and neglected pot-holed roads to play in universities, pubs, village halls and theatres. He wore his hair long then, and smiled enigmatically to the crowd as he played. It had taken him years to master this easy, lazy disinterest.

He was skinny, then. Weren't they all? They had, all five of them, that late-hippie debauched look, dangerously saintly. She sometimes saw the other members of the band, and how was life for them?

Eddy drove long-distance. Fred had been called to the bar. Josh still gigged a little, one-night stands in pubs. He played guitar. He drank. She did what she could. She got by. And Mike? Mike got a Filofax, and now he had a personal organiser. Wasn't there a song like that? Hadn't Lou Reed written it? Or was it Iggy Pop?

After six years (three hundred and twelve Saturday nights, in fact) and too many disappointments to bear, they'd given up. It hadn't been an abrupt or bitter parting of the ways, just the slow fraying of relationships that came with the dawning that life was slipping by and realistic decisions about the future had to be taken.

Mike decided his future was in accountancy. Megs took a job at the mail-order market garden to help keep them whilst he went to college. He emerged a fully qualified accountant with short hair, a trimmed beard and initials after his name. She got broken nails and an astonishing knowledge of plants and herbs that she didn't know was in her head till someone asked, what was a good ground-spreading flower for a shady border? Or, what fertiliser do you put on basil? Or, what's nivalis really called?

'Snowdrops,' she'd say, surprising everybody, especially herself.

Then she'd had Jack, then Hannah and later Thomas. By the time Thomas arrived, she and Mike lived separate lives. She dressed in jeans and T-shirts, wore her hair long and spoke about plants, music, what the children did, what they ate and where they went today.

He got a job with an upmarket firm in Charlotte Square, and had a better relationship with his hairdresser than he had with her. He wore a suit and spoke about clients, expense accounts, deals and how he needed the right suits and shoes if he wanted to be taken at all seriously. He bought a mobile phone and the famous Filofax. She wanted a dishwasher. It was some time before they realised how deep was the gulf that had developed between them. They had stopped speaking to one another. All they did now was say things. 'It's your turn to take Jack to his swim class.' 'We're out of milk.' 'Is there anything decent on telly tonight?' Through these and a hundred other innocuous questions and remarks they managed to express the constant undertow of their dissatisfaction. 'Would you like some coffee?' Megs might ask. But there would be a movement of her lips, a shifting of tone that only Mike would notice. Only he would know the deal of resentment that went into that little question.

Mike found someone new. Denise shared his new enthusiasm. He and Megs parted. He got the car and the record collection. She got the children, the flat and Shameless, the dog – a large, hairy, absurdly friendly impulse buy that she had wanted to call Leroy. However, every time Megs saw him lying sprawled on his back in front of the fire, or guiltlessly licking his genitals or sticking his cold nose up passing skirts, mooching her children's cornflakes, or scratching, sniffing in the kitchen bin for tasty bits, sleeping at full stretch on Hannah's bed, or silently filling the room with sudden, putrid, yellowed air from his guileless, unabashed farting, she called him shameless. In the end that was the name that stuck.

Mike turned into a far better accountant than he was bass guitarist. Time and money were kind to him. Now he and Denise lived in a new house on a small, select estate. They had a new car, a new stereo system and a new daughter. Megs didn't know who he was any more. Still, when Mike came back to the flat to collect the children for the weekend, he would linger longer than necessary. Sitting in Megs's kitchen amidst the mess and music and banter he felt the tension round his neck and shoulders ease. He did not mean to hurt Megs when he casually mentioned that Denise bought Betty Jackson jackets, or that she went once a month to Glasgow to have her hair done at Vidal Sassoon. But he did. Megs did not mean to inflict on herself that emotional wince she felt when she pumped him for information about his new wife and her credit cards. But she did. She couldn't help it. She still wanted a dishwasher.

The Blue Boys backed her at the Glass Bucket. They didn't have the spiralling aspirations of her first band. They were a don't-give-up-the-day-job sort of a bunch. Not that any of them minded. They had long stopped dreaming. Stardom was something to be scoffed at. They were happy with the perks being in the band brought them: a little respect, some compliments that bordered on flattery, free drinks, cash the tax man didn't know about and, for Jim, the drummer, sex his wife didn't know about.

For years Megs had a numbing weekly routine. Weekdays she cleaned for a small group of clients whose lives she found fascinating. Friday nights Vivienne, her mother, would baby-sit whilst she sang at the Glass Bucket. She got by.

Recently, however, she'd been feeling that getting by wasn't enough. The hankering for something better had grown from being a small itchy longing to a festering discontent that kept her awake at nights and plagued her during the day if she did not drive it from her mind with songs she hummed as she furiously wiped other people's kitchens, dusted other people's mantelpieces and picture frames, scrubbed other people's lavatories, baths and showers, changed other people's beds and listened to the small shifts and clicks of other people's houses when they were not at home. She liked the silence of strangers' houses. It was not as disquieting as the silence of her own.

All her life Megs had plans that were really just well-honed dreams. Lorraine got sucked into them. There was something irresistible about Megs's dreams. They were so much juicier than life itself. There had been the starogram dream.

'I'll dress as old dead film stars. Mae West, Joan Crawford, Ginger Rogers sort of thing,' Megs enthused to Lorraine. 'And I'll go along to people's work, parties and pubs and sing, "Always True to You

Darlin' In My Fashion" or "I'm In the Money" or whatever, rip open my frock. Flash my tits. You man the phones.'

Phones, definitely phones, plural. They were going to get inundated with calls. 'We'll make a fortune.' Then, considering the demoralising effect life, its trials and temptations, its chocolate and vodka, had had on her body, Megs said, 'Perhaps not.' The starogram dream had been a five-minute flirtation with success and riches. Once it was spoken out, its flaws – both of them – became obvious. Megs's tits were not up to the challenge. So the starogram plan was abandoned and replaced with the plant shop plan.

'Huge clay pots of marguerites and geraniums on the pavement outside, glistening white and red into the afternoon, so iridescent the redness glows up into the air around them.' Megs had verbal energy. She painted her fancies perfectly, swept Lorraine along. 'A whole wall of herbs, scenting the air – thyme, rosemary, lovage. The blast of basil in the summer, huge succulent leaves and clusters of tiny white flowers, will make people dizzy. They'll just stand outside breathing and sighing. A large plain glass bowl of daisies fresh every morning on the counter . . .'

Now the big plan was the sandwich bar. It was to be called M & L's (Megs and Lorraine's) and it was to look like an early American drug store. 'Norman Rockwell would come by to drink coffee, spin out homey philosophies and observe folk. James Stewart in his younger days would work behind the counter wrapped in a huge white apron that tied round his middle, shyly tripping over his words. The décor will be simple and wholesome.'

'Stripped pine?' asked Lorraine.

'No.' Megs shook her head. 'A glass counter, chrome rails, bar seats with red leather cushions and a bar made of shiny walnut beaded with a dark-red border.' She had it all worked out.

There would be fabulous sandwiches all named after blues singers or famous songs. Irresistible fillings tailored to markets. 'A free-range egg fried in chilli oil – the Satchmo (because you'd really have to get your mouth round it) – for the building site people, or tomato and mozzarella with fresh basil for the women office workers.'

'What'll that be?' Lorraine wanted to know.

'Dunno yet.'

Megs had spent nights and nights sitting about with the band. As they smoked, drank and discussed gigs and how they would handle fame when it came – they were all, except her, convinced it would – she'd read the copious notes on the backs of their albums. The only thing that superseded her knowledge of plants was her knowledge of the blues and the people who played and sang them. 'What about the Lil Hardin? Satchmo's wife. One of them, anyway.'

Lorraine shrugged. 'Perhaps,' she said.

'The Lil Hardin,' Megs glowed, 'will be creamy cheese and ripe fresh tomatoes that explode in your mouth, all peppered and tangy with fresh basil. It'll sing to you.' She paused a moment, considering her dream. The Lil Hardin and the Satchmo were their first sandwiches. There would be others. 'It'll be wonderful.' Megs was sure of this. 'It'll be the making of us.' They stared at each other, slightly embarrassed. They both thought they were far too old to be clutching at daydreams. At their age they ought to be living comfortable, sorted-out lives. It was as if sanity and normality had somehow passed them by. And that was all they'd really wanted.

'What went wrong?' Lorraine asked. They knew each other so well now they had no need to explain the heart-searching that went behind such a gruelling question. They could any time, anywhere, without any sort of lead-in, start the what-went-wrong conversation.

'Dunno,' Megs said. 'How did this happen? How did I end up grubbing about for a living? This isn't what I planned.' She suffered from the sort of recurring angst she considered only chocolate and alcohol could soothe.

Chapter Three

The name Megs was a legacy from that infants' class, all those years ago where she'd first met Lorraine. Actually she was Nina. Nina Megson. As a child Megs hated her name. She considered Nina a name fit only for fat old ladies, and had, therefore, refused to answer to it. She sat at her school desk hands stiffly by her sides, jaw set, refusing to respond to any mention of the word Nina.

'Nina,' her teacher would say. 'Nina, it's your turn to feed the hamster.' Or, 'Nina, hand out the reading books.'

But young Nina would look pudgily defiant, stare out the window, little brow knit, lips puckered. This wasn't happening. Who was Nina? Not her. She would never be Nina, as long as she lived. No. No. No. There was no Nina. 'I'm Megs,' she said. 'Megsy to my friends.' It was another small show of defiance from the infant anarchist.

After she married, the name still stayed. She took Mike's last name, Williams. Nina was not allowed in her life. She became Megs Williams. Now the only person who called her Nina was her mother. And at that only when she wasn't speaking to her.

Megs was the name she'd used when she introduced herself to Hundred-Miles-An-Hour. He, of course, had no notion of his nickname. As far as he was concerned he was Gilbert Christie.

'This is it, then,' he said to her, indicating with a clumsy body swerve, hands firmly stuck in his trouser pockets, the mess his house was in. 'Um,' realising the extent of his untidiness, 'it's got a bit out of hand.'

'So I see,' Megs said, looking glumly round. This man is disgusting, she thought. There was a mouldering mountain of newspapers threatening to take over the sofa. A thick layer of fuzz lined the tops of his pictures and skirting boards. His kitchen floor was sticky. She felt the soles of her shoes rasping against it. She doubted he'd ever thought to wipe the front of his fridge or cooker. A week's dirty dishes were piled on the drainer. She suspected he'd left them as soon as he heard she was coming.

Just-Keep-It-Above-the-Dysentery-Line McGhee had recommended her at a dinner party when he'd complained about not being able to see through his windows. 'I'll send my cleaning lady round to you, Gilbert darling. She's just what you need. Mrs Williams. Megs. You'll love her.'

'You've no washing machine, then?' Megs asked, casting her eye grimly round. The waste bin overflowed. There was an impressive display of empty wine bottles on the floor by the sink.

'Heavens, no.' He looked alarmed at the suggestion. 'Bourgeois things.' Washing machines, dishwashers, videos all horrified him. He felt that if he let any of them into his life a fatuous middle-class-ness that he'd been rebelling against ever since he left home twenty-five years ago would creep over him. After the washing machine came fitted carpets with matching curtains, a cocktail cabinet with bottles of sherry. Then he'd be putting gaudy Van Gogh prints on the wall and a fluffy cover on the lavatory lid. He shuddered. 'Wouldn't give one house room.'

'Right,' she said, bemused. She only mentioned a washing machine, for heaven's sake.

'You can take my things to the laundrette round the corner.'

'And use the bourgeois things there,' she said. 'Perhaps,' she asked, 'you'd prefer it if I took your washing down to the river and beat it against some stones?'

'Hardly,' he said. Was she mocking him? He didn't know. Mockery was hard to recognise, even harder to bear. Especially from a woman – a woman such as this.

He took her upstairs. His living room was worse. There were beer bottles on the floor, old shoes, books – books everywhere, small piles of them on every step of the stairs. 'I kind of let it go when I heard you were coming,' he confessed.

'Let it go,' she mused. This was more than let go. This was years of neglect. He seemed to think she could fix it all with a single wipe with a damp cloth. 'I won't be able to do it in a day. It'll take a bit of cleaning.'

'Whatever,' he said. 'Just come and do it.' He had no interest in anything domestic.

'When?' asked Megs. She studied his face. Faces interested her. Without being too obvious she studied them, tried to see the people within. His was long and slightly forlorn. His eyebrows were on the verge of taking on a life of their own. There was a small scattering of tiny broken veins on his cheeks – he drank too much. She could see that his beard, should he ever grow one, would be flecked grey. She liked that. His eyes would one day be clouded and watery, stained with the reading he did. But for the moment they were clear and deep, brown pools. Taking the face as a whole, the expressions that crossed it naturally, the lines those expressions left – she concluded that Gilbert Christie was perplexed and lonely and confused. But then, wasn't she? 'When?' she asked again.

'Whenever.' He hardly looked at her.

'I can do Wednesday mornings,' she offered.

'Can't you come in twice a week?'

'The only other time I have is Friday afternoons and I like to keep them free. I work Friday night at the Glass Bucket.'

'I don't think a little light housework will interfere with your barkeeping,' he said. He hated himself. God, that was patronising.

'I don't work at the bar,' Megs corrected him. 'I sing.'

'Really?' He looked at her for the first time. It was the first time he showed any interest in her. He imagined her fronting jolly singalong evenings, winding up at the head of a long, weaving, drunken conga line. She'd be wearing a spangly coconut matting sort of a frock. He thought she'd be part of that crazy, hearty world of booze and abandonment he couldn't ever join in, that fascinated him and that scared the pants off him. 'What do you sing?' he asked.

'Whatever,' she said flatly. She didn't think she liked him. 'Will you be here Friday afternoons?'

'No.'

'Well, I'll come then.' She needed the money.

'Um . . . how will I pay you?'

'Money'll do nicely.' She did not meet his eye.

'Not a cheque then?'

She shook her head. 'I'm not a banking sort of person.'

'Ah,' he said. Looking at her closely now, he could see she was the grown-up version of the sort of girl he'd always lusted after from afar when he was at school. She would have worn fashionable clothes, and have dated the most popular boy in class. Not him, definitely not him. He felt, though, he had the measure of her; she cleaned, she avoided banks and she led conga lines. Righto, he could deal with that. He flattered himself he had the common touch. Ordinary people liked him. Look at the way they smiled when he cycled past. It never crossed his mind that the smiles were not for him, but his perpendicular hairstyle.

He showed her to the door, saying he'd look forward to seeing her Wednesday and it would be great to have the place cleaned up. She looked at him and imagined what Lorraine would say about him.

'What was he like?' she'd demand.

'OK,' Megs would say. 'A bit vague.'

'Oh.' Lorraine would swoon expansively, clutching her bosom. 'All he needs is the love of a good woman.'

Whenever they came up against boorish, disinterested or rude men – pushily flirtatious salesmen, obnoxiously rude gynaecologists, irate drivers flashing and tooting wildly at some minor motoring misdemeanour one of them had made – they'd clutch their hearts and cry, 'All he needs is the love of a good woman.' It was their joke, stemming back to when they were teenagers – stars in their eyes, hope in their hearts. Love, they had convinced themselves, would conquer all. They both believed they'd grow into the sort of good woman whose pure and passionate love would sort out wayward, disillusioned, broken-hearted men.

'Were we ever that dumb?' Megs said when that adolescent naïvety came to mind. Thinking about Lorraine's abandoned crowing, Megs fought to keep her face straight. She resisted the urge to put a comforting hand on his arm, gaze soulfully into his eyes and tell him what he needed. She felt a fit of giggles coming on and, staring down at her feet so that she could compose her face without him watching, she noticed the carpet. It was dusty and crumb-ridden. 'You do have a vacuum, don't you?' she anxiously asked.

'Ah now.' He lit up. 'That I do have.' Vacuums, apparently, were not bourgeois. With a grandiose sweep he opened the hall cupboard, giving her an actual view of the beast. Beast indeed. But not to him. He was enthused. 'Behold the vacuum!' he cried, almost embracing it.

It was older than they were. It was brown, vast and cumbersome with a long handle that had a fraying cord wound round and round it. Its large bag would, Megs knew, bloat up with air as soon as it was switched on. Its noise would deafen her. Heaving it from room to room would do nasty things to her back. She hated it.

'Isn't it wonderful?' He was truly excited. 'Got it at an auction a couple of years ago. The Big Hoover Nine Six One. They don't make them like that any more.'

'Well, that's something.'

'Look at the style and the lines. Straight, well defined, no clutter. It makes a real statement about what it is and what it does. It is unpretentious and functional and that gives it a beauty . . .'

'It's a vacuum,' she interrupted him. 'Does it suck up the dirt?'

He looked baffled. 'Haven't a clue,' he told her. 'I've never actually used it.'

Glumly noting the small, round-pinned, two-point plug, she realised he'd never switched it on. He'd bought it because he thought it added a certain utilitarian elegance to his cupboard. 'It says something about domesticity – something sturdy.' It had never occurred to him to clean the floor with it.

'But, dammit' – no cleaning woman was going to cast aspersions on his vacuum – 'they used this very model in stately homes and on ocean liners. *Queen Mary* and such.' Patting it now. 'These things were built to last. It has style.'

'There you go,' Megs sighed. 'A vacuum with style. I'll bring my own.'

She wondered how somebody who considered washing machines bourgeois and thought vacuums should have style actually earned a living. 'What is it you do?' she asked.

'I lecture on the history of design. Right now I'm working on a book about packaging in the twentieth century. *The Theme Pack*.' He'd

285

been working on his book for the past eight years.

The urge to giggle had gone; she could look into his face once more. This time she knew what she saw. She saw a man past forty who, though still confused about his identity, was very precise about the day-to-day details of his life – no washing machine and a vacuum cleaner that didn't actually vacuum but made a statement about vacuuming.

'Just what I need,' she sighed as she made her way out through the main door, and along the quiet, tree-lined street to her car.

The following Wednesday morning he stayed late to let her into his house and give her a key. 'I don't expect we'll be seeing much of each other,' he said.

That's a mercy, she thought.

Then, indicating his home with a sweep of his arm, 'Let yourself in and help yourself to coffee. Make yourself at home.'

'Oh, lovely,' she said. 'I'll have a bath, drink your gin and phone my brother in Melbourne.' And cursed herself inwardly for her sarcasm.

He looked dismayed, didn't know what to make of her. He was used to speaking whilst others listened. In awe, he hoped. Was she making a fool of him? 'Pardon?' he said.

'Oh, don't mind me.' She dismissed herself. Then, instantly bored with seeking the pardon of someone who owned a vacuum with style, 'I've already had a bath, it's far too early for alcohol, and don't worry, I won't phone anybody.'

He looked desperate to get away from her. She knew she was prattling, but couldn't stop herself. It was cleaner's defence. She imagined she was vulnerable to all sorts of humiliation, so before it materialised she got in a swift spot of mockery.

He looked mildly demented, was running his fingers through his hair which was starting to rise, and he hadn't even cycled to work yet. She noted with interest that he started the morning with his hair flat. The trials of his day and his bike journeys made it stand on end. He wasn't looking his usual hundred-miles-an-hour self yet.

After he left she moved slowly from room to room, trailing her hand over his things, observing his life. She spent so much time clearing out the clutter and stains of other people's lives, she had become expert at observing them. Just-Keep-It-Above-the-Dysentery-Line McGhee was, for example, overdrawn at the bank. Megs recognised the letters and overdrawn slips. She got them regularly herself. This was why she preferred to be paid with cash. Money put into her bank account got lost in the vast hole that was her overdraft. Cathy McGhee, however, solved her financial problems by buying wines from South Africa and Australia, tasty things from the delicatessen that she did not eat, and shoes. Megs tried the wines if any was left in an opened bottle in the fridge, and had developed a taste she could not afford to indulge for Rosemount chardonnay. She nibbled sun-dried tomatoes, anchovy-stuffed olives, pastrami and rare cheeses, and tried on the shoes. The soft black leather medium-heeled ones with straps that wound round her ankles were her favourite.

Cathy McGhee took tranquillisers, had problems with her periods and had migraine tablets by her bed. She spent a deal of time watching television, reading magazines, drinking wine. Her CD collection included Paul Simon, Kurt Weill, Marvin Gaye and Joni Mitchell. Sometimes she intensified her pre-menstrual tension by playing Shostakovich. Hidden behind her sofa was a Reebok step and an exercise thing for reducing thighs. Cher's exercise video was amongst the pile of tapes under the television table. Cathy McGhee had a lover who came by at weekends. He had dark hair. Cathy's was auburn. But the man who slept in her bed during the week was grey. Megs knew these things.

The interesting thing about the Pearsons, on the other hand, was their blandness. They had beige rooms, beige walls – they didn't want them white, white was too bold, too bohemian.

'Colours are so – so, well, colourful,' Mrs Pearson said, looking apologetic. They wore beige or beigeish clothes. The carpets throughout the house were beige and immaculate. Their three-piece suite was beige. In the corner a lustrous cheese plant flourished, shinily, almost defiantly, green. Megs could see that its vibrancy pained Mrs Pearson. But there was nothing she could do to mute it down. The only other thing that stood out against all this blandness was their son, Frederick. Called, to his mother's deep displeasure, Freddy by his chums.

In the midst of all this blandness Fred, the teenager, was surprising. His jeans were ripped, ears and nose pierced, his hair hung down rasta-style in long ringlets past his shoulders. There was a tattoo on his left forearm and a ring through his eyebrow. His Doc Martens dug into the perfect carpeting. He seemed at odds with his surroundings, vivid against his plain backdrop. Yet Megs could tell from his diffident, slope-shouldered body movements, his slow, uncertain eye contact and slight, gentle voice that underneath this rebellious exterior a nice boy lurked. In a couple of years he'd be beige like his mummy and daddy. No, the only rebel in the Pearson household was the cheese plant.

Mummy and Daddy Pearson roused Megs's suspicions. She suspected all this beige was a front. They seethed and raged secretly and did not know what to do about it. They hid behind their safe furnishings. Their bland clothing was a camouflage so they'd blend into their living room and nobody would know the turmoil within.

Mrs Pearson washed a lot. Not that she was often around when Megs was there cleaning, but when she was, she washed. Every twenty minutes or so Megs would hear the rush of the bathroom tap and the watery rustle of hands lathering. Mrs Pearson did not like bars of soap. 'Other people have been using them.' She used the liquid sort, from a bottle, camomile-scented. She washed, dried and then carefully, slowly softened her hands with cream. Twice a day she changed the towels. She insisted Megs disinfect the bath, then polish it.

'Polish it?' Megs questioned the order. 'Will that not make it slippy?'

'I like things shiny,' Mrs Pearson insisted. 'I like things neat and clean and shiny.'

The house was numbingly silent. Moving through it, Megs could hear her feet on carpet, or her begrudging exhalations when she bent to wipe the skirting board or remove from the rug a thread that defied the vacuum. It made her nervous. The Pearsons had a busy phone. Megs had strict instructions to let it ring if no actual Pearson was around to attend to it. Often Mrs Pearson stood by as it rang and rang. She'd stare at it and then at Megs. It seemed as if the perfect cleanness and shininess was being polluted by the noisy, vibrating thing. Megs got the impression Mrs Pearson would like her to scrub and polish the air round the phone, to wipe it clean of the insistent *tring-tring*.

Sometimes, when the silence, the blandness and grim tidiness became overwhelming, Megs gave in to screaming and shouting. It was then she addressed the Pearsons' living room. 'Hello, room,' she would say. 'How can people live like this, room? A lifeless life. This is me. And look,' opening her shirt, 'here's all of me. Tits, room. Tits. Haven't seen the like of that before, have you?' She'd put on a favourite blues tape, brought with her specially, Howlin' Wolf, Muddy Waters or the Allman Brothers, and turn up the volume till the ornaments buzzed. 'Boogie,' she'd cry, shimmying over the carpet. 'People do this, room. In the world out there, where colours are allowed, people dance. They play loud music and show themselves to one another. Have that, room.'

'Mrs Pearson.' Megs shook her head, describing the woman to Lorraine. 'Now there's a woman who has never even got within spitting distance of an orgasm.'

'Do you think that's her problem?' Lorraine wanted to know. Other people, even those she hadn't met, fascinated her as much as they did Megs.

'Probably. I don't think she enjoys anything. It hasn't occurred to her that she could. That, and she spends her life walking carefully. She and Mr Pearson walk carefully round each other, calling each other Madge and Don, saying names whenever they can. Reminding each other that they're there. They're treading softly, scared of what they are inside. As if they've seen it once and can't bear it.'

Mrs Terribly-Clean Pearson was an insomniac. She sat up at the kitchen table drinking weak tea, eating digestive biscuits, and often as she sat alone in the silence and chill, she cried. Megs knew this because there were four cups to wash in the morning and only three Pearsons. And Mrs Pearson's dressing gown pocket always contained screwed-up tissues. Once there had been a book Mrs Pearson was reading left open on the table, with damp drops on the page. Besides, Megs knew the symptoms. Here she was facing forty and she couldn't remember when she had last seen it through the night. She sat up at the kitchen table, too. Watching strange night-time television programmes, too. Cried sometimes, too.

'Have you been sitting up half the night again?' Vivienne accused that morning when she popped in for a cup of tea. They were a popping-in sort of family.

'Yes,' said Megs. 'How did you know?'

'The state of you. Baggy-eyed and look at the cups. Do you have to use a fresh cup every time? Could you not just rinse out the one and fill it again?'

Megs shook her head. Staying up half the night was bad enough. Staying up and being tidy was unthinkable.

'Why do you do it anyway? Why can't you sleep?'

'I'm scared.'

'Scared? Nonsense. What are you scared of?'

'Life. Getting old. I'm getting on. I have no prospects and no pension scheme. What's going to happen to me? One day I'll be old. I'll have nobody. The children will be gone and I'll be alone. I'll wear the same baggy cardy day after day. I'll shuffle on my walking frame down to the corner shop for a couple of slices of ham. And I'll shuffle back with them and I'll sit at this table eating them with some peas. Chewing them with a shaky jaw. Staring at the wall. And the house will be silent, and when I'm done I'll wander through empty rooms. Furthermore, I hate peas.'

'Goodness' sake, Megs. Stop it. The rubbish you talk. Stop it,' Vivienne said. The description had set up a chill in her heart. A dread she had not examined, far less come to terms with. 'Old age doesn't have to be like that. You keep yourself busy. Like me . . . I'm sixty-three, you know. And you don't have to eat peas if you don't like them.'

Hundred-Miles-An-Hour had one thing in common with the Pearsons. He was honest. Like the Pearsons he did not hide his life from her. Just-Keep-It-Above-the-Dysentery-Line McGhee and Emotionally-Deranged Davis both shoved their mess, shame, secrets, truth – old shoes, underpants, dirty plates, carry-out trays, magazines, bank statements – their lives, in fact, behind the sofa before she came, as if she wouldn't find them there. As if she had not been hired to clean behind the sofa along with the rest of the house. They were out-of-sight-out-of-mind people.

Giving Up On Ordinary

The pile of dishes in Hundred-Miles-An-Hour's kitchen had grown since her first visit. She turned on the tap and sighed hugely. No hot water. She looked in his cupboards and under the sink. Another sigh. There was nothing to clean with. No cloths, no washing-up liquid, no polish, no scourers, nothing. 'No stuff.' She sighed again.

She went upstairs, lumbered upstairs, stamping as she went, arms dangling by her sides, heaving in her breath. Boring, boring, this was boring. She stripped his bed, gathered towels from the bathroom, shoved everything into a selection of carrier bags, switched on the water heater and went to the laundrette. Medium wash with conditioner, she'd come back to put everything in the drier. Meantime she bought some washing-up liquid, polish and other cleaning things and went to do his dishes.

She walked the long terrace back to Gilbert's house, watching her feet move over the paving slabs. The very pavement here was classier than the pavement outside her own flat. Russian vines thrust up from basement plant pots, waterfalled vibrantly over the railings. She could peek into ground-floor living rooms, elegant high-ceilinged places, and could not imagine anything ordinary happening in any of them. If she did not come to clean, she would never enter any of these rooms. She would be outside, in her old suede jacket, nose pressed against the window panes, watching the beautifully lit, mannerly doings of the people who lived here. If she lived here, she would not worry about Lizzy playing on the pavement outside. Then the Botannical Gardens were only a step away. They could go there, walk hand in hand, Lizzy and her, reading the names of plants, touching leaves. Birds sang. Magpies, long tails trailing, flew on missions to raid dustbins.

Gilbert's house was on two floors. It had a large, elegant drawing room on the upper floor, a study and two bedrooms. Downstairs there was his much-used messy living room, a third bedroom and a bathroom. All those rooms for just one person, and in a crescent where cars purred politely past. Megs envied him.

Three-quarters of an hour later she returned to the laundrette, moved his damp bundle of sheets and towels to the drier and went back to his house to clean his bath and hoover his floors with her own vacuum cleaner. Then grumpily back to the laundrette, collect stuff and back to the house to make up the bed and drape clean towels in the newly clean bathroom. After that she dusted, wiped, gathered newspapers into bundles, emptied the kitchen bin and made an attempt at the kitchen floor. It was after three. She phoned her mother.

'Could you collect Lizzy from the nursery? I won't make it. There's more to do than I thought. It's filthy here . . .'

Gilbert came home, and shutting the front door caught these last words. He walked stiffly past her down the hall, wheeling his bike, a slow tick, tick, tick, said nothing. His hair was sticking up.

She worked on for another hour. Before she left, she found Gilbert in his study.

'I'll be off then.'

'Oh, all right.' He did not turn to look at her.

'Do you want me to take your old newspapers to the dump? I pass it on the way home.'

His newspapers? How dare she? They were his. There was an article on the new Chinese cinema somewhere in that pile, and a piece about an exhibition of French landscape paintings that he hadn't yet got round to. 'There are things I want to read in them,' he huffed.

'Ah.' She nodded. 'You'll have been planning to read them for some time. Some of them are five years old.'

'Nonetheless.' Stiffer now. 'I've left your money in an envelope on the kitchen table.'

'Righto, then.'

Sniffing disdainfully, he said, 'You've made my house awfully smelly. It smells of chemicals in here. I don't like it at all.'

'It's cleaning stuff. Would you prefer I did everything with cold water and elbow grease?' Looking scathingly round, 'It'd take a while.'

'No, of course not. I would, however, prefer it if you didn't use my phone. You said you wouldn't do drastic things to my phone bill. I trust it wasn't your brother in Melbourne.'

'It was my mother. I had to get her to collect my daughter from nursery. It took longer than I thought to clean up here. I had to go to the laundrette and buy washing-up things. I didn't want Lizzy hanging about on her own.' She glared at him, hot red spots flushing on her cheeks.

'Oh.'

'I'll go then. You owe me for the laundrette and the chemicals,' that last said with stinging sarcasm. 'I'll get it next week.'

'Right,' quietly now.

She took her vacuum cleaner and left. She was the sort of person who bought a vacuum cleaner for function not design. She was the sort of person who scrubbed and polished and bustled. She made vulgar smells in his home – crass lemon-scented abrasive things. She felt insensitive. And foolish with it. He watched her carrying her cleaner down to the path to her car. He had not considered she had a child to care for. He felt he was a boor, an insensitive boor. And filthy with it.

Megs drove home staring vilely through the windscreen, repeating, 'Smelly. Smelly. Smelly.' Over and over. A fine bile and bitterness brewed within her. 'Smelly. Smelly. Stupid bugger.'

The things she should have said to him rattled round her head. She longed to drive back, hurtling through the traffic, screech to a halt at his door and burst in on him yelling, 'Ripe nappies. Mushy things at the bottom of the fridge. A decaying hamster corpse amongst training shoes under the bed. Smells. In your precious life you know nothing. I'll show you smells.'

When she got home she was seething and slammed the car keys down on the kitchen unit. Her children were seated round the table eating ham salad and chips her mother had prepared, and stopped to watch her.

'How did it go?' her mother asked.

'Awful,' Megs sulked.

'Awful? Can't be that bad. Can it?'

'He says I made his house smell.'

'Smell!' the children cried in unison. This was their sort of conversation.

'Smell?' Vivienne was horrified. 'Smell? You?'

As far as she was concerned there was nothing worse than smelling. In terms of vileness she ranked it alongside homicide and rape. A deal of her adult life had been devoted to the eradication of all sorts of dubious aromas. One of Megs's abiding childhood memories was of her mother standing in her living room looking manic, sniffing wildly first facing north, then wheeling round, facing south, saying grimly, 'There's a smell in here. A definite smell.' She could set small crowds of people guiltily heaving air deeply into their nostrils in unison, saying, 'Yes. Yes. You're right. Old fish, anchovies type thing.'

'Yes. I made it smell of chemicals. Vim, Flash – the stuff you use to clean with,' Megs confessed. Then, still enraged at her own ineffectualness in dealing with his absurd accusation, she wheeled round on her children, spread her arms and shouted, 'Stop listening. This has nothing to do with you. Eat, eat.'

'Stupid man,' Vivienne scoffed. 'What does he expect his house to smell like?'

'Oh.' Megs gave a cynical wave of her hand.

Her mother folded her arms, pursed her lips. Here she goes, she thought.

'He'd probably like it to smell of lavender polish blending gently with wafts of fresh dark coffee brewing and bread baking in the kitchen. He'd like his bathroom to smell of gentleman's lime cologne and his bedroom to smell of freshly ironed Irish linen. Just so long as he doesn't have to do any of the polishing, brewing, baking or ironing. Stupid shite.'

'There's no need to swear.' Vivienne swore regularly herself but felt it her duty to stop those around her from doing it too.

'There is every need to swear,' said Megs. Then, sharply, to Jack, Hannah and Lizzy, who were still ignoring their food, listening to her expound, 'Don't let that food get cold. Eat, I tell you.' Turning to her mother she continued, 'You should see him. His face is florid. Booze, I thought at first. But now I've got a look at it again, I can see it's flushed with privilege. He comes from generations of beef-eaters. His cheeks are coloured pinkish, and he is arrogant. Not like us pale, wan serfs. Our faces are white, and we are stunted from the thin gruel our forebears ate.' She picked up a chip from Lizzy's plate and wagged it at her mother before stuffing it into her mouth. 'We come from poor stock, our shoulders are hunched, our bones brittle and malformed . . .'

'I beg your pardon,' Vivienne barked. She was enraged. 'Cheek of you. Pale and wan. Years of eating thin gruel.' She pointed a furious accusing finger at Megs. 'You have never eaten gruel in your life. You should learn to watch your tongue, my lass. You always go too far.'

Megs shrugged. 'He's a meat-eater and arrogant.'

'You ate meat. Beef stew with parsley dumplings. Roast chicken. Burgers. Lamb on a Sunday. Or pork. There was nothing wrong with the way I fed you. Gruel indeed.' Incensed, she stormed from the room and started to clear up. Tidying shoes and papers. Taking coats from where they'd been abandoned draped on the back of the sofa and hanging them on the hall stand. Bustling in a furious, don't-meddle-with-me way.

'Bacon and eggs. Sausages. Apple crumble.' She appeared at the kitchen door. 'Jam sponge with custard.' She disappeared again. They could hear her moving about the house, clearing and wiping. Working up a rage.

'Look at what you've done,' Lizzy said. 'She's in a bad mood.'

Megs said nothing. Why didn't she watch what she said? She spoke then she thought. Wrong order. But then she thought no matter what she said she would anger her mother. Their relationship was edgy. Megs could not recall a time when it had been any other way. Megs always felt inadequate in her mother's presence. Her life was never organised enough. Her house was never quite clean enough, her standards never high enough whatever she was doing. Wiping the sink. 'That's never clean.' Naming the dog. 'Shameless. You can't call him that. Imagine standing in the park shouting, "Shameless. Shameless." You'd feel daft.' Choosing a husband. 'You're not marrying him, are you? No good will come of it.' Losing a husband. 'I won't say I told you so. But I told you so.' They seemed doomed to bicker and sigh at each other.

'Fish pie,' her mother yelled from the other room. 'Macaroni cheese with bacony bits in. You used to love that.'

Chapter Four

Dave Roberts's office at the Glass Bucket was small and claustrophobic. A little room at odds with itself. Plainly, the man and his vision of himself did not fit within these four walls. The immaculately cut, soft-shouldered suit, still in its dry cleaner's wrapping, hanging on the back of the door; the computer, fax and palm seemed uncomfortable against the plain, time-stained mushroom walls.

The newly acquired electrical goods sat uneasily on a table made reliable with a paperback copy of *The Day of the Triffids* shoved under one of the legs, and on his chipped metal desk with drawers that rumbled open, clanged shut, under the gruelling glow of a long, fluorescent tube. They were perfect, gleamy things waiting, like Dave was waiting, for this place to smarten itself up for them. Then their proper life could begin.

Backstage at the Glass Bucket was a corridor lined with empty crates and beer casks where the band sat eating carry-out curries before starting work. There was a small, mirrorless lavatory and washroom that on lucky days had actual hot water. So it was in Dave's office that Megs made last-minute repairs to her hair and make-up.

She propped a mirror on his filing cabinet and stared at herself a moment. Her make-up routine was always the same. Didn't take long. She'd worn the same face for years. She moussed her hair, layered on mascara and grey eye shadow and, pouting at her reflection, coloured her lips pale brown. She considered her profiles, left first, then right, and ran her fingers through her hair. 'There,' she said at last, 'that's her.' As if she had created a new person. As if the woman who sang Friday nights at the Glass Bucket was not the same woman who went out cleaning five days a week.

She turned to go and saw the letter lying on Dave's desk. Unusual – for he was an immaculate man who kept everything in its place. Every night, Dave filed all letters and invoices and locked his filing cabinet. He polished his desk, watered his palm, and ran a clean yellow duster over his beloved fax and computer. He emptied his blue plastic waste-paper bin. He kept his affairs, business and personal, in perfect order. So perhaps it was the strangeness of spotting a ripple of disorder from the immaculate one, a rare chance to catch an insight into Dave's life that made Megs pause on her way out the door and pick up and read the letter.

It was written on thick pale-buff paper with a dark-green embossed letterhead. It said expensive. It was from a firm of architects and interior decorators, Ian and Myra Donaldson and Partners.

Dear Dave,

A note to thank you informally for the contract. It means a lot to us. I can't tell you how excited we all are at the prospect of being involved in the revamping of the Glass Bucket. Doesn't the old place need a facelift?

I'm sure you won't regret your decision to go with us.

We'll have plans for the renovations, including the removal of the stage and installation of a disco unit, ready to submit to the council next week . . .

Megs's heart tumbled. She read no more. Replaced the letter and left. She walked down the corridor, saw Dave coming towards her. She knew her dismay was showing on her face and couldn't move her lips into a smile, couldn't hide her shock.

'Dave,' she said as they passed.

'Megs,' he replied. They looked at each other – a lingering bit of meaningful eye contact. He knows I know, she thought. Yet she could say nothing about it, for then she would give herself away. I have been snooping, she confessed to herself. She realised then that he'd left the letter out deliberately, knowing she'd look at it. Knowing she and the band would voluntarily leave rather than lose their jobs to a disco machine.

That's it, then, she thought. Soon I'll only be a cleaner. The singer's for the chop. And she had always sung, all her life.

'We are the last of the singers,' Aunty Betty would say when she and Megs were working in the kitchen of the Seaview Guest House. 'We sing for singing's sake. People don't do that any more. Not like they used to in the old days when the world was still in black and white. Then people sang things like "When the Red Red Robin Comes Bob Bob Bobbin' Along".' She sang, demonstrating, with expansive arm movements, the bobbin' of the robin. 'Now though,' she lamented, 'they sing recordings. Everything's in colour and everyone wants to be a star. They know the drinks stars drink, the clothes stars wear and the exercises stars do to take their bodies to stardom. So they sing like stars. They have pretend microphones, play air guitars, and when they sing they also do the backing. I can't get no satisfaction, doo, di, doo di doo doo. Not the same. There's no innocence there.'

Aunty Betty was keen on innocence. 'We were happy back then,' she'd say, 'in the golden days before hygiene and cholesterol.' An era she pined for. The world, according to Aunty Betty, was not what it once was. People were not as happy as they once were. They no longer sang out loud. Window-cleaners and milkmen no longer whistled in the street. She blamed this loss of happiness on what seemed to her, at least, society's sudden discovery of hygiene and cholesterol. 'We were perfectly happy and healthy when we didn't know about them,' she'd say. 'People sang. Women sang as they cleaned their houses. People sang at work.'

It was true, Megs thought. She remembered years ago, when she and Lorraine were Hannah's age, dreaming of Stevie Wonder. They sang his songs, 'You are the Sunshine of My Life' and 'Superstition', backing and all, arms linked, as they walked the small route through school from French to chemistry. A cappella teenage angst. Lovely.

Tonight, as she sang, she scanned the faces in the Glass Bucket. Over the years they had changed. Familiar faces appeared week after week, Friday after Friday. But some had disappeared. And new ones taken their place. Young faces. These fresh faces did not gather round the small raised platform where she performed, preferring instead to stay at the bar, chatting and drinking. They were young. They had money. They did not want to listen to her youth. They wanted to drink and flirt and do their Friday-night thing to their own sounds.

This noticing of changing faces and haircuts was not new to Megs. In those years of standing before crowds, styles changed. She'd noticed trousers narrow and hair shorten. The sound she heard pouring from passing cars and shopping malls, roaring in pubs, stopped being young and cheeky, became raw and angry. She loved it. Mike hated it.

'We should do stuff like that,' she said, excited by its primitive energy.

'It's rubbish,' Mike dismissed her. 'We wouldn't demean ourselves. It'd be the end of us.'

'It'll be the end of us if we don't,' she said.

'Crap,' he spat and walked off. Now she realised he hadn't changed because he couldn't. Change scared him then, and it still did.

She sang U2, 'With or Without You' and 'I Still Haven't Found What I'm Looking For'. Then, when in the middle of her Bryan Ferry version of 'Smoke Gets In Your Eyes', Frank, the sax player, stepped forward to do a solo, she danced.

When she was little Megs had an invisible friend, Lonnie. She knew exactly what he looked like – dark curly hair, blue eyes. He went everywhere with her, sat beside her at the dinner table, agreed with everything she said. Perfect friends, they rarely argued.

Now she danced with an air man, the perfect partner. She curved her arms round him and they moved in time to the song, dipping and twirling. She loved to dance with her air man. He would never let her down. Not like Dave Roberts with his letter.

She saw him standing at the bar, watching her. He'd changed into a fresh shirt and tie and the suit that had been hanging on the door of his office. She watched him pull his cuffs down the jacket sleeve and brush some imagined something from his trousers. Preening.

Look at him, thought Megs. Three hours ago he was spotless, creaseless. Not a wrinkle in his pants, knife-edge sleeves on his shirt. Now look at him, spotless, creaseless. Knife-edges on his sleeves. And look at me. Make-up melted, lipstick licked off, my skirt all wrinkly round the bum. I guess some people are born to be creaseless. We should simply lie in their shadow, let them pass. We are not worthy, creaseless one. She hated him.

'"God Bless The Child",' she said to the band.

'I don't think so,' said Frank. He was tired. He worked in a garage fixing cars, starting at eight in the morning till five in the evening. Then straight to the Glass Bucket to play till after eleven. He was tired. He wanted to go home.

'Oh yes. I think so,' said Megs.

'The boss won't like it.'

'Exactly,' said Megs. 'If you won't do it, I'll do it alone.'

She started to sing unaccompanied. Everything stopped. Even the new faces turned to watch and listen. Her voice cut through the smoke- and booze-laden room. The till did not chime. Silence. No clink of glasses, no hum of conversation. Dave glared at her, slowly drummed his stubby fingers on the bar, an elaborate gesture of irritation.

Now he really knows I know, Megs thought. And she cursed herself for her weakness. He knows I've been spying on his life, reading his mail. She soared easily into the second verse and the band came up behind her, drifting sorrow. When she'd done she ignored the applause. Dave came across the room and gallantly held out his hand to help her step from the stage. 'Two months,' he said. 'We close for renovations in two months.'

She met his eye. She would not let him see how afraid she was of losing her singing persona, of becoming just a cleaner. 'There you go, then,' she said brightly, as brightly as she could manage. 'Two months.' She turned and went to sit with Lorraine and her husband, Harry.

'What was that all about?' Lorraine asked.

'Oh, nothing,' said Megs.

Oh, nothing. Lorraine knew oh, nothing when she heard it. It meant oh, something. Usually something dire. Megs would bottle it up till she ached. When the ache became intolerable, that something dire would come tumbling furiously out. Meantime, she fixed Megs with a long, knowing stare.

Wincing, Megs stared back. 'Oh shut up,' she said.

'I never said anything,' said Lorraine.

'Shut up your thoughts.'

301

'If only I could,' Lorraine said quietly. 'If only any of us could. How happy we'd be.'

'Yes,' sighed Megs. 'I know. Let's get horribly drunk and do silly things.'

'Alternatively,' Harry joined in the conversation, 'let's not.' Obviously he had firm ideas on the subject of getting horribly drunk and silly, and the man was not for turning.

'OK,' agreed Lorraine. 'Let's not.' She smiled at him.

They are in love, thought Megs. How ghastly of them. She drank slowly, letting the ice cubes move past her lips and chink against her teeth. She watched Lorraine wrap her fingers around Harry's. They had been married for years. Years and years, Megs thought. I was bridesmaid.

'You two have been married forever,' she said. 'When was your wedding?'

'Don't ask.' Harry waved her question away. He looked down into his glass, refusing to meet Lorraine's tipsily adoring gaze. Megs noticed, and wondered if, perhaps, it was only Lorraine who was in love.

'Our wedding was back in the golden days before hygiene and cholesterol, as Aunty Betty would say,' Lorraine offered.

Megs put her elbow on the table, chin in cupped hand, and tried to chase her encroaching depression away with songs in her head. She hummed a little snatch of 'Maggie Mae'. A crass and unsubtle choice since it was about an affair between a boy and an older woman. The poet Lorraine had run off with, her one big adventure, had been sixteen years her junior.

'Sixteen years,' Megs said to her. 'Doesn't it shock you that you're old enough to have someone in the world functioning – smoking and drinking legally, having sex – who is sixteen years younger than you?'

'I love him,' Lorraine said. So she left Harry and her job and climbed into her poet's yellow Mini with its clutter of jackets and boots on the back seat and drove off into the sunset.

To Bristol actually. There they stayed in a squat with a rock musician, a mime artist and a girl called Tasmin who was studying astrotherapy. They lived on brown rice and Guinness. Or so it seemed to Lorraine.

302

'It was wonderful,' Lorraine sighed. Then, sensing Megs's disbelief. 'Well, at first. Then I got indigestion. I mean, how much brown rice can a person my age take? My system isn't up to it. I need things – wine, chocolate. You know. Prawns in garlic and lime butter, peppered steak, crispy duck in black bean sauce, red jelly with hundreds and thousands . . . um.'

'Chips?' suggested Megs.

'Chips,' Lorraine enthused. 'Those little crispy ones at the bottom of the bag all salty and vinegary. I mean . . .' realising she had enthused perhaps a little too loudly, too long, '. . . what's the damn use of being a poet, writing all that poetry, and never mentioning chips?'

'I've always wondered about that,' agreed Megs. 'All that stuff by Byron and Keats at school. Not a chip there.'

'Exactly.' Lorraine nodded. 'Brown rice indeed.' She envied her poet his youth and his digestive system. 'How could he? And there's proper beds with duvets, and chairs and carpets. A person gets to a certain age and needs certain things.'

After a month Harry had turned up at the door of the squat. 'I think it's time to come home,' he said. Lorraine did not argue. She packed her bags and within ten minutes was sitting by his side, leaning back in his Ford Sierra. After insisting he stop at a motorway caff for chicken, bacon and chips followed by apple pie and ice cream, she had slept and cried alternately all the way home.

From the sweet distance of her third vodka Megs watched them. Remembering how Harry had, at the time, forgiven Lorraine everything, and thinking now she could say something to salvage what looked like a floundering relationship, Megs said, 'You are a nice man, Harry. A really nice man.' She was thinking about her air man, dance partner. She thought if she had stuck with an air man things would have been fine for her. Then, she thought, why leave it at an air man? If she had an air mother and air children her life, her dilemma, would be so much more manageable.

'Time to go.' Harry stood up.

'Already?' Lorraine protested. 'Why?'

'Megs has just said I'm a nice man. She's going to get maudlin. Time to go.'

'It will be nice to get home,' said Megs. She was longing to lie

303

down. To be alone in bed, horizontal and warm, in a darkened room, and consider her life. Better yet, to be horizontal and warm in a darkened room and not consider her life.

Chapter Five

At home, alone, she moved through, listening to, her darkened flat. The fridge hummed and clicked in the kitchen. If she stood in the hall she could hear her children sleep: Jack's flat snoring, Hannah's sighs and Lizzy's small moans and childish mumblings.

What will become of me? she thought. What have I done to myself to get to here? How did this happen? When she became a cleaner it never occurred to her that when people looked at her a cleaner would be all they saw. It isn't what I saw when I looked at me, she thought. What do I do? she asked herself. I bustle and crow. I fuss and boss. If I wipe the sink so hard my whole body shakes from elbow to bum with the vibrancy of my wipe, and if I shout the odds loud enough, boss my children hard enough, I can just about blot out the demons. The doubts and fears.

She went to the living room and switched on the television, sound down, and sat amidst its glimmer and flicker. On screen young people in absurd clothes were dancing. Every time they saw the camera watching them they pulled insane faces and waved. They were frantically going through the motions, putting on a show of having a good time. But they are only bustling and crowing, she thought.

Yet she had always been relatively happy with what went on in her head – her observations of other people and their lives, her knowledge of music and plants, her hopes and dreams for her children. But last week something happened. Such a little thing, but it stayed with Megs, rattling round and round inside her head with all the doubts, fears and guilts that kept her awake at night.

Mrs Emotionally-Deranged Davis published the details of her blustery life on a series of Post-It notes pinned to the fridge, her computer in the living room, the bathroom cabinet, the bedroom mirror and the headboards of the four children's beds, and anywhere else likely to catch the eye of those family members she was currently bossing.

'Veronica's veruca – 2.30 at the outpatients!' 'Clive's cello lesson cancelled this week. Doesn't mean you can stop working on the Dvorák.' 'Robert! We have dinner at Johnstones' on Friday, 8.00 sharp. Please remember the Shiraz gives her a headache.' 'Lucinda – that horrible boy phoned. Can't remember when.' 'The downstairs lavatory is not to be used – it's overflowing.' On the wine rack: 'Whoever has been drinking the South African white is grounded.' On the television: 'Not to be switched on till all homework is finished.' On the kitchen cupboard: 'I've counted the KitKats!' On the phone: 'Remember, children, I get details of the bill.' 'Sasha – tidy your room. Find your missing blue sock. Your piano lesson is on Tuesday this week. Your school report is diabolical.' 'Everybody! My PDK test was negative. We can breathe again.'

There it was, Mrs Emotionally-Deranged's autobiography written on yellow notes. The more deranged her life, the more strewn with yellow litter the house became. Julia Davis was a therapist. She was rarely home. Then again, she was omnipresent.

Last week when Megs was there, cleaning, Julia Davis was home supervising verbally. Lucinda was at the kitchen table working on her school project, the Russian Revolution.

'I have to write about Lenin,' she whined, sprawling across the table top, head lolling over her books. 'I don't want to. It's boring. I hate this.'

Mrs Emotionally-Deranged Davis slipped into parental preamble. Megs recognised it. She'd heard herself deliver similar ludicrous preachings when she felt her children were on the verge of failure and defeat. She noticed that her imaginings of her children as adults were two-dimensional. They would succeed or they would fail. They would live in gorgeous homes or they would embrace the gutter. She saw them grandly sweeping through cheering hordes to collect their Nobel prize, or she saw them in green stripy aprons grinning vacuously from behind a counter, asking customers if they wanted a happy hat today. When they did their homework it was glittering prizes here we come, when they sat sideways on armchairs, staring open-jawed at old Bugs Bunny cartoons, it was happy hats ahoy. They gave her hope and she feared for them.

'This isn't about the Russian Revolution.' Mrs Emotionally-Deranged Davis sounded pious. 'This is about you displaying your ability to amass and coherently relate information. This is about you moving forward and getting closer to achieving your goals. You get good grades for this and you are a step nearer to getting more good grades, which will eventually take you to the university you want, and the course you want, and, in time, the job you want, and the life you want. It starts here, at this kitchen table, doing this project.'

Oh, heavy, thought Megs. Emotionally-Deranged Davis was being plagued by images of her daughter dishing out happy hats. Megs did not have to look round. She knew Lucinda would be slumped, chewing gum, staring away from her mother, silently mouthing, 'Shut up. Shut up.'

'I hate Lenin,' Lucinda moaned. 'I hate him. Why did he have to go and start that sodding revolution? If he hadn't I wouldn't have to sit here doing this. Why do I have to know his real name? Difference does it make?'

'It was Ulyanov,' said Megs. She was quoting from Hannah's chewed, chocolate-stained picture book, *Twenty Men Who Changed the World*. She did not turn round or stop squishing lemon cleaner on the kitchen unit doors. 'Vladimir Ilyich Ulyanov. Born at Simbirsk, son of a maths and physics teacher.' She wiped furiously. 'He was the third of seven, though one died. Then again so did his older brother. He was hanged for taking part in a plot against the Tsar when Lenin was only seventeen. Changed his life.' She squished some more. Then paused. 'Lenin's,' she said. 'Not the brother's. Though it would his too, I suppose. On account of getting hung. But that's what got Lenin going. He'd had a comfortable middle-class life. No need to rebel, really. Then again, some might say every reason to rebel.'

She wiped more vigorously, aware of the squall of silence behind her. She knew they were pulling faces behind her back, exchanging astonished, well-fancy-that expressions.

'Goodness, Megs.' Emotionally-Deranged Davis made no effort

to hide her amazement. 'How did you know that?'

'Read it somewhere,' Megs said, not turning, wiping on.

During her singing years she'd sat in the back of the van and read endlessly – books, magazines, comics, the backs of cereal packets, the contents of a can of Coke, the instructions on Mike's condom packs, which she could quote verbatim to this day. She was not a discriminating reader. But information stuck.

Uninvited titbits of information still wormed their way into her brain. Her gleanings included tabloid newspapers, *National Geographic* magazines in the dentist's waiting room, her children's school books, battered cookbooks, old magazines, as well as the books her clients left lying around.

Incensed, she confided in Lorraine. 'It was so insulting. They just stood there gobsmacked. They didn't say, "Well, thanks for your help, Megs." And they just took the information, as if it was part of my job to give it. They seemed so surprised that I knew about Lenin. Why shouldn't I know? I get to know things. From my worm's-eye view from under my stone, I see things. It's allowed.' She knew she was starting to rant. 'Who do they think I am? Just the cleaner?'

Lorraine carefully put her mug of coffee down on the kitchen table and turned to look at Megs. 'Yes,' she said coldly. 'That's what they think. You are just the cleaner. They prefer not to really see you. Then when you show them there's more to you than they thought, it stops them in their tracks.' She tapped the table with a red-lacquered nail as she spoke. 'If you know stuff and cleaning's happened to you, then it could happen to them. They are not so safe as they think.'

'I am wedged in their minds as a small brown person who totes a yellow duster.' Megs winced at the thought, then heaved up her self-image, adding, 'They do not know they are dealing with the leader of the Bucketeers.'

For two years she'd been leader of the Bucketeers, the Glass Bucket quiz team. She regularly dazzled her children with the casual way she fielded questions on *Mastermind*. She mildly came up with answers from behind her newspaper or called them from the kitchen. They regularly came to her trailing homework notebooks.

'Hey, Ma. What was Schubert's first name?'

'Where's Zaire?'

'Who wrote *The Pit and the Pendulum*?'

She rarely let them down.

'You should be on television,' Lizzy said. Little squeaky pronouncement. 'Then you'd win a million pounds and I could have a rabbit.'

'A rabbit?' Her children always surprised Megs.

'Yes. If we had a million pounds I'd have a pair of red shoes and a rabbit.'

'We have nowhere to keep a rabbit,' Megs said. Stupidly.

'If we won a million pounds we could buy it a house.' Lizzy was scathing.

'Of course.' Megs conceded that housing rabbits was not a problem for millionaires.

So now she sat, three o'clock in the morning, staring glumly at the soundless flicker on television, feet tucked under the dog, and fought off her demons. Fear and guilt. She'd lost her singing job. She was just a cleaner. That was how people saw her. And she could not afford a rabbit.

She stumped through to her bedroom, and, on a whim, fetched her old shoebox full of photos from on top of the wardrobe. Clutching it, she slid into bed. She took out some photos of herself years ago and spread them on the duvet. There she was with the band, young, blonde and skinny. She was wearing jeans and a T-shirt with a marijuana leaf on the front. Mike was wearing a hat and grinning. She thought she looked desperate. At the time she'd been convinced she was smiling her best smile.

Wondering if she'd been giving off false signals all her life, she gathered up her memories and put them back in the box. Then she slid down under the covers. 'God, this is good. Prone is good. I was born to be prone, Shameless. Prone suits me.'

She tried to sleep, but ghosts haunted her. Dave Roberts with his perfect suit and his grim smile. He did not think much of her, she knew that. Mrs Emotionally-Deranged Davis and her surprise at Megs's small show of general knowledge. What did Julia Davis think of her? Plainly not a lot. Hundred-Miles-An-Hour, with his flushed face and his distaste for chemical smells. Him and his vacuum. They didn't think much of her.

'We are defined by how old we are, what we look like and where we live. Shite to the lot of you,' Megs called out, chasing off her ghosts. 'Megs is thirty-nine, looks like shite and lives in a second-floor four-roomed flat in Edinburgh. That's all, folks. Good night to you and good night to me. Sod you all. Sod you all. There's more to me than that. I just have to find out what it is.'

She turned over and pulled the duvet up over her head, hoping sleep would come to her. The dog lay on the floor, waiting till the sound of her breathing became heavy and rhythmic. Then he'd sneak on to the bed. In the morning she'd wake in a lather with small child pressed next to her and dog sprawled over her feet.

Chapter Six

'You were always an awkward beggar,' Vivienne said. She was sitting at Megs's kitchen table drinking tea. She meant bugger, but couldn't bring herself to swear in front of her daughter. 'Your father and me often say that.'

'Why?' Megs was indignant. It seemed her father's thoughts and opinions always came second-hand to her, through her mother. She had stopped communicating with him, but couldn't quite say exactly when. Now his wishes were passed on by Vivienne. 'Your father said.' 'Your father won't like this, you know.' 'Your father and me have decided.'

'First there was the business with your name,' Vivienne said. 'There is nothing wrong with Nina.' She shook her head as she spoke. 'Your father and I loved that name.'

Megs said nothing. Recently she'd been reconsidering her decision, taken all those years ago when she was five, not to answer to her given name. Nina was beginning to appeal to her, Megs was beginning to pall. She was feeling foolish for refusing to answer to a perfectly respectable name.

'Then,' Vivienne was warming to her theme, 'you went off with that daft band when you should have been studying. After that there was the cleaning job. And there have been lots of other things along the way, little things.'

'What?' asked Megs, knowing she shouldn't. Her mother's memory was long and horrifyingly accurate.

Vivienne leaned forward. 'There was that hat.'

Megs flinched inwardly. The memory she was dealing with was more than long and accurate, it was vicious. 'Hat?' She tried to sound innocent.

'That green-and-pink-striped hat I bought you when you'd had measles and were going back to school. It was January. It did you no good, no good at all, going out in the cold after the temperature you'd had. But oh no, you did not want to wear it. The fuss you made, crying and stamping your foot. Then you came home without it. It was a lovely hat, too.'

'I have no idea what you are talking about,' Megs lied.

Vivienne glared at her.

'For heaven's sake, you expect me to remember a hat? It was over thirty years ago,' Megs defended herself. She remembered it well. Who could forget such a hat – pink and green stripes with a pink bobble on top. She'd hated it. She could still recall the tantrum, lying on the floor drumming her heels, refusing to leave the house with it on. It was an object of derision. It lacked the sort of style a five-year-old needed to gain playground kudos. In such a hat she would be a mockery. And all her life Megs had known no mockery as fierce and furious as playground mockery.

Her mother had been adamant. 'The hat stays on,' she insisted. She dragged Megs, hat on head, to school. But as soon as she'd disappeared, Megs snatched the hated hat from her head and on the way home stuffed it up a drainpipe.

'Whatever happened to that hat, anyway?' Vivienne asked.

'Dunno,' shrugged Megs. 'Can't remember.'

'Oh yes you can. You can tell me now. What did you do with it?'

Megs looked distractedly out of the window. 'Lost it,' she mumbled.

'I don't believe you.' Vivienne looked at her indignantly. She always felt her good taste was threatened by Megs's rejection of the hat. 'I liked that hat. It was lovely.'

Megs was chagrined. She noticed she was staring at her feet and feeling vaguely sweaty with guilt. Her mother could still do that to her. She still couldn't own up about the loathsome hat. She changed the subject. 'I don't think I'm an awkward beggar.' They stared at each other, mother and daughter, across the chasm they'd created. They were separated by years, a hat and other lies.

Megs was twelve when Vivienne was diagnosed as having TB. In those days it meant a long stay in a sanatorium. Wrapped in a tartan dressing gown, Vivienne would lean on the huge windows, staring out at the grounds, longing for her daughter. The disease brought lines to her face early. She always thought of the hideous spores her breath might carry. She feared that kissing her family might have brought them danger. She rarely put her lips to theirs after she got home. Megs still remembered going to visit every Sunday, wearing her best coat and shiny black shoes with a buckle on the side. She walked the long drive holding her father's hand, huge and rough against hers. He did not say much.

When the disease was first diagnosed, Megs, her brother and father had to go for an X-ray, checking that their lungs were clear. The clinic was huge, chill and empty. Megs hadn't wanted to strip and stood huddled in her vest, clutching herself, refusing to remove it. Her father had smacked the back of her head. 'Get on with it. You're wasting the doctor's time.' It was the only time he ever hit her. It was years before Megs realised how distraught the man had been.

He could not afford to take time off work, so Megs was sent to stay with Aunty Betty. Her brother was old enough to stay home alone. It was summer, and there was a 'No Vacancies' notice in the window of the Seaview Guest House. It was a busy time.

Megs learned to love the smell of hotel breakfasts. She helped serve them. She would tour the tables, politely reciting the morning menu, porridge and kippers, bacon, egg and tomato, and nod with solemn approval of their choice. Cornflakes or krispies? Tea or coffee? Toast?

After breakfast she'd help wash up. As she dried plates and cups she listened to Aunty Betty's stories. There was no doubt in anybody's mind where Megs got her imagination and her vivid vocabulary. Aunty Betty spun tales of her youth. Those long-ago days seemed to her to be the golden age of Bakelite. She could recall vividly the glorious time people had in the years before cholesterol and hygiene. 'They could eat what they liked, no bother. Eggs, chips, butter. White sugar. There was nothing wrong with that stuff, then. And I can remember going to the newsagent's on the corner. There was a big black cat sat on the counter. On the rolls. We just lifted it up and took what we wanted and put it back again. There was no thought of us getting food poisoning. We'd have none of it.'

313

Every morning, before her breakfast recital, Megs would lie listening to the sea and the eiders that came round to coo on the rocks outside her bedroom window. After breakfast and washing-up she'd walk along the sands to the shows. There she'd stand breathing in the greasy air, chips and burgers, candy floss and hot dogs, listening to the Beatles booming out. Hits of the day. In the evenings she always wrote to Vivienne.

Dear Mum,
    I'm fine. The weather is lovely. Hope you're getting better. I'm enjoying being here. I help serve the meals. Aunty Betty says I'm a great help. Aunty Betty says there didn't used to be food poisoning in the olden days when she was young and butter was good for you then.

Vivienne did not see the letters as cheery nonsense from a lonely twelve-year-old. She read them from the depths, the blackness of the depression and anger, the fluctuating moods that came with her disease. Her daughter preferred her sister to her. But then everybody preferred Betty to her. Always had. Betty had always been taller, prettier, cleverer, more popular than her. Betty had the handsomest boyfriends. With a flick of her fingers, Betty could do interesting things with her hair. Betty chose the best clothes, and wore the reddest lipstick. Betty danced in her memories always laughing, always flirting. Vivienne sighed. She had always walked in her sister's shadow. She was small and would never be fabulous – like Betty.

Dear Mum,
    Aunty Betty lets me play her records. I like Duke Ellington best. And Ella Fitzgerald. When we do the dusting we sing stuff like 'With a Song In My Heart' and 'The Lady Is a Tramp'.

With a pang of jealousy Vivienne imagined Megs and her Aunty Betty in yellow frocks, flashing through the housework with an effortless waft of feather dusters, the sunny way Doris Day did – all freckly smiles and shiny songs. She thought they'd be having a wonderful time, and here was she, half a woman, with decaying lungs, in a blue-and-beige-striped winceyette nightie. Vivienne wept.

Dear Mum,

Aunty Betty can dance. She can do the tango and the foxtrot. She says she and Uncle Ron used to be the champions at the Salutation Ballroom. Aunty Betty says that dancing isn't what it used to be. She says that when she and Uncle Ron took to the floor everyone clapped . . .

'Aunty Betty says. Aunty Betty says. Aunty Betty says,' cursed Vivienne. Her condition made her despair. She coughed and spat. Every morning she had to hawk into a stainless-steel tray, her sputum test. She cried hopelessly, and never realised she was reacting to illness and drugs.

Of course it was true. Betty and Ron moved across the floor of the Salutation Ballroom in perfect harmony. They dipped, bobbed and twirled. Ron would lean Betty back and they'd smile to the small line of observers standing at the edge of the floor, dazzled by the show and hindered by their inadequacy from grabbing a partner and joining in.

Aunty Betty's records were thick and broke if you sat on them. Aunty Betty had a huge gramophone that could stack eight LPs and play them one after another. But Megs preferred to put them on one at a time. She liked the business of taking one record off, wiping it, putting it carefully back in its sleeve and taking out another. Megs played Count Basie, Glen Miller and Duke Ellington, and one day she discovered Billie Holiday. 'God hep the chile,' she sang, and it cut through Megs's childhood. This was what she wanted. She wanted to sing like that. More than that. She was on the turn, moving towards being a woman, and, like any sickening adolescent, she'd discovered the joy of being sad.

She was far from home and wanted her mum, who she feared was going to die. Nobody said it like Billie. 'God hep the chile.' She was a chile and she wanted God to hep her. She sat listening to that song over and over. It stopped and she put it on again, lifting the arm, replacing the needle at the beginning of the track. Over and over that song hummed and sighed through the Seaview Guest House

315

till Aunty Betty said that if she ever heard it again she'd scream. And all the summering guests, with their red and peeling faces, smiled grimly and said if they heard that bloody thing again they'd go somewhere else next year.

Dear Mum,
　　Aunty Betty says I can have her Billie Holiday record. Can we get a record player? Please. When I come home. I'll pay for it. Well, you pay for it and I'll pay you back. I am going to be a singer when I grow up. So there's no need for me to bother at school. I am going to sing the blues and rooms will stop at the very sound of my voice. It will cut through the night and break hearts.

Even then, all those years ago, Megs could weave a dream.

When this declaration reached her, Vivienne was at her window, wheezing in air. Imagining its cleanness cutting through the filth in her lungs. She threw the letter across the room. That sudden passionate swing of her arm pained her. She thought she'd never feel better. She'd been reduced to a slow, hunched shuffle that had more to do with her state of mind than her condition. She thought she'd never move across rooms with her old determined stride. She annoyed herself. The smallest undertaking, tying her shoelaces, putting on her bra, reading a magazine, exhausted her. She ached to get home. The intensity of this ache and the frustration at not being able to put her daughter in her place made her weep. She'd listen to the radio on the ward, the disc jockey played jolly tunes, beamed out bass sincerity, and she'd cry. Relentless tears kept coming and coming without her being able to stop them. Her sadness seemed like a tangible thing that followed her from day room to ward, morning and night. All that and she knew for sure she was useless.

　Walter came and went. The shifts he worked formed the rhythm of their lives – ten till six one week, six till two the next, two till ten the week after. Then back to ten till six again. Sometimes he slept in the visitor's chair beside her bed, whilst Vivienne cried. Sometimes he stood by watching not knowing what to do. He found her illness perturbing. It made her flushed and passionate.

'Can I bring you something?' he'd ask, his big hands dangling by his sides. 'Grapes?'

'No. No.' Vivienne dabbed her cheeks. 'Not grapes. Please not grapes.'

When he got home, Walter could not bear to be in the house. So he'd banish himself to his garden shed where he would, making a comforting whistling noise from between clamped teeth, sand things down, glue things together, tinker with things, arrange and rearrange his tools into neat rows and peer out of the window.

Vivienne had convinced herself that Megs preferred the swirling glee of the Seaview Guest House to the drab routine she offered her. When she came home Vivienne never told her daughter how she'd longed for her, and Megs never told her mother that she'd been afraid she would die.

Chapter Seven

'How long has my mother been saying she's sixty-three?' Megs asked. She put down the iron, stared into the distance, considering this,

'Oh God.' Lorraine thought about it too. 'Ages. Years and years.' She'd come round to tell Megs that Clark's Catering had phoned offering them both four hours' work, double time, tonight. 'Yes. Years and years. She's been sixty-three since goodness knows how long.'

'She's been lying.'

'That's not a lie. That's not lying about your age. That's making a legend out of it. We should take note. We should stay forty at least five years, then move on slowly from there.'

'Yes,' Megs agreed. She was ironing her waitress uniform – black skirt, white shirt, white apron – that had been lying crumpled and forgotten at the bottom of the clothes basket for the last two months. 'I don't know if I'll remember. You have to admire my mother for the blatancy of her deceit. Declaring the wrong age loudly by the day is magnificently upfront. She has risen in my estimation.'

'Your mother is OK,' Lorraine said. Then, idly, 'Pork sausages on wholewheat bread spread with mustard then topped with apple sauce. What do you think?'

'That's not bad. Sort of business lunch and workers' lunch at the same time. Yes.' She smoothed out the sleeve of her shirt. Added, 'My mother has her moments.' Admitting Vivienne had moments was as much praise as Megs was going to give. 'When do we have to be there?'

'Seven,' said Lorraine, bored already at the prospect of the evening ahead. 'It's a university dinner.'

'God. Hundred-Miles-An-Hour won't be there, will he?'

Last week Hundred-Miles-An-Hour had walked through his house, arms spread, looking beatific. 'This place is almost human.' He smiled at her. 'You really have made an improvement. I mean, look,' and he strode manfully across his living room, 'I can walk from place to place without tripping over things. And I can see out of the window. There's the garden.' He pointed in wonderment.

'Well,' Megs said. 'Sometimes there is only one way to go. Up. When things get really bad, improvement is all that's left.' She followed his gaze out to the garden. A small tangled area of dried overgrown aubretia and yellowed lawn. She had her eye on that garden.

'No. 'Course he won't be there,' Lorraine answered her. 'Anyway, it'll be over by eleven.' As if that automatically meant Gilbert Christie wouldn't go. As if he never stayed out as late as eleven.

'Home by twelve and up again tomorrow morning to go clean for Mrs Terribly-Clean Pearson. I can hardly wait.'

Across the room the television blared an early-evening quiz show. Hannah and Lizzy were at the kitchen table eating spaghetti, Hannah deftly twirling it round her fork, Lizzy sucking it strand by strand into her mouth, splattering herself with tomato sauce. Jack came in and handed Megs a shirt. 'Iron this, go on? I need it for school tomorrow.'

'What do you mean, iron your shirt? Iron your own shirt, why can't you? Who do you think I am, your mother?'

'Yes. I thought that was the deal.' Jack looked confused.

'Well, that's only because I gave birth to you. Ironing was not mentioned at the time. And, quite frankly, motherhood is not what it's cracked up to be. In fact, if you ask me motherhood is a ruse dreamed up by the Church of Scotland to stop women from . . . from . . .'

'From having orgasms,' Lorraine put in mildly.

Megs looked at her in astonishment. 'We are not in the habit of discussing orgasms at the dinner table,' she said.

'Might be more interesting than ironing,' said Jack.

'What's an orgasm?' Lizzy wanted to know.

'Lorraine will tell you,' Megs told her. She left them to it and went to sit heavily in front of the television, hoping something mindless was on. She got ten brainless minutes of game show before Lizzy came bawling into the room.

'The man at the shop told me to go away and never come back,' she was sobbing.

'Why on earth did he do that?' Megs asked, only mildly interested because across the room the game show host was smiling and asking the contestants if they wanted to stick with their thousand pounds, their colour television set, video and weekend for two in a luxury hotel or did they want to risk everything and go for the four-wheel-drive jeep with CD player, leather seats and electric sunroof. Megs looked at her semi-hysterical daughter, and thought she wouldn't risk anything, she'd take the cash, the electrical goodies and the holiday. Yes, she could do with some of that.

'Because he said I was cheeky. He said I was filthy rude and he's never going to serve me again.'

The game show players chose to risk everything for the jeep. Lizzy was hyperventilating, shuddering with shame. Megs kneeled down, put her arms round her and drew the child to her.

Lizzy threw herself on to her mother, sobbing and wailing. 'I'll never go there again. Where will I buy crisps? I'll have to walk for miles . . . and he didn't even give me the orgasms.'

'What?' said Megs.

'So for the thousand pounds, the television set, the video, the luxury weekend for two and the jeep, name these tunes . . .' The orchestra struck up 'Only the Lonely', 'Fly Me To the Moon' . . .

'"Only the Lonely", "Fly Me To the Moon",' said Megs, rocking the child. Then, 'Orgasms? You asked for orgasms?'

'Yes, Lorraine said they were sweeties with the yummiest filling ever, so I took the milk money from the tin in the kitchen to go buy some. I asked for half a pound of orgasms and the man chased me out. He said I was . . .' she sobbed, gathered her breath and howled, '. . . RUDE!'

The orchestra on the telly played 'Mountain Greenery', 'Dancing In the Dark' and 'Mack the Knife'.

'"Mountain Greenery", "Dancing In the Dark" and . . . Lorraine,' Megs shouted. She heard her friend rattling speedily down the hall. With child wrapped round her front, Megs ran after her. 'Lorraine

. . . LORRAINE!' The front door slammed shut. There was the desperate click of high-heel shoes taking the stairs at a dangerous pace. 'LORRAINE!' Megs yelled again. But her friend was gone. 'I'll get you for this,' Megs said softly. She walked back up the hall. The orchestra was playing 'Gone Fishing' then battered into 'Manhattan'.

'Oh,' cried Megs, still cradling the child and nursing the wounded ego, stroking the little head. Her shoulder was wet with tears. 'That's "Mack the Knife", "Gone Fishing" and "Manhattan". Aunty Betty used to love that.' She sang it, gently dancing across the room, moving back and forth. The child silenced. Thumb went into mouth, little eyes rolled up.

'I'll talk to Mr Hodges in the morning,' Megs whispered. 'It'll be all right.'

But Lizzy was sleeping.

'You got them all. You could have won all that.' Jack was impressed. 'A jeep you could've had. A new telly. A holiday. A thousand pounds. What would you do with it?' Cash always got him going.

'Dunno,' Megs said, sitting down, still cradling Lizzy.

'You could buy yourself pounds and pounds of orgasms with really yummy centres,' Jack mocked.

'Sod off,' Megs said, softly stroking her child's head. 'I'll get that Lorraine, I really will.' She clung to her baby. 'Did Lorraine let her go out alone? She never goes out alone. She's too young.'

Jack sighed, slumped his shoulders, exasperated with her. 'It's only yards. She won't get lost.'

'That's not the point. She had to cross the road. You know I don't like her crossing the road.'

'She has to do it sometime. You can't hang on to her forever.' Then into the heavy silence he said, 'She's not going to get run over.'

'She might,' Megs said quietly. She would never admit she was wrong.

'You have to let go,' Jack said.

'Sod off,' Megs sulked. 'It's bad enough ironing your shirts without you being smarter than me.'

'It's dead easy,' he told her.

'What is?'

'Being smarter than you. Especially when you hide from your

322

smartness.' He chewed gum as he spoke. Looked almost disinterested.

She didn't want to move. They hadn't spoke as much as this in months. 'What do you mean by that?' As if she didn't know.

He sighed. 'I mean you don't have to do the things you do. You're just punishing yourself for Thomas. You could do better than clean.'

She said nothing. If she wasn't so overwhelmed with pride that her son had turned out to be so astute, she might have smacked him on the mouth for his cheek. 'Maybe cleaning's all I deserve,' she said.

His young lip curled. He even stopped chewing. 'Crap,' he said. 'The only thing you ever taught me was that there was no such thing as deserve and no such thing as fair.'

'I taught you more than that.' Relieved to be changing the subject, 'I taught you to eat with a knife and fork. I taught you to tie your shoelaces. And to swim.'

'Anybody could've taught me that stuff – teachers, mates, mates' mums. Deserve and fair – that was you.'

They stared at each other. She knew he'd been thinking this for a long time and had been working up to saying it. He wanted more for her. Also, she suspected, he wanted more for himself than a cleaner for a mother. She searched his face to see if it was numb, like she thought hers had become. And she bit her lip lest she say something to him that would send him reeling into himself, never to be honest with her again.

He was taller than her. His face was forming, emerging a little more every day, it seemed, from its adolescent lumpenness. She had seen that face when it was tiny, tender, innocent, wrinkled and just minutes old. She had watched this boy develop. She could remember him at ten months old heaving himself upright by holding on to the sofa, one hand over the other. Then up, look at me. He'd turned to her. He was wearing little blue dungarees and a striped red and navy jumper. He'd smiled to her, wanting nothing more than her approval and touch. Arms outstretched he'd stepped towards her. His first step. She'd been there. She'd seen it. She wished she had a photograph. But no, she thought, she didn't need one. It was one of her moments, she had it clearly in her mind. It would stay there untouched, uncreased – perfect.

At last she broke the tension between them by handing Lizzy to him. 'Here. Look after your sister. I have to iron a shirt then go off to work. To work,' she said, 'to serve food to people who are all smarter than me.' She did not say that she knew he was right, and it was time she sorted herself out.

Chapter Eight

The tables were laid – starched gleamy-white cloths, glistening glass and polished cutlery. At the top of the hall, stretched broadside, was a long head table where the dignitaries and speakers would sit. It faced half a dozen more that stretched lengthwise to the door.

Megs was on table one. The nearest to the kitchen. Hundred-Miles-An-Hour sat halfway down, facing her as she served. Oh bugger, she thought, it's him. He stared hard at her, trying to place her. He was bad at recognising people out of context. Had Megs been wearing jeans and T-shirt and standing belligerently behind her vacuum, he would have known her immediately. He had come with a woman Megs didn't recognise and they sat opposite Just-Keep-It-Above-the-Dysentery-Line McGhee, who sat, back to Megs, with her weekday grey-haired man. They were ardently discussing design. Megs could hear the forceful thrust of their conversation above the babble and hum, chink and clatter of the other one hundred and ninety-six diners in the hall.

'Style has become incredibly important, almost absurdly so,' Dysentery McGhee said.

'Absolutely,' agreed Hundred-Miles-An-Hour.

Megs moved down the table, reciting, 'Lobster bisque? Melon with port? Terrine of fresh mushrooms?'

'Thing is,' the woman who was with Hundred-Miles-An-Hour said, 'we are so attuned to style statements we can at a glance make judgements on others just by noting the stripes, or lack of stripes, on the side of their training shoe.'

'Exactly,' said Dysentery McGhee.

Hundred-Miles-An-Hour watched Megs approach. Who was that?

Isla Dewar

How come he recognised a waitress? She seemed so familiar. Where had he seen her before?

'Lobster bisque? Melon with port? Terrine of fresh mushrooms?' chanted Megs.

'You become so aware of making the simplest of statements about yourself, even on ordinary trips to the supermarket,' the woman with Hundred-Miles-An-Hour said. 'One glance in my trolley and you know who I am. You know my demographic grouping. My class, my background, even, I suspect, my aspirations.'

Megs reached the group. 'Lobster bisque? Melon with port? Terrine of fresh mushrooms?'

Dysentery McGhee nodded furiously. 'Hmm. I'll have the bisque, please,' without turning. 'Porcini, anchovies, Chilean red, Pellegrino, spinach,' she enthused. 'Says it all.' She spread her hands at this revelation about herself. She was naked and unashamed. They all laughed. Ha. Ha. Ha. How many ways to tell a lie? With make-up. With clothes. With shopping trolley. Dysentery McGhee was master of them all. What a liar she was.

She may buy that stuff, but the woman lives on toast, yoghurt, microwaved Lean Cuisines and wine from a box, Megs thought. Oven chips, bumper size, she thought. Giant packs of cornflakes and toilet rolls – I dare not think what that says about me and my aspirations.

'Good design should be an integral part of all our lives. It should be everywhere.' Gilbert glowed. Several whiskies and half a bottle of Chablis before he left home, he was not as sober as he thought he was. 'We shouldn't even think about it. It should surround us. A spoon,' he pointed to the nearest object, 'for example is a spoon. We all have one. But why shouldn't it be a beautiful spoon? Consider the spoon.' His face reddened as he spoke. He felt enlightened. He was seeing a spoon for the first time in his life. 'In the culinary panoply it's almost a haiku in deconstructive utilitarian design. Its very ordinariness makes it beautiful.' He looked at his companions, making sure they were sharing his enthusiasm. 'Honed by centuries of usage into a simple shape. Like the blade of grass.' He leaned forward meaningfully. 'Who looks at the spoon?' He picked his up and looked at it. Saw himself reflected, club-nosed and concave. Hair sticking on end. Slammed it back on to the table. Why had nobody told him he looked like that?

'Lobster bisque? Melon with port? Terrine of mushrooms?' Megs broke, flat-toned, into his shock.

'Melon,' Gilbert said swiftly. Horrified by what he'd seen, he'd said the first thing he could remember her saying. He hated melon.

He noticed Megs looking at him. 'Who is that?' he asked Dysentery McGhee. 'I'm sure I've seen that waitress somewhere.'

Megs thought, I scrub his bath, change his sheets, wipe his sink and God knows what else, and the arse doesn't even recognise me.

Dysentery McGhee turned to see who he was talking about, but Megs had disappeared into the sweat, rattle and frenetic thrum of the kitchen.

The bisque came from vast catering cans, some rusting along the bottom. It was dolloped into pans, heated and ladled top-speed into bowls, wiped round the rim, decorated with a sworl of cream and hustled out to the tables. Melon was sliced wafer-thin – three slices each plate, one grape, one half-strawberry and one half-ladle port-flavoured fruit sauce spread in the curve of melon. The bisque was salty. Megs had sucked some off her thumb after carelessly grabbing a bowl. The mushroom terrines were not popular. Strange that, Megs thought, she'd had one and liked it. She would take some home to vegetarian Hannah, who, however, had protested foully when offered broccoli. 'I'm not a broccoli sort of vegetarian. I'm just a not-eating-sausages sort of vegetarian.'

Megs laid two melon plates on her arm, then one bisque in her hand, another in the other. Thus laden she headed for the door, kicked it open, held it with her bum and stepped backwards into the hall.

Dysentery McGhee had, at Gilbert's insistence, been watching for her. 'Megs!' she called. 'Good heavens, Megs. How wonderful. Come here and talk to us, Megs.'

Megs looked over and allowed a small smile to flicker across her lips. 'Hi,' she mouthed and with a nod of her head she indicated the top of the table where she was headed with her load.

'Of course, you can't come chat. You're carrying food. How gross of me,' Cathy McGhee scolded herself.

Megs noted sourly that she was wearing the favourite strappy shoes. Probably had a glass or three of that nice wine before she left, too.

'Bisque?' She looked brightly round.

'Here,' said somebody. 'I'm bisque, and she's a melon,' pointing to his companion.

What did I have? she grumped to herself. Lukewarm Nescafé, a wailing child, and a vague confrontation with my son. That he won. Something's not right. *I want to be happy* – the jolly song, transformed into a small dirge, moved uninvited through her brain.

Across the room, Lorraine was flirting outrageously with a mushroom terrine and a bisque. Megs could tell she had her eye on a bottle of South African white that was so far untouched. So had a couple of the wine waiters. But, Megs knew, against Lorraine they hadn't a chance. She and Lorraine would kill that bottle along with their mushroom terrines when they got home.

On her way back to the kitchen she gave Dysentery McGhee a passing wave, a ripple of fingers. She knew that when she took her bisque to her, Dysentery McGhee would take hold of her and patronise her. There was nothing she could do about it. She was doomed.

And she was right. As soon as the soup bowl hit the table, Dysentery McGhee turned and gripped Megs's hand in both of hers.

'How gorgeous,' she thrilled. 'Our very own waitress. You'll be able to advise us.' Then, seizing the opportunity, 'You'll be able to bring us extra-large portions.'

'Even better,' said Megs, 'I'll be able to bring you extra-small portions.'

Hundred-Miles-An-Hour smiled. Ah, Megs thought, didn't think he could do that. He thought he would welcome smaller portions. This melon was absurdly sweet.

Dysentery McGhee refilled her glass, did not bother with any of the others nearby, and drank deeply. Megs watched. Sometimes she thought Dysentery McGhee was even more screwed up than she was. And this puzzled her.

'You would think,' she said to Lorraine once when they were in Megs's kitchen, doing their Saturday-morning review of their week, 'that she has it all. A good job. A nice house. Furniture. Clothes. A car – a natty black two-seater. Lovers. Note the "s". More than one. No children. Still she's screwed up.'

'Maybe it's the no-children bit,' Lorraine offered. She couldn't conceive and always felt that was part of her own screwed-upness.

'No. She's the sort of person who thinks things through. If she hasn't children it's because she's thought about it and taken that decision. Me now, I never thought about it at all. I got all hormonal one night in bed. I was in the right place, and I had the means lying beside me. Nine months later, bingo, a baby. I never thought about it. That's my problem, I never think things through.'

'Well, you know women,' Lorraine said. 'Give us the perfect relationship, perfect home, perfect job, car, whatever, and we'll make a mess of it. If a woman has the perfect man, she'll wonder if some other man isn't more perfect. Or if life would be more exciting with someone less perfect. Or if she could hack it on her own without the perfect man. Or she'll discover she prefers women. Screwing up? Nothing to us. We can do it every time – speciality of the species.'

By the time Megs served the main course the conversation had turned to seriously considering trivia. Trivia, thought Megs, I'm good at that. Hundred-Miles-An-Hour, remembering his spoon eulogy, was squirming. The measure of his discomfort was showing in his flushed cheeks and sticking-up hair.

'Good heavens,' his companion was saying, 'we go over the top at nothing at all these days. Our sense of excellence is diminished. This is brilliant, that is wonderful. Soon they'll be handing out Pulitzer prizes for T-shirt slogans.'

'I know,' agreed Dysentery McGhee. Her weekday grey-haired man was looking groggy and working his way through a second bottle of red. Megs laid his glazed lamb before him and smiled. Not a lot of fun for Dysentery McGhee when she got home tonight.

As they ate the main course Megs stood with her back to the wall, a discreet sort of lean. She slipped her hot and aching foot from her shoe and pressed it into the cool tiled floor. The massed conversations of the diners merged into a frothing babble. She put her cooled foot back into its shoe, and gave her other foot a cooling on the tiles.

Blah. Blah. Blah, thought Megs. From deep within herself she watched these people. How they drank – you never saw them swig hugely from their glasses yet the wine went down, and down. How they ate – they did not launch themselves into their dinners. They raised their heads, and cooed, 'How lovely.' 'Oh, wicked.' 'Asparagus, I cannot resist asparagus. Mmmm.' Megs wondered if they tasted something she didn't.

'It's only a vegetable,' she said to Lorraine. 'And they're getting orgasms over it. What are they like in bed?'

They would cut things up neatly and put down their forks as they chewed. They looked deeply at whoever was talking and listened with apparent unshakeable interest to whatever was being said, no matter how boring. Mostly what was being said was boring. But women put elbow on table, chin in hand and looked riveted. How did they do that without yawning? Or saying, so what? Or, who cares? Megs wanted to know as she put hot foot number two into its shoe and gave hot foot number one another turn on the cool tiles.

Nobody spilled a drop on their posh frocks and nobody wondered what was number one in the charts this week or what had happened in any of the soaps. It was unreal. But who was she to criticise? They were all tucking into glazed roast lamb with dauphinoise potatoes, baby turnips, glazed carrots and petits pois. She was only here to serve the pudding. And a very fine pudding it was too. She'd already had a couple and there were three more in her bag to take to her children.

Gilbert leaned back in his seat, twirled his wine glass on the table and watched Megs. He thought that if he ever mustered the courage to give up his job, this day job of his, he would like to paint her. She had a comfortable face. It had done a deal of living, that face, expressions moved easily across it. He was beginning to like having Megs in his house. Mornings when she came to him, he would linger, pottering with his bike, filling, emptying, then refilling his battered briefcase before strapping it to the carrier behind his saddle. On Fridays he'd come home early. Hers was a calming presence, he liked to sit in his study and hear her moving quietly from room to room. If he came into the kitchen she would smile at him, and gently scold him for some domestic absurdity she'd discovered. 'I cleaned out that drawer on your kitchen unit. Do you know you had three hundred-and-seventy-five wine corks in it? You could lash them together, build a raft and sail off to France. Take them home.' Her tales revealed small glimpses of her home life. 'I averted a major domestic disaster yesterday. Jack was heating up a tin of tomato soup by putting it unopened in the oven. Could've blown us all up.' He was changing his mind about her, starting to like her.

There are sneezes and there are sneezes. Some sneezes are a long time coming and some take the body by storm. Hundred-Miles-An-Hour was listening to his companion, Annette, talking with passion about cultural renaissance. His hand was hovering at his forehead, fingers poised to run through his hair. And he sneezed. He had not known this horrific thing was going to happen. It was as if the sneeze was some external force that overwhelmed him.

'Aaaaah.' Head pushed back, mouth opened. 'Chooo.' Head flung forward. A single pea, still perfectly formed, burst from his mouth and bounced on to the table in front of him. He watched, horrified. Conversations stilled as diners followed the escapee pea's progress down the centre of the table.

Megs put hot foot number one back in its shoe and gave hot foot two its turn on the tiles. She looked at the floor. It did not do for waitresses to giggle. She sucked in her cheeks.

The table silenced. Gilbert Christie stared, mortified, at the pea that had come to a halt some way down the table. All eyes were on it. Round and ebulliently green against the pristine tablecloth. It shamed him. He did not know what to do about it. But he felt its glistening presence was an effrontery to the other diners. And he felt it was his responsibility, his pea. He rose, and muttering apologies to everyone he passed, he mumbled and grovelled his way towards it. 'Sorry. Sorry. 'Scuse me. Sorry.'

Megs watched. Gilbert reached the pea, and apologising profusely to the people directly in front of it, he stretched over and took it gently between finger and thumb. 'My pea,' he explained. Flustered, blushing deeply, he returned to his seat, where he continued to apologise as he wrapped the pea in his paper napkin and put it in his pocket. He was in hell. Megs knew a tortured soul when she saw one. Her heart went out to him.

Chapter Nine

'If only he'd eaten it,' Lorraine said. 'That'd've made my day.'

They were at the kitchen table finishing the procured South African white, eating mushroom terrines and discussing their evening. Shoes off, feet up.

'He'll be scared of peas for the rest of his life,' said Megs.

'Peaphobia,' Lorraine said.

'One day far from now,' Megs said, 'he'll get those trousers from his wardrobe and put them on. He'll put his hand in his pocket and feel the napkin. What's that? he'll think. And he'll draw it out. And there it'll be. The pea. He'll get all hot and bothered remembering. Poor soul.'

'Why poor soul?' Lorraine wanted to know. 'I thought you thought he was a snob. Face flushed with privilege, you said. You've gone soft on him.' She pointed an accusing finger.

'No. No. I haven't. I can sympathise. He was so embarrassed. I know what it's like when your body lets you down. I'd be fine if it wasn't for my body.'

Lorraine's face was unyielding. The accusation stood.

'Oh, come on.' Megs squirmed. 'He's not my type. Right now he'll be snuggled up with his woman.'

'You think?'

'Yes. And when I go to bed I've got Shameless.'

'You need a man. I think you secretly fancy Gilbert.'

'I do not.' Megs denied it.

'I think you fantasise about him. Actually, all that cycling he does. He's got a nice bum. Quite firm and nubby.' She made a bum-groping movement. 'What do you think he's like in bed?'

333

'I can't think. Probably sort of sweet and gentle.'

Lorraine thought about this. 'You don't think he's a secret spanker, then? His type often are.'

'How would you know?'

Lorraine looked into her glass. 'I just know. Some things you know. Some things I know.'

'And you know about spanking?'

'I know more about sex than you.'

'Well, I haven't had your affairs.'

'I just need to know I've still got what it takes. Oooh, did you see that waiter at table three?'

'No.'

'Yes you did. I saw you. I could do with some of him. You could do with some of that, too. Watch you don't become like Terribly-Clean Pearson.'

'I will not. I don't ever want another man. I wouldn't know what to do with one. I've left all that flirting and getting to know somebody and everything behind. I wouldn't even know where to start. Where would I meet somebody?'

'Advertise,' said Lorraine. 'In a lonely hearts column.'

Megs smiled. 'What would I say?'

'You're better at that sort of thing than me.'

'Those columns – they're all lies. I could tell the truth. "Lonely cleaner, three children and smelly dog, seeks uncritical lover to cook her meals, run her baths, massage her feet and split mortgage payments."'

'They'll be battering the door down.' Lorraine refilled their glasses.

Megs regularly read the soulmates column in Dysentery McGhee's paper. 'It's all people wanting other people to share theatre, walks and log fires with lots of wine and conversation. When do I ever get to chat to somebody? Or go to the theatre? Or lie in front of a log fire?' She smiled, sudden inspiration. 'Actually, I have thought what I would write. "Woman seeks chum. Any age, any sex, any size, any shape, any star sign, any colour. Simply must not use the word brill to describe anything. Ever. For any purpose."'

'That's not too much to ask,' Lorraine said. 'That's a brill advert.'

Aunty Betty always said that grief either ravaged women or it graced them. Megs had been lucky. Or at least, in the light of her tragedy, her face had been. Her lips did not fall into a bitter slit, her eyes were not bagged and rendered tearless from too much crying. Her face fell into a soulful sulk when she forgot her front and thought nobody was watching her. She was sulking now.

'I feel,' she said, 'that I don't belong anywhere any more. I've lost my place in the world. I don't understand what's going on. Right now a telltale computer is keying up the fact that I'm three months behind with my credit card. Nobody asked me if it could do that. People are sitting in on courses looking at flip charts, getting the gen they need to sell me soap powders and shampoos I don't want, and to get me to sit down and watch TV shows I don't like. I don't know what's going on. Whilst I was busy with my back turned bringing up kids, doing my crap jobs, the world moved on and left me behind. I'm old and I'm fat and I don't belong any more.'

Lorraine looked at her glumly. Considered this a while. At last she said, 'You're not that fat.'

'Suppose,' said Megs.

Lorraine leaned over and touched her hand. 'C'mon, girl,' she said. 'You got to get on with things.'

Megs smiled. She was numb with exhaustion. Her innards felt as if they were already sleeping. It was two in the morning. Outside occasional cars rattled by. Shameless, under the table, snored and shifted. She felt she had been isolated, standing alone with her grief whilst all around her rushed on with their lives. Her children grew up. Her mother retired. Lorraine danced, laughed, teased her husband, had odd affairs and sometimes leaned across the kitchen table, touched her hand, sympathised. 'C'mon girl. You got to get on with things.'

'What things?'

'Life. You know.'

'No I don't. I don't do life. I've forgotten how. How do you meet someone new? How do you get to know someone? And if I do meet someone, how do you kiss for the first time again? And how do you get into bed with someone you don't know? I couldn't. I'm too old. Too flabby. I don't want a stranger looking at me.'

'Oh, come on. If it came to the bit you'd know what to do. Everybody does.'

'I'd be all right if it wasn't for my body. It lets me down. I fart in supermarket queues. I belch. I get hiccups. Intimacy seems terribly difficult. I'd drink too much and say something stupid. Oh no.' She hid her face in her hands, wallowing in her fear and inadequacy. 'I can't do it. I'll never do it again. I'll never have sex again. I'll never lie beside someone and feel his lips against my neck. Or hear him sleep beside me. I'll never wake with someone and we'll turn to each other, toasting warm, sleep still dripping from us, to enfold each other and love. Make love whilst thrushes gather outside on the lawn and distant buses rumble taking morning people to work. Sparrows chatter in the eaves and my hands are in his hair and down his back, and his cheek is rough against me. Never.' She was making herself cry.

'Stop it,' said Lorraine. 'Stop it. You're wallowing.' Megs's description had set up a longing in her. She wanted to rush home to Harry, to lie beside him. Then in the morning do all the things Megs had just said she would be denied for ever. 'Besides, you don't have a garden.'

'I do in my daydreams.'

'Oh, come on. You never know what treats and goodies are out there waiting for you.'

Lorraine was an optimist. Some people thought that life was something that happened to them. A set of occurrences, mostly miserable, that beset them on their bewildered journey from birth to death. But Lorraine believed that life was something wonderful waiting just outside her window for her to come to it. And this she did anew every day.

She was a receptionist with a large insurance company. She wore her hair piled up on her head. She applied careful make-up. All day she said, 'Will you hold?' And, 'That's Mr Makepeace for you now.' And, 'I'm sorry, Mr Harrower is in a meeting.' She painted her nails. She smiled lavishly at visitors. 'Can I help you?' She walked on perfect carpeting. She watered the plants. She got bored. She would lean into the small microphone on her desk and in a soft, confiding voice ask for Albert Einstein or Rolf Harris to report to front office, please. She had occasional affairs. 'It isn't passion,' she told Megs. 'It's curiosity. I want to know what other people are like. What other women have. It's exciting.'

Being a receptionist made Lorraine, in Megs's opinion, one of the glacé people. There was a time, Megs thought, when you could go to the dentist or hairdresser and meet folk. A whole range of human beings – fat, thin, shy, brassy – were out there in the world ripe for the meeting and chatting to. There were stories to be told. Now you went somewhere and there was behind the reception desk the same chirpy, glossily friendly person you met at the last reception desk. You met people who'd gone on courses to learn how to be people. They were frosted like glacé fruits. Who'd think a glacé cherry had once been a cherry, dark and red and succulent? Where had the cherry gone? Who'd think the woman behind the desk at the building society, who was interchangeable with the woman behind the desk at the hairdresser's, who was interchangeable with the woman behind the desk at the dentist, was in fact a live and functioning woman who cried at night, hated doing the washing-up and read her horoscope. She was a glacé person. Where, Megs wondered, had all the people gone? And where did the real Lorraine go during the day? What became of her? Sometimes she thought Lorraine only came out at night.

'I have to go,' Lorraine said now. 'Poor old Harry will be wondering where I've got to.' She reached for her coat. 'We could do a breakfast sandwich. Egg, bacon and tomato in a warm roll.'

Before she was a receptionist she worked at a make-up counter. One of those terrifying, over-made-up front-of-the-shop people who told you you needed a matt foundation 'for your skin, darling' and made you feel just terrible. Before that she sold cars. And before that something else and before that something else. She couldn't settle. Recently, though, the idea of a sandwich bar appealed to her. 'I'd be my own boss,' she told Harry. 'I could serve sandwiches in a French maid's outfit. That'd go down a treat.'

'No wife of mine . . .' started Harry. Lorraine held up her hand, shushed him. In the end they settled for jeans and a T-shirt. 'Scoop-necked,' said Lorraine, indicating with a sweep of her fingers across her tits the depth of the scoop she had in mind.

'Yes,' said Megs, stirring herself. If she didn't get up now, she'd be too tired to go to bed. 'And a date and cheese and apple might go well mid-morning. I'll never sleep with anyone again. It's over for me.'

'Rubbish. A smoked haddock with mayo and cayenne could go. People are into fish these days. Of course it isn't over for you. You'll find someone. I know you will.'

'Rubbish. Who'd want me? It's over I tell you. Smoked fish repeats on me.'

'Bet it isn't. You don't have to eat it, then.'

'How much?'

'Bet you a fiver.'

'You're on. A fiver that my sex life is over for ever and ever.'

On her way out the door Lorraine said, 'Actually, I don't know what you're on about. You're not fat at all.'

After Lorraine had gone, Megs stared glumly into the fridge. The only thing in there was a pack of bacon with one drying slice in it, a wrinkly tomato, a tiny lump of cheese and several ketchup bottles. She would have to shop tomorrow. She felt vaguely thankful that her diminished supplies saved her from her longing to eat and eat.

It was two-thirty, and Shameless was hovering by the front door, looking guilty. If she did not take him out he would, she knew, disgrace himself. Reluctantly she put on his leash and walked him to the small scrubland park at the end of the road. She hunched herself against her imagination. Muggers, thieves and rapists were about. Every distant step, rustle of wind, slow rattle of empty crisp bag drifting along pavement made her stop. Her stomach chilled. When she stopped, expecting something dreadful to happen, the silence was appalling.

She stood clutching her coat round her, shifting from foot to foot, waiting for Shameless to pee. 'Hurry up. Hurry up.' The dog ran gleefully, nose glued to the ground, tail waving. There were fresh scents, scurryings of urban wildlife on dewy grass. He was in no hurry to go home.

Right now, she thought, everyone I know is in bed curled against a fellow being. And I am alone in this park waiting to be mugged. Lorraine will be snuggling into Harry. Gilbert Hundred-Miles-An-Hour Christie will no doubt be hanging on to that woman, if the sneeze did not put her off for ever. Mrs Terribly-Clean Pearson will be sleeping sensibly next to Mr Terribly-Clean Pearson, both wearing safe, no-nonsense pyjamas. Emotionally-Deranged Davis will be heaving the bed clothes from Mr Emotionally-Deranged Davis, giving him a lecture on duvet sharing and whose bit of bed is whose. Dysentery McGhee will be zonked out next to her weekday grey-haired man. Mike will be lying spoonlike next to Denise. My mother will be lying with my father in the bed they've shared for over forty years. Even their teeth will be companionably soaking side by side in glasses in the bathroom. I'm alone. Alone, she thought. Too late for me. She stood perfectly still, listening to the night: lorries trundling on the main road and a wheezing, a vile snorting and hoarse breathing behind her.

Her stomach curdled. Blood crystallised in her veins. Her breath stopped in her throat. She thought to run, but knew it to be a mistake. Walk, she told herself. Walk naturally. Do not look round. She put Shameless on his leash and headed out of the park. The snorting and wheezing did not stop. It was there. It was real. She moved faster. Shameless, sensing something behind her, turned and lunged.

'Come on, dog,' she ordered. 'Home.'

The vile snufflings got closer. Oh God, she thought, I am going to die. Nobody will miss me. I'll be found in the morning. Savagely beaten, skirt wrapped round my waist and Shameless looming over me, breathing foully. The thing behind coughed and dragged its spluttered breath. How dare someone frighten her? How dare he do this? She should be able to take her dog out unmolested. Suddenly furious, she whirled round. 'Leave me alone.' Nothing. She glared back up the path. Where had he gone? The bastard. How dare he disappear? She was fired up with fury, and ready to berate him for scaring her. Shameless lunged again. She looked down. A hedgehog was shuffling and snorting, a wheezing waddle, making its flea-bitten way along the path.

Humbled, foolish and crying with relief, she ran all the way home, panting and turning, checking for muggers, thieves and rapists. Heart pounding.

Home and straight to bed. Clothes torn off and thrown to the floor. Covers over head, shivering in the dark. All I want is someone who will hold me and tell me I'm wonderful. Someone who will lie to me when I need it, she thought. But this is me – a loveless fool who faces up to hedgehogs.

Chapter Ten

It was summer when it happened. Megs was wearing a short red T-shirt dress, dark tights. She never wore that dress again. A Wednesday. Business was brisk seven days a week at the market garden. So for the gardening months, Megs worked Sundays for double pay and took Wednesdays off.

'I'll collect you from school,' she told Thomas. 'Don't you go setting off without me.'

She would curse herself for saying that. 'I shouldn't've said it. It was a challenge. He thought he would come home on his own and arrive saying, "Look at me. I did it without you." Children are like that. They spend their little lives proving they're not children.' She would agonise and reprimand herself for the rest of her life.

She left the house well after three. A little late, but no hurry really. The school was only ten minutes' walk away and it was such a good day. She'd take her time, a slow stroll through the heat. She bought him a can of Coca-Cola. He would come to her, as children did when set free at the end of the school day, tumbling and tearing across the playground like puppies spilling from their basket. He'd trail his bag along the ground. His school jersey would be tied by the sleeves round his waist. Shirt hanging out of trousers. Hands grubby and sweatily damp after an afternoon wrestling with pencils, paints and school glue.

'Anything to eat?' he'd say. She would hand him his drink and a chocolate bar. It was a routine they went through every Wednesday.

She met Josh. One of those long, slow encounters that last the length of the street. She saw him approach and couldn't decide who he was, or how she knew such a creature. He shambled towards her,

341

smiling slightly. She frowned, chewed her gum – who was that?

'Hello, Megs,' he said. Smiling. Bad teeth.

'Hello,' she said. Trying not to smile too much. Trying to pass by. She stared at him. The features were familiar – where had she met him?

'You don't know me, do you?'

She felt it rude to admit it, but slowly shook her head. 'No. Sorry.'

'Josh,' he told her. 'Remember? With the band?' She could not hide her shock.

'Josh? Josh? Is that you?' This could not be him.

She remembered Josh beautiful. He used to shut his eyes when he played, his lips would move with some song only he knew. He had blond hair that flowed over his face when he leaned down, checking his fingers. Women would gather to watch him with blatant longing. They did not bother to flirt, they just wanted him. Now look at him. He'd spent too much of the five years since she'd last seen him in his head. It was not a pretty place to be. Loneliness, poverty and isolation had ruined him. He was in tatters. His jeans were threadbare and lifeless, raggy at the bottom. His left shoe was open at the tip and a single sad toe stuck grubbily into the daylight. He wore a greying T-shirt that had once been black. Over that a shirt, no buttons, threads hanging from the collar. The cuffs hung out from the sleeves of his denim jacket. His hair was long, tangled. Nicotined fingers, nails rimmed dirty. He hid them in his pockets. He smelled of old booze and cigarettes. Stubble on his chin. He spoke slowly, pausing to swallow every few words, as if he'd lost the knack of casual conversation. They communicated with silences and apologies.

'Sorry,' she said. 'I wasn't thinking about the band. I couldn't place you. You know how it is.' In the distance a siren sounded.

He smiled. 'Sorry,' he said. Indicating himself, all of him. He was a mess. 'Sorry. Things haven't been going so good. How are you? What are you doing?'

'Still at the market garden. Still potting geraniums.' She smiled. Shoved her head to one side. A little apology for not having a grand tale to tell. 'And you?' she asked. As if she needed to. His appearance said it all.

'This and that,' he said. 'I still play, you know.' He shuffled a little, scratched his head, apologising for the lie. 'Are you singing?'

'Friday nights down the Glass Bucket. Come see me. Actually, I quite like it. I do old Bessie Smith numbers and Billie. Stuff I couldn't do with the band. It's good.' She nodded. Yes, it was good. Really it was good.

'Um,' he said. He grinned embarrassment. Hand moving to scratch his head again. Apologising in advance for what he was about to do.

He's going to touch me for a fiver, thought Megs.

'Um.' Again. 'Don't suppose you've any money on you? Only I need a bit right now. Got to see someone about a job. And . . .'

She reached out to touch him, silence him. No need to apologise. When they were young they had sat side by side in the back of a van, day upon day. She had sat moving with the rumble of wheels on the road, sucking Strepsils, staring vacuously at her companions, the way people do when they have travelled too far together and there is nothing left to say.

'Ciggie?' He'd offer her a battered packet of Camels.

She would look at the pack and lift her lazy, empty eyes to his, shaking her head. 'Nope.' Silence again. That small piece of communication was all they could manage.

She remembered he always stood up for her in a way Mike didn't. Mike wanted to be one of the lads during the day and to come to her bed at night. Mike wanted everything. Once on the way from Inverness to Perth, travelling down the A9, they stopped to let her out to pee. Lately, she'd noticed she was always needing to pee.

'Again,' the others complained. She was beginning to suspect there was more to this recurring need to empty her bladder than the amount she'd drunk. Could she be pregnant?

Three o'clock in the morning and chilly. Shivering in the sudden cold, she stepped into the undergrowth, carefully placing her feet, afraid of what unseen ditches and tangled heather roots might do to her ankles. She wandered further than she planned. Outdoor peeing was the only time she ever suffered penis envy, no matter what Freud said. Men had it easy. Squatting in the undergrowth, bum shining white in the night, she worried about lurking strangers in bushes behind her, observing. Then, pulling up her knickers, she felt she'd captured half the insect population in them.

But when she'd done she relaxed and started to like the night. It was soft, sweet. She stood idly scratching her arse before making her way slowly back to the road, trailing her hand on the long grasses. Tiny moths sleepily rose at her touch, seeds and pollen spread. It was not dark, just the textured grey of northern summer. Distant mountains, thunderous, still as lions, shouldered the sky.

She did not want to go back. This silky, cold air was cleansing. She lingered. Tugged up some heather to put on the front bumper of the van. Only when she got back to the road, it was gone. She looked after it, the way it must have gone, then started to slowly walk, sniffing her heather. They were playing a trick. They'd be just round the corner. Waiting. But they weren't. She walked on down the road. A little faster, she could not see the tail lights. She started to run. Alone in this place with nothing for miles and miles. Running, hearing her feet on the tarmac. She was wearing silly shoes – open-toed sling-backs. What had become of them? What could become of them in a few minutes in this place? A small dread started within her. She could feel it. Something had happened and they'd moved on without her. Something had happened to Mike. They were racing him to hospital. She still ran. Still clutching her heather.

They blasted the horn, put on the lights and flooded her with panic. They had been coming slowly behind all that time. Instead of pulling ahead they'd backed up round the corner. Then they followed her. The horn rasped again, they knocked on the windscreen and laughed. It seemed it was them against her. She turned to scream at them. Hated them seeing her like this. Crying because she was alone and afraid. 'Bastards,' she shouted. 'Bastards. Let me in.'

The van pulled past her and stopped. She reached the back door, stretched out for the handle and the van pulled away from her. She chased it. Reached the door, stretched for the handle and again the van moved away. She chased again, stretched again for the door and again they pulled away. She gave up. Let her arms drop miserably to her sides and slouched behind them. Her sweat chilled to goosebumps. 'Stop it. Stop it. Stop it.' They opened the door and called to her. She always remembered Mike's face. It was more than laughing. He was enjoying her pain. 'Let me in,' she said. 'Let me in.' Josh put a stop to it. 'Pack it in,' he called. And reaching out for her, pulled her into the van. 'Let her be.' She was crying, had thrown her precious heather to the side of the road. 'Bastards,' she said. Josh handed her a hankie, 'It was only a joke,' he said. 'We didn't mean nothing.' Three days later the band split up.

She took five pounds from her purse and handed it to him. Apologising. 'Sorry.' Sorry for having some money. For getting by. Sorry for not being true to my ambitions, for selling out. For surviving, when you obviously are not.

He took it. 'Sorry,' he said. 'You were the best.' Genuine admiration. 'It was you. We all knew it was you. Everyone said so. Did Mike ever get round to telling you about the bloke?'

'Bloke? What bloke?'

The distant sirens turned to hyper. A wild panic that clattered and vibrated the air. It became more than a sound. It was a hard and tangible thing that dinned and howled through the air, bouncing off walls, hollering above the rooftops. Clanging and foreboding. Face fraught with dread, she turned in the direction of the uproar. Thomas.

'I have to go,' she said. 'I've to pick up my son.' She turned and fled. Josh held the money up, thanking her. Then he went back to the pub.

Megs ran through the streets to the school. All the way, every step, she knew the sirens were for her. Urgency and horror were stamped on her face. People stepped aside, turned to watch her go. 'Oh no. Oh no. Oh no,' she wheezed. There was scarcely a breath left in her. She was rushing through the noise.

The child was already covered when she arrived. 'No,' was all she could say. 'No. No. No.' Police cars, an ambulance. Whirling lights. The policeman stepped aside to let her past. No need to explain, he could see who she was. She dropped to her knees on the road. Reached out and touched him. It was the last time she ever felt his little body. She leaned over him. Her mouth was open. Hand reaching out. She was gasping. When she looked up, two policemen and an ambulance nurse were standing over her, bending down to her to stop her from collapsing. She put her hand to her face. 'Oh,' she wailed out loud. 'Oh.'

That moment of coming into view, seeing him lying, the policeman holding his school satchel. The way everyone turned to her. That moment kept coming back to her, for years and years it returned. It arrived in her head, always uninvited. And always, always as vividly as it had been when it happened. There it was. Every time she'd look wildly round to find someone who might save her from drowning, from reeling and crying. But every time there was never anybody there.

If only. If only she hadn't met Josh. Or stopped to buy the Coke. Or thought she had lots of time. She would have arrived before school closed. She would have taken him home. He would have told her about his day. What he ate for lunch. The little story he'd written about Captain Scarlet, his hamster. She kept reconstructing that afternoon as it ought to have been. She would have held his hand all the way home. She would never have let it go.

In the evening she sat frozen in grief by the gas fire. It hissed warmth. Megs was cold though summer shimmered outside. People on telly dressed thinly in the heat, frolicked in fountains. Tonight's national news. Vivienne came to her. She carried a yellow plastic basin, warm water clouded with Dettol slapping against the sides. A smell of disinfectant.

'Your knees,' she said. 'I have to fix your knees.'

Megs looked without really seeing. There were two huge holes in her tights where she had dropped down beside Thomas. Her knees shone whitely through them. They were pitted with grit and dried blood. She hadn't noticed. Vivienne gently dipped cotton wool into the cloudy water, squeezed it and drew it across the open wounds. She'd thought her days of wiping and bathing were over. 'What a mess you've got yourself into,' she said.

Chapter Eleven

Gilbert was at home when Megs arrived, carrying her vacuum. He was looking his hundred-miles-an-hour self, hair on end and agitated. She was in good form. The thing about the late-night contretemps with the hedgehog was that it had set her up for a night's undisturbed sleep. Her first in years.

He skulked in his study but still the house was filled with the quiet rage he was working up imagining all the cruel things that were being said about him behind his back. Everybody he knew was laughing at him. He listened to Wagner, always a barometer of his despair. At the moment it was a gnawing drone. But by evening, when his angst reached full howl, it would be roaring, and his neighbours would all know that Gilbert was suffering.

Megs moved mouselike from room to room, going through her routine. She stripped his bed, trying not to notice that he'd slept alone last night. The pea from hell, she thought. He's going to let it ruin his life. The dark hum of German opera battered the walls. Getting louder. When she left for the laundrette she could hear it outside. When she came back she could hear it at the end of the road.

It filled the house as she polished and wiped. She thought that what she did was so mindless nothing could distract her. But she was wrong. There was nothing like Wagner blaring to put a person off life's little mundanities, such as cleaning the bath and doing someone else's pile of dirty dishes, a week's pile. She was in the kitchen, working through the clattering greasy mound, hands encased in pink rubber gloves, when he came in, scowling.

'Is there a cup?' he said. 'I want some coffee.'

She nodded at the neat row of cups in his cupboard. He took one. Put on the kettle and stood waiting for it to boil, hands deep in the pockets of his training pants, staring out at his back garden. Sometimes he switched his gaze back at the kettle. Occasionally he flapped his pants. He did not speak. How could someone fret so much over a small incident?

The kettle boiled. He took a paper filter from its pack, placed it on a jug, scooped out three spilling spoons of Colombian blend and poured boiling water over it. A thick, bitter smell of coffee flooded the room.

His nerves were catching. Megs could feel them round her throat and deep in her nostrils with the coffee. She felt that his nerves and this overwhelming smell of coffee were crowding her out of the room.

'Oh, for heaven's sake.' She could no longer contain herself. 'It was only a pea.'

He glared at her. Cup paused halfway to his lips. The cheek of the woman, scolding him. 'What do you know about peas?' he demanded. 'What do you know about sneezing?'

She snorted. 'A pea,' she said scathingly, 'valuable source of riboflavin, lactoflavin, pyridoxine and magnesium. A sneeze,' she said, 'involuntary expulsion of air from nose and mouth. Caused by cold, allergy and sometimes emotional tension.' She was quoting from *The Bumper Book of Home Medicines*, by Fanny Tryer. A huge, once scarlet but now faded pink, crumbling and extremely dubious reference tome that had been in her family for over fifty years. Vivienne had consulted it often during Megs's childhood. Between its pages old postcards were lovingly preserved and flowers pressed. The advice it offered, however, was dire. It recommended milk of magnesia or caster oil for everything from flu to sprained ankles and duodenal ulcers. The very sight of Vivienne slowly turing its wafer-thin pages was enough to make Megs declare herself cured of whatever had been ailing her. No illness was worse than the effects of a double dose of laxative.

'The longest recorded bout of sneezing,' Megs pushed past Gilbert, pulled a clean dishcloth from the drawer, flapped it open and started to dry his week's cups, 'was a woman in Hereford who sneezed more than two million times over a period of nine hundred and

348

seventy-six days.' 'Startling Stories – Sensneezional', from the tabloid she'd used to line Terribly-Clean Pearson's bin a month ago. 'That's two thousand sneezes a day. Eighty-five an hour and over one a minute.' Hannah and Jack had worked it out with their calculator when she'd told them about it. It was the most interest in anything mathematical they'd ever shown. She dried as she spoke, shoving the red-and-white-striped towel down inside the cups, turning them briskly, squeaking dampness from them. 'Think about that. The mountain of peas you would have left if that had happened to you.' Reaching for another cup, her tenth, 'However bad it seems, it could be worse.' She wished she believed that.

He sipped coffee. Never thought to offer her some. Words formed on his mouth, but came to nothing. Melted instead into the wordless depths of his quandary. He thought he might never go out again.

'My goodness.' Megs was in full flow. An undisturbed night's sleep made her chatty and bossy with it. 'Last night I found myself shouting the odds at a hedgehog.'

'A hedgehog?'

'Yes. It was coming along behind me in the park and I thought it was a man. Snuffling and wheezing. You know, I was sure I was about to be murdered and raped.'

He wondered if that was the right order of ordeals.

'So I turned on him and told him to leave me alone. I really told him.'

'A hedgehog?'

'I thought it was a bloke. A murderer. A rapist.'

He wanted to say that not all blokes were murderers and rapists. He refilled his cup, cradled it between his palms and said nothing. He lived alone. He'd left behind long ago the need to communicate.

So she interpreted his silence for him. Decided what he was thinking. He'd made up his mind that she was a scatter-brain, prone to hysterical impulses. She knew she was a fool. Had rushed home along the street, dog scampering easily beside her as she moved, wheezing and leaden. Her black high heels clicked frantically on the pavement. Fleeing from the hedgehog.

'Well,' she excused herself, 'there you go. Silly me.'

He looked her way, gave her a small, watery smile.

'Good God,' she went on, 'can't you laugh at yourself? What's the good of all your books and your damn education if you can't even laugh at yourself?'

He did not know. He thought he should be working. 'Um,' he told her. 'Um. Help yourself to coffee.'

She turned to the jug, but it was empty.

She cleaned his house. She vacuumed and did not care about the din she made. When he came to her, she shoved the violent machine up and down between them. The great hooing wail a noisy wall to hide behind. He leaned down, switched it off. The silence made her vulnerable.

'Shouldn't you be going?' he asked. 'Isn't your little girl waiting?'

'My mother picks her up.'

'Your money's on the table.'

'Thank you.' She walked stiffly past him, unplugged the vacuum, then returned to the machine, pressed the button and the cord snaked across the room, rattled into the body of the vacuum.

'Goodness,' he said. 'How handy. You won't have the cord trailing.'

'Yes.' She was sarcastic now. 'They do that. Machines made since the nineteen-twenties do that.'

'Can I carry it to your car for you?' he said.

'I can manage.'

'I know. But I can do it for you. Save you.'

She wondered if it was surly of her to refuse. Didn't care if she was surly.

'I'm OK.'

'Only.' His hand moved to his hair, hovered a moment, then plunged in, ruffling it, pushing it upwards. She watched. Felt compelled to copy him. Clenched her fist lest she did.

'Only,' he said, 'I was wondering – what's the point of your damn lecture if you won't let a chap carry your vacuum for you?'

He did not bother with her consent. He lifted the machine and walked down the path, leaning awkwardly to one side against its small weight. Awkwardly, because it was an alien thing to him. He only ever carried books, a briefcase, and occasionally his bike – upside-down, slow wheel ticking round and round.

'Is this your car?' He thought he was hiding his dismay. But it

350

showed. He had long lost the knack of controlling his facial expressions.

The car was fifteen years old and orange. His most hated colour. One of its many previous owners had put a sticker in the back window – WINDSURFERS DO IT STANDING UP. He read and was horrified.

'Dunno who put that there.' Megs read his face. 'I bought it with the car.'

'Ah.' He did not understand why she had not removed it the instant she got it home.

She opened the boot for him. He gently laid the vacuum in beside the vast accumulation of motoring rubbish: maps, welly boots, carrier bags, a selection of various-size anoraks and jerseys, a cracked thermos, towels, a dog bowl and spare leash. A cheap, brightly coloured Indian durry lay over the back seat. It was covered with toys, children's books, clothes, a pair of red canvas shoes and a big silver balloon. For a second he fancied being a child again, being driven in that car, sitting barefoot on that durry playing with the balloon. In a lavish bit of courteous behaviour he took her key and opened the driver's door for her. Paused only a moment to consider, surprise and confusion flickering over his face, the cans of diet Coke, the chocolate wrappers, discarded parking tickets, sunglasses, raincoat, battered copy of Vita Sackville-West, and spilling of cassettes pouring from the rack beside the gear stick on to the floor: Billie Holiday, Bessie Smith, Etta James, Janis Joplin.

'Thank you,' she said, getting in. Though she hated people seeing the inside of her car, she was only vaguely ashamed of the rubbish she carried back and forth daily through the city. She switched on the ignition. 'I'd Rather Go Blind.' Etta blared and soared. The blast widened their eyes.

'Sorry, sorry,' she said, unable to find the volume control for noise and guilt. 'I forgot I had it so loud.'

She calmed the din, shifted into first and smiled goodbye. 'See you next week.'

He stood, watching the car rattle and splutter down the street. She was his cleaning lady. He'd had only small glimpses of her life. Oh, he imagined her leading the conga line, singing jolly songs, or trailing a howling squall of thin-lipped, TV-eyed, pallid children. That

351

was the sort of thing cleaning women did. Wasn't it? This one, however, had a book that had obviously been opened, music she listened to. And yes, he had started to find her domestic presence comforting. But now he was fascinated. Changing his opinion of her was hard work. He fantasised about laying his head on her breast. She would stroke his hair and sort out his turmoil. 'It's all right, Gilbert. It was only a pea, Gilbert.' He stared down the empty street, rearranging his thoughts. His hand moved slowly up to his hair, fingers raked through it, shoving it upwards.

Chapter Twelve

Gilbert was an only child. A precious boy with a silver lonestar gun and a red holster. He rode the range making clip-clop horsy noises on the back of the chesterfield in his daddy's study, alone. His father, a barrister, had died of a stroke when Gilbert was ten. Gilbert had no friends. His parents could find nobody suitable. Other children were too rough, or they had atrocious table manners, or they were too silly, too common or just generally not quite up to snuff. Children, Gilbert's mother noted in horror (and if she'd noted this in time she wouldn't have had one), picked their noses, fiddled with their genitals when they got nervous or excited, had grubby knees, asked silly questions, never sat still at dinner and spoke during *Gardeners' Question Time*. All his life, then, Gilbert had felt conspicuous and uncertain. He apologised when he entered rooms, and again when he left them, even if nobody else was there.

When he was four Gilbert was taken to his first opera – *The Marriage of Figaro*. He took a dislike to the Count, stood up pointing at the stage and screamed, 'I don't like that man.' His mother took his hand and yanked him from his seat and out of the theatre. Once in the street, round the corner and out of sight, she shook him viciously. 'We do not shout at Counts in the opera,' she hissed. Shake. Shake. For days afterwards she mourned that Gilbert was turning into quite an unsuitable sort of person.

When he was eight he was given a giant paintbox. It had a number three sable brush and one hundred colours, each one a tiny square: magenta, crimson, ochre, sepia. His favourite was midnight. A deep, fathomless blue that set up a longing in him. He never knew what it was he longed for. He felt he belonged in this endless blueness, he could plunge into it and be happy. He bought *The Junior World of Watercolours* with his pocket money and taught himself painting. He did washes, letting water then paint flood the page, dark at the top, paling, paling down. He watched the colour flow. He painted skies and hills, then moved on to flowers. When that started to bore him he turned to sketching.

He drew trees, the sea, horses, old buildings, walls covered with ivy in a series of sketch pads that with use grew battered and coated with a fine-powdered skim of charcoal. He taught himself the art of practical staring – he took in what he saw. Trees, he noted, had a rhythm and symmetry. No tip grew out further than the others. As they spread out into the sky, so they spread into the ground – roots reaching out as far below as branches above. He drew all this leaning into his little A5 books, perfectly honed, lovingly tended pencils scrutting over the page. His face twisting and contorting the while, reflecting the moments, passions, pleasures he was drawing. When he drew an old man smiling with unabashed joy, he smiled with unabashed joy. When he drew a tree he imagined to be wise and worn with weather and time, his eyebrows knit, his brow furrowed, mouth slid downwards at the corners, his face became wise and worn with weather and time.

His mother was proud. She turned the attic into a studio for Gilbert, where the boy could be alone and develop his talent. He had, at last, proved himself suitable to be her son.

Gilbert's mother, Muriel Christie, was tall, formidable. She pulled her hair severely from her face and tied it behind. A no-nonsense hairdo that intensified her imperiousness. She never walked. She strode, slapping one sensibly clad foot in front of the other, eyes fixed on the horizon. And when she spoke she threw her voice forward, a great welter of words that boomed across rooms, across shop floors, stations and doctors' surgeries. 'Gilbert has swollen nipples.' There were no secrets, only scarlet shame. She looked power-dressed in bathrobe and slippers.

By the time Gilbert was fourteen he had abandoned watercolours and sketching and turned to oils and acrylics. He worked alone in his cluttered attic, his private space. He painted his name on the door, 'Gilbert's Room – Keep Out'. He dreamed of going to art college when he left school. He would wear paint-splattered jeans and a black T-shirt or a round-neck sweater with the sleeves rolled up. He would grow his hair long, drink beer, talk about art and life and have, he hoped, a small, thin, blonde girlfriend who would sit close to him in the pub. He would keep his arm round her.

Now he painted on canvas that he carried to his loft in great rolls, cut out and stretched over wooden frames he built himself. Every new canvas he started was bigger than the one he'd just finished. He lost his fascination for trees and old men and became interested in surrealism. He bought books on Dali and Magritte. He painted a toad sitting on a roof gloating down at naked women-tadpole creatures dancing, leaping whilst a tall, phantom-like scowl – a severe hairdo, vast flat feet and in between nothing but a womb – stood apart, fearsome and disapproving. He painted that same phantom-scowl standing beside a bath full of naked women-toads, lathering and laughing. As he painted canvas after canvas the naked women-toads dropped their toadishness, became simply women, and larger and larger, whilst the scowl with the intense haircut got smaller and smaller till it was minuscule and hysterical beside the languorous ladies. Then it disappeared. The late works of Gilbert Christie, aged sixteen, showed only huge women, rolling and frolicking, leaping, dancing in rings, hair flying, thunderous thighs rippling. Sometimes they were writhing on a soft forest floor in bacchanalian glee. They were all stark naked. And they were always, always joyous.

Sometimes he was in his paintings, a tiny soul dwarfed between two vast, quivering snow-capped tits, or mountaineering his way along a huge stomach towards a dense forest of pubic hair. In one, an enormous woman was lying on her back, propped on her elbows, legs bent, open slightly. She was a bed – pillows, sheets, eiderdown on her vast, comfortable tummy. Gilbert was tucked up sweetly under the covers, head on pillow, eyes shut and smiling a little soft, smirky smile. Beside him lay another woman, one his own size. She also was smiling. This was to be his last painting.

One day Gilbert came home from school to find the house in turmoil. His mother was in a fury that was so intense he could sense it, feel it in his guts as he walked up the path. It was five o'clock, a summer afternoon in the suburbs. The air was vibrating rage. It came in black waves from the front door, stormed down the path, and the very pansies and lupins growing on the borders trembled. Gilbert stood, hand on door knob, contemplated running away, a notion that haunted him. He could run away. He could just turn now, down the path, out the gate and away. Away, away he could go, running faster and faster. Down the street, round the corner, away for ever. He could disappear in the city, live frugally in a bedsit, earn a crust working in cafés or delivering milk. Or he could find a cave on a hillside somewhere and live wild, eating berries, snaring rabbits. He would sleep on a bed of moss and bracken. He would be free, he had no need of paltry bourgeois comforts. He was an artist. He need never see his mother again.

He went in. She was standing in the hall, blocking the light, glowering the glower of an insane empress. Hands on hips.

'Come through here,' she said. Her voice was soft with menace. She was terrifying. He followed her into the living room. All his paintings were lined up, propped against the wall. All his laughing ladies looking wanton and voluptuous. Their frenzied frolicking made him feel foolish and guilty. His mother had the knack of making him feel smaller than he was. He felt his face slide into an expression of oily sycophancy. He hated himself. She always did that to him.

'I can explain,' he said.

'Explain!' His mother had abandoned the soft menace mode and reverted to her normal boom. 'No need to explain. There is nothing to explain. I do not want an explanation. I want this rubbish out of the house. NOW.' She pointed, arm quivering, finger stiff with intent. 'Burn them, Gilbert,' she demanded.

He should have refused. He should have stood his ground. Put himself defiantly between insane mother and paintings and protected them. All his life, in agonising reruns of that afternoon, he knew that was what he ought to have done. But he didn't. Perhaps if his father had been alive . . .? he wondered. But he wasn't. So Gilbert said nothing. He carried his beloved paintings, one by one, out into the garden, across the long lawn, round behind the hedge, past the vegetable plots to the bonfire patch. His arms were outstretched full width, only his fingertips curled round the edges of his masterworks. Every now and then he had to stop, put down the canvas he was carrying and adjust his grip. Then he would peek over the top, checking his route. Muriel Christie's garden was her passion. Stepping off her official paths across lawn and round edges of vegetable plots was a sin.

Trip after trip he made, placing the canvases one on top of the other. When he was done his mother fetched the old black paraffin can from the shed and grimly handed it to him. He emptied it on to the pile, and, glugging, paraffin rushed over the paint. She gave him a kitchen box of matches. He lit one, watched it fizz into flame, then threw it on to the pile. The fire shot up, a searing blue-yellow whoosh of heat higher than the hedges, spitting and splattering sparks. Gilbert felt his eyes widen, he stepped closer to it. For a moment he thought he might throw himself on to the pyre. But he didn't. He turned and walked back into the house, still saying nothing.

His silence enraged Muriel even more. She stood, hands on hips, glaring at the blaze, then she turned to stride after her son, shouting, 'Trees. Seascapes. Flowers. That's what you said you were doing. Not this . . . this . . .' She groped about in her mind for a word. 'Filth,' she said. She was searching for something to make her behaviour reasonable. Gilbert did not reply.

He went to his room, shut the door and sat on his bed. There would be no art college now. No paint-splattered jeans, no passionate talk of life and art. There would be no little blonde girlfriend who adored him. He could see that now. None of that was for him. How foolish he was to imagine that he could join in such a world. When he left school he studied art history, but found painful this association with art that did not involve him in actual painting. So he switched to studying the history of design. In time he gained a small, specialist, international reputation for his studies on packaging in the twentieth century.

During his last two years at home, Gilbert shut himself off from his mother. He felt shame in her presence. Their conversation was limited to passing comments in the hall. 'Excuse me.' 'Have you seen the evening paper?' 'Take your coat if you're going out, Gilbert. It looks like rain.'

Gilbert studied. His mother gardened. Every afternoon when he came home from school she was kneeling on the lawn, face close to the earth, trowelling, weeding, muttering to herself. She snipped and preened, watered and fertilised. Everything outside the house flourished in vast, spilling bursts of colour. In summer blue tits and chaffinches hopped on the lawns and moved in undulating flights from cherry tree to weeping willow to bird table to feed on the bacon strips and cake crumbs that were lovingly laid out for them. Tamed, they came to Muriel's call. 'Come on, birdies. Tweet, tweet,' raising that dictatorial boom an octave, softening it. 'Tea time.'

Standing at his bedroom window, hands in pockets, Gilbert would watch her. The house turned musty and dank. A thin coating of dust lay on the dressers and along the top of the picture frames. A milky film formed on the windows so that it was hard to see out. Then again, it was also hard to see in – swings and roundabouts. The fridge was empty, biscuits went soft in the tin with a picture of Buckingham Palace on the lid. Gilbert left school, toured France and Italy for six weeks and started university. He hardly ever went home.

It was 1971, the sixties were still buzzing. People wore fabulously silly clothes, headbands, flowered shirts, absurd trousers, Afghan coats. They were gloriously, noisily gaudy, except Gilbert. His sensible, no-nonsense outfit – tweed jacket, flannels and shiny brown brogues – made him conspicuous. It seemed to him that he moved joylessly through crowds of vibrant people arguing politics and feminism, listening to ostentatious music and dancing. When he was invited to join in, he couldn't. He stood on the edge looking on. What was it all about? He couldn't debate. He didn't understand the songs. And dance? He couldn't dance. His legs wouldn't do what his brain told them to do. They took on a life of their own, kicking, tripping people up, stepping on partners' toes. His knees jutted out. They did all their mischief at their own pace. No matter what music was playing, Gilbert always danced to his own clumsy tune.

Chapter Thirteen

It wasn't a good day. Mrs Emotionally-Deranged Davis ran out of money. Again. Mrs Emotionally-Deranged Davis only took her own money seriously. Amounts she owed to other people did not make it into her accounting system. Bills took her by surprise.

'Oh my goodness, Megs,' she said, breezing into the kitchen, stuffing her hand into her wallet, opening it wide, staring into it with affected consternation, 'I seem to have run out of cash. I'll see you next week.' She laid her hand, briskly, briefly on Megs's arm.

'That's what you said last week,' said Megs, looking grimly at the hand on her arm.

'Did I?'

Megs looked round. There were signs of financial frolicking everywhere. Julia Davis never arrived home from any sort of trip without bringing in yet another bag stuffed with some sort of consumer goods. Megs wondered that the house could continue to contain all that was brought into it week by week, day by day: CDs, books, bottles, clothes, cushions, plants – endless things. These people made affluence seem ordinary.

A bottle of wine with a small swilling left at the bottom stood on the kitchen table beside an overflowing fruit bowl. In Megs's house that fruit bowl would contain only stalks and a twiggish skeleton that had once been a bunch of grapes. Food in her house did not last. In this house half-empty packs of smoked chicken, dried up, white-spotted with age, were tossed into the bin. Exotic vegetables bought only out of mild interest and supermarket trolley upmanship were turning to decay in the fridge.

On the wall there was a framed photograph of the family on

359

holiday in Provence. They were sitting round a table on a veranda high up on a hillside, behind them slopes of vines and across the valley in the distance another château where another family was probably doing the same thing – being photographed drinking wine, wearing summer clothes and smiling.

It was the hand on her arm that did it. It was Emotionally-Deranged Davis's assumption that a small piece of physical contact was enough for her. A reassuring little pat would keep her going till next week. This woman plainly thought the small amount she paid Megs hardly worth bothering about. What did she know of managing? Megs had had enough.

'I'm beginning to think, the way you forget to pay me, that you don't think very much of me. Then again, the way you don't pay me, it occurs to me that I don't think much of you.' She fixed Emotionally-Deranged Davis with a furious glare. She was discovering that mutual dislike was liberating. 'Money,' she said. 'I want money. I do not clean your floor for love. I do it for money. I don't do it because I'm good at it. I don't want to be good at it. Money. That's all, money. You don't talk about money, you don't have to. You have it. I don't, so I do. If it offends you, disturbs your middle-class politeness, I'm sorry. There it is, money. MONEY. I want it.'

'It isn't everything.'

'So people like you would have people like me believe. But I don't go for that. There's money and love and music and beautiful things and honesty but without money – where are you? You want a roof over your head, food in your mouth, in your children's mouths. Money. You need money. And sex. You enjoy it. You can have orgasms aplenty because you are warm, comfortable and relatively secure. It's all money, isn't it?'

'I'll pay you next week.'

'I work for money. Do your bosses in the health centre where you work say they'll pay you next month? If they did, what would you say? And I know you love your work. Would you do it for nothing?' She looked desperately round. She was tempted to take the bulging supermarket bag from the kitchen unit, saying that would do instead. But didn't really dare. Besides, she suspected she didn't want anything it contained. She had the feeling she was being absurd. She didn't care. She wanted to shock this woman. She wanted to see the mildly patronising look replaced with one of horror. She hated this. 'Money,' she shrilled instead, shaking with indignation. 'Money. Money. Money.' She slapped a damp cloth helplessly on to the unit she was wiping.

'Well, Megs.' Mrs Emotionally-Deranged Davis slipped into her therapist persona. Dipping freely into skills picked up on courses, role plays with other therapists on training routines. She folded her arms, put her head to one side, deepened her voice, tried to catch the naughty eye of the recalcitrant. She spoke with charming authority. 'Well, Megs . . .'

'How dare you speak to me like that.' Megs picked up the cloth and threw it on the floor. 'How dare you use your cheap, quickie, sort-the-little-person-out routines on me. You don't write case notes on me. I'm your cleaner. You don't turn this situation around. You don't make *me* feel guilty. You *pay* me. And,' turning on the woman, 'furthermore, how dare you reduce me to this . . . this . . . effing fury. How buggery dare you do this to me.'

She did not look round, would not give Emotionally-Deranged Davis a chance to reply. She picked up her denim jacket, her bag and went out the back door. Slamming it. Stood. Still furious. She would have to borrow from her mother to get through the weekend. A lecture coming, there. 'I don't know what you do with your money, Megs.' And, 'If these people don't pay you, why do you work for them?'

She opened the door once again. 'Not enough. Not enough,' she screamed. Slammed the door again. A good slam this time. A satisfying slam. She heard the fruit bowl tumble from the table and smash on the floor. That was better. 'Yes,' she shouted, 'that's the sort of slam. That's what I mean by a slam.'

She walked round the side of the house, down the path, out through the front gate, along the street to the corner – all that way before remorse set in. That was it for sure. They wouldn't want her back. 'Damn and fart and shite,' she cursed, breathed the words out, feet hit the pavement. 'Fuck, sod it,' swearing and striding all the way to the bus stop. 'Bastard, bitch, shite.' The fool she was. She stopped. Stood, staring ahead, lips pursed. Should she go back and apologise? A bit of grovelling? She imagined herself wringing her hands and whingeing, creeping and cringing forward under Mrs Emotionally-Deranged's uppity glare. 'No. Won't. Won't do it,' she said aloud.

Fellow queuers turned away, stared, stiff with politeness, into the distance, pretending not to notice. They had seen and heard her approach. They would have no truck with the potentially unstable. Suddenly aware of how she must appear to her co-queuers, Megs fell silent, humiliated. It's my turn to be the loony on the bus, she thought.

She sat in her favourite place, window seat, halfway down the inside. She could stare at pavements and people, did not like watching cars. She put her head on the window and felt the grumbling whine of wheels drumming tarmac, through her. The vibrations rattled at her, eased the guilt she was now feeling at her outburst. Whenever she remembered her behaviour, her hand rushed to her face. 'Oh God.'

At the West End the bus, caught in the early evening traffic, shuddered and crawled. Megs yawned, felt safely removed from the world she was watching. A newspaper vendor was hollering his wares. A cracked voice, ruined, constantly extended beyond its range. Whatever it was he was actually shouting, it sounded like, 'Left leg. Left leg.'

A busker played guitar in a doorway. He was absurdly thin. His clothes, cheap to begin with, were lifeless now and useless against any kind of weather. His eyes were shut and his blond hair fell over his face. He was playing 'Spoonful' and playing it very well, quite lost in the sound he was making. A quivering sadness that broke through the mindless evening rumble, and soared. But that mastery was lost behind the throaty moanings he made. A deep drunken hum, singing out the music as the song made its way from brain to fingers. He was not aware he was doing it. People only saw a drunk with wild hair, broken shoes and dirty fingernails humming incomprehensively. They gave him a wide berth.

Megs liked people-spotting. It was, along with eavesdropping and staring, her hobby. She loved to look at people's clothes and the rhythm of their movements and speculate about the lives they led.

Years ago, she and Lorraine, on their way home from school,

played the underpants game. They'd pick, from afar, some unsuspecting man, poor soul, and guess what sort of underpants he was wearing. 'Huge flappers,' Megs would whisper, giggling, leaning her head against Lorraine's – two dirty little minds at work.

'Enormous Aertex with skid marks,' Lorraine would add. Lorraine always went further. They'd snort helplessly, eyes watering. They were young and thought the world wondrous and gloriously grubby. Memories. Megs grinned hugely.

The busker looked up and caught the grin. 'Megs!' he shouted, stepping forward to knock on the window where she sat. It was Josh. Oh, please God, no. She did not want to see him like this. She turned. What happened to someone that he could start out dreaming and end up playing exquisitely to commuters who noticed only his dereliction, not the fabulous noise he was making? She rummaged through her handbag, scarlet and mumbling, pretending not to see him. 'Hey, Megs,' he shouted. 'Look at me. Hey, come on out. "God Bless the Child", Megs. Come on.'

Megs did not respond. She was embarrassed to know him. She did not want her fellow passengers to know she mixed with people like this. She wanted their acceptance. She studied her ticket, wishing the bus would move, whisking her away from this moment. When it did she heard him call, surprise in his voice, 'Megs. Hey, Megs. It's me. Josh.' She did not look round, but knew he was standing at the edge of the pavement, watching the bus, and her, go. An apology would be moving on his lips. 'Sorry.'

So what was it that made him apologise when all he'd done was say hello? She remembered when the band broke up. After their last gig he had driven her home. Mike and the others were drinking, smoking some unusually fine dope (mostly they smoked home-grown) and dedicating themselves to getting very, very incomprehensible indeed. She was pregnant, eight weeks, and taking her duties to her unborn seriously. She'd given up alcohol and had stopped smoking. The end of the band depressed her. They were in Eddy's flat.

'That's it,' Mike said. He was enthused. Endings always made him happy. His greatest glories were when making a triumphant show of leaving. Moving on – what to made no matter – was

363

exhilarating. The business of goodbyes thrilled him.

'That's it,' again, reaching out, snapping his fingers. 'Hit me again.' He took a bottle of Jack Daniels and drank. 'Yes. C'mon, Megsy. Have some. Stop being so superior. Are you enjoying sneering at us?'

'I'm not sneering. I'm just watching out for the baby.'

'Oooh,' mocked Mike. 'The baby.' Then, to the others, 'She's been eating lettuce and stuff and drinking milk.'

'Looks good on it.' Josh admired her.

'I've got to go,' Megs said. If she couldn't join in, she didn't want to stay. She fetched her coat, a white Afghan that in a few months would not meet in the middle. After Jack was born it still would not fasten properly. Never again. She came back into the room to say her goodbyes. To kiss everyone and promise to stay in touch. Though they didn't.

The window was open. Mike was standing on the ledge, grinning at her. The others were looking helpless, shuffling their feet. 'Fuck's sake, Mike. Come in. Stop this.'

'See me, Megsy,' Mike leered. 'I can fly too.'

Fly too? Megs looked up, stared quizzically at the driver's back at the front of the bus. What on earth had he meant by that?

'Watch me,' Mike shouted. He turned to watch her watching him. She wondered how it felt. The way he looked back, the expression on his face – a vague, almost bitter triumph about him.

'Look at me. I can do it. I fucking can.'

They were one floor up.

'Christ's sake, Mike,' someone called. 'You're drunk, man.'

He jumped. Or rather spread his arms and embraced the sky. He looked back at her, grinning wildly. Ablaze. Did he really think he could fly? Was there, perhaps, a moment's belief? A full second's rapture – just before the plummet?

They rushed to the window. He was standing on the scrub of lawn below, surrounded by the woman upstairs's washing and a tangle of line. 'See,' he bellowed at them, shaking his fist. 'See. Told you I could do it. I can fucking fly.' Then he fainted.

Eddy and Fred took Mike to hospital to spend the rest of the night waiting in casualty. Josh took her home because she'd been sick, leaning out of the window, on to the scattered laundry.

He did not leave her that night. He stayed, made her tea, sat on her sofa and talked. He was more scared than she was.

'Them others, Eddy, Fred and Mike, they're going to do other things. You can see that. But me, at my age.' He was thirty then, and the oldest among them. Old enough, unnerved enough by too much contact with the really young, to think he was really old. 'I can't do nothing. I'm no good for nothing except playing.'

'Most people would die to play like you,' Megs said.

He smiled and shook his head. 'It's over for me.'

When he left he touched her hair and made to kiss her, then thought better of it. 'Sorry,' he said. Apologising again. 'Sorry. You wouldn't. I mean me.' He scoffed at himself. 'Look at me.' He feebly indicated his worn jeans, once blue, now pale with a dying weave, and T-shirt.

'No.' She touched him. 'It's not that. It's just the baby. And Mike, you know.'

'I know. But we can be friends. We're mates, us.'

'Friends,' she said.

Hers was the next stop. She stood up and made her way, balancing against the movement of the bus, towards the entrance. Another passenger, a man who remembered her from the queue, shot her a mildly sympathetic look. Not a smile, a furtive flicker of the mouth, a gesture of acceptance. Now that she, too, had refused to acknowledge a loony, she was OK. She could join the safe and sane travellers. Megs shot him a hostile glare. What was up with her? She'd sought the acceptance of strangers. Looking for reassurance from transient, fleeting eye-contact relationships with people who sat near her on a bus, she had denied a friend. She was ashamed of herself.

Chapter Fourteen

Lorraine was drinking coffee at the kitchen table when Megs got home.

'Who let you in?'

'Jack. Why are you in such a foul mood?'

'What makes you think I'm in a foul mood?'

'The way you slammed the door. The way you threw your things down. Your face.'

'It's been a day. One of those days.' She opened a jar of Nescafé and gazed ponderously at the small amount of instant left. 'I'll have to shop. Christ.'

Lorraine said nothing.

'First of all Mrs Emotionally-Deranged Davis tells me she's got no money and I'll have to wait till next week. Like I had to wait till next week, which is now this week, last week. Then second of all I took a tantrum, and now third of all she'll probably sack me.'

'I don't think so,' Lorraine soothed her. 'First of all,' she held up a finger indicating number one, 'she's at fault and knows it and she's all liberal. She'll be guilty. And second of all,' another finger, 'finding a good cleaner isn't easy. And third of all . . .' Another finger. She stopped, looked vaguely at finger three, thinking about this. 'There is no third of all,' she said.

Megs brought her coffee across to the table and sat opposite Lorraine. 'My feet hurt, that could be third of all.' She took one of Lorraine's cigarettes from its packet, turned it over, looking at it, then put it back. 'I'm going to have to borrow from my mother. And you know what she'll say?'

Lorraine shook her head.

'She'll say, "I don't know why you need to be forever borrowing money, Megs." No, it'll be Nina. I'm always Nina when she's ticking me off. "I have never, ever borrowed as much as a penny. I have never been in debt my whole life. And . . ."'

'I'm sixty-three, you know.' They chanted Vivienne's catch-phrase in unison.

'You could scupper her argument by telling her you know she's older than that,' Lorraine offered.

'Nah.' Megs shook her head. 'It's all I have over her. I'm saving it for something big.'

'I'll lend you money for the supermarket.'

Megs shook her head. 'No. You need your money to fritter on rubbish. You'll get withdrawal symptoms if you don't squander cash.'

'Come on. Let me.'

'No. I'll get it from Mum. She'll nag and boss and tick me off. She'll complain that I take advantage of her, only go near her when I want a babysitter or some money. Then again, if I borrowed from someone else she'd be offended. You know families. It's all very complex.'

'Was it a good tantrum, then?' Lorraine wanted to know.

'Pretty good, as tantrums go. I didn't writhe about on the floor and drum my heels. You need to be three to get away with that. But I got rid of some steam. My fury swept me along all the way tó the bus stop before I felt silly. Then on the way home I saw Josh busking and I pretended I didn't now him. So that's me. A shameful bitch and snobbish with it . . .'

'Who's a shameful bitch? Who's a snob?' Mike stood in the kitchen doorway, jingling his car keys. He stepped into the room, looking carefully round. For what? Megs wondered. Signs of prosperity? Signs of squalor? Signs of change? He sat at the table next to Lorraine, crossed his legs and brushed an imaginary bit of fluff from a grey-tweeded trouser leg. His brogues were brown and not too shiny. 'A gentleman,' he always insisted, 'does not overshine his shoes.' He knew such things.

'Me,' Megs confessed. 'I'm a shameful bitch and a snob.'

'Oh, you.' He knew her. Didn't want to talk about her. 'Any chance of some coffee?'

She levered herself sorely out of her seat and moved to the kettle. 'What brings you here? This isn't your day. Who let you in anyway?'

'The door wasn't locked. I came to tell you I won't be able to take Hannah on Saturday. We're going away for the weekend.'

'Right,' Megs said, stirring his coffee. Hannah will be pleased, she thought. It was getting increasingly difficult to get either Jack or Hannah to spend time with their father. Saturdays were too precious to them. They had grown from the little children who had spent weekends being spoilt by their daddy and his new wife, to being young adults with their own lives to lead. For years they had spent two weekends a month with Mike and Denise. Megs had at first fretted resentfully at home as her ex-husband and his new wife had given her children a glimpse of a lifestyle she could not possibly match. Not that she needed to bother. Mike forgot how young his children were, and expected them to appreciate his sophisticated new home. To his dismay, the only thing about his wealth that impressed his children was the size of the television set and the electric can-opener in the kitchen. They wanted only to behave at his house as they behaved in their own. Alternate Sunday mornings, then, Mike and Denise were irritably woken at dawn by the explosive sounds of children's television shows. It was not what either of them had planned. But in time Denise found she had learned a lot about a culture – music, television comedy, comics – that would otherwise have passed her by. Denise worked too hard at making friends with her stepchildren. She spent hours making them elaborate meals that they would not eat. At last, she gave in and bought them carry-out pizzas and Chinese. After that Megs complained that her children would start to expect such extravagances from her, and she could not afford them.

When Mike and Denise eventually had a child of their own, everyone worried. Would the children get along? Would Hannah and Jack take exception to the adoration poured on to the new daughter, Sara? Of course they didn't. They thought all the doting absurd. Sara lived an organised life. She had dancing lessons, piano lessons, a reproduction Victorian rocking horse, books and clothes. Before she was even in the world Sara's name was down for an expensive private school. Mike worried that his other children would resent Sara's privileges. But they didn't. Denise worried about the influence Jack and Hannah would have on Sara. She needn't have. Despite the odd dubious word Sara learned from Hannah, having older children around was good for her. Denise knew, though she never admitted, that the mockery Sara received from Jack and Hannah helped sort out a very spoiled child. At last, however, Jack and Hannah started to protest that the weekend visits to Mike and Denise were interrupting their own blossoming social rounds and often refused to go. It seemed to the three adults involved that no sooner had they got the hang of this divorcee-stepparent-children relationship thing than the two children grew up and moved the goalposts.

Megs put Mike's cup on the unit just, annoyingly, out of his reach. Then she leaned on the sink to chat from there. She did not return to her seat. Did not want to sit close to Mike. Recently she'd noticed that in herself. She did not like to get too close to her ex-husband. He was carefully tapping the key to his Audi on the melamine top of the kitchen table. She distracted herself from the niggle of resentment his suit and car keys set up in her by raking through the freezer.

He leaned back and sighed. He liked coming here. There was something easy about this home. No demands were made of him. He felt he could curl up and sleep. There was a huge pot of chrysanthemums on the kitchen windowsill, a smell of coffee and food, the phone rang a lot, in the living room was the bluish flicker and constant babble of television. Music played in the kitchen – Megs's blues, usually. He realised every time he came that he never, ever played his old records. That part of his life was gone for ever. His own home was a showcase of all the things he and Denise had chosen. Everything matched. Everything had its place. There was a well-worked, carefully planned design that somehow left no room for the simple business of hanging out. He could hang out here. The atmosphere was relaxed, uncritical.

Perhaps that was why he kept coming back. He did not mean to return week after week with tales of his new life, but he did. He told her about Denise's trip to New York (she was marketing manager of a whisky firm). He told her about Sara's piano prizes. He told her about Denise's Italian cookery course, and her herb garden. Megs knew how much Mike had paid to have a conservatory built on to his kitchen. She knew, too, the huge amount Denise had inherited when her father died. Megs did not mean to keep hurting herself by probing the details of Mike's home life and the joint bank account he shared with Denise, but she did. She could, of course, have asked Mike for more money. But since most of their wealth came from Denise, this meant asking *her* for more money. Megs thought it enough that Denise had her husband – she would not take her pride as well.

'Well, that's *it*,' Mike said now, placing his hands, fingers spread, on the table.

An indication of how absolutely it *it* was.

Now we hear the real reason he dropped by, Megs thought. She was tempted not to ask what he was talking about. But, 'What's it?'

'I've done it,' Mike said. 'Always wanted to. And now I've done it.'

'What?' Lorraine sounded disinterested. Lorraine was disinterested. Mike bored her.

'I have booked a holiday in Italy. Two months. A villa in Umbria with swimming pool. I've always felt a fortnight is not enough. I'll really get into the mood of the place. Get to know the people. Really experience the life.'

'Oh, goody.' Megs spoke flatly. 'We'll have pizza to celebrate.' She took three flat boxes from the freezer. 'One pepperoni, one mushroom and garlic and one tomato and cheese. There we go.' She thumped them on the unit and turned to switch on the oven.

'Is there anything for eating?' Jack shuffled into the kitchen and looked round without acknowledging his father. 'I'm starving.'

'Pizza in about thirty minutes,' Megs told him.

'Great,' he said. Only someone of seventeen could say it with so little joy.

'Your father has just told us he's going to Italy for two months this summer.'

'Great,' said Jack again. Joylessly again.

'I'll make some salad,' Megs offered.

'Great,' said Jack. Then, 'Only if you're going to eat it yourself. I mean, what's the point of lettuce?'

'You let that boy get away with too much,' Mike criticised.

Megs threw a dish towel at him. 'Don't you come here in your suit, flashing your car keys and holidays and start on me. Do you want some pizza?'

He picked the towel off his head. 'Why not?'

'I saw a good sandwich the other day,' said Lorraine. 'Cream cheese and marmalade. It's sort of cheesecakey.'

'We could do it for a sweet. Then again, some women like sweet things. They'd just have it for lunch. Or it could be a mid-morning snack.'

'And cheese is nutritious.' Lorraine flicked her cigarette ash into the ashtray. A deft movement that added authority to her sandwich suggestion.

'I was thinking, if we could do some chargrilled burgers and chicken, that'd go well. And it'd smell out the place nicely.'

'Good thinking.' Lorraine nodded. 'I'll have to go. That pizza's reminded me, Harry needs feeding.'

The front door slammed. Vivienne complained all the way down the hall into the kitchen. 'Bloody traffic. And this child is getting too wild for me. I should be taking things easy at my age . . .'

'I'm sixty-three, you know,' Megs and Lorraine mouthed at each other.

'It's you.' Vivienne came into the kitchen and shot Mike a filthy look. Everything that had ever gone wrong in her daughter's life was the fault of this man. She loathed him, and let it show. Fact was, she rather enjoyed the display of foul temper she unleashed on him. She, too, had discovered how liberating mutual dislike could be. 'I'll have a cup of tea in the living room with my grandchildren,' she said. 'You won't be staying long, will you?' This was not so much a question as a command. Go away, she was saying.

Lizzy came into the room. Megs swept her up and kissed her. 'Well, hello you. How was this Thursday for you? Good? Did wonderful things happen? Did you ride on elephants in the park? Swing on stars? Play tambourines? Discover the meaning of life?'

Lizzy pushed her away. 'Don't be silly. Put me down. I want to watch telly with Gran. There's cartoons on.'

'The burgers should be garlicky,' said Lorraine. 'And what about smoked salmon on a bagel with cream cheese and watercress?'

'Good one,' said Megs, setting Lizzy down. She leaned once more on the kitchen unit to talk sandwiches and life with Lorraine, ignoring Mike. After an hour she looked round at the oven, alarmed. 'God. The pizzas.' The crisp brown smell of burnt crust filled the room.

'I definitely have to go.' Lorraine picked up her handbag, yanked her leather jacket from the back of her chair and headed into the hall, small steps. Her heels were too high. 'See ya,' she called, waving.

'Yes,' said Megs, opening the oven. A cloud of smoke billowed out.

In the hall Lorraine stopped, took five pounds from her purse and put it in the inside pocket of the old raincoat that always hung by the front door. It was here that Megs kept her secret, emergency funds. Tomorrow, Lorraine knew, she'd find it and think it was money she'd forgotten about.

Jack, Hannah and Lizzy drifted into the kitchen, Lizzy still staring back at the television. They sat round the table. Hannah fetched knives and forks. Jack filled glasses with milk. A silent routine they went through every mealtime.

'Do you two have to?' said Mike.

'What?' said Megs.

'Discuss sandwiches when you're serving food.' He waved his fork at her. 'Hamburgers that are chargrilled and garlicky. Smoked salmon, for chrissakes. And look what you give us. This . . .' he pointed at Hannah's plate, '. . . muck. Think about the children. Talking glowingly about food and serving this . . . what is it?'

'You are well aware of what it is. It started life as a pizza. Now it doesn't know. It's got a complex,' Megs said.

'That's what they'll all have.' He indicated the gathering at the table.

'Jack and Hannah don't care. They just want to eat and go.'

'And I love it,' said Hannah. 'I love pizza with a complex.'

'There you go,' said Megs. 'Do you want your food with or without?'

'With or without what?'

'A plate.' She had a slice of steaming burnt pizza poised in her hand, aimed at him.

'I won't bother.' Remembering her accuracy with the dish towel, he was worried about his suit. 'I'll go.'

She showed him out. 'If you're so damn worried about your children, why don't you make more of an effort to see them?'

'What do you mean? They don't like coming over for the weekend any more.'

'You know what I mean.' Right now she hated him. He was going to Italy. She could not remember when she had last been on holiday. But she recognised the pang his announcement had made. It was that same pang she got when she looked at the picture of the Emotionally-Deranged Davises on their veranda in Provence. It was jealousy. More than that. She hated that she could not provide the children with such exotic things as holidays abroad. Long summer afternoons in rarefied places, breathing in foreign scents, listening to the outlandish clatter of strange languages would not be part of Jack's or Hannah's or Lizzy's memories when they looked back on their childhoods. She was swamped by guilt and envy.

'If you care about Jack and Hannah that much why don't you take them with you? Why don't you give them a holiday of a lifetime too? You could do that instead of criticising me all the time.'

It was always the same. They started out trying to be amicable but their good intentions always dissolved into an acid mix of jealousy, disillusionment, guilt and pain. They could not look at one another without pain. Even for this small moment in the hall. She took a step back. She was standing too close. She found she hated being near him. He stared at her – a defensive grimace that turned to confusion.

You weren't there. It's all your fault. My child is dead, he didn't say.

You were never there. Not for any of his six years, she didn't say.

'All right,' he said, regretting it even as he spoke. 'I'll take them.' They stared some more. 'Hannah and Jack,' he said. 'I'll take them.'

'Too right,' she said. 'You're not getting Lizzy. She's mine.'

Megs went back to her kitchen, slumped into a chair.

Vivienne was making tea. 'You forgot about me.'

'Sorry.' She picked up a piece of pizza crust left untouched on Hannah's plate and chewed it. 'Can you lend me some money? Mrs

Davis didn't pay me again. I'll pay you back.'

Vivienne turned, teapot in hand. 'Why do you work for people if they don't pay you?'

'Good question.'

Vivienne silently poured the tea. Well, she didn't say, I have never borrowed as much as a penny. I have never been in debt my whole life. And I'm sixty-three, you know. 'There's money in my purse,' she said. 'How much do you need?'

'Enough to get me through the weekend,' Megs said. The doorbell rang and she rose to answer it. She returned five minutes later, staring into an envelope, counting the money it contained. 'That was Mrs Davis. She brought me the money she owed me. I must get stroppy more often. It pays off.'

Vivienne sipped her tea, watching Megs. You shouldn't get stroppy with people you work for. You could lose a job that you need, she didn't say. 'That was nice of your Mrs Davis to come all this way,' she said.

'Nice.' Megs was angry. 'What was nice? She didn't pay me, that wasn't nice. And look,' she waved the money, 'she must've had it all the time. Or she must've gone to the cash machine. She could have paid me. Don't tell me about nice. You always think things are nice.'

'What's wrong with nice?' Vivienne asked. 'Nice is all you could want. Ask for nice, and you're not likely to be disappointed.' She meant it. She'd thought about it a lot. Nice was almost her only adjective. They'd have a nice bit of roast on a Sunday. Some days were nice. Some weren't. She liked to have a nice time at her club on a Tuesday afternoon. Bruce Forsythe seemed like an awfully nice man. Nice. If, on her death bed, she considered her life and concluded that, for the most part, it had been nice, she'd die happy. 'What's wrong with you, anyway? You're grumpy today.'

Megs looked at her mother. She was wearing her beloved green tweed skirt that fell roomily over her thighs, though she was thin enough to get away with something a lot more stylish. She had other, smarter skirts, but kept coming back to her green. It offered no challenges. The bad veins on her legs were concealed by thick brown tights. On her feet she wore low-heeled cheap beige shoes. The sort of shoes that cost £10 for two pairs. The shoes of a woman of low self-esteem.

It seemed odd now that this woman had forced her to school in a hideous hat, and had unshakeable faith in the healing properties of milk of magnesia. She also made the best pancakes in the world. Winter evenings when Megs and her father were sitting by the fire, watching early-evening television programmes, *Top of the Pops* or *Tomorrow's World*, Vivienne would bustle in with a tray, cups of tea, and a plate of pancakes heaped and golden, the room filled with the soft, comforting waft of fresh baking. She would complain that nobody was taking any mind of her standing with a heavy tray when the table was covered with papers and Megs's homework jotters. Megs and her father would sheepishly clear the table, making room for the laden tray. Then Vivienne would sit back and secretly watch them indulge. 'Hmm,' they would enthuse, hot butter dripping on to their plates. 'Wonderful. Best pancakes in the world.'

'Nonsense.' Vivienne would dismiss this as an exaggeration. 'Rubbish. Just some leftover eggs I had to use up.'

Yet if they did not say it, did not heap her efforts with praise and make a huge show of enjoyment, she would sulk for days. 'Nobody appreciates me around here.'

They saw each other, Megs and her mother, every day. Lorraine came by most days. Mike called in at least once a week. In the next room she could hear her children bicker as they watched television. Soon their friends would come round. This was the place where her children's friends gathered. This flat was always noisy and always full of people.

'I'm lonely,' Megs said.

Vivienne snorted softly. It was easier than answering. Her sister Betty always criticised her for being too soft, too easy. Only wanting nice when there was so much more. Her husband came and went, pottered in his shed, read the paper in the evening and didn't say much. Her daughter was lost in mists of guilt, grief and regret. She always wanted someone, an easy-going chum, to fancy nice with. She was lonely too.

Chapter Fifteen

'You're going.' Megs thumped a packet of cereal on the kitchen table, and a cloud of krispies spewed from the box, scattered over the table and on to the floor. Lizzy raced the dog to eat them, squatting under the table. Mornings were wretched.

'She's got an identity problem,' Jack scorned, leaning down, looking at Lizzy. He was feeling foul, venomous. He'd been ordered off to Italy for the summer when he'd been looking forward to an indolent stay at home, sitting draped sideways on a chair watching his *Beavis and Butthead* tapes, drinking, eating bowls of cornflakes. And Sharon, he'd just met a girl called Sharon, and suddenly that name would never be the same . . . 'You going to the Glass Bucket tonight?' he asked Megs.

She nodded. 'I've still got a few Fridays left before they switch to disc jockeys.'

'Well, I can baby-sit.'

She looked at him suspiciously. 'Why? Are you planning to have mates in? Will I come home to find a writhing mass of naked sweaty flesh, the air thick with dope? People in the corner snorting forbidden things? And the place awash with beer, cans everywhere . . . music blaring . . .'

'No.' Her accusation made him hostile. 'I just want to stay home. That's all.'

'Fine,' she said, ashamed that she had shown such distrust. 'Why not.'

Hannah's world had ended. Two months with her father and her father's new wife and daughter in a country with a different language when she had a love life to organise and some serious partying, clubbing and gossiping to do. She stormed from the house swinging her bag of school books, wailing that the worst thing about mothers was that they never understood anything. She vowed never to come home again.

Megs phoned Lorraine.

'It's her age,' Lorraine said soothingly. 'Remember?'

'No.' Oh, but Megs did. She was nagging herself that when she was that age she'd been worse. But admitting it would mean understanding her mother, and she wasn't ready for that.

'I have to go,' Lorraine said. 'If I'm late for work one more time they'll fire me.'

Megs dialled her mother's number.

'What's wrong?' asked Vivienne.

'Nothing. What makes you think something's wrong?'

'Why else would you phone this early?'

'Perhaps I just wanted to say hello.'

'Do you?'

'No. Well, yes. But . . .' Why did her conversations with her mother always go like this? 'It's Hannah,' she said. 'She's making a dreadful fuss about going to Italy. She gets this fabulous opportunity to go abroad for two months and all she can do is shout about it. I don't know . . .'

'What did you expect?' asked Vivienne. 'You didn't honestly think a girl that age would want to be uprooted from her friends and banished to some foreign country, did you?'

'What do you mean, banished? Good grief. I wangle this trip for her and she complains.'

'Of course she complains. She wants to manage her own life. Why did you do it anyway?'

'I thought it'd be good for her to be with her father. She needs to know him better. She'd get a sense of family. They both would.'

'She has a family,' Vivienne protested. 'She has us. What more does she need?'

'A father. She might need that. She might find when she gets older that she wishes she'd had one. Then there's me. What about me?'

'What about you?'

'I need things too. I need time to spend by myself. When did I last get that?'

'Why do you need time to yourself? In my day you didn't want things like that. This is modern rubbish. What are you going to do with time to yourself?'

'Think.'

'Think! What do you want to do that for? No good will come of that. Thinking is not good for you. If you start thinking you'll just get unhappy. What are you going to think about?'

'Me. My life. Who I am. What's happened to me without my planning it. Getting my life back on track. What I want.'

'What is all that?' Vivienne was shocked. 'Life. Getting back on track. Wanting. What do you want, anyway?'

'I want,' said Megs. 'I want . . .' She searched desperately for what she wanted. That feeling of being part of something. Of not being completely on her own. Of moving forward with people on ventures, adventures. Life. 'I want . . .' She didn't know how to put it. 'I want to belong again.'

'What!' Vivienne's shock deepened.

Megs held the receiver away from her ear. Oh dear, she thought. Shouldn't have said that.

'What on earth do you mean by that? Belong again? You belong. You've got lots to belong to.' Vivienne rang off, offended. Later, preparing lunch, heating a small tin of mushroom soup, she leaned against the stove, feeling mournful. Gas seethed against the pot, one of her everyday noises. But when she was depressed, ordinary sounds got intrusive. She wants to belong again, Vivienne thought. Don't we all. Don't we bloody, bloody all.

In the Pearson house the discontent was almost tangible. The air was thick with it. Every time Megs went there, winter or summer, blisteringly hot or Arctic cold, she would open the windows. When she left she would, after closing the front door, hold her breath till she got to the gate. Then she'd open her mouth, allowing some cool air on to her tongue. Tasting it. Smelling it. 'I think,' she said to Lorraine once, 'I must hate the smell of perfection.' But as her cleaning years passed, she realised that what she hated was the smell of deceit. That sweet potpourri that poured into the air in every room was part of the great Pearson lie. It was only a pretend sweetness.

Megs knew that houses had smells: coffee, books, old carpet, washing, sickness, yesterday's supper. Her home smelled of feet and instant food, noise, constant laundry and wet dog, with an undertow of craziness that teenage children brought. They were always moving. Her flat smelled used. In Megs's home senses intertwined – smells and sounds, sights and textures. The smell of a child's sleepy head in the morning and the wild halloo of the seven-thirty DJ hollering banter, playing the banshee strummings of this week's hero. A plant, glistening health brimming from its clay pot, spreading exuberant growth down the wall to the old patterned carpet with its soft coating of dog hair.

There were no signs of life in the Pearson house. Cleaning it was boring and perturbing. Start at the top, beds, washing, dusting, clean the bathroom, then the kitchen, into the living room, wipe, clean inside of windows, finish by vacuuming the whole house from top to bottom. Vacuum all the way to front door, doing a backwards shuffle for the last few steps. Put machine in cupboard by front door, then leave. Change shoes in porch, Mrs Pearson didn't like shoes that stomped over pavements to tread her carpets. All the time, from when she opened the front door till when she finally walked through the gate, Megs clamped her lips. Don't breathe till you hit the street, she told herself. Keep this disquieting stench from your lungs.

'It's all so orderly,' Megs complained to Lorraine. 'Stultifyingly orderly. It's not natural. I swear one day that Mrs Pearson is going to start screaming and screaming and never stop.'

Today Mrs Pearson was in the house as Megs cleaned. She sat in the kitchen drinking tea, reading the newspaper and staring into the garden. Every now and then her hand moved to her neck, she would spread her fingers over her throat and mouth her worries over and over.

Megs wiped the sink. Then wiped the windowsill, carefully lifting the pot plant and washing-up liquid, wiping under them. Mrs Pearson watched. The silence between them was neither hostile nor companionable. It was sterile.

The garden beyond the kitchen window was immaculate. The lawn, Wimbledon trim, perfect mower-width stripes. Each shrub and plant was allocated its little bit of border, any insubordinate growing was cut back. The earth was properly brown and crumbly. The weeping willow at the foot of the lawn draped glumly towards the grass it would never be allowed to reach. Megs always imagined that the plants mutinied against their regimented life by growing when the Pearsons were not watching. She thought they'd wait till the first fortnight in August, when the Pearsons always went on holiday, to behave like naughty teenagers. They'd party, indulge in an orgy of growing and spreading, flowering and flourishing. Then when the Pearsons returned their plants would shrink back into the allotted space. It would be the pruning shears for them, punishment for two weeks' abandonment.

Megs watched a sparrow bounce across the lawn. There was nothing the Pearsons could do about the suburban bird life, though they tried. The sparrow cockily strutted across the grass, flew up into the drab little willow and declared himself. This is me. This is mine. A female appeared. The male joined her. Together they bounced on the lawn. Then he was on her. Chittering, flapping, fussing – feathered ecstasy. It lasted all of two seconds. Then the male bounced off. Boing, boing.

'Well,' said Megs. 'I don't think much of that. And from the looks of her neither does she.'

'Who?' Mrs Pearson half-stood and glared out into the garden. 'Is there somebody out there?'

'Only a couple of sparrows having it off on your lawn.' Megs surprised herself. She did not usually chat to Mrs Pearson. And speaking about anything vaguely sexual seemed taboo.

But Mrs Pearson came to join her at the window. 'Where?' she asked.

'There, look.' Megs pointed at the lovers on the lawn. 'Look at him. Shoving out his chest, strutting his stuff. "Hey, babe. How was that for you?"' Megs flapped her elbows, did a swift cock sparrow impersonation. 'And her, she's bewildered. She's looking round saying, "How was what for me? Did something happen?"' Megs looked round in fake innocence and bewilderment.

Mrs Pearson laughed. 'Poor thing,' she said.

Megs looked at her. Sympathy with an unfulfilled sparrow, she thought. There's hope for you, Mrs Pearson.

'When I was a girl,' Megs said, 'I was sent to my Aunty Betty's guest house to help out at holiday times – spring and summer. In April the eiders came round to the rocks outside my bedroom window. They were not like the sparrow bouncing on his little bird legs, chittering and overexcited about a two-second fuck. They made love. I used to hear them woo each other. They cooed and moaned and made love sound fabulous. When I was little I didn't know why they made this joyous noise. Later, when I understood, I always envied them their rapture.'

Mrs Pearson took a tissue from her cardigan pocket, blew her nose, sniffed and dabbed her eyes. Megs did not spot any tears.

Later, after Megs had left, Mrs Pearson went upstairs. She lifted an old shoebox from the shelf in her wardrobe, laid it on the bed and carefully opened it. The watches it contained never failed to give her pleasure. There were three Guccis, two Rolexes, a Breitling chronomat and an Ellesse sports watch. She took her favourite Gucci out and laid it on her wrist. It was a beautiful thing. Its presence in her life, in her shoebox, filled her with a confidence she'd never known before. She felt that she had something in common with the glittering people she read about in her Sunday newspaper. She felt nearer to them. In her drawer was an unworn Betty Jackson shirt and a Nicole Farhi wool rollneck sweater. There were jackets hanging up in the wardrobe, and coats. Hidden about the house, Mrs Pearson had over twenty thousand pounds' worth of clothes, sports equipment (and she did no sports) and jewellery Mr Pearson did not know about, bought with credit cards he did not know about. Buying things made her feel good. She snapped her plastic on the counter, said, 'Do you take these?' and felt thrilled, and wanted. 'Rapture.' She repeated Megs's words. 'Rapture.' Her head had been turned. Fancying a bit of rapture, she thought she might use some of the secret credit cards, and shop.

Megs changed her shoes at the front door, made her breathless way back to the street, gasping at the gate, 'Ah. That's it. Get some pollution into my system, lead in my lungs.' She gulped in a blast of car exhaust, and her recriminations started. Had she said 'fuck' to Mrs Pearson? Oh God, surely not. She had expounded at some length, she recalled, about the sex lives of sparrows and eider ducks. She shook her head, trying to dislodge the memory. 'I must stop speaking,' she promised herself.

She picked Lizzy up from the nursery. Took her home, fed her and dropped her off at Vivienne's for the afternoon whilst she went to Gilbert's.

He was in his living room, waiting for her, standing beside a new vacuum cleaner. He gestured at it with his hand, palm upwards. 'Look.' He was awfully proud of it. 'It's French,' he said. 'I love the colour. Pure Gauguin. And,' he awkwardly tried to open the top, 'when I get this open, it has all the tools inside. A thing for dusting up high and a long thing for . . .' He looked baffled. 'Whatever you use long things for.' He bustled round it. Hair on end. She watched him. He was, she thought, all ego and thumbs.

She noted a birthday card on his mantelpiece. It only took a slight lean to one side to read it. 'To Gilbert, love Annette.' That was all. Still, it was a tasteful card. Unlike the gaudy, glitter-encrusted ones her children sent her. She watched him fuss round his new acquisition. He was a Gemini. Damn, she thought, she did not want to know that. Now she would add him to her horoscope routine.

Megs had a regimented horoscope routine. First she read Vivienne's, then Lorraine's, Jack's, Hannah's, Lizzy's and Mike's. She always hoped Saturn was doing malicious things in Mike's stars, and always forgave herself the sliver of shame she felt when uplifted at any misfortunes the stars had headed his way. Then she read her own, saving the best till last.

Now she knew she would incorporate Gilbert's astrological chart into her routine. Sometimes she read Dysentery McGhee's or Emotionally-Deranged Davis's. She felt it gave her the drop on them. She knew vaguely what was going on in their lives – financial problems, imminent journeys or romantic adventures. The nonsense in all this, of course, was that she didn't believe any of it. 'Horoscopes are just nonsense,' she'd say. Only it mattered to her when some stargazing tabloid guru promised good things. It was a small source of hope – a back-door, black-market, easy-access optimism. Sometimes, that was just what she needed.

'Good, strong primary colours,' Gilbert was saying. 'That is what you need in terms of design of modern household implements. Simple straight lines and bold, uncompromising use of reds or blues. It says function. It says strength.'

'It's a vacuum. Maybe all it says is, "I'm a vacuum",' Megs said. His enthusiasm bewildered her. A vacuum was a vacuum was a vacuum. You took it from its cupboard, plugged it in, switched it on, sucked up the dirt and put it back in its cupboard again. Design never occurred to her.

'Yes.' He stepped back from it. Stuck his hands deep into his pockets and vaguely flapped his trousers. 'Of course. I'm sorry. I'm whiffling. I'm sure it'll do the trick. You won't have to bring yours any more.'

'Oh, don't apologise. It's lovely. It's a beautiful colour.'

'Yes. I've never been fond of reds. But that's a good one. Burgundy, really. Blues and greens interest me more. Greens are endless. You just have to think of young summer lawns or old wooden sports pavilions or the soft melty inside of peppermint chocolate or the steamy brightness of broccoli – hot and crunchily ready to eat – or . . .'

'Lampposts in the rain?'

'Yes.' Bending his knees, clenching his fists with enthusiasm. 'That's green going into grey. An intrinsic grubbiness that's so alluring. It has atmosphere and you think about all the weather this green has seen and the passing hands that have touched it.' He stopped. Oh God, he was speaking too much. He was talking rubbish about greens. 'Sorry,' he said. Brilliant limes in the fruit shop, soft, gentle, translucent olive oil. His mind was buzzing with greens.

'Don't apologise,' Megs advised. Heavens, she thought, he talks so much. When he gets going, he's worse than me. 'Don't explain, don't justify, just get on with things, as my Aunt Betty always says.'

'I think I'd like your Aunt Betty.'

'You'd be joining a majority group.'

He smiled. A majority group, part of the crowd, that would be a first. 'Would you like some coffee before you start?'

'I'd love a cup,' she lied. She'd drunk two cups for lunch and felt awash with the stuff. But this was not a moment to squander. If she said no, he might never offer another. He was so offendable. And, really, she asked herself, if she was going to clean for somebody –

wasn't it best to be friends? So she accepted his cup of Colombian and his questions. How come she was called Megs?

'It's my maiden name.'

'Are you married?'

'Not any more.'

'Ah.'

'My name is Nina Megson, or was. Now it's Nina Williams. Only when I was little I hated Nina so I insisted I be called Megs, or Megsy. It was my playground name. It has stuck.' She shrugged. 'I thought Nina was a name for old ladies with a single wiry hair growing from their chins, and fat upper arms.'

'Nobody calls you Nina, then?'

'Only my mother when she's not speaking to me.'

Nina. He loved that name. It was a Russian princess, a dark-eyed woman in a long white fur, staring at him across a crowded railway platform, with that icy gleam of forbidden passion. It was a torch singer in a Paris nightclub, aching out songs of lost love and lonely nights . . .

'You sing.' He suddenly remembered their first meeting.

'Yes. At the Glass Bucket.' She winced to tell him. 'It has the name in italicised neon at the front with a top hat alongside. It's all in blue. Not the deepening sky at midnight blue but the blue you coloured the sea with your first paintbox when you were little.'

He raised a finger acknowledging the colour. 'Know it.' They exchanged a shy look, mutual childhoods, mutual silly colours from cheap paintboxes, a lifetime ago when they were innocent, knew nothing of shades and tarnishes and stains and thought the sky was always seaside blue and grass was perfect green. 'So what do you sing?' He knew now he was wrong about the spangly coconut matting sort of dress and the conga line.

'The blues. Mostly. Sixties favourites when the manager gets his way.'

'Sixties favourites.' His face fell. Nothing made him more glum than sixties favourites. Rows and rows of jolly-cheeked people, arms linked, a multicoloured human mass swaying, drinking Newcastle Brown Ale, singing 'Itchycoo Park' and reminiscing about old Herman's Hermits' hits. He closed his eyes, cast the vision out.

She noted the shudder. Could not help but take pride in having caused it. 'You can have fun with sixties songs,' she told him. 'If you sing them to a different beat than the one intended. "Let's Twist Again", for example. If you sing it really, really slowly, moronically, really glumly, with your face frozen and your arms dangling by your sides, it makes you laugh.'

She demonstrated. Stood in his kitchen looking chronically depressed, chanting 'Let's Twist Again' in a monotone. Barely an expression moved on his face as he watched. This monotonous singing of a stupid song defined exactly how he felt about the sixties. It started with everyone dancing in absurd clothes singing songs about twisting the night away and ended with people wearing wide-bottomed trousers doing drugs and seeing purple butterflies and love. He'd stood back with his arms dangling by his sides, looking moronic in his funny haircut, feeling vaguely flatulent because smoking anything did that to him. Air sucked in at one end battered through him and came embarrassingly, without any warning, out the other. This wasn't funny. This was painful.

'Gosh,' said Megs, registering his tormented expression. 'I never realised it was that bad. I'll get on.' She scurried from the kitchen to hide her chagrin behind the drone of the vacuum and the officious flap of busy duster.

He watched her from the place he retreated to inside himself when painful memories came visiting. They kept doing that. Kept coming when he wasn't expecting them. It seemed getting older only meant adding more and more painful memories to his already plentiful store. 'I'm sorry,' he said. 'I didn't mean . . .'

But she didn't hear him. One more moment to revisit later, wincing.

Chapter Sixteen

The Glass Bucket never was salubrious. It was conceived to satisfy a distant longing for a long-lost seedy glamour. It reeked of a forgotten long-ago when people went out drinking and played at being worldly-wise. Seen-it-all-and-done-it-all types, Robert Mitchum or Bette Davis in grainy black and white. Movie dreams that were too old, even, for rainy Sunday afternoons, and now played on television in the middle of the night, when only insomniacs and night-watchmen were up. It demanded nothing of its patrons other than that they paid for their drinks and took their fights outside to the car park. Nowadays, grown-ups going out to play went to better places than the Glass Bucket. Places where they wore their best clothes, sipped their drinks, looked around them and, for an hour or so, took pleasure in pretending to be a whole lot richer than they were.

People at the Glass Bucket wore second-best, never cast an eye this way or that – who cared if nobody was looking at them? – there was nobody here to impress. Here they leaned on the bar, or sat at the round glass-topped tables, and spoke with the authority only alcohol can induce about sport, soaps, what was on telly last night and the embroiled relationships of distant superstars, or the folks next door.

But there had always been live music at the Glass Bucket on a Friday night. The people who went would mostly rather have had Country and Western. But they'd grown used to Megs. During her first set anyway, her songs didn't stop the fervent crack. They just slowed it down. People would tap their fingers on their glasses, move their heads in time with the tunes they were hearing, without really noticing they were doing it. It was her second set, when she sang the

387

blues, that set people drifting into little worlds of forgotten dreams and distant memories.

It was her second-last Friday. Megs was wearing her black jeans and white silk shirt. She'd spent more time than usual moussing her hair and putting on one of the lipsticks from Lorraine's vast collection. Never a week passed but Lorraine spent time trailing round make-up counters. She was on a lifetime's quest, a mission that she never abandoned – the search for the perfect lipstick. This would be a red that was too deep to look cheap. A pale brown that didn't turn pink after a couple of gins. It was out there somewhere, on some scented counter, waiting for her.

Megs was coming to the end of the sixties selection, singing 'Me and Bobby McGee', nodding to Lorraine and Harry that she'd be with them after the next chorus, when she saw Gilbert. He was standing at the bar wearing his junior Humphrey Bogart outfit.

He was enveloped in a long raincoat, collar up. People nearby had shifted aside and turned their backs to him. Stranger in our midst, their body language said. He was standing alone, back to the bar, looking down at the whisky in his glass. Every now and then he looked up and gazed sadly ahead. Awkward stranger, his body language said.

Megs watched him as he took the room in. What did a man with his acute sense of shape and colour make of the Glass Bucket? She smiled, imagining his mental turmoil as he surveyed the tartan carpet and walls. She saw him glance at the ceiling. And looked at it too. She hadn't noticed it before. All those years, and she hadn't once considered the ceiling. It was brown from a million or three nicotined exhalations. How long had the ceiling been that colour? And why had nobody ever remarked on it? People round here don't look up. What sort of brown was it, anyway? Sort of yellowed, a baby-diarrhoea brown. Oh God, he's got me at it, she screamed silently. Defining colours.

She stepped from the stage. A little step on to the tartan, she could feel beneath her feet the vague squelch of an industrial-strength twist that had seen too much. It was jaded, the nights, the passions that had been played out on it. The lager it had absorbed.

'This carpet is clapped out,' she said, crossing to Lorraine's table.

'It has to go. Like me.' She nodded towards Gilbert and, grinning sheepishly, moved through the Friday-night crowd to him.

Lorraine squirmed round in her seat. Her skirt and off-the-shoulder top did not allow for much more movement than squirming. 'Told you.' She leaned across to Harry, aglow with gossip. 'She's gone soft on him.'

'So,' said Megs, leaning folded arms on the bar, 'what do you think of the Glass Bucket?' His obvious discomfort amused her.

'Um,' said Gilbert. 'It's . . . um . . .' He could not think of anything tactful to say.

'It's life, Gilbert. But not as you know it.'

'Yes.' He gave her a fragile smile. 'That'd do it. That's what I think.' Then, apologising for himself, 'I just never thought of it.'

'Come meet Lorraine and Harry.' She took his hand, led him across the room in the practised, comfortingly bossy manner of a woman overly accustomed to dealing with children, who has forgotten the ways of adults. It was just what Gilbert needed.

He placed his whisky carefully on the table and sat before it. His hand moved through his hair as he nodded hello.

'What brings you here?' asked Lorraine. She did not like this. Megs was hers.

'I wondered . . . You know . . . I wanted to hear Megs sing.' It was the first time he'd said her name. He'd rather call her Nina. He looked across at her. It seemed so familiar to say someone's name when you hardly knew them. He was not good at familiar. He never usually called someone by name till the third or fourth meeting. It took a little juggling the conversation, but he'd become expert.

'What do you think, then?' Harry wanted to know.

'Wonderful.' His admiration was genuine. 'I've only heard a little. But wonderful.'

Megs finished her drink. 'Time to go fix myself.' She smiled at Gilbert, touched his arm. 'Hope you're going to wait till I'm done.'

'Oh yes.' He was keen. He was drinking with the singer in the band. For the first time in his life, he was in with the in-crowd.

Megs went backstage to reapply Lorraine's cast-off lipstick, Sahara Sundae, and fix her hair. She lingered a while, considering her reflection – the person she preferred to the person she was – the singer in the mirror.

She sang 'Mad about the Boy' and 'Georgia'. She did a little Wilson Pickett, 'Midnight Hour' and U2, 'With or Without You'. When she was halfway through 'I Put a Spell On You' the crowd drifted off into their little worlds of stolen moments and lost chances remembered. People touched, drained handfuls of peanuts into their mouths and allowed themselves a little dreaming. Gilbert forgot he was in the Glass Bucket. He was falling in love with a torch singer called Nina who had a lonely look and a tragic past.

Lorraine looked at Harry, who was looking across the bar at a girl, young, slim, in tight jeans and a shirt that showed her navel. It was the sort of navel that could stand a little showing-off. The girl was looking at Harry. They were smiling that small slip of a knowing smile that said everything. You bastard, Lorraine thought. You're having an affair. Harry, with his balding head, his droopy moustache, his cuddly little beer belly and his lovely liquid brown eyes, was shagging this young thing – how dare he? Lorraine put her hand on the inside of his thigh and looked across at her rival. He's mine. And the younger woman looked away, said something inane to the bartender and laughed gorgeously at her own joke. Her shoulders shook, she put her head on her hand, and turned to look back at Lorraine. Oh no he isn't. And Megs sang on. 'One For the Road'.

When she'd finished, Megs came back to the table. She sat next to Gilbert and took a long swig of the drink he'd bought her.

'You two want to go on somewhere?' Harry was feeling sociable.

Gilbert and Megs smiled they were willing. But Lorraine took Harry's hand and said she was tired. She needed to go home, needed her bed. She put her head on his shoulder and licked the lobe of his ear. Just a flicker of the tongue. She had plans for Harry. She gripped his arm and glanced towards the young, self-assured one sitting at the bar. No chance, girl. Her rival simply sniggered, turned her back. That's what you think, oh old and baggy one.

'He can see you home,' Lorraine told Megs, gesturing with her head to Gilbert. She, too, didn't use people's names. Not when she suspected them of stealing her best friend, anyway.

For a moment Megs imagined herself going home on the back of his bike, wobbling through back streets, legs splayed out, keeping her tights intact. But Gilbert had a car, a 1967 Jaguar.

'I don't use it much,' he explained. 'It keeps needing to be fixed. But it's the shape. I love it. The classic lines. Then the dash isn't cluttered. Nice round dials.' When he switched on the ignition, Schubert played on the cassette deck. He waved his arms as he spoke, as he drove. They hurtled wildly. And Megs worried. Should she invite him in? What would he make of her tasteless clutter? She couldn't relax and enjoy this stylish ride through familiar grey streets, she was having too many doubts about her lifestyle.

She sat back in her seat, reviewing the contents of her home. The fridge and surrounding area alone would bring him out in hives. For the design-conscious, it was six square feet of hell. On top of the fridge was a pale-blue plastic box full of things – an empty can of Mr Sheen, a curler (though nobody used them), some crumpled J-Cloths, a sock waiting for a partner, some postcards and an old Christmas card. Why did she have these useless things? Why hadn't she thrown them out? A tasteful, organised person would have. Next to the box was a pair of Lizzy's wellies, small, bright red, with a sock dangling from one. They were up high, safe from Shameless's chewings. She thought there was a small blue plastic spade next to the wellies. And in behind the frayed wire that snaked up to the electric point was a wad of mail, mostly junk.

'I should've chucked out all that stuff from *Reader's Digest*,' she said into the dark.

'Pardon?' said Gilbert.

'Oh, nothing. Just doing a spot of self-recriminating.'

'Oh, that. I do that in the car, too.'

Then there were the fridge door magnets – two pineapples, a strawberry, a pair of bright-pink plastic feet, a couple of ancient Mr Men, a fried egg, if she remembered correctly. Behind each magnet a note. From Jack: 'Get cornflakes.' From her to Jack: 'Get a job. Buy your own.' From Hannah: 'I hate my school shoes.' That message had been stuck behind the pink feet for the past six months. From Lizzy a series of squiggles and hieroglyphics because she was four and couldn't yet read or write. But she wanted to join in everything. Next to the fridge was a basket filled with filthy potatoes and carrots, because dirty veg were cheaper. Oh God . . . that was just one small area. She considered the rest of her house trying to come up with one item she'd chosen. Everything she now owned, it seemed, had been gifted or donated second-hand by friends or relatives – mostly Vivienne and Lorraine.

He stopped outside her door and switched off the engine. They sat facing ahead, looking through the windscreen, saying nothing. The warmth, Schubert, their vaguely comfortable silence – it was, Megs thought, the most intimate moment she'd had for years.

'Would you like to come up for some coffee?' she asked.

He leaned on the steering wheel, staring up at her building. 'Why not.'

'Only,' she launched into an apology, 'it's messy. Cluttered.'

'My house is cluttered. As you well know.'

'Ah, but you chose your clutter, mine was thrust upon me. Like my life.' She wished she hadn't said that.

The flat was nervily quiet. 'Where is everybody?' Megs looked round. Hannah was staying over with a friend. But there was no sign of Jack. The television was playing silently to an empty room. There was an empty cider bottle on its side by the sofa. Shameless, wagging his tail insanely, intimately sniffed Gilbert's crotch.

'Where's Jack?' Megs looked into the kitchen. Then she checked on Lizzy. The child was in bed, hair spread over the pillow, sleeping effortlessly.

'Jack?' asked Gilbert.

'My son,' said Megs, putting on the kettle, noticing Gilbert taking in, evaluating, her clutter. 'He's meant to be baby-sitting.'

The phone rang. Megs lifted the receiver. 'Hi,' she said.

'How're things?' whispered Lorraine.

'We're about to have coffee,' Megs said. Cupping her hand over the mouthpiece she mouthed, 'Lorraine,' to Gilbert.

He couldn't understand this. They'd parted only ten minutes before. What could they possibly have to say to each other?

'Listen,' Lorraine breathed, 'I can't tell you now, but Harry's having an affair. He's in the loo. I'll phone you tomorrow. I have to see about this.'

'Harry?' Megs didn't believe her. 'Your Harry? Don't be daft.'

'Yes, he is. I know. I saw him. The way he looked at that girl.'

'What girl?'

'At the bar. Ten years old, flat stomach, brainless. I have to go.' She rang off.

'Lorraine,' Megs explained to Gilbert again, as if he would understand why people so soon parted would want to talk. He didn't. In his entire life he had never once phoned someone unless he had something very definite to say.

The phone rang again.

'Hello, Mum,' said Megs before whoever it was on the other end could say a word. 'How did I know it was you? Who else would it be? Yes, everything's fine. No problems. Jack's fine. He's sitting watching telly. Lizzy's fine, sound asleep.'

Gilbert listened to this expert and soothing weaving of truth and lies.

'My mother,' said Megs, putting the phone down. 'If I told her there was no sign of Jack her blood pressure would rocket. She'd explode.' Megs handed him a mug of instant. 'Where is Jack?'

Gilbert shrugged. 'Perhaps he just slipped out for something.'

'He has nothing to slip out for.' Megs stood a moment, listening, sniffing. She knew that smell. She realised she'd been aware of it since she got in. It was one of the smells of her youth. That smell, and the little excitement of entertaining a stranger, a male stranger, had made her heady, and nostalgic with it. Booze, incense, cigarettes and dope. Yes, dope. She stood sniffing violently, thinking: God, this is what my mother does. This suspicious snorting the air. And bath essence. Yes, there was bath essence in with those other decadent scents.

'He's in the bath,' she said to Gilbert.

'There you are. Problem solved,' Gilbert said simply.

'He's in the bath, drinking and smoking.'

'I do that.' Gilbert was quite enthused.

'I'll kill him.' Megs stormed up the hall to the bathroom, stood at the door. 'Jack. Jack. Are you in there?'

Panicked whisperings and tidal waves of splashings from within.

'Jack? What are you doing in there . . .' Megs rattled the door, opening it.

Howls. 'Christ. Get out.'

'Don't tell me to get out.' Megs was furious. 'If you don't want people to come in, you should lock the door. No doubt you were too drunk to think about that.'

The room was dim, thickly fogged with steam, and candlelit. It took a second before Megs's eyes adjusted. A ghetto-blaster on the cistern was playing a mournful Oasis song. There were two strange people in her bath, two young faces frozen in raw stupefaction. The girl was sitting behind the boy, legs curled round his back. They were bald, both of them. Megs gripped the towel rail. Her knees were giving way. My God, Lizzy was sleeping alone in the flat and two bald intruders were having a bath.

'Who the hell are you?' she shouted. 'What the fuck are you doing in my bath? Jack? Jesus, Jack. What have you done?'

Gilbert stood staring vacantly at the fridge. He was not too upset by the yellings to fail to notice its ghastliness. He hated fridge magnets. He did not know what to do. Perhaps he should go. But then he did not like to disappear without saying goodbye. It wasn't polite. He sipped his coffee and waited for Megs.

'What are you smoking?' she was screaming. 'And your hair. My God, your hair.' Then a small, torrid silence. 'And Jesus Christ, Jack. Her hair. Jack, you arse.' Splashings and the squeak of naked flesh against bath enamel. 'Get bloody dressed,' Megs shouted.

Gilbert heard her slam the bathroom door. She reappeared in the kitchen tight-lipped, rabid with rage and still clutching their joint. 'The little bugger,' she said. 'He's in the bath, in candlelight, smoking dope, drinking cider and with Sharon Wallace from round the corner.'

Gilbert smiled wanly. 'Oh well. Teenagers . . .'

'And they're bald,' screamed Megs. 'Bald. The stupid bastards are in there shaving each other's heads. Bald.' She said it again. Couldn't believe it. 'Bald.'

'Bald,' Gilbert repeated.

'Both of them,' Megs said. 'What am I going to say to her mother?' She looked at the joint in her hand. She hadn't realised she'd taken it. Without thinking what she was doing she inhaled deeply on it. 'Two white heads gleaming in the dark.' She took another puff. 'There is something about newly shaven heads and pubes. They always look surprised and sort of innocent. Know what I mean?'

Gilbert shrugged.

Megs felt the tension and strain drizzle from her. She relaxed against the wall. 'Bald,' she said. There was whimsy in her voice. 'See your children, they will always knock the legs from under you. You think you're liberated. But they'll find something. Bald. That'd do it. We were such a hairy generation.' She sat at the kitchen table, cupped her chin in her hand. 'And see parents. Some folks are natural-born parents. The rest of us feel as if our psyches have been taken by storm. The natural-born ones breeze through it. This is the time of their lives. They speak soothingly. I see them in parks, on buses – places. They tie laces, wipe assorted grubby bits on and off the body, make endless plates of custard with chopped banana and think nothing of it. But the rest of us spend the whole time from birth to empty-nest syndrome with surprised, agonised expressions on our faces. We look pale and fraught. Our hair is constantly on end with the strain of it all.'

Realising what she'd said, she looked shyly across at him. But he showed no sign of offence. He had no notion of his hairstyle.

Sounds of semi-hysterical giggling came from the bathroom. Shaking with the effort of trying to appear sane and sober, Jack padded into the kitchen. He wore a towel wrapped round his waist. Megs and Gilbert stared at his head.

'What?' Jack stroked his naked skull defensively. His face looked worn against the newly exposed skin on top. His eyebrows were suddenly huge.

'You know what,' said Megs, smoking freely now, gripping the remaining stub of roll-up between thumb and forefinger. 'Jack, Gilbert. Gilbert, Jack.' She nodded from one to the other, introducing them. Gilbert, reliably awkward, held out his hand. Jack looked at it apologetically. He had one hand on his head, the other gripped his towel. He didn't want to let go of either.

'Sorry,' he said.

Gilbert smiled. This boy spoke his language.

'God.' Voice soft, Megs looked up at Jack. 'There's your head. I haven't seen that in years. You were bald when you were born.'

Jack said, 'Christ, Mother.' And padded out of the room again.

'Are you going to see Sharon home?' Megs called into the hall. 'When did her mother say she had to be back?'

'An hour ago,' Jack confessed. He looked down at his feet, wriggled his toes.

'The woman will be worried. Phone her and explain.' Megs pointed at the phone.

Jack didn't move. 'Couldn't you?'

'Me? What's all this got to do with me? You're the one that's been stupid.'

Still Jack didn't move. He clung to his towel and kept his eyes fixed on his toes. 'Please.'

Megs relented. 'All right. I'll see her home as I'm taking Shameless out. But really, Jack, you should take responsibility. What on earth am I going to say to her mother?'

Jack shrugged.

Gilbert seized the moment. If there were exits being made, he could make one too. 'I should go.'

'Don't go,' said Megs. 'Have some coffee.'

'You already made me some.'

'That's right. I gave you the good cup. You being so tasteful I couldn't decide if I should give you the nice cup, which is dark blue – very Gauguin – but cracked. Or one of the crap cups, which are cheap seaside-resort yellow, but crack-free. In the end taste won.'

'Well, thank heavens for that. You certainly have the measure of me.' He wondered if he should kiss her. They stood feet from one another, making fleeting ducking movements, a choreographed shyness, that did not lead to anything physical. He swallowed. His hand, as if it made its own decisions, went to his hair, hovered a moment at his brow, before it took comfort in ploughing a small row of furrows across his scalp. 'I'll see you soon,' he said.

Chapter Seventeen

'Look at it this way,' said Lorraine. 'You'll laugh at it in years to come. It'll be a family joke.'

Saturday morning, Megs's kitchen table, where for years they'd done documentary reruns and critical reviews of their Friday nights.

'I doubt it,' said Megs.

'What did Sharon's mother say?'

'She seemed to think it was all my fault. Not firm enough with my children. Then, who knows what she said, the amount of brandy she took. Of course I didn't need brandy. I just smoked his dope.'

'Good for you. Was it any good?'

'The best. Wonder where he got it.'

They stared at each other a moment before sniggering wildly.

'Look on the bright side,' said Lorraine. 'It'll be a great saving on shampoo.' Then, because she had to say it, and didn't know how to approach the subject, 'Harry's left me.'

'He hasn't. I don't believe you. Not Harry.'

'Yes.' Lorraine nodded. 'He's gone off with Flat Stomach and Brainless.' The room filled with her despair. She lit a cigarette, snap of lighter, fizz of singeing tobacco. 'I thought I'd take him home. Pour him a glass of malt and give him the best blow-job of his life. Remind him of how good he had things. But, "A blow-job won't fix everything, Lorraine," he says. "You think it will. But not this time." So . . .' she flicked ash into the plant pot, '. . . there you go. A blow-job doesn't fix everything. And here's me thinking it did. More fool me.'

Megs didn't like to fetch an ashtray. This was too dire a moment to be prissy about plants. 'He's left?'

'Yes. He wants a baby. Says he's been thinking about it for a couple of years now. And that's what he really wants – children. Now there's something a blow-job really won't get you.' She moved her tongue across her teeth, clamped her lips. She didn't want to cry. Avoiding Megs's sympathetic gaze, she looked out of the window.

'Well.' Megs was shocked. 'I never thought Harry . . .' Then, reassuringly, 'He'll be back.'

'I don't think so. Flat Stomach and Brainless is two months gone.'

'My God.' Then, stiffly through the gloom, 'Well, brainless she may remain, but the flat stomach's soon to be but a memory.'

Lorraine meant to smile, only grimaced. 'There's that.'

The squeak and honk, rattle and bash of Saturday cartoons battered through from the living room. A tear slid down Lorraine's cheek. 'There you go.' She was resigned. 'Don't people always want the one thing you can't give them?' She'd fought a long, bitter, hormonal battle with her body, cursing its inability to conceive. She hated it. She hated herself. Sometimes she'd lie alone on her bed in the dark on her pink-patterned duvet, under the framed picture of puppies in a basket, quietly punching her stomach, punishment for blocked tubes. 'Damn you.'

For years her monthly cycle brought her out in craziness and rage. She'd sit on the toilet staring with sorrow at bloodied tissue. 'Damn you.' She'd run her fingers tenderly over newspaper pictures of abused children. 'I'd love you. I wouldn't do that.' Sitting, weekday television evenings, side by side on the sofa, Harry would look across at her and she'd be crying. He'd turn back to the screen. There was nothing he could say. Babies were all she thought about. Her obsession made him lonely. 'Pack it in, Lor.'

After a couple of years of precision lovemaking – passion on cue, according to the demands of charts, thermometers, and Lorraine lying frigid when her body wasn't ripe, 'No, no, we must save it for tomorrow. It's my time tomorrow' – Harry had insisted Lorraine get tested. He knew it couldn't be him. His last girlfriend had aborted his child. Now he discovered himself thinking about it. He rather fancied himself as a dad.

When they discovered Lorraine's tubes were blocked, Harry tore up the charts and graphs Lorraine had lovingly drawn up.

'That's my life you're tearing into pieces,' she cried.

'Our life starts now.' He was adamant. 'And while I'm at it . . .' He reached up and took down the puppy picture. 'I fucking hate this.' Lorraine re-hung the puppies and took out a personal loan to pay for IVF treatment. But Harry said, 'I'm not wanking in a cubicle surrounded by porno magazines.' So they applied to adopt.

Then, two days before their interview, Lorraine met her poet. Friday night at the Glass Bucket, there he was at the bar, looking gorgeous. It was chemistry at first sight. He took her back to his flat and Lorraine remembered what sex was about. That fevered fumble, helping him to help her out of her clothes and never getting close enough. She lay on his bed, one hand on his neck in his hair, the other on his bum, and she thought, 'This is me. This is what I am. Sex is what I do best.' She only cried a little bit.

Next day she and her poet and her personal loan took off across the country. They battered and crunched down the motorway, listening to old Neil Young tapes, singing along. 'Hey, hey, my, my . . .' And Lorraine wept buckets for lost years. 'I should've been doing this all along.'

They stopped at motorway caffs, drank foul coffee, ate burgers, listened to the banter of long-distance truckers. Lorraine felt the throb of wheels and the hum of a different life. She borrowed money for the jukebox, played hits, old songs from happy times past before she declared war on her tubes. She breathed greasy wafts of fast food and decadence and she thought, All this life was out here, while I was in my pink bedroom crying for children that would never be born. Hands on the jukebox, back to the room, she danced with herself.

Harry meantime cancelled the adoption interview. Next day, caught in a traffic jam opposite a park, he watched a father playing football with his infant son. The child, knee-high to a white plastic ball, ran with uncertain legs at it, kicked at it wildly, watched it move a full six inches. The father cried, 'Great shot,' and made an absurd display of losing a tiny tackle. Then he lifted his son and gently cast him into the air. 'Away we go.' The child, chuckling wildly, fell back towards his outstretched hands. That wholesome, infantile laughter rang clear through the rattle and irate honk of impatient drivers.

Harry watched, unaware that the snarled knot of traffic had unravelled and the cars in front of him had all moved off. He was smiling, though he didn't realise it. He had never felt such a pang of envy in his life. He wanted a child.

'I wouldn't mind,' Lorraine sniffed, turning to Megs, 'but the bitch looks like I did fifteen years ago. Younger than me. Better-looking than me. And pregnant. I feel like shit. And everybody must've known about it except me. They must all have been laughing at me.'

'No,' said Megs.

'Is this how you felt when you discovered Mike and Denise?'

'Yes. Sort of futile and a failure and betrayed. Tricked out in old, worn, child-stained clothes, with lank hair and no make-up.'

From through the house came the cry, 'Baldy! Baldy!' Something was thrown. Something crashed. 'Shut up, Lizzy.' Jack's voice. Lizzy howled.

'You two stop it through there,' Megs hollered, leaning as far back in her chair as she could so that she could look into the living room without actually getting up.

'They were in bed when I got back. I just stood there at the door, looking at them. I think I said something cryptic like, "Having fun?"'

'Were they actually doing it?' Lorraine wanted details, though she'd heard them all before. Nothing soothed like other people's wounds.

'No. They'd not long done, though. She was getting up. Her clothes were on the chair by the window, all folded nicely. His suit was hanging up on the back of the door.'

'Oh, the tidy bitch. I hate that. How was she?'

'Cellulite. Fat arse. Droopy tits. A grippable roll of fat.' They grinned. 'Nah,' said Megs, 'she's got a great body. Mike was lying back, smoking. She was at my side of the bed. I can still see it. And now I realise they'd been doing it for ages. They had a routine.'

'What did you say then?' Lorraine prompted.

'Nothing. I just stood there. I don't even think my mouth was moving, the way it does, with all the insults that your brain is too shocked to let go of. I was leaning on the doorpost and I think my face was all torn with hurt and betrayal. Denise was horrified. But Mike was just lying there. Know what I think? I think he planned it.

400

I think he wanted me to find them. Then he wouldn't have to tell me about the affair. He wouldn't have to say he was leaving me. I had to throw him out.'

'I wouldn't be surprised,' said Lorraine.

'Know what I did?' said Megs.

'No,' said Lorraine. But she did. Of course she did. She'd been through this story often.

'I stripped the bed. Even though they were still there. I stripped it, and I was going to wash the sheets. But I threw them out. I ran down to the bin at the back and stuffed them in whilst Mike and Denise were struggling to get dressed.' She rubbed her face, and yawned. 'Then of course I had to buy more sheets. We only had one set.'

Megs gathered their empty mugs and took them to the sink, rinsed them under the tap and pressed the button on the kettle. 'More?' she said, lifting the coffee jar.

Lorraine nodded, and lit another cigarette. 'Harry and Brainless did it at her flat.' She pursed her lips. Considered her new identity as a cuckold. 'I suppose I had it coming. The affairs I've had. What goes around comes around. You can't say I didn't deserve it.'

Megs didn't answer that. It was bad enough for Lorraine to admit the truth without someone agreeing with her. She switched back to her own vile moments. 'I didn't want to ever sleep in that bed again. But of course I couldn't afford to throw it out.'

The word 'afford' started fear in Lorraine. She would have to manage on her own. The whole world of alone was looming before her. One little chicken breast under the grill, one plate to wash. No obliging bum to warm her cold feet on in bed. Nobody to chat to. Nobody to turn to after a night slumped before the telly and say, 'Well, that wasn't worth watching.' She never found any solace in silence. It scared her. Then again, if being alone was her future, she thought she ought to go home, lock the door and get on with it.

The front door slammed, Hannah was home. Megs heard her go straight to her room, shut the door, then to the bathroom, rush of water, rattle of toothbrush, back to bedroom, shut door again. 'Signs of a guilty conscience,' she said to Lorraine. 'Remember all that?'

'Do I ever. God, scrubbing your teeth, sucking Polos, smiling

401

dutifully through a stinking hangover. At least I don't have to lie like that any more.'

'Be back in a minute.' Megs reluctantly rose and went to speak to her daughter.

Hannah flushed, and hurriedly stuffed something under her duvet as Megs came into the room.

'Did you have a nice time?' Megs said.

'Great,' Hannah enthused. 'Brilliant.'

'Who was it you stayed with?'

'Chrissy.'

'It was Lisa when you went out last night.'

Hannah flushed deeper. Was it? She couldn't remember. She was so hungover last night's lie seemed a lifetime away. 'No,' she said weakly. 'Chrissy.'

'Who have you been with?' Megs said, sweeping back the duvet cover to reveal a crumpled heap of scanty black underwear. 'Who is he?'

'Chrissy.' Hannah wasn't giving up on her lie. 'These are Chrissy's.'

'I like that lie, it's in the true child-to-parent tradition. Your belief in it is touching. I used to lie like that to my parents. I had parents too. You know, a matching set. Evenings they sat either side of the fireplace reading the *Mail* and I came home to them and told them lies. You have not let the family down. Who is he?'

'David.'

'How old?'

'Twenty,' said with hope.

'How old?' Megs folded her arms. She wasn't moving till she got the truth.

'Twenty-eight.'

'And you're sixteen. It's not on, Hannah. We'll talk about this later.' Megs returned to the kitchen. 'Lorraine,' she sighed, sitting down, 'I do believe the girl is worse than you.'

'Surely not. God help her.'

'Someone has to. She's seeing a man almost twice her age.'

Lorraine raised her eyes. Sipped her coffee and said, 'You'll have to get Aunty Betty and her wooden spoon to him.'

Megs smiled. Years ago, when she'd worked at the Seaview Guest

House, a tattooed man had came into her bedroom, naked. It had taken Megs a minute to see his nakedness through the blaze of decorations all over his body. But when she had, she screamed. Aunty Betty rushed from the kitchen wielding the first thing that came to hand – a wooden spoon. But her fury made it seem like some fearsome cleaver. The interloper had fled, down the stairs and out the door, naked and ashamed. Hours later the police found him cowering on the beach and came to collect his clothes for him. He was too scared to come himself.

'Aunty Betty,' Megs said softly, 'we need you.'

She folded her arms on the table, laid her head on them. 'Lorraine,' she said, 'I don't know – what is it about parents and children that we deny all sexual activity to each other? As if that isn't how they got here in the first place. Parents have silent, stifled sex and children sit suddenly bolt upright and stare ahead in feigned innocence. And I, who just entered the room, pretend not to notice the fumblings and dishevelled hair and rumpled clothing. Sometimes it seems that's all we do to each other, parents and children, lie and lie and lie.'

Lizzy came through. 'I want a drink.' She handed Megs a pink plastic mug. Which was handed back half-filled with orange juice.

'There's nothing in the house,' said Megs. 'I'll have to shop.'

'I'll come with you,' offered Lorraine. She decided to put off being alone for an hour or so. In fact, for as long as possible. She turned in her seat to watch Lizzy in her dungarees and huge dog's-face slippers pad back to the living room, clutching her mug in both hands. She smiled when she heard Lizzy's full-throated roar, 'Get off my seat,' and Jack's huge, resigned sigh as he heaved himself from chair to sofa.

'That one will have no problems when she grows up. Nobody will dump her. Nobody would dare.' She adored the child.

'It's Jack who'll have trouble,' Megs sighed. 'His sisters run rings round him.'

'I'll have to buy him a new baseball cap.'

'Lorraine.' Megs put a mug of coffee in front of her. 'You can't afford to indulge my children any more. You have to watch your cash.'

'I know. I should look for a new job. But who'd have me? What can I do? What am I good at?' She lifted her mug to her lips, blew on it, decided against taking a sip and put it down again. 'Well, there's that.' She shoved her mouth into a wan little smile. 'But we know now that doesn't solve everything.'

'You could put it on your CV,' suggested Megs. '"Gives a great blow-job."'

'Harry said last night that Brainless was better. Better at that. Better at anything you can think of, in fact. He says she really, really loves him. And she listens to him. Which apparently is more than I ever do. He says she makes him feel good about himself for the first time in years.'

'People hurt each other. We always come to that.' Megs cupped her hands round her mug and stared across the kitchen. The crazed cartoon blather and stramash still ricocheted through the living room. The fridge purred. There was a thin haze of dirt on the fake tile lino. The unit was strewn with crumbs, dollops of marg and jam, cornflakes, drops of milk and a scattering of sugar. There was a pile of dirty dishes in the sink and a crumpled tea towel beside the kettle. She should clean up. All her best fights had taken place in this kitchen. The one with Mike when she first had him alone after discovering him with Denise. That night, long after the children were in bed, he appeared in the kitchen to pick up his things.

'You bastard,' she said. 'I've been going out to work, looking after the kids,' she waved her arms – her grievances were too many to list – 'and you were fucking that cow. You were coming home here, moaning at me. Nagging me. "Can't you make an effort, Megs?"' She imitated him, whiny voice. 'Being all nicey-nicey to the neighbours, "Good morning, Mrs Thing. Lovely day, Mr Whatsit." Ignoring your children and . . .' she ran to him, to hit him. But he caught her arm, so she kicked his ankle, '. . . me!' she yelled.

'Bitch,' he spat. Clenched his fist and raised it. His face was knotted with loathing. 'Cunt.' He said it as hard as he could, for he couldn't bring himself to land the blow.

She picked up a plate. Glaring at him, she threw it to the floor. It splattered, scattering china pieces across the kitchen. Years later she was to find bits under the fridge.

'That's right.' His lip curled in scorn. 'Take it out on the crockery.'

She threw a cup at him. Missed. It shattered against the wall and a flying fragment missiled into his cheek. He put his hand over the pain and blood.

'You sodding boor.' Her voice was lowered. She opened her mouth but was too overwhelmed to speak. Her lips and lower jaw were loose, shaking with hurt and fury. When at last she found her voice, it came trembling from her throat. 'You wear your sodding suit and you shut me out. I'm not good enough for you any more, am I? I wear this old stuff and you're ashamed of me, aren't you? But you dump on me. Take your frustrations and tensions out on me. I am so handy for that. You're charming at work and come home to snap at me. Bastard.' She kicked him again. He did not move. 'Behind every successful man is a woman. BOLLOCKS!' Her voice returned. She screamed at him, waving two fingers. 'You fuck,' she shouted. 'Arse.' She was screaming, leaning forward at him, shoving a single, stiff middle finger in his face. Her face was nasty, contorted with pain and shame and disgust. Eyes puffed, swollen with tears. What must I have looked like? she mused. 'I hate you. I hate you. I hate you,' she screamed till her voice cracked. Cords bulged in her throat. She rushed at him, kicking and slapping. 'Hate. Hate. Hate,' she cried. In some recessed layer of untapped feeling beneath the heaving surge of fury, she realised, oh, the relief it was to tell him her true feelings, at last. He did nothing. He stood still under the raining blows, letting her let go. His hand was raised, but not to protect himself from her beating. It was the vile rush of her saliva that he couldn't bear.

'Behind every successful man is a woman with a brush and shovel, cleaning up the shit he's too full of himself to notice. Bastard. Bastard. Bastard.' But now she was not kicking him. She was knocking her own sorry, unloved head on the doorpost and weeping. Choking. She turned. Jack and Hannah were standing watching her. They were hand in hand, wearing matching bright-red tracksuit pyjamas, and they were staring at her with huge, sleepless eyes. Hannah was clutching her favourite toy, an ancient duck called Harvey. They were absorbing everything they saw, every detail of the scene that confronted them. They had seen her fury. She had never felt so ashamed. She thought she had ruined their innocence.

Mike went through to the bedroom to pack. When he came back

into the kitchen to tell her he was finally going she noticed he'd taken her favourite case but thought better of mentioning it. Besides, she had cast around looking for something to use to wipe her face and blow her nose, and finding nothing she had lifted her T-shirt up. Now she'd exposed her stomach and grubby bra, and he pointedly noticed.

'I have to get the children back to bed,' she said.

'I never knew you could be so rude.' That glimpse of sagging underwear and flab had given him the upper hand. His stomach was still smooth and flat.

'Oh, for goodness' sake, Mike,' she scoffed. Her throat hurt – too much shouting. Her voice was still shaking – too much emotion. 'Everybody can be rude. I was always rude. I was just too polite to let it show.'

It was three months before they could communicate again. Divorce. Maintenance. Visiting rights. After Thomas died Mike drifted back, lingering in this kitchen. She could not look at him without noticing the scar on his cheek.

How she hated to remember that night, her loss of control. She still recoiled from that hideous moment when she realised that her children had seen it all. She wondered if they remembered it too, and if they secretly hated her for it. She covered her face with her hands, protecting herself from her memories.

In the living room Lizzy and Jack started to quarrel. 'Leave me. Leave me,' Lizzy shouted. Then, hollering above the television, 'That's mine.'

'Will you two stop it,' Megs said. 'Please.' She did not want to shout. She did not want to move. Though she knew she ought to get up and go through to check that nobody was actually getting beaten up. Lizzy bullied Jack horribly.

'I'm just trying to show her how to make her Lego into something other than a little gun.'

'Lizzy,' Megs ordered, 'let Jack show you how to build something out of the Lego.'

'Don't want him to,' Lizzy sulked.

'Yes you do,' Megs said. 'You want to build things, don't you?'

'No.' Little pouty voice from behind the sofa.

'Oh well. Don't, then. Stick with making little guns. Don't advance yourself. Don't expand your mind to greater and greater things. But don't come crying to me when you're thirty and are still sitting behind the sofa in your silly slippers making Lego guns when all your friends are doctors, lawyers, architects or proper bricklayers complete with bum cleavage.'

Lorraine tutted. 'You shouldn't speak to her like that.'

Jack laughed.

Lizzy relented. 'All right. Show me. You do it.'

'Chip butties,' Megs's eyes lit up. She sat straight in her seat, face brimming with glee. 'Chip butties,' she said again, leaning across the table, gripping Lorraine's arms. 'It came to me just now, when my brain emptied. That's when the best ideas come to you. When you're not doing anything specific with your brain. Forget all the marinated chicken, the tomatoes, ham, cheeses, all the fancy sandwiches. We could open the world's first chip butty bar. The only thing we'll serve is chip sandwiches. Fat chips, thin chips, little crispy chips – whatever you fancy. With a selection of sauces. We'll make a fortune. Days of heaven and cholesterol. Aunty Betty would be proud. Return to the golden fries of yesteryear.'

For a moment Lorraine joined the fantasy. 'Chiparama,' she glowed. 'Chips a-gogo. Don't ask what we can do with your fries, ask what our fries will do for you. Salt, vinegar, ketchup. Mayonnaise, even.' She spread her hands, pardoning already misguided customers who might make this choice. 'They'll come for miles.' Then the truth snuck up and hit her. She shouldn't be dreaming. She couldn't dream any more. She had her life to sort out. And she didn't think chip butties were the answer to her prayers. 'We'll smell of fat all the time. Our hair will go all greasy and lifeless. Our pores will open. Our skin will be grey and flaccid.'

'Don't tell me. The face that launched a thousand chips.'

Grinning, Lorraine said, 'That was very Big Bill Broonzy of you, shouting out like that.'

'God,' Megs shrieked, hands flying to face, shielding it as long-gone expressions from a forsaken slice of her life spread across it. 'I'd forgotten all about that.' Memories. She let them flow. 'God,' she whispered. 'Big Bill Broonzy.'

It was their last tour. They'd done Amsterdam, Copenhagen, Marseilles and Paris. Small, hazy, smoke-filled back-street clubs where people gathered late, drank and listened to the blues. Megs loved it. There was nothing she didn't enthuse about: the buildings, the coffee, the clothes, the beer, the food. 'There are even strange colours. Every morning smells of coffee and fresh baking. And nobody knows who I am. I love being a stranger. All around me I hear the rhythm of strange words. I don't understand what people are saying. If I'm doing something as simple as ordering a beer I have to think about what words to use.'

'You play at home, at least you get ripped off in English. You come over here and it happens to you in a language you don't speak. I just love that,' Mike complained.

Walking in Montmartre she gripped his arm. 'We could come live here. In Paris.'

'Don't be daft,' he said.

'We could,' she said. 'We could play small bars, just you and me. You playing, me singing. We wouldn't need much. I love you.' She didn't mean it. She meant, I love this place. I love this moment. He didn't answer.

'Think of the people who have been here. Lived here. Worked here. Hemingway. James Joyce. Nina Simone. Maybe one of them walked down this street. Maybe their feet . . .' She pointed at the worn paving slabs. She was young enough to be dreamy about fame. To indulge in thinking that if she stepped on the very ground where one of her heroes once trod some of his fabulous gift would seep up through her shoes, through her. She stopped, spread her arms, felt the Parisian air, shut her eyes. She imagined them all here, in this street, walking in a long row, arms linked. Though she knew their times in the city did not coincide. 'Louis Armstrong, T.S. Eliot, F. Scott Fitzgerald, Gertrude Stein, Django Reinhardt. And all those blues singers, sons and daughters of slaves who learned their songs in fields and in Southern bars with wonderful names like the Dreamland Café or Pete Lala's, like' – the name escaped her – 'thing.'

'Who?'

'You know. Tall guy. Deep voice. Swore he ate two pork chops and three fried eggs for his breakfast every morning. You know. Thing.'

'I haven't the vaguest idea who you are talking about.' He was envious of her vast knowledge of the blues, its singers and their biographies. Besides, this was to be his last tour. He'd decided. He was tired of being poor. He felt poor and shoddy in an increasingly gleamy world. He was starting to look with longing at expensive cars and electrical goods. He lingered over adverts in supplements that showed richer men than him lounging on extravagantly comfortable sofas with fabulous women, drinking smart drinks, laughing and looking cool. He wanted that. He'd signed up two months ago to start an accountancy course. He just didn't know how to tell the others.

They came home and returned to their reality, the round of small venues – village halls, pubs, greasy food and bladder-torturing hours heaped and crumpled in the van with the radio on. Miles and miles, with Megs dreaming of Paris every inch. Now and then she'd sit up, staring quizzically ahead. 'Who was that guy? What was his name? Big, handsome face. Oh, I can see it.' The others chipped in to her quandary, sometimes offering names from their smattering knowledge of blues men. 'Blind Lemon Jefferson?' 'Furry Lewis?' 'Scrapper Blackwell?' 'Leroy Carr?' But Megs always shook her head. 'Nah.'

June. They gigged in Aberdeen, boozed, and played old hippie songs – 'Spoonful' and 'Red Rooster' – to students and oil men. Next night Inverness, then up to Nairn and down the west coast, heading for Oban, chewing gum, smoking, drinking lager and Jack Daniels and hardly talking at all.

They took a detour to Gairloch. Eddy said the lobsters were worth the drive. But Megs thought the drive was worth the drive. Trundling down through pine forests, looking over treetops to the sea. The smell of fresh air, intoxicating peaty draughts, dark-green pine scents seeped through the rusting gaps and holes in their van, cut their cleansing way through the fug of smoke, joss sticks, musk, forgotten carry-outs, sweat and old farts.

They fell silent, gazing out at the distant swell of blue, distracted from their usual travelogue: easy tabloid crosswords, small bickerings about old *Bonanza* plots or discontinued chocolate bars, to a constant musical backdrop of Bruce Springsteen or Bob Seger. 'Night moves,' that nicotined, booze-raddled voice would cry. 'Night moves,' they'd join in, even if they only lipped the words. They didn't sing much and they no longer planned or wove dreams out of spangled, elaborated stories of other people's success that floated to them on the musicians' grapevine. They were disillusioned.

They drove to the small quay and decanted, blinking, into a blistering summer day. They'd forgotten the weather. It was for ever late February in the back of that gaudy painted van. People watched as they shuffled out of it, stretching and scratching. People always watched, and they always performed. They looked like a bunch of deranged plumbers. But they were a band. They acted cool. They didn't look at anybody.

They walked the length of the quay. Four blokes and a girl. Mike draped his arm round her. She was his. That was how they always walked together – until they got married. After that she was usually three paces behind him.

Of course, they did not get a lobster. They stood watching as two lorries piled high with them drove off the quay, and south. Then they bought corned beef, bread, crisps, biscuits and beer to eat on the beach.

One o'clock in the morning, Mike and Megs sat alone by the sea. The others, zipped into sleeping bags, slept drunkenly in the back of the van. Megs dug her toes into the sand. They had one last tin of Carlsberg that they handed back and forth between them – a swig apiece.

There was pink campion growing up the bank behind them. The breeze shoved through it. The tide crept towards them, sucking and sighing back, dragging shells and shingle. A late tern called – a scraping cry.

'We could live here,' Megs said. 'We could stop touring and live here. We could grow our own stuff and be self-sufficient.'

'Last week you were going to live in Paris.'

'That was that dream. This is this one.'

'I'm going to be an accountant,' he said. 'I'm giving up the band and going to college in October.'

She stared at him. Couldn't believe it. 'You never said.'

410

'I'm saying now.'

'But why?'

'Why! Why do you think? We've been doing this for years and we're nowhere. We're nothing. We have nothing. It costs as much as we earn to keep going. I'm going to end up an old man with no decent home, no car. Nothing. I'm getting out.'

'But . . .' was all she could say.

Seeing how shaken she was, he put his arm round her. 'Marry me,' he said. 'We'll have our own house done out the way we want it. Kids even. We'll stop all this touring. All this sitting in the van. I can't stand it any more. I can't stand having nothing. No money.'

She didn't answer. Marriage hadn't really occurred to her. She wanted to keep going. She didn't think it through – she never thought anything through – but somehow she believed if she kept on going all the things she wanted would come to her. It was just a matter of time.

He did not know what to make of her silence. So he kissed her. 'Marry me,' he said again. 'I'll make you happy. I'll make you so rich you'll never want for anything.'

She didn't think she was wanting for anything now. But she kissed him back and felt that flicker of his tongue against hers, and she wanted him. They made love on the sand, with the campion moving behind them and the sea sneaking nearer and nearer. She wrapped her legs round him, clung to him. And then, oh joy, it came to her. It came the way things that have been evading an overenquiring mind always come – at that sweet moment when the mind stops enquiring, when it idles and is vacant. Just when Mike was starting to moan, and rapture was on its way to him, Megs remembered the name she'd been seeking.

'BIG BILL BROONZY!' she screamed. 'That's the guy. Big Bill Broonzy.'

Mike's ardour wilted. 'What do you mean by that? Is that what you're thinking about?'

'No.' She knew she'd hurt him.

'Don't you think about me when we're doing it?' He withdrew from her. Sat up. Turned his back.

'Of course I do. I think about you all the time. I love you.' She

411

didn't but she thought she ought to say it. 'It was just that I've been trying to remember his name. Then when I relaxed it came to me. That's all.'

Mike huffed. He lit a cigarette. 'You don't really care about me. Do you?'

'I do. I do. I love you. I want to marry you. I really do.' Anything, anything. She would say anything to cover the fact that she was lying to him, and to hide from the fact that he might be lying to her, too.

'Do you?' He reached out to stroke her hair.

'Yes.' She met his eyes. 'Yes.' For a moment she just about believed it herself. She stripped off what little she was wearing. 'Let's celebrate with a swim.'

'Too cold,' said Mike. 'And I'm too drunk.'

She ran the few steps to the sea alone and tiptoed in, gasping as she went deeper, arms above her head. 'C'mon.'

Mike wouldn't move. So she swam alone. Slowly up and down past him. The night was soft on her face, a small breeze drifting over the surface ruffled against her, chill against her damp cheeks. She turned, eyes level with the water. The sea seemed endless. She thought she could swim out into the Atlantic and keep going and going and going. She turned on to her back, spread-eagled, and floated. She could feel the swell and drift of the water beneath her, and above a dusting of stars, summer constellations. She was truly happy. At the time she thought it was because Mike wanted to marry her. But thinking about it now, she realised it was because he was not with her.

'Betrayed,' she said softly. 'Talk about betrayed. Look what I did. I betrayed myself and Mike.'

'Why?' Lorraine couldn't believe this. 'What did you do?'

'I married him. I was afraid of having nothing. When he said he was going to be an accountant, I couldn't think what I would do next. So I married him. What a shit.'

'No you're not. Don't say that. Rubbish. You and Mike had been together for such a long time, everyone was tired of waiting for you to marry.'

'I didn't love him, though. Did I? I'd been part of something for so long, I was scared of being alone.'

'Ah, that,' said Lorraine. 'I know that. But it's not all your fault. You can't go blaming yourself.'

'Oh well, Big Bill Broonzy.' Megs smiled. 'Better blame him, then. It's all his fault. All of this. Everything.' A wave of her hand indicated the flat and all her past life.

'You gotta blame someone,' said Lorraine.

'It's as well Big Bill Broonzy as anyone.'

Lizzy came into the kitchen, teetering on her high heels, scraping them on the lino. Tiny, naked feet making big boats of her mother's size five shoes. 'Who is Big Bill Broonzy?'

'He was a singer. He's dead. I was just remembering something that happened years ago on a beach. That's all,' Megs told her.

'Did you know him?' Lizzy hobbled dangerously towards her.

'No. It was just something I said.'

'What did you say?'

'I said his name. I'd been trying to remember it. It was at Gairloch. Years and years ago.'

Lizzy considered this. Then her face lit up. 'I remember,' she said. 'I remember that.'

'You can't possibly,' Megs scolded. 'It was before you were born.'

'I was always born.' Lizzy couldn't bear to think of Megs doing anything without her. 'I was there. You just didn't see me. I was hiding.'

'Ah.' Megs softened. 'That'll be it.' She watched the child wobble across the kitchen and felt her expression change. The love she felt. Sometimes it shook her. Sometimes just seeing her daughter made something within her tremble. Her mother often accused her of loving Lizzy too much. But Megs doubted anyone could love someone so small too much. This love was the purest thing Megs had ever known, but still it made her guilty. She thought that Lizzy was a child who was never meant to be. If Thomas hadn't died, Lizzy would never have been born.

The child made her precarious way back to the living room. 'I'm going to have to wear these shoes if we're going out. I can't tie my laces.'

'What?' Megs acted incensed. 'How old are you?'

'Four.'

'Four and you can't tie your own laces. Good heavens, when I was four I had a milk round *and* I was offered a job as head of British Industry.'

'You shouldn't speak to her like that,' said Lorraine. 'You'll give her a complex.'

Lizzy turned and shot Megs a mocking look. 'It's not my fault I can't tie my laces,' she said.

'Whose fault is it, then?' Lorraine wanted to know.

Lizzy looked surprised she had to ask. 'Big Bill Broonzy's,' she said.

Chapter Eighteen

They ordered pizza, hired videos and drank too much wine. Lorraine decided she'd drunk too much to drive home, and stayed over. Drinking too much and staying over suited her. It not only delayed that moment of going home and facing the great alone, but for a while she actually forgot about it. But Megs worried that she would take up residence on the sofa. She couldn't blame her. All those years ago on that beach she had found herself agreeing to marry because she too was afraid of being alone.

They'd slept on the beach that night, squeezed side by side in their double sleeping bag, under the stars. Megs woke early, roused by the rustle of wind through the grasses and campion in the dunes behind them, and the white swish of restless seagulls floating in the half-dark, knowing that something was about to happen. Dawn was going to break. When the first light appeared, a searing glimmer along the horizon, the gulls rose, shrieking. A callous clamour resounding across the morning. The new day seemed to take them by storm, the din they made. Maybe, Megs thought, resentfully lifting herself on to one elbow, in their tiny seagull minds they'd forgotten that this same thing happened yesterday, and the day before, and every single day before that. Maybe each new day scared them stiff. They saw that distant glare in its moments of blinding whiteness before it glowed into reds and golds, and they decided the end had come. 'End of the world, end of the world,' they screamed, a wild, clanging cacophony. Their uproar didn't last long. But Megs was awake. She felt hungover and filthy. Sand lined the secret recesses of her body and made her scalp crawl. She went back into the sea, to cleanse herself.

It was even colder than last night, but when she had grown accustomed to the chill she spread herself into the water and started to swim towards the new light. When she turned, she was surprised at how far she'd come. There was a vast expanse of choppy water between her and the shore. The wind out here was harsh. She rolled in the water and swam again, out towards that white glare, tempted again to keep going. Fear made her stop. She looked down, could hardly see her legs waving in the deep keeping her afloat. 'I'm scared of this, and scared of that. Scared of everything.' Scared of the grey murk below her, scared of the new dawn and scared of life on her own. Years and years she'd gone everywhere, done her growing up as part of a group. She'd forgotten what it was like to be an individual. She was afraid the individual couldn't cope on her own. She didn't trust herself to manage without Mike. Now he'd decided to go off on his own, she wanted to know what was going to happen to her. She couldn't wait to let life happen naturally, so she'd manipulated her future. She'd agreed to marry Mike. 'End of the world. End of the world,' she'd sang to herself as she swam ashore. Remembering that now, Lorraine's reluctance to go home seemed trivial. Still, Megs worried that she'd lose what little privacy she had.

It was a handy worry that distracted her from her main worries – money, work, her children. She lay in the dark, at her feet Shameless fidgeted in his sleep, whiffing, whining, paws scurrying over dreamland parks, chasing dreamland rabbits. Lizzy, clutching a purple toy Transit van that dug into Megs's side, slept noisily, breathing chokily, snorting slightly. Had she been an old man and not her beautiful daughter, Megs would have been deeply irritated. Megs stroked her perfect cheek and said, 'Wonder what Gilbert is doing now?' She surprised herself. Until that moment she had not been aware of thinking about him.

Gilbert was in bed with Annette. They always slept together at his place on Saturday nights, at hers on Thursdays. She liked the right-hand side near the window and kept a pair of ivory silk pyjamas in the top right-hand drawer of the chest next to the bed. She had a toothbrush in the bathroom cabinet and insisted Gilbert kept baking soda toothpaste, for she liked no other. She brought free-range eggs and fresh orange juice for breakfast. They drank Colombian coffee –

black, no sugar. They read the *Sunday Times*, swapping supplements. They didn't speak much. They thought they had a perfect arrangement. A marriage that had no legal bindings, no bickering about who had drunk all the Earl Grey and who should buy the toilet roll. A commitment that did not involve anybody's bank account.

Saturday nights, if they did not go out, Gilbert cooked. Saturday mornings he shopped, cycling – hair on end – between delicatessen, fruit shop, Italian bakers and Oddbins, where he spent a happy half-hour selecting the wine with the most tasteful label.

In the afternoon, wearing a vast butcher's apron with ties that twice circled his waist and knotted over his tummy, he'd set to. He laid out his Sabatier knives, and his best pots, cookbook propped open. For the past three Saturdays he'd done saltimbocca alla romana. This week was no different. He had veal, fresh sage and ham – he was perfecting the dish. He splashed a great deal, drank a great deal, hummed snatches of Verdi and Puccini. The more he drank, the more he splashed, the louder he hummed. He was happy. His hair was flat. Not once did fretful fingers reach towards his scalp.

Annette usually sat, legs curled, on his sofa, watching videos – always with subtitles, often in black and white. She drank white wine. Sometimes she read. And sometimes she came, leaned on the doorpost, not quite entering the cook's domain. Wine in hand, little smile – was she being patronising? Gilbert wondered – she'd watch. 'I'm rubbish in the kitchen,' she told him.

Once a month she ate out with her chums. Over pasta, salad and white wine they'd discuss their lives. The more wine they ordered, the more deranged, gigglish and critical the conversation. Gilbert was a favourite topic. They all agreed Annette should take him in hand. 'Sort him out,' someone always said. 'Get him a decent haircut. And his trousers.' Giggles. Gilbert's trousers were not what he thought them to be.

'I know,' Annette would sigh. 'They're sort of flappy.' She'd make flappy movements with drunken hands. Gilbert's trousers, they unanimously decided, flapped where they ought to be snug, and were snug where a bit of flapping would be the thing. Poor Gilbert.

He invoked such criticism, and all he thought he was doing was living his life.

Today, after he'd bought his Italian rice, fresh Parmesan and porcini, and packed them carefully in his rucksack, he cycled miles out of his way to where Megs lived. He pedalled past her building, looking up at her window. What was she doing? he desperately wanted to know. She would be up there behind her window, answering the phone, fending off friends and admirers. People would be constantly ringing her up with invitations, or perhaps just to say hello. People did things like that to someone like Megs. But not, he knew, to him. Then again, he never phoned anybody just to say hello. He was scared they might be annoyed at him and not want to say hello back.

Megs fascinated him. He imagined her to be a lot wilder and bawdier than she actually was. Suddenly scared that she might throw open her window and lean out, tits pressed on folded arms, to make saucy comments to passers-by, like Melina Mercouri in *Never on a Sunday*, and notice him gazing fondly up at her, he took off. Wheels whirring, feet a blur, he felt a fool. A passing child, exuberantly cheeky, shouted, 'Burn rubber, baby.' Gilbert squirmed. He hadn't done anything like this since he was fourteen and wildly in love with Virginia Watson, who was a precocious thirteen, wildly sophisticated. She drank Pimm's, smoked black Sobranie cigarettes and had a twenty-year-old boyfriend, but she thought him sweet and called him Silly Gilly. God, what was happening to him? He hadn't thought about her in years.

Gilbert and Annette had made love every Saturday night since their routine started. It wasn't ever anything spectacular, just enjoyable and comforting. They both knew they'd slipped into having the sort of orderly sex life they mocked in other people, married people, but neither liked to say.

Annette rolled over to look at him. 'How long have you been sitting awake?'

'Not long.' It was two-thirty. He'd been staring at the end of the bed since before one.

'Are you worrying about your book?'

'No.' He was. Though this bout of sleeplessness was also spent thinking about Megs.

'How's it going?'

'Very well.' It wasn't. Until this moment he hadn't realised how easily he lied to her. He lied as easily as Megs had on the phone to her mother.

'You should go up to your cottage for the summer. You'll get on with it there.'

'Yes,' he said slowly, mulling this over. 'The cottage.' He turned to her. 'Will you come?'

'Gilbert,' she scolded. 'You know I'm going to America.'

'Oh yes,' he said slowly, turning this over. He'd forgotten she'd be away for the summer. 'Pity,' he said. But he felt a little tug of joy. He thought about Megs. What was she doing now? How was she coping with her shaven son, her absurdly friendly dog, her girls and her gossipy chum? Was she in that kitchen? And wasn't it interesting what happened when clutter turned into a home? How individual items, ghastly on their own, somehow collectively became endearing. Maybe they took on the identity of their owner. Who would have thought that this discerning heart would shudder and jolt at the thought of a pink-plastic-feet fridge magnet?

'If you shave off all your hair,' he asked Annette absently, 'how long does it take to grow in?'

'Weeks. Months. Depends. Why? Gilbert.' She sat up. 'You're not thinking of shaving your head, are you?'

'Heavens, no.' Gilbert cupped a protective hand over his head. 'Never,' he said. He lay down. Perfecting his sleeping position, he tugged his pillow round his shoulders, a nightly ritual that ensured draught-free slumber. He relaxed. 'Nina.' He said her name. It spilled, unexpected, from his lips, surprising him.

'What was that?' Annette wanted to know.

'Oh, nothing,' said Gilbert. 'I was just falling to sleep. Dunno what I said.' Then, 'Sorry,' he apologised. For just saying that name in Annette's presence, the feelings it stirred in him, was to betray her.

Chapter Nineteen

Megs was washing his dishes when Gilbert asked her out to dinner. He stood at the door of the kitchen, watching her from behind. The slight wiggle of her bustling body as she wiped cups and plates, scrubbed out dirty pots and placed them on the draining board pleased him. Watching her, he was filled with a joy he hadn't known before. He caught himself smiling. He hated that. It was something his face did when he was happy. He wished it wouldn't. It had a life of its own. She turned and saw the expression on the undisciplined face.

'Something's made you happy.' She smiled back at him.

Something extraordinary happened to him, an exultation within. A bursting of some sort of internal blessedness. He put his hand on his stomach to control it. You, he thought. You have made me happy. 'Can't imagine what,' he said. 'Nothing to be happy about.'

'You can say that again.'

'How are things with the hairless one?'

She laughed. 'Oh, fine. We've all got used to him now. And the first prickle of hair is starting to appear. I still get a shock every time I look at him. But among his friends he's a hero. Shaven heads are the thing, apparently.' She wiped her hands on a tea towel as she spoke.

He was silent a moment, working up some courage. 'Do you eat?'

'As a matter of fact, I do,' she told him. 'Actual food at least once a day.'

'What sort of food do you like?'

'Anything hot that I haven't cooked myself.'

'Do you like Italian? Only, there's a new place not far from here. A small family-run restaurant. I thought we might go. Try it out. Tonight.' It would have to be tonight. Tomorrow was Thursday, and Thursday was Annette. On Friday Megs sang at the Glass Bucket. What am I saying? he thought. We can't go out. What would we talk about?

'Me?' She pointed to herself. 'You want to go out with me? All right. Why not?' she said. I can't go out with you, she thought. What would we talk about?

They spoke about themselves, and Gauguin. They spoke about children, childhood and Billie Holiday. They spoke about music, movies, soap operas, bad habits, school days, mothers and food. They started speaking at eight o'clock when they first sat down and did not stop till eleven when they left. They confessed embarrassing moments and secret, junk-food cravings.

It was a small restaurant, very Italian. White tablecloths, lamps on tables, trellising on one wall, plastic grapes and framed pictures of Italian football teams. Well, thought Megs, looking round, he can hardly criticise the Glass Bucket if this is his sort of décor. Waiters in white aprons breezed past them, and every time one of them pushed open the door to the kitchen the room filled with the rush of Italian babble and banter, the aromas of garlic, olive oil, basil and fresh bread baking.

'Smells promising,' said Gilbert, sniffing deeply. 'What shall we order?'

She stared at the menu, realising how long it had been since she'd been out. She was no longer used to choices.

'What do you like?' he asked. He was wearing a denim shirt, open at the neck, black jacket. His hair was flattish, she noted. This outing mustn't have caused him too much angst. She considered his face anew, she saw things she hadn't seen on her first scrutiny. She saw kindness, uncertainty and a deeper unhappiness than she'd really realised. That underlying sadness was so obvious she could almost reach out and touch it.

'Seafood,' she said. 'I like anything seafoody.'

'Pasta con frutti di mare,' he told the waiter. Bursting, badly, into a strange language, whilst tweaking his fingers in the air in a certain flamboyant continental manner, did not bother him. 'And I'll have osso bucco with risotto alla milanese.' This was what he planned to master next. He was working through the classic Italian dishes. 'Garlic bread, a carafe of house white. And salad.' He handed back the menus and smiling, turned to her. He liked to eat. 'Some places in Venice do your seafood pasta with champagne and cream,' he told her. 'I'll cook it for you, sometime.'

'You cook?' she asked. She wished people wouldn't make promises they had no intention of keeping.

'Love it. I cook every Saturday. Spend hours in the kitchen. What about you?'

'I cook every day. Fish fingers, baked potatoes, spaghetti. I spent as little time in the kitchen as possible. I must say, though, that I do a mean bacon sandwich.' She was tempted to add that she'd cook it for him sometime, but felt there was something morningish about bacon which suggested something all-nightish would have to happen before he got it.

'You got here all right?' he asked. 'No problem with baby-sitters?'

She shook her head. 'You remember Lorraine?'

He nodded.

'She and Harry have split up. She's staying with me for the moment. She can't face her empty house. She hates being alone.'

'I've lived alone for so long, I don't know how I'd take to having someone around. You get set in your ways.'

'I've been surrounded by children for so long I've forgotten any ways I might have liked to get set in.'

Lorraine stayed on Saturday night, then lingered all the next day. At eight o'clock on Sunday evening, Megs asked, 'Aren't you going home, then?' They were standing in the kitchen, Lorraine was wiping the draining board, making it cleaner than it had been in years. Guilt?

'Do I have to go home?' She did not look at Megs. 'I hate it there. It's empty.'

Megs did not have a chance to reply.

'I know. I know,' Lorraine protested against any criticism Megs might be about to offer. 'I was awful to Harry when I had him. And now I don't have him, I want him. All I do when I'm at home is sit in front of the television flicking from station to station because I can't concentrate on anything. I'm too sorry for myself. Then I eat biscuits.

I flick stations and I walk back and forward to the biscuit tin.' She stopped wiping and pointed an imaginary remote control at an imaginary television set. 'What's going to happen to me? How'm I going to get by? And that's another thing I do. I think. God, I hate doing that. Better to let life happen to you without thinking about what might happen.' She stopped flicking stations and returned to wiping. 'I mean,' she said, back to Megs, 'you think all the time. You're good at it. But me, I'm scared of thinking. You never know what awful thing you're going to find in your head.'

'Oh, stay,' Megs said. 'The sofa's yours for as long as you need it. I can't help you with what's going to happen to you – that sort of stuff. But my children won't put up with idle station-flicking when they're watching, and they eat everything that comes into the house. That'll solve your television and biscuit problems, anyway.' She made to go back into the living room. But stopped. 'Lorraine?' she said. 'You were only alone for one night. At that you got in after midnight and were here with me by ten in the morning. You've hardly had any time alone.'

'I know. But I stayed up all night, and it was awful.'

Megs went to tell her family that Lorraine would be staying for a few days.

'Thought so,' said Hannah.

'Yeah,' said Jack.

Now that Lorraine was part of her household, Megs saw those little ways she might have liked to develop slipping further and further from her. She sat across from Gilbert, each considering the other anew – the vast differences in their lives.

'Do you enjoy your job?' she asked.

'I used to. I've sort of gone off it. Recently, I must admit, I've been fascinated by Gauguin.'

'Why?'

'He did what he wanted, I suppose. I don't think I ever have.'

'Why not?'

To his surprise, he told her about his painting, his mother, the great bonfire. He had never told anyone about this before. Not even Annette. 'Do you get along with your mother?' he asked.

'Oh, goodness, don't ask that. We have mastered the art of quality

424

bickering. We don't see eye to eye on any subject under the sun, yet we see each other almost every day – you'd think we'd come up with something we could agree on. She's incredibly good to my children. I think she'd do anything for them. Will you ever draw again?'

He shook his head. 'No.' He didn't mean this. He always intended to start painting again one day. He secretly fancied he had talent.

It was near midnight when he drove her home. 'Do you want to come up?' Megs asked. 'Only I have to warn you, Lorraine's there and she'll quiz you.'

'What about?'

'Where you come from. What you do. How much you earn. What sort of underpants you wear. Just the business of being you.'

'She's a gossip?'

'Well, maybe. She's a woman. She's curious to know what makes different folk tick.'

Gilbert was keen to see Megs at home again. He wanted to know everything about her. 'OK. I'll risk it.'

Lorraine was curled up on the sofa, dunking a biscuit into a cup of hot chocolate. She, Jack and Hannah were watching television, and they turned as Gilbert came into the room. Hand on hair. He felt like an intruder. The room was small, painted white. On the walls, in clipframes, were pictures of blues singers – Robert Johnson, Bessie Smith and Ma Rainey, with her gorgeous smile and defiant dentistry. Plants dripped from bookshelves that were packed with battered second-hand paperbacks. There was a plastic box filled with toys beside the sofa, and beside each chair, shoes that had been kicked off.

The only light was a table lamp in the corner. But the dimness was scattered against flickering blue on the television. An advert for spaghetti hoops spilled into the room, a freckled wide-faced child, mouth smeared with tomato juices, scooped forkfuls from the plate as a gleeful acrylic family fussed round him.

Stepping towards the sofa, Gilbert tripped over the vacuum wire. He was a stranger here. He did not know the domestic obstacles. Megs constantly left her vacuum lying. Having cleaned, she found it too much effort to put it away. Shameless leaped and whirled, pattered his front paws and joyously threw himself at Megs. Gilbert found it difficult to move. He felt overpowered by the heat and the prattle of television adverts. He could not sit down. Lizzy was lying sleeping under her Thomas the Tank Engine duvet.

'What's she doing here?' Megs asked.

'She wouldn't go to bed,' Lorraine told her. 'She wanted to sleep on the sofa like me.'

Megs scooped up child and duvet together and gestured Gilbert to sit in the space she'd just cleared. 'I'll just put Lizzy to bed, then I'll make you coffee.'

The adverts stopped, and the film came back on.

A fully clothed cop was leaning on a doorpost, drinking coffee and chatting to a woman in her underwear. 'You can't fool me, honey,' the cop was saying. 'I know all about you.'

'Oh, doesn't he make you sick,' Lorraine said. 'He's so full of himself.'

'I hate men like that,' Hannah said. She had a huge mug of hot chocolate too.

The cop put his coffee down on the kitchen unit and moved across the room to the woman in her underwear. 'Yeah. I know what you want.'

Megs looked into the room. 'I'll get your coffee now. Back in a sec.'

'Thanks,' said Gilbert.

'Leave me alone, Billy,' said the woman in the film. 'I don't want you.'

'Yes you do,' the cop told her.

Gilbert leaned forward, drummed the heel of his shoe. Idly stared at the screen.

'Did you have a nice time?' Lorraine asked him.

'Oh, yes,' Gilbert told her.

'Don't you touch me,' the woman in her underwear screamed.

Jack got up, walked to the window and looked into the street. 'Is that your car? The Jag?'

'Yes,' said Gilbert.

'Cool,' said Jack.

'It isn't really.' Gilbert casually dismissed the compliment. 'It regularly refuses to start.'

'Doesn't matter,' Jack said. 'That's seriously cool.'

426

Gilbert was secretly pleased. He had never been called cool before.

'Good meal?' Lorraine asked.

Gilbert nodded. 'Yes.'

Lorraine considered his answer. She'd seen adverts for the restaurant they'd been to. She thought he could have taken Megs somewhere a little more expensive for their first date. He should want to impress her. 'What did you have to eat?'

Gilbert told her.

'Not bad.' Lorraine nodded.

The cop lunged at the woman, ripped off her underwear. Her tits tumbled out. She screamed. The two fell on the floor, taking some crockery with them, smashing a chair. The woman struggled. The cop yanked off her scant panties.

'She's got great thighs,' Lorraine said mildly. 'Do you suppose she works out?'

'Yeah,' said Hannah. 'She'll never eat Toblerones.'

'It's all make-up,' said Jack. 'They've got stuff to cover the cellulite.'

Hannah and Lorraine nodded. They liked that theory.

The cop held the woman's hands over her head with one hand, unbuckled his trousers with the other. Then he fell on her, licking her nipples, whilst she beat his back, small, useless fists. At last, weeping, she gave in to him, her legs curled round him. Yielding, she said, 'Billy, Billy, you bastard.' Their sex was crude and noisy.

Gilbert, Lorraine, Jack and Hannah watched, silently bovine. Their faces were all without expression.

'What's this?' Megs came in with the coffee. 'What are you watching?' She crossed the room, switched off the set.

'I was enjoying that,' Hannah protested. 'You think you can come in and switch it off because you've got someone with you.'

'Yes,' said Megs. 'I do.'

Hannah got up and flung herself towards the door. She always did a good flounce, Megs thought. She seemed to propel herself forward with her shoulders and elbows rather than her legs.

'Don't mind her,' Jack told Gilbert. 'She's all premenstrual today.'

'Jack.' Megs frowned at him to be quiet.

'It's true.' Jack would not be silenced. 'She's been a cow all night. And she's drunk two mugs of chocolate and eaten a

427

whole Toblerone. Never gave me any.'

'True,' Lorraine said. 'She's been in good form. Vile.'

Drinking his coffee, Gilbert wondered if it would be flippant of him to say that he liked Toblerones too. 'I think I ought to go,' he said instead. 'It's late.' He got up. With a small foot shuffle, he awkwardly bade Lorraine and Jack good night. As he walked down the hall he called goodbye to Hannah.

''Bye,' she called tonelessly, as if indifference was an art form.

Gilbert flushed slightly. Megs watched. His discomfort surprised her. She'd thought that dealing with students all day he'd be more used to mild tantrums than he was.

She walked back to his car with him. He leaned against it. 'Thanks for coming. I enjoyed it.'

'Me too.' She nodded. 'Sorry about Hannah.'

'I like seeing you at home,' he told her. 'You have a real family. It's good. I like your kids.'

Megs looked at him. 'I doubt that.'

'No, really. They're honest. Like you.' He reached out and stroked her hair. When she didn't object, he kissed her. Or rather he leaned over and placed his lips on hers. 'Sorry,' he said when they pulled apart.

'Why sorry?'

'For kissing you.'

The wine had made her bold. 'That was not a kiss,' she said. 'This is a kiss.' She took his head in her hands and kissed him properly, deeply. Halfway through it, she doubted herself. He must think me a tart, she decided. 'Sorry,' she said when they'd done.

'Oh, don't be,' he said to her back as she headed for the main door of her building. 'Really, don't be.' He watched her go, sat staring at her window long after she'd disappeared. He imagined her up there in her flat amidst her gaudy clutter. She'd be making coffee, laughing with Lorraine, bossing her son, sorting out her premenstrual daughter. Her clutter, he realised, extended far beyond the messy area around her fridge. It spread throughout her whole life.

It delighted him, though he couldn't imagine why.

Hannah was back watching her awful film when Megs returned. 'Is that him?' she asked.

428

'What do you mean by that?' Megs wanted to know.

'I mean you should watch yourself with him. He's a man. You know nothing about men.'

'What?' Megs couldn't believe what she was hearing. 'You think you know more about men than me?'

'That's obvious.'

'Perhaps you should have asked him what his intentions were?' Megs offered.

'Well, someone has to.' Hannah was even sitting knees together, arms folded. So schoolmarmish, Megs wanted to laugh.

'She thinks she knows more about men than you,' Lorraine said. She patted the sofa eagerly. 'C'mon, tell us all about it. I liked his jacket.'

'Yes,' Hannah said. 'Shame about his hair.'

'Poor bloke.' Jack got up. 'I don't want to hear this. I'm off to bed.'

'Me too.' Megs followed him. 'I don't suppose anybody has taken Shameless out?'

Guilty silence. 'Oh, great,' said Megs. She put Shameless on his leash, shoved on her coat and left. She couldn't slam the door in a display of displeasure for fear of waking Lizzy. Wishing she'd changed into flat shoes, she stumbled clumsily down the stairs and down the main hall, yanked by Shameless, who had gone into hyperpant. She heaved open the main door and saw Gilbert. He was leaning out of his car, staring up at her window.

'Hello again.' She smiled.

He reddened, reached for his hair. 'Hello.'

'I have to take Shameless out,' she explained.

'I'll come with you. Protect you from hedgehogs.'

'That'll be a comfort.'

They walked side by side down the street, Shameless pulling her. The sky turned to sludge somewhere above the sodium lights. It was going to rain. A gritty wind worried round them, flapping their clothes, chilling their cheeks, pushing their hair at angles to their faces. They both shivered.

'It's a lovely night,' said Gilbert.

'Yes,' Megs agreed. 'Lovely.'

Chapter Twenty

Megs woke, stared at the sun-bleached curtains. Six o'clock on the morning of the Friday she'd been dreading for weeks. After tonight it's a lifetime of cleaning for me. She let dismay swim through her. I'll be forever picking up after all sorts of people. A professional picker-upper. It's the end for me. She did not spare herself any sorrow, embraced instead the full gloom ahead.

She imagined her descent into misery. Getting older and older, wider and wider, fat-ankled in thick, wrinkled stockings, she'd shuffle from home to home, nagging and wiping. 'You'll be needing that bathroom of yours done today, Mrs Pearshon,' she'd say, squeezing her 's' through ill-fitting National Health dentures. Shuffling fatly through the awful tidiness with a bottle of Domestos and a can of Jif bathroom mousse, 'Oh God, no,' she cried out loud, sitting up. Shameless raised a sleepy head and looked glumly round, ears only half pricked. It was far too early for him to start leaping, panting and being friendly.

Megs lay down again. It wasn't just her last night at the Glass Bucket that she was dreading. It was Gilbert. The loveliness of the evening she'd spent with him had worn off now that she was running through it. She remembered stupid things she'd said. What did he think of her, her home and her family? She'd come into the room and found him sitting with Lorraine, Jack and Hannah watching a noisily explicit sex scene. What had he made of that? And what had he made of Hannah's mini-tantrum? What would he make of one of the girl's major outbursts? How could she face him, clean for him when she'd so passionately kissed him? That was not a kiss, she'd said. This is a kiss. 'Oh God,' she cried out loud, covering her face. She chastised herself. I will never drink again, she vowed for the umpteenth time. She knew she didn't mean it.

Considering the day ahead, cleaning for Terribly-Clean Pearson seemed a breeze. But then, Terribly-Clean Pearson had been easier to get along with recently. Her hair was less demented. Not so much a helmet that topped her head, more loose, like actual hair, in fact, Megs thought. Then last week there had been some mess to clean up. There had been crumbs on the kitchen table, and a ring round the bath, cigarette stubs in the ashtrays, a newspaper read and badly folded. Signs of life. Anyway, it seemed to Megs that Mrs Pearson was on the road to recovery from whatever ailed her. Whatever sent her scurrying to hide behind that perfection of hers. Megs pulled the duvet over her head and rubbed her feet together. Bed was the place to be. But she had a dire afternoon and evening to get through before she got to come back to bed, and hide again.

Gilbert was waiting for her when she arrived. He was leaning on the wall by the front door, looking sheepish. His hair gave his mood away. It was on its way to upright. He had his hands thrust in the pockets of his old black training pants. His sweatshirt had 'University of Ohio' on the front and needed washing. He was doing his grinning thing. His face was smiling, and he was wishing it wouldn't. It kept giving him away.

'Well, hello,' he said. 'And how are you?'

'Fine,' she said.

'And how's the family?'

'Fine,' she said. First lie of the day, she thought. Thinking of Hannah.

He offered her coffee. She accepted. But looking round at the mess thought it best any sort of small talk be cut short. There was a lot to do. Whistling toothily, he moved about his kitchen. He made fresh coffee and laid some dark-chocolate ginger biscuits on a plate. She didn't sit down, drank the cup he gave her leaning against the sink.

'Thank you for the other night,' she said. 'I enjoyed it.' Considering this, she found it to be true.

'Good.' He smiled. 'Do it again? Soon?' He was keen.

She wanted to say no. But couldn't bring herself to. It seemed, somehow, rude.

'Good,' he said again. He stepped towards her, took her cup, laid it on the sink unit and kissed her. It was a spur-of-the-moment move. Had he planned it he might not have spilled her coffee, pressed the small of her back into the draining board and crushed her nose against his cheek so that she couldn't breathe. 'I messed that up.' He let go of her.

'No you didn't.' He looked so ashamed of himself, she stroked his cheek, repeated, 'You make me think you only did that to be polite, or something stupid like that.'

'Oh no. No, really.' He gripped her arms. 'I wanted to. I want to.' He held her to him. She looked over his shoulder at all that was to be done in the kitchen. Really she should get started.

She always thought that if he hadn't made such a mess of that kiss, if it hadn't been so chokingly clumsy, he wouldn't have made such a meal of saying sorry. 'Though, heaven's sake,' she said to Lorraine later, 'my nose got crushed, my back bruised.' Nonetheless, if he hadn't seemed so sorry for himself, she wouldn't have tried so hard to comfort him. Her sympathy extended all the way from his kitchen, through his living room, up the stairs to his bed.

She lay on the sheets she ought to be washing and made love to him. He tasted of coffee, smelled of cologne. She felt she smelled of all the chemicals he so hated, and couldn't relax. She kept chastising herself for what she was doing, or about to do. What would her mother say if she could see her?

His room was light, huge windows, level with the tops of the trees. There were books on the floor and books on the chest of drawers by his bed. An anglepoise lamp *circa* 1950 loomed over her head. It needed dusting, she noted. She turned to him. He touched her face, then trailed a slow hand up her thigh. He lured her from her guilt, till she wrapped herself round him, clung to him. Sweating sweetly, breathing his name, she moved with him into those few precious moments when she forgot about everything. Absolutely everything.

There had, of course, been others. There had been a woman – a cycling enthusiast – who worked at the bike shop, a barmaid from the pub where he drank after work, the wife of one of his postgrad students, his hairdresser. If his long-time love, Annette, was as uncommitted as he was, all of his lovers were caught up in the same intense, boiling family involvement as Megs.

'It wasn't joyous,' she told Lorraine, 'just sort of comforting, passionately comforting. I slept after. And it wasn't embarrassing getting my kit off. That came naturally enough. Getting it back on again, though, was awful. Still, it'll teach me not to go out with old underwear on.'

Lorraine looked unimpressed. 'You owe me a fiver,' she said.

Megs slept till four o'clock, when summer had settled into the day outside, heat filled the streets. She hated summer. 'Oh my,' she said, sitting bolt upright, flapping the duvet. 'Look at the time. And look at me. I have done nothing.' She leaped from the bed. Naked, she stood gazing helplessly round, raising and lowering her arms. 'I have to go to the laundrette. And the dishes – I haven't touched them. And,' she touched her throat, which had reddened, '. . . I have to get home.'

Aware of how she looked with nothing on, she reached for her clothes, bundled at the end of the bed. The elastic of her knickers was escaping from its seam, her bra was torn at the fasteners, and, though clean, it gave the impression of being tired, overly worn. Underwear was not high on her list of priorities, since she reckoned nobody but her would ever see it. She rushed to cover the body and underclothes she so disliked with her shirt and jeans. She rarely bought anything for herself. 'Oh God . . . oh God . . . oh God . . .' she said. 'I must . . . I shouldn't . . . this is wrong . . . I have to . . .' She was distraught, sentences flooded her mind – too many of them to finish one.

Hopping, she yanked on her shoes. She fled the bedroom with him, skipping and tripping, heaving himself into his training pants, running after her. She saw her envelope on the table and turned from it.

'Take it,' he insisted.

'I can't. How can I? I haven't done anything.' She wheeled round, arms spread, displaying openly the work she had not done. The mess intact. The wages she would not accept. 'If I took your money for what I've just done – what would that make me?'

He did not know what to say. Stood forlornly holding his envelope, neatly sealed with her name on the front in his best writing, watching her flee down the steps, two at a time, to her car. And she was so lovely to him. She held his head, kissed his cheek, licked his lobes, and said his name. He loved it when women said his name like that. It cut clean through his loneliness – all the way to his heart.

'It was that messed-up kiss,' Megs said to Lorraine. 'That's what did it.'

For if she'd cleaned and vacuumed and wiped as she ought to have done, she'd have taken his money. When she didn't, it alarmed him. He hadn't considered this. He was not used to honesty. He felt more guilty than ever.

'See,' Megs said to Lorraine during their Saturday-morning review of their lives, 'it was just down to one screwed-up moment. When I moved my face a fraction too far to the left, and he moved his a fraction too far to the right. And we missed. It's all down to that.'

She drove home. He sat considering, for the first time in his life, the full implications of his actions. She would not have enough money to feed her children. If she would not take his money, she would damn well take his food. He would go to the supermarket and shop for her. He would take her food.

She went home, cooked burgers and fed her family as she ran a bath. She washed, and changed into her singing clothes. 'Last night, tonight,' she said to Lorraine. 'I can't stand it. I won't be able to do it. I'll cry.'

'Well, cry,' said Lorraine. 'You're the best crier I know. You're almost as good as me.' Only this afternoon Lorraine had done some crying. She'd gone home to collect some things. She had shoved into a matching set of cases clothes, shoes, CDs, make-up, jewellery, a couple of photograph albums and a threadbare toy spaniel called Fluff that was almost as old as she was – he'd been with her since she was two, had seen her through affairs, her marriage, umpteen jobs, more affairs – her helter skelter life.

Vivienne came to baby-sit. On her way to the kitchen she stepped over Lorraine's luggage. This was not a good sign. She thought Megs's house overcrowded enough. They would egg each other on into mischief like they had when they were little. They were not to be trusted. They'd stay up all hours talking and giggling. Lorraine would set Megs off on wild dreams when she should be settling down. All that, and she wanted her daughter to herself. She went into the kitchen where Jack was doing the washing-up. Vivienne considered his gleaming head and sighed. 'There's your head. You were bald when you were born,' she said, a slight throb of longing for younger, easier times in her voice.

Lorraine and Megs left. Giggling, high heels clicking down the stairs, along the street, through the evening.

It was the best night ever at the Glass Bucket. It was so fine, takings so high, that Dave, the manager, wondered if he'd done the right thing cancelling the band. Megs sang 'God Bless the Child', did three encores, spread her arms, yelled, 'That's it, folks. It's over. Me and the band are going to catch up with Friday-night sitcoms on telly.' She jumped from the stage on to the squelchy tartan carpet and set about getting drunk.

'See,' she said to Lorraine when they were considering the long-term consequences of that blundered kiss, 'if it hadn't been my last night, I wouldn't have had so much to drink. I wouldn't have been so drunk when I got home. And if I hadn't been so drunk, I wouldn't have agreed to anything.' They'd stayed late at the Glass Bucket, drinking and saying goodbye. Round after round they bought and had bought for them. 'Goodbye,' Megs said over and over, tears in her eyes. She sang snatches of favourite songs, closing her eyes, concentrating, making her phrasing perfect, easily reaching notes that needed all her concentration, knowing they were coming, breathing for them in advance.

She told people she'd never seen before in her life that she loved them and they were her dearest friends. She had a lovely time. At last she understood the thrill Mike got from breaking up the band, from walking out on the marriage and from all the other goodbyes he'd said over the years together. All the hugging and promising to stay in touch. It wasn't the new beginning that excited him. The great triumph was simply in leaving.

They staggered, giggling, home sometime after two o'clock. Vivienne was sitting on the sofa chatting to Gilbert, who was in the armchair that Jack usually occupied. They were, to Megs's astonishment, discussing Gauguin.

'I'd have gone,' Vivienne was saying passionately. 'I wouldn't have let him walk out on my five children. I'd have gone. Five children! They need a father. He wouldn't have got away with that with me. Oh no.'

'No, sorry,' Gilbert was saying. He was no longer apologising for himself. Now he was apologising for Gauguin, as if he had some personal involvement in the man's decision to leave his wife and family to go painting in Tahiti. Gauguin interested him. He'd abandoned his career as a stockbroker to paint. Why, the man had been in his forties – the exact age Gilbert was now – when he finally left his wife. Still fancying he had some ability as an artist, he comforted himself with thoughts of Gauguin. Forty was not too late.

'And it would have been good for the kids.' Vivienne was beginning to enthuse. 'All that fruit. And it's quiet. You wouldn't have had to worry about them going off on their bikes.'

'What are you doing here?' Megs said, clutching the doorpost. She wanted to look like she could keep upright on her own. She hated her mother to see her drunk.

'We've been having a good old chat,' Vivienne told her. 'We've been talking about packaging. Gilbert's writing a book about it. Fancy, you'd never have thought there was enough in packaging to fill a whole book. I was telling him that in my day you went to the shops, and the grocer or whoever would pop your things in a paper bag and give it a twirl.' She held her arms out, demonstrating bag-twirling as performed in shops in the fifties, giving Megs a rerun of the conversation before the Gauguin conversation.

'I brought food,' Gilbert told her. 'In the kitchen.'

Megs went through to look. 'Goodness.' She could not hide her surprise. 'Look at this.' Laid across the units were packets of cereal (Gilbert, not knowing what her children would eat, had bought a selection), a variety of cheeses, loaves of bread, six bottles of wine, a bottle of whisky, biscuits, two chickens, steaks, pork chops, oven chips, pizzas, Coca-Cola, Evian, bags of apples, oranges, bananas, papayas, mangoes – fruit she couldn't afford to taste. There was Marmite, thick marmalade and strawberry jam, cocoa, coffee, a selection of teas, Ovaltine. Gilbert's indecision showed, and she could see that it had cost him three times what he would have paid her.

'You didn't need to do this,' she said.

437

'Oh, I think I did.' He'd been to the supermarket for her. Did he have to do anything else to prove his good intentions? He thought not. He took her hand. 'You didn't take your pay.'

'Look at this.' Lorraine held up some lollo rosso. 'Posh lettuce. And tomatoes on the vine.'

Vivienne did not look at the groceries. She had already cast her critical eye over them. She watched Gilbert and her daughter. 'Why didn't you take your pay?' she wanted to know.

'Because,' Megs confessed, 'I didn't clean his house. I slept with him. Didn't I?' She grinned alcoholicly at her mother. 'And I couldn't take any money for that, could I?'

Vivienne tutted. But not, as Megs imagined, with horror. More at her childish attempt to shock.

'See,' said Megs, 'I can't take your money. I can't work for you now.'

'Well, don't,' Gilbert said, taking her hand. 'Don't work for me. Come away with me for the summer. Come to my cottage. Be with me.' He was feeling wildly romantic.

'I can't do that,' Megs protested. 'I work.'

'Stop,' said Gilbert. 'You can't go on cleaning for people. There's more to you than that.'

'You tell her,' said Vivienne. 'She won't listen to me.'

Lorraine ripped a leaf from the lollo rosso, munched it, and watched.

'Come to my cottage. Be with me. It'll just be us. You and me.'

'Me?' Megs leaned on her unit for support. 'You can't just have me. I'm not me any more.' She considered her bustling life. There was Jack, Hannah, Lizzy, Shameless, Lorraine, Vivienne and Mike, who came to her kitchen trailing tales of his wife and new daughter. 'I'm not me any more,' Megs complained. 'I'm a crowd.'

'Come,' Gilbert insisted. 'All of you. Bring the gang.'

'Hannah and Jack are going to Italy with Mike for the summer,' Lorraine said.

Vivienne watched them. She watched Gilbert take Megs's hand, the expression on his face as he looked at her. 'I'd go,' she said. 'If a man asked me to go to his cottage, I'd go. There'd be no stopping me.'

Broken down, drunk, afraid of her future, Megs said, 'Yes. I'll come for the weekend at least.'

'See,' she said to Lorraine later, when they were running through the fine details of the nonsense that had taken place. 'It's a farce. My nose got crushed, my back ricked and I sympathised with him. "It's all right," I said. "I don't mind." If I'd said, "Get off. Leave me alone," I'd be fine. But that's me. That's my life. I go along being ordinary. Ordinary day following ordinary day, and now and then I have forays into tragedy or folly. That's me.'

Lorraine opened a packet of Penguins, chose a red one. 'What?' she said. She had no idea what Megs was talking about. 'I wouldn't mind a little stay in some remote cottage. Even if it was with Hundred-Miles-An-Hour. Seems fine to me.'

Chapter Twenty-One

It was after four when Megs left Edinburgh. She did not take journeys lightly. The boot of her car was packed, as if she was setting off to circumnavigate the globe.

'Just in case,' she said as she jammed in welly boots and jumpers. 'You never know,' she said as she folded up her best frock and laid it carefully on top of the heap of clothes in her suitcase. 'We might need these,' she said, adding anoraks and raincoats. 'Lizzy might get bored,' shoving in books, crayons and Lego. 'Gilbert might not have anything suitable,' putting in Shameless's bowls. 'You know Shameless. He's bound to let us down,' just managing to find space to squeeze in his towel and some extra toilet roll. She fetched Lizzy's duvet and pillow and put them on the back seat. 'She might sleep.' Megs hoped.

Lorraine and Vivienne stood side by side waving, watching them go. 'Don't know what she sees in him.' Lorraine sounded sour. Still, she made an effort. When Megs looked in the driving mirror, she saw Lorraine smiling.

'They're soulmates,' Vivienne offered.

'Lost souls.' Lorraine loved a romance.

'Floundering's the word I'd choose.' Vivienne had long left romance behind.

It took over an hour to get through the Friday-evening traffic to the Forth Bridge, and another hour up the motorway to Perth. 'Are we there yet?' Lizzy asked not long after they turned out of the street where they lived. She seemed to repeat the question at regular ten-minute intervals. But Megs was too thrilled by her journey north to be bothered. She played Roberta Flack, 'The First Time Ever I Saw

441

Your Face', and sang along. Gilbert had drawn a map and given Megs detailed instructions on the road to take after the Perth ring route. But Megs never could follow instructions. She always made up her own.

Lizzy was sleeping. The little roads that turned off the long, boring stretch Megs was driving and wound towards the blue and distant became irresistible. She knew Gilbert's cottage was up there somewhere in those hills and felt she was getting close to him, faster, when she was pointed towards them. Besides, she found the narrow roads, with their unkempt, burgeoning hedgerows, a delight. June, it seemed to her, was unashamedly yellow. 'Tawdry month, June,' she said. 'A bit brazen for me.' Rape shimmered in fields bounded by dry-stone dykes. Six o'clock pheasants croaked from pinewood copses, and Lizzy woke. She demanded Roberta Flack be replaced by Disney's greatest hits. So to the saccharine strains of 'Wish Upon a Star' they battered through Alyth. Across the bridge, up the hill and nearer to Gilbert, Megs thought.

'I need a pee,' Lizzy complained.

'Can't you wait?'

'No.' A protesting squeal.

They found a garage where a man with a black beret pulled low over his forehead gave them the key to the toilet, and, when Lizzy had done, sold them oil for the car, which needed to be topped up every couple of hundred miles. Lizzy also insisted on a tin of Pepsi, an apple, Smarties and a pack of assorted lollies. Megs looked round the shop. They sold everything here. Socks, newspapers, clothes pegs, homemade tablet, jam pot covers. 'Goodness.' Megs picked them up. 'Jam pot covers. You hardly see them these days.' A couple of miles down the road Megs opened the bag of goodies and found she'd been sold two packs.

She drove down endless tiny roads. Stopped to let Shameless out. He sniffed gleefully, peed, then rushed excitedly halfway across a field, starting up a hare. Yipping wildly, he took off after it, disappearing full hurtle into the field beyond. Hands hanging helplessly by her sides, Megs bellowed him to come back. She looked at her watch – seven o'clock. Gilbert was expecting her sometime after five. At last, realising the futility of hare-chasing, Shameless, ears pricked, sat mid-field, watched his quarry go, then turned and returned to Megs. She noted glumly that he had one of Lizzy's lollies, a green one, sticking to his back.

Back in the car they played 'Hi-Ho Hi-Ho It's Off To Work We Go', sped past fields, woods, cottages set back against the road. Tiny-windowed, they were cowering in a vast landscape against a huge sky. They pressed themselves into the roadside, letting tractors past. Megs scrunged behind the steering wheel, arms over her head. How to behave when mighty-wheeled tractors shoved you to the side of the road was not covered in the Highway Code – this seemed the sanest way to cope. Several times they passed signs that pointed to Alyth. Each sign they passed said that Alyth was in another direction. Sometimes it was ten miles away, sometimes only two. The third time they passed the jam pot garage, Megs admitted to herself that they were lost. The tremblings in her stomach were not in the least thrilling. 'Bare Necessities' had never been more irritating, and Lizzy was needing to pee again. They stopped once more at the jam pot garage. Returning the lavatory key to the man in the black beret, Megs asked directions.

'Thocht youze were lost,' he said, shoving the hat up slightly, revealing a deep red weal mid-forehead. 'Third time I seen ye pass I says to masel', "They're lost."' He demonstrated not so much with arm movements, more by leaning his whole body in the direction Megs ought to travel. 'Go this way,' leaning forward, 'an' keep turning this way,' leaning left. It worked. Following the directions, Megs began to notice, at last, the names recited to her by the leaner in the beret. Airlie, Lintrathen, Cortachy – she said the words out loud. They sounded romantic, historic, mystic to her. Ancient Celtic kings and Pictish storytellers wandering here centuries ago. 'King of the Swingers' blared on the tape deck.

Megs drove slowly. The car had climbed into the hills. Megs stared out across the valley. She could see the great gulfs and hollows that glaciers had left aeons ago. Lights shone in cottages miles away. She wondered what people who lived in them did. She wished Lorraine was with her. Lorraine would have a theory or two about how people in remote places passed the time. 'They're all smoking dope,' she'd say. Or, 'They're into bondage, or they're bank robbers hiding from the law.' Sometimes Megs thought Lorraine had no notion of ordinary.

'What do you suppose the people in these little houses all the way across the valley are doing?' she asked Lizzy.

Lizzy had no doubts. 'They're watching their television programmes.'

'Oh no,' cried Megs. 'Don't say it. Don't say it.'

But Lizzy said it. 'When are we going to get there?'

It was late evening. Change of day, a small wind chilled down from the peaks. Still not sure of the way, Megs wound up the window and leaned over the steering wheel. Hills covered with conifers folded out of each other, each one higher than the next, till in the distance – they were mountains. Greens and forest greys. The sun slid low, turned the sky a deeper blue that bleached white far away where the mountains rimmed the dusk. The road was narrow, wound and dipped suddenly and absurdly. A curlew called, shrilled a broken cry.

Lizzy dug small fists into Shameless and cried in anguish, 'When are we going to get there?'

'Soon,' said Megs. 'Very soon.' She stared up at the hills, breathed the night scents. She was on the right road, at last. That earlier fear, which hadn't been in the least thrilling at the time, now seemed exciting. Getting lost had been a small adventure. 'This is it,' she said. 'What I was on about. Where I belong. Watching new colours, listening to sounds I've never heard before. I'm slightly afraid. And if I wasn't in this damn car, I'd be rushing.'

They found the sign at last – Lisdon Cottage – and turned down a narrow track, deeply rutted at either side. The grasses that grew up the centre rattled against the exhaust, whilst Megs, Lizzy and Shameless were pitched from side to side as the car's suspension heaved against unseen pot-holes.

Gilbert heard them coming and came out to greet them – sliding his hand through his hair. He grinned. His face again, working on its own again. He wore his apron.

'Who's that?' Peering from the back of the car, Lizzy considered him with suspicion. She did not take kindly to new people.

'It's Gilbert,' said Megs. 'I've told you all about him.'

'He's got funny hair,' Lizzy said.

'Don't you dare tell him that.' Megs was also tempted to tell her daughter not to pester him, but felt she'd just be putting notions into the child's head.

Megs clambered from the car, and stood unkinking herself from her stiffened travelling position. She scratched her bum, working some circulation into it. 'Nice place,' she said, nodding to the cottage.

It was two crumbling storeys, peeling window frames, huddled against a small, dense conifer wood. The smell of pines. A wave of honeysuckle swam up against and flooded a small wooden porch at the front door. The lawns, overgrown and daisied, grew right up to the wall. The kitchen looked like a lean-to afterthought, but the windows were lit against the dusk. Megs could see a huge scrubbed table, wine bottles, glasses and books. Yes, Gilbert lives here. A thin drift of smoke spiralled into the air, burning wood. The day turned deeper indigo, darkness getting granular against the trees. First bats flickered through the gloom.

'Good journey?' Gilbert asked.

'I enjoyed it. Shameless and Lizzy complained all the way. So did the car. Actually,' she confessed, 'we got lost.' Then, grinning, 'But no mind, here we are.'

Lizzy tumbled from the back seat and stood staring at Gilbert.

'This is Gilbert,' Megs told her again. 'Gilbert, this is Lizzy.'

'Pleased to meet you.' He bent to the child, extending his hand.

Gazing at him intently, Lizzy shook it. 'You've got funny hair,' she said.

'Lizzy!' Megs scolded.

'Have I?' Gilbert reached up to pat it into place. He looked pleadingly across at Megs.

'It's fine,' Megs lied. 'I'm sorry.' She nodded to the child, who was headed for the cottage door. All the excuses she knew she ought to offer spilled into her mind. Her brother died, and I fear for her. I let her get away with too much. She's become too precious. Precocious. She offered none of them, however. 'I don't know what gets into her,' she said.

'She's lovely,' said Gilbert. He meant it. 'Come on in. I've cooked a stew. Cutturiddi.' He raised enthusiastic fingers and snapped the air. He was very pleased with himself. 'Lamb, baby onions, chilli pepper, wine.' Then he glanced at Lizzy. 'Does she eat that sort of thing?'

'She hasn't had the chance,' Megs said, feeling mildly guilty about her child's limited diet.

But Lizzy ate everything she was given. She's playing at being good, Megs thought. Flirting with Gilbert. Little girls are all the same. Was I? She remembered Uncle Ron when she'd visit the Seaview Guest House, before his second fatal heart attack. She remembered how she'd unashamedly flaunt herself before him when Aunty Betty was clearing up the supper dishes. He'd grab her by the waist and thrust his rough, evening chin over her cheek till she squealed. Yes, she thought. I was the same. Uncle Ron would put her feet on his feet, size three stocking soles on his polished size ten brown brogues, and, arm round her, hands clasped high, he'd dance her round the room.

'This is a dance,' he'd say. 'Relax. I'm doing all the work.' But she never could let go and let him dance her. She giggled and wriggled. 'It's a waltz. Good old-fashioned dance.' They'd glide fabulously over the blue-and-pink-patterned carpet, past the red moquette sofa, sailing, twirling over to the cocktail cabinet with the lime-green interior that played 'The Banana Boat Song' when you opened the doors. 'Now when you get yourself a young man of your own, you'll be able to show him what to do.' Of course, she never did.

'Why are you smiling?' Gilbert asked. After Lizzy's comment on his hairstyle, he was ready to be offended. He might have other mockable idiosyncrasies that he hadn't noticed.

'Oh. I was just remembering my Aunty Betty's living room. Blue and pink carpet, red sofa, lime-green cocktail cabinet. I was imagining what you'd make of it.'

'I might've quite liked it. There is something comforting about bold bad taste. You know you're in the company of someone who doesn't doubt herself.'

'That's Aunt Betty,' said Megs. She poured them both some more wine. 'Do you dance, Gilbert?'

'No. I have never mastered dancing. I think there's a link missing between my brain and my feet. Why, do you?' Faint horror that she might drag him off to ballrooms and clubs to entwine themselves in

446

some flamboyant tango with body-checks and head-tossing.

She shook her head. 'Always wanted to. But no, I can't. Well, I can jiggle to music. But actual dancing. No.' She continued shaking her head, reaffirming her failing.

She twirled her glass and looked out at the dark. The kitchen door was open, spreading light, attracting night-time insects that bruised themselves frantically against the window pane. Lizzy slid from her seat and went outside. Then came back in again. Out again. Stepping out on her own was more freedom than she'd ever known. The whole wide world was out there, she could see it – shapes in the darkness. But light and warmth and her mother were just a jump away – a small leap back into the kitchen.

She stood holding Shameless by the collar, taking in the night sounds and scents: an ineffectual wind pushing through the pines, the rattle of ivy leaves, a curlew's late whimpering, the insistent thud of rave music inside a car miles away up the glen – village boys with nothing to do but their Friday-night hurtle, driving up one side of the glen, down the other, passing the end of the road every two hours, thoom, thoom thoom – and honeysuckle, grass, pines and soft air blowing down from the peaks. It was a wonder to the child.

'It's the first time she's been able to come and go on her own,' Megs said, watching her. 'Living in a flat inhibits children. We should have a garden.' She wondered if this moment would stay in Lizzy's memory. There were, Megs realised, thousands of moments imprinted on her own memory. Some things were retained for obvious reasons – her mother in her blue and white winceyette nightie and tartan dressing gown standing by her bed in the sanatorium, waving a slow goodbye, galloping behind Aunty Betty through the house, waving a feather duster, singing 'Sipping Soda'. But some things slipped away and had to be forced back with vicious proddings from her mother. There was, in the family album, a photo of Megs and her brother standing ankle deep in the sea. She was wearing a skirted swimming costume that left little square marks on her bottom. He wore woolly trunks that sagged when wet. She had chubby knees. They were carrying buckets and spades and their faces were puckered against the sun.

'This is us on holiday at Southport, remember?' Vivienne said.

'No,' said Megs. 'I don't remember going to Southport.'

'Remember.' Vivienne was irritated. 'You had a crab in that bucket. And you got stung by a wasp. We bought you a big strawberry ice cream to stop you crying.'

'No.' Megs shook her head. 'I don't remember that.'

'We walked along the pier. We hired deckchairs. We went to see *Mary Poppins*.'

'Did we?'

'We stayed at a small guest house. The landlady had a cocker spaniel called Daniel.'

'A spaniel? A black one?'

'Yes.'

'Daniel the spaniel I do remember. Vaguely. But I don't remember that.' Pointing to the photograph.

Would Lizzy remember this? Or would this trip come back only as some trivial detail? A fleeting flashback of Gilbert's hair?

They went to bed as soon as Lizzy was sleeping. She had the room across the landing from Gilbert's. It had a sloping ceiling. Checked curtains moved against an open window. She lay clutching her purple transit van, Shameless at her feet.

Megs and Gilbert lay in his big cast-iron bedstead, patchwork quilt pulled over them. 'Do you remember your childhood, Gilbert? Or do you look at photos and find yourself forced to recall something long gone?' Megs asked. 'That weird feeling of having the evidence of your being somewhere but you can't remember a moment of it.'

'Yes. I suppose. I remember my teenage more.'

'I had a good teenage. I fell in love. The first time you hold a boy's hand. That first touch palm against palm – first thrill. That's the most romantic thing that ever happens to you. It's never like that again.' She reached for his hand under the covers. Her fingers entwined his. 'I remember the first time I ever got touched by someone a different sex from me that I wasn't related to. It was wonderful. It was Jimmy Sutherland. He had black hair that our English teacher kept telling him to get cut. He was a year older than me, fourteen. He took my hand on the way home from the cinema. Early-evening showing of *Alice's Restaurant*. His hand was dry and rough, chewed nails. Mine was all sweaty. We walked all the way home like that, neither of us mentioned that my hand was in his. If we spoke about it, it would stop. The thrill of it spread from my palm all the way up my arm and right through me. Frankly, that simple handhold reached parts of me American cream soda and raspberry ripple ice cream never got to. Things happened in bits I didn't realise things could happen in. Secret places. God. I was overwhelmed by Jimmy Sutherland. I thought about him all the time. Couldn't sleep. Stopped eating Mars Bars. His name was all over my French jotter. Love, did you say? It lasted a full three weeks. Had to end, something that intense. It'll never be like that again.'

Gilbert felt helpless, quite upset that he would never rouse her to such peaks of ecstasy with a simple meeting of palms. He'd never put anybody off their Mars Bars. He was positive nobody had scrawled his name over a French jotter. He was suddenly insanely jealous of Jimmy Sutherland. Wherever he was, Gilbert hated him. His free hand came out from beneath the quilt, reached for his hair. By the time he'd come out of his jealous haze, Megs, overcome by her journey and the wine, was sleeping. He frowned, cursed himself for being so stupid. This wasn't what he'd planned.

Chapter Twenty-Two

The grumpiness that had befallen him when he fell asleep was still with him when he woke. He stared across at the empty pillow next to his, imagining sourly that she'd left. For a bewildering moment he thought he was alone again. But he realised that the humming sound that had brought him from his sleep was Lizzy driving her van across the floorboards, providing her own sound effects of crunching gears and screeching brakes. He propped himself on his elbows and watched her. 'Where's your mother?'

'In the garden,' Lizzy told him. She did not take her eyes from her van.

He felt irritated. This was definitely not what he'd planned. They would wake together, lie sleepily warm, make love again. He'd rise, go barefoot to cook breakfast – smoked fish, bacon, toast and fresh coffee – whilst she washed and dressed. This child had not been cast in his daydreams. Of course, he'd known Megs was bringing her daughter for the weekend. But when he imagined their time together he had not as much as given the child a walk-on part. Now here she was, vrooming a hideous vehicle on his polished floor, and he was desperate to get up. Last night's wine was heavy in his bladder, he ached to relieve himself. But he did not want to get out of bed letting Lizzy see him wearing nothing but his boxer shorts.

'Why don't you go find her?' he suggested.

'No,' said Lizzy.

'Pl-ee-se.' The word spilled pleadingly from him. He did not know he was going to say it. He was in pain. 'Oh God. Please go see her.'

Lizzy got up, looked mildly at him and left.

Ten minutes later, washed, dressed and relieved, he joined them.

Megs was sitting on the kitchen doorstep drinking coffee. His eyes skimmed the plate beside her. She'd made toast. This wasn't right.

'Sorry.' She smiled at him. 'I was starving after I took Shameless for his walk. I just made some toast. Shall I get you some?'

He shook his head. Walk? Toast? He felt more disgruntled than ever. She'd taken his Schubert from his kitchen tape deck, and some popular American-type music was playing. Definitely things were not going to plan. 'I'll get myself some coffee. Then we'll have to go to the village. I have things I must buy.' It was never like this with Annette.

With Annette he didn't have to discuss plans, they just fitted together without discussion. He'd get up and she'd yawn, stretch, turn over. 'Lovely, I've got the bed to myself. Make us some wonderful breakfast, there's a love.' He'd go rattle and bustle in the kitchen, listening to the news, or Schubert if he'd a mind. Then Annette would come, sit opposite him and read her paper. He'd read his. They were rarely together. And when they were they hardly spoke. No wonder they got along. Perfect relationship, he thought. Trouble with these people was they spoke, they touched, they mingled. Scary.

It was after eleven when they got to the village. Lizzy, in the back of the Jaguar, was sitting, hands folded in her lap, legs sticking straight out in front of her, playing, Megs thought uneasily, at being good. Shameless, to his dismay, was ordered to lie on the floor. Gilbert did not have to say what he felt about dogs on his leather upholstery. The state of his eyebrows – halfway up his forehead – said it all. When they arrived at the village, Shameless, Lizzy and Megs tumbled out on to the pavement and looked about them.

'I have one or two things I have to get,' Gilbert said. 'Do you want to explore and meet up in an hour?'

'Sounds fine to me,' said Megs. She extended her hand to Lizzy. 'Let's have a look round, shall we?'

Lizzy shook her head. 'I want to go with Gilbert. I want to see what he's going to buy.'

'You come with me,' Megs insisted. 'Let Gilbert shop on his own.'

'No.' Lizzy put her hands behind her back. They were not available for Megs to take, lead her off.

'Come on, Lizzy.' Megs dreaded a scene.

'She can come with me if she wants,' Gilbert said. Had he said that? He couldn't believe it. He didn't want Lizzy with him. He wasn't sure about children. They seemed unstable to him. It wasn't just their unrestrained emotional outbursts, there was the business of their bladders and bowels. Children, it seemed to him, had unreliable digestive systems. Lizzy, to his amazement, took his hand. She stepped forward, leading him away from Megs. Things were getting out of control.

'Do you mind?' Megs asked.

'No. No. Not at all,' he said. But I do mind, he thought. Help me.

'Well, I'll take Shameless,' Megs said. 'Nobody should be burdened with him. Don't let her boss you,' she warned Gilbert, nodding at Lizzy.

They parted. Gilbert and Lizzy headed across the square to the shops, Megs and Shameless wandered. She walked up old lanes, high crumbling walls dripping ivy and stock. High above the rush and squeal of swallows. She looked up, Shameless sniffed at doorways, found fascinating patches of ground that he would not be dragged from, peed on lampposts. From open windows Megs heard that same insane chatter and scream of Saturday-morning television as would, she knew, be going on in her own home.

Every lane, every wynd she walked down led back to the square. Not that she minded. The little shops tucked up the lanes sold mostly craftwork – hand-made spoons, plaques, pokerwork name plates and homilies on highly varnished slabs of wood. 'Never borrower or lender be.' 'Home sweet home.' No, the square was more interesting. No more than ten shops facing a tall market cross. A grocer's, where, no doubt, Lizzy was bossing Gilbert and choosing things he didn't want to buy. Do him good. Megs smiled, imagining it. A butcher's painted yellow, with FRESH MEAT in huge lettering on the window. Next to that the Sunset Boulevard video shop, with several posters of Fred Astaire in mid-swirl, tails flying, in the window. It was closed. A wool shop, a fruit-and-veg shop, an ironmonger's, a sweet shop, a newsagent's and post office, an antique shop and the Blue Kettle bakery and café which had, propped on the pavement by the front door, a lopsided painting of a blue kettle. TEAS, the sign said.

Megs could not resist it. She crossed the square and stared in the window. What an array of vibrant cakes, such abandoned use of cochineal. These cakes looked like they'd been crayoned by children in primary school – there was no subtlety here. Megs bent forward to peer into the café. It seemed to be full of women, and it looked like they were all laughing. In years to come, when Megs thought back to the Blue Kettle Café, she would remember it to be filled with women in thick tweed suits – no matter what the weather – twin sets and pearls. They would all be fat-kneed, laughing and toothless. Of course it wasn't true. It was a fleeting first impression that would last forever.

She had to pull herself away from that window. She left these guffawing, hooting women and shyly stuck her head into the butcher's. 'Is it all right to come in here?'

The butcher, in his white overall and blue-and-white apron, sharpening a knife with wide arm movements, said above the rasp of steel on steel, 'Are you thinking of buying something?'

'Oh yes, eggs. It's just the dog. It's not very hygienic to bring him in.'

'Are you a health inspector?' the butcher wanted to know. He was bald, red-cheeked and chubby. He looked like a beef-eating man.

'No.'

'Well, come on in then.' The knife sliced air as he waved her inside. 'We'll forget about the hygiene.'

'Just want a dozen eggs,' Megs excused herself.

'The lad'll get them for you.' He leaned back and hollered into the back shop, 'BILLY!'

Billy appeared, knotting his apron. He was small, thinning hair pasted to his scalp, nervous, definitely past fifty. 'Yes?'

'A dozen eggs,' Megs said again.

The lad flapped open a couple of egg boxes and deftly filled them, lifting eggs four at a time from the basket in the window. 'You'll not mind a few feathers, will you?'

'Oh no. In fact I'd be disappointed if I didn't get a few.'

'Well, I'll pop in a few more.' He lifted some extra and let them sail the small distance from his fingertips to the box. 'There you go. New here? Just passing through?'

'Staying the weekend with a friend.'

'Who's that?'

The curiosity was so finely tuned, the question fired with such precision, it didn't occur to Megs not to answer it.

'Gilbert Christie.'

The lad frowned. 'There's nobody of that name here.' Aha, he'd caught her out.

'He has a cottage up the glen. Lisdon?'

'Him. The professor.' He turned to his boss, who was serving a woman, an obvious Blue Kettle regular. Not that he needed to. They were openly eavesdropping. They lived here, they had a right to know who was who. 'She's staying with pork chops and *Fitzcarraldo,*' he told them.

'Ah.' They nodded in unison. Now they knew about her.

'Say when,' the butcher said to his customer, holding his knife on a large fillet. 'You want thick steaks, or are you not giving your man much this week?'

'Oh,' said the Blue Kettle woman. 'He gets plenty. Ha ha. Make them thick, Kynoch.'

Kynoch. Megs looked at him. A good name for a butcher, she thought. And, indeed, he was robust, assured. Being addressed by his last name suited him. 'Pork chops and *Fitzcarraldo*?' she repeated, bemused.

'I do the video shop evenings and Sundays. If you want a film delivered I can bring it with your meat.' The lad nodded to the pile of videos by the door. Each had a slip showing membership number, film and meat order. Member 52, *Diehard,* 1 lb stew steak, ½ sweet-cure bacon. Member 44, *Three Colours Red,* venison sausages, 3 lb shoulder lamb, 1 doz eggs.

'I miss the old days. Before videos, the Sunset Boulevard used to be our picture house. It was always a good night out at the movies,' Kynoch lamented.

'You got a cup of tea, proper in a china cup, a sandwich and a film. *Song of the South, From Here To Eternity, The Philadelphia Story* – you don't get them like that any more.' The Blue Kettle lady joined him.

'You got a lot more than that if you sat in the golden divans,' Kynoch remembered.

They all drifted into a minute's silence in respectful memory of

455

old movies, sandwiches, tea in real china cups and juicy adventures on the golden divans. Megs took her eggs and left them to it.

Gilbert and Lizzy were standing beside the car, waiting for her. 'I got eggs,' she told them. 'And I had a peek at the Blue Kettle Café.' She was enthused.

Gilbert wasn't. 'I can't go in there.' He imagined Annette bursting in and finding him ensconced at a plastic table, munching a bright-red coconut-encrusted cake with a glacé cherry on top. 'Good heavens. Gilbert. What are you doing?'

'Why not? It's wonderful.'

'No.' Gilbert was adamant. 'We'll go to the Stag and have a beer and sandwich.'

'It's that painting of the blue kettle, isn't it? It offends your fine-tuned artistic sensibilities.'

'No,' he lied. 'I just feel like a beer.'

'It's the women. All that screeching laughter. And the cakes. They're too vivid for you. Seaside-promenade yellow, fifties-lipstick red.'

'Nonsense.' He squirmed.

How could she know the ghosts that were with him? He imagined Annette's astonished sneer should she, in her Jasper Conran, appear at the door of the Blue Kettle Café, and spot him sitting with Megs and child, laughing loudly at some inane but naughty comment, mouth agape, flaunting a half-chewed gaudy cake. 'Gilbert?' She'd raise her prescription Calvin Kleins, peering at him, making sure her eyes didn't deceive her. 'Gilbert? Is that you?'

Oh God, he shuddered.

They went to the Stag, where, despite the heat outside, the fire was lit, Barry Manilow was playing on the jukebox and the landlord called Megs 'lass'. She could see it had its merits, but her heart was with the steaming ladies in the Blue Kettle.

They got back to the cottage after two. Megs watched as Gilbert unpacked the shopping and put on his green apron – his cottage cooking outfit.

'Chicken tonight,' he said. 'Chicken stuffed with soft cheese and herbs. Tomato and olive salad and some potatoes baked with rosemary and garlic.' He spread things out, putting corn-fed chicken, cheese, milk, herbs, tomatoes, olive oil, garlic in easy reach order. He considered a bottle of South African wine with a giraffe on the label. It was not his usual taste in wine labels, but Lizzy had insisted, and he didn't know how to refuse her.

One of his basic life rules was to avoid confrontations, yet every decade or so they came up. A confrontation with a child, however, was unthinkable. Sensing this weakness, Lizzy had come out of their shopping trip with some M&Ms, four white chocolate puddings, a packet of animal biscuits and a kite. This last Gilbert didn't mind at all. It was a traditional-shaped kite, blue and green with a long flagged tail. He imagined himself flying it, standing on some lush, mildly breezy meadow, cowslips at his feet, holding the string, Megs and Lizzy at his side. All of them watching the sky. The wine, however, was something else. He didn't trust it. He had no intention of drinking it.

Whilst he cooked, Megs, Lizzy and Shameless went for a walk through the woods at the back of the house. Gently kneading the chicken, easing the skin away from the breast, so that he could stuff the gap between loosened skin and bird with a soft paste of cheese, basil, oregano and sage, he realised that in his kite vision, Lizzy had been dressed in button boots and leggings. She'd had a straw bonnet on her head. She wasn't saying a word. The dog had been given a shampoo and blow-dry. Behind them was a field of lavender, fusing into the distance, muted indigo. It was, he realised, pure Merchant-Ivory. Standing stooped over the kitchen table, hands, encrusted with cheesy paste, stuffed up the chicken, staring straight ahead, he was horror-struck. Reining in his imagination, he realised that in his kite picture Annette had been leaning on the gate watching them, slightly approving, and more than slightly envious.

Megs, Lizzy and Shameless went carefully along the narrow path in the woods, avoiding the nettles, ignoring rusting cans, empty crisp bags, the abandoned bits of car and barbed wire and the furious spilling of brambles that engulfed them. Once through the woods, they waded waist deep through bracken to the river, staining their clothes. Burrs in Shameless's coat.

It was well after three o'clock. They started to wander, walking slowly along the river bank, staring down at the water, looking for movement – fish, frogs, otters. 'Anything living would please us city folks,' said Megs. They saw nothing, nobody. The river, sometimes a trickle, sometimes deep enough, wide enough to allow a small swim, ran the length of the glen.

Megs felt the silence, rubbed her arms against the chill she imagined it brought. The day was warm. Lizzy carefully ate her sweets, biting off the thick coating so that the soft chocolate centre was left. It stickied her hands, which she wiped on her T-shirt, smearing chocolate. She swore she saw a giant eel. Shameless rolled in a cowpat and came running to them, smelling foul. 'Oh well,' said Megs. 'You two are happy.' She knew there was misery in store – they'd walked too far and for too long. Had, therefore, to go all the way back again.

At the top of the glen, a small hump-backed bridge crossed the river. They climbed up the verge and through the fence to walk over it, to lean on the parapet, watch the water from above. Across the bridge, on the other side of the road, was a small hotel, next to that a hall. It was a wooden building with notices in the window. SCOUT MEETING 7.00 THIS THURSDAY. And ROAD IMPROVEMENT COMMITTEE MEETING, 8.00 TUES, TEA AND SANDWICHES. And DOES ANYONE WANT A KITTEN? OLAF HAS HAD SIX, FREE TO GOOD HOMES. IN FACT, FREE TO ANY HOME. And JEAN WATSON'S APPLE AND DATE CHUTNEY IS NOW SOLD OUT. A BATCH OF PEAR AND RED WINE JELLY IS NOW READY, CALL AT THE CREGGANS'. ALL PROFITS TO NEW HALL FUND.

There were more, Megs did not read them. It would be dark soon. A lone crow rasped from the telegraph wire. A grim call that heightened her worry. She thought to go into the hotel to buy Lizzy a drink and phone Gilbert, ask him to come get them, but she realised she hadn't brought her purse. City folks didn't go into hotels with empty pockets, especially when they were torn by brambles, blackened by bracken, reeking of cow dung and smeared with chocolate. She turned to walk down the road.

It took only a few steps on tarmac before Lizzy realised she was miserable. She dragged her feet, complained of the heat and hunger. Every two or three yards she sat on the verge, crying. Wiped her eyes with filthy fingers, grubbied her cheeks. Megs lifted her on to her back, and set off down the road again. 'Soon be there. Not far to go.' The lie was to soothe herself as much as her daughter.

When the van slowed up beside them, Megs ignored it. It did not do to encourage strangers, far less get into their vans. She strode ahead, refusing to give its occupant a glance. So it crawled beside them for a few yards before the butcher's boy rolled down the window and yelled, 'Are ye not speaking?' Megs turned, recognised a familiar face and smiled. 'Oh, sorry. I didn't realise it was you. Only, you know, a stranger in a car. You have to be careful these days.'

He leaned out of the window, teeth clenched, thinking about this. He was not a man to let clichés slide past him. 'Seems to me, if you're away from home, strangers are all you've got.'

'That's true,' Megs agreed.

'So,' he asked, 'are you wanting a lift or not?'

'Yes please. Very much. I do want a lift. We all want a lift.'

He leaned over to open the passenger door, then gathered some movie magazines and put them behind him, clearing the seat for Megs. She climbed in, sat Lizzy on her knee and put Shameless at her feet. 'Oh bliss,' she said. 'I'll never walk anywhere again. Have you been delivering?'

'Four steak pies, fillet steaks, bacon and *It's a Wonderful Life* and *Presumed Innocent* to the hotel.'

'Interesting,' she said.

'Your dog's smelly,' he said.

'I know, he rolled in some cow dung.'

'That's a dog for you. They'll do that.'

They had nothing more to say to each other. Megs was too tired to speak, and he was not in the habit of speaking for speaking's sake. They drove in silence till they got to the end of the track leading to Lisdon cottage. 'This'll be you,' he said.

'Yes. Thank you very much. You saved my life.'

'Aye, well. Sitting's better than walking. Usually anyway.'

She climbed out, thanked him again. He raised his hand, dismissing her gratitude, then drove off. Nothing more to say.

The air on the way down the track to the cottage was heavily succulent with wafts of Gilbert's cooking. When at last Megs entered his kitchen, she saw the table he'd prepared. A glass stand filled with fruit, dripping grapes in the centre, wine bottles, gleaming glasses, chicken cooked golden, a bowl of green salad, a white linen tablecloth. With a single flickering candle holding off the dusk, it was perfect.

'Good God,' he cried when he saw her. 'Where have you been? I was worried.'

'We walked to the top of the glen. Up the river to the hotel.'

'But that's miles.'

'I know.' She sank on to a chair.

He'd been worried about her. For the last hour, as he basted his chicken and prodded his potatoes, he'd imagined her lying at the foot of a ravine, both legs broken, unable to move. Or perhaps they'd wandered from the path and were lost, were plunging wildly through the heather, unable to find their way back, panicking and crying. Should he call Mountain Rescue? He thought not, best wait till she'd been missing for longer than sixty minutes. Instead, he fretted.

Emerging now from his worry, he saw how tired and filthy they were. He caught a whiff of Shameless. Annette, he knew, would be wearing spotless jeans, Italian canvas deck shoes – probably navy – and a linen shirt, with a cashmere sweater draped over her shoulders. What she would make of these smelly, bracken-blackened, chocolate- and tear-smeared guests – interlopers bruising his perfection – he didn't dare think.

He pushed his hand through his hair, making it stick up. His shirt was splattered with olive oil and cheesy paste. A thick sweat spread over him. His face glowed from working in his hot, low-ceilinged kitchen and a surfeit of wine. The knackered and grubby, then, congregated to worship the glistening glamour of Gilbert's efforts. Gilbert, meantime, looked sheepishly across at the chair where his imagined, impeccable ghost, Annette, sat hardly able to contain her disdain. He shrugged an apology to her.

'My goodness, Gilbert.' Megs broke into his despairing reverie. 'What a fabulous meal. And doesn't it all look wonderful? And look at us. The mess we're in. Will it wait till we go make ourselves presentable?'

'I think,' Gilbert said, 'it's going to have to.'

She put Shameless out into the garden, threw a bucket of water over him and put his dish, filled with dog food, at the door. Then she took Lizzy upstairs to the bathroom, where they stripped and climbed into the shower together. Gilbert, on his way to put on a fresh shirt, paused by the door to listen to them giggling and lathering one another. He wasn't sure about such intimacy. It made him feel squeamish. Yet it was Megs in his shower having fun, and he could not help the rush of envy that swept through him.

They reappeared half an hour later, looking clean and, in Lizzy's case, shiny. Megs, Gilbert noted approvingly, wore black jeans with a plain white cotton shirt. Her toenails were painted a soft pink-brown. She came to his table barefoot. She smelled of vanilla.

He was not used to such eating. His meals were normally savoured rather than devoured. But his guests tonight were ravenous. They ate. They saved the conversation for afters, with coffee.

'This is wonderful,' Megs enthused. 'Where did you learn to cook like this?'

'In the kitchen.' Gilbert was modest about his achievements. But he nodded towards the cooking area of the room, which was in chaos. The crazed debris of the enthusiastic amateur cook.

When Lizzy had eaten, the trials and physical efforts of her day caught up with her. She climbed on to her mother and fell asleep. Megs carried her upstairs to bed. When she came back Gilbert had opened a second bottle of wine and refilled their glasses.

She sank sighing into her seat. 'Oh, lovely,' she said. 'Peace.' She drank. 'Your wine is lovely. It's a one-glasser, your wine.'

'What do you mean by that?'

'I mean it only takes one glass, one sip, and you know it's good stuff. I buy three-glasser wine. You take a drink and you feel it scrape the back of your throat and corrode your tooth enamel. You make a face, a grimace. The sort of look you make when countering a force-nine gale.' She contorted her face into a post-swig-of-nasty-plonk grimace. 'Like this.'

'Right,' he said, leaning towards her. Making the face too.

'One glass you make the face and say, "This is vile." So you have another. 'Cos you're human and you have to check, also it's probably all you have. Second glass and your throat is already coated with the

461

stuff and your system knows what's coming, so you say, "It's not that bad." So you have another glass and you say, "This is quite nice." My wine takes three glasses.'

'Ah.' He smiled. 'I've had wine like that.' He poured her some more of his one-glasser wine. It made her loosen up. He liked her when she loosened up. 'Tell me about you,' he said, chastising himself as he spoke. He thought he sounded like some stereotype Lothario working on his seduction technique.

'I live such a brittle life,' she said. 'I'm constantly waiting for something awful to happen. I drive to the supermarket in my car and all the way there I'm filled with a small fear that it is going to break down. I hear some jangle and I think, "That's it. Something's wrong. Huge bill for me." Then I realise it's only a sound effect on some song on the radio. But for a moment, my heart reels. That's my mood these days – trepidation. Then I get to the supermarket and I'm obsessed with parking as near to the door as I can. I eye other drivers lest they steal a place I'm after. That's me now, trepidation and competition. And I'm only shopping.

'What does a supermarket look like? Some Middle Eastern hacienda sort of building with a vast car park and a filling station. It smells of bread baking. But that's not bread – it's only a contrived smell. Now what have we?' She spread out her fingers to count her feelings. 'Trepidation, competition, cynicism. That's me these days. Not just on Saturday mornings at the supermarket. But all the time, really.' She poured another glass. Drank it.

'Do you think we've lost our sensuality, Gilbert? Do you ever do anything completely and utterly with all of you? Smell, taste, touch? When I was little, Aunty Betty used to send me out to the greenhouse for tomatoes. I'd go barefoot across the lawn, and I could feel and smell the grass. I could hear birds in the hedge. The greenhouse old and wooden, peeling faded paint. You had to lean on the door to open it. It creaked when it moved. You could hear it scrape on the terracotta tiles. Every summer they planted tomatoes in that greenhouse. Huge plants.' She lifted her hands above her head. A demonstration of hugeness. 'It was full of them. I could stand and feel cracks in the warm tiles on the soles of my feet. And I could smell that green, tangy, tomatoey smell. I was bathed in heat and scent. I could hold a tomato to my nose and breathe it in. I could bite into one and the sweetness of it burst into me. They were ripe and red. And they grew as the sun touched them. No one was a clone of the other. Not like supermarket tomatoes. They are cosmetic tomatoes. Red as red can be, every one perfect. "Look at me," they say. "I'm a tomato." Tomatoes with attitude. Not like real tomatoes in Aunty Betty's greenhouse.' She sprawled on the table, fully wined and slightly crazy.

Gilbert could only drink and listen. He'd had no idea she was so verbose.

'And sex.' Megs was at full steam now. 'In the cinema, I sit in the dark, one hand in my popcorn box, and I watch two people fuck. I sit amidst absolute strangers, and I watch amazing intimacies with them. Things we might do in the dark when we get home. Or not in the dark. Or not at all. It's perfect, cinema sex. Cosmeticised sex. Oooh and ahhs and choreographed rolling on top of each other. Shapely, well-lit bums in the glamorous dark. She never cries, "Get off, get off. I can't breathe." Or, "You're stopping the circulation in my arm." He never gets cramp. They never turn to find a little person, eyes level with the top of the mattress, saying, "What are you two doing?" Too perfect.' She scoffed, 'I do not trust perfection.' She lifted a slice of tomato from the salad dish, held it to her nose a moment, then to her lips. 'This is not a tomato,' she said. 'And that stuff on the screen. That's not sex.' She drank some more. Put down her glass. 'Do you fancy shagging me? Do you fancy having sex with me? All of me. All of you. Everything. Do you fancy the feel of me? The sight of me across the pillow? Would you put your tongue in me, taste me? Would you like to do that together, Gilbert Christie? Would you like to smell the soapy cleanness of the sheets and the breeze on the curtains coming down from the hills across the room, and the salty scent of what we're doing? Would you like to hear my breath in your ear and the sounds outside of grass moving and bushes shoving against each other in the wind? And the call of some late bird through the dark? And our cries when we come? Would you like to feel all over you our mutual sweatiness, and my hands on you, and . . . ?'

He reached over and took her hand. He could hardly bear his

urgency. He felt the warmth of her palm pressing against his. 'Yes,' he said. 'Yes.' Again. When he looked across the room, his ghost, Annette, had gone.

Chapter Twenty-Three

He woke. It was raining, bells were ringing far away. Sunday, and some folks in the glen were going to church. But he was lathered in sweat, and some small, irritatingly insistent hissing noise had pierced his dreams, brought him to consciousness. He did not want to open his eyes. He resisted the light. He reached across for Megs. She was not there. That did it. He lifted himself on to one elbow and looked around, trying to take in what he saw.

Shameless was lying sprawled at the foot of the bed, pinning down the eiderdown, causing his sweat. Lizzy was next to him, squishing mousse from a can. She had already plastered quite a handful on to his head.

'There,' she said, fussing over him. 'That's better. Your hair's always sticking up. I've fixed it. Look.'

Before he could stop her, she held up a mirror. This was not what he wanted to see first thing. He was glazed, looking, he thought, insane. His face was flushed, and his hair was glued to his skull. 'Oh God,' he said. 'Where's Megs?'

'In the kitchen. Washing the dishes.' She got bolder. She sat on top of him, smoothing down his hair. Little hands busy on his head. 'There. You look pretty now.'

'Shall we go find her?' he said, sliding clumsily into his boxer shorts under the covers.

She nodded, and as he climbed from the bed, reached up to take his hand. She led him downstairs. 'Here's Gilbert,' she told Megs, entering the kitchen. 'He's awake now.' Then, to Gilbert, 'Can we fly the kite now?'

He did not know how to refuse her. It was not in his nature to refuse anybody anything.

'Let him get dressed and have some coffee before you start nagging, Lizzy,' Megs intervened. Turning to Gilbert, she scolded, 'Don't let her bully you.'

'I'm not used to children. I never know what to say to them,' he excused himself. 'Goodness, this kitchen's clean. You shouldn't've bothered.'

She shrugged. 'It didn't take long. I'm used to it.'

It was the first time she'd referred to the beginnings of their affair, and the routine she was about to go back to. He was a university lecturer, and she was his cleaner. He didn't think he was comfortable with that. What would his friends say? Gilbert looked across the kitchen. Annette was back.

They walked in silence the way down the track to the field, open enough, breezy enough to fly the kite. Still saying nothing, they climbed the gate, whilst Shameless wriggled through the lower spars.

The kite staggered into the wind, taking slowly to the sky. Gilbert showed Lizzy how to tug the string. 'Play the wind,' he said, squatting beside her, so that her face was close to his. He could see her small lips pulled tight, concentrating. 'You can feel the wind on the end of the string. You can feel the gusts and thermals up there.' He let her hold the kite, stood watching till she could manage it before he sat down on the grass beside Megs.

'She picks things up quickly.' He admired the child.

'Which isn't always a good thing,' she said.

He smiled. 'Were you a smart kid?'

'I suspect I was a pain in the arse. I insisted on being called Megs. I never did what anybody told me. You?'

'I always did what I was told.' Realising he'd hung his head as he said that, he played with a daisy. This wasn't a small movement of shame. He was interested in the ground.

'Your mother was a tyrant?'

'She made me give up painting. She had some idea of respectability she couldn't properly pass on except by inflicting silences and spreading a thick atmosphere of disapproval. You could breathe it.'

They looked over at Lizzy, tugging her kite, watching it jiggle and shake ten feet high.

'I often wonder,' Megs said, 'how people get to be the way they are. I had a boss once, at a market garden where I worked, who was a bully and a loud-mouth in a suit. I'm sure when he was six he must've wanted to be a train driver or an astronaut. How did that happen to him? I'm sure your mother never planned to be the way she was.'

He shrugged. 'She's dead now. I'll never be able to ask her.'

'Yes. That's the thing about death. It's the only thing that lasts and lasts. I remember when Thomas died I thought: this will go on for ever, this death, this never seeing him again.' It was her turn to study the daisies. 'I kept seeing him places. You know, in parks playing, or walking along the street. My heart would stop – literally stop. That's Thomas, I'd think, though I knew it couldn't possibly be.'

A week after the funeral she was passing the park on a bus. Sitting looking out of the window, her face frozen in an expression of grief that staved off fellow passengers. The bus was full, but nobody would sit beside her. Staring across the park at a group of boys kicking a ball about, she saw Thomas. 'That's him.' She was sure she had shouted it out. She got up, struggled up the aisle, past the straphangers, and jumped from the platform, though the bus was travelling at some speed.

She ran back to the park gate, then across the grass, waving wildly, shouting, 'Thomas. Thomas.' The children stopped playing, turned to stare at her. Their mothers, standing in a group nearby, did so too. The boys, young and tactless, made faces, screwed their fingers into the side of their foreheads. 'A loony,' they called. The mothers moved instinctively nearer to their children. You never knew with folks these days. Seeing this, reading the language of the bodies, emotional semaphore, Megs stopped running. Stopped waving. Stopped smiling. 'Sorry,' she said. 'I thought I saw somebody I knew.' She walked quickly away, feeling foolish and desolate.

'After my mother died,' Gilbert told her, 'I kept seeing her on the tube. I was in London doing some research. I'd be standing on the platform, and she'd be on a train hurtling past me. Then, sometimes, it was the other way round.'

Gilbert remembered standing on the tube, halfway up the aisle, five o'clock Friday night, no seats available. The train was leaving Piccadilly Circus, gathering speed, when he saw his mother standing on the platform. She was wearing her old tweed coat and black leather gloves and was carrying her brown shopping bag with her handbag tucked inside it for safety. She looked surprised. Gilbert stopped gripping the rail overhead and reached for her. 'My God,' he said out loud. People nearby pretended they did not hear him. He ran his fingers through his hair. 'A ghost,' he said. 'The ghost of my mother is waiting on that platform for the train to Kensington.' People about him pretended even harder not to notice him. The only person who looked ghostly was Gilbert.

'I'd better get my things,' Megs said. 'I want to get back before dark.'

'Must you go?' He reached for her hand. 'Why don't you stay longer?'

'I have to get home. I've work in the morning. Terribly-Clean Pearson.' She was adamant.

'Who?'

'Terribly-Clean Pearson. I clean for her. I have names for people I clean for. It's part of my survival. Terribly-Clean Pearson, Dysentery McGhee and Emotionally-Deranged Davis.'

'Do you have a name for me?'

'No,' she said, considering the daisies rather than meet his eye. He didn't believe her.

Lizzy screamed. Her kite had escaped and was soaring away from her. By the time Megs and Gilbert reached her, it was above the trees at the top of the field and heading for the hills. A multicoloured blob.

'You get it,' Lizzy commanded Megs.

'I can't,' Megs said.

'You get it.' Lizzy turned to Gilbert.

'I can't either.' He felt just awful about this.

'I want my kite.' The child clenched her fists, threw back her head and howled.

'Well, it's gone. Nobody can reach it. We'll get you another,' Megs said.

'I want that one.'

'That one's gone. C'mon.' Megs picked Lizzy up and headed towards the gate. 'Time to go.'

'Will you come back?' Gilbert sounded desperate.

They climbed back over the gate. Halfway down, Lizzy got stuck and refused to climb any further.

'I can't get down,' she wailed.

'I'll lift you,' Megs said.

'No.' Lizzy shook her head. 'Not you. I want Gilbert to lift me.'

Feeling absurdly pleased at being the preferred one, Gilbert swept Lizzy from the gate, whirled her high in the air before putting her down. 'There you go.'

'I think she's jealous of the attention you're giving me,' Megs told him.

'Right,' said Gilbert. 'I never thought. I'm not used to children. I haven't learned their little ways.'

Megs watched him as he took Lizzy's hand and headed home. So whose little ways have you learned, Gilbert? she thought. Who is it you are thinking of when you gaze into the distance, the way you do? And will you ever accept my little ways?

It was after seven when she got home. 'Are you still here?' she said to Lorraine, who was lying on the sofa reading the horoscopes on Teletext.

'Seems like it,' said Lorraine. 'You are going to have a shock tomorrow, it says here.'

'Well, thanks for that. Is everything fine here?'

'Nothing to report. Jack's hair is growing. Hannah's still in love. And your mother has phoned twice to see if you're back.'

'Everything's normal, then.'

'Yes. Did you have a good time? What did you do?'

'I'll never tell you.'

'That good, eh? You are looking healthy. Skin's smooth. Fresh air, food and sex, though not necessarily in that order, I'll bet.'

'Bet away. Make us some coffee, that'd be useful.' Megs sat on the armchair. Rose again. 'Jack has ruined this. You have to be under twenty with a teenagy flexible spine, to get comfortable on it. It's become a Beavis and Butthead chair.' She moved on to the sofa.

469

The phone rang. Megs picked it up. She knew who it was. 'Hello, Mum.'

'How did it go? Did you get back all right? How was the traffic? I don't like you going about in that car of yours.'

'I'm back. Traffic wasn't bad. The car's fine. Lizzy had a good time. She flew a kite. Shameless was, as ever, shameless. And I had a long walk and got a lift back from the butcher's boy. Gilbert cooked a lovely meal. That's all you need to know.'

'That's all I'm getting to know, anyway. Are you going back?'

'He wants me to.'

'You should go. It'll do you good. A man like that, with his education, could bring you to your senses.'

'What do you mean by that?'

'I mean he could show you that there's more to life than cleaning.'

'I already know that.'

'He could make you do something about it.'

'Are you coming round tomorrow?' Megs changed the subject.

'If you want me to.'

'I want you to. You can nag me then, in person, face to face.'

'I will. Good night.'

'Good night.'

Lorraine brought them coffee. 'Don't tell me. That was your mother.'

'She approves of Gilbert.'

'Goodness. As far as you're concerned, that's the worst thing that could happen to Gilbert.'

Megs smiled. 'Maybe not this time.'

Chapter Twenty-Four

A weekend away made it harder than ever to get up and face the day. Megs lay glumly staring at the ceiling. She wondered what Gilbert was doing. Did he have the kitchen door open, letting the soft hill air mix with the smell of brewing coffee? Was he sitting at that kitchen table she'd sat at, and was he mildly staring at today's batch of junk mail? How odd that the red postie's van moved through that exquisite landscape bearing the same rubbish that clattered daily through her own letter box – urgently gushing offers from the *Reader's Digest*, pension plan and loan fliers, breathlessly sincere firms proposing to develop two rolls of films for the price of one.

She could hear Lorraine moving about, switching on the radio, making coffee, before she disappeared pasty-faced and lank-haired in a faded blue dressing gown and reappeared half an hour later, glowing, mincing down the hall in high heels, shirt and tight skirt. A different woman. As soon as she vacated the bathroom, Jack would barge in, leaving Hannah to bang on the door shouting that she had to get in. Then Jack would appear washed and splashed, in multi-reek mode – aftershave, gel (when he had hair to gel), deodorant. After that, Hannah would go in to spray and mousse and fuss.

'It's seven-thirty,' Megs said to Shameless. 'All over the world people are listening to insanity on the radio, pushing mousse through their hair, making the first-sip-of-coffee-in-the-morning face as they hold the cup to their lips. And here's me. As ever, desperate for a pee and wishing I was somewhere else.'

But things were moving on. Now she knew where she wished she was.

She arrived late at the Pearsons'. Hurrying down the path, she

471

did not notice that the front room curtains were still drawn. Had she seen this small break from the norm on the outside, she might have been prepared for the devastation inside.

The mess spread down the hall, strewn torn books, clothes and drifting squalls of feathers coming from the bedroom. Making her careful way to what had been the centre of the storm, Megs peered into the bedroom. The wardrobe was on its side, the dresser had been yanked apart – drawers pulled out, contents spilled on to the floor, make-up, hairspray, jewellery had been thrown at the mirror, which was smashed. The mattress was upturned on the bed, and the duvet slashed, hence the feathers, which billowed and spread in the smallest breeze. But the devastation reached full, catastrophic proportions in the living room and kitchen. Furniture was broken, food furiously splattered against walls, the fridge door swung open, dishes were smashed on the floor. The walls were scarred with the force of hurled crockery and cutlery. The hi-fi was in bits, and CDs, out of their cases, lay covered with coffee and tea poured from their glass storage jars. Tupperware and its contents – lentils, biscuits, flour, rice – spilled everywhere. The vast shiny rebel plant was uprooted, lay centre stage, wilting.

Terribly-Clean was sitting on the sofa. When she looked up, Megs could see her face was bloodied, bruised and swollen. Her eyes were red with more than sobbing – hysteria.

'Good God.' Megs couldn't take in what she was seeing. 'What happened here? Shall I call the police?'

'No. Please don't.' Mrs Pearson's swollen face hurt with every emotion that flickered across it. She raised a hand in protest rather than risk having to use her lips any more.

'Who did this?'

'My husband.' Terribly-Clean put her hand to her mouth.

'Your husband? Did this?' Megs looked round. 'But why?'

Mrs Pearson got up and went through to the bathroom. She returned holding a cloth soaked in cold water to her face. 'I suppose I should tell you. I've got us into terrible debt. He found out about it. He saw me with my credit card. He was on his way back to the office after a business lunch, and he saw me in the jeweller's buying a watch. Another Gucci, I'm afraid. I already have three. But I like them best. I have a thing about watches.'

'You?'

'Yes. Perhaps if he'd done something when he saw me, it wouldn't have been so bad. As it was . . .' she nodded at the room, 'he waited. He waited and checked up on me. He found out about my credit cards. He's known about the debt for a fortnight.' She turned to meet Megs's gaze. 'I have ten credit cards. I owe over twenty thousand pounds.'

'You?' Megs said again. It was all she could think to say.

'Well, last night Access phoned to ask when I was going to make a payment. I'm three months behind with them. And that was it. It set him off.' She blew air into her aching cheeks. 'He went berserk. He hit me in the face with the phone. And then . . . this. I just stood as he wrecked the house. He tore our lives apart. He destroyed everything.' She went back to the bathroom to soak her cloth in cold water again. 'It was awful.' She returned to slump on the sofa, sat back soothed by the chill against her face. 'I had no idea he had such passion. He said he'd worked all those years doing a job he hated just to support us. And I'd blown it all away. We're going to have to sell the house. He went on the rampage, ripping things apart, yelling about his wasted life.'

'Shall I make you a cup of tea?' Megs suggested.

'Yes please. I think the tea bags landed on the floor beside the washing machine. A place for everything and everything in its place. I did a domestic science course. That was one of the first things I learned.'

When Megs brought the tea through from the kitchen, Terribly-Clean Pearson was standing in the debris, crying.

'Never mind the mess for the moment,' Megs said. 'Sit down, drink this. Have you been here all night?'

'I was on the sofa for hours and hours, just staring. It must have been all night. Yes. He stormed out of the house. I haven't heard from him since.'

'He'll be all right, I'm sure.'

'I don't know if I care. I never knew he had such rage.' She looked slowly round at the mess. 'This, of course, is about more than my spending. It's about how bored he's been. Do you know? I think he

Isla Dewar

was jealous that I'd been spending and not him.' She snorted. 'I had
given up, you know. Then that day you started to speak about ducks,
about rapture, I felt so desolate I got my card and hit the shops.
That's when Mr Pearson saw me.'

'So it's all my fault?'

Mrs Pearson put out her hand to touch Megs's. 'Oh no. I didn't
mean that. It would've come out one way or another.'

'You need some sleep.'

'How do I do that?'

'Normally I wouldn't be able to tell you. But in your case I think if
you just lay down it'd come to you.'

'All those years,' Terribly-Clean said, 'and he's been utterly
miserable. If only he'd said. I've been miserable too. I mean, I clean.
I cook. I teach part-time, domestic science, showing young people
how to cook. How many first-year pupils have I taught to make
macaroni and cheese? God.' Then, really thinking about it, 'Probably
thousands. I hate macaroni and cheese. Then I come home here and
go through little lifeless routines. I make supper, he washes up. We
watch television. At eleven we get ready for bed. I make a cup of
tea and a digestive biscuit. We were doing all this and we were both
utterly unhappy. What liars we were.' She sipped her tea. And
winced. 'I have been sitting in this house whilst the whole world
happened outside. Not like you, Megs. I don't have a fabulous life
like you. I don't sing. I don't do the things you do. I don't wear
dark colours.'

'What things?'

Mrs Pearson had no idea. She just imagined things. She hadn't
even come to grips with what her imaginings were. 'Just things,' she
said.

'I don't have a fabulous life,' Megs protested.

'Oh, I bet you have lovers.' The distressed creases in Mrs Pearson's
face dispersed a moment as she imagined Megs's lovers. Her passion.

'I don't have lovers. I haven't had a lover for years and years. I
sleep with my daughter and my dog,' Megs confessed. 'You are
making up a life for me.'

'You haven't had a lover for years?'

'Well, not until last weekend.'

'Now you have one. Who is it?' The eagerness to know swooned out of her.

'He's someone I met.'

'What does he do?'

'He's a lecturer. He's writing a book at the moment.'

'There you go. He must be so interesting. So clever.'

'He's clever.' Megs nodded, musing. 'But he's not wise. He only knows what he knows. He has no intuition. People puzzle him. Life puzzles him.'

'The creative type.'

Megs wanted to laugh. 'Hmm. Perhaps. If he's creative he hasn't let go enough to create anything interesting yet.'

Mrs Pearson would not be dissuaded. She was convinced Megs led a complex, outré life. 'I bet you have lots of friends, though.'

'No.' Megs shook her head. 'Only Lorraine. I see quite a bit of my mother. Otherwise it's just odd folks at the Glass Bucket, though I won't be seeing them any more. And the band.'

'The band. That sounds interesting.'

'Believe me, they're not. They play Friday nights to make ends meet. Like me. They're ordinary, ordinary, ordinary.' There, that should convince her.

'Not as ordinary as me, as I've been all these years. It's what I wanted to be, nothing fancy, safe and ordinary.'

'Daft when you think about it,' said Megs. 'I think ordinary makes women cry more than lost love, being dumped, silent phones or any of that stuff. Women sit alone in absurdly clean living rooms, crying because they're ordinary. And they can't blame anyone but themselves, because it's what they thought they wanted.'

'Yes,' said Mrs Pearson.

'Yes,' Megs agreed with herself. 'Ordinary ain't what it's cut up to be. Still.' She looked round. 'You seem to have rather given up on ordinary,' she said.

'What am I going to do?'

'Drink your tea. Start cleaning up.'

'Yes.' Terribly-Clean Pearson nodded reluctantly.

But they did not move. They sat side by side, quietly companionable. A blackbird shrilled in the garden. Megs looked idly round. 'What a mess,' she said. 'What a lot of stuff we gather. If we didn't buy half the stuff we have, we wouldn't notice we didn't have it.'

'Exactly,' agreed Terribly-Clean. 'See that chicken brick that's smashed in bits over by the television, or what used to be the television. Well, I really wanted that. Used it twice.'

'I have a sandwich toaster – same thing,' Megs said. 'We really should make a start,' she nagged herself.

'Yes. We should,' Terribly-Clean agreed dreamily. 'We could have another cup of tea first.'

'Yes, that'd get us going.'

Still they sat. There was some mutual relief at seeing such a loveless life so passionately wrecked. They sighed. Megs began to idly sing. 'Gimme money. That's what I want,' she sang. Without really noticing she was doing it. She had the knack of plucking totally inappropriate songs from her repertoire.

'Oh, I never really liked that one,' Terribly-Clean Pearson said, taking no offence at all. 'Tell you what I used to love. "Dock of the Bay". Do you know that?'

'Oh, I love that.'

So they sang it.

'Do you know any old Rod Stewart numbers? I had a crush on him.'

Megs sang 'Tonight's the Night', getting into it. Moving and shaking on the sofa. Though not actually standing up. Terribly-Clean joined in the chorus. When they'd finished that one, they started on 'Every Picture Tells a Story'. And when they'd demolished that, Megs said, '"Mandolin Wind", God, remember that one?' So they tore into 'Mandolin Wind'. They bawled, hands waving over their heads.

Passers on the pavement looked mildly bemused at the crescendo blasting from the house at the end of the perfect garden path.

'. . . ah luv ya . . . oooh . . . hooo.'

Chapter Twenty-Five

Vivienne could hardly contain her glee when she heard about Terribly-Clean Pearson. When Megs told her, she got up from her seat by the fire (for such good news made sitting still impossible) and strode into the kitchen. 'Yes,' she said, jubilantly switching on the kettle. 'Yes,' again. Then, keeping her voice under control, 'You'll be wanting a cup of tea, then?'

'Suppose,' said Megs. Though she had a hankering for something stronger.

'You won't be working there any more, then?' Vivienne hoped the question sounded more mildly interested than celebratory.

'Nope,' said Megs. 'They're selling the house. They can't afford me.'

'So what are you going to do?'

'Worry. Gilbert wants me to spend the whole summer with him in his cottage. But I'll have to spend it looking for a job.'

'Go. Why don't you? It'd do you good.'

'I have to find work. I have kids to feed.'

'Your kids will be away all summer. At least two of them will be.'

Megs said, 'I have a mortgage to pay. At least half of one. Mike pays the other half.'

'Let Lorraine chip in. She's living with you. She's got more money than you. She ought to pay her way. Goodness, you haven't had a holiday in years. When you come back you'll be charged up. You'll find a job no problem.' Vivienne had high hopes of Gilbert. She thought he was the best thing that had ever happened to Megs. He would, she was sure, rescue her daughter from this nonsensical life she led and set her on the right track.

477

Megs said, 'Hmm . . .' And nothing else. She knew she'd reached a point when decisions had to be taken. She'd recently read an advert for business courses for women. She'd thought of applying. But hadn't. She worried that all the other women would be shoulder-padded in business suits, and she'd just be a cleaner.

Still, Vivienne took her noncommittal answer as a good sign. It was not, after all, a downright no.

Megs left her mother's in time to walk to the nursery to pick up Lizzy. It was a perfect day. Too good, Megs thought, to spend clearing up other people's debris. She stepped out to the hum of her worries. They stopped being tangible thoughts, became, instead, a mood she was in. A certain despair that, she realised, had been with her, unacknowledged, for some time now.

She tried to empty her mind, to listen to her feet on the pavement instead. She was unaware that she was walking towards Josh.

He stuck his head in front of hers. 'Are you not speaking?'

'Oh, sorry.' She started. 'I didn't see you. I was miles away.'

'Where are you going?'

'I have to pick up Lizzy.'

'Well, I'll not keep you.'

She started to walk away from him, but he turned, came with her. 'What are you doing now?' he wanted to know.

'Worrying, mostly.'

'I do that.' He considered his feet. Watched them moving over the ground. He was looking worse than ever. Tired, filthy, underfed and longing for a drink. Megs tried to disown him. She didn't know how to politely ask him not to walk beside her. She breathed her discomfort. 'Look. Don't ask me for money. I just don't have any.'

'I wasn't going to.' They walked on in silence. Megs tried to outpace him. But he kept up. 'I know it was my fault,' he said at last. 'I've been feeling guilty about it for years.'

'What was your fault?'

'Your wee lad. The one that died. I shouldn't've kept you talking.'

'It wasn't your fault, Josh. Don't blame yourself. It was my fault. I should have been there.'

'Have you stopped singing, then?'

'Yes, Josh.' It sighed out of her. 'I have.'

'So Mike never told you about that deal, then.'

'What deal?'

'Remember the night we slept on the beach at Gairloch? Remember that night? The night before at Inverness there was a bloke came to see you.'

That night at Gairloch had been a turning point in her life. She'd hollered Big Bill Broonzy in the middle of lovemaking. Mike had asked her to marry him. And, consumed with shame and guilt, she'd accepted. She'd swum as far out into the sea as she dared, circling gulls screamed, 'End of the world! End of the world!' How could she forget that night? It was a night that had the makings of magic, but she'd turned it to nonsense.

'He thought you had potential,' Josh told her. 'He wanted to build you a career.'

'I don't believe you,' Megs said.

'It wasn't much. He wasn't any big shakes. I think he wanted you to sing adverts. You know, like for chocolate and that. Well,' reconsidering this, 'maybe more double-glazing sort of thing. You had a selling voice.'

'It would have been better than cleaning.' Megs felt bitter.

'Is that what you do now?' he said. Not without sadness. 'We all knew and nobody told you. Mike said he'd do it. But he never did.'

'No,' said Megs. Staring glumly at the pavement. 'He didn't. And now I'm ordinary.' She wallowed. 'Bruised and ordinary.' She turned and ran.

'Oh no,' Josh called after her. 'You're not that. You're never that.'

For days after that conversation with Josh, Megs carried on her normal life. She went to work. She made supper. She watched television. She phoned her mother and nagged Lorraine about leaving dirty cups lying on the floor and folding towels in the bathroom and burning the dresser in the bedroom when she left her curling tongs on – all as if nothing had happened, as if there wasn't that little bomb of knowledge ticking inside her waiting to explode. She thought she was in control. But she wasn't really a bottling-things-up sort of a person.

She was in the living room, drinking coffee with Lorraine, talking, as they did, about nothing in particular with endless ease. Vivienne and Jack were watching the early-evening news, Vivienne saying the while that she ought to be going. Megs started to cry. Small tears at first that nobody noticed. She sniffed, pulled a pink tissue from the box on the television shelf, dabbed her eyes and wiped her nose.

'Are you crying?' Lorraine looked worried.

'Me? Oh, no. I'm just catching a bit of a cold.' Megs wiped her nose ostentatiously, demonstrating her ailment.

Vivienne looked round, eyed her suspiciously. 'Looks like tears to me,' she said.

'Oh, no,' Megs protested. Crying, her? She denied the charge. But more tears spilled over. She gulped, took a deep breath. No use. The tears kept coming till she was howling, sobbing, shuddering with sorrow. She covered her face with her hands.

'What's wrong?' Lorraine moved across the room to put her arm round her.

'Nothing,' Megs sobbed.

'Doesn't look like nothing to me.' Vivienne could spot a broken heart a mile away. 'Gilbert hasn't dumped you, has he?'

Megs shook her head. 'No. It isn't him,' she choked as she scrubbed at her nose with her sodden tissue.

'What is it then?'

'It's Mike.'

'Mike?' Lorraine and Vivienne cried in unison.

'Yes, Mike. Seems when we were in the band some bloke tried to sign me. He wanted to mould my career. Mike never, ever told me.' She slumped back, gasping and sniffing. 'Who knows what could have happened.' She gazed ahead, letting what might have been drift through her. 'He's all right. He got his nice job, his nice house in that nice scheme, his nice daughter and his nice car. Look at me – I scrub floors and I could have been a star.' The truth blistered out. 'A star,' she wailed.

'A star?' The word caught Jack's interest. 'You couldn't be a star. You're my mother.'

'Mothers can be stars,' Megs protested. 'Besides, I wasn't always your mother. There was life before you were born.'

He snorted. He doubted that.

'The bastard,' said Lorraine. 'The absolute bastard.' She patted

Megs. 'What a terrible thing to find out. It's awful.'

'I know, awful,' Megs sobbed. 'Years and years. Floors and baths I've wiped. Things I've put up with, and I had a chance I didn't even know about. A star. I could have been a star.'

Vivienne had been silent a long time. 'You don't know that,' she said. 'You don't know what might have happened. What did this person want you to do, exactly?'

'Sing.' Megs's voice moved up a note or two. She wasn't comfortable with this line of questioning.

'What sort of singing?' Vivienne persisted, watching Megs carefully.

'Adverts and that,' Megs said.

'Ah,' Vivienne scoffed. 'Adverts. Well, there you are.'

'What does that mean? "Well, there you are." People make lots of money singing adverts.'

'What sort of adverts?'

'Who knows?' Megs knew better than to confess to double-glazing. 'I would have been a star.' She was convinced. 'I'd have had fabulous clothes. Shoes made exclusively for me in Italy. A Mercedes. Not one of those big ones, one of those small two-seater convertibles.'

'Where would we have sat?' asked Jack.

She was indignant. 'What makes you think you're getting into my Mercedes? I'd have a big family people-carrier VW thing for you folks to follow me around in. It'd have "Friends and Family of Megs" on the side in swirling purple lettering.'

'She's got it all mapped out then,' Vivienne said. 'We're all cramped up in the smelly van whilst she's swanning in front in the flash car.'

'I'd have houses in London, Monte Carlo and San Francisco, and a flat in New York. Plastic surgery on the bags under my eyes, tits lifted, bum sorted.' Megs sighed.

'Nina Megson, superstar.' Vivienne folded her arms. This took some coming to terms with.

'Nina Megson,' Megs scoffed. 'Nina Megson. I wouldn't be Nina Megson. You know I hate my name. I'd be Roberta Bennett, or . . . or . . . Mamie Smith.' Softly she corrected herself. 'No, there's been a Mamie Smith. Josephine Sinatra . . .' she mused.

'I think someone's beaten you to Sinatra,' Lorraine said. 'Just a hunch, but I think so.'

'Well, I'd be incredibly sexy, a woman of mystery who the nation loves. A woman with a tragic past, whose romances come to nothing, who can't find love but is adored by her fans.'

'Oh, good,' said Vivienne. 'I'm glad there's some compensation for your messed-up love life. Of course, you have the car, the houses, the plastic surgery, not forgetting the van.'

Megs ignored her. 'I'd pick some sort of name that implies innocence, even though my image is of passion and longing for true love . . .'

'She's got it all worked out,' Vivienne went on.

'Victoria,' Megs suggested. 'Victoria . . .'

'Cross?' Lorraine offered. She didn't mean to be sarcastic. It just popped into her head, so she said it out loud. Then regretted it.

'Oh, funny,' Megs countered. 'Very witty – Victoria Cross, star of stage and screen.'

'What about Pearl Barley?' Vivienne joined in. 'Or Penny Farthing?'

'Iona Bike.' Lorraine started to giggle.

'Nan Bread,' Jack offered.

'Isla Alcatraz.' Vivienne screamed with laughter. Lorraine and Jack joined in, falling about.

'Oh, very funny. Very funny.' Megs was incensed. How dare they laugh at her? 'I lose my big chance in life, I could have been somebody, and all you do is mock. Huh. What do any of you know anyway?' She stumped through to the kitchen. Chastised, Jack, Lorraine and Vivienne stared shamefaced at each other a moment.

Then Lorraine shouted, 'Rosie Cheeks.'

Vivienne howled.

In the kitchen, Megs wiped her nose on her beef stroganoff recipe dish towel and thought, Oh, pathetic, pathetic.

'It could be worse than all that.' Lorraine teetered into the kitchen after her. She'd had a new vile thought she was anxious to share. 'You might've been a one-hit wonder and ended up as a question on Trivial Pursuit.'

That remark stopped Megs mid-dream. She looked up from the tea towel. 'Oh God, no,' she said. 'The horror. The horror.' Then, tossing the towel into the washing machine, 'Tell you what, Lorraine,' she said. 'If you're going to stay here, how would you like to pay your way? How do you feel about chipping in towards the mortgage? Let me get away for a few weeks.'

'Don't mind.' Lorraine shrugged. 'Where are you going?'

'I thought I might go live with Gilbert for the summer. Of course, you'd be alone here. And I know you hate being on your own.'

'I don't mind being alone in your house. I just mind it in my house.' There was such life in Megs's home, Lorraine never felt alone. In fact she began to relish having it to herself, then she could really enjoy it uninterrupted. 'Are you taking Lizzy?'

'Naturally. And Shameless. You'd only have yourself to bother about. And you know my mother will still come by to check on you. You're never alone with a Vivienne. Anyway, it'd only be for six weeks. Two months tops. No longer. Then I'd be back, and . . . There's gas, electricity, insurance. All my standing orders. I can't go.' The savage truth of her finances crept up on her.

'Go.' Lorraine stopped her. She waved Megs off in the direction she imagined would lead to Gilbert. 'You deserve a holiday. Need one.' She was enjoying being generous, she warmed towards herself. She was quite likeable, really. This surprised her. 'I'll pay your half of the mortgage. I was going to anyway. We can work out the rest. Go. For God's sake, go. You couldn't stop me if I had the chance. Shag yourselves to a standstill. Rip your clothes off and run through the heather.'

'A bit nippy, that,' said Megs.

'Well, roll about in front of blazing log fires, drinking vintage port and listening to old Billie Holiday songs. Get all sweaty and rude.'

'Right now,' said Megs, 'I feel like all I'll do when I get there is sleep. I'll sleep and sleep for weeks.'

Gilbert was thinking of Megs. It was better than thinking about his book, which was not going well. When he'd conceived it he'd been sure it would be a masterpiece. A minor masterpiece, perhaps, but a masterpiece nonetheless. He was working on chapter ten and had a sinking feeling that he was repeating himself. In fact, he thought he'd said all he had to say in the first chapter.

What would Megs be doing? He wished he could phone her, but he had nothing in particular to say. He envied Megs her family. He wanted to belong in that deep, entrenched way he thought Megs belonged. She was part of a family that folded round her. He knew now why she phoned her mother when there was nothing to say. She was keeping in touch, firming her bonds. It came naturally to her. It never occurred to her that she was phoning with nothing to say. Saying something was of no importance at all. It was the phoning that mattered, speaking, a voice down the line. He thought he could never do that. Yet tonight, sitting by his fire, tapping blandly at his laptop, he could no longer bear just thinking about Megs. He'd been thinking about her all week since she left, now he wanted to hear her.

He dialled her number and fretted. What if she wasn't in? What if she was busy with her family and they were all gathered round the kitchen table laughing and joking and she didn't want to be bothered with him? The phone rang. He almost replaced the receiver. Megs answered.

'Hello, Megs.' Gilbert said her name shyly.

'Gilbert.' She sounded joyous to hear him.

'Yes. I just wondered how you were.'

'I'm fine.'

He could hear laughter in the background, imagined her sitting with Lorraine and family drinking tea out of blue-and-white-striped mugs, eating thick slices of bread and jam, cosily bonded. He nearly put the phone down. He was intruding. She didn't want him.

'Listen, Gilbert,' Megs said. 'Do you still want me to come and stay for the summer?'

'Of course I do.'

'Then I've decided. It'll do me good. I'd love to come.'

In the living room, Vivienne smirked and silently thanked Josh. He'd made Megs angry and reckless. Now she'd go to her fancy man, and maybe even marry him. Vivienne had a deep-rooted belief in educated people. She thought teachers, doctors and lawyers to be in control of their lives and beyond ordinary dilemmas. They would not get overdrawn at the bank or drink too much and act silly like Megs did with Lorraine. Vivienne was convinced that this new man of Megs's would help her climb from her wrecked life and start afresh. He'd take her in hand. She'd become a mature student, then a teacher, or possibly a lawyer. The way she ran off at the mouth, she'd be good at that. Yes, Vivienne thought, things were working out fine.

Chapter Twenty-Six

Over the next two weeks, as she prepared to go off for what she now thought of as her summer idyll, Megs indulged in dreams of revenge on Mike. She imagined small scenarios where she emerged the triumphant, misunderstood, hard-working mother and he was exposed as the self-seeking father.

She thought she might phone Denise and tell her who Lizzy's father really was. No, better, she would hand her over to him at the airport when she was seeing Hannah and Jack off, telling him to look after the daughter he would not own up to for a moment. Naturally, this would be within Denise's earshot. Then, again, she could just arrange for Lizzy to stand close to Mike – the resemblance said it all.

In the end, though, her scheming came to nothing. She wandered over to the bookshop at the airport, looking for something for Hannah to read. Mike joined her flicking through paperbacks.

'I don't feel comfortable buying anything for Hannah these days,' said Megs.

'Teenagers have such precise ideas of what they like and what they don't. It's hard. You were the same when you were her age.'

'Hmm,' said Megs. She felt he had no right to criticise. 'I know all about that bloke who wanted to sign me, you know.' She needed to confront him and couldn't wait to manoeuvre the conversation into an argument.

'What bloke?'

'You know fine what bloke.'

'Oh, that.' He'd been feeling mildly guilty about this for years. 'He was a chancer. Not nice. He just wanted you to sing jingles for

485

double-glazing companies, carpet warehouses and such. Local advertising. It was beneath you.'

'And cleaning isn't?'

He said nothing.

'It was my decision whether or not to do it. Nothing to do with you.'

'I know. I know.' Then, to her astonishment, 'I'm sorry.'

'I've been plotting my revenge,' she confessed without lifting her eyes from the book she wasn't reading. 'I planned to tell Denise about Lizzy.'

'She already knows. It's a bit obvious, isn't it?'

'She doesn't mind?'

'Minding doesn't come into it. She understands, that's all.'

'Goodness. I believe, Mike, the woman loves you.'

'Yes.' Mike nodded. 'She does. And I love her.'

Megs felt unbearably peeved at this. 'Did you ever love me? You didn't ever love me, did you?' she said.

'Of course I did,' said Mike. No, he thought, I don't think I did. 'Did you love me?'

She pursed her lips. She longed to kick him, to slap him. She wanted to yell that he'd ruined her life, stolen her best chance. Yet here she was in the airport bookshop being stiflingly polite. 'Yes,' she lied.

After they'd boarded the plane, she stood holding Lizzy's hand, waving goodbye, wishing them well. At least she wished Hannah and Jack well, and she hoped they'd behave normally – smoke a little dope, fall in love with revoltingly unsuitable people, disappear just before meal times, have dubious bits of their bodies pierced – which would, at least, give Mike a glimpse of all the angst he'd missed over the years.

She put Lizzy in the back of the car with Shameless and set off to Lisdon Cottage, to Gilbert. Lizzy said nothing. Mile after mile she said nothing. At last Megs asked, 'You don't mind Jack and Hannah going off in an aeroplane without you?'

'I don't want Jack and Hannah to go in an aeroplane. I'm never going in an aeroplane,' Lizzy told her. 'I don't want to get smaller and smaller.'

'What do you mean, smaller and smaller?'

'I've seen planes when they're in the sky. They're teeny. I don't want Jack and Hannah to get teeny. Will they get big again?' She started to cry.

Megs pulled in to the side of the road. Turned round to take the child to her. 'They don't get smaller and smaller. They stay the same size. The aeroplane just looks small because it's so far away. High, high in the sky.' She had the feeling Lizzy wasn't convinced. She pointed to trees and houses in the distance. 'Look at them. You know how big a tree is, and how big a house is. They're not little. They're just far away. Remember the people at the airport? Some of them had just got off a plane. They weren't teeny. They were the same size they were when they got on.'

Lizzy stared solemnly out at trees on the mountainside.

'We're going on our own holiday. We're going to stay with Gilbert. We'll walk up the glen and play in the garden and . . .'

'Get all sweaty and rude?'

Megs put Lizzy back beside Shameless. 'You shouldn't eavesdrop,' she said.

She drove to Gilbert, to her summer idyll. Actually, when she closely examined it, she had no idea what anybody on an idyll did. She imagined it entailed a lot of wafting in and out of the cottage in a long frock. She did not know how long she could waft without becoming totally bored. Ten minutes max, she thought.

Gilbert was standing by the door waiting for her when she arrived. He was wearing his cottage apron and waving. Though waving made him sheepish, and he stopped as soon as he found himself doing it. 'It's wonderful to see you.' He smiled. Then, 'Why not pop your car round the side, out of sight.' He didn't want any friends dropping by and finding a car at his door with a nodding dog and WINDSURFERS DO IT STANDING UP in the back window. Megs obliged.

She came into his living room, dropped her cases on the floor, flopped into the sofa with the tartan throw and said, 'Well, Gilbert, here I am.'

He smiled. 'Good to see you.' He meant it. 'Really good.' They beamed at each other. Let the idyll begin, thought Megs.

'Have you thought about what you are going to do whilst I'm working?' Gilbert asked, bringing her a cup of coffee.

'I shall walk. I shall garden. I shall spend time with my daughter. I shall enjoy myself.'

'Sounds good to me.'

At first it worked. They were delighted with each other. It took a week for their differences to emerge. It started to seem to Megs that it wasn't just her children who were experiencing a whole new culture. She and Lizzy were too.

They moved into little routines. In the morning she rose first, tuned the radio to a rock station whilst she made instant coffee for herself, and a boiled egg for Lizzy. He got up after her, couldn't bear the noise coming from his radio, retuned to Radio Four. Whilst Lizzy played under the table, bossing Shameless, running her purple van over his paws, Gilbert would listen to the news and read the morning paper. Every now and then, if some feature that interested him came on, he'd stop reading and gaze at the radio whilst listening.

Megs, however, joined in. She'd expound. 'Oh, I don't agree with that.' Or, 'What a pompous arse he is.' She repeated things he'd heard, just to make sure he'd heard them. 'Did you hear that, Gilbert? It's going to be fine all day. But rain coming in from the west this evening. That'll do the garden good.'

'I heard.' He was irritated that her opinions and quotations drowned out the broadcast. He was not used to other voices in his life.

Once or twice a week they'd drive to the village to shop. He went to the grocer's to buy extra virgin olive oil, fresh parmesan, espresso coffee, focaccia bread. She went to Tesco and loaded her trolley with rice krispies, tins of beans, Jammy Dodgers and Coca-Cola for Lizzy, and Pedigree Chum for Shameless. The vivid presence of these things in his careful larder made him wince. Food for him was part of his lifestyle statement. Food for her was what you produced at regular times in vast quantities because fed children were easier to cope with than hungry ones.

Every evening Megs would clear the supper dishes, remove the linen tablecloth from Gilbert's table, toss the crumbs she'd swept into her cupped hand out the door for the birds and place the fruit bowl dead centre. Every day Gilbert would tactfully move it slightly to the left. Dead centre was, he considered, tacky. He was constantly rearranging the little groupings of his *objets trouvés* that Megs would dust and put back wrongly. The seventeenth-century green glass wine flask went next to the two candles, not – good heavens, did the woman see nothing? – in between them.

Then there was the gardening. In his dream of Megs gardening, Gilbert had her in full waft, wandering about the lawn in a long white floaty thing, carrying a trug basket filled with lupins. Megs wore jeans. Megs dug. She yanked out weeds, freed tangled shrubs, she filled her watering can at the kitchen sink and carried it slopping water out the door. She got messy, sweaty. Lizzy busied after her, chatting, taking the trowel to dig little holes. She took the watering can, spilling pools on to the kitchen floor, and outside she watered the plants, the path, the clothes poles, the sun dial, Shameless, everything. There was mud under both Megs's and Lizzy's nails.

Gilbert had no experience of children. He understood that Lizzy had to eat, and tried not to mind seeing the odd hardened bean on his kitchen table, or finding half-eaten, slightly soggy chocolate biscuits lying on the arm of the sofa. He knew her clothes had to be washed daily and hung out to dry, and, on rainy days, draped over the heater in the kitchen. Still, he found it hard to come to terms with the clutter and noise a child brought into his house. Then there was the dog. Shameless stole his socks from the laundry basket and gathered them in a secret hoard under the bed. Gilbert swore foully to himself as he squeezed and stretched to get them. The dog, always delighted to find a face level with his own, licked him mercilessly.

No matter how much they were irritated by each other's habits, Gilbert and Megs worked hard at avoiding confrontation. Neither of them wanted to argue.

'Shall I switch the station?' she asked when he came into the living room and found her watching her favourite soap. 'Only I know you hate this.'

'No. Please don't.' Though he found the programme offensive. 'I've never watched this before. It's interesting.'

At times like this a look came over Gilbert. He seemed blank, bemused, bewildered. His arms would hang by his sides and he would turn, checking, Megs always thought, that there was nobody else in the room. Megs had no idea who he was looking out for, but whoever it was, it was a she. And Gilbert was hers.

Once they walked down to the river and sat on the bank whilst Lizzy tried to catch sticklebacks. They watched the flies on the water. Flitting, leaping, skating the surface, teasing the fish.

'I'll never dance like that,' Megs said. 'I'd like to dance.'

'I don't ever dance. But these flies only live for a day. They've got to do something.' He was level-headed. He did not long to be dancing on water.

'They've got a nice day for it, then.'

'For what?'

'Their lives. If you've only got a day, this'd be a good one. What sort of a day has it been for you? For your life?'

He did not know what to say. He did not usually field questions like this. He hated this sort of esoteric talk. Had not the gumption to take her hand and tell her the sun had come out. 'Fine, I suppose.'

'I've had a lot of freezing fog, cloud and drizzle. But I'm hoping for a ridge of high pressure – lots of wiggly lines.' She smiled at him. At last he smiled back.

After this, they started to enjoy each other. Gilbert slowly stopped minding all the attention he was denied whilst Megs looked after Lizzy, and started to love watching her face as she leaned close to the child, helping her out of her clothes, coming into the room with Lizzy, freshly soaped and bathed, enveloped in one of his huge bath towels. It amused him that she had a dog that looked blank when told to sit or stay – normal canine commands – but responded eagerly to the words cuddle or chocolate. 'Children,' Megs would shrug by way of an explanation. The idyll started to come together. They'd be sitting by the fire, window open, and the night scents – honeysuckle, wood smoke, pine trees, peaty mountain air – drifted in. They'd talk.

'Gilbert,' Megs said, 'you tell a better class of lie than me. I tell ordinary lies.'

'What do you mean by that?'

'All that stuff you buy. Focaccia bread and that. All this stuff you have, the groupings of objects, the way you like things, the fear you have of people discovering me here. Common as muck, me. It's part of the lie you tell. I'm not ordinary, you say. You don't have to work so hard at it. Nobody thinks you are. Not like me.'

'You're not ordinary.' He came across the room to her. Stroked her hair. 'Ordinary is the last thing you are.' They kissed.

In bed she clung to him. Wrapped herself round him. Pulled him into her. She pressed her cheek against his unshaven cheek, tasted him. 'I love you,' she said.

When they'd done he said, 'Don't love me. I don't want you to love me.'

'Don't worry about it, Gilbert. It's just something I say to someone who happens to be in bed with me, lying on top of me with my legs curled round his waist. Don't read anything into it.'

Once, in his kitchen, she found a little piece of ginger with a thick green shoot sprouting from it.

'Gilbert, I shall plant this for you and put it on your windowsill. Then, whenever you look at it, you'll think of me.'

'I'll think of you anyway.'

'You'll see it and think of me when she comes back.'

'Who?'

'The ghost that lives with us. The woman you fear will discover you with me.'

'My love?' He was scornful.

'No. I'm your love. But she'll get you in the end.' Megs touched his cheek. Then stood up on tiptoe and kissed him.

She went out to walk along the track. The night was soft on her arms; far away a curlew called. The moon was waxing, had soft circles round it. A harvest moon. A white owl behind her broke from the trees and flew, silent as snow, down the field where, only weeks ago, Lizzy had lost her kite. She watched it swoop and glide. She thought perhaps she ought to be upset that Gilbert did not deny the ghost he glanced at. But she wasn't. Shameless stuck his nose down a small hole he'd found – some tiny creature's nest – and snorted in excitement. 'What are you doing?' she asked fondly. The dog looked at her, bright brown eyes. Megs reached for him, scratched his head. She rather liked this new woman she was, who was not going to allow herself to get broken-hearted. Who was wise enough not to let a little bit of melancholy ruin an exquisite night.

In her time with Gilbert, Megs had felt her face unfold, relax. The muscles that grief and worry had knotted eased. She shut her eyes. She had the feeling that she'd been running very fast, very hard for a long time, and now it was over. She could stop. 'It's over,' she said to herself. 'It's over and I'm all right.' She went back down the track to Gilbert, to his bed, to let her tongue linger with his tongue, to move her fingers through the greying hair on his chest, to run her hand over his soft stomach and feel him next to her, in her.

When Gilbert felt Megs and her radio rock'n'roll too much for him, or when his work knotted him up, and words froze in his brain, he walked. Megs watched him go. He'll be back, she'd think. He'll be back with an apology on his lips. But Lizzy was not used to letting people go. She was little and liked everyone to be together. When Gilbert strode out, she strode after him. At first she stalked behind him, in her denim dungarees and striped T-shirt, imitating his walk. Gilbert always knew she was there and tried to ignore her. Eventually, however, Lizzy was allowed to stride alongside him. She'd try to take huge steps and would, from time to time, look up at him for approval. He could not resist her. After a while she was allowed to hold his hand. Gilbert was not used to physical contact and hated the feel of her soft and innocent palm against his, mostly because it made his hand feel huge and rough. But after a while he came to love that little hand. He'd squeeze it and look down smiling at her small, serious face as she tried to match his strides. Chatting to her, he visited conversations he had left far behind him in his childhood.

'What's your favourite thing to eat, Gilbert? Is it chips dipped in bean juice?'

'Bean juice?'

'You know, the sauce beans come in. Or is it pizza?'

'Um . . .' Gilbert pretended to think. 'Pizza.'

'Yes,' Lizzy agreed, nodding. 'Pizza's my favourite, too.'

'Look, Lizzy.' Gilbert pointed up at a plane tree. 'Look at the leaves. The dark shapes they make against the sky.'

Lizzy stared. 'How do you know it's the leaves making the shape? How do you know it isn't the sky? The sky is peeping through the leaves. It's watching us.'

492

He looked again. Why hadn't he thought of that? She saw more than he did. He stood gazing at the light shimmering through the trees. For days he thought about it, shapes and light. He started to draw again.

Chapter Twenty-Seven

After three weeks together they relaxed. Gilbert no longer glared spikily at Megs's gross additions to his gourmet kitchen. He found himself solemnly dunking a chocolate Hobnob in his coffee whilst humming along with Sting on the radio's Golden Oldie spot. 'Roxanne, you don't have to . . . dum . . . dum . . . any more. I like that one.' Megs no longer deliberately put the fruit bowl in the middle of Gilbert's round dining table then stood back watching him sigh and cross the room to place it left of centre. They started to trust each other enough to turn their small confidences and confessions into jokes and banter.

He bought her an art nouveau dragonfly pendant he found in one of the village craft shops. 'There,' he said, putting it round her neck, 'for you. If you don't like it you can always shove it up the drainpipe to keep your green and pink hat company.'

The garden started to flourish. It no longer looked as if it was recovering from the ravages of some cruel barber. Lunch times they picnicked on the lawn. After twenty minutes Gilbert always started to fidget and look worriedly across at the living room window. His desk and laptop were in there, waiting for him. *The Theme Pack* beckoned.

Megs reached over and stroked his ear with a blade of grass. 'You have no concept of sloth, Gilbert.'

Slapping away the irritating tickle at his ear, 'I don't think that's true.' He could hardly believe this. He was defending himself. He hated loafing about.

'I have never seen you sitting about doing nothing,' she accused.

'I often do nothing,' he said hotly. 'I sleep.'

'Sleeping isn't doing nothing,' she scoffed. 'Sleep's important. You rest. You dream. It's restorative. No.' He wasn't getting away with this. 'Sleeping doesn't count.'

'I watch television. I read,' he whined.

'That's being entertained, that's gathering information. That's not sloth.'

'Even if it's a programme I hate, or it's information I don't want?' The worst sort of information as far as he was concerned. Unwanted information somehow always stuck.

'No.' She was adamant. 'Being slothful, truly slothful, is lying prone on a chair, legs splayed, large tummy openly on view, arms dangling and not a constructive thought in your head. I've never seen you do that. You're always anxious about your work.'

'I could do that.' It was a challenge, and he never could resist a challenge.

'No you couldn't. You couldn't just sit and watch drivel on television, eating crisps.'

'I hate crisps. I'd have pork crackling. I'd have a flask of coffee to save me getting up to make more when my cup was empty. I'd wear two pairs of socks to keep my feet warm.'

'Ugh, not coffee from a flask. It's horrible from a flask. Pork crackling – how vile.'

He felt gleeful that he'd disgusted her. He'd broken down his defences, allowed a little trivia into his life. He'd won a point or two here, though he didn't really understand how. He continued, 'Of course I'd not wear any trousers. No trousers, luxury. I'd pull a travelling rug over my knees to protect myself from crackling crumbs and hot coffee spillages.'

'Gross,' she cried.

He felt oddly triumphant. It made her mediocre television programme and crisps seem polite and tame. He'd always considered himself to be the polite and tame one. 'There, how's that for sloth?'

'I feel sick thinking about it.' She made a sour face.

He matched her expression. He felt quite sickened by his slothfulness too. But he lay down beside her. 'Maybe you're right. I'll lie here. It's quite good, isn't it? Doing nothing. I could get into sloth.'

'There you go. See, I've taught you something.'

Every night after supper, they walked together across the field in front of the cottage. The summer grass was high and lush. There were wild lilies growing in the damp of the ditch, and campion. The hawthorn bloomed. Megs watched him walk in front of her. He wore corduroy trousers and walking boots, carried Lizzy on his shoulders. She felt a rush of love for him.

On the way back to the cottage, Lizzy curled into Gilbert's shoulders, put her face on his head and slept.

Megs reached out and steadied her as they walked. 'See me,' she said as they walked. 'My life is full of nonsense. I used to think stuff and nonsense. But the other day I decided it was more grief and nonsense.'

'What do you mean by that?'

'Well, I've had the most dreadful things happen to me. But they're matched by some utterly nonsensical, embarrassing things.'

'Like running over the park to the boys playing, looking for your son?'

'Yeah. Sort of.' Then, checking Lizzy was sleeping, she continued, lowering her voice. 'I never wanted Lizzy. I denied my pregnancy for the whole nine months. I went to the clinic. But I sort of hid it from myself. As if it would go away. Then when she was born I told them to take her away. I didn't want her. I wanted Thomas back. I felt she was pushing Thomas out. So I lay looking at her as she bawled her head off.'

The ward sister had come by. 'Baby's crying, Mum.'

'Who is Mum?' Megs asked bleakly. 'Don't call me Mum. I'm not your mother.'

Gilbert adjusted her sleeping child on his shoulders. 'But you obviously love her now.'

'Oh yes.' Megs nodded. 'That was the grief bit. Now for the nonsense. It was just before Christmas. She was weeks old, still in her carrying basket, and we were at the supermarket. I was unloading my trolley into the car. I didn't put her on the back seat. I just popped her on the roof as I put all my stuff in the boot. Then I got in and drove off with her still on there. I forgot about her. People in the car park flashed their lights and tooted their horns. People pointed and shouted and I thought, Look at these silly people. What's all the fuss about? I thought they were after my parking place, it was so busy. Bastards, I thought, can't wait. Then someone ran after me and banged on the car window. So I stopped. And that's when I discovered her.'

'So she wasn't hurt?'

Megs remembered the silhouetted figures in the car park, running through the dark waving and yelling. When she discovered what she'd done she felt shamed and foolish. 'No, she was fine. But I got such a shock. I could hardly drive home I was shaking so much. I nearly lost her, too. It was close.'

'Your life is a tragi-comedy,' he said gently.

'Yes.' She liked that.

Next day it rained. Gilbert wanted to cook a loin of pork in milk. 'Maiale al latte,' he said. 'I need white wine vinegar for my marinade. And we're out of coffee, garlic and those hideous jam biscuits that you buy.'

Megs agreed to drive to the village to shop whilst Gilbert would stay home, work and look after Lizzy. He enjoyed having the child to himself. Her quiet, deliberate presence pleased him. She would sit on the floor by his desk with a pile of his A4 paper and some crayons, drawing whilst he frowned at his screen, fretting over his book.

It was the first time Megs had been alone since she'd come to Gilbert's cottage. She relished it. She had decided to go to the Blue Kettle Café. She had longed to go there ever since her first visit, but whenever she mentioned it, Gilbert could hardly contain his scorn. Now, at last, she could go without him. She would shop first, then go. She would, as always, save the best till last. She bought Gilbert's wine vinegar and some sage. Then to the butcher's, where she ordered a chicken and asked Billy to deliver two videos for the weekend.

She always walked slowly past the Blue Kettle Café, longing to go in. The windows steamed, and laughter poured out into the street. There were cake stands in the window and cakes sat fatly on perfect doilies. Bright-red tower-shaped cakes covered with coconut, with cherries on top, meringues, Belgian biscuits and marzipan-covered Battenbergs – she didn't care which one she had. It wasn't the cake really. It was the steamy atmosphere, thick with cigarette smoke and gossip.

At last she went in. Waitresses bustled and prattled, far too busy laying out cakes and making sandwiches to bother with customers, especially ones they didn't know. Megs ordered tea and watched as it was poured from a vast stainless-steel teapot into a thick white cup. She took that, a cheese sandwich and a red coconut cake to a far corner, where she sat at a fake wood Formica table, hoping she'd go unnoticed. She looked round at the bad perms and anoraks, thinking that there was a lot of water being retained in the Blue Kettle Café today.

She sat with the fat-kneed ladies amidst their swelling laughter and prepared herself for a homey treat. The sort of gooey cakes Aunty Betty used to bake. But the tea was dishwater vile, the cake musty and tired and the sandwich was a slice of supermarket bread thick with marg, two flaccid tomatoes and a glum, lumpen slice of cheese. It was a loveless thing. A that'll-do thing. The waitress had smacked the bread down, beefily slapped it with marg, shoved on the cheese. That'll do. It was how they did things. That'll do. No need for fancy.

The longed-for gossip almost broke her heart. 'Has anyone seen Ina?' someone said.

'No,' someone else said. 'I saw her yesterday but I haven't seen her today.'

Was that it? Where was the steamy talk of love and death? The bawdy exchanges? Megs couldn't remember when she'd last been so disappointed. This'll do for a conversation. This'll do for a cake. This'll do for a life. She left her tea and food and never went back. She walked, hunched against the rain, back to her car, trying not to think that she was the same as the fat-kneed Blue Kettle ladies. She lived a this'll-do life.

She drove slowly home, too saddened by the café experience to play the radio. The doleful creak of her windscreen wipers was soundtrack enough for her disappointment. She almost drove past the butcher's van. It was parked by the side of the road, indicators flashing, hood up, with the boy peering glumly in at the engine.

She pulled over. 'Anything wrong?' she asked, winding down her window.

'She's broke.' The boy patted the van. 'Don't know anything about car innards, do you?'

Megs shook her head. 'They're a mystery to me. Can I take you anywhere? Back to the village? I owe you a lift.'

'You could take me to the hotel. I have to deliver these steaks, lamb chops and *Mad Dog and Glory* and *Casino*. I like a bit of Robert de Niro, don't you?'

'Yes,' she agreed.

'Then I can phone the garage from there and they'll come and get me.'

'I could bring you back.'

'Nah. I can get stuck up there and have a pint.'

He transferred his meat and videos into her boot and got in beside her. 'You think this is just a glen, don't you?'

She shrugged. Didn't know what to answer.

'But it's different to me. See that wall.' Pointing to a long, smashed dry-stone dyke. 'That's Will's wall. Every Friday he'd drive home drunk and miss this corner and drive into that wall. So they stopped fixin' it. Better to leave it broken. Then his car would just crash into the gap. Safer.' Then, a few miles further on, 'That's the lay-by where the dentist killed himself. He borrowed the farmer's shotgun and drove here. Blew his brains out.'

'Why?'

'Fed up looking at folk's teeth, probably. That, and his wife left him. See that cottage.' He leaned over, pointing at a damp and dilapidated cottage on the hillside. 'I was brought up there. Lived there with my father till he died over forty years ago, now. Yes.' He drifted off, remembering. 'My father died in that cottage forty-four years ago yesterday.'

She was so engrossed leaning over the steering wheel, staring up at the cottage, she almost did not notice the pheasant. Yards ahead a female pheasant craned out of the undergrowth, cast a beady and vaguely insane eye around and decided now was the time to make a dash to the other side of the road. She hurtled, startled and squawking, a wild hen's run in front of the car, and behind her came two crazed babies. Two tiny fist-sized balls of golden-brown fluff, squeaking hysterically, shot out in front of the car.

'Babies,' screamed Megs. 'Oh no. Babies.' She stamped on the brakes. The car screeched forward, wheels locked. 'Babies, babies,' Megs yelled. 'Watch out, babies.'

The car behind, a red Volvo that Megs had not noticed till now, braked furiously too and the driver put his fist on the horn – a rude, glaring wall of noise.

'Babies,' Megs yelled, turning in her seat, enraged at the tooting. But one foul toot did not satisfy the Volvo driver's rage. He blasted again and again.

'Babies,' Megs screamed, waving at the now empty road in front. The Volvo continued its furious honking. Blast. Blast. Blast. That was it. Megs got out of the car, leaving her passenger to heave himself upright from his sudden jolt forward.

'Babies,' Megs yelled at the driver behind. 'Didn't you see them?'

'Oh, I saw them,' the insane tooter called. 'I saw them before you did. Christ! You nearly killed us all! When something runs out like that you have to keep going.'

'That's just like a man. Squish everything in sight. Mow them down. Let me past. Out of the way. Mr Toad coming through in his shiny red automobile with the really loud horn. Fucking kill everything. Arse,' she bawled. 'Arse. Arse. Arse. You don't give a fucking fart about fucking life, do you? Just kill. Kill. Babies, they were babies.'

Two pressed and pristine children in the back of the Volvo palely peered at her through tinted windows. The driver touched the side of his forehead with his finger, gesturing that he thought her too insane to bother communicating with, put his car into gear and drove slowly past. Megs responded with another finger gesture, a single defiant digit raised aloft against all Mr Toads in all red automobiles everywhere.

'Arse,' she shouted after him. 'Arse. Arse. Arse.' Then, returning to her car, 'Did you see him? The arse he is. Going to squish the babies. What a fuck. What an absolute fuck.'

She sat gripping the wheel, sighing, not breathing. At last, realising the fool she'd made of herself, she turned to the butcher's boy. 'I'm sorry,' she apologised. 'You must think me terrible.' She sighed again. 'My little boy was run over. Just when I think I'm getting over it, something happens and I realise I'm not.' She put her hand to her mouth. 'Thing is,' she didn't know why she was telling him this, 'I always thought it was my fault. I was late picking him up from school and he set off alone. I should have been there.'

He did not answer. He sat staring at the cottage on the hill till they turned a bend and it was lost from sight. 'Aye,' he said then. 'Guilt'll do that to you.'

'Do what?' Megs asked.

'Make you daft.'

She was late getting back. She thought Gilbert would be standing anxiously at the door, gazing up the track. But he wasn't. He was inside, sitting on the floor with a sketch pad on his knees. He was surrounded by drawings of Lizzy. Lizzy drawing. Lizzy drinking orange juice. Lizzy with a ball. Lizzy twirling round and round on his chair. 'She won't keep still,' he complained. His hair was on end.

'She's still enough now.' Megs nodded at the child, who was curled on the sofa, sound asleep and covered with chocolate.

'I had to give her four chocolate puddings to get her to sleep.'

'Wonderful,' said Megs, not even trying to hide her sarcasm. She picked up his sketch pad and looked at the drawing of Lizzy sleeping. 'This is good, though; I have to admit. You really have caught her. The way she sleeps.'

'Yes,' looking at his drawing. 'She pouts, and she's got a little double chin.'

No matter how good Megs thought his drawings, Gilbert knew they were that most dreadful of things – mediocre. It was years since he'd drawn anything. Most of those years had been spent appraising and criticising artists more skilful than he was. Now he had a better idea of how good he was. He was not as good as he'd thought he was all those years ago, when his mother had made him set fire to his work. He felt furious at his failing. It was, after all, such a simple failing. He could not place the lines he was drawing exactly where he wanted them. The shapes he made on the page were not the shapes he saw, either out here in the room, or in his head. His frustration showed in his hairstyle.

'She's good at sleeping, isn't she?' Megs said.

'Yes.' Gilbert nodded. They stood watching Lizzy lying there, doing

502

her childish trick that Megs so envied – making sleep seem simple.

'So where have you been all this time?' he asked.

'Don't ask. I had one of those traumatic shopping trips where you set out to buy something ordinary and end up having one of those pivotal life experiences that changes your destiny. Know what I mean?'

'No,' he said. Sometimes she made him feel so shallow.

'Well,' she sighed, 'I got a guided tour of the glen from the butcher's boy. And . . .'

'And?'

'I went to the Blue Kettle. You were right. It was awful. You and your damn gourmet cooking, you've spoilt me for the rubbish I used to like. You've ruined my punter's palate.'

'Ruined? I thought I'd developed it.'

'Sometimes a person gets nostalgic for food they've left in their past. Cake stands vividly laden, an egg chopped with butter in a cup. You think you can bite into such things and be whisked back to the magic summers of your youth. But all you taste is lard. It'll have to be the Manilow and Coal Scuttle from now on.'

'The what?'

'The hotel we usually go to. The first is always playing on the jukebox and the second is always right in the middle of the floor where people will trip over it.'

'All right,' he said, punching the air. 'It's the Manilow and Coal Scuttle for us.'

A couple of days later they went. They had game pie and Guinness and sang Lizzy's version of the song on the jukebox all the way home. 'The Copabanana'.

Chapter Twenty-Eight

It was inevitable that someone would show up and disturb the drifting calm of their perfect summer. The interloper was Lorraine. She arrived, mincing and squealing, wearing sling-back shoes and a skirt that scarcely covered her bum. She had come to show off her new toy, Jason, who sheepishly shadowed her. He was nineteen. He seemed to regard Megs and Gilbert as grown-ups, and, therefore, felt uncomfortable with them. Every time someone asked him to do something – sit down, carry some glasses from kitchen to living room – he politely did what he was told, which made the grown-ups uncomfortable around him.

'Isn't he gorgeous?' said Lorraine, linking arms with him. Leaning over to kiss him.

If he hadn't been standing two feet away, Megs would have said, 'No.' But he was, so she shrugged a reply instead. 'Is he staying with you?' she asked. As if Jason wasn't standing next to her.

'Yes.' Lorraine drooled, thinking of it. The juicy nights she'd had.

'At my house?'

'Well, yes.' Lorraine seemed shifty. 'But only because we can't go to his house. He still lives with his mum.'

Megs and Gilbert exchanged God-help-us looks.

'I'll be home next Friday,' said Megs. 'Normal life resumes on Monday. Know what I mean, Lorraine?'

'Yes.' A flat reply.

'Is there no chance of you going back to your own house?' Megs pleaded.

'Harry's moved back with his girlfriend. He's going to buy my half of the house from me. When the money comes through I'll get my own place.' She squeezed Jason's arm, thinking of it.

'Well,' said Megs. 'We can make room for you. But not for your love life. I do not want any of my children to come across you frolicking in some abandoned fashion in the living room. They frolic enough as it is without you encouraging them.' She opened a bottle of wine and took them through to the living room, where they sat side by side on the sofa like two children visiting their aunty, being good.

'Good heavens,' said Lorraine, looking round. 'This place is full of drawings.' She picked one up. 'This is of you, Megs. And you've nothing on. That's not very nice.'

'Well, thanks for that.' Megs never expected tact from Lorraine.

Now that Gilbert had started drawing, it seemed he couldn't stop. Megs had spent the last few nights naked. She lay on the sofa trying to remember to keep her tummy hauled in, and pressing the soles of her feet against some cushions. She did not want him to draw them, for she feared they were filthy. Their intimacy worked only when they were alone together. It did not stand up to Lorraine's squealing interest, which made it seem, somehow, silly. Silly and chilly.

Gilbert had become obsessed with his art. He was a man possessed. His inability – that he kept private – to put the things he had in his head on paper made him bad-tempered. 'Don't move,' he'd snap. 'Put your hand up to your face. Turn into the light. Straighten your fingers, they look like a pound of sausages.' Then he'd throw down his sketch pad, pace about a bit, run his fingers through his hair, pour some whisky and come back. 'You've moved.'

'Of course I've moved. You went off to pout and flounce. Don't I get any whisky?'

'Not till I've finished.' She hadn't known he could be so bossy.

'Ooh.' Lorraine gripped Megs's elbow. 'Weren't you cold? He didn't draw your goosebumps. So, apart from sitting around in the buff, what've you been doing, anyway?' she wanted to know.

'Walking. Talking. Eating. Drinking wine. Staring at things. We go to the village now and then. I have slept all night for the last three weeks.'

'You look well on it. The food, the sleep. The sex more like.' Lorraine knew what it took to get a good night's sleep. 'See me, since

Jason. I haven't given Harry a thought. And sleep. God . . . well . . . you can imagine.'

'Yes.' Megs nodded.

Lorraine leaned closer. 'Is he any good, then?'

Megs looked towards the kitchen door. Gilbert was hovering, eavesdropping, running his fingers through his hair. 'Mind your own business,' she said.

'Oh well.' Then, 'I'll get it out of you. You know I will.'

Megs snorted. She knew she would.

After a plate of pasta, two bottles of wine and a whingeing stagger along the path complaining about the likelihood of encountering weasels and bats, Lorraine left.

Her exit was as intrusively noisy as her arrival. Jason opened the car door for her and watched as she squeezed, giggling, into his passenger seat – a deep-sided racing seat. Lorraine got in but her left leg, long, thin, mud-splattered, complete with red patent shoe, let her down. She somehow couldn't manage to wedge it in. Jason helped scoop her into place.

Megs leaned forward to say goodbye and caught a glimpse of the car's customised interior. It seemed to be completely velour. My God, she thought, a pimpmobile. Lorraine, chewing gum vigorously, caught her expression and grinned.

'Great spot,' Jason said shyly, indicating with a slight movement of his head the garden and glen beyond. 'Peaceful,' he said, walking round to the driver's seat. He got in, switched on the engine, a deep macho growl of tuned engine roaring through twin carbs, and leaned out the open window, obviously politely thanking them for the food, wine and peace. Neither Megs nor Gilbert could make out a word. The car's tape deck started with the ignition, a raging techno howl erupted. Jason turned up the volume. The louder the music the wilder Lorraine's gum-chewing. The car shuddered and slithered on fat wheels down the track, both Jason and Lorraine concealed behind blackened windows. But the noise they made lingered long after they were out of sight. Their rave and thump sounded round the glen.

'Do you think it will last?' Megs asked Gilbert when at last they could speak. Birds started to sing again.

'I have no idea,' Gilbert said. 'Does she really like all that stuff? That car? That music?'

'I don't expect so. You just won't get her to admit it.'

After Lizzy was sleeping, Megs and Gilbert stood outside in the garden. The night was at a standstill. She felt as if she was at the very edge of it, under huge static clouds, breathing in the drifting scent of woodsmoke.

'I feel as if I have been invaded,' he said, starting to walk towards the woods.

'You don't like my friends.' She walked with him.

'I have never actively sought the company of women who are all thigh and no brain, who talk about the doings in soap operas as if they're real life. I get confused.'

'Gilbert, how scathing. Actually, she'd be quite chuffed. She takes care of her thighs. Her brain makes its own way.'

'I feel she's criticising me.'

'She's not. She just cares about me.'

'Is that why she asked what I was like in bed?'

'Oh, don't mind about that.'

'But I do.'

'I didn't reply.'

'No. But you will.'

'Then I'll tell her you're a stud. Is that OK?'

He said nothing.

'Please don't fight. I have to go home in a few days. I don't want to argue with you now. Please. I don't want to hear what you think of Lorraine. She's my friend.' Megs leaned against a tree. Avoiding Gilbert's gaze, she looked up through the trees. The wood was like a cathedral tonight. A huge harvest moon was floating up towards mid-heaven. Long, long shafts of light filtered down through the dense weaving of boughs high above. They could smell musk. Deer had been here, minutes before. They would have raised their heads, ears twitching, when they heard Megs and Gilbert approach. 'Please,' said Megs. 'Please, I don't want to argue.'

It was by unspoken mutual consent that they made love. They seemed to fall into one another, sinking down on to the moss. Even the initial clumsy fumbling with underwear and zips seemed natural

508

and joyous. Neither of them said sorry, or wait a minute, my arm's trapped. No buttons got stuck in their needy clamour to feel each other's skin. They moved against each other, trying to get closer and closer, to get to the core of one another. Megs clung to him, tasted him – she wanted to climb into his skin. She smelled the moss and ancient wood. She smelled him, his lime cologne and the carbonara he'd made for Lorraine. She did not say the word love. Whispered his name instead, 'Gilbert.' He lay on her, his lips on her ear, and said, 'Megs.' The sound of her name on his breath thrilled her. She realised how rarely he ever said it.

There was a moment afterwards when she was still beneath him, breathing in the darkness and damp of the ground they lay on. She had her fingers in his hair and her other arm spread. 'Oh God,' she said. 'Wonderful.' Then she remembered Lizzy alone in the house. She wrestled him from her, grabbed her clothes and stumbled away from him, still half naked. 'Lizzy. Lizzy,' she cried. 'What if she wakes and I'm not there? What if something happens?'

'No, wait,' Gilbert called, reaching for her. Shyly watching her white bum and thighs clumsily disappearing through the dense greenness. 'Wait. Lizzy will be all right. I want you. I think . . . I love . . .' but he didn't finish what he wanted to say. Besides, Megs was too far away to hear. Besides, he didn't really want to say it.

On the day that Megs left to go home, Gilbert got a letter from America.

Well, hello, Gilbert, Annette wrote. Her script was curved and polite. *How are you? And how's the book? Progressing in leaps and bounds, I'll bet.*

Gilbert glanced guiltily at his desk and at the drawings that now crowded his little living room.

My research is going well. I've been invited to stay for another few months, till the end of December, in fact. I will be back in the New Year. Looking forward enormously to seeing you then, and to reading the work in progress.
    Fondly,
    Annette

'Who's your letter from?' Megs said.

'Nobody,' said Gilbert, stuffing it into his back pocket. 'Just work. It's not important.'

Megs shrugged. She wished she didn't know he was lying.

Chapter Twenty-Nine

Megs returned, unwillingly, to her old routine. She hadn't much liked her life before her stay with Gilbert. Now that she'd had a glimpse of something better, it was harder to live than ever.

Gilbert wasn't home, and therefore did not need a cleaner. Terribly-Clean Pearson had parted from her husband, put her house on the market and was teaching full-time. She not only couldn't afford a cleaner, she didn't want one. She was enjoying being messy. It was, she told Megs on the phone, a phase she'd missed whilst growing up. She was making up for it now. 'I teach kids hygiene and neatness. I tell them how to have a balanced diet, then I come home, smoke a couple of fags, make a nice long gin and tonic, heat up something quick and hopefully nasty and eat in front of the telly. Freddy' – calling her son by the name she used to loathe – 'cleans up.'

Now that there was only Dysentery McGhee and Emotionally-Deranged Davis to clean for, Megs made up the difference in her earnings working nights, waitressing at private functions.

She'd come home, smelling, she suspected, of sweat and cooking fat. She'd slump on the sofa, too tired to take off her coat and kick her shoes on to the pile of assorted kicked-off shoes on the other side of the room – Jack's, Hannah's, Lizzy's and Lorraine's. 'Oh God,' she'd say, 'this has got to stop. What do you think, Lor? How do we sort out our lives? Failing that, how do we sort out that pile of shoes?'

The day after Megs got home from her stay with Gilbert, Jack and Hannah arrived back from Italy. Mike dropped them off on his way home. They were all delighted to see one another. How long, Megs wondered, would this delight last? Reunions were lovely, though.

Jack and Hannah crowded into the kitchen, looking tanned, slightly taller and older than when they'd left. Or maybe, Megs thought, they'd just got stuck in her memory as smaller, younger and paler than they actually were. 'How was it?' she asked, trying not to fuss round them. 'I want to hear all about it.'

'It was fine,' said Jack. 'Great.' He laid out the olive oil and wine he'd brought with him. 'Here's some Italian stuff.' Clutching a small parcel, he edged towards the door. 'I'll just go see if Sharon's in.' He disappeared.

Hannah brought Megs a red silk shirt.

'You shouldn't have,' said Megs, holding it up. 'This must have taken all your money.'

'Mike helped.' Hannah shrugged.

'How did you all get on?' Megs wanted to know.

'All right.' Small silence. 'In the end.'

'Did you and Denise hit it off?' Megs was hoping for a no.

'Yeah.' Hannah seemed surprised when she thought about it. 'She's OK, Denise.' She looked around. 'This is nice, isn't it?'

'What is?' Megs looked round, wondering what she meant. What precisely was nice?

'Here. Home. This kitchen. It's good.' She looked round at the morning cereal bowls propped on the draining board, the clothes half-hauled out of the tumble-drier, the overflowing bin. The sunlight caught in relief the crumbs scattered beside the bread bin. Music rattled from the radio. 'It's really nice. Isn't it?'

Megs didn't know what to say. In terms of describing her kitchen, nice had never occurred to her. She put the kettle on. 'I want to hear all about it? Tell me all the things you got up to.'

'There's lots to tell,' said Hannah. 'I just can't remember any of it now. I'll tell you bits when I think of them. Actually, Sarah's expecting me. I phoned her last night.'

'Well go,' said Megs. 'We'll have a proper chat later tonight.'

'I've got a date tonight.'

'Well, tomorrow.'

'Fine. Um . . . can I borrow that shirt?'

'Which shirt?'

'The one I bought you. Only I've got nothing to wear. Everything's dirty.'

'Go on then.' Megs handed the red shirt over.

Hannah smiled. On her way out, looking gorgeous, she asked if Megs could possibly wash some clothes. 'Everything's dirty,' she explained again.

When Vivienne arrived to see her grandchildren, they were long gone. 'Where are they?'

'Gone out,' said Megs. 'Come and gone.' She pointed to the teapot. 'There's tea if you want it.'

Vivienne poured herself a cup. 'So did they enjoy themselves?'

'Seemed to,' Megs said.

'And what about you? What about your stay with Gilbert? What did you get up to?'

Megs looked into the cup. She raked through her memories of the past weeks, trying to find something she could actually tell her mother about. It wasn't as if she'd done anything particularly naughty, but when she leafed through her days with Gilbert, all she could remember was being in bed with him, or having conversations with him that she could not pass on to Vivienne. She wondered if this was how, just half an hour ago, Hannah had felt when she'd been asked the same question. 'Do you know,' she said suddenly, 'it's lovely to see them both again. I missed them. I didn't realise how much till I saw them. Fleetingly, I admit. But there you go, I missed them. And I missed you.' She saw the surprise in Vivienne's face. 'No, really. I missed you. And I missed them. And I missed Lorraine. I missed everybody. It's good to be back.'

The family settled back into their routine. Hannah complained about the coffee. 'Denise has bought an actual espresso machine,' she told Megs. 'She brought it back with her. It's got a long handle that you pull.'

'That's what you'd do with a handle,' Megs said. 'Perhaps we should all go round for a cup. Denise would love that. Hannah, I can't afford an espresso machine. When you're out in the world making a fortune, buy me one.'

'OK,' Hannah said brightly. 'I will.'

'That girl is becoming likeable,' Megs told Lorraine. 'Do you suppose she's got some terrible secret she's working up to telling me? Or is this a lull? She'll get back to being her normal unsufferable self soon.'

'She's always been likeable,' said Lorraine. 'You just had to spend time away from her before you noticed.'

The bustling return of Megs and family bothered Lorraine. She had enjoyed having Megs's house to herself. She and Jason had stretched on the sofa watching films on telly. Then, when that wasn't quite comfortable enough, they'd moved the television into Megs's bedroom to watch it whilst lying, semi-clothed, on Megs's bed. Lorraine was missing that bed. 'I'm taking badly to sleeping on the sofa,' she said. 'There's no privacy. Your children wander to and from the kitchen all hours. Then I wake with Lizzy sleeping at the other end of the sofa. At my feet. I need a bed to myself,' she decided.

'Hold that thought,' Megs said. 'And expand it. You need a bed to yourself. What about a lavatory to yourself. A kitchen to yourself. A living room to yourself. In fact, what about a whole flat to yourself?'

'I know. I know.' Unable to meet Megs's eye, Lorraine made an elaborate play of stubbing out her cigarette. 'Shut up,' she said.

'Shut up what? I never said anything.'

'Speaking is just a technicality. I can see what you're thinking. You're thinking that I'm in the way. My stuff is taking over the place. My clothes are pushing yours out of your wardrobe. I'm always in the bath. Or hogging the bathroom one way or another. My moisturisers and toners and make-up have taken over the bathroom shelf. I never fold the towels. The backlog of laundry for five people is horrendous. Nobody can get into the living room to watch telly, 'cos I'm always there. When I bring food in, I always buy the wrong things. And I'm always making coffee. I use it all up, and I never bring back the cups. You are always going on cup hunts, finding my little cache of them beside the sofa . . .'

Lizzy came in. 'Can I have a biscuit?'

'Ask Lorraine,' Megs told her. 'She knows what I'm thinking.'

Lizzy looked at Lorraine. 'Can I have a biscuit?'

'It's nearly time for lunch.' Lorraine would normally have given the child what she wanted, but thought it time to be sensible. 'You don't want to spoil your appetite.'

'That was what I was thinking,' Megs congratulated her. 'As for the rest. Yes, you are the messiest person in the world. But I don't mind.' Then, 'Well, I do mind. But since it's you, be messy. Stay. But please bring your cups back to the kitchen. Oh, and fold a towel. Just one. Just once. So I don't have to.'

Lizzy returned. 'Shameless wants a biscuit,' she told Lorraine. Megs watched.

'Does he?' Lorraine made an elaborate show of fetching the pack of dog biscuits.

'No,' said Lizzy. 'He doesn't want one of them. He's gone off them. He wants a chocolate biscuit. He told me.'

'Did he?' Lorraine smiled. 'What did he say?'

'He said, "Fetch us a biscuit, Lizzy. Be a pal." He said he wanted an animal-shaped one. So's he could lick off the chocolate, then eat the biscuit.'

Lorraine brought the animal-shaped biscuits from the cupboard. Handed Lizzy a lion one.

'No,' Lizzy protested. 'He wants a elephant. Elephants are best.' Then, realising she must have overplayed her ruse, 'Shameless thinks so, anyway.'

'Righto.' Lorraine couldn't resist the girl. 'An elephant for Shameless. Shall I give it to him?'

'No.' Lizzy kept her cool. 'He wants me to do it.' She took the elephant and left. After a small while, from behind the door, 'Shameless wants another one.'

In unison Megs and Lorraine shouted, 'No.'

Lizzy said, 'Oh, bugger.'

'What did you say?' Megs called.

'Shameless said it, Shameless said it.' Lizzy was repentant. 'Shameless, you're a bad boy saying bad words.'

'Lorraine, my daughter is picking up your language,' Megs accused.

'I know. Sorry.' Lorraine put the animal biscuits beside the dog biscuits on the kitchen unit, boiled the kettle, took the last mug, made coffee and disappeared to sit with Lizzy and Shameless.

'Well, thanks for this,' Megs said. She put both packs of biscuits away. Then emptied Lorraine's ashtray. There were no cups left. Sighing, she went through to the living room to find one. 'And you

515

leave overflowing ashtrays everywhere,' she said to Lorraine as she gathered half a dozen assorted cups and mugs from down the side of the sofa.

'Sorry,' said Lorraine.

'You're not really,' Megs said.

'I know,' Lorraine agreed. 'Sorry about that.'

In the middle of all the cleaning and domestic clutter and small family squabbles, Megs got offered a lifeline. Late one Friday night Josh turned up at her door.

'Hi, Megs,' shuffling a little. He was here to ask a favour. Megs knew that shuffle well.

'Josh.' She smiled. 'Come in.'

They went into the kitchen. 'I'll make you some coffee,' she told him. 'You could do with some the way you're shaking.'

'Oh, it's not the drink,' Josh said. 'I'm off the drink. I want a favour. I want a huge favour. And I hate asking for things.'

'What do you want?' She leaned against the sink, waiting for the kettle to boil. In the living room the sounds of Friday-night television nonsense went quiet. Lorraine and Hannah were listening in.

Josh's hands were deep in the pockets of his reefer jacket. A new jacket, Megs noted. He is sorting himself out.

'Will you come sing with me?' Josh asked. He did not look at her. 'There's a new place started up, a blues club, and I play there. I do at least one night a week. But if you came, I'd get two nights. I've asked the guys from the old band. They're thinking about it. They will if you will.'

'What is this place?'

'Yazoo City. It's after a place in the South where Robert Johnson played. He played a place called Inverness, too. Did y'know that? 'Course, not our Inverness.'

'No,' said Megs. 'Fancy.' She made coffee. Handed Josh a cup.

'Cheers.' He nodded thanks at the cup, couldn't look at Megs.

'I think I'd love that, Josh. I think that would just about save my life right now.'

So on Thursday nights Megs sang the blues again. She got out her black jeans and her white silk shirt and stood before a small crowd who drank Miller's and Rolling Rock and looked at her with the longing of people who wished they could do what she could do. She sang Etta James, 'Mad About the Boy', and she sang Robert Johnson, 'Rambling On My Mind'. She sang Bessie Smith, 'Kitchen Man' and 'I'm Wild About That Thing'. 'Ya-da, ya-da,' she almost shouted it. Smiling. Flashing those perfect ceramic caps. She sang 'Gimme a Pigfoot' and 'A Good Man Is Hard to Find'.

'Ain't that the truth,' Lorraine called, holding up a bottle of Bud. 'You tell 'em.'

Whenever she could, Megs spent time with Gilbert. It seemed that without missing a beat, they resumed their little world together. He would hear her car clanking down the path and come out to greet her, waving and smiling. He did not even make that small movement of his head as he looked round, checking he was not being observed being childishly excited. She would come into his living room, the smells of the night, cold and the city, clinging to her coat. The older the year got, the more the journey north pleased her. It coloured yellows and ochre. The trees got stark. Farmers burnt the corn stubble. Flames and spiralling smoke under a mellow moon.

They moved closer to each other. Keeping out the cold, she thought. They made a small ritual of building log fires, constructing them carefully, discussing which log to put on next, and where to lie it on the embers for best effect. They spoke about anything to ward off any actual discussions about themselves and their future together. The bedroom window would not shut properly, they'd wake to find a crusting of frost on the eiderdown. In this cold, the icy air burned down their throats and it hurt to breathe. In the chill and the dark, three in the morning, she heard mice scratching at the walls and deer moving about the garden. Megs and Lizzy spent their mornings in bed, keeping warm, hardly daring to creep out into the chill, whilst Gilbert moved about downstairs, making breakfast and lighting the fire in the living room.

Sometimes she ached to wake him, asking what they were going to do. What was to become of them? Yet she felt if she asked this, he'd feel pressured to answer. She didn't think she wanted to hear what he had to say. If only he was a better liar. Then again, were he to ask her about their future together, what would she say to him? She suspected he would not like to hear her reply to that question either. She was beginning to realise she didn't want commitment. Being loved a little, pampered a lot was more than enough.

She wore Gilbert's navy fisherman's sweater, as none of her clothes were made to combat the kind of cold she met here. 'It'll get worse,' the butcher's boy told her when she went into the village for bacon and free-range eggs. 'Febrerry's the worst. Ten feet of snow. You'll see real weather then, Megs.'

Gilbert resented these conversations. He was jealous of Megs's success in the village and at the hotel at the top of the Glen. Everyone called her Megs, or Megsy. He was still that professory guy in the cottage. He envied how Megs could burst into a room, oozing friendliness. Like a puppy, she'd come to people whilst he stood back, shifting slightly from foot to foot, trying to make his smile seem spontaneous. Smiling, he felt, didn't work for him.

'Hi, Megs,' the barman at the Manilow and Coal Scuttle would call. 'Back again? Can't keep away, can you? Vodka and tonic, is it?'

'That's me,' she'd say, collecting empty glasses from a table and bringing them to the bar. 'Look, am I not good to you, saving you a trip?'

Gilbert couldn't do that. He'd take glasses over, saying, 'Um . . . glasses.' The barman would look at him as if he was insane. But Megs's friendships seemed seamless. Gilbert could not remember when everyone started calling her by name, though nobody seemed to know, or care, what he was called.

'What are you doing for Christmas?' he asked Megs. They were sitting on the floor by his fire. He knew she'd be too embroiled with her family to come see him.

'The usual. Spending money I have not got. Standing in shops looking at Argyle pattern socks whilst listening to some musak version of "Jesu, Joy of Man's Desiring". Then come the day getting woken in the pre-dawn gloom by one overexcited child, whilst two underexcited teenage children pretend not to be bothered. Then my folks will come round and we'll eat too much, drink too much, steam the windows getting hot and fall asleep in front of the telly. What are you doing?'

'Oh, I'll be here. I'll probably cook a steak or maybe some pheasant. Drink some claret and listen to some Schubert.'

'Don't stay on your own. Come to us.'

He didn't need to consider this. 'I can't,' he said. 'Not really. I like being on my own.' He couldn't go to her house. Lorraine would be there and she terrified him. 'Will you come for New Year, then?' he asked.

'I don't know if I can. My mother usually has a party, and anyone who doesn't go doesn't get spoken to till next New Year. It's a traumatic time. I'll come for the weekend in between Christmas and New Year. I'll leave Lizzy with Lorraine. It'll be just us and Shameless. I can't leave him, people forget to take him out. But us, we'll drink too much and do naughty things to each other.'

Chapter Thirty

December the 28th she arrived, teeth chittering. The heater in her car wasn't working. The cold stiffened her bones, gnawed her fingers and toes. She could not wait to get warm, stood in the kitchen complaining shrilly, stamping her feet and rubbing her arms. 'Oh God. Freezing. Freezing.'

He fussed round her, lacing her coffee with brandy, edging her towards the fire. 'It might snow.'

'Too cold for snow,' she told him. 'That's the verdict in the butcher's shop.'

He felt a stupid stab of anger that she should have stopped and spoken to other people on the way to him. He fancied her sitting in her car, pale face behind the windscreen, clutching the wheel, rushing through the cold and dark to get to him.

She laid his Christmas gift on the kitchen table. It was carefully wrapped (by Lorraine – wrapping gifts was not one of Megs's skills) in dark-blue paper with a multi-looped red bow. He eyed it.

'Oh no. After we eat. We'll sit by the fire and exchange gifts properly. I want the full love-nest treat. I've seen it in the movies. We drink wine from huge glasses, lie in front of a roasting fire, wearing comfy jerseys and exchange gifts. I want that. My Christmases have always been a rammy – noisy children, noisy toys, noisy relatives, noisy shows on the telly. I want a bit of class.'

She had bought him a checked cashmere scarf, chosen from Lorraine's catalogue. It cost her £45 – thirty-six weeks at £1.50 a week – that she couldn't afford. She was aware that £1.50 for thirty-six weeks worked out at £54. But that was how it was. Not having enough money cost more money.

He'd bought her a huge black rollneck sweater, a battered copy of Paul Oliver's *Blues Fell This Morning* that he'd found in a second-hand bookshop months ago, and a box set of *La Traviata*. 'I know. I know – opera. Not your scene. But give it a go. You'll love it.'

They lay on the floor, staring into the fire, drinking. The night outside was jagged and chill. The freeze crept in under the door, round the window frame, till Megs and Gilbert found they were sitting, joints stiffened and locked against the cold. Megs rubbed her nose. 'We'd be warmer in bed.' They ran upstairs, ripping off their clothes, shivering and eager to get under the covers. They clung to one another, complaining and giggling about each other's frozen feet and bum.

Megs pulled the eiderdown over her head, drummed her heels and cried out, 'Oh God, cold . . . cold . . . cold.' She took Gilbert's hand. 'Dance with me.'

'I don't dance.'

'Come on. We're under the eiderdown. There's nobody for miles. Dance with me. I won't tell a soul.'

But Gilbert wouldn't. He couldn't, even then, let go. Megs didn't care. The wine, the food – she was all sorts of drunk. She did an on-the-mattress strut. Waving her hands. Shameless joined in, jumping on the bed, nuzzling her. Gilbert felt his face go out of control – he was smiling wildly.

Her hangover woke Megs. 'Oh God, champagne. Never again.' Her head was in a throbbing cloud. She longed for someone to bring her a bucket filled with iced orange juice. She felt foul and she fretted about Lizzy. It was the first time they'd been apart.

Six in the morning, she wandered the cottage wearing only Gilbert's old jersey. She pressed her face on the window and stared out into the garden that had taken up so much of her time in hotter days. Her breath steamed the glass, and every so often she had to slip the sleeve of the jersey over her hand and rub it clean again. She remembered Lizzy out there on that lawn, struggling with the watering can, bossing the pansies. 'You're not getting any more. You'll get a sore tummy.' She wondered if Lorraine would be really mad, or only irritated, if she phoned to ask how they were. She dialled the number.

'Hello. Um . . .' She heard Lorraine's sleep-soaked voice. 'Time is it? Who's this phoning?'

'It's me,' Megs said.

'What are you doing? It's the middle of the night.'

'It's six in the morning.'

'That's what I said. The middle of the night. Why are you phoning? Is everything OK? Are you all right?'

'Yes. 'Course. I was just up. And thinking about Lizzy. How is she?'

'Sleeping. In your bed with me. She's fine. She had a great day. We went to the zoo.'

'The zoo?'

'Yes. It's great in winter. There's nobody about. We had a good time. We took a flask of soup.'

'Soup.' Megs repeated it slowly, peevishly. She felt jealous. She wished she'd taken Lizzy to the zoo. 'What else have you been doing?'

'Oh. I sat about with Hannah, talking about things. Stuff. You know. You, mostly. We spoke about you.'

'Me?' Megs didn't like this. She wanted to be home having a heart-to-heart with Hannah. 'What did you say about me?'

'Oh, just what a tough time you've had. How you've managed. How you deserve this time to yourself, to be with Gilbert. Hannah's decided she'll be nice to him in future.'

'Oh.' Megs still did not like the thought of her best friend and daughter discussing her.

'Then,' Lorraine went on, 'Hannah went out. She borrowed my red top.'

'Not your red top. That's a bit low-cut, isn't it? There's hardly anything of it. She's still young, you know.'

'She looked great,' Lorraine soothed her. 'Then Jack came home early to watch football. But he got cross with me because I kept saying things about the players' thighs and bums. So he went off to bed.'

'What are you meant to watch in football if not the blokes' bums?' Megs asked.

'Dunno.'

'I mean,' said Megs, 'if it was women running about the field in shorts, would men be watching the match?'

"Zactly.' Lorraine lit a cigarette. Megs could hear the snap of her lighter. She imagined her in the kitchen, leaning on the fridge, flicking her ash into the bin. Missing.

'Wipe up your flicked ash, will you.'

'What ash?'

'The ash you'll flick into the bin and miss.'

'If you emptied your bin occasionally, I wouldn't miss.'

'Where was Jason through all this going to the zoo and having heart-to-heart chats?'

'We've split up.'

'Oh, Lorraine, I'm sorry. What happened? Was his life too fast and loud for you? He wanted to go clubbing, and you wanted to stay home and behave like the sedate lady you secretly are.'

'No,' said Lorraine. 'No, wrong. He wanted to stay in. He wanted to watch telly and settle down sort of thing. But I've done that. I wasn't very good at it. I wanted something else. I want to go out clubbing and have a good time. So we split up.'

'Sorry about that. How are you? Are you upset?'

'Nah. Well, a bit. But not really. We hadn't a lot to say to each other.'

'I didn't think speaking was part of your relationship.'

'It wasn't at first. But when we at last got round to it, we realised we had nothing to say to each other. His mother hated me. Said I was mutton dressed as lamb.'

'Cheek. What does she look like? Mutton dressed as mutton?'

'Ha, ha. I'll remember that if I see her again.'

Megs got up from the rush-seated chair she was on. She scratched her bum, which was deeply marked, rush-seated. 'Oooh, my bum's gone all funny. It's imprinted with the chair. It's freezing here. I'm starting to shiver. I better go back to bed. See you soon.'

'OK,' said Lorraine. 'Phone you tomorrow, eh? Or today more like. It is today.'

'Yeah, it's today now. Phone you today.' Megs put down the receiver. She longed to be home having serious chats to Hannah, watching football with Jack, and taking Lizzy to the zoo with a flask of soup. 'Dammit,' she said out loud. 'They're having a fine time without me.'

The cold drove her back to bed. She ran up the stairs, Shameless running ahead of her. They both bounced on to the bed, waking Gilbert. 'Cuddle me,' she said. 'I miss Lizzy.'

He turned to her, took her to him.

'I can tell,' she said, 'this is developing into more than a cuddle.'

They spent most of that day in bed. Megs got up to take Shameless round the garden and came rushing in, bent and bundled, complaining about the weather. A slow wind started and shifted round the cottage.

'I think the temperature's gone up,' Megs said, stamping in through the door. 'I think I can smell snow coming.' She breathed in. Outside in the garden she'd sipped some air, tested it on her tongue. Dampness made it heavy. Snow, she thought. The air tasted dirty with approaching snow.

'You could be right.'

'Good time for you to get cooking, then. What're we getting?'

'Steaks and salad and Australian red.' They were city-born and bred, both of them. The dire implications of snow didn't occur to them.

They ate by the fire. And, lulled by too much wine, they went to bed to sleep some more, and sweat some more in each other's arms.

The light woke Megs. The light and the silence. A new grey translucence filled the room, a damp film of white coated the windowsill. Megs rose and looked out. The garden had been sculpted – the shrubs and trees were reshaped with snow. It was white out there, endlessly, endlessly white. 'Snow,' said Megs. 'Hey, Gilbert, it's snowed.'

Gilbert moved, lumpen, into a new sleeping position, yanked the eiderdown over his head, and said, 'Uh. Good.'

'No, Gilbert.' Megs came over to the bed and shook him. 'It has seriously snowed.'

He rose, pulled the duvet from the bed and wrapped them both in it before moving to the window. 'Christ. So it has.'

Outside the sky had cleared, turned indigo. Small, strident stars gleamed.

'Christ,' Gilbert breathed. 'It's beautiful. I've never seen it so beautiful.'

They stood side by side, gazing out. He thought they were like a couple of wide-eyed babes in a fairy story.

'Do you think I'll get home?' Megs asked.

'No problem.' Gilbert was sure of this. 'Snow never lasts.'

Later in the morning they walked, snow squeaking beneath their feet, to the end of the track. Shameless plunged ahead. Every few yards he would stop and roll joyously. There was something thrilling about all this sudden white. Megs stooped against the cold, hands deep in her pockets. The morning was icy against her cheeks. 'Isn't this beautiful?' she said, sticking her tongue out into the air. 'I have never tasted anything so pure, so clean.' She took some snow from the top of the dyke and put it to her lips. 'When you were little, Gilbert, did you eat snow?'

'No.'

'It still tastes the same as it did when I was little, which is more than you can say for American cream soda or Heinz Sandwich Spread or . . .'

'What does it taste of?' Gilbert lifted a handful and carefully licked it.

'Of being white and cold. It tastes snowy.'

'Yes.' He gave a gourmet's verdict. 'Snowy.' He turned, considering the world in wonder. 'Isn't it marvellous? It changes everything. You see everything anew. Reshaped as the snow hit it. Look, small layers along the wire fence, and the branches. It's amazing.'

Megs scooped up a fistful of snow that she moulded in numbing hands into a ball to hurl at Gilbert. She missed. It fell, disappeared into a drift. Shameless bounded after it, then stood looking vacantly round. Where had it gone? Megs made another and threw it for him. Then Gilbert. They had a small flurry of a fight, throwing armfuls of snow at each other. Iced and damp, they reached the road, stood in the chill and the silence, looked up, then down. There was not a tyre track to be seen.

'It's Sunday,' Gilbert said. 'Nobody goes out on Sundays. Well, not this time of year. It's too good on telly. You'll get home tomorrow, no trouble.' His breath spanned out in verbal bursts, his face glowed. He stuck his hands in his pockets. The cold was a deeper chill than he'd ever known. 'Oh yes,' he said. 'No trouble.' His voice trailed into disbelief.

Megs watched him. The glorious sparkle, the glittering morning had turned bitter. She shivered, not a lowering-of-temperature ripple, but a whole shaking of her body. Her teeth clattered. Her nose was running, she sniffed. Her clothes were acrylic. There was not a lot between her and the weather. 'I think I'd prefer to observe this gorgeousness from inside.'

They passed the day by the fire. Every now and then one of them would wander to the window to stare out. They watched the new world turn into evening. That glimmer gleamed against the evening, and took on the night. It didn't quite get dark.

It thawed in the morning. Ice on the guttering turned watery, dripped, leaving huge pockmarks in the snow below. On the lawn they could see where deer had wandered, looking for food, and a small scuttly track – little feet and a traily tail – a mouse out and about.

'I have to go,' Megs said over breakfast. 'I should leave before it ices over.'

'Stay.' He wanted to beg, but didn't dare.

'I want to. You know that. But it's New Year's Eve. I have to be home. I must bring in the New Year with my family. My mother will never speak to me again if I'm not there. It's traditional, we go to her house. Come with me, why don't you?'

'No.' He shook his head, emphasising his refusal. He felt awkward with her family.

She shrugged. 'Well, don't think you're not welcome.'

Driving, slithering slowly, down the glen, she could see mountainous clouds, heavy-bellied with snow, moving in, but ignored them. Calamities for her were bank statements, broken appliances, bruised children, an empty fridge. Weather never occurred to her.

The usual twenty-minute journey from Gilbert's cottage to the village took her over an hour. It was after midday when she got there, and snowing. She stopped at the butcher's shop to buy some steaks for New Year's Day dinner.

'You'd better get on home.' Billy, the butcher's boy, appeared from the back shop. 'Else you'll be stuck.'

'I was going back to town.'

'Not today you're not. Road's closed.'

'But . . .' protested Megs, as if this man behind the counter was in some way responsible. As if a nod from him would make the ten-foot drifts passable.

'If you don't hurry, you'll not even get back up the glen.'

'But . . .' Megs said again. 'It's New Year. I go to my mother's. I always go.'

He leaned on the counter. 'This year you'll just have to go to the party in the glen hall.'

She wanted to say that she didn't want to go to the party in the glen hall. She wanted home. She wanted to see Lizzy. She wanted to stamp her foot and cry. 'I better head back.' She sighed. 'I actually came in to buy some steaks to take home. I'll take something up to Gilbert. Is that a goose?' Megs pointed at a huge bird, plucked and glistening beneath the glass counter.

'It is that,' said Billy. 'This goose, this goose,' slapping it bitterly, 'this goose was ordered by Lady Morven herself. Wanted it for Hogmanay. I took it out this morning on my bike.'

'Bike?' Megs turned towards the weather. Snow, fat, freezing, penny-size flakes, freewheeled and blew past the window. She could not see across to the other side of the road. Gears crunching, cars crawled past, moving into the grey, lights on. 'Bike?' she said again.

'Aye. Ten mile. Five here an' five back again. Ten mile an' she said she'd changed her mind. Didn't want the bloody goose.' He pointed furiously at the beast as if it was all its fault. Well, it couldn't possibly be Lady Morven's, could it? She was a lady. She lived in the big house at the foot of the glen.

This morning, at seven, before the shop opened, he had put on his enormous brown slab-shouldered, double-breasted herringbone tweed coat. Wrapped his checked scarf round and round his neck, shoved the goose into the huge basket on the front of his delivery bike and set off. Saddle creaking, pedalling slowly. Contemplating the chill. He moved painfully into a bitter wind that left him gasping and turned his throat raw. His breath heaved and steamed before him, misting his glasses as he went. Grunting with effort. 'Too old for this. Too bleddy old for this.'

He was three miles out of the village, on the road cleared by the plough, when the snow started. Small, scudding flakes at first. He did not stop. 'Be there before it really comes down,' he promised himself. Wading ancient cycle through the morning. He did not look at the sky that bulged above him. It was pouring down when he reached Morven Hall. He banged the huge knocker. Moving it slowly against the door, staring at his feet. The Lady herself answered the door.

'Brought the goose,' said Billy.

'Goose?' Lady Morven withered. 'Goose? I didn't say anything about a goose.'

'Ordered one, three weeks ago. Wanted it for Hogmanay,' he pleadingly reminded her.

'No I didn't.'

'Did,' said Billy. 'Answered the phone myself. Said I'd bring it out. And here it is.'

'Well, I don't want it now. Take it away.' Lady Morven slammed the door.

Sadly, and without complaint, Billy turned. Trudged down the steps back to his bike, put the goose back in the basket and slowly, slowly pedalled back. By now the sky was emptying. It took him two hours of monotonous, deliberate pedalling to get back. The bike swished slowly over whitened roads. From the little battery a wan, wavering yellow light glimmered into the sheeting grey-blue weather. When he got back he was white. White like an iced man. There were tiny drops of ice clinging to his eyebrows. Snow formed layers on his trousers and filled the turn-ups. Snow lined the creases in his scarf, and caked his coat, melted and ran down the back of his neck. He moved one stiff, frozen leg at a time, like a robot into the shop, the goose straddling his spread arms that he held as if they were still gripping a pair of handlebars. Everyone stopped. Ignoring them, he continued his chilled shuffle through to the back and laid the goose on the table. 'Didn't want it,' he said. Then, 'Still, she answered the door herself. Her very self. Must've fallen on hard times.' He didn't actually know what the gentry did. But they certainly did not answer their own doors. 'I have had enough.'

'Enough of what?' Kynoch, his boss, asked.

'Enough of everything. Delivering geese. Being me.' Looking glumly down at his frozen coat, holding his hands, stiff fingers iced

529

into the clench with which he grasped his bike, over the buttons. 'Undo me, someone,' he said slowly. For speaking was tricky. 'I'm froze.'

'I'll buy the goose,' Megs offered. 'If nobody else wants it.'

Kynoch wrapped it, smiling pleasantly. He thought he was going to be stuck with the thing. Hated goose.

'Um,' said Megs. 'Do you know how I cook it?'

Billy stepped forward. 'Rub it with salt.'

'Billy'll keep you right,' Kynoch said, nodding. 'He's right fond of cooking.'

'Prick it all over with a fork. Let the fat out. Then stand it on some sort of grill and put grill and goose into a baking tray. Keep it out of the fat. Don't want the bugger swimming in fat as it cooks,' Billy said, patting the beast softly as he spoke. Must've bonded on the long bike ride, thought Megs.

So with goose on passenger seat, safe from Shameless, she drove back. Gripping the steering wheel and hunched over till her face was close to the windscreen, she inched her way up the glen. Every now and then she'd rub a small viewing hole on the steamy windscreen with the back of her glove. Then she'd drag the same damp glove across her eyes, wiping her tears.

'I hate this,' she told the goose. 'I hate it.' She could not see the way ahead. The unending whiteness covered road and verge, filled ditches. The car whined forward in third gear. If she moved up into fourth, she felt it slip out of control, skate on frozen snow. 'It's all right for you, goose. You're already dead.'

The journey back took even longer than the journey down. Three hours after setting out, she opened the door and found Gilbert sitting at his kitchen table, head in hands.

'I'm back,' she said. 'And I've brought a goose.'

Chapter Thirty-One

Gilbert jumped when she burst in. He'd been agonising, confronting himself with some difficult truths and trying to come to a decision. There were three things in life that Gilbert wasn't good at – dancing, emotions and decisions.

In the time Megs had been slithering on ice-packed roads, Annette had phoned.

'I'll be back on the fifth of January,' she said. 'Can't wait. How are you, anyway?'

'Oh, fine.'

'And how's the book?'

'Um.'

'Oh, for heaven's sake, Gilbert, don't tell me you've been tucked away at your cottage all these months and haven't finished it.'

'Well.'

'What have you been doing?'

'Actually, I've started to paint again.'

'Really? That's wonderful. That is such good news, Gilbert.'

'Yes,' weakly said.

'I can hardly wait to see what you've done. Oh, I'm so glad.'

'Yes. I find it very soothing, calming just manipulating, juxtaposing light and shape. It's done me a lot of good. I've come to terms with myself.'

He had spent hours and hours drawing, then painting Megs. What he saw as the simple business of laying down the lines where he wanted them to go evaded him. He only knew the line was wrong when it was in place, so he'd redraw it. Still it wasn't right. Again and again he tried. He could never get his drawings on paper to match the vision in his head. His frustration became an ache. He drank. He threw his pencil, then his brush across the room. He ran both hands at once through his hair. In other words, as he tried to explain it to Annette, his paintings weren't as good as he thought they'd be. He was not the artist he'd always thought he was. His secret conceit had floundered.

A long pause. 'Well, that's reassuring. A term of self-discovery, eh?' Annette sighed down the line.

He could imagine that little wry smile of hers. It annoyed him that there never was any fooling her. 'I enjoy,' he said, trying to convince her, and enjoying also the first chance to expound pretentiously in months, 'the tiny nuances involved in artistic honesty. Searching for some kind of technical perfection is humbling. I feel I am finding a new humility. The actual act of laying on paint . . .'

'Gilbert,' she interrupted him, 'I have to go. I have a meeting. Will you pick me up at the airport? I get in at four o'clock on the afternoon of the fifth.'

'Yes,' he said, meekly.

After she'd rung off, Gilbert sat at the kitchen table, head in hands. He didn't know what to do. He did not want to lose Annette. The companionable life they'd built over the years suited him. Yet there was Megs. She intrigued and excited him. Then again, he felt that if his friends and colleagues knew he was having an affair with his cleaner, they'd laugh at him.

He imagined them all in the pub, drinking and discussing him. 'Oh no,' he cried, burying his face in his folded arms. There was also the business of his sketches and paintings. People would want to see them. Not only would they see who he'd been sketching and painting, they would see that he was not the undiscovered talent he'd quietly given the impression he was. Burn them, he thought. Yes. People would just think he was a poor tortured soul. Which, when he thought about it, he was.

Then Megs burst in, frozen stiff and carrying a goose. She could hardly move for Shameless leaping, eager to investigate the beast in her arms. 'I can't get home,' she wailed. 'The road's closed. I want to go home.' She dumped the goose on the table. 'I want to see Lizzy. I want to be there at midnight.'

His heart went out to her. He went to hold her. 'Phone home. Tell them what's happened. They'll be worried.'

'I wanted to be there. I'm always there for New Year.'

'Well, this year you'll be with me.'

She just stopped herself saying that she didn't want to be with him. She wanted her family.

'We'll go to the dance at the village hall.' He tried to enthuse. He was saying this for her. He knew he'd hate it. 'We'll boogie.' And he danced. He hadn't done such a thing since he was ten. He'd turned up at a birthday party wearing shiny shoes, pants with immaculate creases, white shirt and velvet bow tie. Everyone else was John Lennon. That afternoon he'd done the twist. So that was what he did now, a slow, clumsy hip-swivel. The dance of a man who did not dance. His body moved, but his clothes stayed still. Megs watched him in dismay.

She phoned home, but Vivienne was out panic-buying bread because the shops would be shut for the next two days. Lorraine thought it wildly romantic that Megs was snowed in with Gilbert. 'Just like *Doctor Zhivago*,' she swooned. 'That snowy bit with Omar Sharif and Julie Christie. You lucky bugger.' Lizzy, however, when she eventually got to the phone, was not as impressed as Lorraine and wanted to speak to Shameless. She missed him. Megs dutifully held the receiver to Shameless's ear whilst Lizzy spoke to him. Then she told Lizzy that Shameless was missing her too, and had said she should be good.

At ten-thirty they left Shameless locked in the cottage and set out for the glen hall. It had stopped snowing.

'It's Good King Wenceslas snow,' said Megs, stamping tracks in the pristine white. 'Deep and crisp and even.'

The cars that had gone ahead of them had rutted the road. Gilbert slid into a track and grimly crawled forward. Rubbled snow, churned by earlier travellers, gleamed in the headlights. Gilbert gripped the wheel, trying not to complain or let his fear of ice show. He didn't think terror manly.

They heard the party long before they got to it. The hooch and skirl of abandon echoed across the frozen evening. It cheered Megs up and added to Gilbert's terror.

533

The hall inside was wood-lined, overly lit. Ancient chairs with concave seats long carved into the shape of the thousands of bums that had descended on them lined the walls. On the stage at the far end the Purple Haze Trio – a Hammond organ, drums and a guitar – played something Jimmy Shand-ish. Everyone danced. The Purple Haze Trio were wearing their yellow-sequinned jackets, that's how folks knew who they were tonight. Wednesday nights, when they played the Manilow and Coal Scuttle, they wore tartan jackets. Then they were the Tartan Trio.

The guitar player stepped forward to the mike. 'Gonney change the mood now with something a wee bit more up-to-date.' They plodded into something that sounded deliberate and familiar to Megs, though she couldn't place it. She stood, head to one side, gazing quizzically ahead. 'My God, Gilbert, they're playing "Dark Star". Oh, I love it. All the way up here, Jerry Garcia in the middle of nowhere. Don't you love it?' She dipped her knees, did a little jiggle. Something familiar, she felt better already. Though she noted she was the only one moving. Older people did not want anything a wee bit more up-to-date. Younger people had a younger idea of up-to-date.

'No, I do not love it,' said Gilbert. He'd never heard of Jerry Garcia. He hated this already. He'd only suggested coming to make Megs happy and now he was regretting it. He spotted a lone chair by the door and resolved to spend the evening there. He fetched them both a drink, then settled into his hideaway spot. Megs left him to be sour and unsociable and joined the fray.

She danced with a man who beamed hello to her. It was New Year, everyone had come to party, locals and incomers. Megs slowly recognised the man she was dancing with. She'd seen him often driving his tractor on the cottage track. Then he would nod brusquely before ignoring her. He crossed the dance floor with that same furrow-straddling stride he used to cross fields. It took her a moment or two to recognise him without his bonnet. His face below the bonnet-line was ruddy, weathered. Above the bonnet-line, it was pasty white, sweat-beaded. Every now and then he would nervously slap it. It was obviously part of his body that he felt he'd rather keep to himself.

From his shy little corner, Gilbert watched and surreptitiously consulted his watch. Half past eleven, how long before they could politely leave? If another person came up to him and beamed, 'Smile, it might never happen,' he thought he might go insane. The friendliness was overwhelming. Strangers, stooped with concern, would lean into Megs, face inches from her face. 'Is yer glass empty? Sees it here. I'll get ye another.' Her glass would be whisked from her hand, and brought back refilled with whisky, advocaat, vodka or rum and coke – whatever the solicitous one thought she ought to be drinking. Megs knew she was getting absurdly drunk, but was sucked in. This party was infectious. The band played jigs and reels, old Beatles medleys, George Gershwin and anything that was requested. Megs, breathless from dancing, sank on to Gilbert's knee. 'This band has the repertoire from hell,' she said.

At midnight they reached new peaks in abandon. There was frenzied hugging and kissing and weeping. People linked hands, singing, 'Auld Lang Syne'. They clutched each other, saying one another's names with passion.

By now Megs was, to everybody present, Megs. But Gilbert, to his resentment, was still That Professorish Bloke Who Has the Cottage at the End of the Track. Despite that, several strange women lunged at him and wetly kissed him. Men slapped his shoulder and shook his hand.

'They don't like me,' he complained to Megs, who had fought through the sway to kiss him as the clock struck twelve.

'It seems to them that you don't like them,' she told him. 'You are being a tad stand-offish.'

'It's not my sort of do.' He fetched another drink and settled into his chair once more. 'When are we going?'

'Oh, come on, Gilbert. It's not long past midnight. The party's just hotting up.'

'Hotting up?' he cried, dismayed. 'I thought it already was as hot as it could get. I want to go home.'

'I don't.' She left him to be miserable.

She went out into the foyer to cool off. Stood pressing a cold beer can to her cheeks.

'Hot, isn't it?' The butcher's boy came to stand beside her. He wore an ancient, carefully tended tuxedo, starched shirt and black bow tie.

535

'My goodness, Billy.' Megs smiled to him. 'Aren't you smart?'

'I like to dress up. I wear an apron all day.'

'Yes.' Megs wondered if she'd been patronising him.

'So how do you like New Year all the way up here?'

'I think it's wonderful. I'm having a wonderful time.'

'It's different. Year after year it changes. Year after year there's more newcomers taking over the glen. As the locals leave to find work, strangers move into their cottages. They buy them as holiday homes. Or they come live here. The old school's a home now. New folk. They try to fit in, you have to hand it to them. Look at them.' He pointed back into the hall. A moving sway of dancers, whirling and hooching. 'They even do the dances better than we do. They've been to classes.'

Megs remembered her school days, thundering about the gym whilst Mrs Leadbetter, the teacher, bawled instructions. 'Skip, change of step, gels. Link arms with the person to your right and dance into the middle, then back.' She remembered them barging into one another, tripping and hysterical with giggles.

'Aye,' Billy said. 'You best change yoursel' before change changes ye. If y'see what I mean. So,' he said, suspecting he was depressing her, 'are you not dancing with your man?'

'It's not his sort of thing.'

'Right.'

They stood in silence, drinking and cooling off.

'Dunno what you see in him,' the butcher's boy said. 'He's not your type.'

Megs looked at him. She was tempted to tell him to mind his own business, but defended Gilbert instead. 'He makes me see a bit of myself I actually like. I feel less guilty when I'm round him.'

'Guilty? What've you got to be guilty about?' He was, she realised, terribly drunk.

'My little boy,' she said. 'Remember I told you? He was run over when I should've been there to bring him home. I was late.'

He shook his head. 'I'll tell you guilt. I killed my father. There's guilt.'

Megs felt a chill creeping over her scalp. 'I don't believe you.'

'Oh, it's true. My father was not a nice man.' He said the words carefully, sounding each one. 'He beat me. Used anything that came to hand. He hit me for nothin'. Couldn't find a match to light the gas, so I got it.' He did a drunken punch at the air that would have been ineffectual, but for the venom in his face. He rolled up his sleeve, showed a cluster of round white scars. 'Stubbed his fags out on me.' He hated these arms of his, stained as they were with parental rage. 'He had a look that came over his face. It started with his lips. The way he moved them. An' you knew what was coming. It's only these past couple of years I realised it wasn't me he hated. It was hisself. Only he couldn't hit hisself, could he?' He leaned into her again. She watched his face, deeply etched lines round his eyes, round his mouth. This face had been a long time miserable. 'I peed the bed every night till I was twelve. That's when I killed him. There, that's terrible. That's guilt.'

Megs didn't know what to say. 'I don't believe you did that,' she said when at last words came to her. 'How did you do that?'

'He took a heart attack.' He sniffed, swigged his whisky. 'He was in the living room. He just gripped his chest and fell down. He was gaspin' with pain. He lay on the floor and told me to go to the farm. Phone the doctor. His face was all twisted, and he couldn't hardly speak. He said to hurry up.' Billy looked at Megs, piercing, honest eyes. 'But when I got out the door I dawdled. Don't know why. It was a lovely afternoon and I felt so peaceful. I don't think I took him seriously.'

That afternoon forty-four years ago would never leave him. Every colour: the soft purples on the hill hazing into sunlit distance, the dank green moss on the damp at the foot of the wall of the cottage. Every scent: the blast of manure passing the byre, the sour curdle of dairy cows. He'd been a stick of a boy, refugee thin. His hair was heartlessly barbered, shaved up the sides and back, leaving a tuft atop. His face, white with mistrust, looked wizened, childishly wizened. The smattering of freckles over his nose and cheeks looked odd against his permanently worried expression. Puny pale legs stuck out from hand-me-down school shorts, two sizes too big. Scabbed knees. He wore a grey shirt, huge tails stuck into grubby underpants. His shoes, scuffed toes, had metal segs in the heels. He'd been an underfed sparrow of a child. He had not known he appeared like a starved fledgling to others. He'd thought that was how things were.

Hands in pockets, he'd taken two hours to walk the fifty yards from the cottage he shared with his father to the farm. He'd stopped to pick moss from the dyke with his grubby, chewed nails. He'd found a centipede and watched it scurry into a crack. He'd kicked at a stone embedded in the dried mud till it came loose. Then he'd overturned it and squatted, watching the wildlife beneath scatter and wriggle in the sudden flooding of light. He'd picked up a stick and dragged it after him. At last he'd knocked on the back door of the farmhouse. 'My father's ill. He asked me to get you to phone the doctor. He's lyin' on the floor.' After that, he'd been shoved aside whilst grown-ups took over. The farmer's wife had phoned for an ambulance, then run up the path to the cottage.

'But when she got there my father was dead.'

'Where was your mother?'

'She walked out years before.'

Megs shook. 'I'd like to say I don't believe you. But I think I do.'

'So after that Kynoch took me in. I was meant to go to a home, but I just stayed with him. Now I still work for him. I was the butcher's boy then, still am. So don't talk to me about guilt. Guilt'll make y'daft.' He walked to the door and stared out into the bitter dark.

'Why are you telling me this?' Megs asked.

'Always wanted to tell somebody. And you're the only person I know that I don't know. You can't pass it on to anybody local.'

'Why didn't you leave?'

'I belong here. I get excused here.'

'Excused?'

'For day-dreamin' my life away. It's not the thing to do, y'know. Folk'll take advantage. You'll end up tired and cold, standing in the snow with a goose and a door slammed in your face.'

'What do you day-dream about?' Megs touched his arm.

'Freddy. Freddy Stair. He would've danced with you, not like old misery guts back there.'

She stared at him. Then it came to her. 'Fred Astaire.' She glowed.

'Aye, him. He's dead, you know.'

'Yes.' She joined him at the door. The air was frosty clear. The sky deep and starry. The frost purified the air, every scent came to them.

Someone somewhere nearby was smoking dope. Megs wished she had some.

'When my boy was run down, when I kneeled beside him, I heard this awful noise. A terrible, terrible wailing. Demented. The noise was coming from me. I was making it. Do you think we all have a noise like that inside?'

'Aye.' The word came out on an inward breath.

'There.' Megs put her head next to his. 'I've told you something I have never told anybody else. I have always been horrified at that noise I made. And I don't think you killed your father. If he went quickly, it's unlikely an ambulance would have arrived in time. Then there's the trip to hospital. That would've taken over an hour. Don't blame yourself.'

He looked up, nodding. 'Sometimes I hate they stars. They're so buggery belligerent. All they do is shine.' He took her hand. 'C'mon inside.' A brusque order. 'I'll give you a dance.'

They took to the floor. Him with one hand on her waist, the other holding hers aloft. As the band ached out a drunken rendition of 'Hotel California' they waltzed. All her life Megs had dreamed of her perfect partner. Someone who would take her dipping and twirling across the dance floor. A man who could dance like Freddy Stair. Now here it was happening to her. She hated it. She felt controlled, manoeuvred into doing things she didn't want to do. Her feet weren't up to the task. Twirling, she was, beyond her abilities.

Chapter Thirty-Two

Megs and Gilbert got home after four. Megs was drunk. Gilbert was grumpy. On the drive back to the cottage he'd asked Megs why she had spent so long talking to the bloke who worked in the butcher's shop, and she had accused him of being jealous.

'Me?' Hand flying from steering wheel to point to himself. 'Jealous? I don't think so.'

They stopped speaking. Their silence thickened when they got in and found Shameless chewing Gilbert's briefcase. Shameless had had a busy night. He had climbed on to the kitchen table and eaten a bowl of olives and a packet of New York Cheddar crisps. He'd spilled a carton of milk and what contents he hadn't lapped up dripped on to the kitchen floor. He'd found the pheasant Gilbert was planning for his New Year Day dinner and eaten enough of it to ruin it. Then the olives, crisps, milk and pheasant had taken their toll. The mess was beside the door. He'd left the goose untouched.

In the living room Shameless had sought comfort by chewing a pair of Megs's shoes. Then he'd dragged a pair of Gilbert's boxer shorts from the laundry basket and lain on them as he chewed his briefcase. The contents, his book, *The Theme Pack*, were spread across the floor.

'Christ,' said Gilbert. He spoke with no emotion. He was too tired for emotion. 'Now I remember why I never wanted a dog.' He stared at the regurgitated pheasant carcass. 'Now we'll have to have the goose.' He hated goose, but hadn't liked to mention it to Megs. He went to bed.

What a sobering for Megs, cleaning up. She cleaned up the turds and sick, wiped and disinfected the floor. She gathered Gilbert's notes and put them on his work table. She put her dismembered shoes in the bin with the pheasant, milk carton, broken olive bowl and crisp bag. She picked up Gilbert's stolen underpants, thought to wash them, then said, 'Oh, stuff him, grumpy bastard.' And put them back with the clean laundry. It was five-thirty when she'd finished. She was no longer tired, and took Shameless out into the garden. He was too ashamed to bound ahead of her, walked instead at her heel, head down. 'It's a bit late to put on a show of good behaviour,' she told him. 'You have surpassed yourself. The New Year situation is now beyond redemption.' Still, when she, at last, flopped into bed beside Gilbert, she made sure the dog was at her feet. It was the only comfort either of them was going to get.

Next morning they moved stiffly round each other, each making deliberate movements, hoping the other would notice they weren't being spoken to. At last Gilbert broke the hostilities.

'What *were* you doing talking to the butcher's boy for such a long time?'

Megs shrugged. 'We were just talking about what it's like to live here all the time. He says it's not so nice as it looks.' She had no intention of telling him the truth. It had left her feeling depressed and raw. Then she was still tired from cleaning up after Shameless.

Gilbert made a testy sound, 'Nymph,' and disappeared into the kitchen to wrestle with the goose. Megs sat by the fire, reading the same page of a book over and over. During the afternoon and evening they drank too much. But alcohol did not mellow them. They were just boozily irritated with each other. The goose did not cook well; perhaps it was too travelled. Now they both had indigestion. They made odd, sharp exchanges whilst trying not to fart, hiccup or belch.

'I think the sprouts were a bit underdone,' Megs said.

'Well, you should've cooked them yourself.'

'Do you think I'll get down the road tomorrow?' she asked later.

'Should do.' He hoped his disgruntled tone hid how much he really wanted her to stay. He was too proud to end the argument. Besides, he still hadn't forgiven Shameless.

They went to bed early, still tired from the night before. Megs hadn't followed her usual habit of clearing up the kitchen after him. They left the sink piled with dirty dishes, the hob splattered with grease. The table was cluttered with dishes, wine-stained glasses and a half-demolished goose.

They slept sweatily, as deep as their exhausted digestive systems would let them. Voices, ringing shrill from the snowy garden, woke them. They lay a moment listening to footsteps crunching on the path outside and the quizzical surprise of people examining her car.

'Good heavens, whose is this?'

'It isn't Gilbert's.'

'No. That's his over there.'

'There must be someone with him.'

There was rapping at the door and window. 'Coo-hoo Gilbert.' They could hear someone rattling the letterbox.

He squirmed. Clambered from bed, and in his red nightshirt (his Wee Willie Winkie outfit, Megs thought) went to the window. 'Oh Christ. Oh Christ, no.'

'Who is it?' Megs sat up.

'Cathy McGhee.'

'Dysentery?'

'Yes,' he snapped. 'Dysentery McGhee is here. Outside. Wanting in.' He stared in horror at Cathy McGhee in jeans, boots and flying jacket, hopping about outside clutching a couple of bottles of wine. This was the moment he'd dreaded. 'She'll definitely be wanting in.'

'Gilbert,' came the voice from outside. 'I see you, Gilbert. Let us in. It's bloody freezing out here.'

'She's been looking at your car.' Gilbert looked at Megs crossly. 'Why didn't I get you to move it round the corner?'

'Ashamed of it, are you?' said Megs flatly. As if she hadn't always known that.

But Gilbert didn't hear her. He was in misery. 'Oh my God,' he moaned. 'Oh God. Oh God. Oh God.' He rushed downstairs.

Megs could hear him thundering about the living room as she pulled on her jeans and a sweater. When she got into the kitchen, Gilbert still hadn't opened the door, so she let Cathy McGhee and her boyfriend in.

'Megs,' Cathy cried when at last the door opened. 'Megs. What are you doing here?'

Megs could see that for a full two seconds Cathy thought she was here to clean for Gilbert. Then the truth dawned.

'Megs?' Knowingly said, finger moving between Megs and an imaginary Gilbert. 'Are you and Gilbert . . . ? My goodness.'

Megs could tell that Cathy McGhee desperately wanted to turn and drive immediately back to town to phone round with this snippet of gossip. Instead she burst past her into the kitchen, calling, 'Gilbert. Gilbert. Show yourself. We've brought goodies. And want fed.'

She found him by the fire in the living room, still in his Wee Willie Winkie outfit, looking shifty. The devastation of last night's meal was still untouched, but he'd cleared the room of all his drawings and paintings. Megs looked at him sharply, said nothing, thought, so that's what you think of me.

She went upstairs to shower. Still dripping, wrapped in a towel, she stopped on the landing on her way to the bedroom. She stood listening to the cries and guffaws as Gilbert, in his red nightshirt, held court.

'C'mon, Gilbert. Get into the kitchen, do your magic. We're famished.'

'In a second. I'm not quite ready. The culinary muse isn't on me this time in the morning.'

'It's half past eleven. What's this you've been eating last night, anyway?'

'Goose.'

'Well, you can rustle us up something. I'm sure a man of your abilities must know a million things to do with an old goose. Ha, ha.'

They started to talk about people Megs didn't know.

'Martin and Lucy are expecting again.'

'For heaven's sake, don't they know when to stop?' Gilbert boomed sanctimoniously. 'How many sprogs is that they've brought into the world?'

Sprogs, Megs thought. There was something dismissive about the word. It was a description of children from people who didn't have any. Did Gilbert think Lizzy was a sprog?

'So, Gilbert,' Cathy McGhee's companion said, 'how's the book?'

'Ha, don't ask.' Gilbert sighed. 'Actually, I put it aside and started to paint again.'

'That's wonderful.' Cathy's voice. 'Anything you can let us see?'

'No. Not yet.' Gilbert was defensive. 'It's not what I'm painting that matters. It's the actual act of doing it that's so exciting. The small technical decisions as you move through the canvas, trying to achieve some sort of perfection that's in the end exhilarating and humbling. I paint and I think about nothing else but the job in hand. There's a purity in that sort of concentration that's cleansing.'

Megs heard the snap of a lighter and the small fizz of flame licking cigarette end. 'I know what you mean. I feel the same when I work on my novel.'

'Right. You'd know,' said Gilbert. The sound of a whisky bottle being opened, glasses laid out on the table and filled. 'Water?'

'Hmm, please.' Voice lowered, but not lowered enough. 'So, Gilbert, what's this with you and Megs?'

'Oh, it's just . . .' Gilbert stopped. Megs knew he'd be looking vaguely round, running his fingers through his hair.

'A dalliance?' Cathy's boyfriend asked.

'Ha, ha. A pleasant dalliance?' Cathy pursued him.

Megs could tell Gilbert was squirming. 'Pleasant . . .' His voice drifted. 'Yes, pleasant.'

Megs went into the bedroom to finish drying herself, dress and pack. Ten minutes later she stood leaning slightly on the living room doorpost. 'I'll be off then, Gilbert.'

He looked shocked. 'You're not going, are you?'

'Looks like it.'

Cathy McGhee smiled and said, 'You're not leaving on account of us, are you?'

Megs shook her head. 'I have to get back. If you got here it must mean the roads are clear. We've been snowed in for the last few days.'

'How wildly romantic.' Cathy beamed.

Megs moved her lips into what should have been a smile. But she only grimaced. 'You could say that.'

'Wait till I get something on,' Gilbert pleaded. He ran upstairs.

By the time he'd yanked on a pair of pants, socks and boots, Megs had thrown her case in the boot, put Shameless in the back seat and was letting the engine idle.

'I don't want you to go like this,' Gilbert said.

'How do you want me to go?'

'Not like this.'

'I heard you, Gilbert. You denied me. I'm a dalliance, am I?' She could not hide her hurt.

'No. No. I just didn't know what to say. You know how it is.'

'No. No, I don't.' She pressed the accelerator and moved slowly towards the track.

He grabbed the car, ran alongside it. 'Oh please, please. Don't be like this.'

'How am I meant to be? Would you like me to bustle, clean up and smile whilst you and your friends hoot loudly and drink?'

'No.' His hand went to his hair. 'No. Really no.'

'You're ashamed of me, aren't you?'

He shook his head. 'Of course I'm not. I . . .' He couldn't tell her how much he cared. 'Megs, please don't be like this.'

His hurt, his pleading made her feel powerful. It eased her pain. 'You are so clever, Gilbert. You know so much about things I'll never understand. But sometimes, when it comes to people, I think you're just God's gift to stupid.' She pressed the accelerator. 'I'll let you get back to your friends. Go. Go back to your ghost woman. The one you think about and secretly glance at. Her. I won't bother you any more. Don't worry, when the phone rings it won't be me.'

Nightshirt flapping, he stood in the middle of the track, watching her car slip and shove towards the road.

She drove off. All the way home, driving over wet black roads, great dirty cliffs of drifts either side of her, she cried, wishing her parting words to him had been kinder.

Chapter Thirty-Three

When Megs got home Lorraine was curled up on the sofa watching television, drinking vodka and Coke. 'You're back,' she said.

'You always had a knack with the obvious,' Megs told her. 'Where is everybody?'

'Lizzy's with your folks. Hannah with one of her friends, forgotten which one. Jack is having dinner with Sharon's parents.'

'Goodness,' said Megs. 'They have forgiven the haircut, then?'

'Seems like,' said Lorraine. 'Wasn't expecting you till tomorrow. How was it being snowed up?'

'Don't ask.' Megs hung up her coat, kicked off her shoes, and walked through to the kitchen. Lorraine said nothing. Megs wheeled round, reappeared waving her arms. 'All right then, ask.'

'OK. How was it being snowed up?'

'Awful,' said Megs. 'We argued. We went to the dance up the glen. I got horribly drunk, spent too long talking to Billy who works in the butcher's. Then when we got home Shameless had wrecked the cottage. Then Dysentery McGhee turned up and I overheard them talking and I realised I didn't belong with them. So I came home. That was it.'

Lorraine said, 'Do you want a drink? Or a cup of tea?'

'A drink,' said Megs. 'Though the hangover I had after that dance, I was never going to touch alcohol again.'

'So what were you talking to the butcher's boy about?' Lorraine handed her a glass of vodka and Coke.

'Why did you pinpoint that?'

'Just call it instinct. I watched your face.'

'We spoke about guilt,' Megs told her. 'He has this terrible idea

547

that because he took too long to go fetch help when his father had a heart attack, he killed him.'

'That's awful. Do you think he did?'

'No. He was just being a kid. That's all.' Megs lay back on the sofa, forcing Lorraine on to the chair. 'But it was horrible. I looked at him, at his weary old face, and he's only in his fifties, and I saw myself. I saw me in a few years, racked with pain and grief and guilt. Know what I was thinking all the time he spoke? I thought what a waste. What a waste of a person, waste of a life.' She put her glass on her forehead. 'Why do we do it?'

'Everyone feels guilty. You can't be blamed.' Lorraine spoke gently.

'No,' said Megs. 'Lie back and put your glass on your forehead.'

'Because you're daft?' suggested Lorraine.

'That'll be it. Sometimes doing something completely moronic is sort of soothing. Then when your mind's empty you realise you have to fix your life. But what can I do? Sing? Haven't made money doing that.'

'You can make sandwiches,' Lorraine said. 'We could open your sandwich bar. Of all your daft schemes, that's my favourite. My money from Harry came through,' she said.

'When?' Megs asked.

'The other day. We could do it, we really could.'

'Yes,' Megs said. Though the idea made her nervous. 'I'd rather just spend my life lying here on this sofa with a glass of something on my forehead. But I don't suppose it'd work out.' Then, after a while, she asked, 'Do you think my forehead's huge and flat?'

The room got dark, the television flickered silently. Their conversation roamed over past times, old loves, distant memories. Every now and then they tentatively explored the sandwich bar notion.

'I suppose,' said Lorraine, 'we're going to have to do it.'

'Scary though,' said Megs. 'There's only one thing scarier than doing it.'

'What's that?'

'Not doing it,' said Megs.

They were still exchanging reminiscences, anecdotes, snippets of their different New Year celebrations when Gilbert phoned. Megs picked up the receiver.

'Hello.' Gilbert sounded apologetic. 'Did you get home all right?'

'Yes,' said Megs. 'The roads were fine. And once I got on the motorway there was no sign of snow. There's nothing here in town.'

'Good,' said Gilbert. 'I'm coming home on the fifth. I've got to see someone.' He wasn't going to own up to Annette. 'And then a couple of days later I go back to work. My sabbatical's over.'

'Life goes on, eh?'

'Yes.' He sounded sad. 'I'm so sorry if I insulted you. I didn't mean anything I said to Cathy. I was trying to impress them. I was awful.'

She knew he'd been reliving this morning, and had been hard on himself. 'Gilbert.' She said his name softly. 'Don't blame yourself. I was as bad. I just stormed out. I should have come down and chatted. But I felt suddenly out of place. Know what I mean?'

'I know. That's how I felt at that dance.'

'You had the courage not to hide it, too.'

'Will . . . ? Are you . . . ?'

'We'll see each other again, Gilbert. You can bet on that. And no, Gilbert, I won't be cleaning for you any more. Not a good idea. I don't think I'll be cleaning for anybody soon enough, anyway.'

'Good for you,' he said. 'Is there anything I can do? Is there anything you want? Anything.'

She wished she could think of something. It would make them both feel better, she thought. 'If ever there's anything you can do, I'll let you know. Bet on it,' she said.

After she'd rung off, Gilbert sat alone. He had thought that once Cathy McGhee left to go home he would take all his sketches and paintings of Megs out into the garden and burn them. But now the moment had come, he couldn't do it. Instead he bundled them together and put them in his loft. When he'd done he poured himself a drink. He thought the silence in the cottage was hideous. It was filled with his longing.

Megs went back into the living room. Lorraine was lying on the sofa, glass on forehead. 'It is good,' she agreed. 'Putting a glass on your forehead. It's sort of mindless.'

Megs decided. 'I will start a sandwich bar. If you will.'

'I'm for it. I'll go for that.'

'We'll have to get our act together. We have to know what we're doing. Go on courses. Accountancy, hygiene and that.'

'You do accountancy. I'll do hygiene,' Lorraine offered.

'No, you do accountancy. You passed maths. I failed miserably. I got English and music.'

'I don't want to do accountancy.'

'Into every life,' Megs said wisely, 'a little accountancy must fall. See that box of wine we just finished? If you take the bag out and squeeze it, there's a glass in there. You do accountancy and you can have it.'

'OK,' said Lorraine. It seemed like a fair deal to her. 'But I want to work behind the counter. I want to look at the customers and flirt with the men.'

'Of course you can do that. I'll be in the back making sandwiches. Bacon, lettuce and tomato and such.'

'I like flirting,' said Lorraine. 'It's friendly. And flattering. It's good for you.' Then, wistfully, 'There'll be young boys. First job. Wearing their new suits, looking all shiny-faced and eager to please.'

'A good old-fashioned cheese sandwich,' said Megs. 'Thick bread, and chutney.'

'Or flirty men from building sites who call you darlin' and take their shirts off on hot days.'

'Nuts are good. Though some people are allergic to them. Chicken and walnuts. Or toasted pine kernels. Gilbert used to put them through things. Salads.'

'Older men, with comfy faces that have done a lot of laughing. With grey bits at the side of their hair. Who get drunk and sing to you. Romantic songs like "Fly Me To the Moon". Who take your hand and pat it and tell you you're lovely.'

'Yes,' said Megs. 'I like them. Next man I have, I'll have one like that.'

When Vivienne arrived with Lizzy she found Megs and Lorraine lying at each end of the sofa, each with a glass on her forehead, still talking about sandwiches and men. Mostly men.

'What are you two doing?' she asked.

'Being silly,' said Megs. 'How are you? Did you have a good New Year? And did you miss me?'

'Yes on both counts, as it happens.' Vivienne collected their glasses. 'I think you two could do with some coffee.'

Lizzy came into the room. 'You're back.' She posed dramatically a moment before rushing across the room, arms wide. For a moment Megs thought, goodness, the welcome I deserve, at last. But Lizzy passed her, fell on her knees. 'Shameless, my best friend. You're back.'

And Megs said, 'Oh well.'

Chapter Thirty-Four

On the fifth of January, the day Gilbert collected Annette from the airport, Aunty Betty died.

'She just drifted out of living in the middle of the night,' Vivienne said. 'According to the doctor she never felt a thing.'

The day after the funeral she and Megs went to clear out Aunty Betty's house. They collected her clothes into bundles suitable for Oxfam and bundles to be thrown out. They stripped her bed. Collected what they wanted to keep, and what was to be sent to auction. They sat at her kitchen table, looking through old family photos.

'Look,' Megs said. 'Here's one of me taken that summer when you were in the sanatorium.'

'Don't you look miserable?'

'I was miserable. Some of the time anyway. I was homesick.'

'I never knew that. I always thought . . .' Vivienne didn't finish the sentence. She always thought Megs preferred being with Aunty Betty to her.

'Look, here's one of her in the tracksuit after she took up jogging.'

'What, after the hysterectomy?'

They giggled.

Aunty Betty's hysterectomy was a family legend. It turned her from interesting relative to heroine. She did not suffer gynaecologists gladly. Constant bleeding, sore breasts, tiredness had sent her to her doctor, who had passed her to a consultant. As soon as she sat in his room, before he even laid a chilled hand on her, or pulled on the dread surgical gloves, he said, 'I think we'll have to give you a wee hysterectomy.'

Isla Dewar

'You do them in sizes?' Aunty Betty asked. 'You have hysterectomies in trial packs and large economy?'

The consultant raised his hand, dismissing this. Nobody, patients especially, questioned his judgement. 'We can remove just the womb, or we can whip out the works. At your age you'll hardly be needing it.'

'It has always been my intention,' Aunty Betty said, 'to part this world with everything I came into it with. Teeth and all.' She shot him a revealing smile. Sixty and still a perfect shiny set.

Nonetheless, the bleeding persisted. Eventually Aunty Betty gave in to medical pressure and ended up labelled, shaved and tranquillised, lying on a trolley in a corridor leading to the operating theatre of the local hospital. She was wearing a backless gown, a cap and large white socks. Her gynaecologist passed by and patted her arm, 'Soon be done,' he said briskly. 'You're third up this afternoon.'

'Sod this,' said Aunty Betty. She lay watching a small piece of afternoon through the little window opposite where her trolley was parked. She thought about her life. The children she always meant to have. Dancing on Friday nights, loves she'd known. Kisses. Nobody would kiss her again. And that moment in bed when you turned to someone you loved and he turned to you. 'That's a grand moment,' she cried out. Two passing nurses giggled. 'Now my face is chewed with time and worry and too much port and lemon.' She lay. The afternoon still drifted past. She watched it. Two doctors passed, talking about a boat they shared. 'Took her up the Sound of Jura. Lovely sailing. Drinks on the deck. That's the life.'

It seemed to Aunty Betty that the wombs of sorry women, lying on trolleys with bald pubes, paid for such treats. 'Sod this,' she cried. And got up. In fabulous, backless hospital wear she wandered down the corridor. Nobody said a word. She walked back to the ward, fished her shoes from the locker. Then, fearing someone might find her and force her into the operating theatre, she stole a coat from the back of a visitor's chair. And left.

She walked out of the hospital, down to the local taxi office, and arrived at the Seaview Guest House at four-thirty, just when afternoon tea was being cleared off the tables and dinner started in the kitchen.

'Bastards,' she cried, throwing off the stolen coat, revealing her

554

bum through the diabolical hospital outfit to a gobsmacked clientele. The cap and white socks had been left at the hospital. 'Bastards,' she cried again. 'Shaved my privates. Were going to cut me up. I look like Telly Savalas down there. Buggers.' She thundered to the drinks cabinet, poured a huge whisky. Knocked it back. Went to bed and slept for two days.

She took up jogging. In a pink tracksuit she stumped daily along the beach at low tide. She started to eat broccoli and spinach and swore that greens and exercise were her salvation, along with whisky and port and lemon. She never went to the doctor again.

'There was nobody like her,' said Megs.

'No,' said Vivienne. 'She was a one-off.' Then, taking advantage of this moment of mutual mellowness, 'What happened between you and that man of yours? He was the best thing that ever happened to you. Why did you dump him?'

'I don't think either of us did any dumping. But I think we both knew it would have to end. Our lives were too far apart. He was so different from me.' She leaned over, touched Vivienne's arm. Smiling hugely, she said, 'He told a better class of lie than me. His bullshit was class.'

Vivienne tutted. 'Don't know what you mean.'

They moved to empty the food cupboards.

'Oh God,' Megs squealed, taking out a jar of Heinz Sandwich Spread. 'Sandwich Spread, I used to love that. You never bought it. I always vowed that when I grew up I would buy jars and jars of it and eat it all myself. Then I grew up, and it wasn't the same. I didn't like it any more.'

Vivienne objected to any criticism of her mothering skills. 'So that's why you ended up the way you did. I never bought you Sandwich Spread.'

'That'll be it,' said Megs.

'I never heard the like in my life. And I'm sixty-three, you know.'

Megs's heart turned over. She had to look away lest her mother saw her smile. Well, hello, old lie, she thought, haven't heard you in ages.

'You were always so obstinate,' Vivienne said. 'Not liking your name. Saying things like, "I didn't ask to be born." You were a trial.

Then there was that hat.' Vivienne still felt bitter about the hat.

'What hat?' Megs hoped she sounded innocent.

'That lovely pink and green hat I knitted you for school. You came home without it. What happened to that hat?'

Megs looked at her, swallowed and said, 'I lost it.'

'No you didn't, you stuffed it up a drainpipe,' Vivienne snorted.

Megs burst out laughing. 'I didn't know you knew that.'

'I know lots of things.'

'What do you know?'

'I know that if you open that sandwich bar of yours – and it looks like you actually will – you'll need as much money as you can get.'

'I know that too.'

'Your father and me will give you some. We'll match what Lorraine puts in.'

'I can't take your money. You'll need it for your old age.'

'This is my old age. And it'd be going a lot better if I saw you settled. Take the money. For my grandchildren, if nothing else. Your father and me want to chip in. We want to be part of it. A new lease of life. And after all Lorraine's done, it's the least we can do.'

Lorraine went on the accountancy course. It lasted three weeks, long enough for her to master bookkeeping, basic computing, the language of business plans, and, as she put it, the body language of someone who actually believed all this bloody business-speak – projected figures, meetings, business plans. 'That's mostly what business is about. Being cocky,' she told Megs. 'That and having a good jacket when you need it.'

Megs enrolled on a course learning hygiene standards. 'Aunty Betty would not approve.' Whilst she learned the importance of wearing a hairnet, keeping raw and cooked food separately, sterilising work surfaces and knives, Lorraine found a property just up from Stockbridge. 'On the edge of the business belt,' she enthused. 'We'll get the business trade, and the local trade too. We'll make squillions of pounds. I'll have a huge flat with high ceilings, a flash kitchen.'

'With an espresso machine with a handle,' Megs said.

'Two of them.' Lorraine was going to spare no expense. 'And a jacuzzi.'

When they found that Lorraine's money, with the money Megs's parents put up, was not quite enough, Lorraine went to see the bank manager. She bought a navy suit, borrowed Megs's white shirt and Mike's briefcase and promised not to giggle. 'I won't giggle,' she protested, hurt at the accusation that she might. 'I am actually starting to believe this is going to happen.'

She managed the interview well. 'Of course I'm sure it's a paying proposition,' she enthused. 'There's no competition around. Not everybody wants to walk miles for some lunch. A lot of people just send out. Then we plan to stay open late for folks who work late and folks who live round about. Look at this bank.' She waved her arms. 'How many people have you got working here?' And before she got a reply, 'Thirty?' she suggested. 'Well, if thirty people bought a sandwich costing say one pound fifty, that'd be . . .' she removed her calculator from Mike's briefcase, tapped the buttons with polished nails, 'Forty-five pounds a day. Two hundred and twenty-five pounds a week, which is . . .' she thought about this, '. . . not enough to run a business. But,' dismissing this failing, 'we can build on that.' Her energy and enthusiasm got her a loan and a promise of an overdraft facility when they knew how much they might need.

Lorraine emerged triumphantly from the bank, waving to Megs, who had been waiting across the road, because their raising-cash-and-meeting-people budget wouldn't run to two suits.

'We got it. We got it,' Lorraine screamed. She did a small knee-dip, fists clenched. 'Five grand.' She ran down the pavement, shouting, 'Five grand. Five grand. Five grand.'

She and Megs held each other, bouncing round and round. 'Let's get drunk,' said Lorraine. 'We've got five grand. We can spend a little of it. He wants to meet you, though.'

'Will he notice I'm wearing the same suit?'

'Nah, they all wear suits like this.'

'I know,' said Megs. 'Sod work, sod families, sod guilt, let's take the money and run away.'

'Ooh, tempting,' said Lorraine.

Chapter Thirty-Five

A week later, Megs phoned Emotionally-Deranged Davis to tell her she would not be back. The conversation was swift and polite.

'We're sorry to see you go, Megs.'

'Thank you.'

'Best of luck with your new venture.'

'Thank you.'

She went to see Dysentery McGhee personally.

'I thought this was coming,' Dysentery said. 'Is it me? Were we horrible to you at New Year?'

'No. It's nothing to do with that. Actually, I rather think I was horrible to Gilbert.'

'He is sweet really. He's actually a really nice man.'

'I know,' Megs said. 'You don't have to tell me. No, I just won't be cleaning any more. Not for him, or you, or Emotionally-Deranged Davis.'

'Who?'

'Emotionally-Deranged Davis. Julia Davis. That's what I call her. I found it easier to clean for people if they had nicknames. It's less personal.'

'So what did you call Gilbert?'

'Hundred-Miles-An-Hour, on account of his hair.'

'Oh yes. Very good. I like that. And,' lighting a cigarette, 'what did you call me?'

Megs looked away. 'Dysentery McGhee.'

'What! Why?'

'You said, "Just keep it above the dysentery line." So you became Dysentery McGhee.'

'I sound like something out of a bad Western. Dysentery McGhee. Actually I quite like that. It's a bit of rough. So, what are you going to do now, Megs?'

'Open a sandwich bar. I've been working it out with my friend.'

'I like that. I've always wanted to do something like that. Something that requires movement and meeting people.'

Megs looked round. 'You always seem to have the perfect life to me.'

'There you go. You never know what people are thinking,' said Cathy. 'Would you like some coffee?'

Megs nodded.

'What I always fancied,' said Cathy, bringing two cups to the table, 'was being a barmaid. You know, one of those lovable and worldly-wise women who lean on the bar. Big tits.' She indicated the size of tit she fancied, considerably larger than what was actually there. 'I'd lean on the bar and people would tell me their worries, and I'd say, "Never mind, my love. Here's your gin and tonic," or whisky or whatever. I'm just not the sort of woman who can call strangers love, or darling. You are.'

'Me? I have never called anybody I don't know darling.'

'You could.'

'I haven't got the tits for it either,' said Megs, pulling out her T-shirt and surveying her inadequacies.

'Yours are better than mine.' Cathy McGhee pulled out her T-shirt too, and looked at the failings within.

'Will you come for a sandwich?' said Megs.

'Try and keep me away. Do me a favour,' still looking, double-chinned, down her T-shirt.

'Sure. What?'

'Give me a shot at serving. Will you have aprons? And little hats? Let me try calling folk darling.'

'We're going to have matching T-shirts. Lorraine wants them low-cut. She's got the equipment to call people my love and darling, though.'

'I hate her already.' Cathy smiled. 'Go on, let me serve sandwiches sometime, please.'

'OK.' Megs laughed. 'Why not.'

When she left, Cathy kissed her. 'Take care, Megs. Best of luck. And keep in touch. Oh, and phone Gilbert sometime. I know he thinks about you a lot.'

That evening, when Lizzy was sleeping and Lorraine was poring over her projected figures, Megs phoned Gilbert. 'Just wondered how you are,' she said.

'I'm fine. Back to work. Quite enjoying it.'

'Still cycling back and forth.'

'Still cycling.'

'I'm going into business with Lorraine,' she told him. 'We're opening a sandwich bar.'

'I heard, Dysentery McGhee told me,' he said. 'And she told me about Hundred-Miles-An-Hour. Guess what? I've had a haircut. Not as drastic as your Jack's, but you can't call me that any more.'

'Pity. You suited it.'

She heard a woman's voice in the background call his name. 'Gilbert, who's that you're speaking to?'

That's her, Megs thought. The ghost in the corner.

'I have to go,' Gilbert said. 'I'll see you.'

'Yes,' said Megs. 'See you. Will you come for a sandwich?'

'Of course I will.'

But Megs knew he wouldn't.

After Gilbert had rung off, Annette quizzed him. 'Who was that on the phone?'

'Nobody.' He shrugged, not meeting her eye. 'Nothing. Just work. It's not important.' He was ashamed of himself. Looked apologetically across the room to his new ghost in the corner. Annette trailed her gaze after his. He kept doing that these days, looking across the room as if somebody was there, somebody he was saying sorry to.

Chapter Thirty-Six

They called it the Dreamland Café, after the café where Louis Armstrong first played. They spent the spring fitting out the bar and kitchen. They opened for business at the beginning of July. They called their sandwiches after blues singers and tunes. They had never been so tired in their lives. Megs's hands were raw from wiping surfaces and cutting up lettuce, tomatoes and onions. 'I never knew grating cheese could be so draining.' But by the end of the month they'd made more than their projected figure and were wildly pleased with themselves.

'I'll soon be able to afford a place of my own,' said Lorraine. 'Big flat, jacuzzi, here I come.'

It was late August, early evening. Lizzy, in her new school outfit, was home with Vivienne, who regularly came in to help, to boss and to tell customers she was sixty-three, you know. Megs and Lorraine had just locked the door and were walking down the hill towards Stockbridge. Laughing.

Gilbert and Annette were in a taxi, going back to Annette's, where she would cook a light supper before they went to the Filmhouse.

'We'll just have some smoked duck and a tomato salad before we go,' Annette said.

Gilbert reached into her supermarket bag, pulled out a tomato and held it to his nose. 'Fine.' He saw Megs and Lorraine walking down the hill, heard their laughter cannon up the street. 'Oh God,' he said. He knew he'd bump into her one day.

Seeing his expression, Annette followed his gaze. 'That's her, isn't it?'

Gilbert said nothing.

'I know there was someone, Gilbert,' Annette said. 'And I know she wasn't the first.' She fixed him with a look. One of her looks.

The taxi passed the two as they walked.

'Thank heavens,' Gilbert said.

The taxi stopped at the lights. 'Oh, change. Change, please.' Gilbert silently pleaded.

Megs and Lorraine drew level, turned to cross the road. For the first time in months, Megs and Gilbert were face to face.

She did not know what to do. Smile? Look away? Stick out her tongue? Oh no, not that. He had, in the end, denied her. But then he only got there first. How long would it have been before she denied him? He'd been good for her. Perhaps she'd even been good for him. She remembered summer evenings, things they'd done. They'd walked across the field. Him with Lizzy on his shoulders, her hand in his. Shameless running ahead. They'd sat together on the kitchen doorstep long after midnight, talking, rambling conversations. She'd told him some of her secrets. These things she'd done with him were favourite memories. Pictures she'd keep in her head.

She grinned at him. Leaned forward, knocked at the taxi window. Shook a scolding finger. 'Hey, Gilbert. That is *not* a tomato.'